# Atlas Snubbed

## An Unsanctioned Pastiche Parody

# Ken V. Krawchuk

*To Brigid,*

*Excellent narrator on*
*The Pennsylvania Project*

*Enjoy!*

*Ken Krawchuk 6-25-2020*

**Atlas Snubbed**
Copyright 2011 by Ken V. Krawchuk
All rights reserved.

ISBN 978-0-6156-0002-4

Version W.0
February 3, 2012
10.5-point Garamond
230,443 words total

Cover art:
Desert scene courtesy of Michael Davis (mdpub.com)
Train pictures courtesy of Barry F. Krawchuk

Publisher and Licensed Distributor:
Ken Krawchuk & Associates, Ltd.
c/o PO Box 260
Cheltenham, Penna., 19012
info@AtlasSnubbed.com

# Table of Contents

Preface ......................................................................................... 1

Book One: Who Is John Galt? ........................................................ 3

    Section 1 – The First Hours ..................................................... 4

    Section II – The First Days ...................................................... 21

    Section III – The First Weeks .................................................. 60

    Section IV – The First Months ............................................... 157

    Section V – The First Years ................................................... 222

Book Two: Who Is Eddie Willers? ................................................ 283

    Section I – The Final Days .................................................... 284

    Section II – The Final Weeks ................................................ 304

    Section III – The Final Months .............................................. 399

    Section IV – The Final Years ................................................. 405

*I dedicate this book in grateful appreciation to the memory of Alisa Rosenbaum, self-styled as Ayn Rand. Through her writings, she taught me how to argue with fools—and the first fool I had to argue with was myself. You'll have to decide for yourself who won that argument.*

# Preface

The United States was falling.

Beginning with the nineteenth century conflict known variously as the War Between the States, the Civil War, or the War of Northern Aggression—depending on the allegiance of the observer—the nation had embarked upon a path which took it further and further from its philosophical underpinnings of personal liberty and individual rights, drifting oh-so-slowly toward a society rife with over-regulation and collectivism. Over the years, petty thieves, looters, and thugs assumed greater and greater control over the machinery of State, and with predictable results: more and more of the nation's productive output found itself routed into the pockets of those in power rather than those who had earned it. Unavoidably, the promise of tax-paid riches attracted the unscrupulous, much as a bright light shining in the night draws obnoxious insects. Before long, leadership positions were increasingly awarded not to the most able, but rather to the most ruthless, in a cycle that rapidly worsened with each iteration.

Perhaps America would have realized in time the grave error she was committing and eventually returned to the moral code she had abandoned, if not for the deliberate efforts of one man: the Worker.

"Who is the Worker?" one must ask. Like the fictional John Galt, the Worker was an engineer, inventor, and philosopher, a man of humble beginnings who ultimately graduated from the most prestigious academic institution in the nation. After earning a dual degree in physics and philosophy, he began a promising career as a researcher for the Century Motor Company in Starnesville, Wisconsin, the best motor manufacturer in the nation at that time. But after the company's founder passed away, his heirs forsook their father's individualist management style in favor of a blatantly collectivist approach, "from each according to his ability, to each according to his need." The inevitable result was the rapid decline of the firm, and within four years the Century went bankrupt.

But there was one enduring legacy from the company's collectivist experiment. Upon hearing the unspeakable evil of collectivism spoken by the heirs in a tone of high moral righteousness, the Worker finally realized the root of the world's tragedy—the moral code of collectivism—the key to it, and the solution: a brand new moral code, one that was rooted not in some collectivist creed, but rather in individual rights. The summation of his new code fit neatly into a twenty-nine-word oath: "I swear by my life and my love of it that I will never live for the sake of another man, nor ask another man to live for mine."

The Worker did not stay on to witness the destruction of the Century Motor Company. On the night the heirs took over the Factory, at a massive meeting of the entire company, the Worker quit—or, more precisely, commenced a one man strike. As he walked off the job, he vowed to his collectivist co-workers, "I will put an end to this once and for all. I will stop the motor of the world."

His was no idle threat. Armed only with his unique philosophy, he set forth to scout out the men of ability, the men of the mind. When he found them, his message to them was always the same: stop supporting your destroyers! One by one, one after another, the Worker convinced the nation's best and brightest to join him in his strike, to withhold from society the fruits of the superlative ability of their minds. Only by withdrawing their support from the collectivist society could they defeat it. Only by consistently treating their life as their own would they finally come to truly own it. Only by refusing to sanction the collectivist's moral code would the men of ability finally be free. And time after time, in one business after another, the call was heard; and as the years passed, his roster of recruits swelled from dozens, to hundreds, to thousands.

Although the Worker pursued his goals in secret, oddly enough the men of America well knew him by name. Without conscious orchestration, whenever people saw the lights go out in the great factories, their gates closed and conveyor belts stilled, when the roads began to grow empty, or when they saw another collapse in the world which no one could explain, when they took another blow or lost another hope, they would habitually ask the rhetorical question: "Who is John Galt" that he could stop the motor of the world? The question was asked at first by the Worker's fellow employees at Century, but the pseudonym soon spontaneously spread throughout the nation; and the citizens of America were destined to have their answer.

With economic inevitability, as each man of ability joined the Worker's strike, the productive output of the nation declined, sometimes only marginally, other times quite significantly. But regardless of the size of the reduction, the result was always the same: fewer goods and services, and a greater strain on the nation's economy and on the poor souls left behind. Infrastructure—and nerves—became more and more frayed with each successive blow.

At long last, after twelve years of uncompromising effort, the Worker's dream of the total collapse of the collectivist state was finally poised to come to pass, and that collapse promised to be a horrible one. The declining economic situation had attained dire proportions, and the nation found itself teetering on the brink of disaster and starvation. Armed fighting broke out between men, between cities, and between states as they battled over the last remnants of food and the hulks of abandoned factories. The greatest nation the world had ever known was about to come to a nasty, bloody end.

But at the last minute, the Worker was unwittingly betrayed by the woman he loved, and captured by government agents. They both flattered and tortured him in an attempt to break his will and force him to abandon his strike and rescue the crumbling nation. But before long, his fellow strikers staged a dramatic rescue and they escaped with the Worker to their secret stronghold high in the Colorado Rockies.

Safe in their mountain redoubt, the men of the mind waited patiently for the last remnants of the collectivist state to crumble before they could or would consider returning to the world Outside. But they did not have long to wait. With her last hope abruptly snatched out from beneath her, the United States of America entered her final death throes, and in a fury of fighting, finally perished from the face of the Earth. The once great nation had been relegated to the dustbin of history, the last victim of her own flawed moral code.

With the complete collapse of the collectivists, the course was now clear for the strikers to return. But the world that they ultimately inherited was nothing at all like the world they had originally left behind. Nor was the reception they received quite what they expected, once they did return.

For among the survivors still clinging to life in obscure niches of the four corners of the world, there was one cliché that could not be uttered. No longer could people idly bear to hear the name, the phrase, the apocryphal cry of despair, "Who is John Galt?"

Because now, they knew.

# Book One:
# Who Is John Galt?

# SECTION 1 – THE FIRST HOURS

February 25, 1953

## CHAPTER 1 – UNDERTURE

Eddie smiled in his sleep.

His smile was not so much due to any chance dream, but rather in instinctive response to the slight tickle of perspiration trickling down his cheek. In an ironic twist, the persistent tickling caused the smile to fade, along with the last traces of sleep.

Waking, he felt the cold reality of the warm metal floor of the Diesel's cab pressing against his cheek, its angled, grey flatness filling half his field of view. With a start, he realized he was still aboard Transcontinental Railroad's *Meteor*, the fastest train in the nation, but stalled and stranded somewhere in the middle of an Arizona desert. His back and neck were sore from having slept for hours on the bare metal floor.

Even though the desert sun had not yet risen very far above the horizon, it was already oppressively hot inside the cab. His clothes were drenched with perspiration. When he climbed into the engine the night before, he distinctly recalled closing the cab's hatch against the night's chill. But right now if he spent another half hour inside the enclosed Diesel, he feared he would melt like a tallow candle on a hotplate.

Eddie lifted himself painfully, opened the hatch, and climbed down the still-shadowed side of the silent *Meteor*. The flinty odor of dry sand hung in the breezeless air. Shading his eyes with his hand, he gazed out across the vast, unimpeded expanse of lonely desert. Except for occasional dots of cacti and scrub, the only feature on the limitless gravelly sand was the dusty road at his feet, running parallel to the track. It was the same road that had brought the covered wagons the night before—*covered wagons!*—that had carried away the last passengers to ever ride the *Meteor*. All the passengers except him, that is.

He looked back along the length of the train, back toward San Francisco from which the *Meteor* had recently departed. The train stretched in a straight line away from him: a mail car, two baggage cars, a sleeper, two day coaches, and an ornate observation car coupled to its end. Waves of heat streamed from their roofs, wavering starkly against the featureless crystal blue sky. A growing menagerie of mice, rabbits and prairie dogs had taken refuge from the sun in the shadow of the train. The nearer ones eyed Eddie nervously.

"I am a fool," he told himself out loud, carefully enunciating each word. He knew now that he should have accepted the wagonmaster's offer the night before to join up with their wagon train rather than remaining alone aboard the train. In the light of the new day, he saw the naked folly of his grand gesture to the *Meteor* and to Transcontinental Railroad. He took a deep breath and pulled himself together. *No! Not a fool!* he reminded himself sternly within the confines of his mind. *I am the Special Assistant to the Vice-President in Charge of Operations for Transcontinental Railroad, and this train is my responsibility!* Despite his proud words, there was no denying that he and the *Meteor* were stranded together, and it was becoming increasingly clear that they would likely die together as he went down with his ship. His shoulders slumped perceptibly. *But still a fool...*

His mind refused to accept the unbelievable news that the wagonmaster had brought him the night before, news that the famous Transcontinental Bridge which had once spanned the mighty Mississippi River was now gone, blasted to bits by some unimaginable mishap at the secretive X Project in Iowa. He looked eastward, past the silent Diesel, his gaze following the track across the nondescript desert stretching beyond his ability to see. He shook his head; the *Meteor* had originally set out for New York City, but even the waypoint of Chicago was now unattainable. Eddie and the *Meteor* were left to fend for themselves.

A rumble from his stomach interrupted his reverie, but he gave it no further thought. He knew there was no food on board; diner service on all Transcontinental trains had been "temporarily suspended" months ago; in fact, he had personally relayed the order suspending service. Still, while there may be no food, he knew there would be plenty of potable water in the lavatory holding tanks of the sleeper and day coaches. He might starve, but he certainly wouldn't die of thirst. Looking again at the living smorgasbord still eying him warily from behind the safety of the train's wheels, he considered that perhaps he wouldn't starve either.

Suddenly aware of his thirst, Eddie turned his back on thoughts of unreachable destinations and climbed aboard the sleeper car, ignoring the scuttling of creatures scrambling at his approach. Heat poured out of the sleeper's door as he opened it, almost a physical wall pressing hot against his sweaty clothes. Entering the sweltering car, he walked down the corridor to the porter's cubbyhole, opened an access panel, and pulled a dipstick from the main water holding tank. The expertly-calibrated, scored stick indicated that almost ninety gallons remained. He nodded with satisfaction. After replacing the dipstick and conscientiously closing the access panel, he walked further down the hot corridor to the first lavatory, entered it, and turned on the faucet over the sink. Driven by the immutable force of gravity, lukewarm water splashed cheerfully into the bottom of the basin, down the drain, and onto the trackbed below. Eddie pulled a paper cup from its dispenser alongside the sink and felt no guilt as he drank heavily. Ninety gallons would last him for many weeks, maybe months; and there was likely even more water in the day coaches. He knew his bigger problem would be food.

Rather than filling the void in his stomach, drinking so much water made him more acutely aware of the lack of solid food. Inevitably, he found his thoughts returning to the creatures outside. How could he go about catching one? Skinning one? Cooking one? The realization suddenly came to him that he didn't even have a penknife, let alone any matches to build a fire. What would he do? It appeared he was about to learn, or perhaps die trying.

Searching the entire train, he could find neither a knife nor anything else with a sharp edge. He did, however, discover some watery ice cubes in a refrigerator that was softly humming on fading battery power in an elegantly-paneled recess aboard the observation car. But the best and only weapons he could locate were a screwdriver and a rusted hammer; he wondered how he would be able to get close enough to any animal to be able to use either of them effectively.

Eddie knew it would be no use, but also knew he had to try. He constructed a crude, screwdriver-tipped spear out of a broom handle and some hemp twine he found on board, but it quickly became obvious that he lacked the hunting skills necessary to use it capably; none of his thrusts came anywhere close to his prey. They would always maintain a respectful distance, whiskers twitching, sitting in the shade of the train, easily scurrying out of the path of his ineffectual lunges. Frustrated, he would throw his homemade weapon aside, only to pick it up a short while later to try his hand once again. But the end result always remained the same, and his hunger mounted.

As the desert day wore on, Eddie took occasional breaks from his fruitless hunting to tinker equally in vain with the dead Diesel. In his long career with Transcontinental, he had learned much about Diesels. He put that knowledge to use by making up lengthy lists of items to check, proceeded to check every single thing on his list, then check them all again. But for all his experience, checking, and lists, he could not discover the reason for the engine's untimely demise. It simply would not start.

Frustrated, Eddie plopped into the engineer's seat; it creaked geriatrically under the sudden weight. He sat immobile for several minutes when something in front of the train caught his eye. Through the windshield, ahead he could see a prairie dog standing upright in the middle of the track, the sun glinting off its copper-colored fur. Several of its species gathered fearlessly behind it. The lead prairie dog eyed Eddie dispassionately, nose twitching slightly, its tiny arms protruding at ease from its copper pelage. Eddie watched the critter's tiny whiskers with an almost morbid interest before finally tearing his gaze away. *No!* he cried silently. *We can't let it go! Not the Meteor!* Angrily, he turned his attention back to the task at hand with a renewed vigor, as if the prairie dog's very existence was an affront to him, driving him on. But the inspiration proved to be a hollow promise; the motor that could save his life persisted in remaining silent.

Come evening, it became impossible for him to ignore the hunger pangs which wracked him. He felt miserable. When the cold of the winter desert night started him shivering, he retired to a sleeper compartment and the shelter of worn, woolen blankets. Remembering how his day had begun in the oven of the Diesel's cab, he left both the cabin's window and its door open to the night air. Pulling the covers tightly about his neck, his hunger, fatigue, and frustration quickly drove him into a fitful sleep.

## CHAPTER 2 – I LEFT MY HEART IN SAN FRANCISCO

Ma cried.

*So many dead!* she thought, crying. *So many more were dying, and all for what?* she asked herself. *For what?*

Ma and the Buddhist adherents of her "Party of the People" were hurriedly regrouping on the north side of the Golden Gate Bridge. They had recently been routed from their stronghold in the Transcontinental terminal in San Francisco, driven northward, and finally from the besieged city itself. Worst of all, their main force lay south of the city. They had been cut off.

*So many comrades abandoned along the way*, she cried to herself. *So many dead!* The tears poured down her dirt-streaked face and showed no signs of slowing. She was at a loss to explain how things had reached such a deadly stage. What had started as an innocent fling with Asian mysticism and Oriental asceticism had somehow ended up as a full-scale religious war engulfing the entire West Coast. *They were the ones who started it*, she told herself, *those fanatics and some First Commandment or other!*

After weeks of fierce factional fighting, the religious movement known as Back For God now controlled the entire city, plus most of California between the ocean and the Sierras, from San Francisco halfway to Big Sur; and the territory they controlled was still expanding. Though no strategist herself, her top lieutenant maintained that their isolated band of followers should be able to make an effective defensive stand here at the northern terminus of the Golden Gate. And if things turned sour yet again, he figured they could always blow up the bridge—assuming their men had enough time to finish planting the explosive charges.

She thought of her son, Kip, and her already-voluminous flow of tears actually increased. Kip had died only a few months earlier, killed in a train accident caused by the failure of the famous Transcontinental Tunnel in Colorado. It was that disaster which had somehow catapulted her to the forefront of the nation's leadership, an unexpected legacy inadvertently bestowed upon her by the untimely demise of her bureaucrat son. But all she had wanted to do with her newfound celebrity was bring good things to the greatest number, only good. The sound of small arms fire from across the bridge reached her ears. *Only good? Only the good die young!* she quoted bitterly to herself as she pushed back a damp lock of her grey hair. She turned to look back across the bridge at the smoldering, smoky city. The fires appeared to be growing.

"All for what?" she wailed out loud this time, then sighed heavily at the naked despair reflected in her words. She turned to her top lieutenant who was crouched next to her, reloading a large-caliber weapon.

He looked up at her, not taking her question as rhetorical. "For what? Because we're all godless heathens, that's why!" he replied with his characteristic theatrical sarcasm. His four-year hitch in the Army a decade ago had left him with a modicum of military skills, but had also solidified and reinforced a sharp, cynical outlook on life. "Behold!" he mocked, waving a sweeping hand toward the burning city. "The holy ones are merely fulfilling their divine duty to wipe us off the face of the mortal world!"

Ma wiped tears from her face with a dirty sleeve. *And they're doing a good job of it!* she thought to herself. She had only wanted to help, but now she found herself marked for death. Looking back across the bridge to the lost city, out loud she quoted to herself, "'What makes a person so poisonously righteous that they'd think less of anyone who just disagreed?'"

Her lieutenant gave a short snort of derision. "Who is John Galt?"

Turning away from his dark mood, Ma gaped as a flare burst into bright flame high above the Golden Gate. At first she could not help but admire its brilliant beauty, but terror suddenly stopped her admiration cold. For the flare had been a signal, and now she could see a teeming mob beginning its charge across the bridge toward them, many wearing identical red robes adorned with a fist-sized orange flame embroidered over the left breast, the emblem of the acolyte soldier in the army of Back For God.

"To Mount Tam!" she screamed to her followers. "Quickly! Regroup on Mount Tam!" She turned to run with the rest, but only to halt immediately. Ahead of them, coming from the north, she saw a second host of red-robed figures.

"Flanked!" cried her lieutenant.

A startled Ma turned quickly to look at him quizzically, an offended look on her face. Not knowing what the word meant, she was not entirely sure she had heard him correctly. But it no longer mattered. The first of the red robes from the north were almost upon them, driving them into the arms of the red robes rising from the south.

*What makes a person so poisonously righteous...,*" she thought one last time as the red tides swept over them.

## Chapter 3 – We Just Disagree

Dwight smiled wearily.

It had been not only a busy February day at the airfield in the Gulch, but also a memorable one. The morning had seen the triumphant return of the strikers who had accomplished the daring rescue of the Worker from the hands of the looters, and the entire valley was nothing short of jubilant.

The fleet of rescuers had returned from the State's Science Institute with the Worker shortly after dawn, and while that meant a day for the liberators to celebrate, for Dwight it meant work. He was the valley's airfield attendant—in addition to his careers as aircraft manufacturer and hog farmer—and as such, it was his responsibility to see to the dozens of airplanes that had to be hangared, and those without galtmotors refueled. It took a great deal of effort, more time consuming than it was difficult, and the sheer volume of busywork made his day pass quickly. But he didn't mind at all; he thoroughly enjoyed the responsibilities of his profession; besides, he was no fan of jubilant celebrations, no matter how warranted. The superlative performance of his duties was all the celebration of life he had ever desired or needed.

Although it was still light out, the winter sun had already set behind the snow-covered mountain peaks that surrounded the Colorado valley. He sat at his desk in the quarter of the airfield's administration building which had not been given over to temporary housing, humming to himself as he updated the last of the maintenance logs of the airplanes for which he was responsible. Of course, there were dozens of logs, one per airplane; more busywork.

When his task was finally completed and the last of the logs returned to its niche above his desk, he was more than ready to head home for dinner; but much to his surprise, the airfield radio burst into life.

"Atlantis tower, Atlantis tower, this is Wandering Premise. Request clearance for landing. Over."

Dwight grinned like a kid on Christmas morning. "Owen?" he asked himself in excited disbelief. Still grinning, he picked up the microphone, keyed his transmitter and replied, "Atlantis tower here. Owen! Is that you? Over."

"Is there another premise that wanders?" he kidded. "Of course it's me, Dwight! Over."

"Man, but it's good to hear your voice! With the outside world taking its final nose dive, we feared the worst! Over."

"Come on, Dwight; you know I'm harder to kill than that. Over."

Dwight paused a moment; something was tickling the edges of his awareness. "What's wrong with your radio? Your voice sounds odd. Over."

"A long story, Dwight. I may be hard to kill, but the slings and arrows of outrageous fortune sometimes score upon this too, too solid flesh," he misquoted. "Over."

"If you insist," he replied jokingly, the smile obvious in his voice. "I'm looking forward to hearing all about it." With practiced ease, he shifted to a professional, no-nonsense tone of voice. "Wandering Premise this is Atlantis tower. You are cleared to land. Winds are from the northwest at twenty-four knots with gusts to forty, so keep an eye out. Over."

"Roger that; cleared to land, twenty-four knots from the northwest pushing forty. Over and out."

"Roger. Over and out."

Dwight stood at the window of his office watching with a professional eye as Owen swung his airplane around to the eastern end of the airstrip to avoid the worst of the winds. Although Dwight could not discern any noticeable visual effect from his vantage point on the ground, he knew that Owen had momentarily keyed off the ray screen that floated over the valley.

That screen was one of the many inventions created by the men of the Gulch. It protected them from prying eyes by ensuring that anyone flying overhead would see only the refracted image of giant boulders, not the sprawling enclave of the men of the mind. Not that there were many prying eyes flitting about the skies in these dark days; even so, the screen was kept active and in place, just in case. But the ray screen wasn't merely an optical illusion meant to fool the uninitiated; it possessed another, more dangerous property as well; for any unwary pilot who attempted to physically penetrate it would find themselves momentarily blinded and the circuits of their airplane scrambled. The only person to ever successfully navigate that particular hazard was Dagny, the Vice-President of Operations for Transcontinental Railroad. Although she had survived the attempt, she happened to flatten one of Dwight's brand-new monoplanes in the process. The unfortunate aircraft had been stationed at an emergency landing field owned by Friendship Airlines, not far from the Gulch, to be used as a ferry aircraft by residents of the valley. Through an unbelievable coincidence, Dagny had chanced upon the airplane, rented it from someone who had absolutely no authority over it, then used it to literally crash the gate into the strikers' valley.

Dwight smiled and shook his head at the memory. Dagny was some woman, that was sure. She had just returned to the valley that morning, a part of the victorious fleet that had rescued the Worker. Dwight was overjoyed to hear that she had finally decided to come home to the valley for good.

Still smiling, he donned his fleece jacket, covering up the brightly-colored cowboy shirt he liked to wear, and headed outside to greet Owen. He stood hatless in the cold breeze on the shoveled walkway, ignoring the two long rows of olive-drab Army tents that stretched alongside the hangar and the campfires that blazed among them. He watched as Owen's airplane touched down expertly and rolled along the airstrip, shedding speed. Reaching the far end of the runway, the aircraft swung around onto the plowed taxiway which would bring it back to where Dwight stood. Smiling, he waited eagerly as the aircraft approached.

A loud, brief screeching of tires behind him took Dwight by surprise. His head snapped around and his jaw dropped in disbelief. There, rolling along his runway was a second airplane, a twin-engine sightseeing model, it's elongated canopy consisting entirely of segmented panes of glass. Both of its motors were shut down, which explained why he hadn't heard it approach until its tires had scuffed the tarmac. The strange airplane rolled to a halt a little beyond the administration building, almost even with where Dwight stood. The aircraft was large enough to seat several people, but it appeared that only the pilot was on board. The intruder sat on the runway and did not immediately emerge from his aircraft.

Owen's airplane was closing in on the administration building, the impressive drone of its oversized propeller increasing in pitch and volume as it approached. It stopped between Dwight and the runway, blocking somewhat his view of the intruder. The engine fell silent, and the door impatiently swung open. Grinning from ear to ear, Owen disembarked and strode briskly in Dwight's direction.

"Hey, Dwight!" he called out, but he received no reply. Owen's smile faltered and his step slowed in confusion. It appeared to him that Dwight was looking right through him; but as he came closer, he realized that Dwight wasn't so much looking through him as he was looking past him. He turned his head around to see what was so captivating, and his jaw fell open in shocked surprise, for there on the runway was the very airplane he had left behind that morning in Wisconsin. The two men stared as the front portion of the canopy popped open, and a familiar face was revealed.

"Hello-o-o-o-o, O-o-o-o-owen!" called a deep bass voice. He stood on his seat and leapt with gusto directly from the cabin onto the runway, landing on both feet simultaneously, his bending knees absorbing the shock. He immediately headed in their direction, sporting a big, friendly grin.

Dwight turned his head slightly to face Owen. "You *know* this guy?"

He closed his still-gaping mouth and answered without even a glance toward Dwight. "I saved his life yesterday," he admitted.

"Outrageous fortune indeed! You should have let me know you were bringing company in behind you, if only for safety's sake." His eyes darted skywards out of professional habit, then returned to Owen, a quizzical expression on his face. "Why didn't you leave the ray screen turned off for him? Looks like you killed his motors."

"I didn't know he was following me," he replied flatly, still staring at the approaching intruder.

"What? He tailed you here?"

"Apparently."

"From where?"

"Wisconsin." He finally turned to face his questioner. "Madison, Wisconsin. He told me he was heading back to the State's Science Institute. I guess he didn't."

"He was heading *where?*" he cried incredulously. Too many successive shocks were shaking Dwight.

"The State's Science Institute in New Hampshire. He works as a pilot for the Institute's top co-ordinator, Dr. Floyd."

Dwight was thoroughly flabbergasted, and it showed plainly on his face. He took a deep breath and tried to hold his voice steady. "Am I to understand that one of Dr. Floyd's men—the same Dr. Floyd who kidnapped and tortured the Worker!—followed you *here?*"

Owen sighed. "That about sums it up."

Dwight nervously licked his lips; he had no weapon handy. He glanced at the approaching pilot, then back to Owen. "Are we in danger, do you think?"

"Danger? No, I don't think so." Recalling the animated discussions he and the pilot had had the night before regarding Directive 289-10, he predicted, "But it could get interesting."

An obvious fact finally penetrated Dwight's confused consciousness. "What's wrong with your voice? Why is it so deep?"

He smiled. "The slings and arrows of the X Project."

"The X Project? You mean the looters' killer sound ray machine?" Agitated, he ran his fingers through his hair like a comb. "Didn't that blow up a few days ago?" Clearly, he was still having trouble keeping up.

"I told you it was a long story."

But there was no chance to tell it just then, for the pilot strode up to the two waiting men. "Hello, Owen. Sorry I dropped in unannounced, but I had second thoughts about continuing my employment with Dr. Floyd."

Owen smiled mockingly. "Did you ask the Unificating Board for permission to quit? No man can be hired, fired, or change jobs without their permission, remember. Directive 289-10 was very clear about the sweeping powers granted to the Board—a Directive you said you approved of, as I recall. Last night you called it 'a victory for us common folks.'"

The pilot shrugged. "Maybe I'm having second thoughts about that as well." Dismissing the subject, he looked around appreciatively. "What is this place?"

"'Home.'"

"Nice view," he opined as he gazed at the snow-covered panorama surrounding them. "Look at those mountains!" Returning his attention to the two men standing in front of him, he stated the obvious. "I seem to be having engine troubles again. Can I impose upon you gentlemen to help me move my airplane off of the runway?"

Dwight's addled wits finally caught up with events. "What are you doing here?" he demanded angrily.

The pilot appraised him in turn with a touch of disdain on his face. "In case you hadn't heard, the United States of America died yesterday. I saw for myself the lights of New York City go out. Didn't you hear the news?"

Dwight refused to be diverted. "Yes, yes. Everybody knows all about that. About time, too. But that doesn't answer my question."

"Well, where else was I to go?" he retorted testily, then continued in a calmer voice. "So I figured I'd impose upon Captain Owen and his friends for a little charity in these hard times."

Dwight burst into loud guffaws. "Brother, have *you* come to the wrong place!"

The pilot misunderstood Dwight's logic. "What, does Captain Owen have no friends here?"

Dwight and Owen exchanged glances, then Dwight chuckled. "Check your premises and guess again."

The pilot put on airs and replied, in his best fake British accent, "Which premises could you possibly mean?" His unusually-deep voice added depth to his dramatics.

"All of them, it would seem." He looked away from the pilot to the stalled airplane. "Never mind; no time for all this gay banter. Right now, we have to get your airplane off that runway. I'm not expecting anyone else tonight, but with the world crumbling the way it is, you never know."

The pilot smiled. "I see you *do* understand why I'm here." Neither listener deigned to reply as they began walking the short distance to the disabled airplane. After a few paces, the pilot spoke again. "Once we get my girl out of your way, I could sure use some liquid refreshment. Is it far to the nearest taproom?"

Dwight laughed. "Yes, it is. I believe the nearest one is in Denver."

The pilot halted. "Denver?" he exclaimed.

"Could be Provo or Albuquerque," came the offhanded reply as he kept walking. "I'd have to check a map before I could say for sure."

"Probably not Provo," mumbled Owen, suppressing a smile.

The pilot shook his head and started walking again. "No taproom!" He glanced heavenward and asked rhetorically, "*What* have I gotten myself into?"

"The real world. Deal with it."

\* \* \*

The three men took seats.

Dwight had led them into his office in the airfield's administration building—at least the one corner of it that hadn't been given over to temporary lodging—to discuss their next moves. Domestic noises drifted out from behind the artificial and inadequate barriers of file cabinets, mobile corkboards, and old cotton sheets that walled off Dwight's corner of the expansive room. Smells of cooking filled the air, an olfactory amalgam of numerous, radically-differing dishes underpinned by the tang of stale cigarette smoke. A large Franklin stove dominated the middle of the room, hence one corner of their immediate space, but it sat cold. Nevertheless, the room was quite comfortable despite the wintry chill outside.

"It's been a long day," the pilot needlessly observed. "I shouldn't be staying overly long. Is there a hotel nearby?"

Once again, Owen and Dwight exchanged glances knowingly. "No," they replied simultaneously.

"Maybe Provo," Owen suggested quietly, a hint of a smile in his deep voice.

"What?"

"Nothing."

Seconds passed before Dwight took up an answer. "No, there are no hotels here, per se. People tend to stay with the people who invited them in."

The pilot turned to face Owen.

"Don't look at me! I didn't invite you!"

"I can pay my own way, sir," the pilot interjected proudly. The two men looked at him, as at the boast of a beggar, then exchanged knowing glances again. The pilot looked on, perplexed.

"You'll have to," asserted Dwight. "And speaking of which, you already owe me a landing fee. Do you plan on paying your own way there, too?"

"Depends," he replied cautiously, sensing it to be a trick question. "How much is it?"

"Three cents," Dwight pronounced solemnly.

"Three cents?" He was stunned. The price was far too low.

"Three cents."

He looked at Dwight blankly for a brief moment, then scowled. "All right. What's the catch?"

Dwight smiled. "In gold."

The pilot did not react. After a brief moment, "I see," was all he said. The silence that followed lasted a long time: no one wanted to be next to speak. Voices came to them from over the barriers: a man and wife discussing his day at work; half a conversation being held via telephone; the rhythmic sounds of a concerto serving as an undercurrent to the audioscape. The comparative silence extended itself.

Finally, the pilot spoke. "Well, since I'm the one who needs food and shelter, let me ask again: where can I spend the night?"

"I don't know," Owen responded quickly.

"Me neither," Dwight chimed in.

"Well, *someone's* got to help me!"

From across a wall, a woman's voice replied to her husband's unrelated question: "Must we?" she asked petulantly. Her question hung immobile in the air.

13

"What did you do to my airplane?" demanded the pilot, shifting the subject. "How did you shoot me down?"

"Ray screen," Dwight replied offhandedly. The brief explanation was the least he could do, and he did it.

"What kind of ray screen?"

His two listeners exchanged knowing glances once again.

"Knock that off," he huffed. He folded his arms defensively. "I don't give a damn anyhow." He paused, then asked again. "Tell me: where do I spend the night?"

Both men looked away.

The silence dragged on.

Finally, Owen looked back and offered, "In your airplane?"

"But I'll freeze!"

"Nobody asked you to follow me here," he pointed out needlessly.

The pilot snorted a sharp, short breath and fell back in his chair, deflated. He looked first from one man then to the other. "I don't get it," he finally declared, tossing his hands in the air and letting them fall with a dual slap onto his knees. "Here I am, a man in need, and you guys play games!"

Yet again, the other two men exchanged their knowing look.

"Stop that!" yelled the pilot.

"Stop that yelling!" came the quick reply from over one of the barriers. All three sets of eyes turned toward the unexpected intrusion; but only two sets were accompanied by a smile.

The pilot folded his arms again and looked away, none too happy. "So what's the deal?" he finally hissed, his deep voice theatrically low.

"You want to tell him?" Owen suggested to Dwight.

"Me? It was you he was following!"

Owen shrugged.

Dwight took a deep breath, glancing sidelong at the pilot. "All right, I'll tell him." Turning to the pilot, he plunged into his narrative, "Okay, here's how it is... Have you ever heard of the Worker?"

The pilot's only reply was a sardonic glare; and the tableau held for several seconds. Owen looked from one man to the other and decided it simpler if he offered Dwight a brief summary. "He's the pilot who flew the Worker up to the State's Science Institute the other day," explained Owen. "And that was the airplane." He jerked a thumb over his shoulder in the general direction of the hangar.

The pilot smiled grimly and said nothing, arms still folded.

Dwight's eyebrows went up in surprise; he stared at Owen for several seconds, then turned back to face the pilot. "Well, I guess someone had to be the one to do it." He took a deep breath before continuing. "You may have flown him up there, but he's escaped; he's back here now. This is the Worker's home. We call it the Gulch."

The pilot did not act surprised, but Owen did. "He's back! When did he get here?"

"Just this morning. Francisco led a raiding party on the State's Science Institute the day before yesterday. And Dagny's come home to stay, too. Lots of changes in the week you've been gone."

The pilot listened to their exchange knowingly. "So this is the Worker's place. I figured you were headed to one of those enclaves he talked about on the radio," he confided, looking at Owen. "But I didn't suspect this particular one was the Worker's home turf." He chuckled, then added, "No wonder it doesn't have a taproom!"

Dwight hesitated uncertainly. "Huh? Why do you say that?"

The pilot shrugged. "I heard his big speech on the radio a few months ago. Seems to me that the Worker is the sort of man who doesn't know how to have a good time. No sense of humor, either." After a moment, he added derisively, "And it looks like the same goes for you, too, pal."

Dwight held his temper and proffered a meaningful response instead. "Those of us who live here conduct our lives according to the philosophy the Worker taught us, and every person who stays here must first take his striker's oath. Believe it or not, there *are* some of us here who do drink, but not to the point of—"

"Striker's oath?" interjected the pilot.

Dwight drew himself up proudly. "Yes, the striker's oath." He continued without being prompted. "'I swear, by my life and my love of it, that I will never live for the sake of another man, nor ask another man to live for mine.'" His eyes shone as he recited the words, as if it were a sacred prayer. "The striker's oath. We, the men of the mind, are on strike against your society, and have been for the last twelve years. It is because of our strike that your society has collapsed. About time, too!" Some of his anger edged out into the open, and reflected itself in his strident tone of voice. "You, who did not know how to value us, have now learned the hard way about the value we once provided. You, who once persecuted us, now have only yourselves to persecute. You—"

"Yeah, yeah, I get the idea," the pilot interrupted again. "So this Johnnie-boy had it up to here—" His hand flew in a chopping motion over the top of his head. "—with men like me, so him and the rest of you Johnnies went and hid up here in the mountains. Save your breath—I heard the big speech, I tell you."

"—who took everything we had to offer, yet gave us no value in return," he continued steadily, as if the pilot had not spoken, "are now denied any value that we might give. We, the men of the mind, are on strike."

"Okay, okay, I get it. No taproom, no hotel, no fun, no help. Thanks for nothing, pal!"

Dwight pushed his chair backwards in disgust, its legs scraping loudly across the wooden floor. His mouth opened in preparation to speak, but Owen stretched his arm out in front of Dwight to restrain him, although not touching him. "Why should we help you?" Owen cut in, speaking to the pilot.

"Because I'm in need, I tell you!" the pilot cried aloud without pause. "Because I'm thousands of miles from home with no place else to go!" He lurched to his feet, his chair clattering over onto the floor behind him. Through clenched teeth, he ended angrily, "Because you killed my goddamn *airplane!*"

"Knock it off!" came the cry from over the impromptu wall. Again, no one apologized.

"It's just your coils," Owen explained calmly, his deep voice low. "No big deal to replace them."

"And just how am I supposed to *pay* for it?" He pulled a billfold out of his pocket and jerkily extracted a wad of useless cash. Grey dust puffed out from within the wallet as he did so, leaving a small cloud hanging immobile in the air. He brandished the bills and thrust them at the man. "With this?" A few dusty notes fluttered to the floor trailing a thin scarf of dust that first hung twisting in the air, then slowly began to drift downward. No one bothered to retrieve the fallen cash, not even the pilot. "Or are you going to break your oh-so-holy oath and just *give* the parts to me?" The pilot stood red-faced with emotion, and he strained to keep his deep voice low.

Having weathered the pilot's anger the night before, Owen knew to take a different tack. "No I'm not going to buy the coils for you," he replied, his voice still calm. "But you are."

"Me? What do you mean? I have no gold! Owning gold's illegal, in case you forgot."

"Not here, it isn't. And I'll bet you must've brought something with you that someone here will find worth exchanging for some gold. What do you think I was doing in Madison? There are all sorts of things we need here in the valley that can only be found Outside. Surely you have something of value with you?"

"I wish! I used up all my whiskey against the damned dust." He gestured angrily to the curtain of grey dust still hanging in mid-air in front of him. "What else do I have left? Nothing!"

"The dust?" inquired Dwight, his confusion surfacing again.

"The du-u-u-u-ust," intoned the pilot in a deep bass voice, gesturing again at the slowly-settling swirl "Where do you think we got this manly voice?"

"He's right," explained Owen, his own voice reflecting the same bass note. "It's because of the X Project—I started to tell you when we were outside. The dust kicked up from its disintegration clogged our vocal chords and changed the tonal qualities of our voices. Much more and it would have killed us." He paused a second, his eyes downcast. "It did kill Wesley and Gene."

"Wesley and Eugene? Two of the top leaders of the nation?" Dwight shrugged. "Can't say as I really care."

"*Formerly* two of the top leaders," corrected the pilot, interrupting. "We left their bodies in Wisconsin—and almost left mine there, too! Captain Owen here saved my life. Saved me from the dust, he did. And I used up all my whiskey following his advice."

Dwight reassumed his confused countenance and looked up at the pilot. "How does whiskey enter into it?"

"I soaked a shirttail with it," the pilot explained, "then used it as a mask to filter out the dust." He turned and held Owen's eye. "Saved my life," he repeated, then turned back to face Dwight and sigh mightily. "So now I have my life, but nothing left to sell." He bent over to right his fallen chair.

"No other cargo?"

The pilot reclaimed his seat with a plop. "Nope."

"No supplies?"

"Nope," he repeated. "And probably not even enough fuel to get me the hell out of here."

The silence dragged on for several seconds, then Dwight slowly suggested, "Well, you do have an airplane..."

The pilot's eyes darted to meet his. "Yes. I do," he enunciated very clearly. "And she's mine," he stated slowly and firmly.

"But she's worth some fraction of her weight in gold, isn't she?"

The pilot held Dwight's gaze, but did not reply. The seconds passed.

"And you say you don't have enough fuel to get yourself out of here?"

Still, the pilot did not answer.

"Doesn't sound like you have a whole lot of options."

Silence.

"I'd be willing to buy her from you."

No reply.

"We don't have any airplanes here like yours, and I could sure use one." As an afterthought, he added, "Not that I couldn't outfit it with a galtmotor and it wouldn't need hardly a thimbleful of fuel ever again."

The pilot retained his stony silence, but tilted his head at Dwight's final remark. The silence stretched on, until finally he replied. "A galtmotor?"

"Yep. They run on atmospheric electricity."

"I think I heard the Worker mention that on the radio." He paused again reflectively. "You'd put one of those in my girl?" He tossed his head lightly in the direction of the hangar.

Dwight nodded once in silence.

"But you'd own her."

Another nod.

"Would you sell her back to me afterwards?"

Dwight shrugged.

The pilot assimilated the situation as the silent seconds dragged into mute minutes. *Well, there's no going back for me—and no place else to go, either! Like it or not, this'll have to be my home for now.* The pilot shrugged mentally as he reached a decision. *Might as well roll with it...* Finally, aloud he broached the forbidden subject. "How much will you give me for her," he stammered. It was not easy for him.

"That depends. Tell me everything about her; I want to know cycles, hours, gross weight, load, seating, the works."

For the next several minutes, the pilot divulged the intimate secrets of his lady to the man he had just met. As he spoke, Dwight compiled a detailed inventory of her salient features. When finally the inventory was complete, he contemplated his notes for a moment, jotted some calculations, then named his price.

A stunned Owen faced Dwight open-mouthed. "How much did you say?" He turned to the pilot. "I'll give you twice that!"

Dwight held both hands in front of him, palms forward, fingers splayed. "Okay, Okay! Let me think for a minute." He glowered briefly at Owen, then turned to make some additional calculations alongside his previous ones. He stared at the ceiling for a moment, then named a new price many times higher than his previous offer, one with two more zeroes to the left of the decimal point. This time, Owen remained silent.

The pilot considered the answer for a moment, then leaned over to whisper in Owen's ear. "Is that enough?"

Owen sat back while folding his arms, and nodded knowingly. "More than enough," he rumbled.

The pilot remained silent for the better part of a minute; his two chance companions allowed him the time to think. Finally, he spoke again, his eyes narrowing. "Enough for me to buy a house?"

"Oh, yes," affirmed Dwight. "Enough and then some. Even in our current tight housing market." He extended his hand to indicate the file cabinets and cork boards that surrounded them.

The pilot looked to Owen again. "And that's a good price?"

"I could use a big airplane like that myself, but he'd have to offer a whole lot less before I'd consider bidding on it. At that price, it's out of my league."

The pilot sighed; they continued to wait him out. "Like you say, it doesn't seem like I have much of a choice. Can't fly her out, can't stay without selling her." He fell silent again, then repeated, "You sure it's a good price?"

Owen merely nodded.

"And it's a lot?" he persisted.

"You'll be relatively well off, compared to other new residents—including me, and I've been living here for a while."

The pilot sighed again. Clearly, he did not want to sell, but he saw just as clearly that he had no other option. But on the positive side, the cache of gold would give him the resources he'd need to establish himself in the valley. Coming to a decision, he stretched out a hand to Dwight. "Okay. Deal."

The two men shook hands.

"Great. Let me write you out a warehouse receipt for the gold." He fetched a small card from a niche above his desk and made some notations upon it before handing it to the pilot. "You can cash it at the Midas Bank in town..." He turned to Owen, concern appearing on his face. "Speaking of which, did you hear about Midas?"

"Did I hear what about Midas?"

Dwight's face fell, then his head dropped. Obviously, the news was not good. Looking up, he took a deep breath. "Let me tell you later, okay?"

"Hey, are you telling me this check's no good?" interrupted the pilot, gesturing angrily with the card. "What are you trying to pull here?"

"There's nothing wrong with the check," Dwight explained slowly, his words like drops of lead, his emotions barely held in check.

The pilot carefully examined the warehouse receipt, then pocketed it within his flight jacket. "I'll be back if it bounces," he warned.

"It won't."

None of the men said anything for a brief while, then the pilot spoke again. "So now that I have some credit in this God-forsaken valley, let me ask again: where can I spend the night?"

Pulling himself back together again, Dwight took a deep breath, then glanced around his quadrant of the administration building, finally suggesting, "Why not stay right here? Just for tonight, though," he added quickly. "It'll only cost you another nickel."

The pilot snorted in mock laughter, his mouth pinched shut. "Does that come with room service?" he added sarcastically in his best British accent, playing the faux-Sassenach.

Dwight ignored the jab and simply answered, "It's another dime a day for meals, if you want them. At least that's what I hear the going rate is. But you'll have to negotiate that with the fishwife, not me. And I couldn't say if she'd want to take on any more customers right now. Remember, we're pretty strained these days. You'll have to ask her."

"Does she sell whiskey?"

"No," Dwight replied flatly. "And now that I think about it, I don't think she'd deal with a scab in any case." As an afterthought, he added, "Nobody here distills whiskey, not that I know of. Our pianist composer Richard does lay down a pretty respectable wine, though."

The pilot snorted again. "It sounds like what this place needs is a decent taproom!" He paused at the thought, then his eyes went wide. "Yeah... A taproom! And I know just the guy who can do it!" He smiled in reflection. *And maybe I can meet a sweet little thing here in this God-forsaken Gulch...*

"Good luck finding a decent place to build it. As I said, housing is tight, and you're not the only unexpected guest here in town, not by a long shot."

The pilot continued smiling, wrapped in his own thoughts and only half listening. *Yep, the future is definitely looking up.*

# Chapter 4 – Peace Train

The Transcontinental terminal manager fled.

The fire in San Francisco had quickly spread from the beleaguered Transcontinental terminal to the surrounding structures. No one was battling the blaze; they were too busy battling each other. No fireman could be convinced to take a stand in the No Man's Land that once was the busiest district in the City By The Bay, nor could anyone make a full, comprehensive list of the factions who had fought over the terminal, nor why. Granted, the terminal manager possessed a signed truce with three of those factions, painstakingly negotiated only a few days earlier by some Transcontinental executive from New York, a serious-looking fellow named Mr. Eddie. The negotiations had ultimately succeeded and trains began to move once more, but it quickly became a hollow victory, for the peace treaties now sat in the terminal manager's office—on the second floor of the blazing building. *Fittingly enough*, he thought bitterly.

The terminal manager found himself a man without a job and a manager without a terminal, trudging south along Transcontinental's coastal tracks, destination unknown. Behind him billowed huge clouds of black smoke that rose from the burning city, a sky-blotting fog that slowly drifted inland. Hundreds of other refugees from the fighting paraded on the tracks all around him, all heading south. Some wore overstuffed backpacks, a few others pushed overloaded wheelbarrows, but the vast majority had only the clothes on their backs. Like him, they had no destination in mind, no plan of action to follow, their only goal to put distance between themselves and the fighting.

As he walked, the terminal manager took stock of his location. Steep mountains rose dramatically on his left; to his right, only scrub growth and a rocky cliff separated the railroad from the ocean. Mountain and cliff conspired together to funnel the two tracks onto a narrow, slowly-winding shelf squeezed precariously between land and sea. In other circumstances, he would have considered the scenery stupendous; but today, he could muster no appreciation for such luxuries.

Ahead, he could see that a large crowd had gathered on the tracks, the gradual flow of refugees from the north slowly adding to its size. Upon reaching the blob of humanity, he halted momentarily, then elbowed and shouldered his way through the mob until he saw the reason for the holdup: two parallel coils of barbed wire, six feet apart, stretched across both tracks and off into the underbrush on either side of the right of way. Behind the barriers were armed men, some carrying only shotguns or pistols, but others perched in menacing machine gun emplacements surrounded by sandbags. Some wore uniforms he did not recognize; the others were dressed in random fashion. A large sign in the middle of the track loudly proclaimed in large, crudely-painted capitals, "YOU CANNOT PASS," signed semi-legibly in the name of some organization whose name he could not quite make out, "The Party of something-or-other." The terminal manager scanned the armed tableau before him with a sinking feeling of terror in the pit of his stomach. Up until now, walking had given him the illusion of activity, of purpose, an impression that he was actually accomplishing something. But all of his illusions vanished in the cold reality of the impenetrable barrier blocking his way. "Now what do we do?" he pled wide-eyed to the unshaven stranger standing next to him. It was almost a cry.

The stranger was facing south, a far look in his eye, also seeing the track, the barbed wire, and the armed men. Looking closer, the terminal manager noticed that the man was weeping.

Without turning, the stranger chuckled through his tears. "Who is John Galt?"

A growing disturbance to their left cut off any response that the terminal manager might have made. A sudden growl rose from the crowd; some of the voices were shouting curses. Without further preamble, the mob surged toward the barrier, leaping over the barbed wire; first one coil, then the next. The nearest of the patrolling soldiers were caught off guard and quickly fell to the hands of the advancing horde. Gunfire erupted from both sides, then the loud staccato rattle of one of the machine guns split the air, followed by another, then a third. The front line of the mob's advance fell before the hail of bullets like a row of rag dolls. Another wave fell, then a third as the machine guns played back and forth across the face of the surging mob. At first the mayhem was only directed at the vanguard of the advance, but now the people standing around the terminal manager started to fall as well. In panic, he dropped to his belly, hearing the bullets whizzing over his head. Bodies of the dead and dying fell across him, pinning him down, while the incredible cacophony of the machine guns crashed in his ears.

At last, when it seemed as if the noise would go on forever, the gunfire abruptly halted. He heard moaning from the wounded around him, and felt the warm blood of some unfortunate as it trickled over his own head and stained his hair. Bloodied though he was, the terminal manager was unhurt. He lifted his head as far as he could, given the weight of the bodies on top of him. Scanning the scene, it appeared to the terminal manager that almost the entire mob had been mowed down. He could see a precious few in the distance who had survived, running back north as if their lives depended on it; which, of course, they did.

He lay there for a moment pinned to the ground, stunned by the sudden mass death that had swept the crowd. As he lay there, he heard the loud report of an occasional single gunshot, perhaps once every second or two. In terror, he suddenly saw its source. Soldiers were climbing through the downed mob putting the wounded out of their misery, one by one.

With all his might, he tried pushing away the dead bodies that lay on top of him, grunting loudly at the effort. But he stopped, petrified by terror at the sight of a soldier suddenly standing over him, gun in hand.

"Poor fellow," commiserated the soldier, seeing the blood all over the terminal manager's face. "Let me help..."

# Section II – The First Days

Late February, 1953

# Chapter 1 – On the Road Again

Eddie awoke.

His second day stranded in the desert was much like the first, and just as fruitless. No matter what he tried, the Diesel could not be started. He would often pause from his tinkering to gaze distantly up and down the sandy road that paralleled the track, looking for some new passerby, maybe even another train. But he knew the idea of a rescue train to be a pipe dream; this was the track of the Pacific Southern, and they no longer operated any trains at all in this part of the country. The only train to use this rail these days was the *Meteor*. The setting sun found him as alone as he was at its dawn, and no less hungry.

One after another, the days quickly slipped past for Eddie, not only because of the time of the year, but also because he kept himself busy with the single-mindedness of someone who buries himself in his work. Yet all his best efforts bore no fruit. The only metric that marked the passing of his days was an increasing weakness from a lack of food. He had begun to nap more, and it became increasingly difficult for him to concentrate; his eyes would no longer focus readily, and the strength in his fingers had diminished so badly that he sometimes found it to be a challenge merely holding onto a cup of water. He had originally considered keeping a tally of the disappearing days, but had immediately dismissed the thought—it smacked too much of being a prisoner in a cell, and unnecessary as well. But now he wished he had; due to his fading faculties he had completely lost track.

One morning like all the others, he awoke around dawn, thirsty and undeniably weak with hunger. He tossed off the blankets, feeling the cool morning air that nevertheless held the promise of yet another scorcher to come. As he sat on the edge of the bed, his head swam wildly for a moment; but he steadied himself, and was eventually able to muster sufficient strength and composure to complete the mundane task of dressing. Emerging from the sleeper car into the morning shade, in his weakness he staggered, stumbled down the last two steps, slipped, and fell face first into the desert sand alongside the track. Several rabbits bolted from the scene, startled by his sudden, dramatic entrance, but a copper-colored prairie dog stood its ground, studying Eddie impassively. Weakly, Eddie lifted his head, spitting some of the gritty sand from his mouth in the direction of the indifferent animal. Ignoring its pitiless scrutiny, he scanned the terrain slowly, first left, then right. Nothing had changed from the days before; there was nothing *to* change. He laid his head back down, the shaded sand coarse and cool against his cheek.

"If I don't do something besides just sitting here, I'm going to be a dead man really soon," he observed out loud, his voice raspy from disuse. Raising his head slightly to face his animal audience, he repeated more loudly, "A sitting dead man!" partly in defiance, partly out of light-headedness. The prairie dog watched his soliloquy in silence, without pity and without mercy, as Eddie laid his face once again against the cool sand. "A dead man...," he trailed off.

In one swift motion, Eddie suddenly snapped to a kneeling position on all fours, fatigue forgotten, his head turned sharply toward the engine, his eyes wide. "*A sitting dead man!*" he yelled hoarsely, startling the pitiless prairie dog into a quick retreat to the safety of the shadow of the *Meteor*.

Eddie scrambled to his feet, fell, scrambled up again, fell again, finally settling on a half-crawl, half stumble, through the shifting sands as he hastened to reach the silent Diesel. Starting from all fours, he clambered weakly up the ladder into the cab, and fell panting to the floor, pausing briefly to catch his breath and muster his meager strength. He rolled over, sat up on crossed legs, and grabbed the shabby, scruffy seat cushion of the engineer's chair that floated in front of his face, not to pull himself up, but rather to pull it down. He rocked the chair back and forth on its hollow cylindrical pedestal, back and forth, the rivets at its base losing more and more of their iron grip on the floor with every push. Then with one final effort, he crashed his shoulder against the side of the chair, the force ripping it from the last of its moorings. Together, Eddie and the chair toppled to the cab floor. Shaking slightly from the effort, his weakened hands groped around inside the chair's pedestal. With a quick jerk, he pulled two copper wires out of the seat's cushion, wires which led to the dead man's switch installed inside the worn padding of the cushion.

The dead man's switch was a crucial safety device installed inside the engineer's chair on every Transcontinental train engine, its purpose to verify the presence of a living man sitting at the controls. If the engineer should slump unconscious in his seat, the dead man's switch would take note of the shift in weight and automatically halt the train. But this particular switch had served the safety of its masters for far too many miles; it was beyond repair and had become the enemy of motion rather than its ally.

Despite his hunger-induced handicaps, Eddie swiftly and expertly stripped the lead wires and shorted the circuit around the defective switch. The vital surgery completed, he pushed the broken seat out of his way. Kneeling now in front of the Diesel's control panel, like some acolyte performing a ritual at a religious shrine, Eddie quickly performed the start-up sequence for the Diesel one more time, flipping switches, turning knobs, and pulling levers in a deliberate, planned sequence. When the crucial moment came to engage the motor generators, he paused, took a deep breath, and punched the final button. Without hesitation, and with the banality of the ordinary, the Diesel roared to life. The black smoke of half-combusted hydrocarbons darkened the air around the Diesel, the acrid odor of exhaust permeating the cab. Startled animals fled in all directions from the unexpectedly-reincarnated behemoth.

A triumphant Eddie righted the engineer's seat as best could be done, and sat himself properly in front of the controls to complete the start-up procedure. As the Diesel warmed up, its black exhaust rapidly transitioned to grey, then thinned to transparency. The quivering needles on the gauges and the green lights winking across the control panel confirmed that all was well inside the engine. The *Meteor* was coming to life once again, and with more than enough fuel to reach distant Denver.

*Denver?* Eddie peered ahead down the track, out to the East, trying to force his hunger-befuddled mind to think. The *Meteor* sat about halfway between San Francisco and Denver, with the tallest mountains still to come. It was somewhere around the end of February, or perhaps early March—at least he *thought* it might be!—and he knew from past experience that the mountain passes would all be choked with snow—and an avalanche could always bring more without warning. Even if he made it as far as Denver, beyond that was the ultimate barrier of the destroyed Transcontinental Bridge barring his path into Illinois. *No*, he thought. *Not Denver. It'll have to be back to San Francisco for now.* He knew the risk it would pose, running the train in reverse safely, but he was confident he would be up to the challenge.

For the first time in weeks, he began to feel he was once again in control of his world.

He rose to his feet easily now. Starting the Diesel had started something inside Eddie as well. He found he was able to walk steadily through the train as he readied each car for departure. As he passed through the mail car, a glimpse of motion caught his eye. In one corner huddled a stowaway: the copper-haired prairie dog. Eddie froze, his eyes casting about for a weapon, any weapon. No luck; except for a few meager sacks of mail, the car was empty.

Without thinking, without waiting, working purely on instinct, Eddie immediately lunged at the frightened, cornered creature. So lightning quick was his blitz that he had both hands wrapped firmly around its fuzzy body before its tiny brain even registered that Eddie had started moving. Without stopping or even thinking about the fact that he had caught his prey, his hands continued their flight and twisted in their arc to hurl his prize at a nearby wall, crushing the animal's skull on impact. It fell to the floor with a tiny thump, lifeless and defeated. Surprised at himself, Eddie gawked wide-eyed at the dead creature lying on the floor. The entire episode had taken less than two seconds; and not many minutes later, with the help of a porter's hotplate, Eddie sat down to a welcome breakfast of boiled prairie dog. No Thanksgiving feast ever tasted so good, he told himself as he gnawed at the animal's gamy carcass.

Rejuvenated physically by the meal and mentally by the restarting of the engine, Eddie turned to completing the task of preparing the train for departure. Before long all was ready, and with a final loud hiss, the train's air brakes released their iron grip on the steel rails. The *Meteor* was ready to roll once more.

Hanging precariously out of the engineer's window to improve his view toward the rear of the train, he set the Diesel's throttle into a slow reverse. The *Meteor* began to move in response to Eddie's hand, slowly at first, then a little faster. The sharp *clack-clack* of the wheels could be heard clearly over the droning of the Diesel, a percussive reminder of the train's steady progress; and as the sun rose high over the Arizona desert, the *Meteor* began to retrace its path back toward San Francisco, the scenario resembling more a movie played in reverse than the stark reality it was; and for the first time since the *Meteor* stalled so many uncounted days ago, Eddie felt somewhat at peace.

It was exactly what he was looking for, and he saw it coming long before the train reached it—a passing track branching off to parallel the main line. He parked the *Meteor* next to the siding, uncoupled the engine, then used the passing track to move the engine to the other end of the train, re-coupling it behind the curved railing of the observation car. Moments later he was underway once again. With the Diesel now in the lead, albeit still facing backwards, forward visibility improved to the point where Eddie was able to safely increase his speed to the fastest that the worn track of the Pacific Southern would allow. The pace of his journey to San Francisco increased markedly.

The hours passed without incident. As he traversed the miles back toward California, Eddie caught sight of no other travelers on the parallel road or at the infrequent grade crossings, neither automobile nor pedestrian, not even a covered wagon. He realized what an incredible coincidence it must have been to run across that wagon train on the night the *Meteor* died, the sort of coincidence that only happened in second-rate, dime store novels and pathetic, contemptible movies.

The backward Diesel continued its return journey uneventfully. Sunset found the *Meteor* crossing the state line from Arizona back into Nevada. With the coming of darkness Eddie was surprised to see the electric glow of Las Vegas far ahead on the horizon. His own plight had led him to believe that the entire world had perished, not merely one safety switch. *Of course they'd have electricity*, he told himself. *Boulder Dam isn't about to crumble!* He recalled how Las Vegas was a growing tourist town, and the image of its bright lights and the thought of him having a feast in one of their fine restaurants brought a physical pain to his long-empty stomach. He briefly considered halting the Diesel for the night and resting, but immediately dismissed the idea. He felt himself the master of his fate, the captain of not only his own soul but also that of the *Meteor*, and the exhilarating feeling imparted to him a near-superhuman strength. He resolved to continue his journey until he reached at least Las Vegas, or for however long his abused physical body could hold out.

* * *

Eddie held out.

Dawn found the *Meteor* at the junction where the track of the Pacific Southern met that of Transcontinental. The train wheels clattered noisily over the track switch which marked the connection between the two railroads, the noise of the wheels diminishing noticeably once they shifted to the higher-quality Transcontinental rail. It felt good to be back on his own track again, its Miracle Metal rails glittering greenish-blue in the early morning sun, and Eddie's spirits lifted even more.

As the day wore on, he began to encounter signs of civilized life: pedestrians, horse traffic, even an occasional automobile. Most people just watched dully as the inverted train passed them by. Some folks waved to him, friendly-like, and Eddie waved back. Others tried desperately to flag him down, but Eddie ignored them. At one point, gunfire erupted from a lonely freight station as he passed it, shattering several windows in one of the day coaches, and pocking its metal flank. *A nice welcome back*, he thought bitterly, recalling his recent visit to San Francisco and the widespread fighting there. Idly, he wondered how the new terminal manager there was getting along, and if the truce he had brokered for the Transcontinental terminal in San Francisco still held. But with all the factions that were warring in California, he seriously doubted that it did.

It was late afternoon when Eddie finally pulled the *Meteor* into Transcontinental's Las Vegas station, and brought the train to a halt. The tracks and platforms of the station were deserted; he was not surprised, as few trains ran nowadays. As he performed the motions to idle the powerful motor, Eddie caught sight of a stout stationmaster tottering in the direction of the backward Diesel, eyes wide and wondering. The very ordinary sight of the stationmaster wearing the livery of a Transcontinental trainman instilled an illusion of normalcy in Eddie; but the illusion lasted for only a brief moment. With an almost physical impact, all the recent events descended upon his consciousness in a massive heap: his hunger, his personal brush with death, the *Meteor's* near-demise, and the deserted Las Vegas station reminding him of the wider, continuing collapse of Transcontinental Railroad, of the nation, and the entire world. It was suddenly too much for any one man to bear. With a loud moan, Eddie simply crumbled and broke, like an overstressed dam, his body sinking slowly against the Diesel's control panel, his head falling across his arm.

25

Adding one final, impersonal insult, with the slumping of Eddie's shoulders, the unsecured base of the uprooted engineer's chair suddenly slid sideways across the smooth metal surface of the floor, shifting swiftly and dumping him unceremoniously onto the hard, unyielding metal floor of the Diesel's cab.

It was there that the stationmaster found him, sobbing softly.

## CHAPTER 2 – GOING UP THE COUNTRY

Gwen daydreamed.

It was difficult not to; the picture postcard perfect scenery of the towering Colorado Rockies could not help but to set her thoughts free to wander. Admiring the encircling crown of glistening granite peaks encouraged a mellow mood, especially now that evening was coming on. Golden sunlight from the westering sun set the rocky, snow-capped crown ablaze with a fierce orange light, a fire made brighter still when contrasted against the clear blue sky above and the steel-blue shadow of the snowy slopes below.

The calm beauty of the winter mountain scene did much to calm her concerns, of which she had many. Chief among them was the news of the devastating explosion at the X Project and the death of New York City along with the subsequent collapse of the rest of the eastern seaboard, a heartbreaking bulletin whose details had reached the valley only that morning. The unimaginable horror of the twin disasters had left her numb. Conservative estimates for the number of dead ran into the thousands, with a virtual certainty that millions would die in the coming weeks—*millions!*— and there was no way for anyone to stop it. Her troubled eyes misted over at the unthinkable thought as she sat looking out her bedroom window, numbed by the sheer scope of the unfolding disaster, a sedentary receptor rather than an active participant, the mind-boggling magnitude of the tragedy repeatedly wrenching her attention away from her daydreaming. Not for the first time, she shook her head; the triumphant rescue of the Worker seemed insignificant in the face of the looming doom that was swallowing the world beyond the borders of the valley. But at least his rescue was something, a solitary bright spot in these darkest of times.

Thinking of the world Outside and watching the fiery coloration of the mountain scene, Gwen was reminded of a similar ruddy radiance that was once the hallmark of the blast furnaces at the mills of the Hank Steel Company in Pennsylvania. There she had worked there as Mr. Hank's executive secretary, back in the days before he had brought her and her father here to the valley. The recollection triggered a fleeting nostalgic smile across her face, vanishing before it could take noticeable shape; for with the disintegration of the world beyond the glowing orange crown, she knew for certain that *that* world was now gone forever—the mills, her home, her friends and family, all of it—and that she would never return to it. The only future left to her now remained within the tight confines of this mountain redoubt known colloquially as the Gulch.

With a pang, she recalled once again how even *that* future could also soon be denied her—no; how it *would* be denied her! Again she shook her head. Even though she had only been living here in the valley a mere four months, she felt that this had always been her home; and irrespective of the widespread disasters unfolding Outside, her mind automatically shied away from any thought of leaving. But leave it she must, her and her father both, unless they could find a way to accept the striker's inflexible moral code which underpinned the valley's existence. But after months of total immersion in their unique philosophy, she was far from certain that she was up to the challenge of honestly accepting it and taking the striker's oath; but on the other hand, she was more than certain that her father was not.

Gwen sighed almost imperceptibly. Thoughts of her father and her prior life in Pennsylvania invariably brought to mind that fateful November day four months ago when Mr. Hank had first brought the two of them here to the Gulch. The intervening months had not dimmed the memory one bit. Unbidden, she could recall the events surrounding her arrival in the valley as clearly as if they had happened only yesterday...

* * *

Gwen remembered.

She had arrived at work early that day, much earlier than her usual practice. The late autumn sun was barely peering over the flat eastern horizon of Pennsylvania, giving the sprawling structures of Hank Steel an orange tinge, as if the cranes and mills were bathed in a bright rust. She had made it a point to arrive for work earlier than usual, for a bloody battle had been fought there the day before; and now that the thugs' attack on the mills had been successfully beaten back, it was time to turn her imperturbable attention to their reconstruction. *It's going to be a very busy morning*, she told herself, *and there's much to be done before Mr. Hank arrives.* Without flourish or emotion, she finished typing the third of three contracts she was preparing for his signature, and stacked it neatly to one side along with the other two.

Despite her outward calm efficiency, the unprecedented events of the previous day troubled her greatly. She could not understand why the mills had been attacked, the once-ubiquitous bureaucrat they called "the Nursemaid" murdered, or Mr. Hank himself knocked unconscious by some mindless thug. If their furnace foreman, Frankie Addams, hadn't taken charge of the mills' defense, she was certain the battle would have been lost. *And such a good looking fellow!* she noted with an invisible smile.

Humming happily to herself without realizing the reason why, she organized Mr. Hank's calendar for the day, scheduled several appointments over the telephone, and sorted through some mail she hadn't had the chance to attack the day before. She was about to contact their preferred contractors to obtain estimates for repairs to buildings and equipment damaged during the battle, when Mr. Hank walked in, an uncharacteristic smile on his usually-austere face. His bonhomie contrasted sharply with the clean, white bandage that graced one side of his scalp, a sorry souvenir of the skirmish the day before.

"Good morning, Gwen. When you have a moment, there's something important I'd like to discuss." He continued into his office without breaking stride, as if in a hurry—another action out of character for him—leaving the door open for her to follow.

She entered a moment later, her appointment book and the three contracts in hand, to find him sitting behind his expansive desk rummaging through its drawers one by one. A collection of odds and ends sat on the desktop in front of him: a thin stack of papers, his jade vase, several odd-shaped samples of metal, and other uncategorizable flotsam. He looked up at her entrance and smiled again.

From the look on his face, Gwen could tell that something fundamental had changed within him. He appeared younger, more relaxed,

27

as if a great weight had been lifted from his shoulders. Considering the mayhem at the mills the day before, his mood seemed completely incongruous and out of place.

He closed the last drawer and extended a hand in the direction of a chair, inviting her to have a seat. He rose deliberately from his own, walked around to stand in front of his desk, and leaned against it in an abnormally informal pose, legs crossed, again acting out of character.

Without preamble, the smile still on his face, he announced, "Gwen, I'm quitting."

Time stopped as the room swooned around her. She couldn't believe her ears. "Quitting?" was all she could finally manage to say.

"Yes, I'm quitting Hank Steel. I wanted you to be one of the first to know."

She did not move; *could* not move. The three contracts fell from her limp fingers, their pages scattering across the floor like autumn leaves. The appointment book followed two seconds later, hitting the carpeted floor with a muffled thump. Still in shock, she finally stammered, "When?"

"This morning. Right now, in fact. I just need to gather a few items here and from my apartment in Philadelphia, and then I'm leaving—and I do not expect I'll ever return."

Gwen sat speechless and stunned, not knowing what to say. Her typically-imperturbable mind was in turmoil.

"I'm only telling a few people: our doctor, the mills' superintendent Pete, the chief metallurgist, and chief engineer; but that's it. And you, of course."

"But where will you go, Mr. Hank? What will you do?"

He smiled more broadly. "Me? I'm going to run Hank Steel."

She looked at him askance, perplexed.

"Gwen, you're not going to believe this, but..."

In fine detail, Hank told her the truth about the Worker, his strike, and the secret stronghold in the Colorado Rockies where the men of the mind were patiently awaiting the collapse of the looter state before they would consider returning. He spoke of his plans to rebuild Hank Steel in the hidden valley under the protection of the Worker's moral code of life. She made no comment as she absorbed all he had to say.

Hank concluded his narrative. "I'm going to join the strikers, Gwen. I'm through supporting my own destroyers in a game where they're setting the rules, a game I cannot win."

Gwen did not speak for some time; he continued to lean against his desk as he waited her out. Without a doubt it was a lot to assimilate, and he knew from personal experience that the process could not be rushed.

Presently he saw a look of decision on her face, a tightening of the jaw that he recognized from long association. She stared up into his eyes with a hard resolve.

"Take me with you!"

Hank smiled again. "I was hoping you'd say that." He stood up straight. "The ferry flight will be taking off from Philadelphia this evening around dusk. Before that, you'll have to pack whatever you want to take along. I'll pick you up on my way to the airfield around three this afternoon. Then we can—"

"Wait!" she interrupted, the life fading from her eyes. "I just remembered—I... I can't go."

"What do you mean? Why not?"

"It's my father. He's getting on in years, and there's no one else to take care of him if I go. I can't leave him behind, Mr. Hank."

Without pausing, he suggested, "Then why don't you bring him along?"

"Oh, could I?" she asked, the hope plain in her voice.

"I don't know how big the airplane is," he confessed. "But Francisco did say there'd be plenty of room for all of us plus our luggage. I'd imagine another passenger shouldn't be a problem. And Pete is bringing his wife; so sure, I'd say you could bring your father."

Gwen brightened. "I'm so glad! And it'll be the first time I've ever flown, too." At a sudden thought her face clouded again. "But what will happen to your mills?"

"My mills?" Hank turned to gaze out of his office window, likely for the last time, at the vast expanse of cranes, furnaces, and structures that together comprised the Pennsylvania home of Hank Steel. He looked on silently for a moment, head held high, as if he were paying final homage to them and to their lost purpose, then turned back to face her. She could plainly read the emotion on his face: it was love.

"My mills?" he repeated, the smile returning. "They're to be redeemed."

\* \* \*

Tires squealed.

Gwen and her father involuntarily shifted sideways in the back seat of the sleek Lawrence limousine as Hank swung the automobile to a brisk halt alongside the gaping door of a private hangar at the Philadelphia airfield. Bright lights illuminated a large airplane within as several men in coveralls readied it for the long flight West. Next to the airplane were Hank's co-workers who had agreed to accompany him, busily loading luggage through a hatch under one of the wings. One of the coveralled mechanics approached the automobile as Hank and his passengers were getting out.

"Good evening, Mr. Hank. We're completing our preflight checkout and we should be ready to leave in about half an hour, maybe a little sooner."

"Good. By the way, we have an additional passenger we're taking with us. Will there be enough room for him?"

"Sure! And we can always come back for stragglers if we have to. But I'm sure we can carry the whole group of you and your gear in one trip. The airplane's motor is definitely up to the task," he added with a wink.

"A galtmotor?"

The mechanic smiled broadly, nodding. "You bet!"

"Let me get our baggage aboard." He turned away and began transferring luggage from the limousine to a stack alongside the airplane's underwing hatch. As he worked, Gwen's father shuffled over to the aircraft, cane in hand.

"Joining the strikers, gramps?" the mechanic asked conversationally, the bulk of his attention concentrated on his preflight checklist.

"What do you mean? I'm not on any strike. My striking days are over; I'm retired now. My Gwen has to take care of me, so I have to go along with her."

The mechanic looked up from his checklist. "What do you mean? You're not a striker?"

"What strike?"

"The Worker's strike. Didn't you take the oath?"

"What oath?"

"The striker's oath: that you'll never live your life for another man, or ask another to live for yours."

"Nope, sonny, I haven't, and I don't know that I'd care to take it, either. Like I said, I need my Gwen to look after me. I'm not as young as I used to be, you know, so Gwen and I are living for each other these days. Besides, I wouldn't take that oath anyway. I'm a union man over forty years, and proud of it! We union brothers stick together, no matter what. That's what makes us strong!"

"Then I can't take you," the mechanic asserted flatly, both hands and the checklist falling to his side. "Everyone in the valley has to take the striker's oath."

Gwen came up to stand beside her father, a suitcase in either hand. She had heard a little of their conversation, enough to comprehend its tone, but not enough to understand its content. "What's the problem, Dad?"

"He says I can't go!" he answered angrily, stabbing his cane in the direction of the mechanic, his thrusts coming dangerously close.

"That's right," confirmed the mechanic, pointedly ignoring the old man's menacing fencing. "I can't take scabs into the valley. If he hasn't taken the oath, he can't go."

"What oath?" she inquired, setting down the heavy suitcases.

"What, another scab?" the mechanic asked mockingly, eyeing her suspiciously.

"What oath?" she repeated firmly, hands on her hips, her voice revealing a sharp, no nonsense edge she usually reserved for unwanted salesmen. Hank walked past unnoticing, a suitcase in each hand, heading for the airplane. Gwen stopped him with a hand on his arm.

"Mr. Hank, he says we can't go with you."

"What? Why not?" he asked bewildered, setting his own suitcases down.

Again, the mechanic explained the need for the oath.

"But they're my co-workers from the mill," Hank informed him. "They're with me."

"That's as may be, but they still have to take the oath before they can get into the valley."

Turning to Hank, hands still on her hips, Gwen firmly informed him, "I'm not taking any oath to abandon my father!"

"And I'm not disowning my union buddies!" her father added with finality.

Hank looked from Gwen to her father to his co-workers as they stowed gear under the wing, then turned back to the mechanic. "None of them have taken the oath," he admitted. "Francisco didn't mention that they were required to do so."

"Well, they are."

The seconds ticked by. Finally, Hank asked, "Can we get in touch with Francisco?"

"It sounds like we'd better," the mechanic suggested grimly. "But I'm not sure what good it might do you."

The two men entered a small office alongside the hangar, and Hank waited as the mechanic placed several long-distance calls in an attempt to reach Francisco; but in the end, it was the erstwhile pirate Ragnar who answered the telephone. The two men exchanged greetings, then the mechanic provided a pocket outline of the situation, ending with his mantra: "If they don't take the oath, they can't get into the valley."

The mechanic listened for a moment, then answered, "Eight, counting Mr. Hank. They were his co-workers at Hank Steel." He looked outside the office window to Gwen and her father, still standing by the airplane. "And one of them wants to bring her father, an old union man." He listened for a moment longer, his face gradually revealing that he was none too pleased with what he heard. "Conferences and seminars, you say? How would that help?" After a moment he took a deep breath, almost theatrically. "Okay, but I hope you know what you're doing," he concluded with resigned finality. "And those seminars better be good!" He brusquely hung up the telephone.

The mechanic faced Hank, none too happy. "Apparently I was laboring under a false premise. What I said is technically correct: everyone who remains in the valley must take the striker's oath. But I hear we're allowing newcomers to come in to the valley, then let them correct their error of knowledge in their own good time." He scowled and glanced down at the telephone. "From what Ragnar tells me, we started tolerating scabs last June when Miss Dagny crashed her airplane there." He shook his head, clearly not liking the idea of scabs in the valley. "And it didn't end with her— Ragnar also tells me that Francisco brought in a whole cadre of his co-workers from Francisco Copper a few months ago, none of whom had taken the oath. Then a lot of other people started bringing in their families and friends, and not all of them had taken the oath, either. So you're not alone, I'm told. You can bring your scab co-workers along—" His face twisted in disapproval. "—for now. Not that I approve of it, mind you!"

Relieved that there would be no immediate complications, Hank replied, "I'm glad to hear they'll have their chance. It would be a lot more difficult for me to resurrect Hank Steel without help from the people I've worked with all these years."

The mechanic wagged a sharp finger in Hank's face. "But remember: they'll have to take the oath soon! Nobody can remain in the valley who hasn't taken the striker's oath!" Without another word, he abruptly spun away and stalked out the office door. After a few seconds' pause, Hank followed to face Gwen's waiting, concerned scrutiny and her father's belligerent stance.

"There's no problem," Hank told them. "We all go. It'll all work out in the end."

The mechanic stood to one side, his arms folded defensively across his chest. "We'll see," he grumbled, unconvinced.

Gwen's father glared menacingly at the mechanic. "Union buster!" he hissed.

* * *

The hours passed.

It was mid-morning the next day when their airplane arrived at the Gulch in Colorado. They crossed the jagged crown of snow-covered mountains that towered over the valley, circling several times as they shed altitude. At first, only jumbled boulders were visible on the forbidding terrain below, but suddenly the entire valley burst into plain view as they penetrated the ray screen that hid it from prying eyes.

The scene that opened below them was too much to take in all at once. One side of the wide, circular valley exhibited all the signs of an industrial neighborhood, replete with factories, smokestacks, and storage yards randomly grouped together. At the other end of the valley lay a broad spread of farmlands, their expansive, rolling pastures enclosed in thin lines of wooden fencing. Midway between farms and factories lay a collection of tiny homes and other buildings situated at irregular intervals over the rises and hollows of the valley floor spread out below them, too dispersed to be called a town, yet too concentrated to be considered anything else. Thin wisps of smoke curled from a few of their chimneys, with snow-dusted pines interspersed throughout. From their aerial vantage, the valley more resembled a miniature Christmas display in a department store window than an actual town; the only touch missing was a toy train. The first snows had already covered the ground in a light blanket; a half-frozen lake near the center of the valley gleamed with weak sunlight reflecting off its ice, but the roads and walkways that meandered among the hillocks remained clear. As the airplane banked, the newcomers could see a large golden object apparently floating over the center of the town, glinting brightly in the late autumn sun. As they came closer, they discerned the icon for what it was: a giant golden dollar sign.

The airplane swooped around and leveled off for landing, the last of its altitude dissipating as it approached the leading edge of the runway. With a light bounce that belied the airplane's great mass, they touched down on the valley's concrete airstrip and rolled to a halt. Ground crews ran from a nearby hangar to meet them.

"Dagny never mentioned how pretty this place is," Hank mused out loud. "Look at those mountains!"

"It's like a toy village," breathed Gwen, somewhat in awe.

"Looks cold to me!" her father broke in, his face in a scowl.

His daughter smiled at him and squeezed his hand affectionately. "Oh, Dad!"

A chill breeze floated into the airplane's cabin as the door was opened to the wintry mountain air. The travelers quickly gathered up their belongings and stepped outside into the cold. An olive-skinned man in a long leather coat stood outside the door helping each of the travelers step down onto the plowed airstrip.

"Welcome to the Gulch!" he announced, a Spanish accent unmistakable in his voice. "Welcome, welcome! Let's get you out of the wind and inside where it's warm." He indicated the boxy one-story administration building next to the control tower. "Go on, go on! I'll be along in a moment." They hurried to comply, hastened by the cold.

Inside the expansive, one-room building, it was toasty warm. Desks and filing cabinets were arranged along the walls, and a fair-sized Franklin stove stood in the middle of the floor, its welcome warmth permeating the large, high-ceilinged room. A tinge of wood smoke scented the space surrounding the stove, sweetening the smell of the stale cigarette smoke that suffused the air. Pairs of tall, paned windows on each of the four walls presented a grand vista of the mountains that surrounded the valley, drenching the room with the brilliant morning sunlight. The travelers dropped their baggage near the door and instinctively gathered around the warmth of the stove.

"'Andrew Foundry, Colorado,'" commented the metallurgist, reading the raised letters on its side. "I wonder if it was made here in the valley or in the old abandoned foundry down along Transcontinental's Rio branch?"

"More likely made here," Hank weighed in. He examined it with a critical eye. "It's definitely high-quality work."

"That's for sure. Look at that fancy scrollwork in the corners," complimented the metallurgist. He continued to inspect the stove closely out of professional curiosity. A small clunk sounded from within the Franklin stove as a piece of coaling wood tumbled inside.

"A Franklin stove! Reminds me of when I was a kid." Gwen's father stretched his hands over the warm stovetop. "Hey, is there a union bug printed on that nameplate, sonny?"

"A what?"

"A union bug." He held up his cane and indicated a miniature, ornate seal on its side. "It shows that it was union made. I don't buy nothing without the union bug." He swung his cane to the floor, spiking it with a loud thud to drive home his point. "We union brothers stick together!"

The metallurgist examined one side of the stove, then another, his expert gaze searching for the telltale bug, but he saw nothing. Taking a step back, the raised scrollwork in all four corners of each side unexpectedly snapped into perspective. Close up each one resembled a scroll; but from further away, there was no mistaking it. It wasn't a scroll at all. It was the sign of the dollar.

"Hank!" a voice called from the doorway. Hank turned to see the slim figure of Francisco sporting a huge grin and a fur parka worn loosely, its hood thrown back. "Welcome to Atlantis!" he called. Hank grinned broadly.

"Atlantis?" groused Gwen's father. He gestured with his cane in the general direction of the airplane. "I thought the man said this was the Gulch."

The two men glanced briefly in his direction, but paid him no mind. Rather, Francisco quickly closed the distance between him and Hank, his hand outstretched. The scene was that of a father greeting the return of a prodigal son. They shook hands warmly for a brief moment, then embraced.

"Welcome home, Hank!" declared Francisco, now holding Hank at arm's length, the strong emotion plain in his voice. This moment was the culmination of many years' worth of effort; his greatest conquest had finally arrived.

At first Hank said nothing in return, but the look on his face said it all. "Thank you, Francisco," he finally managed.

After a pause, the two men turned their attention to the other travelers.

"Let me introduce you to my men," offered Hank. One by one, he presented his co-workers, giving their names and the position they held at Hank Steel. Lastly, he introduced his secretary Gwen and her father.

"Wait a minute! I know you!" exclaimed Gwen with a sudden start. "You're Frankie Addams, our furnace foreman!"

"At your service," replied Francisco, taking a graceful bow. "But here in the valley I prefer to be known by my family name: Francisco Domingo Carlos Andres Sebastian." Again he bowed, took her hand, and lightly kissed it. Gwen blushed fetchingly at the attention.

"Get your hands off my daughter!" interrupted her father, raising his cane in mock attack. "And quit trying to show off with all them fancy names!"

"Oh, Dad," Gwen demurred with a small smile. She looked at Francisco and shrugged. "My father is quite a nice person, once you get to know him."

"We'll have all the time in the world to get acquainted," Francisco assured her. Turning full toward her father, he added, "I look forward to the pleasure of getting to know you better, sir," again giving a short bow.

"We'll see," he muttered, reluctantly lowering his cane. "Just watch it with my Gwen." He glared at Francisco to underscore his words.

"Come on," Francisco replied to the group. "Let's get you folks settled."

\* \* \*

Francisco bowed.

"Welcome home!" he announced with a flourish as he held the front door of his log cabin open to the newcomers. The dwelling was a humble, two-story retreat, its weathered walls beaten in dark streaks by the tears of many rains that imparted an aura of its having been built in loneliness. He stood to one side as his guests passed under the worn, silver coat of arms of his ancestors hanging over the door. One by one they filed in: Hank, Gwen, then her father. A brief, but strong gust of chilly air swirled into the room before Francisco was able to close the stout door behind them, its icy embrace hastening their step. His guests and their luggage crowded into the undersized living room; they peered around self-consciously, standing almost elbow to elbow among the room's furniture.

"We've been experiencing something of a population boom recently," explained their host with a smile. "While your quarters here can best be labeled as Spartan, at least they'll make do until you've had a chance to find a more permanent home. And you won't find anyplace nearly as nice for the fifty cents a night that I'll be charging for the three of you."

Hank nodded; Gwen looked away; her father seemed not to have heard; he stared at nothing as he leaned on his cane.

Turning, Francisco escorted them to their rooms, and they found that he had neither exaggerated nor minimized; their lodging promised to be adequate, yet crowded. Hank and Gwen's father were to become roommates, sharing a double bed in one of Francisco's two spare bedrooms upstairs, while Gwen would take up residence in the other. The newcomers found they were not the only guests at Francisco's homestead: two of his co-workers from Francisco Copper had been using those guest rooms since their arrival in September, but would now be relegated to less comfortable hay mattresses on the floor of a cramped storage room off the kitchen. Together the six of them occupied all the volume in the house that could be secured behind a closed door. Only the kitchen and the pint-sized living room remained as public space, and only Francisco and Gwen would sleep alone.

If any of the new houseguests felt that they had not fared so well, they might take some cold comfort in knowing that Hank's co-workers fared far worse. For Hank's mill superintendent and his wife, home became one corner of the airstrip's administration building, where the desks and file cabinets were rearranged to form some semi-private living space that bordered on the Franklin stove. At the distant opposite end of the housing spectrum, the hospital doctor from Hank Steel found he fared much better than any of them: he was fortunate enough to join the medical practice of the eminent Dr. Thomas, which earned him a private apartment adjacent to the valley's modest hospital.

Similar crowding existed in residences and industrial concerns throughout the valley. As recently as summer, the amount of available living space was not even remotely considered to be an issue; everyone had a place to live, and only a few dozen new strikers had been expected to trickle in before winter. But that trickle quickly broadened into a brook after Francisco closed Francisco Copper in early September. For several weeks afterward, there was a steady stream of executives, mineralogists, engineers, superintendents, and other former employees who emigrated to the Gulch from the doomed outside world. Many brought their wives or husbands and even some young children as well, not wanting to be separated from their families. Predictably, the meager supply of available accommodations quickly dried up, leaving some of the Johnnies-come-lately to reside temporarily in a makeshift tent city near the valley's airstrip. At first, only a few canvas dwellings were required, but their number began to rise inexorably as the immigrants continued to arrive faster than new housing could be constructed. Before the end of September, communal tent kitchens and latrines had been established, and the new neighborhood near the airstrip resembled something more akin to the early days of the Wild West rather than a hearkening to the promised bright future. Fortunately, the September days were warm enough for the tent dwellers' comfort; but as autumn settled in, the mountain nights became increasingly chilly.

As the collapse of the outside world accelerated, the stream of newcomers swelled into a torrent, with new arrivals landing almost daily. Following Francisco's lead, some of the other valley residents began inviting like-minded fellow co-workers and family members to take refuge in the valley before the looters' game reached its inevitable, incipient end; and the tiny society strained beyond its limits to accommodate them all. But the worst was yet to come, for the torrent swelled into a deluge as the population of the valley doubled, then doubled again, and for the first time ever, the residents of the Gulch had to deal with a significant and growing cadre of the homeless unemployed.

Many entrepreneurs, both long-term residents and new immigrants alike, attempted to take advantage of the excess available labor and the boom in demand for housing by establishing themselves in the building trades. However, several barriers arose which thwarted their plans. The first obstacle was that most of the newcomers proved to be unemployable as construction workers, lacking the necessary skills sufficient to fill any position other than that of a lowly day laborer. Another impediment involved the onset of the heavy winter snows, which put many construction plans on hold. But even had the weather cooperated and a pool of skilled workers existed, the result would not have changed: the unexpected demand for housing had exhausted certain critical building supplies. As a result, the construction of new homes progressed sluggishly at best despite the demand, while the supply chain struggled mightily to catch up. To help meet that demand, importing became a boom business. Those residents who were proficient at flying took to the skies, ferrying in those items that were in the shortest supply. Sadly, there was an insufficient number of available pilots to relieve the pressure much, so the shortages persisted.

Aside from shelter and employment concerns, there were other problems in the Gulch that grew along with the population. One of the most notable was brought on by the residents of the valley themselves: inflation. For whenever the residents brought a new immigrant into the valley, they would offer them not only shelter, much as Francisco had done with his friends and co-workers, but would also grant them loans until the newcomers could become established in their chosen lines of business. More critically, a substantial number of the immigrants needed no such loans; they brought their own supply of precious metals, some bringing along quite a hoard. So it was no surprise to anyone that as the tide of refugees grew sharply, so did the amount of money in circulation. Inevitably, the combination of a sudden expansion of the money supply, the shortage of certain goods, and the influx of additional inhabitants placed a noticeable, asymmetrical strain on the valley's economy. Inflationary pressures coupled with the inexorable law of supply and demand began to push up dramatically the prices of everything: from food, to lumber, to industrial supplies, to clothing and more, while simultaneously depressing the value of the gold and silver coins which purchased them. While most people found themselves with ample gold in their pocket, they also found themselves unable to find at any price many of the commodities they needed; and when they could, the price was always higher than the time before.

It did not take long for some of the valley's industrial concerns to begin to feel the pinch, especially when it came to business loans. As the demand for capital continued to grow, the number of residents willing to back new or existing ventures continued to shrink, until Midas was the only person in the valley still loaning and investing; but even he began to exhibit an unusual caution as to how he allocated his wealth, so much so that some suspected the aging banker was considering retirement. It came as no surprise that interest rates began to rise on the rumor along with prices and inflation, feeding the cycle's growth.

In spite of any fiscal pressures on businesses or imbalances in the housing market, still more important was the impact that the higher demand had on consumables. Given that certain foodstuffs and common household items, such as light bulbs and cookware, were suddenly in short supply, most of the valley's merchants instituted rationing of purchases among the newcomers to better accommodate the needs of their existing customer base, and some began refusing to take on any new customers at all. Still, the pressure on the valley's economy grew. And grew.

But in the end, it wasn't food, shelter, or economics that caught up with the valley's residents; it was philosophy. With the figurative lowering of the drawbridge into the Gulch during America's final days, among the arrivals were a significant number of immigrants who had never heard, let alone taken, the striker's oath proudly carved in stone above the door of the powerplant of the Gulch. From the very start, some of the long-standing residents began to take loud exception to the flood of immigrants, not so much because of any shortages or overcrowding, but more so because of the rising number of scabs who had not yet taken the oath. But their protestations did not travel far; precedent had first been set by Dagny's unanticipated gate crashing the prior June, then expanded upon by Francisco bringing in so many of his co-workers in September. By November, scabs in the valley sporting an "error of knowledge" had become more of the rule rather than the exception, and still the population grew, producing a problematical philosophical predicament clamoring for a solution.

## CHAPTER 3 – A DAY IN THE LIFE

Hank lost no time.

He had been in the valley not one hour before he embarked on the task of rebuilding Hank Steel; and he fitted himself into the local economy with the ease of water pouring into a glass. Once he had dropped his baggage at

Francisco's house, his first action was to head straight to the Midas Bank; it wasn't a long walk, and he was there in a few moments.

When he entered the bank, he saw Midas himself standing behind the teller's window, intent upon some task; he moved his lips once in a while, as if reciting a memorized lesson. After a moment, Midas glanced up briefly, then lifted his stunned face, his expression ecstatic and wide eyed.

"Hank! You old dog!" He almost danced out from behind the teller's window, and quickly swallowed Hank in a bear hug embrace. "It's sure great to see you!" he exclaimed as he released the taller man. "How long has it been? What, twenty years since I gave you that loan to start Hank Steel? God, but the years went by quickly! How are you doing? Boy, they sure gave you hell Outside. I'm glad we've got you now. You didn't deserve a penny's worth of the trouble they handed you every day. And that battle at your mills the other day! We don't always get the news right away..." Midas prattled on excitedly.

Hank smiled as he listened; the old banker hadn't changed one iota in all those intervening years. His exuberance reminded Hank quite a lot of Francisco's energy, only less refined; more like Ellis, the oil tycoon. Thinking of Francisco made him realize how good it had been to see him again. With a start, he suddenly realized all the people he could expect to see again; not just Midas and Francisco, but also Ken the coal miner, Roger the electronics wizard, Lawrence the auto manufacturer, Ragnar the former pirate, and so many others he thought lost forever. *But I won't be seeing Dagny anytime soon!* With a conscious effort, Hank brought his attention back to the speaker, lest he miss some of his words.

"...and Francisco kept us up to date as best he could. But enough of my rambling. I assume you're here to claim your account."

"Yes, of course. I met Ragnar in Philadelphia back in May, and he told me all about it. Even left me a down payment..." Hank handed over a heavy, paper-wrapped bundle about the size of a carton of cigarettes. From long association, Midas recognized it from its heft; it was a bar of solid gold.

"And there's a hell of a lot more than this," the banker informed him with a broad smile, gesturing clumsily with the heavy bundle. He returned to his station behind the teller's window and leafed through some records. "Let's see here... Dwight... Ellsworth... Francisco... Howard... Hey, where the hell'd you go? Ah! Here you are: Hank." He retrieved two small passbooks from an envelope and handed one of them over. "This copy is yours."

Hank accepted the slim document, opened it, and scanned its pages. Listed in a neat hand were the amounts and dates of scores of deposits ranging back over the last dozen years. He flipped to the most recent entry and checked the account balance. His eyebrows shot up in an uncharacteristic gesture of surprise; the balance was staggering. Without otherwise moving a muscle, he lifted his astounded gaze to Midas, dropped it to consult the balance again, then unconsciously stepped back slightly in dumbfounded shock.

Again, Midas smiled broadly. "A big number, isn't it? All your income taxes for the last twelve years, as I'm sure Ragnar told you. Plus interest and minus storage fees, of course." He took the passbook from Hank's numbed fingers. "Let me record your latest deposit and you can have this back." He weighed the gold on a large, triple-beam balance, then recorded the supplement in each passbook as well as his daily deposits log.

"I imagine I'll be needing some spending money," Hank reminded him. "But I'm not quite sure how much."

"Certainly. I can help with that." Midas made another notation in the passbooks and in his log, counted out a pile of gold and silver coins, then slid them through the teller's window. "That should be enough to hold you over for now, until you can get a better feel for your normal needs." He handed over a small stack of forms, each about the size of an index card. "And here are some blank warehouse receipts in case you want to buy or sell anything big. You can use them to transfer gold from your account to anyone else's, or vice versa."

Recovering his normal calm, Hank accepted the papers and coins, placing them in his breast and pants pockets, respectively. "Good. This will be the seed money I need for the rebirth of Hank Steel. Now all I need is a place to build it."

"I can help you with that, too!" He turned as he spoke and opened a broad, flat drawer, producing a detailed map of the valley. "I've been holding onto this property with Hank Steel in mind." He stretched the map on a nearby desk and bent over it, a questing finger hovering in the air several inches above it. "Let's see..." The finger finally landed among a neat tracery of property lines, roads, and buildings. "This is the valley's industrial neighborhood, and here..." His finger sliced a vertical line, "...are the western mountains. This area..." His finger traced a circle between the two. "...is a broad, flat meadow that I believe would be an ideal location for your mills. The bedrock is deep enough that you'll have no problems with digging basements or burying plumbing, but close enough to the surface to give you the solid foundation your heavy work will need. And when you have to expand... See this second parcel of land, further north along the foot of the mountains? Right through this broad pass?" His finger slid up the mountains in the direction away from the existing settlement, then between the two whorls of contour lines that represented the pass, to a large, open area nestled in the northwest corner of the valley. "The second parcel is about the same size as the first, so there's enough room to double your operations whenever you're ready."

Hank nodded. "It looks good. What are your terms for the properties?"

Midas pointed to each parcel of land and named his prices and terms. "I'll sell you the first piece of land outright, and take a deposit to hold your claim on the second until you're ready for it, an option you can exercise anytime over the next six months. If you don't buy it before then, we'll need to renegotiate the price."

"All right. Can I get a look at the properties first?"

"Of course." Midas pulled out his pocket watch—a priceless heirloom, from the looks of it—and examined it briefly. "I close for lunch at noon, and it's almost that now." He pocketed the watch. "Do you have the time right now?"

"Yes. At the moment, there's nothing else more important that I could be doing."

"There are a lot of people in this valley who'd agree with that," opined Midas, more to himself than to Hank as he returned the map to its drawer.

"How is the supply of raw materials here?"

Midas closed the map drawer, but his hands still held onto its two, widely-spaced handles. He looked Hank in the eye. "The latest wave of immigrants is taking its toll—no offense intended. A lot of household items are in short stock, but Owen tells me he'll be heading back out on another one of his supply runs later this week. Just let him know what you need, and he'll take care of it."

"Household items?" Hank was confused. "I mean raw materials for my mills."

"Oh, sorry; I misunderstood. Copper you can get from Francisco, but if you want iron ore and limestone in any quantity, you'll have to prospect for it yourself, like Andrew does for his foundry. But that shouldn't be a big problem; I had some preliminary surveys made before I bought this valley, and they mention both limestone and iron ore. So I know it's out there, and I can give you some idea of where to start looking." He paused, then added. "There are a lot of other things you can find in those mountains, if one knows where to dig."

"Good. I'd be interested in mining the copper myself as well."

"Copper? *Copper?*" Gales of laughter came from Midas.

Again, Hank was confused. "What's so funny about copper?"

"Poor Francisco! The joke's on him! He's been trying for years to get you into this valley, and here you are on your first day—your first day!—talking about how you're going to become his competitor! What a hoot!"

Hank did not react to Midas' mirth; he replied in a serious tone, "I like to have control of my own raw materials, that's all. I haven't been able to do that since they passed that Equalization of Opportunities Bill. It forced me to sell off all of my enterprises except Hank Steel."

Midas wiped the tears from the corners of his eyes. "Have it your way." He took a deep breath before continuing. "I'll drive us to the new mills' site, but let me warn you that you'll have to rent a mule to check out those ore deposits. Once we get back, I'll introduce you to the man who can make arrangements for the mule." He grabbed his hat and coat, crossed the lobby and flipped the sign on the bank door to display, "Out to Lunch." He held the door open for Hank. "Okay, let's go."

For the next two hours, the two men tromped around the snow-dusted meadows that were destined to become the new home of Hank Steel. The pastoral scene was nothing short of gorgeous, with tall tan grasses protruding from a thin covering of snow, their seed-laden tops waving artfully in the light breeze. The broad, white-and-tan field was punctuated by the occasional impossibly-green coniferous tree, with the entire Eden backdropped in the near distance by the majestic, snow-capped Rockies that surrounded their corner of the valley. But in their mind's eye, the men saw none of Nature's beauty, but rather spoke only of the cranes, furnaces, railroad sidings, and laboratories that were to come. The time passed quickly and enjoyably.

When they finally returned to Midas' automobile, Hank summed up his evaluation. "You were right: the site is ideal, Midas. Not a lot of land to be cleared, and it even has flowing water. This will do fine; I'll buy it, both parcels, right now. Draw up the papers as soon as you can and let's get them signed."

"Fine."

"I'll get back to you regarding the mines after I've taken that mule ride."

"Okay. Let me know if there's anything else I can do to help."

"Of course." The men shook hands, then climbed back into Midas' automobile.

"By the way," Hank mentioned, "someone else I need to speak with right away is Andrew. Do you know where I might be able to find him?"

"Probably in his foundry, this time of day."

"Would you mind dropping me off on our way back?"

"Not at all." He turned and smiled at Hank, both hands on the wheel. "And I'll ask only a nickel for the ride, just because it's for you."

\* \* \*

Andrew grinned.

"Hank!" he cried, as he pulled off his massive asbestos gloves and set them next to the tabletop kiln he had been adjusting. He half ran across the foundry floor and met Hank before the man had a chance to close the door. "This is great seeing you again! Come on in! Welcome to the Gulch!" He extended a large, well-muscled hand in welcome.

Hank couldn't help but return the smile along with the handshake. "Thanks. It's good to finally be here, too. I'm looking forward to re-establishing Hank Steel as soon as I can."

Andrew grinned in mocking mischievousness. "What, a new competitor for me, perhaps?"

Hank did not think to return the grin. "In a few areas, perhaps," he mimicked unconsciously. "But I expect most of my work to focus on producing Miracle Metal and products made from it."

Andrew added a tilted head to his smile. "And what makes you think I won't be gearing up to work with Miracle Metal, too?" he teased. "What good is being in business if I don't offer the best product on the market?"

Hank remained serious, not noticing Andrew's playful tone. "I wouldn't go to too much expense yet, Andrew. Miracle Metal II is on the way, and you'd only have to re-tool. Wait'll you see it! I finished up the preliminary experiments just last month and found that I can raise the normal melting point for Miracle Metal a lot higher than the four thousand degrees it is now; it's only a question of how much higher. I still have some research to finish up first, but MM-II will be here before you know it."

"That's great!" laughed Andrew, thumping Hank on the shoulder. "Congratulations! I guess we'll have to merge our operations if I'm going to be able to make any money in this valley."

Again, Hank answered seriously. "Maybe someday, but not today. What I actually came to see you about is renting some space temporarily. I'd like to be able to use your foundry until my new mills are built. I'm sure there's a lot of pent-up demand for articles made of Miracle Metal, and I'd like to start meeting that demand as soon as I can."

"What exactly do you need?"

"Access to your facilities, tools, and equipment, plus enough working space for me and four of my co-workers from Hank Steel."

"Starting when?"

"Today?"

Andrew chuckled. "I should have guessed that. For how long?"

"However long it takes before the new mills are sufficiently finished that we can move our operations there. By late summer, I'm hoping."

"Okay. I should have enough extra capacity to accommodate that. Let me work up a quote for you. I guess you want that quote today, too?" he suggested with a smile.

Once more, Hank did not think to smile in return. "Yes, of course. What time can I bring my people over?"

Andrew shrugged at the omission of the smile and became serious in turn. He looked over his shoulder at the foundry floor, taking a brief mental inventory of what needed to be done. "Uh... Later this afternoon, I'd say.

Or maybe tomorrow morning would actually be better. Yes, it would. I have some things I need to finish up. Let's call it tomorrow morning."

"Tomorrow morning it is. I'll be here with my co-workers at eight. You can give me your quote then."

"But what if you don't like it?"

Hank unconsciously raised his hand to cover his breast pocket where the bank passbook nestled, and this time he did smile. "Don't worry. I'll like it."

Andrew returned the smile, and after a pause, he continued. "Oh, yes—there's something else I think you'll like." He turned around, cupped his hands around his mouth to form a makeshift megaphone, and bellowed out, "Hey, Tom! Get down here!" From the foundry loft above them came a muffled acknowledgement. Hank looked quizzically at Andrew, but Andrew merely held his gaze and continued to smile mischievously, saying nothing. They heard footsteps coming down a ladder, then, rubbing his hands on a towel, in walked Tom, Hank's former rolling mill foreman. Tom had quit his job at Hank Steel months ago, on the morning Directive 289-10 had gone into effect, emigrating directly from Pennsylvania to the Gulch.

When Tom saw who was standing alongside Andrew, he halted dead in his tracks, mouth simultaneously agape and smiling. He quickly closed the distance between them, a grimy hand extended in warm greeting. Hank shook the proffered hand without considering the stains.

"I warned you you'd end up right alongside of me, Mr. Hank. And I was right. Welcome home!"

"You work here?" Hank observed needlessly.

"Why, is something bigger coming along?" he asked with an innocent smile. The three men laughed together in long-delayed camaraderie.

Hank turned to Andrew, a serious expression on his face. "How much are you paying him?"

Andrew laughed again. "Not as much as I think you will!"

The next morning, meeting in their new makeshift offices, Tom, Gwen, Hank, and the men who accompanied him into the valley formulated the plan of action needed to transform his newly-acquired open fields into the new home of Hank Steel. Before lunch, they had their strategy outlined in broad detail. Through the afternoon, one by one they visited the craftsmen and contractors who would build the furnaces, cranes, and tools they would require. Contracts and timetables were set up in short order, any argument cut short by the businessman's credo: "Price no object." By the time the sun had set on Hank's second day in the Gulch, everything was in place; the seeds had been sown. Hank Steel had been redeemed.

All it needed now was time to grow.

* * *

Midas parked.

He did not drive directly to the bank after he dropped off Hank, but instead made a detour to visit Dr. Thomas. Walking into the doctor's office, he found the man sitting behind his desk, reading

Dr. Thomas looked up as the door opened. "Good afternoon, Midas. How are you feeling?"

"I live," he snapped. "You said you wanted to go over the results of those tests you did last week."

"I do," Dr. Thomas replied grimly.

Midas could tell from Dr. Thomas' manner that the news could not be good. "Well, skip the preambles and just tell me. What's the story?"

"I'm sorry, Midas," he said gravely. "It's inoperable."

Seconds passed in heavy silence. The news plainly deflated Midas. His eyes became unfocused and he stared off into the distance, looking at nothing. He suddenly seemed many years older than his actual advanced age. "So how long do I have?" he finally managed to ask.

"Three months? Maybe five."

Midas walked over to the window and looked out at the snow-dusted valley, his head held high, the orange autumn sun full on his face. He spoke to the window. "So there will be no spring for me, is that what you're saying?"

Dr. Thomas took a deep breath. "Yes; I guess you could put it that way."

"And in the meantime?"

"It will likely progress along the lines we discussed last week. Almost certainly, in fact."

Midas remained silent for a moment. Still speaking to the window, he added softly, "Do you know how much I've always loved it—being alive?" A shadow of a smile flickered across his face, but it faded quickly. Shaking off his melancholy, he tossed a brief glance at Dr. Thomas. "I'll guess I'll have to accelerate my efforts to find someone to take over the bank; that and the mint. I've already been cutting back on my outstanding loan portfolio and working on getting the bank records all shipshape."

"Do you have someone in mind?"

"Not for the bank. All of us old-timers are already busy with our own careers, and none of the newcomers seem to have the background or temperament for a bank job. I shouldn't have any problem getting rid of the mint, though. Anyone with half a brain can run that."

After a brief silence, Dr. Thomas prompted, "So when do you plan to break the news to your friends?"

Midas turned away from the window to face the doctor full on. "I'm not," he replied flatly. "Let's let it ride for now: don't tell anyone. I don't want anybody to start fawning over me every minute! I'd prefer to wait until we can't hide it anymore."

"As you wish."

"Just make sure I get the best care possible," he warned, wagging a finger at the doctor and wearing a wry smile to take the sting out of his words. "I've already signed the papers to triple your retainer, and the next time you look at your account, you'll find there's a little something extra in the grouch bag for you."

"Now, Midas, that's really not necess—"

"No, no; I insist. I want the best doctoring I can get—and I don't want anyone bidding your services away from me!"

Dr. Thomas allowed himself a small, half-smile. "I doubt anyone could match your original retainer, let alone the tripled amount."

"Well, you deserve it anyway. You've always taken good care of me, Tom. It's the least I can do to take good care of you in return."

Dr. Thomas smiled again. "Altruism, Midas?"

"Nope," he fired back sternly. "It's value for value, and you know it! You didn't think you could trap me with that old looters' line, did you?"

"If I did, it wouldn't be the first time!" he laughed.

Midas laughed, too, remembering. "It seems I'll never be able to live that one down!"

His accidentally apropos wording sobered the two men instantly. After an awkward silence, Dr. Thomas became all business again. He handed an opaque vial to Midas, its contents rattling audibly. "Take one of these according to the directions on the label whenever you feel you need it. It'll help minimize your discomfort."

"I don't feel so bad yet."

Dr. Thomas did not comment.

Midas sighed. "Well, I should probably be on my way. I've already taken an overly-long lunch break, and I need to get back to the bank. Probably run into an annoyed customer or two along the way." He headed for the door, but turned to squint an eye and shake a finger again at Dr. Thomas before leaving. "And remember: no squealing!"

"No, of course not."

Midas walked out of the office into the afternoon sunshine, closing the door behind him.

## CHAPTER 4 – HELLO, GOODBYE

Gwen's father complained.

"Whaddaya mean, I have to go to school? I'm too old to learn. Besides, I was already learned everything anyway."

"Now, Dad; it's not school. Frankie told me it'll be a radio show about how the valley works, about their philosophy, and their striker's oath. All of us newcomers are getting together to listen to it."

"And that's another thing! I don't like no oath about abandoning my union buddies. And I won't be afraid to say that to no teacher!" He moved as if to gesture angrily with his cane, but slowly realized it wasn't in his hand. "Heh?" he muttered to himself, peered around, then bent over to pick it up from the hassock where he had left it.

"Now, Dad! I'm sure Frankie can explain it all to you."

"And I'm tired of hearing about that over-named smoothie!" he warned, brandishing the cane, now in hand. "If I ever catch him—"

"Now, Dad," she interrupted again, her face reddening slightly. "Don't try to embarrass me, because it won't work. Stop your grousing, put on your coat, and let's get to the meeting."

"Hey, wait a minute! Why doesn't that Hank guy gotta go, too?"

Gwen stood her ground and did not answer, except through the unwavering determination in her eyes; she held his coat out toward him.

Her father paused, looked down at the coat in her hand, avoiding her stern gaze as he reluctantly took the garment, muttering, "When the shop steward speaks..."

"That's better. Now come on or we'll be late."

It was a typically cold evening for late November in the high Colorado Rockies, with occasional icy gusts that cut right through their bulky winter clothes. Father and daughter both were quite happy once they finally reached Dwight's large, well-heated hangar at the valley's airstrip. The hangar had been chosen as the venue for the broadcast primarily because there wasn't another heated space large enough to hold all of the newcomers at one time, and there was room to spare. Gwen and her father found themselves among the last to arrive, and as a result, were forced to take seats in the front row.

The hangar was not overly crowded, but there were well over a hundred people of varying sex, age, and ethnicity, including many couples and a lanky teenaged boy, but no young children. Most sat on folding chairs which faced four radio receivers, a dozen rows of ten chairs each, but a number had chosen to sit on desks or tables around the periphery.

A strikingly handsome man with golden hair stood in front of the arrayed chairs, glanced at his wristwatch, and announced, "The broadcast will begin in a few moments, so let's get settled." He waited a moment for silence, then introduced himself. "My name is Ragnar, and I'll—"

A collective gasp burst from the assembly; they all recognized the infamous pirate's name. Frightened murmurs rippled through the crowd.

His laughter forced an instant change of mood. "You don't have to be frightened. I'm not dangerous—to anyone here in the Gulch, that is! Besides, I have retired from my pirating days." He smiled warmly to put them at ease before continuing. "Instead, I have chosen to become a philosopher. Along those lines, and as you know, the reason you are here tonight is to learn all about the philosophy that supports this valley. This is critically important—"

Gwen's father leaned over to her and whispered, "I thought you said this wasn't going to be school!"

"Shhh! Pay attention and listen."

"—because the oath is the key to our society. If you decide to remain here in the Gulch, you will all be required to take the striker's oath because—"

"*Not me!*" interrupted Gwen's father, standing. All heads turned his way. He folded his arms, held his head high, and proclaimed, "I'm not abandoning my union buddies!" Light laughter rippled through the room; but the teenager applauded loudly, earning him several dirty looks.

"Dad!" hissed Gwen, unsuccessfully trying to pull him back into his seat.

But Ragnar remained unruffled; he addressed the old man respectfully. "No one is asking you to abandon anyone, sir. What you'll learn here is that our strike actually helps your union buddies."

Gwen's father eyed him warily. "Yeah? How?" He did not trust the pirate-turned-philosopher, and did not try to hide it.

"What would your union do if you were forced to work for no pay?"

"Why, we'd go on *strike!*" he replied with gusto.

Again, the teenager clapped long and loud. It was obvious that he was a union man as well.

Ragnar shifted his gaze to include the rest of the room. "That is exactly what we have done. We, the men of the mind, have gone on strike against our destroyers. They demanded that we work as their slaves. They demanded the unearned, with us as the supplier of their needs. We refused. Rather than submit, we went on strike; and a successful strike it has been. Today their society is on the brink of falling to pieces on top of their own heads."

"Hey," Gwen's father whispered to his daughter as he re-seated himself, the admiration plain in his hushed voice. "You didn't tell me he was a union brother. This guy is all right!"

"I told you he was. Now shhh."

Ragnar bowed slightly at the overheard compliment before continuing. "Tonight we will be exploring the meaning and implications of the striker's oath we have taken, and the philosophy that makes this valley possible."

A hand went up; it was the teenager. "The striker's oath? What is that? I'm proud to say I just joined my first union a few months ago, but this is the first I've heard of it."

Ragnar drew himself up solemnly, locking eyes with the young man. "I swear, by my life and my love of it, that I will never live for the sake of another man, nor ask another man to live for mine," reciting the words as if his vow were a prayer, a thing of reverence. The teenager did not reply, but his jaw was set firmly.

Ragnar paused respectfully when he had finished. "Who among you is willing to take that oath today?" Not a single hand went up. "Why won't you?" He pointed to a woman in the back row, the wife of Hank's mill superintendent.

"Because I love my husband," she declared confidently and without hesitation. She turned to the man sitting in the seat next to her and patted his hand affectionately. "Pete and I have been married over fourteen years, and I'm not going to stop living for him now."

"And you?" Ragnar pointed to another member of the audience.

"I don't see why I should have to."

"You?" he asked, indicating a stern-faced man with his arms folded defensively across his chest.

"I don't agree with it."

"And you?" he asked a pretty blonde sitting by herself on a large chest.

"I'm not sure I understand what it means."

One by one, Ragnar continued to poll the audience, receiving a diverse range of answers, none affirmative. When he was done, he sighed. "It would appear that we have our work cut out for us. Fortunately you'll have the best of teachers—" Gwen's father pointedly faced his daughter, but she refused to react. "—to guide your understanding, starting in about two minutes..." He glanced at his wristwatch, and his eyebrows went up as he amended, "...no, in two seconds. Sit down, folks, and listen."

On cue, when the hands of his wristwatch reached the dot of six, the four large radios flanking him came to life. "Ladies and gentlemen...," they blared, flawlessly reproducing a man's clear, calm, implacable voice. Ragnar needlessly adjusted the volume on each of the four receivers, then sat down to listen, a blissful smile on his face.

*  *  *

Gwen's father snored.

He had fallen sound asleep less than fifteen minutes into the epic speech, and Gwen had given up trying to rouse him, choosing instead to focus on the content of the broadcast and take shorthand notes. Only when his snoring became overly loud would she nudge him into silence.

As she listened, Gwen found her emotional and intellectual reactions to the broadcast rising and falling like some philosophical roller coaster. Certain things that the speaker said were so crystal clear, so startlingly true, that she wondered why she had never seen things that way before. But on other topics she was clearly lost, becoming too enmeshed in the details to grasp the bigger picture. Sections of it seemed repetitive, as if the speaker were trying to cover every possible aspect of the issue at hand. Although the speaker had a good deal of public speaking talent, it was obvious he was no Toastmaster. Aside from any flaws in its presentation, she felt that the subject matter itself was ill-suited to a spoken broadcast, especially such a long one; and it would have been easier to understand if she had an outline to follow. Further, the speech was scattered with many words unfamiliar to her; a dictionary of some of the specialized terms would also have been helpful. But overall she comprehended more than enough to understand the basics, and the sum total was that she was impressed.

She also found interesting the reactions of those around her, not counting her father's. Many others' overt responses mirrored her own—confusion interspersed with wonder—and curiously, the timing of their reactions did not always coincide with hers. But everyone reacted positively to the part where the speaker exhorted people to take to the hills and establish hidden enclaves; there were many exchanged smiles and nods among the listeners.

Finally, and in some cases thankfully, it was over; and Ragnar took center stage again. "Well, that's it in a rather large nutshell. What did you think?" His eyes moved around the silent room. "Anybody? I just want to hear some initial reactions right now. No big speeches, just a few words about what we just heard."

Seconds passed in heavy silence, softly punctuated by light snoring from Gwen's father. Nobody wanted to be the first to speak. Ragnar decided to give matters a small push. He caught the eye of the teenager.

"What did you think of it?"

"Too long," he replied instantly, an edge of typical teenaged insolence in his voice.

"I meant, what did you think of what he said?"

"Well, he used a lot of words I never heard before, so I don't know about that. But I liked the part about enclaves in the mountains. That's what we are, aren't we?"

"Indeed we are." He scanned the faces of the audience. "Anyone else want to comment?" Most avoided eye contact, clearly not wanting to be singled out as the teenager had been. Gwen's father continued to snore hollowly, a little louder than before. "How about you?" Ragnar indicated the stern-faced man who had expressed his dislike for the oath prior to the broadcast.

"I think it's a bunch of malarkey. Non-existence, savages, looters, and blank-outs? Good God! Who could understand the half of it! Just what kind of soap is that guy peddling?"

It was a credit to Ragnar's upbringing that he maintained his poise. "An interesting observation that certainly requires more inquiry," he replied noncommittally. "Anyone else?"

Gwen raised her hand sheepishly. "I have a few questions."

"Go ahead."

In her neat, efficient manner, she consulted her notes and ticked off each of her concerns and questions one by one, like a clerk reporting on a manifest. She continued on for several minutes, point after point, then concluded with a final question: "...and I saved the most important for last: I'm not sure what happens to my father when I stop living for him." As if in support of his daughter, Gwen's father let loose with a particularly loud snort.

From one side of the room, a voice called out, "Now there's someone who paid attention!" Light laughter sprinkled through the crowd; some thought he was referring to Gwen's father, others, to Gwen.

"Those are some good questions," Ragnar told her. "Suppose we discuss it later, you and I? Right now, let's see if anyone else has something they'd like to say."

Again a thick silence descended on the room, broken only by the continued snoring.

"I know it's a lot to take in all at once," admitted Ragnar. "And it's getting late. Let's call it a night and give each of you a chance to think it over. If you have any questions about the striker's oath or anything else that you heard tonight, feel free to contact me. I teach philosophy classes, conduct seminars, and hold conferences. I have many exciting offerings scheduled to begin over the next few weeks, so please take one of my advertising circulars on your way out. Usually I charge a penny a piece for them, but for tonight only they're free."

A buzz of conversation started amid the rustle of coats and scrapes of chairs as everyone prepared to leave.

"Wait a minute!" the teenager called out over the din. "I still have a question!"

"Yes?" Ragnar called in return, raising his voice to be heard.

The room quieted down somewhat to better hear what the teenager had to say, but it was obvious he was reluctant to speak.

"If something needs to be said, say it!" Ragnar prompted.

Finally the teenager posed his troubling question. "What happens if we don't take the oath?"

The room became much quieter very quickly, as if a heavy, wet woolen blanket had been thrown over a roaring campfire.

Ragnar paused briefly for effect, and to let the last of the noises die away. A silence formed around him into which he might drop his words. "Then you can't stay in the valley," he stated flatly, his face deadly serious. "This is private property, and anyone who chooses to remain here must take the striker's oath." As he spoke, his aura was suddenly no longer that of Ragnar the philosopher, but rather Ragnar the pirate: steel in his eyes, chin held high, body taut in preparation to enforce his mandate. The room became deathly still under the weight of his words and the power of his persona.

After a few seconds, the teenager summoned up the courage to continue, his nervous voice cracking badly. "Bu... bu... but if we don't take the oath, where else would we go?"

"Well, where did you come from?"

The teenager paused again, his face pale, then stammered. "San... San Francisco." His shoulders slumped, and his eyes fell. Many in the room looked away from him in unease; the latest news about the fierce fighting and religious rebellion in California was well known to them all.

More seconds passed in silence before Ragnar continued, philosopher again rather than pirate. "Don't worry." He flashed a friendly smile. "We'll give everyone plenty of time to think things through, ask questions, learn about our philosophy, and make your own decision." His eyes took on a distant look, as he studied a calendar in his mind's eye. Bringing his attention back to the assembly, he continued cheerily. "Tell you what: we'll give you until winter is over. Let's set a deadline for everyone to take the oath by the end of March, about four months from now. Plenty of time for everyone to take the proper classes and attend the seminars. How does that sound?"

The silence weighed heavily in the air; no one looked at his neighbor, spoke, or moved. A brief gust of wind whistled outside past the massive hangar doors, moaning eerily. It was a terrible night for any person to be caught unprotected outside.

"Any other questions?"

There were none.

* * *

Gwen daydreamed still.

The fiery orange circle of mountain peaks around her had dimmed with the setting of the sun, and the steel-blue shadow on the snowy slopes had spread upward to swallow the tops of the mountains. Recalling the night of the Worker's epic speech four months ago, she shook her head in wonder at how quickly those months had passed. Here it was, already the beginning of March, and only four short weeks remained until Ragnar's deadline. Over and over in her mind, she had rolled the possibility of taking the striker's oath, but had to admit that she was no closer to embracing it today as she had been when she first arrived in the valley last November. If her reluctance to take the oath had not changed, her father's blank refusal had changed even less, which is to say: not at all.

It wasn't as if she hadn't tried to understand, to accept; it was more that she lacked some basic sense which the other strikers possessed, an Olympian point of view denied to her that they took for granted. Time after time, she found herself making some statement that they found clearly wrong—she could tell by the lifting of an eyebrow in mild surprise, or by the exchange of knowing glances between two strikers. Repeatedly, she felt like an outsider in her own home; as in fact, she was.

Ignoring the nervous knot of concern in her stomach, Gwen turned away from the darkening window and her troubled thoughts. There was no point in worrying. As with the millions Outside who were doomed to die in the coming weeks, there was nothing she could do about it in any case.

## CHAPTER 5 – WHAT NOW MY LOVE?

Eddie sighed contentedly.

He sat at a corner table in the cafeteria of Transcontinental's Las Vegas station, dawdling over his second cup of coffee. The meal he had just finished was undoubtedly one of the best of his entire life; and had the world not been crashing down around his ears, he was certain he would have enjoyed it all the more. But he felt a nagging disquiet, not stemming merely from all his recent troubles or those of the world around him, but rather from recalling with whom he had last shared a meal in a Transcontinental cafeteria—the Worker.

But it wasn't the Worker who now sat across the table from him; it was the Transcontinental stationmaster, his dour, chubby face reflecting the same doom that Eddie knew was on his own. Together they sat pooling what meager knowledge of the outside world they possessed.

"It's not a pretty picture, Mr. Eddie," warned the stationmaster. "Not pretty at all. The whole town is nervous and on edge. Nobody knows what's going on, and that makes them even more nervous. All the tourists have long gone, and people are quitting their jobs and leaving town— important people, too. Even the Mayor's gone!"

Eddie only nodded. The story was a familiar one. Similar tales spanned the nation.

"Some of them up and quit, just like that, claiming they're going to join up with a secret enclave up in the mountains someplace, and we never see or hear from them again. Others go off looking for jobs they say the Unificating Board doesn't know about. I know a lot of people worried about their kinfolk out in California, and some of them go off looking to help." He paused momentarily, then looked directly into Eddie's eyes. "Is it as bad as they say it is out there, Mr. Eddie? You know, with the fighting and all? You were there."

Eddie sighed; the news he knew was not good. "I don't know about the rest of California, but it was pretty bad in San Francisco."

"Real bad?" the stationmaster asked worriedly, his jaw slack. It was obvious that he was one of those who had family there.

Eddie considered briefly that he should put the best face on the fighting—as if such a thing were possible!—but decided honesty was the best policy, even when the truth was hard to bear. He paused respectfully before continuing in a flat voice, "I'm sorry. Yes, it is bad. Very bad. When I left, there were three factions warring over our terminal there—actually shooting at each other! I had to pay tribute to get the *Meteor* out of town."

The stationmaster hung his head. "I see," he said.

"There's more bad news," cautioned Eddie, placing a sympathetic hand on the stationmaster's slumping shoulder. "But not about California. I was told that the Transcontinental Bridge over the Mississippi is gone. 'Blasted to bits,' I heard."

The stationmaster looked up again, his face still full of concern. "That, we knew about, Mr. Eddie. We heard about it on the radio—before they stopped broadcasting, that is. They said that the X Project blew up the whole middle of the country!"

"Then it's true?" asked Eddie, slowly retracting his hand from the stationmaster's shoulder. "The Transcontinental Bridge is gone?"

"Radio said so, Mr. Eddie."

Eddie did not speak for several seconds before he mounted the courage to ask the question that had hovered at the edge of his consciousness since the night the *Meteor* had died. "And what of New York City?"

The stationmaster shook his head. "No word since the night the X Project blew up. We heard the broadcast about the Worker's plan, then nothing since."

"No word from New York, you say?"

"No, sir."

"Not at all?"

"No, sir, not at all. No radio, no television, no long-distance, not for almost two weeks now." He shook his head. "And it's not just New York—the rest of the country is silent, too. And now even our local telephones are starting to go."

*No word!* Eddie had stopped listening to the stationmaster, stunned into a shocked silence. His mind was a whirl in the face of the unimaginable conclusion: *New York City blasted to bits!* His mind balked at the horrendous scene he visualized; then his eyes widened as he followed the horror to its ultimate conclusion: *Dagny!*

The thought of her fell upon Eddie like a physical blow, and he reeled under its impact, falling back in his chair. His ears rang as the room tilted out from under him; his arms and legs felt remote and rubbery. His field of vision swiftly narrowed until perception vanished entirely, leaving him a motionless rock sitting in his chair, his brain numbed into rejecting any sensory inputs. Only a single thought seared itself echoingly across his mind: *Dagny!*

"Mr. Eddie? Are you all right?"

Unbidden, memories poured into his consciousness, like water rushing through a breached levee, recollections of Dagny's formal debut ball at New

York's exclusive Falkland Hotel when she was seventeen, and Eddie two years her junior. Although he had known her since early childhood, he had never before imagined her so elegantly clad as she was that evening; and without a doubt she was stunning. The little girl he had known had clearly grown up—and so had Eddie. For days afterwards, his thoughts were dominated by her enchanting image and the intimacy of the single dance that they had shared; he could think of nothing else except the touch of his bare hand against her naked back as they danced, the soft pressure of her breasts flattened against his chest, the way her natural scent flooded his awareness, her soft, brown hair gently tickling his ear. Eddie had stopped the moment in his mind that night, the very picture of paradise, a precious mixture of both bliss and torture; bliss for the pure perfection of the moment, yet torture for its ephemeral transience. He carried that cherished moment with him throughout his life; for never again in the intervening decades did they share such close physical contact—even their final parting last month had been consummated by a mere handshake. Yet the memory of the dance had remained, sharp and clear, untarnished by time despite the frequent handling it received. But with a sharp *crack!* the mental image of the bright lights of the ballroom at the Falkland suddenly shattered, blasted to bits, splinters flying in all directions as the city around the hotel disintegrated, another victim of the destructive energies of the X Project. *Dagny!* he screamed wordlessly in his mind, again and again. *Dagny!* Tears welled up in his eyes, driven by his certainty regarding her fate. He felt drained and hollow, crushed by an anguished despair, his distress reverberating dazzlingly inside his head. *Gone! She's gone!* Eddie had never felt so utterly alone in his entire life. *Gone! Oh my God! Dagny, Dagny!*

"Mr. Eddie?"

Awareness of his surroundings returned slowly: first, the feel of the warm cup of coffee in his hand, next its invigorating aroma, followed by the blurry figure of the stationmaster finally swimming into view. Once, then twice, Eddie blinked before the tears in his eyes cleared sufficiently to discern the stationmaster's concerned gaze. Taking a ragged, deep breath, Eddie needlessly pushed back his short blonde hair with his free hand and replied weakly, his voice shaking, "I... I haven't eaten much in... in... what, over a week?" he temporized. "I guess I'm still pretty weak." Finding the coffee in his hand, he took another sip without thinking and without tasting it; the paralyzing vision of Dagny's demise still dominated his consciousness.

"You ought to get some sleep, Mr. Eddie."

Again, he sighed heavily, looking at but not seeing the coffee in his hand. *Get a grip!* he scolded himself. *Maybe she survived!* he told himself, although he couldn't imagine how. With a Herculean effort, and with limited success, he set aside his turmoil and grief, his thoughts turning back to matters at hand. With a start, Eddie's ears finally caught up with his stunned mind.

"The Worker's plan? What do you mean, the Worker's plan? What broadcast?" He set his coffee down, his eyes suddenly wide. "Has he given in to them? What was his plan?"

"You mean the Worker's Plan for Profit, Prosperity, and Peace?"

"Is that what he called it?"

The stationmaster shrugged. "Radio said so," he repeated.

"What was the plan?"

The stationmaster smiled for the first time since Eddie's arrival. "'Get the hell out of my way,'" he quoted.

"What?" Eddie was perplexed, with traces of an offended expression flickering across his face.

"'Get the hell out of my way!' That was his plan. They did this big build-up at some gala event, and that was all he had to say."

As the words sunk in, Eddie found himself incapable of smiling in return. "Just that?"

The stationmaster nodded, the smile on his own face broadening. "Just that."

Eddie did not react to the stationmaster's mirth. "And then the X Project blew up."

"Yes, sir," he replied, his smile disintegrating. "The same night. Right after, in fact."

Eddie returned his attention to his coffee. Reluctantly, he was forced to face the unimaginable truth that much, if not most of the nation lay in ruins. Las Vegas would likely be left to its own devices, at least for the next few weeks, perhaps longer. But that brought to mind a whole host of new concerns; he glanced at the remnants of the meal in front of him, then pursued a new tangent. "How reliable is the food supply here?"

"The food supply?" The sudden shift of subject took the stationmaster by surprise. He considered the question a moment before replying. "I guess it's a mixed bag, Mr. Eddie. There's an awful lot of cattle and sheep all around the city, and a lot of fruit, too. Most people grow their own vegetables—I've got my own truck patch, too, you know—but there's not much in the way of grain or flour. Most of that used to come in by train, but we haven't seen a shipment in months. I think it's due to all that trouble on our Minnesota Division back in September. Less than half the wheat harvest made it to the mills, I hear, and we haven't seen hardly any of it. At least it didn't come in by train, or I'd have heard about it."

Eddie assimilated the news, then nodded. If Las Vegas were left to her own devices, the fare may become monotonous, but they wouldn't likely starve. And water and electricity shouldn't be a problem; so long as the massive Boulder Dam remained, there would be enough of both to last a hundred lifetimes. Eddie stared into space as he considered their tactical situation. "People are leaving town, you say? How many do you think are left?"

The stationmaster barely hesitated. "I've lived here all my life, and I'd guess almost half of them have already gone, and more are leaving all the time, especially since the X Project blew up a few weeks ago. Some neighborhoods are like ghost towns—especially in the worst parts of town. Last census put us around eight or nine thousand, so it could be three, maybe five thousand left? Hard to say. The tourists always made the town seem more crowded than it really is."

"Many people coming into town?"

He spread his pudgy hands and raised his eyebrows in surprise. "From where? How would they get here? The nearest big city is a hundred miles away!"

Eddie nodded again; the stationmaster's surprise made sense. The chances of Las Vegas being invaded from across the desert were slim to none, and being located in the middle of a desert would give them a badly-needed, strategic remoteness from the fighting to their west.

It seemed as if the stationmaster was reading Eddie's thoughts, saying, "There is a big Army base not too far north of here if we need help, although the telephones aren't working that far out any more."

"What about Transcontinental Railroad? What sort of motive power do we have here?"

Again, the stationmaster shook his head. "Nothing near like the Diesel you brought in with you, that's for sure! She's a real beauty! The only motive power left around here is a switcher and a yard engine, both of them steam powered—and I wouldn't trust either one of them one inch beyond the yard limit. I can't see either one of them making it over the Rockies or the Sierras now, not after all the winter snows."

"Do you have any fuel for the Diesel?"

The stationmaster's eyes lit up. "That, we have, Mr. Eddie. Lots of it, too! There are over a dozen tank cars full of diesel fuel out in the yard!" He chuckled without mirth. "If you ask me, I think those tank cars got forgotten. And I wasn't going to stick my neck out and tell anyone about them..." He trailed off, remembering the presence of his superior sitting across the table from him. "...not unless someone asked, that is."

Eddie let it ride. "What about the men? Are there crews to run a train? Mechanics? Clerks? Who's left? How many?"

The stationmaster shook his head slowly. "Not many, Mr. Eddie. Not many at all. Out of the forty-two we had last May when Directive 289-10 went into effect, we're down to an even dozen men who haven't deserted, and none of them are mechanics. Most are the sort who aren't good for much, if you know what I mean, and the rest only show up out of habit. None of them are engineers either, and I don't know that any of them could actually run a train if they wanted to—not that there's anyplace for a train to go to these days."

Neither man said anything for most of a minute. Coming to a decision, Eddie unconsciously sat up straight and squared his shoulders, abandoning for the first time his original plan to return to San Francisco. "You're right. There's nowhere else *to* go. We'll have to make our stand here as best we can until the country can get back on its feet."

The stationmaster had long since come to the same conclusion, but for different reasons. Although intelligent, he was no leader of men, nor imaginative enough to even make the attempt to lead; and leaving Las Vegas was inconceivable for this town's native son. With Eddie's unexpected appearance on the scene, the stationmaster felt the great, unwanted burden of responsibility dissipating, as if a great weight had been lifted from his shoulders. He had always been better at taking orders than giving them, so he welcomed Eddie's leadership gratefully, blindly, and with open arms.

"There's no point in keeping the station open without any trains," continued Eddie. "But we can use it as our base of operations." He stared off into space for a moment, considering how best he could utilize the dozen men of uncertain talents left to him.

*What would Dagny do?* he asked himself; but he knew the question was rhetorical as well as unnecessary. Through his long association with the Vice-President of Operations for Transcontinental Railroad, Eddie knew precisely what Dagny would do, and in fine detail, even down to the expression on her face when she'd give the orders. *Dagny, Dagny!* he thought with another sudden surge of emotion, his eyes clouding. Pulling himself together once again, he turned his attention back to the stationmaster. "Send two men up to the Army base. We need to find out what's happening with the rest of the country." He sipped at his coffee, taking a moment to think, and more became clear to him. "As I recall, there are only four roads leading into town."

"That's right—except for a few dirt tracks through the mountains here and there."

"Station one man on each of the main roads just outside of town and have them keep an eye on what's going on. They shouldn't interfere with anyone, probably stay out of sight, too. Tell them to keep their eyes and ears open. Put them on two twelve-hour shifts, and give them the train crew's walkie-talkies from the *Meteor* so they can keep in touch with us. Use your own judgment who's best for each task."

"Yes, sir," replied the stationmaster, relieved that someone else had taken charge.

But Eddie did not notice. He was looking out the tall, wide windows of the cafeteria at the westering sun, the end of a long day. It was no surprise that he felt exhausted; he had been up all night the night before guiding the *Meteor* back to Las Vegas. "I'll find someplace here where I can catch some sleep," he continued. "We'll get together again after breakfast tomorrow morning and go over what's next."

The stationmaster stood up with a measure of confidence. "I'll get on it right away, Mr. Eddie," he assured him as he turned to go, the relief still obvious in his voice.

After the stationmaster had left, Eddie remained at the table, swirling the dregs of coffee in his cup and watching the brown grounds spin. He hadn't felt the pressure of command weigh this heavily upon him since Dagny had taken a month-long hiatus from the railroad last May and retreated to her cabin in the Berkshires, leaving him to run the Operating Department of Transcontinental Railroad all on his own. But he had coped during her absence then, he reminded himself, and he would cope now. Should he and Dagny chance to finally meet again, he wanted her to be proud of him, of how he lived up to his childhood promise to her, to do "whatever is right."

With great difficulty, Eddie tried in vain to put all thoughts of Dagny out of his mind. He drained what was left of his coffee, made a bitter face that matched its bottom-of-the-cup taste, then rose wearily to his feet. Once he completed shutting down the still-idling Diesel, he'd retire to his compartment in the *Meteor's* sleeper car for some badly-needed rest.

## CHAPTER 6 – IT DON'T MATTER ANY MORE

Fish fried.

The woman stood before a battered, borrowed hotplate and poked a tiny, borrowed cocktail fork at their dinner as it sizzled in an overly-large, borrowed pan, finding herself in a borrowed situation of what seemed to be a borrowed life.

A scant three feet away, her husband sat against the wall on a makeshift chair constructed out of a discarded wooden box and several mismatched pillows of varying shape, size, and color. He leaned smiling against the pillowed wall, hands behind his head, gazing idly out the tall window of their compact, crowded corner of the airstrip's administration building. On the other side of an improvised partition delineating their private space came the murmur of men talking, something about airplanes. No surprise; a quarter of the building still served its original purpose. It was difficult to make out their words over the sound of music that drifted from behind another temporary wall. But then, that was the music's purpose.

"So how was your day, Pete?" she inquired conversationally, her voice unintentionally revealing that something was troubling her. Unconsciously, she sought the diversion of small talk.

"Pretty good!" he replied with enthusiasm, not noticing her tribulations, and more than eager to talk about his work. "Hank and I were out to visit the site of the new mills again today."

"That so?" she asked indifferently, her attention focused more on her cooking.

"Yep!" He stretched lazily, extending his arms high in the air, fists balled, making a guttural sound before continuing. "The place is really starting to take shape. They poured the second foundation for the furnaces today, and the surveyor finally got the last of the other buildings staked out. At the rate things are moving, the mills should be ready for the first heat by September. Maybe sooner!"

The woman hesitated briefly, then resumed poking at the contents of the big pan.

"What?" he asked pointedly, recognizing the pause for what it was. Fourteen years of marriage had well schooled him as to when his wife held unspoken words on her tongue.

She hesitated again before answering, cautious; the years had educated her as well. "Will we really be staying here that long, do you think?"

Her husband laughed, completely misunderstanding her concern and unwittingly feeding her fears. "Honey, where else is there to go? You heard the news that came in this morning—New York City finally died last night, and the X Project blew up, too! Assuming California's finished killing itself off by now, which is a good bet, that means it's all over for the United States of America!"

Silently she continued to poke at their dinner, a little more forcefully than before.

Reading the figurative tea leaves without understanding their message, her husband lost some of his exuberance; nevertheless, he continued to press his lack of understanding. "Aw, come on, honey. We're lucky to even *be* here. You know that!"

She did not deign to reply or even look in his direction; her cold aloofness was not a good sign.

"And where else would we go?" he persisted patiently, again naming exactly the wrong thing. "We certainly can't go back to Pennsylvania! Don't you see? We have no choice! We *had* to come here! And with things Outside falling apart left and right, we'll have to stay."

Enough was enough for the poor woman. She slammed down her tiny fork without letting it go and whirled to face him. "Must we?" she whined petulantly, her voice sharp and loud.

He held her angry gaze for several seconds before deciding on a different tack, inadvertently stumbling yet again into the heart of her fears. "Well, what's the matter with staying?"

Without even a half second delay, an answer tumbled out, as if long held prisoner and waiting for the chance to escape, even though the words went wide of her true concerns. "What's the matter? Huh! *I'll* tell you what's the matter!" Her hand swept angrily across the contents of their primitive domicile. "We had a beautiful home in Elkins Park, not a crowded corner of someone's office!" She shook the tiny fork at him. "I had a kitchen and pots and pans I could call my own, and a real stove, too! We had a decent place to sleep!" She gestured angrily to the straw mat on the floor that served as their bed; it was carefully and expertly made. "I had friends, a place in society, and we were well respected in our congregation! Where is that all now? Where?" Her breath came rapidly. "And there are people here who won't even *talk* to me!"

"Stop that!" a man's deep voice yelled out from over one of the makeshift barriers, obviously addressing someone else. "Stop that yelling!" immediately cried another voice. Both their heads turned in the direction of the intrusion, momentarily stunned. Fortunately, her husband successfully suppressed a slight smile before she could turn back to see it; he had found the incongruous rejoinders somehow amusing, if not apropos. But his amusement did not matter; she had returned her attention to her cooking, again poking with unnecessary force, not noticing his momentary transgression.

"Aw, honey, we've talked about this before. We'll have our house just as soon as the builders can get around to building it. Everybody's waiting for houses, not just us. We're not the only homeless ones in the valley. It won't be long—June at the latest, they tell me." He gestured at the line of canvas structures outside their window. "You're lucky we're not living in one of those tents! If I weren't Hank's mill superintendent, it's likely we would be, you know!"

She still did not look in his direction. "*I'm* lucky?" she asked the pan, her voice dripping with irritation.

He did not reply right away, there being no safe answer. Shifting the subject back slightly, he picked up his prior thread. "It'll be a bigger house than our old one, and prettier, too! You were at the site: a broad hump of grass overlooking the valley, and the Colorado Rockies in the background. Why, all our old neighbors would *die* for such a beautiful spot!"

Cold silence filled their corner of the room.

"What's wrong with so nice a home?" he pleaded, still barreling down the wrong track at full speed. "June's not that far off—only three months! Why can't you just accept that we'll have to wait a little longer?"

She whirled on him as if to speak, but before she could more than take in a deep breath, words boomed out from across the partition, impressive in their deep bass tones: "Because I'm in need, I tell you! Because I'm thousands of miles from home with no place else to go!" The crash of tumbling furniture masked some final few words.

At hearing her own fears restated so bluntly and authoritatively, the overstressed woman's face scrunched up in naked hurt; she fell to her knees and threw herself onto her husband's lap, sobbing.

"Knock it off!" her husband cried out to the unseen voice, lashing out at the messenger and not yet understanding the message. He stroked his wife's hair softly. "There, there," he soothed. "There, there."

After a moment her crying subsided; she lifted her head and looked up at him with a fierce intensity, her eyes red and moist. "June?" Her voice was high and brittle. Finally, she found she was able to name her nightmare outright. "June, you say? That's a laugh! You know as well as I do there'll *be* no June for me—they're going to throw me out of this damn valley *long* before that! Tell me they won't!" Wide-eyed and unblinking, she watched in silence for his reaction.

Dawn broke on his consciousness bit by bit. His mouth opened in surprise, then slowly closed. Several seconds passed as he collected his scattered wits and swallowed his embarrassment. Finally, fully, he understood; and softly, he asked, "It's that striker's oath, isn't it?"

She looked away, and after a long moment nodded once, then laid her head back onto his lap. "They're going to throw me out," she moaned softly to his knees. The tears had started again; he could feel their warm dampness seeping through his pant leg. "Throw me out to die," she whispered as she broke down completely. His knees rocked in sympathy with the force of her sobs.

"There, there," he repeated, stroking her hair. "There, there." Chastised, he didn't know what else to say, or what he could possibly do. He knew her words to be true.

"There, there."

## CHAPTER 7 – LISTEN TO THE MUSIC

The silence was deafening.

The woman pulled away from him reluctantly. "If we play some more music," she theorized, "perhaps they won't be able to hear us?"

The man did not reply; he was not in the mood to argue, and there was no need. Her premise was correct. He rose and placed another record on the phonograph. "Good thinking," he agreed as he returned to their improvised bed.

Strands of a pleasant symphony filled the air of the airfield's administration building, muffling the sounds that crawled to them over and around the makeshift barriers that separated their quarter of the building from their housemates. Just as those external sounds were being muffled by the music, they assumed and prayed their own sounds were being similarly masked.

Their ersatz solitude persevered for not long enough, when there came from over the walls a plaintive whine, "Must we?" that rose above the delightful harmonies of the music. The man and woman locked gazes; given the context in which they found themselves, the answer in their eyes could be nothing other than an emphatic "Yes!" They successfully suppressed an almost uncontrollable urge to burst out laughing, but the bright sparkle in their eyes amounted to the same thing.

"We need to move out of this place!" the man observed needlessly, his voice a whisper almost swallowed up by the music.

"Not now!" she sighed emphatically, her eyes wide.

## CHAPTER 8 – MARGARITAVILLE

The pilot grinned.

Not two hours after landing in the Gulch, he stood hands on his hips in the middle of the lobby of the building he had just purchased, the former Midas Bank; it was destined to become the home of his new taproom. The structure was a squat block of rough granite consisting of two stories in the shape of a smaller cube placed asymmetrically on top of the larger one. It was sturdy, solid, and neatly built, the lines of its dual-rectangular bulk as severely precise as the creases of a formal garment. Although it had cost the pilot the bulk of the gold he had received in exchange for his airplane, he knew that the investment would be more than worth it. Despite being a stranger to the world of real estate, he knew a killing when he saw it, and this was definitely a big one. In a masterstroke of lucky timing, he had come on the scene just as Midas was selling all of his enterprises, including the bank. Its location was impeccable: it sat in the middle of the commercial district of the valley, in the shadow of the floating golden dollar sign, with virtually all of the other commercial establishments in the valley within a few hundred yards of him, placing him squarely in the center of the growing town. Within a year, just the land itself would be worth ten times the price he had just paid, he was sure.

While he held clear title to the bank building, he had not purchased the banking business itself; that had gone to another newcomer. Even if the pilot had demonstrated one speck of interest in becoming a banker, it wouldn't have mattered; Midas had refused to sell the bank to anyone but a sworn striker. That was fine by the pilot; he wasn't interested in counting gold, but rather in enjoying its fruits.

In his mind's eye, he envisioned the future décor of his fledgling establishment: the location of the bar, the shelves for the spirits, tables and chairs for the patrons, and a modest kitchen for his cook to prepare their meals, perhaps even a stage for some burlesque theatre. He smiled broadly at that last thought. *I'll teach these stuffy Johnnies how to have a little fun!* he promised himself. His enjoyment of his new possession drowned out, for the moment, the pangs of loss he suffered over the clipping of his wings. He loved flying; it was his life, and he knew he would sorely miss it.

Although securing such a worthy establishment was a fortuitous accomplishment in itself, he knew the real work would now begin. He was no handyman himself, and he quickly found that real handymen were in short supply. Because of the recent rapid growth in the valley's population, all of them were committed to one assignment or another for months to come; and even if they were available, there were those who simply refused to deal with scabs like him at all. In the end, he was left to his own ingenuity and abilities to transform bank to bar.

Another unanticipated challenge was locating consumables for his establishment. He had found only two ready sources for spirits: Richard, the famous composer and pianist who was the sole local vintner, and Owen, who was the sole importer who would deal with him; the former required much lead time, and the latter, much gold. But there was little else he could do beyond placing his orders, setting his prices accordingly, then letting the free market take its course.

The more he did for his new venture, the more he saw that needed to be done, and there never seemed to be anyone available or willing to do any of it, not at any price. Out of desperation, he was forced to devise a novel scheme for obtaining the bulk of the unavailable skills and services he needed. Seeing how the pool of available labor was quite large—particularly among immigrants such as himself who had not taken the striker's oath— and still growing larger every day, he discovered that one sure-fire way to inspire the unemployed was to suggest a direction for their future careers, then offer to become their first customer. With surprising enthusiasm they would gladly comply; there was little enough gainful employment available to scabs. Thus, the pilot created his own supply chain among the unsworn merely by using the power of suggestion. In this manner, he was responsible for launching two distillers, three brewers, a delivery service, a custodial service, many of their supporting vendors, and a host of other minor businesses. His meager orders would not constitute a full-time job for any of them, but he hoped it would allow them to set themselves up in a business to bring them some beer money. At least it would help to bring in *his* beer money! And as an added side bonus, the newcomers would feel a debt of gratitude to him, something he counted on to help boost business.

To his amazement, he discovered that his tactic of suggesting careers worked not only on the newcomers, but also on some of the long-established residents. As the most notable example, he found the empathetic pianist Richard more than willing to expand his wine production in support of the pilot's taproom, despite its scab owner; and on consignment, no less.

The pilot could not fathom their reasons, but he knew for a fact that there were some human beings on the planet Earth who did not drink alcohol. From that premise, he correctly reasoned that he would have to create another draw to bring that sort of person into his establishment. Toward that end, he turned again to Richard, suggesting that he may want to take advantage of this opportunity to expand his universe of possible audiences. Again, surprisingly, Richard agreed; but as a condition to the bargain, Richard requested the addition of a piano to the taproom's furnishings. To this, the pilot readily agreed. Although the piano would have to be imported into the valley at great price and peril, it promised to pay for itself in short order.

He commissioned his brother-in-vocal-chords Owen to ferry in a piano, and Owen in turn rented the pilot's former airplane from Dwight to transport the instrument into the valley. Dwight had to temporarily remove the rear seats from the sightseeing craft to make room for the ungainly instrument, but in less than an hour the modifications were complete, and Owen departed on his mission. He was gone for a mere three hours before he returned with a beautiful upright piano, its unmarred wooden surface polished to a high sheen. The pilot was shocked, more so at the quick turnaround time than at the high quality of the workmanship.

"Where did you find such a fine instrument, and so quickly? Or is it a family heirloom that was stashed away in your grandmother's garage waiting for you?"

"Abandoned churches," explained Owen. "The smaller ones never have pipe organs; they always have an upright. So I flew eastward at low altitude following some of the main back roads. When I saw the first church, I landed. The church was abandoned, and sure enough, there was this piano inside."

The pilot stared at him as two long seconds passed. "You have no problem with looting churches?"

Owen shrugged. "I wouldn't call it looting if the church is abandoned. And it is a beautiful instrument, isn't it? Someone might as well get some use out of the thing."

The pilot had to agree on all counts. He admired it for a moment, but soon his professional pilot's mind took over and he began calculating centers of gravity, moment arms, and weight estimates, especially how they related to his once-and-future airplane. At a sudden thought, he turned back to Owen. "What did you do, land my airplane in their graveyard? How did you get the piano into her?"

"I landed on the highway in front, then walked the piano out using a hoist I brought with me. I set up the hoist, moved the piano as far as I could, then moved the hoist, then moved the piano again, and eventually got it out to the street and into the airplane. Didn't even nick it, as you can see. And it's not your airplane, by the way."

The pilot scowled. "Don't worry. It will be."

If finding a piano took an unbelievably short time, it was balanced out by the protracted period that the pilot spent agonizing over a name for his new enterprise, first falling in love with, then ultimately eliminating clever name after clever name. At first he just called it "Bar," but his choices grew into a series of discarded monikers which he kept returning to, only to discard yet again. Some of the possible names were personal references, such as The Surly Scab, The Scabby Bird, and Crash Landing II. Others referred to the valley or its philosophy, such as The Gold Standard, Prometheus' Pub, and the corresponding British version: the Rock And Chain. Others were acronyms that perhaps only he would understand, among them being TANSTAAFL, SOL, ARI, TOC, TAS, and BWAIN. Some of his potential names were on the humorous side, and these he reluctantly discarded only after long thought. Among those that fell by that wayside were Beer Is Beer, The Last Straw, The Faulty Premise, and his clear favorite, Galt's Gulp. But he doubted that *that* philosophically-prissy striker would ever darken his scabby doorway, so that particular pearl of a name would surely be wasted on the swine of the valley.

In the end, he opted for a subtly suggestive title which paid homage to the valley, the building's original purpose, its former owner, and the pilot's own love of the ladies: *The Golden Touch*. He hoped it would prove prophetic as well, and serve him as an amorous good luck charm, if not also as a reputation.

With a decent name finally in hand, the pilot turned his attention to constructing a sign. However, the owner of the valley's dry goods store was of that ilk who would not sell anything to scabs, so the pilot had to hire Owen to import a bolt of red velvet and some yellow paint from the store up the road. With these tools and his meager skill, the pilot created several serviceable banners that would hang in his windows and on his walls to advertise the name of his establishment to the world. In less than a week—much sooner than he had thought possible—everything was ready for the grand opening.

With great fanfare, *The Golden Touch* opened its doors. Richard himself was the featured act for the evening, playing the imported piano as a draw for customers. The pianist had even written a lively tune specifically to commemorate the grand opening, much to the surprised delight of the pilot; Richard played it once an hour, every hour, but the pilot never tired of hearing it. Many of the patrons came strictly to hear the famous pianist, deliberately purchasing nothing, but a large percentage of the listeners willingly bought a glass of his wine or sampled some of the simple fare that the pilot served at the board. The inaugural event was a tremendous success, and at the end of his first evening in business, the pilot counted his gold with glee. *And*, he gloated, *no Income Tax!*

While Richard's talent and genius helped to break open the gates for the pilot's business, keeping that momentum going turned out to be a completely different matter. While many residents of the valley were eager for top-notch entertainment, the universe of potential regular patrons for a mere taproom proved limited. Many strikers, such as the owner of the dry goods store, refused to deal with scabs at all, preferring to be discriminating in their choice of associations regardless of draws like Richard. Others had little reason to frequent such a place at all, given that they did not imbibe, or perhaps merely chose not to do so in public. Ultimately, the bulk of his regular customers turned out to be scabs like himself, and younger residents who may have taken the oath but were looking for a place to socialize with their peers. Since some of them were the very pretty young things whose company the pilot had first targeted, he catered more and more toward the younger set while still watching out that he kept his scab regulars happy.

As a result, as the valley's population continued to grow through the rest of March, so also did his clientele; and as the weeks passed, *The Golden Touch* prospered.

# SECTION III – THE FIRST WEEKS

Late Winter, 1953

## CHAPTER 1 – I FEEL THE EARTH MOVE

Gwen gaped.

She was a Jersey girl, born and raised, accustomed to spending muggy summers "down the shore" in Wildwood and enduring bland winters punctuated by occasional Nor'easter storms that inexplicably alternated with balmy, spring-like days. She remembered from her childhood the occasional epic snowfall where the schools would close and an impromptu holiday be declared; but she also recalled how people shoveled out quickly, and within a day or two life would inevitably return to normal. With so provincial a background in the realm of winter weather, it was no surprise that she was not at all prepared for the size and ferocity of the storm that descended upon the Colorado enclave.

The storm began gathering two full days before the snow started to fall. On the first day, high, wispy cirrus clouds gradually materialized, stretching in smoky, hazy lines across the blue winter sky. Slowly, throughout the day, the lines fattened, blurred, and merged together into a uniform grey, not thick enough to hide the sun, but dense enough to banish the blue that surrounded it. By the time the sun finally set, its disc was no longer visible at all, although the clouds did take on the slight reddish hue of sunset just before dark. It had been cold enough a day, but that night the temperature plummeted far below zero.

The second day dawned a leaden grey, and the existence of the sun could only be inferred by the presence of a diffuse light that oozed from behind the featureless grey wall that floated overhead, neatly decapitating the tall peaks that surrounded the valley. With no sun to help drive it back, the bitter cold remained firmly entrenched. The thick clouds thickened further and sank lower, slowly swallowing the mountains as the morning wore on; and despite the sun rising higher in the sky, the gloom on the ground of the Gulch only deepened. By noon, the low light levels rivaled that of a typical early evening, and still the storm clouds gathered. Sunset began hours early that day, its sluggish progression marked only by the color of the sky shifting imperceptibly from a gloomy grey to a murky grey, to a grey too dim to be perceived, before finally fading to an impenetrable black. But no one was out and about on that biting, bitter evening who could notice or appreciate the nuances in transitions of non-color. Rather, on this darkest of nights, they knew the nature of the behemoth that was bearing down upon them; and in silence, they waited for the storm.

It began sometime in the dark of night, descending upon the vulnerable valley with an unbelievable ferocity. Heavy snow fell in huge, bushy flakes that drove visibility to virtually zero as it accumulated an inch or two every hour, hour after hour.

The next morning, the light of dawn broke across the valley with all of the speed of molasses in January, revealing the ground to be already blanketed in a foot of snow. The feeble light of an invisible sun did not even remotely rival the gloomy grey of the day before; and throughout this new dim day, more snow fell. By dusk, three feet of snow blanketed the valley, and still more fell, all through the night.

Dawn on the following day could only be distinguished from its predecessor by the greater amount of snow that was present upon the ground. Five feet of snow had accrued, and still more came. For those of the valley's residents who may have become accustomed to this particular storm's character, a new treat awaited them; for before noon the wind gusts began to pick up dramatically, and by the end of the day they were whipping through the valley with the force and fury of a flying freight train. Snowdrifts mounded up and clung to whatever lee they could find, rearing taller than the objects they engulfed, swallowing automobiles, trees, and even houses in their enormity. In random places, the wind paradoxically stripped the ground bare of all snow, leaving some streets and walks inexplicably swept clean. As the sun slowly set yet again on the tireless storm, still it kept snowing and blowing.

Thankfully, the new morning dawned bright, blue, and clear. The icy winds still howled, but snow no longer fell from the sky. Instead it was whipped off the ground and tossed into a whirling frenzy high in the air by the force of fierce gales, then abruptly abandoned by the fickle breeze to flitter back down to re-blanket the already-smothered surface far below. Sometimes the wind merely howled, other times it roared; and in between came the occasional distant subsonic rumble of a minor avalanche tumbling down one or another of the surrounding mountainsides. While the noise from the white tremors was not enough to rattle dishes in the cupboard, it was more than sufficient to be felt through the floor, more than enough to wake the Jersey girl Gwen.

Leaping to her feet and throwing open the curtains of her bedroom window, all she could do was gape. All appearances were that Frankie's house had sunk into the Earth during the storm, that somehow some supernatural spell had raised the ground level outside to meet her second-story window. She felt she could step out that window and simply walk straightaway across the pristine white landscape.

Pressing her cheek to the icy glass, she peered sideways into the distance toward the bulk of settlements in the valley. From her angled vantage, she could see a few rooftops barely protruding from the deep drifts, some of them sporting smoking chimneys. There were snow devils rising and falling in the air, and in one place not too far away she saw a column of white smoke boiling out of the drifts; but there was no sign of human activity.

She grabbed her robe and ran downstairs with all the excitement of a child staying home from school on a New Jersey snow day. She pulled back the curtains from the living room window, but only darkened white panes of glass met her eye; the house was buried in snow. She reached for the latch on the front door, stopped to consider for a moment the wisdom of her contemplated action, then cracked the door slowly open anyway. A few flakes dislodged to fall onto the interior doormat, but the white wall of snow in front of her held firm, reflecting a perfect impression of the outside of Frankie's front door. Still wrapped in disbelief and smiling with child-like wonder, she poked a single finger at the white wall; prosaically, it merely penetrated the cold snow, soft as a feather. She pulled out her finger, ineffectually shook the snow off it, and gently closed the door. She jumped, startled at the sound of someone coming up behind her.

"So how do you like our new outdoor décor?" Francisco announced gaily as he strode into the living room, sporting a smile as bright as the blue morning outside.

"I don't know what to make of it!" she answered excitedly. She held up her snowy finger, watching as the clinging snowflakes slowly melted back into the water it was. "It's so... so..." Words failed her. "Well, it's just that there's so *much* of it!"

"Well, this particular storm was unusually persistent, but we've learned to get used to them."

"How could you get used to a wall of snow blocking your door?"

"We won't have to. It'll be gone soon enough."

"Gone? Didn't you see how deep it is? It'll take *weeks* just to clear the front walk!"

Francisco glanced casually at the mantle clock and answered innocently, "Actually, it should be about two hours."

Gwen's expression shifted to one of bewilderment. "Two hours?"

"Maybe less; it depends on what time Lawrence got out of bed this morning."

"Lawrence?" Gwen was clearly at a total loss, and her face reflected it. "You mean the grocer, Lawrence?"

"Yes—and the automobile manufacturer Lawrence, by the way. He also runs the snow plow he built."

"The snow plow," she echoed, half understanding. "But how can you plow—" Her hand waved toward the front door. "—all that snow!"

Francisco smiled again. "You should see the plow's motor."

Although the comprehension had started slowly, it coalesced quickly. "The plow has a galtmotor in it."

"Of course. A relatively big one, too. Lawrence built a special plow for our type of snowstorms. It uses massive electric heaters driven by the galtmotor to instantly vaporize the snow. You should see it run—it has a snow scoop on the front of it that's twelve feet high! Lawrence just drives it once or twice around the valley roads and that's that. The heat it generates also cauterizes the snow on either side of the pathways he carves, so the walls don't collapse back onto the plowed portion. Not too often, at least. Once he's done the main roads, he sends a couple of his employees out with junior versions of the plow to clean the walkways and any tight spots. I'm one of Lawrence's customers, and my contract says he's supposed be here within three hours of the snow stopping, or no later than three hours after daybreak if the snow stops during the night." He looked at the mantle clock again. "It's eight o'clock now, and sunrise was about seven, so he's contractually required to be done around ten. But he's usually early."

Gwen jumped again, startled by a completely unexpected knock at the front door. Her head turned sharply, eyes wide with surprise, but Francisco just smiled.

"Come in!" he called.

The door latch rattled, and in stepped Lawrence, snow and icicles clinging to him so heavily that he appeared to be a walking snowdrift himself. The wall of snow that had been blocking the doorway only moments earlier was gone.

"We were just talking about you. You're early."

"Yes, I know. I have a busy day ahead of me, and sitting on my scupper these last two days waiting for the storm to pass has knocked my production schedule way off. We've lost a few days work on the new Lawrence limousine we're building, and now we'll have to make up the time, although I can't rightly say how. At least we got Hank's delivered before the storm hit. Anyway, I made it a point to start my rounds long before dawn today, just as soon as Dwight told me that his radar showed the main body of the storm had passed. Fortunately, you're the last ones on my rounds. Except for the powerhouse, all my other customers are already dug out."

"Is everyone in the valley your customer?" asked Gwen.

63

He smiled. "Just about; but there are a few holdouts: Richard, that scab who runs the taproom, a few others."

"What do they do on days like today?"

Lawrence smiled grimly. "They burrow a tunnel to one of my paths. Either that, or wait for the spring thaw."

Gwen brow furrowed. "But don't you ever help people out when it snows like this?"

"Sure I do. I came here to help you, didn't I? I always help my customers."

"I meant the people who aren't your customers, like the taproom owner."

"But he's not my customer," he countered, his own brow now furrowing in turn. "I'm running a business here. Why would I plow for him when he hasn't hired me?"

"But he's snowed in!"

"Yes he is," he agreed. He tilted his head slightly and added mockingly, "I'm not sure I follow your drift."

Listening to their exchange, Francisco had long since grasped the source of Gwen's confusion. "She's had enough shocks for today, Lawrence. Let me explain things to her later. Why don't you get your route finished?"

"All right. Thanks, Francisco." He turned to leave with a final wave. "Enjoy the snow!"

The instant the door closed, Gwen whirled to face Francisco. "So he won't help out the other people?" she asked curtly.

Francisco shrugged good-naturedly, his bonhomie a sharp contrast to Gwen's exasperation "If they want his help, they can always hire him."

"Good heavens! Couldn't he just give them the service this one time as a courtesy? Look at all that snow!"

Although Francisco held his smile as his only answer, it was enough to jar something in Gwen's memory, something Ragnar had said during one of the many three-cent philosophical lectures he held for the newcomers. Her eyes fell, a burst of blood coloring the skin on her cheekbones revealing the realization that she had once again said the wrong thing—and she realized, in the same instant, that she already knew the answer to her question. She could even hear Ragnar's uncompromising voice echoing inside her head: *'Give' is a word that is forbidden in this valley.*

"You're right," she finally replied, not looking up, her flushed cheeks regaining their normal hue. "I'm sorry; I forgot."

"You don't sound too convinced," he chided playfully.

As she looked up to him, there appeared in her eyes a brief flash of fire that faded quickly. "Well, I know that I was raised to try to help people when they're in trouble." Her eyes fell again, as if she were ashamed of a confession.

"And you *can* help them, so long as it's not motivated by altruism or done by force." He indicated the doorway with a tilt of the head. "Think about what you said to Lawrence: you were demanding that he work free for others, that somehow their need of him trumped his own right to his own life. It is that sort of unearned help, the kind that is demanded of others, which is forbidden here."

She nodded weakly, still not looking at him; presently she was struck by a sudden thought. She shook her head slightly to help clear it, but it would not be denied; not that she would want to deny it. As she did with the snowdrift behind the front door, so also did she proceed here with caution.

Measuring each word, she looked up to Francisco and asked, "Can I ask why are you taking the time to help me to understand? Is it altruism? I don't think I'm forcing you, so if you're not answering my questions out of altruism or force, then why *are* you doing it?" She held his gaze steadily, boldly, almost brazenly. "Is this all part of our fifty cents a night?" she asked pointedly. "Or is there another reason?"

Without hesitation, Francisco opened his mouth to answer, but never had the chance to speak..

"Would you look at all that snow!" exclaimed Gwen's father as he hobbled into the room, his cane thumping the lead. "Never saw nothin' like it in all my days! It'll take us all day just to dig out the front porch! Guess we'll have to get the neighbors to come over and lend us a hand, don't you think?"

He looked from Gwen to Francisco and back. The look on their faces must have given them away.

"Heh! Hey, what's the matter with you two? What did I say?"

She sighed. "Nothing, Dad."

"What is it? No, wait! I know: you're going to want me to help shovel, aren't you."

"No, Dad. It's not a good idea to exert yourself that much. You know that." Recognizing that he would immediately complain about the constraint, strategically she changed the subject. "Come on and let me make your breakfast. I have to get to work." She escorted her father into the kitchen, leaving her question to Francisco unanswered.

* * *

Gwen shivered.

Bundled against the icy winds that still raged through the mountain hamlet, she trekked to her temporary office at the Andrew Foundry. If a snowstorm had just dumped ten feet of snow on the Gulch, you could not tell it from the impact it had on its citizens, for the activities of everyday life went on as if the storm had never happened. Along her way to work she exchanged greetings with all the usual people; every shop along her route was completely dug out and open for business—except for the taproom. All that could be seen of it was the top part of its sign: "The Golden—" with the noun buried in white. Incongruously, the street a few feet in front of the establishment was free of snow. Had Mr. Lawrence swerved his massive plow only a few yards to one side, the front of the taproom would have been cleared as well. In fact, he had to swerve to *avoid* plowing it! She shook her head in disbelief. *These people!*

As she continued her journey into work, she noticed how no one seemed either put off or amazed by the outrageous snowscape surrounding them; they behaved as if the huge walls of white were just illusions that had no power to dare deflect the productive ability of men. Again, she found herself amazed how the valley's society always seemed to function at such high efficiency. Just look at Mr. Lawrence: automobile manufacturer, grocer, and plow boy, all in one morning. So many people in the valley wore so many hats that she confessed to a slight tinge of guilt for having only a single career. Although she was not yet convinced that the tenets of the valley's philosophy were correct, there was no denying that it made for one vibrant community.

Regardless of the philosophy's successes, she had to admit that she still did not understand it fully, as her episode with Mr. Lawrence that morning had so bluntly revealed. Time and time again she found herself playing the part of a blind child in a room full of sighted adults, not noticing her own blindness or immaturity until in ignorance she stumbled over some piece of philosophical baggage she never suspected she carried. It was disquieting; for how often are men forced to question the very foundations of their own thinking?

Part of her disquiet came from the realization of the nature of her affliction—and that she would even refer to it as an affliction at all!—but a larger part had its root in the mandate that she and all the other newcomers must soon take the striker's oath. There were only a few weeks left before the deadline, yet she knew she could not personally take that oath today in all honesty. *And will they throw me out on my ear if I don't?* she asked herself, and not for the first time. With Mr. Lawrence's unconscious intransigence still fresh in her mind, the question took on a chilling urgency. That a deadline existed at all was an indication of how the valley would react. *Perhaps I can pretend to agree?* she wondered briefly before instantly tossing the idea aside. *I'd give myself away in a minute! Just like this morning.* Again, she felt herself playing the role of the blind child; she could never get away with feigning agreement to that which she did not understand. A chill touched her as she came to a startling realization: *I'm not one of them!* Nor was she sure she could transform herself into one of them—certainly not in the next few weeks.

And what of her father? Her eyes misted over, thinking of him. She knew he'd never take the oath—and so did everyone else in the valley! He had proclaimed it often enough at too many inappropriate places that it was impossible for anyone not to know. *Will they throw Dad out on his ear, too?* She brushed the bristly back of her woolen glove against her face to wipe away the nascent tear before it froze there.

And where would they abandon her, if—no, not "if," *when*—when they threw her out? Would they take her back to Philadelphia? From what news they heard on the shortwave radio, there *was* no Philadelphia any longer, or a New York City, a Chicago, or even a Wildwood. Perhaps other cities still harbored human life, but word had been received from only a precious few of them. Several of the cities in the South still possessed shortwave communications, but a growing number of them reported being overrun by successive waves of starving refugees—usually before falling silent forever. Of all the larger cities, only Washington had somehow managed to hold off the endless attackers. Perhaps she and her father could get dropped off in Washington? Apparently there was no other place to go. She had heard that part of California had also survived, but as a religious dictatorship that shunned all technology. Even if they were accepting new immigrants, Gwen was certain that she did not want to live that way. Peasant values held no appeal for this steel mill's executive secretary. She sighed out loud. There were few choices open to her, none of them good.

Thoughts of banishment were driven from her mind as she walked up to the side door of the Stockton Foundry, the entrance nearest her secretary's desk inside. She had assumed the little-used entranceway would have been blocked by the snow, but not only were all the entrances to the foundry open and clear, so also was the expansive lot out back where Andrew set up most of his heavy work. With the squared, white walls towering over her on all sides, the illusion was great that she stood in the bottom of a tremendous white box, with a maze of passages snaking off in all directions. The clean competency in how well the valley dealt with the storm somehow frightened her, as if the society were a machine running of its own volition, and without an off switch.

With a shiver and a sigh, she walked inside and into her warm office, hung up her coat, and sat down at her desk alongside the window. She noted that Hank's coat was not hanging on its usual peg; of course he would be out visiting the new mills, supervising the next stage of their construction. She had wanted to discuss the impact of the storm with him, but apparently he had already left; tending to her father that morning had delayed her departure.

It was toasty warm in her office despite the sub-zero winds whistling outside. Surprisingly, the telephone and electric lines had not blown down during the storm, another efficiency revealed, but she paid it no mind it as she busied herself with her work. Prior to the arrival of the storm, they had been several days ahead of schedule with the construction of their first furnace. But now their entire timetable would have to be juggled to restore the balance between deliveries, available workers, financing, and all the other odds and ends that were the myriad tasks which, woven together, encompassed the rebuilding of Hank Steel. She turned to it with her characteristic, unflappable efficiency, forgetting, for the moment, any thoughts of banishment or philosophies.

The morning passed quickly for her; she remained busy answering the telephone, typing up contracts and purchase orders, and a host of other everyday activities. So it was understandable that at first she did not take notice of the subsonic rumble being transmitted to her feet through the floorboards, but it grew in volume and intensity until it eventually grasped her attention.

Interrupted, Gwen finally glanced up in curiosity and looked out the window; and for the second time that day, she gaped. For coming down the mountainside toward the foundry she saw an immense, boiling, rumbling wall of white rearing up in a gigantic cloud of snow reaching hundreds of feet into the air. Uprooted trees, massive rocks, and other debris churned in its grip as it seethed inexorably downhill.

"Avalanche!" she screamed, not knowing what else to do. "Avalanche!"

Andrew came running out of his office, saw the approaching maelstrom, and added his voice to hers. "Avalanche! Quick! Everybody outside! Use the front door! Out the front door!" People appeared from offices and other parts of the building, running for their lives toward the indicated exit.

They congregated outside in front of the building, most of them coatless and hatless standing in the bitter cold as the roar of the approaching avalanche grew. But they could not see its approach; Andrew's selection of an exit was a deliberate one, for it placed the bulk of the foundry between the fragile humans and the onrushing, killing mass of snow and debris. All they could do was huddle together to keep warm, to listen, and to wait.

Now the ground began shaking in serious harmony with the growing, rumbling din. Flakes of snow began falling all around them as the leading edge of the avalanche cloud arrived, with a crescendo so loud that speech was impossible. Without order or coordination, everyone drew close to the foundry wall, flattening themselves against it in preparation for the blow.

But it never came. With an abruptness that seemed almost unnatural, the rumblings ceased. Snow still drifted down out of the air, making small, raspy sounds as it settled, but the valley was otherwise completely silent. Presently they heard voices rising in the near distance, some of them shouting, others wailing. Andrew cautiously made his way to the side of the foundry, slowly edging around the corner of the building, then stopped dead still. Gwen and the foundry workers came up alongside him, the cold forgotten, stunned into silence by what they saw.

The rear lot of the foundry, previously a large plain clear of snow, now held an unbelievably tall, snowy mountain hundreds of feet tall bristling with trees canted at odd angles, with a few large pieces of foundry equipment jutting from its foot. Barely twenty feet of clearance separated the new mountain from the building. The last of the snow cloud fell from the air and settled onto the hair and shoulders of the onlookers.

Finally, someone spoke; it was Gwen. "Dad!" she screamed. Like a ballerina, she spun on her toe, bolted for the door, and ran back into her office, in her haste leaving the outside door open to the bitter cold. She almost knocked the telephone off of her desk before she finally got a firm grasp on the receiver. She simultaneously lifted it to her ear and began dialing before she realized that the instrument was not functioning. She paused only for a short moment, dropped the dead device, and without stopping to think, grabbed her coat and ran from the foundry.

She was unable to make her way back to Francisco's house. Before she was even halfway home, she found her way blocked by a massive arm of snow lying squarely across her route, mounding up dozens of feet high. No one else was there with her in the impromptu cul-de-sac, no crews digging open a channel for her, no one to ask for help. She paused for a second, uncertain as to what to do. Abruptly, again the unintentional ballerina, she spun on one toe and took off in the other direction in search of an adequate detour. She explored one channel after another, like a cold rat in an icy maze, until she realized that *all* the channels were blocked, that she could not reach her father. Almost without pause, spinning again, she bolted for Lawrence's Grocery Market, hoping that a channel would be open to her.

Her luck held. When she arrived, she found a stark "closed" sign hanging in the door's window. She tried the knob anyway; it was locked. Again without pausing, Gwen ran around back, stopped, and breathed a sigh of relief. There, climbing the ladder up the side of his massive snow plow, was Mr. Lawrence.

"Mr. Lawrence! Mr. Lawrence!"

He turned at the call. "Hi, Gwen!" He plopped into the elevated driver's seat high above the ground, his hand on the cabin's door handle, ready to pull it shut behind him.

Gwen screamed up at him. "You have to clear the path back to Frankie's house! My father was there all alone and I can't reach him to find out if he's okay."

"Sorry, Gwen," he called back. "I've got other customers I have to take care of first." When she did not respond, he continued. "You know I have to service my best customers first."

Momentarily confused, she asked, "But isn't Frankie one of your best customers?"

"Huh? Not him, the curmudgeon! He chose not to match the price that most of my other customers offered. That's why he has a 'three hours after sunrise' contract; that was as high as he bid."

Gwen found her mind in a whirl. "But my father may be in trouble!"

"That's as may be, but unless you can overbid half the valley, which I doubt, then you'll just have to wait your turn."

"But my father—"

Lawrence turned his attention to the dashboard in front of him and began manipulating switches and knobs. "For twenty-five cents I'll get to him as soon as I can, but according to my contract with Francisco, I don't have to be there for another three hours. Tell you what: go back to work. I'll telephone you from his place when I get there, only two cents. Okay? But right now I have to get a move on."

Not waiting for an answer, he waved perfunctorily and slammed the cabin door shut. The huge plow lurched forward, heading directly into a white wall, instantly vaporizing it upon contact, turning it into a billowing cloud of puffy white superheated steam that shot swiftly skyward. The plow proceeded through the drift as if the snow were air. In seconds, he was dozens of feet distant along a newly carved channel, made a turn, and was out of sight. Only the pillar of a white cloud marked his departing location as he threaded his way away.

"But the telephones don't work," she said softly, with only herself to hear.

Gwen stood for a moment, not understanding why her pleas meant nothing to Mr. Lawrence. Didn't he understand? It was her *father!* She stood in the cold mid-morning sunshine, still staring after the vanished plow, blinking back the tears. This was the second time that day Mr. Lawrence had inadvertently taught her a lesson in the valley's philosophy. The first was an impersonal lesson involving his plow and some random third person. But when the issue becomes first hand, when she personally had to live and sleep under the foul shadow of dread, when it wasn't someone else's father, but rather *her* father, somehow everything changed. *But not in the opinion of Mr. Lawrence and the men of the valley!* Her lips pursed in hurt anger.

Intellectually, she understood the issue: the free market drives the process. She even understood, again intellectually, why Mr. Lawrence had refused to help. Ragnar had explained the concept to her just the other night with a parable at one of his seminars. With her mind's ear, she could still hear his voice:

"Once there was a terrible hurricane that ravaged the East Coast seashore communities, leaving thousands without power and many homeless. Without modern refrigeration, they found their food supply was in dire peril. But some ice men from outside of the disaster area saw their chance: they drove in with truckloads of ice, charging ten times the normal price—and people paid it! The merchants were happy to get the ice at any price; the food supply had been saved.

"But the authorities soon caught wind of the operation and assumed emergency powers to commandeer the ice. The ice men were ordered to sell their ice at the normal price, no more than two blocks to a customer, and stood guard to enforce their order. All the newspapers hailed the solution as a model program for helping the disadvantaged. Newsreels touted stories featuring one Man On The Street who could finally find a cold beer again. But the newsreels did not talk about the fish factory that failed because the owner could no longer get enough ice to keep the day's catch cold, or the milk that went bad without refrigeration, or the damage done to the region's blood supply.

"Ironically, there were many, many ice men who would have been more than willing to come into the disaster area and help alleviate the ice shortage—for a price—and they would have done so, too, had the authorities not stepped in and cut them short. The free market system had already begun to save the victims of the storm, but too soon was stopped by force; and people suffered. Worse yet, without the unsolicited assistance of the ice men, the authorities were forced to bring in the ice themselves, with the cost being passed along to the taxpayers—at several times the normal price! Adding more injury, the governmental distribution system was so inefficient that a great deal of the ice melted en route, bringing the total cost of a delivered block much higher than what the ice men were originally charging. The moral of the story is that when it comes to helping people, the free market is the most compassionate and efficient system there is."

*The greatest good for the greatest number?* she wondered. But that couldn't be it. It's fine to say that everything works out when you only look at the bigger picture, but when it's *you* who doesn't get that block of ice, you're just as much the victim as if a looter had stolen the ice right out of your cold hands

Gwen's mood broke; she giggled. Here she stood in the freezing cold behind Mr. Lawrence's store, surrounded by giant mounds of snow, and all she could think about was ice blocks. *It's all the same thing!* she laughed, half in mirth, half in bitterness. *Cold is cold!* But her gaiety vanished instantly as a mental connection suddenly snapped into place. *But it IS all the same!* she realized. It didn't matter whether you were the fish factory owner or the Man On The Street—the basic fact remained that she or anyone else had *no right* to step in and help either the Man *or* the factory owner, if that help has to come at the expense of the other. The authorities helping the Man on the Street created one set of victims, and the free market helping the ice men and their customers created another; but it was an undeniable fact that both philosophies left victims in their wake. *It's all the same!* There was no difference between the two, she concluded, if you were to judge them by their final results. Granted, one used evil means and the other good means, but each produced that same evil end: victims. The victim Gwen nodded to herself in understanding; it *was* all the same. Both philosophies had the same inherent flaw: their practitioners did not care about what happened to certain people.

With a sharp mental click, another piece of the puzzle abruptly fell into place. If she would still create victims regardless of her choice, if it truly was all the same in the end, then, by definition, it didn't matter *what* she did. The choice of means wasn't so important when the evil end remained the same. A victim was a victim no matter how you created him. A was A.

*But what does the oath say about creating victims?* she wondered. She examined the words in her mind. "I swear by my life and my love of it—" *A good basis, although a selfish one—like not wanting to be a victim?* "—that I will never live for the sake of another man—" *Even if I make him a victim?* "—nor ask another man to live for mine." *Even when I'm being made to play the victim?* Slowly, she repeated the words to herself, but it was obvious that the oath made no mention of victims, nor why they must be created—or more importantly, why their creation should be avoided, or how. It was as if the strikers had no sympathy at all for the pain of the innocent.

She scrutinized the oath from every angle she could imagine, but the study left Gwen feeling empty; the words triggered nothing within her. All she could feel was the cold slowly seeping into her toes as she continued to stand deep in thought behind Mr. Lawrence's store. In spite of the cold, she remained standing where she was; she desperately wanted to reach her father, but could think of nothing that she could do to reach him; she had no possibility of a plan, no suggested course of action she could follow, nothing. The emptiness filled her completely. She felt as if she wasn't living her life for anyone at all at the moment, not even herself.

Gwen gasped out loud as yet another connection fell into place. It was no wonder that she felt so empty! With a sudden clarity, she grasped the dilemma that was inherent in their striker's oath: it didn't *say* anything! Once again, she examined the words of the oath carefully, but the conclusion was inescapable: it did not say what to do. Rather, it said what one must *not* do. It didn't say what you should live your life *for*; it only told you what *not* to live it for. It prescribed no action, but rather *inaction*. Living your life for someone else was an action, a "something." But not living your life for someone else was a negation, a not-action; and a negation neglects to instruct exactly what action it is that you should be performing; yet action was the most necessary attribute of life. To live for someone, or to not live for someone, that was the question; two questions, actually, with two completely different answers and two orthogonal frames of reference: one wanted to help; the other, not to hinder. One was an action; the other, an inaction. One a something; the other, a nothing; a zero, two completely different, opposite approaches.

But how could a zero hold a mortgage over her life? She began experimenting with the words of the oath, seeing if she could somehow invert them into a positive statement, to tease the words into taking an affirmative stand. *I will live my life for me? I will tell others not to live for me?* She shook her head; she found no insights or guidance in her word games. Following the best of the inverted advice would just as surely leave the metaphorical gate open to creating victims.

Somehow, she felt that there must be some third path she was not visualizing, some philosopher's stone that would spare humanity the necessity of creating any victims at all. But while she could sense the dim outline of the path untraveled, the details of its direction eluded her. Somehow, the taproom could be plowed out without inconveniencing Mr. Lawrence. Somehow, the Man On The Street would have a cold beer with his fish dinner. Somehow, she could take care of her father without doing so. She shook her head at the maze of contradictions. She concluded that there was no third way, *could be* no third way; there must always be victims. All that remained was to determine how one created them. But should she agree to the method of the strikers? More importantly, could she?

With a start, she realized that by agreeing to come into the valley, she had already accepted the striker's oath; she had already become one of them. Her survival was now inextricably bound up in theirs, even though neither she nor they would live their lives for each other. Rather, the binding was based in the nature of how they chose their victims. Like a fan of some secretly demented sports team, she had unthinkingly donned their jersey without realizing the package deal that would come with it. Fully, she grasped how she had already inadvertently chosen sides, and in the process implicitly condoned the strikers' method for choosing victims. She saw that there was no going back for her now, neither in the physical sense nor in the philosophical sense.

Again she experienced a mental hiccough as she realized she could now honestly swear to their striker's oath, and it honestly wouldn't matter. It didn't make any difference if you never lived your life for another or not, because someone was still going to be forced to play the victim, that was certain. Today, Gwen happened to be that victim; it was her fears for her father's safety that were to be sacrificed to the gods of the free market. And that was exactly how it should be. After all, this was the Gulch, and the free market was their way of choosing victims.

She lifted her gaze to the insurmountable granite mountains that encircled the deep blue sky that arched over the valley, feeling as if her future courses of action were similarly circumscribed. But she knew for certain that the imprisoning peaks were more than mere symbolism; she had no other choice but to accept the tenets of the Worker's philosophy, considering the alternative. She knew all too well the means and ends of the code of the looters, and recoiled from it in understandable horror. But in backing off of one philosophy, she somehow found herself pushed into the arms of another. If she wouldn't choose victims in the manner of Mr. Wesley, should she then be forced to choose them in the manner of the Worker? She sighed silently. Had she had her choice, she would rather choose to create no victims at all.

*But no*, she concluded, there was no third path; only the mountains, the sky, and the figure of the Worker. Given a choice, there was no choice. She was here in the valley; there was nowhere else to go. It was a fact, a *fait accompli*, and that was that. A was already A.

With that, she knew exactly what it was that was required of her in these times of uncertain troubles. It was if a great weight had been lifted from her shoulders. Her choice of sides had long-since been made, and she would have to live with the consequences of that choice, inadvertent though it may have been. Now events would play themselves out, as they will, in spite of her second-guessing and wishes. She felt relief in knowing her place in the grander scheme of things, and that she could have chosen no better alternative, given the choices—but she didn't have to like it.

With the matter finally settled in her own mind, she held her head high, thought lovingly of her father, spun once more on a cold toe, and headed back to work, as she should.

* * *

Gwen started.

The unexpected ringing of the telephone on her desk caught her completely by surprise. It had been dead all morning, but apparently it was back in service. Answering the device, she was not surprised to hear the voice of Mr. Lawrence.

"Hi, Gwen. I'm calling to let you know that there should be a clear path back to Francisco's. You'll have to swing past the airstrip and walk along the taxiway, but at least you'll be able to get home."

"Did you stop in to see my father?" she asked anxiously.

"No, I didn't. I'm still at the airstrip. I just finished clearing the runway, and my reports tell me that there's no other plowing needing to be done between here and Francisco's. So the way is probably open and you should be able to check on him yourself. I could do it for you for another nickel, if you like. I'd be happy to help."

There was a noticeable pause. "Thank you, Mr. Lawrence," she finally replied in a crisp, professional tone, but with an almost imperceptible edge to it. "I'll take care of it myself." After hanging up from Mr. Lawrence, she immediately dialed Francisco's house, but the call would not go through. Two, three, four times she tried, but apparently some of the lines had not yet been repaired. She glanced at her wristwatch; it was almost noon. The impetus was great to drop the task she was doing and run to check on her father. *But it's all the same!* She told herself she could wait the ten minutes until her lunch hour began, but despite her new certainty somehow she would not listen to herself. Without another moment's hesitation, she grabbed her coat and headed home to learn what she might.

As she threaded the serpentine path back to Frankie's house, she found that the snows had drifted appreciably over more than one of the plowed paths she had traversed just that morning, with some drifts rearing up several feet. But Mr. Lawrence had spoken rightly; she was able to navigate the berms successfully, and soon arrived.

With her field of vision limited by the towering walls of snow on either side, the first thing she saw when she came around the last bend was the prosaic sight of Francisco shoveling some minor amounts of new snow from their front walk. Catching sight of her out of the corner of his eye, he paused in his labors, leaned on his shovel, and smiled. "Half day, Gwen?"

"Don't you play your games with me, Frankie! How is my father?"

"At the moment, he's a little dismayed because I won't let him help shovel, but otherwise in his usual cantankerous spirits. At his age, I know it's not a good idea for him to take that sort of chance."

Gwen brightened noticeably, a great relief washing over her. Without another word, she maneuvered past the smiling man and entered the house. She found her father sitting at the kitchen table daydreaming over a cup of hot tea. He turned at her approach.

"Hi, Gwen! What are you doing here? Did Hank give you a snow day?"

"No, Dad. I'm on my lunch break and just wanted to check in on you."

"Well I'm fine, even if that damn smoothie won't let me help!" He gestured brusquely with the teacup in the direction of the shoveling copper magnate. "He even insisted he make my tea for me! He treats me like I can't do nothing for myself, like I'm a baby. Says it's all part of my room and board—not that I'd ask him to do it!" He seethed in his chair. "Why, if I were a younger man, I'd—"

"Now, Dad; he means well."

"I guess," he grumbled.

"And so do I. Now give me a kiss. I'm sorry I can't stay; I have to get back to work. But I did want to check in on you." She bent over him and offered a cheek, but the ringing of the phone halted her midway. She turned to answer it.

"No, no!" cried her father. "Let me get it! Let me be good for at least one thing around here." He raised himself slowly and carefully from the kitchen chair, leaning heavily on his cane, and ambled over to the telephone, finally answering it on its fourth ring.

"Hello?... Oh, hang on a minute. He's out front shoveling the walk." He set the receiver on the counter and faced Gwen's inquisitive glance. "It's for Mister Smoothie."

"I'll let him know on my way out."

"No! I'll tell him!"

Gwen shrugged. "Have it your way. But here—let me help you get your coat on. It's far too cold outside." She helped him with his heavy coat, pecked him on the cheek, and together the two of them headed out the front door. Gwen continued silently on her way, as her father slowly approached Francisco.

"Hey, Frankie! Telephone call for you. It's that pirate fellow. Can't remember how you say his name!"

Francisco set the shovel aside. "Thank you. And it's pronounced 'Ragnar.'" He headed into the house to take the call, leaving Gwen's father alone.

The old man stood in the cold for a moment, leaning on his cane, then brightened. He saw his chance, and seized the opportunity. "Tell me I can't help, will ya?" He angrily speared his cane into a snow pile, snatched up the abandoned shovel, and clumsily began shoveling. Although he made slow progress, it was progress nonetheless; and by the time Francisco returned he had cleared the newly-drifted snow from several feet of walkway.

Francisco stepped in immediately. "Sir! You shouldn't be doing that! Give me that! Give me that shovel, sir!"

"No! I'm doing fine," he insisted, using the shovel as a clumsy pointer to indicate his handiwork in clearing the path. "Look at that walk!" he bragged. He held the pose for a moment, but the shovel's metal blade proved to be too much of a weight for his slight frame to counterbalance. Without his making a sound, both his feet abruptly swung out from under him, and he landed on his belly on the cold ground. He grunted softly on contact.

"Dang it!" he shouted, wiggling fruitlessly from his prone position. "Frankie! Help me! I've fallen and I can't get up!"

Francisco hurried over and knelt by his side. "Are you hurt?" he asked anxiously.

"Nope; just banged my head a little." He rubbed a spot above his temple for a moment. "No harm done."

"Please, sir!" He gently helped the old man to his feet. "Get back into the house where you'll be safe."

"No! I want to help! We strikers have to stick together!"

Francisco pulled the cane from the snow pile. "And we do. You've done your fair share, and I can finish up from here. Now you can help best by staying out of the way." He held him insistently by elbow, offering the cane with his other hand.

"I guess," he finally grumbled. He snatched his cane brusquely from Francisco's outstretched hand and shuffled back toward the house, rubbing his temple and muttering to himself all the way.

Francisco kept an eye on the retreating back until it vanished behind the closed door. With a small smile and a shake of the head, he returned to his work.

When he entered the living room a short time later, he found Gwen's father asleep on the sofa, his gentle snoring keeping time with the slow ticking of the mantle clock. Obviously, the unusual effort of the day had tuckered out the old man. Francisco smiled at the reclining form and retired to his room upstairs to resume working on plans for his new copper smelter.

\* \* \*

Hank rubbed his eyes.

It had long since grown dark outside of his small office in the Andrew Foundry, and he was more than ready to call it a night. The day had been a long one, and despite the interrupting avalanche and interrupted telephone service, he and Gwen had still managed to accomplish much. Before the sun had set, they had been able to orchestrate all of the necessary alterations to their construction schedule to accommodate the delays introduced by the two-day snowstorm and the subsequent avalanche. The net result was that the date for the firing of the first heat of Miracle Metal in the Gulch would be delayed by only a single day, and they still remained far ahead of their original target of late September. Hank took pride in his day's accomplishments; and while he may have been weary in body, he was exuberant in spirit.

He gathered some papers that would serve as his reading material for the evening, and stuffed them into his inside jacket pocket. He put on his hat and overcoat, and snapped off the light. Emerging from his office, he saw that Gwen was still sitting at her desk, reviewing some paperwork. "Plenty of time to worry about that tomorrow, Gwen. It's late. Why not close up shop? I'll walk home with you."

"Yes, Mr. Hank," she replied with her usual formal efficiency. In a moment her desk was clear, and he was helping her with her coat. Together, they emerged into the frigid March darkness, navigating in silence the deserted, deeply-plowed ravines that led back to Francisco's house.

With the distraction of her workday behind her, Gwen's thoughts turned again to questions of philosophy, and the epiphany she had experienced that morning, picking up right where she had left off. *It's all the same—there are always victims—the striker's oath prescribes no action—there is no third path—I can honestly swear to the oath, because it makes no difference.* But something about her conclusions still felt incomplete, as if there were some greater epiphany that hovered somewhere in the wings, waiting upon a chance discovery. With characteristic curiosity, she plunged into deep speculations on the subject, ignoring the presence of her boss at her side.

As they walked, she pondered the alternative philosophical avenues that had opened up before her that morning. If there were no effective differences between the results of living your life for someone versus not living your life for someone—both ways still created victims—then there must be some higher truth which could guide a person in choosing one approach over another, providing some rationale for damning a certain victim or crowning a particular champion, or—hopefully!—driving the decision in some third, as yet unknown direction. As to what that method might be, or how the selection might be done, or where it may lead, she had few clues. She had sought guidance in the striker's oath, but found no philosopher's stone there. What good, then, was the oath? The strikers' willing, long-winded explanations nibbled at the edges of her questions, but did nothing to satisfy her intellectual appetite. What value did the strikers see in it? With a start, she realized there was a striker at hand whom she could ask.

"Mr. Hank?" she ventured, breaking the silence between them.

Hank heard an unusual tone in Gwen's voice; not her normal tone of quiet efficiency, but rather an unprotected innocence that he rarely heard from her. "What is it, Gwen?" he replied softly, unconsciously mirroring her manner.

"Pardon me for getting personal, but may I ask you a question?"

"Sure."

"You've taken the striker's oath, haven't you?"

He nodded to himself, understanding now the reason for her unusual tone of voice. "Yes. I took it the day before we came to the valley, the same night the mills were attacked."

"What made you take it?"

He smiled in the dark. "That's a big question, with an even bigger answer." He remained silent for a few paces, gathering his thoughts, then began. "I had embraced the oath's essence for a long time before I actually heard it verbalized. Although I had practiced it ruthlessly in my work, my discussions with Francisco helped me to understand that I wasn't living it in my personal life. I didn't even realize I wasn't! It took a long time for me to understand what was out of kilter with how I did live my life. But little by little, I puzzled it out."

"How?"

"Well, the beginnings of my understanding started not too long after I had invented Miracle Metal. Remember how the State's Science Institute insisted that I sell them some of my Metal, but I refused? They wanted me to pretend that it was merely a normal business transaction when obviously it wasn't. They could have simply passed another directive and taken the Metal out of my hands at any time, but they needed my participation to make their pretense complete. They needed the sanction of the victim. That was my first step toward understanding, when I realized that it takes my sanction to make their looters' game work. Any power they have, it is because I gave it to them; and it has always been mine to either grant or take away. When they put me on trial for selling my Metal to Ken to shore up his coal mines, that's how I won: by refusing to give them my sanction."

Gwen considered his words carefully, but could not match them up with her new understanding. Were victims determined by circumstance or by sanction? "I'm not sure I follow what you mean," she interjected. "How does that relate to the striker's oath?"

"Think of it this way: what is the real reason why you do anything in life, whether it's getting up in the morning, working at Hank Steel, or even doing something simple, such as having this conversation? For me, the reason is the same: to share my mind, my creativity, and my life with other rational men such as myself, and to have them share theirs with me. It's a trade that makes us both richer for it. But last November I reached the point where I was finally forced to admit to myself that those sort of men no longer existed, except here in the Gulch, so the reason behind the existence of my mills Outside no longer existed either; the only thing that remained to hold it all together was my sanction. Once I withdrew that sanction, there was nothing left to keep it going. The only thing I had to do was to stop living my life for the looters, and all the rest followed almost automatically. Witness how operations of the old Hank Steel were 'temporarily suspended' soon after we left. The soul had gone out of it—my sanction—along with all the reasons why I created Hank Steel, and so it died. But here in the valley, all of my reasons are still valid. The looters' code does not reign here. So I'm able to share and be shared with again, which is the way it should have always been. The soul of Hank Steel lies here, and it's here that it will be reborn. So you see, there was really no other rational choice but to abandon the looters, join the strikers, and take their oath. Do you understand now?"

She did not. "But it's all the same!" she blurted blindly, going for broke. If she couldn't understand him, she would have to make him understand her.

"What? What's all the same?"

"Why should it matter to you who you produce your Metal for?"

Now it was Hank's turn to be confused. "What do you mean? I just told you."

"But isn't it all just a choice of victims? Maybe the looters chose you to be their victim, but didn't you choose them to be yours? You withdrew your sanction and now the Hank Steel they knew is gone. You left them all in the lurch, making them your victim just as surely as they had made you theirs. So isn't it all the same? You both created victims. You just did it for different reasons."

Hank did not reply immediately. He could understand her words, but the rationale behind them was elusive; he saw that she was concentrating on results, not on reasons, on effects rather than causes. While she had not presented a formal, philosophical statement, he could still see that within a certain scope she was correct; the end result was simply a different choice of victims. But the reasons behind the choices were vastly different, and that constituted the heart of his answer. Finally, he spoke. "The difference is in the means. Looters use evil means; the strikers use good means."

"I can accept that, but did you ever stop and think about your ends? What about the victims you create? Isn't that still an evil end?" He had no ready reply, so she pressed on. "Are you telling me the difference between the strikers and the looters is that the looters use evil means to an evil end, but you strikers use good means to an evil end?"

"No! We strive for a good end!" he riposted automatically. He swept an arm across their path and around behind them, indicating all of the Gulch. "Isn't this a good end?"

*I wonder!* she exclaimed to herself. "But aren't you forgetting the effect your strike has had on the looters' world?"

Hank chortled. "The looters will climb on your shoulders to keep from drowning, regardless of their effect upon others."

"And we don't?"

"No! In the world Outside, I had to jump through hoops to keep my mills open—*you* of all people know that! But here in the valley we're protected against their meddling."

"In exchange for a different sort of meddling?"

"What meddling? Different how?"

"Well, the striker's oath, for one thing. You have to take it, and live by it."

"Of course I do. Why wouldn't I?"

"Because it's just another way of choosing the victims: the Worker's way."

Again Hank did not reply immediately, so Gwen continued. "Mr. Lawrence spent the day choosing victims, didn't he?"

"What do you mean? He plowed out the valley twice today, I hear. Which victims did he choose?"

"He chose several: the pilot who runs the taproom. Richard. My father. All those people who don't pay him the—I don't know what to call it—the 'snow tribute.' He left them at the mercy of the storm."

"But plowing snow is his business!"

"Yes! And so is choosing victims!"

Hank shook his head. "It's a choice of who Lawrence helps, not a choice of who he doesn't help. His 'victims' choose themselves."

"But he could have still chosen to help the victims of the storm, couldn't he?"

"But they're not his customers!"

"Regardless! Couldn't he?" she pressed.

"Yes," he conceded, then qualified, "But they chose not to hire him."

"But they were snowed in!"

"Yes, but he chose to help his customers instead."

She could see she was not getting through to him. "But how is choosing who to help different from choosing who not to help, Mr. Hank? The logical result of the choice is still the same: Mr. X gets help. Mr. Y does not. Is a difference that makes no difference a real difference?"

"But it's the basis for that choice that matters!"

"Yes!" she agreed vehemently, "But what *is* that basis?"

"The striker's oath," he asserted automatically.

"That's what I've heard a lot of people here saying. But the oath is not a basis at all. It's not a statement of what you or I *should* do. It's a negation of things that we *don't* want to do! Listen to the words: 'I won't live for others or ask them to live for me.' There's no substance to it! All that it has is the choice of victims, the person you won't live for. Even the Boy Scout oath has more substance than that! What was it? Trustworthy, loyal, helpful, happy... I forget the rest." She giggled incongruously, her hand held to her mouth in embarrassment. "I was never a Boy Scout, Mr. Hank."

"Neither was I. I was too busy with my work, even as a teen."

"But do you see my point about creating victims?"

"Yes, but you have to realize that there's much more to the Worker's philosophy than merely the oath. That's just the ethics, not the metaphysics or epistemology."

"If the metaphysics and epistemology cared about preventing victims, then why isn't that reflected in the oath, too?"

"Isn't it?" wondered Hank out loud to himself.

"Where is it, then?" pressed Gwen. "It's not! Why does the oath say what you *won't* do rather than what you *should* do? Such an oath is not an act of defining, but rather one of wiping out. Why use a negation?" She paused briefly in thought, then again giggled incongruously.

Hank walked alongside her, a puzzled expression on his face, then impatiently prompted, "Well? What's funny now?"

"I was just wondering what the strikers say when they get married. Instead of saying *I do*, do they say, *I don't?*" She ended her sentence with laughter plain in her voice.

Hank did not smile.

Gwen picked up her reasoning where she had left off, her tone serious again. "Excuse me, Mr. Hank; I was digressing. However, my point is still a valid one: why not say what you will do rather than what you won't do?"

"Good question." Hank considered the implications and mused out loud. "Now that I think about it, you may be on to something." He thought for a moment longer, then went on. "Or maybe not. The first half of the oath can easily be phrased positively, such as 'I swear to live my life for myself.' But that ignores the second half, which is to not ask others to live for mine." He paused thoughtfully, then suggested, "How about, 'I swear not to be a victim?'—wait, that's still a negation. Or 'I swear I'll leave you alone?' No, that's a negation, too—"

"Wait a minute, Mr. Hank," she interrupted, stopping dead in her tracks, light dawning on her. "Now that I think about it, the second part of the oath can't be made to work at all!"

Hank halted uncertainly. "How's that?"

"The problem is that I have no power to order you how to run your life, none at all!"

"True, but to refrain from asking *is* in one's power."

She waved his words aside. "It doesn't matter if I ask or not; the burden remains on others to choose for themselves whether or not they live their life for my sake, or if you want to phrase it positively, that it's *they* who should decide to live their lives for themselves and not for me. But that's not within my power, and how can I swear to do something I know that's outside of my power? What's the value in such an oath? And if men are just living their lives for themselves, then everything else—everything!—is left without a rudder. All they're doing after that is living for themselves, like some spoiled brat, and, in the process, choosing victims. But by what standard?"

Hank replied instantly. "The standard is life. '...by my life and my love of it...' And man is the measure."

"'...and *victims* are the measure', you mean."

A hint of distress fleeting crossed Hank's face. "I don't like to think of it as 'choosing victims.'"

Gwen shrugged, the movement barely visible under her bulky winter coat. "You could call it 'choosing champions' instead, but what difference would it make? It's the choosing that matters." Gwen's eyes were bright in the darkness with their emotional intensity.

"That implies there must be some broader principle that determines which champions to choose," he suggested.

"Yes! Yes! That's exactly what I told myself! But what is it?"

"Not living your life for others", he replied immediately.

"Phrased positively," she insisted.

Hank stood in the starlight alongside her, but did not immediately reply. "Is it the non-initiation of force? No, wait; that's another negation." He stood in thought for a moment longer, then shook his head. "How else would you want to phrase it, besides not living your life for others? Because that's key."

"Key? Is it really? We do live our lives for others, Mr. Hank," she pointed out. "We're rebuilding Hank Steel so others can benefit from it."

"In a sense that's true," he agreed. "But not the looters!"

"So we're still choosing victims? Excuse me, 'choosing champions?'"

He stood silently with no reply.

She went on, the words tumbling from her quickly in her excitement. "Do you remember Mr. Harvester from a few years ago? We had to juggle our schedule for weeks to get him the extra steel he needed, and we succeeded. He was able to keep his plant operating, when otherwise he would have had to shut it down for good."

"I remember. That was right about the same time that they passed that damnable Equalization of Opportunities Bill."

She ignored his aside, instead driving home her point. "But we stretched our schedules, increased our workers' overtime, delayed some of our other customers' deliveries, but in the end we managed to deliver for Mr. Harvester, our champion."

Neither of them mentioned that Mr. Harvester had gone out of business anyway a year later, but the memory was on both of their minds.

"But Mr. Harvester wasn't a looter," Hank quickly interjected. "He's just the sort of person we would want to help."

"Then shouldn't the oath reflect that? Something like, 'I swear by my life and my love of it that I will help people like Mr. Harvester and not people like Mr. James, the president of Transcontinental Railroad?'"

"From what I've been hearing, James has just turned over a new leaf."

"All the more reason we need the principle and not the people. But what is that principle?"

Riposting, Hank replied, "Then what would you call someone who selfishly lives for himself, yet sets up a business that does good things for other people by selling them things they need? Or conversely, someone who refuses to demand that others live for him, but freely accepts their help when offered?"

Gwen stood silently and considered the question for a moment before making an obvious observation. "It's cold out. Let's get home."

The roaring, gusty winds from earlier in the day had mercifully vanished to be replaced by a starry silence, an ear-ringing quiet heightened by the sound-dampening effects of the ubiquitous snow and the thin mountain air. The brilliant pinpoints of the stars reeled overhead in a moonless sky, their dim light still sufficient to vaguely illuminate the surrounding snow-covered mountain peaks. The dry, icy air stung in their nostrils and seeped into their exposed skin, making their cheeks numb to the touch. But neither noticed either the beauty of the winter night, or the minor ills it spawned; they were too deep in thought.

Gwen finally spoke. "Would you call them traders? Or capitalists? I'm not sure."

"Perhaps. Either word could describe anyone here in the valley."

She laughed sarcastically, something that Hank had never heard her do before. "Traders? No, I think it goes far beyond traders. Take the case of the pilot who runs the taproom. He may not have taken the oath yet, but he's not a bad sort. Yet there are some folks here in the valley who refuse to trade with him at all, either as buyer or seller. Some won't even sell to people who re-sell to him. They call him rude names and make fun of him behind his back. Yet there are others in the valley who treat him decently. Obviously there's a noteworthy difference there—especially if you're the poor pilot!"

They continued in silence for a short distance, then she added pensively, "You'd think there could be a system or philosophy where it wouldn't be necessary to choose among victims. Arguments about good means versus evil means are useless, so long as the ends remain evil. Why should it be a necessary evil to always have a victim, Mr. Hank? Why should we be choosing victims at all?"

He remained silent a moment before summing up his thoughts. "I cannot see any way to prevent it."

She sighed sorrowfully. "Nor I."

They walked on in silence through the cold night, contemplating the conundrum. Ahead they could see the lights of Francisco's house, then Gwen spoke again. "What did it feel like, Mr. Hank?"

"What's that?"

"When you finally accepted the truth behind the striker's oath?"

Hank's pace slowed unconsciously, and Gwen slowed deliberately in turn. He looked up to the sky as he considered the question. He appeared deeply moved at the memory. Finally he spoke, almost in awe. "It was as if the proverbial scales had fallen from my eyes," he confessed. "I found I suddenly understood the great questions of the universe. And the answers. No task seemed beyond my ability, no question unanswerable to my reasoning, or hidden from my intellect. All of the follies of my life abruptly snapped into perspective, and I realized with a clarity that I had never felt before that I was finally rid of them, and that they no longer had to matter. It was as if a great weight had been lifted from my shoulders and I had been set free for the first time in my life. It was a single answer to a thousand questions, and they all fell into place all at once and in the proper order. It was something that had been building for a long time, but then suddenly flipped, like a light switch. One minute I was one person; the next, I was another."

Gwen nodded in understanding. "That's a lot like how I felt," she said softly, more to herself than to him.

Hank glanced at her in the dark, stunned. "You're ready to take the oath, then?"

They had reached Francisco's house. She stopped at the front door and turned to face him, a shocked expression on her face. "Me? Heavens, no! Haven't we just been talking about how meaningless it is?"

"Then what happened that made you feel that way?"

"It happened this morning; I realized that it didn't matter whether or not I took the oath, because all we were doing was choosing victims—or champions, if you will." She waited in silence for a few seconds, then looked up at his dim countenance in the dark and spoke softly. "It's a powerful feeling, isn't it, Mr. Hank? That certainty, I mean. It's very liberating and energizing, even a little frightening, when you realize that your life is completely in your own hands, and absolutely under your own control, isn't it?" Her voice fell to a soft whisper, yet he plainly heard her words hanging in the quiet winter air. "Almost... godlike... Isn't it?"

They held each other's eye firmly for several seconds, then she blinked twice, quickly, uncertainly, then turned away from him and opened the door. Together they entered the warm, brightly-lit living room, closing the door against the night's chill. Gwen's father lay on the sofa silently sleeping, his chest rhythmically rising and falling in a slow cadence. His nose had been running as he slept, forming a thin, dry crust of mucous across one cheek. Hank helped her out of her coat, removed his own, hung them up on their usual pegs in the closet, then headed upstairs.

"Why isn't he in bed at this hour?" Gwen wondered aloud, a mite perturbed. She knelt down at his side and shook him gently. "Dad? Dad? Wake up. You should be upstairs sleeping in your own bed." But the old man did not stir. Gwen shook him a little less gently. "Dad?" His head lolled slightly to one side, revealing an ugly, purplish bruise above his temple, the blotchy patch of discolored skin plainly visible through his thinning hair. She drew a sharp inward breath, then let out with a yell. "Mr. Hank! Frankie! Somebody!" Despite the shrillness of her cries, her father did not stir.

From upstairs she heard the sound of hurrying feet. Francisco bounded down the steps, followed soon after by Hank.

"How long has he been asleep?" she demanded.

"I don't know," confessed Francisco. "I've been upstairs working all day."

"Did you see this?" She pointed to the nasty bruise.

"My God, no!" Francisco was at his side in a second, gently examining the bruise. "This can't be good!" he asserted. "I'm going to telephone Dr. Thomas!"

"But what happened?" she pressed.

Francisco was already clutching the telephone, the violent whirl of its dial punctuating his distracted words. "He fell on the front walk just after you left... Said he banged his—" Francisco focused his attention on the voice at the other end of the line. "Dr. Thomas?... Oh. This is Francisco. Let me speak with Dr. Thomas please... Yes, I know how busy he is, but I need to speak with him immediately. Gwen's father fell and banged his head," he explained, glancing at the unconscious man. "He's asleep and we can't wake him. My guess is that it's at least a concussion, maybe an epidural hematoma... Yes, we can bring him right over... Good... All right. Goodbye." He hung up the telephone, turning his anxious glance to Gwen. "We have to take him to the hospital right away!"

"I'll bring my Lawrence around," Hank offered. "The roads are clear enough that we can drive him there."

"Good." Francisco hastened to a closet. "I'll grab a couple of blankets to keep him warm."

Hank returned shortly, and the two men had little difficulty carrying the slight form of Gwen's father out to the waiting automobile. They laid him in the back seat, and the three of them squeezed into the front. It was not a long drive, and in a few moments they reached the hospital.

Outside the building all was quiet, but inside bedlam reigned. The injured from the avalanche still filled the waiting room and lined the corridors, bundled two to a bed. Several nurses and Hank's mill doctor moved among them, administering what aid they could.

Francisco lightly grabbed the arm of one of the passing nurses. "Gwen's father is unconscious out in the car. Where can I put him?"

The nurse stopped and blinked at him myopically. "What? What? Her father? Can't you leave him where he is? We simply don't have the room for him!"

Francisco held his calm. "Only for a short while; he's in the back seat, and it's a cold night."

"Well, you can see for yourself that we're up to our ears with the injured. I don't know what we can do with him." As an afterthought, she added warily, "Is he on retainer?"

"No," admitted Francisco. "Not to my knowledge."

"Then he'll have to wait," she snapped. "There's another man who's not on retainer already in the cellar. For twenty-five cents a day you can put your patient downstairs with him, if you like; there should be more than enough room. Did you bring blankets and a pillow? Two cents a day more, if you want us to supply them. It's a little chilly down there, but not as cold as it is in your automobile. Maybe if you put him close to the furnace, he'll keep warmer." She turned and walked away, calling one final sentence over her shoulder as she left, "And I'm not sure how soon we'll be able to get around to him!" Without another word, she left the room.

Francisco took Hank by the arm. "Come on. Give me a hand getting him in."

Gwen stepped in front of the two men, hands on her hips. "In the cellar?" she asked incredulously.

"In the cellar," agreed Francisco.

"With the furnace?"

"With the furnace."

"No!" She turned her steel-eyed gaze from one man to the other. "No! This is taking things too far! He's my *father*! We can't put him in the cellar!"

"Nor can we leave him in the back seat," countered Francisco. He turned to Hank. "Come on, Hank."

"No!" she cried yet again.

Hank placed a compassionate hand on her shoulder. "Gwen. Please. We must do whatever we can for our champion."

After two heartbeats, she let out an exasperated sigh. Some of the fire went out of her eyes as she stepped aside. "Yes, Mr. Hank."

* * *

Gwen was crestfallen.

"There's nothing I can do for him short of immediate surgery," Dr. Thomas told her flatly, an edge of irritation plain in his voice, "but my time is completely taken up with my retainer customers. Maybe your company doctor could handle it, but he was on duty all night last night, then worked the entire day today treating victims of the avalanche. He finally got to bed not a half an hour ago, and *I'm* not going to try to wake him. I'm not even sure it would be possible at this point! And even if we could rouse him, would you want him performing brain surgery?"

Gwen's father lay on the cellar floor alongside the furnace, his blankets giving him an illusory bulk. Gwen knelt on the hard floor alongside him, her back to an injured man also lying on the floor, a scab victim of the avalanche. The man moaned eerily in his sleep every few breaths, but no one paid him any mind.

"Even if I had the time to look at your father, I already have Midas and two others lying under a death watch upstairs, not to mention corridors lined with other priority patients. I'll be working through the night tonight if I'm lucky, and all day tomorrow, too, if I'm not. The only way I could possibly be able to help your father now is if you could overbid one of the patients who I'm already treating, which I know you can't. Otherwise I can't afford to spend any time with your father at all. Gods, woman! I can't even afford to take the time to explain it all to you!" With that, Dr. Thomas spun on his heel to leave.

He was not halfway across the room when Gwen burst into tears, her face falling, sobbing, onto her father's chest. The injured man behind her moaned once in ghoulish harmony.

"Dr. Thomas," Hank called softly to the retreating form.

The doctor's hand grasped the doorknob before he glanced back. He turned only slightly, not facing Hank, with one eyebrow going up. "Yes?" he asked in a weary voice.

"Please. Do whatever it takes to save her father. Do it now. Send me the bill for whatever it costs."

Dr. Thomas stood at the cellar exit, hand on the knob, still not turning full to face Hank or even meeting his eyes, but rather merely looking over his shoulder in Hank's general direction. In the silence, they heard the avalanche victim behind Gwen moan again. Dr. Thomas looked at the blank door in front of him and sighed inaudibly. "All right," he finally assented, not turning. "I'll do what I can. But at this point I'm not sure how much anyone can do for him." He turned the knob, opened the door, and left.

Ignored in the exchange and still crouching on the floor was Gwen. Her sobs still filled the room, but they were now tears of joy. Her father was going to live!

Hank reached down to her and moved his hand gently across her forehead, a rare break in the formality that had always existed between them. She looked up to him gratefully with red, wet eyes. He smiled at her and asked, "We must do what we can for our champion, mustn't we?"

She forced a smile in return and nodded vigorously, shaking tears loose to sprinkle across her father's still form.

Behind her, the injured scab moaned yet again, ignored.

\* \* \*

The Gulch mourned.

On the third day following the disastrous avalanche, funeral ceremonies were held for the dead. Literally the entire valley turned out to pay their final respects—the first time there had been a complete town gathering in the history of the valley—and there was not a person among them who wasn't surprised by the sheer size of the crowd. There had never been any official census taken, so the valley's population had previously been mere conjecture, but no longer. They found they numbered over two thousand strong, where less than a year ago there had been barely a few hundred.

The dead fortunately represented a substantially smaller number: a mere baker's dozen. Death had come in the guise of a democrat, for among the dead were Atlanteans both young and old, famous and anonymous, rich and poor, striker and scab. The most notable among the deceased was Midas himself, the longest resident of the valley, whose cancer had finally taken its ultimate course. Despite the fact that his demise was unrelated to the catastrophe, forever after it ironically became known as "Midas' Avalanche." Least notable among the victims was the reclusive scab wife of Hank's mill superintendent, she being known only to her mourning widower. A horrified Lawrence had discovered her charred remains jammed within his snowplow's massive maw. Apparently she had been buried by the avalanche, and he had unwittingly scooped up her trapped form while plowing.

Also mustered among the remaining eleven victims lay Gwen's father, the oldest of the lot. True to his word, Dr. Thomas had done everything he could for the poor man, from administering rare antibiotics that had been ferried into the valley at great expense, to drilling tiny surgical holes in cranial bones to relieve the pressure of built-up fluids. He had brought to bear all of the valley's technologies, both the unique and the mundane, but in the end the effort proved to be in vain. The long delay between concussion and treatment had taken too great a toll, exceeding even Dr. Thomas' ability to rectify. Similar stories could be told for several others of Midas' honor guard. Demand had far outstripped supply, with predictable, tragic results.

In-ground interment was the order of the day, there being no facilities for cremation more sophisticated than a makeshift pinewood bonfire, so funerary grounds were hastily established midway between the valley's industrial and residential sections, to the immediate profit of one quick-thinking immigrant striker who gladly accepted the ferryman's fee from both striker and scab. It was there in the new necropolis that the survivors gathered, standing in the cold March sun upon the hastily-cleared, frozen Earth. One by one, thirteen different ceremonies were held, each according to their own light; some religious, some atheistic, some an unwieldy amalgam of the two. Everyone stood in respectful silence through them all, finally dispersing in a murmur of quiet words, comforts, and tears.

Their first dead having been buried, life in the valley known as the Gulch moved on, as it must.

* * *

Rumors ran rampant.

Following the funerals, one of the first orders of business was the reading of Midas' will, and curiosity was keen among the strikers as to what would become of the late mogul's immense fortune. Many presumed themselves to be potential beneficiaries of a portion of the proceeds, while others questioned the very idea of the dead dictating to the living what must be done with real property. But Midas had appointed an incorruptible striker jurist as executor—the Judge, they called him—and the Judge lived up to his promise to abide by the bequeathing, leaving philosophical arguments for another day.

All conjecture as to the fortune's disposition was quickly laid to rest with the reading of the will. Ultimately, Midas left his riches to everyone and to no one. His will directed that the Judge establish two Foundations, each at opposite ends of the financial spectrum. The first Foundation was to take possession of the valley itself with the mission to sell land to would-be residents—with the crucial caveat that the properties be sold solely to sworn strikers—and once all of the land had been sold, the first Foundation would dissolve, with all proceeds of the sales merging into the rest of Midas' wealth.

On the other hand, the second Foundation would live on, presumably forever. It was to this Foundation that Midas had assigned his riches, bestowing upon it a mission similar to the one the banker had pursued in life: that of helping the men of ability to succeed. Rather than simply acquiring capital, as the first Foundation did, it would be a distributor of capital through loans and investments. Remarkably, Midas decreed that a certain percentage of those investments would look far beyond the range of the moment, plan in terms of decades, invest in terms of generations, and undertake ninety-nine year contracts. Whether or not the trustees of the Foundation would be as successful as their sponsor in triggering unexpected, spectacular bullets of industrial success shooting across the country, only time would tell—perhaps centuries, in some cases.

Given their goals, the establishment of the two Foundations was met with universal acceptance. However, it was just as widely noted in exasperated annoyance that Midas had recently sold his bank building to a scab, of all people, a transaction that the first Foundation would never be permitted to perform. Privately, many felt it an indication that the late banker's faculties had already been slipping; nevertheless, the dastardly deed was a done deal, and to violate the sanctity of either the contract or private property precluded any reconsideration, scab or no scab, all of which suited the scab pilot immensely.

## Chapter 2 – All By Myself

Eddie set up housekeeping.

Even though there was an overabundance of vacant houses readily available throughout Las Vegas that were his for the taking, he continued to spend his nights in the largest of the compartments in the sleeper car on the *Meteor*, still parked in the Transcontinental station. Although he inspected several abandoned dwellings in one of the nicer parts of town with an eye toward making one of them his home, he felt himself the trespasser, whereas the *Meteor* somehow seemed more "his." In the end, he decided to retain the *Meteor* as his permanent address, rationalizing his claiming of the boon by considering it a part of his salary; he felt more at home on board in any case. So the sleeper car became his bedroom and kitchen, the baggage car his attic, and the observation car his parlor and dining room. The mail car, day coaches, and the second baggage car he left empty and parked, for now, on one of the more out-of-the-way platforms. He kept the Diesel uncoupled from the rest of the train, and once every week he would start it up and let it idle for several hours, sometimes running it out to the yard limit and back, just to reassure himself that it still functioned. Beyond that, he had no plan to run the *Meteor* any further than that, nor any idea as to where he might go, nor why. But his sense of duty to Transcontinental Railroad was strong, and keeping the Diesel in an operational state gave the feeling an outlet. It was only late at night that he would admit to himself that his underlying reason was to keep alive a portion of his life that he knew for certain was forever dead. His only wish was that he could do more for her memory.

* * *

Eddie was perplexed.

"Closed? What do you mean, closed?"

"That's what they told me, Mr. Eddie," the stationmaster insisted none too patiently, gesturing at the walkie-talkie base station. "Last time they checked in, they told me there's this big sign in front of the Army base, and that's what they said it says, and it says, 'Closed.'"

Eddie took a deep breath, suddenly realizing how vulnerable Las Vegas lay. *Closed!* A precious few refugees from the fighting on the West Coast had survived the trek across the desert to wander into town, and their stories were not for the faint-hearted; even Eddie had a few of his own nasty tales he could tell. He hadn't realized how much he had been depending on the defensive prop of the Army base until it had been abruptly kicked out from under them. The last thing they needed was a full-scale invasion of Las Vegas with no means to repel it. Or even a small-scale invasion!

"Anything new from our sentries watching the roads?" asked Eddie, shifting the subject, not wanting to dwell further on their vulnerabilities.

"They're reporting the same thing they reported when you first put them out there two weeks ago, Mr. Eddie," the stationmaster summarized, an impatient edge remaining in his voice. "It's all one way traffic. Still a few people leaving, and no one's coming back. They say not nearly as many are leaving as when you first put them out there, though."

Eddie couldn't understand why people would leave; there was really nowhere else to go. While it was no New York City, life in Las Vegas had proved relatively comfortable; still, its character had changed dramatically in the few weeks since he had first arrived in town. The most noticeable transformation was how quickly horse traffic had displaced motorized vehicles as the fuel supply evaporated.

One thing hadn't changed, though, and that was electricity. It continued to flow from the turbines at the massive Boulder Dam southeast of town, even though regular maintenance of the equipment and transmission wires had long since fallen by the wayside. Although the Dam itself still stood strong and tall, figurative cracks were beginning to show. Some portions of town had been without electricity since before Eddie arrived, mostly due to downed wires which no one had bothered to repair. More ominously, the control room of the Dam and its powerplant went frequently unattended as more and more of the technicians walked off the job. The situation was increasingly ripe for disaster, and it was not long after the last technician quit that calamity fell.

It started with a minor temperature rise within one of the electric turbines, owing to a lack of proper periodic lubrication. As its temperature slowly rose unchecked, the governor on the turbine began to slip, allowing the turbine's speed to increase well beyond its design limit until finally its bearings overheated and melted into a worthless lump of metal. No one had been on duty at the Dam when the mishap occurred; only the automatic failsafe mechanisms noted the failure and dutifully shut down both banks of turbines. The Dam's powerplant had saved itself, but Las Vegas was left without electricity.

It was early evening when the lights died. Eddie was awake, wrestling with some new plumbing for his sleeper car. As with the turbines, it was a situation that sorely needed attention. Ordinarily, lavatory effluvia from the sleeper would simply dump out on the trackbed, but since it appeared the *Meteor* wasn't going anywhere anytime soon, a more permanent hookup was definitely in order. He wasn't half completed his task when the lights unexpectedly flickered once; he glanced up and watched them slowly fade to orange, to brown, then vanish to nothing. A ghostly twilight seeped through the windows of the sleeper, barely enough to make out dim shapes, and surely not enough for installing the rest of his new plumbing. Eddie set down his tools, grateful for the mandatory rest break, and waited patiently for the power to return. Almost an hour later, now sitting in total darkness, he decided he may as well call it a night.

He awoke the next morning later than he expected—the sleeper's electric alarm clock did not sound; the electricity had still not returned. He dressed, stepped down from his sleeper car, and walked up the long, sloping tunnel into the station building, then into the stationmaster's office. The stationmaster was already there, sitting at his desk doing nothing—not that there was much to do in any case, even when the electricity was flowing.

"Morning, Mr. Eddie."

"Good morning. Any word when the electricity is coming back on?"

"No, sir. Matter of fact, I'm wondering if anyone's even trying to fix it."

"What? What do you mean?"

"Let me say rather that I'm not sure there's anyone who *can* fix it! Like I told you, most of the technicians quit back when they passed Directive 289-10, and the ones who stayed on weren't exactly the brightest bulbs on the marquis, if you know what I mean. Not sure they'd know how to fix things if they broke." He snorted his derision. "They're more like caretakers who would be helpless if a single tube in all that vast structure burnt out." He shrugged. "Doesn't matter what'd break, though, because it'd stay broken."

"Even so, do you know if anyone's out there to try to fix the problem?"

The stationmaster spread his pudgy hands helplessly and stared at Eddie owlishly. "How could I know? It's thirty-five miles away!"

"Use the telephone?" Eddie suggested blankly.

"Out," he replied simply. "No electricity, remember?"

"Oh."

The seconds passed in silence. Eddie found himself at a complete loss. *No electricity, and probably no one fixing it. Worse yet, there may be no one TO fix it!* Finally, he spoke again, the despair evident in his voice. "What are we going to do?" It was almost a cry.

Again the stationmaster shrugged. "Who is John Galt?"

Eddie's mind remained stubbornly blank. In the past there had always been men whose responsibility it was to keep the electricity flowing. But where were they now? Were they all gone for good? And if they were indeed gone for good, where did that leave Eddie and the rest of Las Vegas? In the dark forever? His shoulders drooped dejectedly; he had no idea how to proceed. Unbidden, a bittersweet notion crossed his mind. *Dagny would have known what to do. She'd never allow random happenstance to divert her from her goals. And if something like this happened to her, she'd—* His reverie halted at a sudden realization. Pursuing it, Eddie thoughts raced down familiar paths for a moment, then he nodded. *She'd take matters into her own hands, that's what!*

He stood in thought for a moment longer, then faced the stationmaster. "All right, here's what we'll do. Send your best man out to the Dam on horseback immediately to see if there's a technician on duty. If there is, find out if he needs help to restore electricity. Send another man along to act as a messenger to come back immediately and report to me once they see what the situation is."

"Yes, sir."

"And have two other men search the city for any of the old Dam technicians who may still be around. We've got to get this fixed!"

"Yes sir, Mr. Eddie." He turned to comply.

Eddie remained standing in the stationmaster's office a while longer, then unceremoniously turned to go. It would take all day for the messenger to reach the Dam on horseback and return, perhaps longer; Eddie figured he may as well take advantage of the daylight and complete his plumbing task. But something tickled at the back of his mind for a moment before he finally recognized the thought: listening to himself giving orders to the stationmaster, he realized with a start that he had sounded just like Dagny. He would have smiled, if he could.

* * *

The news was mixed.

It was mid-afternoon the following day before the messenger returned from the Dam—and he did not return alone. His companion who had gone out with him had also returned. They had discovered that the Dam powerplant was silent and deserted; no one was on site effecting repairs. Lacking the ability to troubleshoot the turbines' troubles themselves, and with no one more knowledgeable on the scene to direct the repair activities, both men had no other choice but to return to Las Vegas together.

Fortunately, the men who were searching the city for technicians had better luck; they had found one—apparently the only one left in town—but the man wanted nothing more to do with the Dam. He had long since tired of his lonely vigil so far from his home in the city, a solitude made unbearable by the recent loss of mechanized transportation to and from the distant Dam. For a while he had persevered at his job despite being abandoned by all his co-workers; but when his regular paychecks had ceased to arrive, that was the final straw. The man quit out of necessity to seek his sustenance elsewhere.

Again taking matters into his own hands, Eddie decided to pay the technician a visit. Drawing on the technician's limited civic virtue, Eddie was able to convince him to at least make an attempt to repair the damage. The next morning, he personally accompanied the man to the Dam, riding on horseback the entire thirty-five-mile distance—a first for Eddie—and together the two of them were quickly able to isolate the troubled turbine and bring the remaining ones back on line. In short order electricity flowed once again through the copper wires that stretched across the desert to light the homes and shops of Las Vegas.

On the long ride back, Eddie tried in vain to convince the technician to man his post on a regular basis, or at least to begin training others in his craft; Eddie knew that if anything were to happen to the technician before he passed on his knowledge, Las Vegas would be sunk. But the technician was adamant; it was simply too much responsibility for any one man. Besides, he had a new job now, and could not leave it behind. He had a family to support!

Driven by need, Eddie devised a questionable method to re-establish some semblance of responsible stewardship over the Dam and its electric powerplant. Although he was well aware that he had no real right to do so, he appointed himself in charge of the Dam and commissioned the printing of ten thousand shares of stock, a hundred crude-looking, one-hundred-share certificates that represented not shares of ownership in the Dam—that was not his to give—but rather shares of the responsibility for keeping the electricity flowing, and an entitlement to a share of the rewards. Half of the certificates Eddie simply gave to the technician as an incentive for him to re-assume his post. Unsurprisingly, the incentive worked. The thought of being effectively half-owner of the massive Boulder Dam—and entitled to half the revenue it generated—eliminated any objections the technician could possibly conjure up.

To raise capital for the maintenance of the Dam, the other half of the shares Eddie offered for sale to the citizens of Las Vegas; the sale would also serve as a vehicle to add a measure of legitimacy to his dubious scheme by increasing its constituency.

From behind the ornate railing of the observation platform at the rear of the *Meteor*, Eddie inaugurated the town's first stock exchange. Checkbooks in hand, potential investors lined up on the station platform to bid for the shares; and for his trouble, Eddie retained a small percentage of the certificates for himself. With the capital raised through the sale, he and the technician were able to hire and train the assistants needed to perform regular maintenance and billing. Within the month, electric service to the town became as reliable as it was inexpensive, and with profits mounting, a modest dividend for shareholders was soon declared.

Eddie was pleased with the outcome of his efforts. With only a trivial amount of initiative on his part, he was able to establish a reliable routine to ensure that electricity continued to flow—plus he had turned a smart profit by collecting his broker's fee on the stock transactions, and now received dividends as well. Everyone won, and it was one less worry for Eddie and Las Vegas.

## CHAPTER 3 – REVOLUTION

The drunken scab groused.

It was late in the evening at *The Golden Touch*; he was on his fourth glass of potato vodka—the variety of distilled beverages available in the valley remained severely limited—and the alcohol was having its desired, undeniable effect. "Damn their oath, I say! Damn it to HELL!" In time with his final word, he slammed his fist against the surface of the bar. "You'll never catch *me* swearing, that's for *damn* sure!"

The scab woman sitting five empty seats up from him paid him no mind, not even so much as a glance in the drunk's direction. She continued her conversation unabated, as if she were used to ignoring sudden sharp noises. "—don't have much time left before Ragnar's deadline to take the striker's oath, and I ask you: does it really matter whether or not I swear?"

"Of course it does," warned her chance companion, his drawl revealing his Texan origin. He drained the beer in the bottom of his glass and made a sour face before continuing. "They'll throw us out of here at precisely midnight the last day of the month if we don't. Count on it!"

"That's not what I meant," she countered. "For sure, they'll throw us out if we don't swear. No one would argue with that! What I meant was, why shouldn't I just swear the oath?"

"Because you don't mean it, that's why!"

"So what? I'll just swear anyway and be done with it."

"They'll know you're lying," he warned.

"So what?" she repeated. "What are they going to do, take away my birthday?"

"They'll throw you out just as soon as they find you lied, that's what! You know how the strikers feel about integrity!"

"Maybe," she agreed, not knowing exactly what the word meant. "But at least I'll be able to stay in this nice, warm valley a little later in the year than the end of March. Do you want to face the rest of the winter Outside?"

"Depends on where they drop me off, doesn't it? I can't go back home to Dallas, that's for sure! Not after the fires. Florida's still got some civilization, last I heard. So does the People's State of Mexico, and the People's State of Canada."

"What, you want to live in a People's State?"

"What, you want to live here?" he mimicked.

"This is a lot better than any People's State, and you know it. It's even better than the good old U.S.A. back in the days when it was still the good old U.S.A. This place is a dream world in comparison! No taxes, no crime, no bureaucrats, no religion, no raiders, no—"

"Right!" he interrupted. "In the good old U.S.A., Ragnar would stay offshore and bother the looter ships, not threaten to throw regular people like you and me out of their homes."

"Oh, do you own your own home?" she asked, suddenly more interested.

"Me? Nah, I'm living in a tent down at the airstrip." He shivered involuntarily at the thought.

"Ragnar might be doing you a favor to throw you out," she jibed, her interest dimming. "Must get pretty cold in there at night."

He reddened faintly. "You know what I mean."

"And no one has said anything about giving anybody an actual ride out of town either," she continued. "Getting evicted might just consist of an armed escort to the foot of the nearest mountain."

"I bet they charge you for the escort, too," he predicted grumpily.

She paid his dark mood no more mind than she had the drunk's. "I'm just planning to lie about it and then let them try to prove it."

"You'll slip up, and you know it. They'll catch you doing something they consider an 'error.' Hasn't it already happened to you? It sure has to *me!* More than once, too!"

"Of course it has. But all I have to do is call it an 'error of knowledge,' say my Act of Contrition, go my way and sin no more." As she concluded the ejaculation, her eyes took on a distant stare, as if she were reliving some other past prayer.

He remained unconvinced. "Yeah, but how many times can you slip up before they call in the eviction squad?"

After a few seconds more of silence, she sat up perkily. "Ask me in April—assuming you're still here to ask. But I know I'll be here to answer!"

"You think so? They're just letting you get away with it for now because you're new here. And let me tell you another thing: back in Texas, we would..."

The pilot stood behind the bar in silence, appearing attentive but only half listening to their exchange. He had heard too many conversations just like theirs in the last few weeks to consider becoming embroiled in its details. So he kept his thoughts to himself and an idle ear on their words in the off chance that they might stumble upon a dodge that his other scab patrons hadn't considered. But this pair showed no promise at all. Lying! The pilot was no Plato, but he was smart enough to know that you can't lie about philosophy. You tend to live it, which means it always tends to stick out like a sore thumb. *Just look at Gwen's old man,* he thought. *Better yet, let's look at Gwen!* he corrected himself. *Sure would be nice to take her with me on a trip for two to Vegas!* He smiled evilly at the thought. The woman who sat at his bar wasn't quite as pretty as Gwen, but she'd certainly serve as a fine companion for a cold winter's night. *She should dump this tent-man so I can make some time here! Maybe I could take her upstairs and show her my nice, warm apartment?* But his patrons' conversation showed no signs of flagging anytime soon. He scowled behind a featureless face. It was bad enough that the ratio of women to men in this God-forsaken gulch was badly skewed—and in the wrong direction!—adding to the difficulty of securing feminine companionship. But worse yet, tonight this simpering rotter prattled on and on, mouthing his bland, shabby tripe as if he would never cease, thereby pre-empting any possible progress the pilot might have made with the only available woman in sight.

"...and that's the truth!" the man finally concluded.

"Maybe," she demurred absently. It was obvious that her thoughts were elsewhere.

"Why, what is it you're thinking?"

She did not answer right away. "About Sacramento," she finally admitted, offering no further explanation.

The man did not follow up with any questions; but it wasn't that he respected her obviously touchy feelings on the subject, rather he was merely a terrible conversationalist.

The woman had long since noted his lack of social skills, and unconsciously ignored his latest faux pas; she was still deep in thought. "You know...," she began slowly, unsure of herself.

"Do I know what?" prompted her companion.

"...we could always revolt?" It sounded more a question than a statement.

"Revolt? What do you mean, revolt?"

The pilot's ears twitched at the suggestion. *Now here's something new!* He retained his passive pose, but his brain shifted into high gear behind his best poker face.

"I don't know exactly," she admitted. "But isn't that what oppressed people are supposed to do?"

Her companion was intrigued. "But who is it we'd revolt against?" he mused. "There's not really any government here, just a philosophy. There's no single enemy and no villain. It's everyone and it's no one."

"Not 'who,' '*what!*' The philosophy! We'd revolt against their philosophy!" She was warming to the subject as she talked.

"How does one attack a philosophy?"

She considered the question intently for a moment, but soon her shoulders slumped. Not understanding what philosophy was, or the need for one, she had no clue how to battle one. "I don't know," she finally confessed.

"Maybe we could just shoot all its adherents," he suggested grimly, only half in jest. "Show them you don't mess with us Texans!"

She took a small sip of her wine feigning nonchalance. "Before you go shooting up the town, cowboy, tell me how that snow plow works."

91

"The snow plow? But I thought... You said we should revolt!" Clearly, he was not following her train of thought.

She did not look back to him as she replied. "Yes, I did. But before you start shooting innocent people, tell me what makes you think that *you* won't go floating off as some big white cloud?"

"What do you mean?" he replied in confusion.

She ignored his question. Talk of shooting up the town did not sit well with her, especially given her recent history.

"C'mon. What do you mean?" he prodded.

Again without facing him, she pointed out, "I mean, what other secret inventions might they have which could be used against you if you were to revolt?"

"Beats me. Probably nothing."

The pilot saw his chance. "Wait a minute!" he interrupted, his deep voice sounding impressively authoritative. "She's right, you know!" Both of them turned to him, startled. He had been silent for so long that they had forgotten his presence, even though he had been standing right there in front of them all along. "They shot my airplane out of the sky the day I got here," he explained indignantly. "They killed both my engines with some sort of 'ray screen,' they called it, but that's all they'd say. Burned out my motors' coils from a mile away. Damned if I know how they did it." He looked from one face to the other intently, eyes wide. "A ray screen, they said."

The woman readily clung to the intellectual lifeline the pilot had tossed her. "Hey, I heard about that," she lied—she had arrived in the valley only days ago, and knew nothing of the pilot or his history. "And your episode with the ray screen proves my point."

"It proves nothing!" retorted her companion, miffed at being upstaged in front of the woman. "Let me explain..." He feebly attempted to justify himself, but it was obvious that the woman was no longer listening; she had completely lost interest in both the conversation and her chance companion. Whenever he spoke, she replied in monosyllables if at all, and she never initiated conversation, preferring instead to sit in silence. Soon, the poor man got the message, paid his tab, and left with a mumbled good-bye.

Alone now, the woman continued to nurse her wine in silence, her face reflecting some deep, troubled thought as she stared into its ruby depths.

*The eyes...*, the pilot observed. *You can see it in their eyes!* All of the new arrivals had that wild look in their eyes, as if they had seen far too much. *Things must be getting pretty bad Outside!*

After a respectful pause, the pilot pushed his advantage. "Can you believe that guy!" he opined, shaking his head.

She shrugged, adding a small smile. "Cowboys. What else would you expect?"

"That's an interesting idea you had. Revolution, I mean. I've heard a lot of suggestions about what to do about the oath, but that's the first time I've heard that one."

She sipped her wine again, her mannerisms revealing that she was pleased at the compliment. "I only wish I knew how to make it happen. There's really no government here, so there's nothing to fight. It's like everybody and nobody is responsible."

"I know what you mean," he commiserated. "But there *is* a way to attack a philosophy, you know."

"How?" she breathed.

"With another philosophy," he replied matter-of-factly.

She looked at him blankly, not understanding. "What other philosophy?"

He hesitated. "That, I don't know," he apologized. "Maybe with some kind of religion?"

The woman's eyes went wide. "No!" she replied vehemently. "No religion! Not that kind of world! Their striker's oath is bad enough without bringing in religion!"

The pilot did not reply to her outburst. He harbored no love for religion himself, or for the striker's oath, for that matter; he was merely using religion as an example. But remembering her California origins, he could readily understand her horror at the thought of introducing religion.

"Are you going to take the oath?" she asked, deliberately shifting the subject away from religion.

"Me? No way!"

"Aren't you concerned?" she asked, her voice all concern. "They'll throw you out!"

The pilot held his chin bravely high. "They're bluffing. Nobody would send someone back Outside with things the way they are, especially in winter. It'd be a death sentence!"

"That's for sure!" she asserted. She fell silent as her eyes again took on that distant, vacant stare. The pilot could tell that she was reliving some moment in her recent past, and from the look on her face, it was not a pleasant one.

"Where're you from?" he interrupted, even though he already knew.

"Sacramento," she replied absently, still lost in thought. She suddenly sat up with a start, and refocused her attention within the room. "At least I *was* from Sacramento—I'm not certain if Sacramento even exists anymore!"

"I hear it's pretty bad out that way," he sympathized, deliberately stoking the memory flames.

Her eyes lost their focus again. Images of bloody fighting, red-robed fanatics, and dying friends overcame her. Tears welled up in the corners of her eyes and began to trickle down her cheeks. She nodded.

He handed her a paper napkin. "Sorry," he lied. Having bonded with her through his understanding of her recent dangers, his next move was to strategically change the subject. *I am so much the expert at this!* he congratulated himself. "So how long have you been in the Gulch?"

She dabbed at her tears. "Almost a week."

"Like it here?"

She nodded.

"What brought you here?"

"It wasn't so much a 'what' as a 'who.' It was the janitor at our toaster factory. We'd both worked there for years. When he told me he was coming here, I jumped at the chance to—" She paused, her mouth hanging slightly open, as if she had suddenly forgotten she was speaking. Without warning, again she burst into tears.

"What? What's the matter?" asked the pilot, perplexed.

"My cat!" she cried. "It's my cat!" Her face reflected a deep, fierce agony; tears streamed unheeded from eyes stretched open unnaturally wide. "He made me leave my cat behind!" With signs of the effort plainly visible on her face, she slowly regained control of her ragged emotions. Tight lipped, she tossed her hair back, sprinkling loose tears on the surface of the bar. She wiped her eyes one last time, balled up the tear-soaked napkin and threw it in mock disgust onto the surface of the bar, exclaiming, "As if I would have stayed in Sacramento for a damn cat!" She lifted her wine glass and looked at it appreciatively, then laughed without mirth. "The Bishop's acolytes don't approve of drinking, you know." She drained the little amount remaining.

"Damn them damn do-gooders!" the drunken scab suddenly chimed in. "Damn them! Who're they to tell anybody what to drink?" He reached for his own drink with limited success. "Stand still," he mumbled to the stationary glass.

The pilot chuckled at the interruption. Hooking a thumb at the drunk, he informed the woman, "He's a living example of the truth of that old bromide, 'Limit your intoxicants before they limit you.'" Turning to the drunk, in jest he called back, "Hey, maybe we should send Ragnar out there to straighten them out, don't you think?"

The drunk was far too inebriated to recognize the humor in the pilot's voice. "Yep. Send in the pirate!" He raised his half-full glass clumsily. "To Ragnar!" he toasted. "He'll force those damn fanatics to stop forcing people!" He slowly finished off the remaining vodka and set down the glass with remarkable gentleness.

Neither the pilot nor the woman spoke for several seconds. Both of them were taken aback by the profound contradiction inherent in the drunk's convoluted, off-handed toast.

"From the mouths of babes...," the pilot needlessly observed.

The woman had started crying again. "But he's right!" she sobbed. "Don't you see? He's right! They're still trying to tell me what to think! First it was the acolytes, and now it's Ragnar! Who wants to live in that sort of a world? Not me! Not that sort of world!"

"Course I'm right," mumbled the drunk, his head falling onto the surface of the bar with an audible thud.

She looked at the drunk with a new intensity. "No, I'm serious! You're right, don't you see? Why should I be forced to believe in Back For God's religion—or in Ragnar's philosophy? Why should I be forced? He's just as bad as they are, initiating force like that!" She was almost shrieking now. "Why must they force people to believe? Why can't they just leave us be?"

The drunken oracle did not reply.

She turned back to the pilot, repeating her unanswered question with the same wide-eyed intensity she exhibited when she spoke of her cat. "Why can't they leave us be?" she cried, the tears still falling down her cheeks.

"There, there," soothed the pilot, handing her another paper napkin. "There's nothing to worry about. I told you they're bluffing. It'll come out okay. You'll see."

Slowly, her outburst subsided. "I hope you're right," she sniffed, dabbing the tears away yet again.

*I'm definitely going to score with this one!* the pilot congratulated himself. "Hey, would you like another glass of wine? On the house."

She nodded gratefully, giving him a small, red-eyed smile.

He poured a glass for each of them. "It's almost closing time. After we finish our drinks, let me throw out Mr. Potato Head here, and I can walk you home. Everything will be all right. You'll see. So relax! Life is too important to be taken seriously. Now tell me, where did you grow up?"

* * *

Word came down.

To the shock and surprise of many, the date for taking the striker's oath had been moved up almost two weeks. Rather than March 31st, the new date would be March 20th, a mere three days hence.

The rationale behind the accelerated date could be considered, in some ways, charitable. The stated goal was to help the strikers to identify those who might need special guidance; and for those who would choose not to swear, the earlier deadline would allow them additional time to wrap up their affairs in an orderly fashion before they were forced to leave. Those who refused to take the oath the first time around would be given one final opportunity on the last day of the month; if they declined again, they would be ferried outside of the valley.

The hard-core scabs immediately pounced on the decision, calling it Directive 3-20, but their cause had no support at all among the strikers. Whenever questioned about it, the strikers' replies were strikingly similar, spanning the spectrum of civility:

"We have no rules of any kind except one: everyone must take the oath to remain in this valley."

"We never demand agreement. This is a voluntary society. All you need do is volunteer."

"We've sworn not to give the outside world anything of our ability, and until you take the oath, you are of that world."

"The mistakes of a child we treat with loving forbearance. But toward evil, we have no mercy."

"I've taken an oath not to live for you. Would you do the same for me as I would for you?"

"Everyone else in this valley has taken the oath except you. So you must leave."

"We are not asking your consent. You did not ask ours before you came here."

"I left the looter world behind, and will not have you bring it back."

"We've already done you a favor by letting you stay this long!"

"You broke our rules coming in here at all!"

"I choose not to support my destroyers."

"Get a life—but not mine!"

"Self-sacrificer!"

"Altruist!"

"Looter!"

"Scab!"

\* \* \*

The hangar was packed.

The men of the mind were crowded together on temporary bleachers built up to the rafters of Dwight's largest hangar. Almost the entire valley, some two thousand strong, had turned out to witness the oath-taking for the first deadline. The strikers sat calmly in their seats, but many of the newcomers were in an edgy sort of mood, some of them talking too loudly or making too much noise. White arclights beat down on the crowd, leaving some of the scabs feeling touchy and raw. While the gathering could not be described as dangerous, the atmosphere was far from cordial.

Ragnar hammered a gavel for order, and the congregation quieted down some. Still, some people moved restlessly from side to side, like water in a pan that is being rocked. He adjusted the microphone and began to speak. "This is a crucial moment in the history of our valley," he proclaimed. "Remember that none can remain in this place, except those who have taken the striker's oath, which is a moral code that we all accept."

"I don't!" cried out one small voice.

Heads swiveled to zero in on the dissenter. A teenager stood up, and the room turned dead-still. Without a word, the teen started to walk out. He stalked down the length of the hangar in the white light, not hurrying and not noticing anyone else. Nobody moved to stop him.

Ragnar broke the silence, calling after him, "You! Why not?"

The teen faced the pirate and answered slowly and deliberately, "Out of respect for the memory of Gwen's father—not that I expect you could understand." With that, he turned and walked out.

The pirate looked out across the sea of faces and shrugged. "Okay by me. Anyone else?"

At first no one moved. But like rats deserting a sinking ship, people stood and walked out, at first one or two at a time, then swelling into a shuffling tide. Some called out names as they left, much as the teenager had done, and others slunk out in deep embarrassment. While the dissenters formed an appreciable fraction of the newcomers, the vast majority remained in their seats.

After the last dissenter had departed, Ragnar continued from where he had left off. "Welcome to reality!" he intoned solemnly. The room burst into loud applause and cheers. When the rally faded, he spoke again. "Will the remaining newcomers please rise."

A rustle swept through the hangar as they rose to their feet, some five hundred strong.

"My rational men, it is time for you to enter Atlantis! Come! Let us swear the striker's oath together!" He paused briefly, dramatically, then began. "I swear..."

Five hundred voices joined him as he spoke, the sounds of their combined pledge rocking the hangar walls. Ten seconds was all it took, and when they had finished, again the audience burst into spontaneous applause, rising to their feet to give the former scabs a standing ovation.

"Welcome to Atlantis!" the pirate-philosopher shouted again over the swaying sea of applause. "This is now the most rational place on Earth! Two thousand minds, all dedicated to the ideal that their fellow man is *not* their slave!"

The applause thundered even louder in the air, rivaling the sounds of the avalanche from the week before. Finally, everyone reclaimed their seats, and the room fell quiet again.

"We must remember that today is but a dress rehearsal," he reminded them. "The main event happens here in exactly eleven days, when each one of the newcomers will step up to this podium to take the pledge individually, which is the way it should properly be done."

Again, they burst into applause without a cue. No surprise, that; for nowhere else on the entire planet Earth was there so large a crowd of a like mind. Soon, they were silent again.

For effect, Ragnar let the silence drag on for a moment before continuing. "It is a frightening world outside our valley," he observed darkly, dramatically pausing again. "To avoid suffering the consequences of their flawed moral code, there are looters among us who would lie, cheat, and steal to save themselves, scabs who would trade their priceless integrity for a short-term advantage. They forget that integrity is something that can never be taken from a man, it can only be surrendered. But what sort of man hands over his most potent weapon to his destroyers? The worst sort! Do we want this sort of man polluting our valley?"

"*NO!*" the crowd cheered as one.

"The threat to our moral code is a real one," he continued. "One that must be guarded against with all our might using all our abilities. When we reconvene at the end of this month, we will utilize all of the unique capabilities of our science to help guard against these looters of the soul, to expose the man of no integrity. So, as each man takes the oath, he will place his hands here..." He theatrically placed a hand on either side of the top of the lectern, exaggerating his motions. "...on the electrode plates of the lie detector installed in this lectern, then swear the striker's oath. To insure that the device is operating properly, its inventor, Dr. Thomas, will personally preside over its use. Let me show you how it works..."

The room fell silent as Ragnar again recited the striker's oath. When he had completed, a tiny light on the front of the lectern winked a bright, piercing green. In the same solemn tone, he intoned, "Looting is good." The light winked blood red. Still leaning on the lectern, his gaze swept like a lighthouse searchlight shining across the sea of faces arrayed in front of him, as if seeking out the unfaithful using only the power of his gaze. "I declare this meeting in recess for eleven days. If any of you newcomers have any last-minute questions about the striker's oath or anything else that you've heard tonight, please feel free to contact me. I teach philosophy classes, conduct seminars, and hold conferences. I have many exciting offerings scheduled to begin over the next few weeks, so please take one of my advertising circulars on your way out. Usually I charge a penny apiece for them, but for tonight only they're free."

Unnoticed by the pirate, the light on the lectern glowed a steady red.

* * *

*The Golden Touch* was jammed.

The pilot was not surprised at the unprecedented turnout; after all, it was mostly his fault. When those who refused to take the oath abandoned the hangar, the pilot was among the first out the door. He stood there alongside the entrance bellowing out in his deepest voice, "Town meeting in ten minutes! Town meeting at *The Golden Touch*! Town meeting in ten minutes!" over and over. Most of the scabs were uncertain what they would be doing next, so it was an easy task to convince them to attend. Besides, they had just cut their own philosophical jugulars, the pilot included. They had nowhere else to go.

Once they reached the taproom, the pilot was never so busy in his life. Drink after drink he poured, and the demand showed no signs of slowing. People stood three deep at the bar, crowded across the floor of the lobby of the old bank, and poured out into the cold street. At first he was able to keep up with the demands of the crowd. Almost a hundred newcomers had initially walked out of the tent revival, refusing to take the striker's oath, and most of them had heeded the pilot's exhortations to come to his taproom. But the revival had broken up not fifteen minutes later, and many from the second wave also followed, further swelling the number of patrons. Soon he ran out of glasses and resorted to paper cups. On the spot he hired his Sacramento friend and dispatched her to take orders and bring back empty glasses. He fervently hoped his supply of spirits would hold out better than his supply of glasses had.

The din was deafening. Emotions were running understandably high, and loudly reflected in everyone's voice. No surprise, others in turn spoke all the louder to make themselves heard over the hubbub, feeding the rising noise level all the more. Soon it was difficult for anyone to hear anyone, and still the commotion continued.

The pilot decided to take matters into his own hands. "Ladies and gentlemen!" he bellowed in his deepest, dust-scarred voice. "Ladies and gentlemen!" Presently those closest to him suspended their conversations, and a cone of silence spread from that point outward. Just as the high noise level had encouraged more noise, so also did the spreading silence encourage more silence. In seconds *The Golden Touch* was quiet as a church.

"Ladies and gentlemen!" he repeated one final time into the silence he had created. "This is supposed to be a town meeting to discuss what we're going to do. Who wants to be the Chairman?"

"You do it!" someone called out.

The pilot looked at him askance. "And who's going to pour your beer? Tell you what: why don't *you* get up there, Mr. Chairman! You've shown enough initiative to deserve the position." The crowd cheered and jeered its assent. Red-faced, the man climbed awkwardly onto his chair.

"Okay," he began uncertainly, "First things first. Nobody speaks unless I recognize him. Got it?" The crowd murmured its assent, fueling the chariman's self-assurance by their faith in his impromptu leadership. With some measure of confidence, he continued to address the crowd. "Now I think I speak for all of us when I say that this idea of banishment cannot be allowed to stand!" His words were met with a roar of approval, which augmented his confidence all the more. "The question becomes," he continued belligerently, "what are we going to do about it?" He cast a defiant gaze across the sea of faces looking up to him.

Silence answered him.

"Well, what do we do?" he roared in impatient irritation with the anger of a man declaring their silence to be a personal affront to him.

Silence.

Suddenly unsure of himself, he looked down to the pilot, who just shrugged. Looking back to the crowd, he implored weakly, "Well, doesn't anyone have any ideas?"

"Revolt!" instantly came a woman's voice. Everyone turned to identify the speaker: standing in the middle of the crowd with a trayful of dirty glasses in her hands was the woman from Sacramento. "Revolt!" she shouted again with deep feeling, fire in her eyes. Again, the crowd roared its approval.

"Okay, now we're getting somewhere," the Chairman approved. "Revolt how?" he asked her.

But his question only served to knock the wind out of her sails just as completely as the question had done to her the other night.

"I... I don't know," she admitted, the fire in her eyes instantly extinguished—and she certainly wasn't going to suggest *religion!* She was no closer to an answer now as she was then.

"They're trying to kick us out of our homes!" shouted a man from just outside the taproom's front door, his Texan accent prominent. It was the woman's jilted companion. "That means we have the right to defend ourselves! Let's line them up against the wall and shoot them!"

"Yeah? You and who's army?" shouted another.

"They outnumber us ten to one!" shouted a third.

"Closer to twenty to one!" interjected a fourth.

With that, everyone tried to speak at once, some in approval, some in shocked anger, everyone wanting to be heard, with the result that no one was heard. The meeting broke down into boisterous anarchistic disorder, despite the Chairman's ineffectual, unheard protestations. Soon the booming baritone of the pilot's voice reasserted control of the conversation with repeated calls of "ladies and gentlemen!"

A modicum of quiet descended on the crowd, but there was still much low murmuring among them. The Chairman stepped in to fill the void that had been opened for him. "Okay, okay. Just out of curiosity, how many of you brought a firearm into the valley? The hands that were raised in response were few and far between. "So much for armed revolt," he sighed. "Any other ideas?"

Again, a near-perfect silence descended upon the would-be revolutionaries. The seconds ticked by.

"Anyone?"

More seconds ticked by.

"Anyone?"

Silence.

"Pardon me, please!" came a quiet voice from along the far wall of the taproom. Every head turned to scry out its source. Seated at the piano was a tall, emaciated man with graying hair. He did not smile, but just sat there looking at the crowd. His face had the quiet, earnest look of a man staring at a question. They recognized him in an instant; it was the striker-pianist, Richard. "Perhaps we strikers are not quite so monolithic in the application of our philosophy as you might imagine," he suggested.

Three full seconds passed before the full import of his words sank in, and once it did, *The Golden Touch* burst into cheers and applause. It took a long time for the ruckus to dissipate.

"What is it you're suggesting we do?" inquired the chairman, once some semblance of silence returned.

"Why, the obvious, of course," Richard replied enigmatically.

"Which is...?" prompted the chairman.

"Join us!"

"But none of us are willing or able to take your oath!"

"Granted, but now that the world Outside has collapsed, we strikers have achieved our purpose. In many ways our strike has become moot. So perhaps there are now other ways to placate my philosophical brethren."

"Such as...? the chairman prompted again.

"Any one of a number of ways. For example, what about presenting yourself not as a scab, but rather as 'not a looter?'"

The chairman hesitated. "I'm not sure I understand what you mean."

"Look at it this way," he offered. "What is the goal of the striker's oath?" When no one ventured a guess, Richard continued. "It's one way of ensuring that a man does not demand—or receive—the unearned. Why not devise your *own* oath that accomplishes the same goal—one based on a principle you can honestly believe in—then swear to it?"

"Such as...?" prompted the chairman one more time. Clearly, he was completely at sea. Philosophy was not his forte any more than was chairing a town meeting. Regardless, he felt it incumbent upon himself to ask the question; Richard's characteristically-halting exposition almost demanded the participation of a foil.

"Oh, I don't know...," mused the pianist. "How about something taken from the big radio speech? The strikers might react more favorably to something like that."

"Such as...?" he repeated, still floundering, still prompting.

Richard pondered the question for a moment, then his eyes lit up. "I know! We can use the initiation of force!"

The chairman was perplexed. "You mean we should attack?"

"No, no! I meant as a topic for the oath!" He pondered a moment longer. "How about this? 'I swear that I do not advocate the initiation of force to achieve political or social goals?' No room for looters there, is there?"

A murmur rose from the audience as they puzzled out its meaning.

"'Force or fraud,'" I should say," Richard corrected himself. "Integrity is important, too, you know."

The chairman pulled at his chin. "But will the strikers accept that?"

Richard shrugged. "Who knows for certain until you try? *I* certainly accept it. That's why—" He raised his half-full glass of wine in silent toast to the pilot. "—I am happy and proud to patronize and support this establishment. The owner and I reject the initiation of force, and as a result, we each benefit from our peaceful dealings with one another. In that, we are philosophical brothers—but *not*, be it noted, fellow strikers." He lowered his glass and stared for a moment into the golden liquid before continuing, unprompted. "You must always remember that this is a philosophical battle you are waging, and such a battle can only be fought by philosophy." He lifted his gaze and let it wander across the sea of faces that surrounded him. "So this confrontation will be a battle of words; and not merely words, but more importantly the meaning behind them."

The chairman paused in an unsuccessful attempt to assimilate the essence of Richard's suggestion, then looked about uncertainly in a clear appeal to the assembled scabs. "What say you, people? Anyone have a problem with that sort of an oath?"

"Yeah," a voice called out. "What's it mean?"

The chairman peered around myopically, unsure himself as to its meaning.

"You're just swearing you won't toss the first punch," explained Richard, coming to the chairman's rescue.

There was a general nodding of heads, but also a significant, persistent number of blank stares. Like their chairman, many of them were hopelessly adrift in deep philosophical waters. Yet despite their uncertainties, they clung desperately to the lifeline Richard had tossed them, even if they did not understand it, nor where it might lead. But anything was better than certain eviction.

"All right, now we're getting somewhere!" the chairman called out, regaining a sense of hope. He glanced about eagerly. "Who's got a paper and pencil?"

"I do!" boomed a deep, resonant voice. From behind the bar, the pilot produced the requested items; he set the paper on the surface of the bar and looked up eagerly, pencil in hand, prepared to take dictation. "Read that off to me again, would you Richard?"

The pianist did so, enunciating each word slowly, which the pilot faithfully reproduced. As the room watched on in silence, he strode to the far wall and tacked the makeshift petition at eye level. Theatrically he held out the pencil to the chairman.

Following the pilot's lead, the chairman stepped down from his perch, accepted the pencil, and signed. One by one, the scabs lined up behind him for their own turn to sign the replacement oath. Soon a second sheet was required; then a third; then a fourth. The buzz of conversation resumed, and the mood became markedly much more upbeat. The scabs felt their fortunes had taken a turn for the better, although few of them could put into words exactly how.

Among those few was the pilot, one of the few who had chosen not to sign. He observed in silence as the endorsements continued, then muttered to himself, "Now let's see if the damn thing works."

## Chapter 4 – Riders on the Storm

The radio blared.

"Raiders! Raiders!" came the startled cry from the speaker grille. It echoed menacingly within the vaulted confines of the Las Vegas station of Transcontinental Railroad.

Eddie was working in the station's cafeteria when the warning arrived, in the process of converting its windowed side into a vast greenhouse. He froze, eyes wide in alarm, then dropped his tools and ran to the ticket booth where the walkie-talkie's base station was installed. He grabbed the microphone clumsily, almost dropping it twice. His thumb finally found the talk button; he pressed it savagely and called out, "Report!"

The stationmaster emerged from his office and hurried up behind him, his face reflecting the same alarm that was on Eddie's.

"Mr. Eddie!" echoed the booming electronic voice. "There's about a dozen men riding up from the south. Ain't got no automobiles or wagons, just men on horses headed this way. Can't say for sure how many—it's tough to make out all the details with these pathetic hockshop field glasses."

"Stay out of sight!" he warned. "And I'll get help. Meet us on the road at the edge of town, if you can."

"I'll try, sir."

Eddie set the microphone down, lost in worried thought for the moment.

"It sure does sound like it could be raiders, Mr. Eddie," prompted the stationmaster anxiously. "What'll we do?"

"We'll have to be ready for them!" he cried. "Follow me!" He grabbed his hat and rifle from their perch alongside the front door of the station, and bursting out onto the street, he stopped the first man he saw. "Raiders riding up from the south!" he cried. "Get your rifle and some more men and meet me at the edge of town! Spread the word!" Without a word, the man reared his horse around and galloped away as Eddie raced off to the south, repeating his call to arms to each man he passed, and meeting with similar reactions.

Soon he reached the south end of town; he was the second to arrive; the lookout was already waiting for him. Out across the desert Eddie could plainly see the cluster of mounted men even though they were still almost a mile away. The group was not moving; it appeared they were waiting for something.

"Thirteen of them, Mr. Eddie," reported the lookout, gesturing with the field glasses. "And it looks like every one of them is only carrying a rifle, saddlebags, and not much else. Doesn't look good!"

Eddie nodded. Behind him he heard the sound of hoof beats. His makeshift militia was starting to arrive, at first by ones and twos, then by fours and fives. Soon there was a large crowd, over fifty men assembled, and still more came. Eddie assumed command.

"Okay, listen up!" he called out. "We have to be sure if they mean us good or ill before we—" Gunshots could be heard in the distance along with whoops and catcalls; the raiders were closing in on the town at a gallop. Eddie's face turned grim. There could be no parlay with the likes of men who fired first. "Okay, listen up!" he began again. "We don't have much time! Here's what we'll do..."

* * *

The raiders approached.

They had been riding hard for several days now, their food gone, their water low, and their tempers short. They had fled the Arizona town where they had once been part of a vicious ruling clique; but their fortunes had abruptly taken a turn for the worse when outlaws even more vicious than they had laid siege to the town, driving them out in a hasty retreat, leaving behind many casualties. They had chosen Las Vegas as a destination in desperation, that being the only town of size within a hundred miles. They had nowhere else to go.

As they approached, they could see the homes and shops of Las Vegas appearing as if they were sprouting out of the gravelly desert sands. Their leader held up a dusty, gloved hand, halting the motley crew. For a moment he eyed the edge of town from under the broad brim of a battered hat. Two riders came up beside him; identical twins riding completely dissimilar horses.

"How's it look, boss?" one of them asked eagerly.

Seconds passed before he murmured gruffly, "Quiet." It wasn't clear if it were an answer or a command.

"Deserted?" the twin prodded.

He pointed to a larger structure toward the eastern edge of town. "Nah—see that smoke?" He turned to the twin and snickered. "Don't worry. There's people there."

"Women, too, ya think?" His eyes glowed.

The boss did not reply; he returned his attention to the town in the distance.

The twin pulled out his revolver in one quick, practiced motion, its barrel angled toward the clear blue sky. "Let's take over, boss!" he hissed eagerly, eyes large.

The boss rested his hands unhurriedly on the saddle horn and slowly faced the twin. He was weary to the bone, and it showed in his voice. "Not so fast, pal. I'm thinking maybe we should take it slow. Ride in like we're tourists or something. Look around first, then get the drop on them."

The other twin chimed in. "But the men are hungry, boss! We got no time for them subtle niceties." He pulled out his own revolver with a speed that rivaled his brother's. "Let's just grab some hostages and take over!"

The boss pointedly turned his attention back toward the town and spat upon the sand; but that was the limit of any display of his disdain for their opinion. Had he been more secure in his status as "boss," he would have berated them in angry exasperation and simply followed his own counsel. But the brothers were birds of a feather, hotheads through and through, more inclined to take than to ask, to shoot than to talk, and never a regret afterward. He was all too aware that it was only through their tacit support that he held his command; one major disagreement between him and them and that would be that; there would be a new boss—and he could already sense the seeds of their discontent with his leadership. So it was no surprise that as he kept a watchful eye on the town ahead, he could feel his authority ebbing away; in its place a knot of dread coalesced in his stomach. It was the same feeling he would experience back in the old days when he worked as a bureaucrat for the Unificating Board, and the feeling had a similar cause: his superiors were always countermanding his orders without rhyme or reason until it reached the point where the flunkies under his command would no longer pay him any heed. Rather, they would look at him askance with closed faces plainly revealing their lack of faith in his authority. He had hated the feeling then, and he hated it just as much now; but making matters worse, there was no Directive 289-10 here and now to guarantee him a continued position as boss. In this new world, he had to be flexible above all else. Cornered, he reacted as he always had—he stifled his exasperation and capitulated.

Still facing town, the decision made, the boss forced a wide, false grin. "Well, let's take over, then!" Louder, so the others could plainly hear, he reared his horse around and cried out, "Welcome to your new home, boys!" He let out with a loud whoop, pulled out his revolver, and fired several shots in the air. His horse reared again with a loud neighing. "And it's time we move in!"

Whooping in imitation, without hesitation the raiders charged toward town, guns blazing, the twins taking the lead. In short order they closed the distance, galloping along the main boulevard into town.

They encountered no one on the street; the town appeared deserted. Soon, guns still blazing, they reached the first traffic signal. It glowed red, but the lead riders paid its command no mind, nor, for that matter, did they note its presence even when a chance shot exploded the brightly-lit bulb into a thousand sparkling fragments. The raiders burst through the empty intersection and up the broad boulevard heading for the heart of town, but they never reached the end of the next block. From every alley, window, and rooftop along the right side of the street the makeshift militia's guns suddenly blazed. It took less than five seconds before the cacophony of gunshots ended as abruptly as it had begun; there were no targets left. Every single raider was down; to a man, they had all been slain, each felled by multiple bullets of varying caliber. Many horses also lay among the dead, innocent victims of some poorly-aimed shot, while an unhurt minority aimlessly ambled about, riderless and apparently unconcerned, as if they were accustomed to sudden bursts of gunfire.

Slowly, silently, the members of the militia peered out from behind their cover, then made their way cautiously into the street. Eddie was there at their head, taking in the gruesome, hushed scene. He swayed a little, and had to turn away from the slaughter; he had begun to feel sick at his stomach. Having turned, in front of him stood the men of Las Vegas. They studied Eddie in silence for a moment, then someone in the back of the crowd cried suddenly, with enthusiasm, "Three cheers for Eddie!"

An explosion answered him. The men laughed, they cheered, they broke into applause; they surged forward to surround Eddie, mobbing him, slapping him on the back, shaking his free hand, almost shaking his rifle out of the other.

"God bless you, Mr. Eddie!"

"They were going to eat us alive!"

"I'll never think it's hopeless again!"

They continued to crowd around him, pressing close. Eddie wasn't sure how it happened, but one second he was standing firmly on the ground on his own two feet, the next he found himself held high, perched on the shoulders of two burly militiamen. He became aware of a rhythmic, repeated shout that was spreading from a small beginning and pulsing into what Eddie could only call insanity. Spontaneously, the crowd began to chant: *"Long live Eddie... Long live Eddie...,"* over and over. It was like watching an old movie, from back in the days when the stories were still about heroes, except that this story was real.

Eddie winced, embarrassed and red-faced. He was a railroad executive, the Special Assistant to the Vice-President of Operations for Transcontinental Railroad, not some barrel-chested champion from the Saturday matinees. But seeing the triumphant sea of jubilant faces that surrounded him, he was forced to face his true self and the hero's role he had played in their victory. Giving himself up to it, deliberately and self-consciously he forced a wan smile and waved back, sparking all the more fervor in their cheers. Eventually the rally wound down, but still with scattered backslapping, laughter, and excited discussion.

"Well done, men!" cried Eddie, still seated on the militiamen's shoulders. "Well done!" The crowd roared their agreement, then fell silent to hear his words. "Let's be honest—we got lucky today." Grumbling murmurs rose from the crowd; clearly, they were not convinced, but Eddie charged ahead nonetheless. "I say we need to be better organized so that the next time this sort of thing happens, we'll be ready. We need to set up squads and lines of communication so that we can get into action on a moment's notice." This time it was nodding heads and a rumble of assent that drifted up to him. "No more of this 'seat of the pants' planning. Let's meet at the Transcontinental station tonight at sunset and we'll see what we can do to get ourselves better organized. Any questions?"

After a pause, some wiseacre yelled out, "Eddie for Mayor!" The crowd laughed at Eddie's manifest embarrassment amid scattered applause.

"Then I'll see you all tonight," Eddie called out in reply, as if he hadn't heard, then slid clumsily from his human perch.

Slowly, the militia began to disperse, and their hero turned away to return to tending his garden.

"Hey, wait a minute!" called out an angry voice.

The exodus halted. Heads turned in the direction of the cry. Standing in the doorway of a modest butcher shop stood a balding shopkeeper, his little remaining hair a frazzled, dark-grey fringe. He wore a stained, full-length white apron and held a long rifle by the end of the barrel in one hand as if it were a broom. He swept his free hand across the carnage lying in the street and demanded, "Who's gonna clean up this mess?" He set his jaw firm and his eyes scanned the crowd. When no one volunteered an answer, he pressed the issue. "Well?"

Instinctively, every eye turned to Eddie.

Taking his cue from the crowd, the butcher put his free hand on his hip, glared at Eddie as well and repeated, "Well? How am I supposed to run a business here when you leave such an awful mess behind?" Clearly agitated, his hand swept the street again.

Eddie's eyes followed the gesture to its subject, but his stomach rose again and he was forced to quickly look away. "I... I don't know," he admitted uncertainly.

"Well, somebody better do *something!*"

Doubtfully, Eddie suggested, "Call the police?"

The butcher snorted. "What planet are *you* from, kid? Ain't been no real policing in this town since long before the Mayor left." He leaned on his rifle, again as if leaning on a broom. "Fat chance they'd do anything about anything! And let me tell you another thing—" He was warming to his audience. "—I've been robbed twice in the last month, and ain't nobody done nothing about it, police or otherwise. As if I didn't have enough troubles! Now *you* come in here, guns blazing, and you want to leave *me* with the mess to clean up? What do you have to say for yourself?"

Eddie was dumbfounded. Here he had just saved countless innocent lives, and was now being called on the carpet for his initiative. Instinctively, from long practice, Eddie turned the problem over in the back of his mind; unsurprisingly, it produced an answer; with a small start, he realized how he might rectify things. "Do you own a horse?" he asked incongruously.

"A what?" The butcher was taken aback by the sudden turn of conversation.

"A horse."

"Nope. Can't afford one. But what's that got to do with—" He stopped abruptly, as if his mother had caught him uttering a naughty word. Silently, the butcher pulled at his chin; his keen shopkeeper's mind had already gotten the drift, and was quickly running far ahead of Eddie's.

"Tell you what," barked the butcher in a businesslike tone, raising his voice and taking in the entire crowd. "Why don't you fellows just leave this to me, and I'll take care of everything. An altruistic public service!" As he spoke, his eyes were surreptitiously scanning the battlefield, mentally tallying the number of unhurt animals and multiplying that number by the market price for a horse. He saw numerous rifles held by cold, dead hands, and his calculations skyrocketed. He began to sweep off the crowd with broom-like motions of the stock of his rifle. "Go on, boys, go on. You did your part, now I'll do mine. This is a butcher's job. You just leave it to me."

"What about their—," Eddie began.

"No, no! Not another word!" The butcher feared someone else might catch on and cut into his bounty. "On your way, now. Off! Just leave it to me, I tell you." His eyes shone gleefully. "Git!"

* * *

Darkness came.

The inaugural meeting of the makeshift militia had gone well. A crowd almost three times the number of defenders had converged on the Transcontinental station, a worthy troop, staunch and strong. So many had gathered that the waiting room could not accommodate them all, and they were forced to gather on the large boulevard in front of the station. Eddie wished there were some large structure that could house everyone, something the size of an airplane hangar, but the streets in front of Transcontinental station were the best they had. Regardless, in short order, lines of communication were established, leaders chosen, stock strategies hammered out, and training scheduled. With only a single meeting, Eddie felt that they were far better prepared to face the next challenge, whether it came from raiders, religious radicals, or any random rabble who might make the mistake of invading Las Vegas.

In spite of his confidence, it was no contradiction that Eddie returned to the scene of the day's skirmish with some trepidation. He steeled himself for the worst when he rounded the last corner, but the precaution was not necessary. Aside from scattered splotches of blood, the overhead street lights revealed no overt evidence that a deadly confrontation had taken place earlier that day.

No one was about. As he walked down the lamp-lit, empty street, he heard the sound of neighs escaping from a darkened garage. It was locked with an oversized padlock; in fact, the lock was so large and out of proportion that it appeared as if the owner were deliberately advertising the fact that the garage was locked. Curious, Eddie peered through a dusty, eye-level window; several horses stood in close formation, their reins secured to a long piece of lumber crudely nailed along the rear wall. He nodded to himself and turned away. Alongside the garage, electric lights burned within the butcher's shop; the neighboring buildings were dark at this late hour. Eddie walked up to the door; it was unlocked. He let himself in, a tiny bell affixed to the inside of the door cheerfully announcing his entrance.

The butcher was crouching at the back of the store, his back to the door. He whirled around and bolted stiffly upright at the sound, eyes wide, as if expecting the worst, his hand shooting to the weapon at his hip. Behind the startled shopkeeper, Eddie could see a broad array of rifles leaning against the back wall, and several boxes brimming with revolvers, holsters, ammunition, saddlebags, and random livery.

The proprietor lowered his hand when he recognized Eddie. "Thought you might be that bandit fellow come back for more," he explained nervously.

"No. It's just me. I wanted to see how you were coming along cleaning up, and I had a couple of questions besides."

The butcher beamed a broad smile and swept a hand across the array of armaments behind him. "I'm doing quite well, as you can see. *Quite* well, thank you!"

"Are those your horses locked up in the garage next door?"

"They are now," he laughed, slapping his hip. He was in high humor. "That was a good idea you had there, kid."

"Thanks. You deserve it." After a respectful pause, he added, "What happened to our raider friends?"

"Loaded them into an old wagon and hauled them up into the mountains."

"The mountains?" Eddie looked confused. "Why bury them in the mountains? Isn't the ground a lot rockier up there?"

"Bury them?" The butcher barked a short laugh. "Who said anything about burying them? I just carted them up there and *dumped* them!" He swirled an index finger at the ceiling. "It's the buzzards for their like! And more's the pity!" Sporting a wicked grin, he glared at Eddie with eyes unnaturally wide.

Eddie took a reeling step backwards. He was shaken by the sheer barbarism of the butcher's solution, yet somehow could not find it in himself to condemn it. In the weeks since he had come to Las Vegas he had noticed innumerable other such small changes in himself—not to mention several larger ones! Surviving the collapse of civilization could tend to change a man—and here he faced yet another change, but he let it pass with only the mental note. He wondered how soon the mental notes might also pass. Recovering his composure, he managed to keep his voice level. "How about the dead horses?" he asked reluctantly, not wanting to know.

The butcher eyed him warily, his strange smile quickly fading. "You look like you don't really want to know," he offered generously.

Moments passed in silence before Eddie finally mustered an answer. "You're an interesting fellow," was all he could manage.

"Let's just say that I recognize a bargain when I see one." He turned to face the wall of rifles, hands on his hips.

Gratefully changing the subject, Eddie interjected, "Not meaning to change the subject, but I wanted to ask you about something you said this morning about bandits."

"What about 'em?" he asked apprehensively.

"You've been held up?"

"Twice. This month. So far." He was plainly angry.

"Who was it?"

The butcher shrugged.

"You said the police were no help?"

"The police!" He made as if to spit on the floor of his own shop, but caught himself. "The police?" he repeated. He stalked over to the counter and seized his telephone with both hands. "Go on, try to telephone them!" Angrily he shoved the device at Eddie. When Eddie hesitated, he gestured again. "Go on and call them, I tell you!"

Slowly, Eddie took the instrument from the butcher's outstretched hands and dialed the number posted alongside the cash register. He heard the repeated burring on the line: once, twice, three times. On the sixth ring, he hung up and handed the device back. "I see," he said.

"And let me tell you another thing: even when they do answer—which ain't often!—they still won't come!"

"Why not?"

"Busy... scared... lost... How the hell should I know? Maybe it's because I'm all the way down here on the south side of town." He chucked dryly. "It's not like I'm living in one of them abandoned neighborhoods. All I know is that they don't come."

"Maybe I ought to go and have a talk with them."

"Why not?" The butcher chuckled dryly. "You already have your finger in a lot of pies, kid. What's one more?"

\* \* \*

The policeman prevaricated.

"Now, Mr. Eddie, be reasonable! There are only three of us for... For what? Oh, I don't know, thousands of people? Of course we're not here all the time!"

"Did you know that the butcher on the south side has been robbed twice this month?"

The policeman sighed. He knew what was coming. "Yes, sir. I knew."

"Have you any leads?"

The policeman looked down, reddening slightly. "Well, really, we haven't had the time to do much about it." He looked up again. "Not that there were many clues! Whoever did it pulled it off real smooth—a real smooth smarty, he is. The only thing we know is that he was average height and wore jeans, work shirt and a mask over his entire head. It could have been anybody... or nobody!"

"Nobody? You doubt the butcher's word?"

"No, no," he retreated. "I'm just saying we have nothing to go on."

"But it's happened twice. Maybe there'll be a third time. Couldn't you post a watch?"

From under the brim of his blue cap he looked up at Eddie reproachfully. "Every night? There are only three of us, Mr. Eddie. Nobody wants to sit out all night waiting for something that'll probably never happen." He took a deep breath bordering on a sigh. "Besides," he explained patiently. "We're in the business of law enforcement. Crime prevention is something else entirely."

Eddie was struck momentarily speechless. He had never stopped to consider the nuance before. "But wouldn't you want to try to prevent crime, too?"

The comment struck a chord in the policeman. His eyes brightened, but the fire immediately died, as if someone had poured a large bucket of water over a small match. "The short answer is that we would love to, Mr. Eddie. But the reality is that the Mayor always held us back. Our job devolved into crime *reporting* rather than law enforcement—and the last year or two we were under orders to stop even the reporting, and ignore way too many illegal doings." He shook his head at the memory.

"But the Mayor's left town, I hear. What's holding you back?"

This time he did sigh. "It's too late to matter, Mr. Eddie. We just don't have the manpower these days. Most of those on the force that didn't light out with the Mayor have up and quit. Like I said, there's only three of us left."

"Why not hire deputies, then?" He gestured to the telephone. "Or a dispatcher to take calls?"

The question struck another chord; it was just what the policeman had wanted to hear, a pet peeve he longed to slaughter, and he seized the chance. Theatrically, he scratched the back of his head, tipping his cap forward a little in the process. "Well, now, you touch upon something there that's becoming a real issue with me and the men." He paused for effect, waiting to be prompted.

Eddie was still distracted considering the difference between enforcement and prevention; unconsciously, he did the officer the favor. "What issue? Crime prevention?"

"Huh? No, no. Hiring deputies. We should have at least a score of officers for a town this size, but..." He paused and looked upward as if seeking strength. "...but it seems we haven't been paid in over a month!"

"Not paid?" Recalling his experiences with the Dam technician, Eddie was only half surprised.

"Over a month, Mr. Eddie. That's why we're down to three—everyone else quit. When a man isn't getting paid, it's nigh on impossible to get him to stay. And there's no way to stop anyone from quitting these days—Directive 289-10 doesn't mean anything anymore—and we're the ones who are supposed to be enforcing it!"

Eddie let the observation pass. "Who's supposed to be paying you?"

"The Mayor, of course." He chuckled dryly. "But if you go down to City Hall, you won't find anyone there—or any *thing!* Maybe I shouldn't be telling tales out of school, but when the Mayor bugged out of town last month, he loaded everything into his limousine that wasn't nailed down. Like the best furniture. Like the artwork off the walls. Like the entire city treasury."

"But that's against the law!"

"Yes, I suppose it is," he responded wearily.

"Well, what did you do about it? Why didn't you arrest him?"

The policeman shrugged. "Who is John Galt?"

Eddie blinked twice before deciding to let that pass as well. Instead, he repeated his question. "So who's paying you now?"

Again, the policeman shrugged. "Nobody! That's why there are only three of us left, each pulling an eight hour shift. If any of us happens to be here at the station when the phone rings, we answer it. But fact is we're out more than in. You were lucky to catch me here tonight at all, Mr. Eddie. We're stretched pretty thin."

"But you have a town to protect! How will you do it?"

The policeman sighed. "Mr. Eddie, I'm only a little guy. I do what I'm told and get what I can, just like everyone else. But let me tell you: the wife won't let me keep up this job much longer unless I start getting paid real soon. Same's for the other men, too. We love police work, or we wouldn't still be here. But a man's got to eat, you know."

Again, Eddie could think of nothing to say. As with most people, to him policemen were a constant presence that required no thought, like breathing the air. The police force simply *was*, a prosaic commodity always taken for granted, like electricity or street lights, but here the officer was calmly predicting its demise. Eddie couldn't imagine a world without police; but apparently he was to experience it for himself soon enough. *No!* he shouted to himself inside his head. *Not if I have anything to say about it!* To the policeman, he replied evenly, "Don't worry. I'll think of something."

"Somebody better," the policeman warned darkly. "And soon."

\* \* \*

The Diesel rumbled.

Eddie sat at the controls of the throbbing engine and piloted it slowly along the rails of Las Vegas at restricted speed, its yard bell clanking a rhythmic, flat, off-key warning of his approach. Before long the buildings of the town fell behind him, as did the need for caution. He flipped an overhead toggle switch to kill the bell, then advanced the throttle further, increasing his velocity first to medium speed then to limited speed; it was the fastest he had operated the Diesel since arriving in Las Vegas. In no time the town fell far behind, leaving him alone with the moving desert under his clicking wheels as his only companion.

Eddie reveled in the moment. His bonhomie came from a mixture of joys: the feel of the powerful, living engine tamed to his whim, the stark splendor of the desert landscape, the beautiful blue sky, and the blessed solitude. It was the last which he had sought this day; he needed time to think, and indulging himself, for the first time since his arrival he took the last living remnant of Transcontinental Railroad out on the road it no longer served.

Many miles north of town, he came to a track switch where the rails split into two directions: northwest toward what used to be San Francisco, and northeast into the uncrossable, snow-clogged Colorado Rockies. Rolling a little beyond the switch in the northwesterly direction, he brought the Diesel to a gentle halt, dumped air to set the brake, and climbed out, letting it idle noisily. He slogged the short distance through the shifting sands back to the switch, and with a great heave on its lever, flipped it to the other track. His maps told him that a spur track connected the left and right branches less than a mile further up, forming a triangle of track; Eddie planned to back the Diesel along the spur to the easterly track, then head back to town facing forward again. The track switch would already be correctly positioned for his return when he reached it.

He trudged through the gravelly sand back to the Diesel, but did not climb aboard. He knew from personal experience that the Diesel's cab would quickly become as hot as an oven if it sat immobile for very long under the unforgiving desert sun. Instead he perched on a ladder rung on the shadowed side of the idling train admiring the scenery, taking the time to sit and think.

In the hazy distance, he could make out the jagged mountain range that surrounded the tan flatness of the featureless desert. The towering ring gave him the impression that he sat in the bottom of a gigantic sandy saucer many miles in diameter, the massive granite arms of the mountains protecting him and all Las Vegas from the multitude of disasters that had apparently befallen the outside world. But raiders and other troubles still managed to seep in, with the police situation being the latest and most urgent incarnation.

He felt that his conversation with the policeman—and the butcher before that—had opened up a hornets' nest of interrelated troubles. He knew that what made the issue complex wasn't merely paying policemen; it spanned all that those payments implied: setting tax rates, collecting the taxes, and enforcing compliance, not to mention all the other functions once performed by the now-defunct Las Vegas government. Even if he had the authority—which he knew he hadn't—he wasn't eager to see the old status quo re-established in any case. Death and taxes, it was said, were inescapable evils; but Eddie by nature was unable to accept any evil, inescapable or otherwise. Neither choice was a course of action he would wish to initiate; in fact, the very idea of re-instituting taxation revolted him. Although he never entertained any second thoughts about the authority of government to levy taxes, when it became personal—when it was *he* who had to levy them—and *collect* them!—it became another matter entirely. What right did he have to take money from one person and give it to another, even for something as important as police protection? He felt that if he should ever attempt to enforce a tax, he would thereby become a thief himself. Nor was he willing to accept the idea of letting people vote to authorize him to collect a tax; it only diffused the blame and made everyone who voted for him a thief as well, partners in crime, with Eddie as their patsy. What right did a group of people have to take money from others when none of the individual members of that group had that right?

He shook his head in weariness. *Are taxes really necessary?* he asked himself, but he knew the question to be rhetorical. Because if not through taxation, how else could the police possibly be paid? He briefly considered establishing a volunteer police force modeled after the town's volunteer firemen, but the problem was an inherently different one—firemen only served active duty once in a while; they could go about their everyday lives even while they remained on alert. The same could be said for the newly-formed Las Vegas militia. But police work was completely different; they needed to be on the job around the clock. He also considered but immediately dismissed a Boulder Dam style of solution; he knew there would be no income to cover expenses, no dividends to distribute.

Eddie sighed. He was fresh out of ideas. Where, then, was the money to pay the police to come from? What else was there besides coercive taxation? He halted, wide eyes staring unseeing at the distant desert horizon, his mind grasping an unexpected corollary statement—what about *non*-coercive taxation?

Excited now, he unconsciously stood up and took two steps forward into the bright sunshine, his eyes still unfocused as his mind focused on the unusual concept. Details of its implementation clicked neatly together of their own accord, one after another, all of the pieces falling into their proper place. It simply stood to reason, and he wouldn't have to rob anyone.

He lingered another moment in the sunshine, his eyes refocusing on the distant mountains. Satisfied with his answer, he climbed aboard the steamy, idling Diesel, released the brakes, advanced the throttle, and slowly began to navigate the triangle of track to head back into town. There was much to do.

* * *

The butcher complained.

"What do you mean, I have to pay for police protection?" he demanded. "What do I pay taxes for?"

"You're not paying taxes anymore, now are you?" Eddie pointed out. The butcher did not reply; they both knew that Las Vegas had not bothered with tax collection since the Mayor had left town; besides, there was no one left in City Hall to pay the taxes to.

"So who are you, the new taxman?"

"No!" cried Eddie with an unexpected vehemence. "I'm only a citizen who believes in law enforcement." After a pause, he added, "Don't you?"

The answer was quick in coming. "A fat lot of protection I got when I was robbed twice in the last month!"

"That's crime prevention," Eddie pointed out, just as quickly. "Not law enforcement. But with my new approach you'll get that and enforcement, too." When the shopkeeper did not immediately reply, he prompted, "So are you on board?"

Apprehensively, the butcher countered, "And what if I'm not?"

"Then you're not," he replied flatly. "But if you're not and you want the police to investigate a crime, you'll have to pay the going rate. Crime prevention is billed per hour. The cost of law enforcement depends upon the crime." He brandished a sheet of paper listing the various rates, gesturing slightly in emphasis. "It's all spelled out here in detail."

The butcher threw up his hands in exaggerated, exasperated anger. "This is extortion!"

"No it isn't. Nobody is going to beat you up or anything. You don't have to pay."

"Yes I do! I either have to pay in advance or pay after the fact."

"True—if you want the service. But you could always do it yourself."

The butcher scoffed. "Who, me? Chase crooks?" He ran his fingers through what was left of his grey fringe. "Maybe once upon a time, but I ain't as young as I used to be, you know."

"All the more reason why you should sign up. And by paying in advance, it's an awful lot cheaper."

The butcher eyed him warily. "Yeah? How much cheaper?"

Hearing that question, Eddie felt he was on the home stretch. Once he moved beyond the question of whether or not police services were needed, it became only a question of price; and the rates he established were deliberately set far lower than the taxes the butcher once paid to the city. The benevolent trap was set; Eddie moved in to close the deal, naming his price. "For that low monthly fee, you get unlimited law enforcement, plus prevention at a ninety percent discount."

"Ninety percent!" The butcher pulled on his chin thoughtfully for a moment, then sarcastically added, "Will the police bother to answer the phone?"

"Guaranteed," Eddie replied easily. "One month of enforcement free if they don't answer by the third ring." He waved the paper in his hand. "Like I said: it's all spelled out here in black and white."

Running out of arguments, the butcher retreated into innuendo. "But this is nothing but a protection racket!"

Eddie was momentarily shocked; he hadn't thought of putting it into those exact words, but what the butcher said was true. "Yes... I guess it is..." he said softly to himself.

"And what if I want to start my own protection racket?" he demanded belligerently.

"Go ahead," Eddie replied unreservedly. "I'd think that the more men this town has protecting us from crooks, the better. No one should have a monopoly on chasing crooks." He paused a moment, considering a tangential notion. "And I'm not sure where they would get such a monopolistic power anyhow," he murmured to himself. Shaking off the thought, he returned to the issue at hand. "Yes, you could always do it yourself, but don't you think it would be better to hire experts to handle it for you?"

The butcher stood mute and stared at Eddie with a stone face. Obviously the man had finished arguing.

Eddie sighed. He had done all he could. "As you wish." He turned to leave, but before he could reach the door, the butcher came back to life.

"No, wait!"

Patiently, Eddie halted and faced the shopkeeper.

The butcher said nothing for a moment, then asked, "Will you catch my bandit?"

"We can try."

"At a ninety percent discount, remember!"

Eddie nodded.

The butcher stood silent for another moment, then threw up his hands again, this time in surrender. "All right, all right! Sign me up! And good luck, kid—you're going to need it!"

\* \* \*

Sponsorship grew.

Starting with the butcher had been a good idea, Eddie told himself. He was a man whose keen business sense would make him the most difficult of the lot, to be sure. But the man had inadvertently helped define for him the pattern of people's resistance, and that gave Eddie an accurate map to navigate around the more obvious obstacles with subsequent recalcitrants.

At first Eddie had gone door to door peddling his scheme, a practice he found that he loathed—he had never done it before—but fortunately it did not take him long to solicit sufficient seed capital. With that, he hired several former policemen to spread the word. That solved three problems for him simultaneously—putting more policemen on the pay rolls, spreading the new gospel, and sparing Eddie the embarrassing drudgery of knocking on the doors of strangers.

He had no idea in advance how many people would take him up on his commercialized police protection. He had priced his business model on the assumption that one out of ten would buy into his scheme, and he was astonished when he surpassed that goal with the first week's subscriptions. Ultimately, more than half of those who were approached accepted Eddie's "protection racket." There was money for salaries and equipment, and to spare.

Truth be told, he had an unaffiliated salesman drumming up business for him, namely the anonymous local bandit who had twice robbed the butcher and many other merchants and homes; and he was still prowling the streets, striking one unfortunate victim after another, once or twice a week. In response to his illegal activities, Eddie's venture boomed. Given the number of policemen he could now afford to put on the streets, it came as no surprise that it didn't take long for his crime prevention unit to present a suspect for his law enforcement unit.

## CHAPTER 5 – EASY TO BE HARD

Tempers flared.

"What do you mean, you won't serve me?" the scab demanded.

"I don't serve no stinking looter!" the clerk retorted vehemently.

"But I'm no looter!" countered the scab. "I've taken an oath never to initiate the use of force or fraud! Go look—it's posted on the wall inside *The Golden Touch*!"

"Yes...? And...?" the clerk asked in mock innocence, an eyebrow going up in spiteful anticipation of an answer he knew would not be forthcoming.

"So you should serve me!"

"A logical fallacy, scab. I serve whom I please, and I do not serve scabs."

"But all I want is two pounds of galvanized nails!"

"Another logical fallacy, scab. If you haven't taken the oath, it doesn't matter one whit *what* you want; you're not getting it here!"

"But I've taken an oath, I tell you! The words are right out of the Worker's speech!"

"That's inarguably true," the clerk admitted ominously. "Because they are indeed taken *right out* of his speech—literally! And when you take away the support of the philosophy he outlined in the rest of his speech, all you have left is a floating, disembodied ideology." He threw his hands in the air. "It's not an oath! It's a meaningless bromide!"

"No it isn't!"

"Oh, yeah? Then what's its basis? What values underlie your oath? Why those values and not others? How did you choose them?"

"The value is that it allows men to live together in peace."

"And that is a value because...?" he prompted.

The scab harrumphed. "What kind of question is that? It's self-evident!"

"Maybe to someone who's abandoned reason, it is. But not to me."

"Huh? I haven't abandoned reason."

"Sure you have. Look at your oath! It rests upon nothing except your whim. *Why* should you not initiate force? Where is the reasoning that defends your whim? Why, even the definition of your words is suspect."

"Suspect? But I already told you! It lets men live together in peace!"

"Think again, scab. If you abandon reason, you endorse force."

"Huh!" He took a half step backward. "How's that?"

"Without reason, how else would you propose that men settle issues?"

"Peacefully!"

"Really? Like your fellow scab who said that we strikers should be lined up against the wall and shot? Oh, yes, I heard about that! He's signed your oath, too, but somehow he's rationalized the words to justify his whim to shoot first."

"Well, he doesn't speak for me!"

"That's true—because your oath has already spoken for both of you, and it's using the language of looters! That's why two men can derive two diametrically opposed morals starting from the same oath! Now do you see why it's meaningless?"

"But—"

The clerk cut him off. "Bah! This is a waste of time! On your way! I have work to do."

"But—"

"Get out before I *throw* you out!"

"But—"

"I said *git!*"

Checkmated, the scab left in a huff.

The clerk muttered a curse under his breath, grumbled about the infernal gall of some people, and returned to his interrupted task. Moments later, a striker entered.

"Can I help you?" the clerk inquired politely, recognizing the man as a fellow philosophical traveler.

"Two pounds of galvanized nails and a screwdriver, please."

The politeness vanished. The clerk studied him with narrowed eyes for a moment, then asked ominously, "What do you want them nails for?"

Reddening faintly, the striker prevaricated. "What do you mean? I just want some nails."

"You're not buying them for some scab, are you?" he probed suspiciously.

The striker hesitated uneasily. "What if I were?"

"Then you're not getting them from me, that's what! I don't deal with scabs!"

"Hey, wait a minute! You know me! I'm a sworn striker, same as you!"

"Maybe. But like I said, I don't deal with scabs—or strikers who deal with scabs!" An awkward silence hung in the air as the proprietor scrutinized the striker carefully. Without taking his angry eyes off the man, he reached under the counter and retrieved a clipboard, dropping it squarely onto the countertop with a loud smack. "Sign this first and maybe I'll serve you." His eyes narrowed further. "Maybe," he stressed.

The striker glanced down at clipboard. It held a sheet of paper formatted as a petition; there was a very short paragraph at the top, with scores of signatures scribbled under it.

"Sign it."

The striker spun the petition around so as to better make out the paragraph at the top. It read: "I hereby certify that my purchase will not be used for the benefit of scabs." He recognized the names of many of his fellow strikers beneath it.

The striker looked up. "This is ridiculous! It's none of your business how I choose to run my affairs! I refuse to sign it!"

"Then I refuse to serve you."

"But—"

"I'm running a hardware store here, not a looter's charity. Now get out!"

"How about that screwdriver? That's for me!"

"Get... Out...!" he commanded, enunciating each word separately and equally.

Chastised, the striker left empty-handed.

\* \* \*

The striker returned.

It was a little after noon that same day; he knew the surly clerk would be away having lunch, and taking his place behind the counter would be his second assistant bookkeeper. Boldly, the striker strode into the store. Sure enough, the bookkeeper was behind the counter; he looked up from his novel—over a thousand pages long, from the heft of it. If he felt put out by the intrusion on his reading, it did not reflect itself in his demeanor; in fact, he seemed almost eager to help, as if he were seeking a reason to abandon the oversized volume.

"Can I help you?"

"Ah... yes. I was walking by and I thought I'd... uh... stop in," he stammered clumsily. He was nervous and it showed, but the bookkeeper took no notice. He only marked his page and set the ponderous tome aside.

"Certainly, sir. What can I get for—" He stopped himself as he remembered, slapping his forehead theatrically. "Almost forgot," he chided himself with an awkward smile. Reaching under the counter, he pulled out the clipboard.

"That's all right," the striker replied easily, holding up a palm, surprising himself with his fast thinking. "I was here earlier, and was already asked to sign." *And that's the absolute truth, too!* he reminded himself, taking mental note to the exception.

The bookkeeper stopped in mid-motion and put away the clipboard. "Good! It's a bother, to be sure, but a necessary one."

"I can see what you mean!" replied the striker, again skirting the edge of the truth. "The looters have already taken far too much from us."

"Now, what can I get for you?" the second assistant bookkeeper asked again, still smiling.

"A screwdriver," replied the striker. "Just a screwdriver. That's all."

## Chapter 6 – Exodus

The banishments began.

Although the philosophical counterrevolution staged by the clerk and other hard-core strikers was unofficial, unorganized and by no means comprehensive, its adherents occupied a sufficiently strategic segment of the valley's economy to more than assure its effectiveness. For the first time in history, the hard-core producers found themselves in command of the moral high ground over the looters, and they pressed their advantage assiduously. Scab and sympathetic striker alike were left with no alternative but to comply. Within the short span of only a few days, the scabs' revolution had materialized, flourished, and died.

With the revolt crushed, there followed much debate among the strikers regarding the disposition of the soon-to-be-banished scabs, with their key concern being where to send them. There was no question that the location of the valley still had to be kept secret, for the world Outside, dying though it was, was still incomparably mighty. It could still destroy the fledging enclave, if only it decided to do so. Precautions had to be taken.

Many options were explored which might safely implement the banishment, ranging from setting up a scab enclave in the nearby foothills a few miles north of the Gulch, to ferrying the entire scab population out of the country. In the end, a clever scheme to protect the valley's privacy was proposed, its reasoning based upon the valley's experience with their first scab, Dagny: the idea was that one by one, those who had refused to take the oath would be marched up to the lie-detecting lectern and asked a signal question: "Do you solemnly swear never to divulge the location of the valley prior to our return?" Those who truthfully answered "Yes" would be offered the option of being ferried to the location of their choice anywhere west of the Mississippi.

However, this option turned out to offer no option at all. According to the latest reports received over the shortwave, most American cities had not survived the initial collapse of the intricate infrastructure that had made their existence possible, and the prognosis for the few surviving cities was bleak. Remaining in America was simply too dangerous a proposition for the scabs—not that it mattered to the strikers.

Many other alternatives were debated, but ultimately the only viable option for the banished scabs was for them to settle in an obscure corner of Central America where they knew they wouldn't be engulfed by massive tides of refugees or blanketed by ten-foot snowfalls. Although the quality of the infrastructure in the foreign land would be far from sophisticated, it would at least be operational. As an added bonus, the choice of Central America would help both striker and scab: striker, because the secret of the valley would be better protected by the greater distance; and scab, because the expansive bulk of Mexico lay between them and the teeming hordes of refugees still seeking to escape the former United States. Both scab and secret would be relatively safe.

If a solution had quickly been found for those who promised to keep the valley a secret, a solution was just as quickly proposed for those who would not. For there was only one place in the western hemisphere where the strikers knew their secret would not spread even if revealed, one place from which the deadly knowledge could not inadvertently be leaked, a destination which would best serve the needs of the strikers, although not necessarily the scabs, and that place was California. Between its ban on electricity, the complete lack of communications facilities, its geographic separation from the rest of the nation, and its indigenous Luddite ruling clique, loose-lipped scabs would pose no danger to their former hosts.

Needless to say, this decision was not popular with the imminent emigrants who might choose not to promise secrecy, and ultimately was the direct cause of a change of heart in every single one of them. Rather than face life in a religious dictatorship, they decided that the price offered for their silence was one they could willingly accept after all.

Although this compromise proved acceptable to the scabs, there was one critically-important striker who vehemently opposed any scheme to ferry any scab out of the valley whatsoever: Dwight.

"Who's going to pay for the fuel?" he demanded. "Who's going to fly my airplanes? Who's going to pay for the wear and tear, and for the added maintenance? Who's going to insure them against accidental loss? Who's going to develop and administer the evacuation plan? Who's going to pay for it all? Not me!" But he was quick to add, "However, I *am* available for hire."

News of Dwight's determined recalcitrance spread like wildfire among the scabs, giving some a false hope that their banishments would not be carried out. But almost as soon as the news reached the scabs, a solution to the funding issue quickly followed: those strikers who invited any scabs into the valley would be responsible for underwriting their trip back out. It was a compromise that any oath-taker could readily understand and embrace. Among those whose opinions mattered, there was no dissent.

Dwight certainly loved the arrangement. He smiled happily at the thought of renting out so many of his aircraft. He was already planning on how he would spend his windfall of gold: for months he had been drafting plans for a revolutionary new type of aircraft—a galtmotor-powered hypersonic craft constructed entirely of the much more capable Miracle Metal II—and the profits he expected to earn shuttling scabs would more than cover the cost of its construction. He was almost glad the scabs had appeared on the scene—almost, but not quite. Nevertheless, he still appreciated the windfall.

With compromises in hand, and in short order, pilots were hired, aircraft scheduled, and manifests of scab passengers compiled in preparation for the mass exile. There being no reason to wait, long before the end of March the ferry trips began; and with so many scabs leaving, the transplanting promised to stretch well into April.

And so the exodus began.

# Chapter 7 – Did You Ever Have To Make Up Your Mind?

All was quiet.

The bandit peeked out from behind a dusty curtain to make certain the coast was clear. Satisfied, he donned his mask and slunk out the back door of the abandoned house, soundlessly closing the door behind him. He was a careful bandit, intelligent far beyond his ilk, the type of man to leave nothing to chance. Weak and disorganized though they were, there was still an off chance that the Las Vegas police might accidentally stumble across him. Instinctively and consciously, by carefully cultivated habit and by deliberate intent, he took every opportunity not to get caught. That had once been an easily-attained goal, but not any longer; times had changed. Back in the days when tourists had outnumbered residents many times over, there were a great number of easy opportunities for petty banditry. But in these new times, the pool of potential prey had grown paltry indeed, pressing him to pursue more perilous plans, including robbing the same establishments multiple times or stretching far beyond his usual territory, as was the case tonight.

He slithered easily into the overgrown bushes that ringed the unkempt yard. It wasn't a large yard; but the bushes were high, and he was confident no one would see him shift. But then, they weren't supposed to see him at all. To help make sure that everything happened according to his careful plan, he had practiced his motions there in the wee hours twice in the past week, several times each night, aiming to be the epitome of the master in action. He was honed; he was ready.

He was also hungry and sober, a bad combination, and he knew it. Either of them would be sufficient reason to drive him to the streets to seek his next victim, something he was always reluctant to chance, but the overpowering combination of needs easily removed his reluctance, as usual. But insistent though the twin drives were, they could not remove his inherent caution and predisposition to meticulous planning and orchestrated execution.

From his hiding place in the bushes, he studied the street through the gaps between the houses trying to catch a glimpse of any foot traffic, but as expected, there was none. It was an average residential neighborhood, its streets deserted, and given the hour he knew they would remain that way until the last lone pedestrian came by. *A pretty lady*, he predicted. *And all alone, too!* He knew the residents and their schedules; he knew there'd be no one to see.

As time passed, the street empty, he waited patiently according to his plan. *There she is!* In the crack of unobstructed vision between the third and fourth houses distant he saw his quarry momentarily appear then disappear. She was an unusually beautiful woman in her late twenties, shapely, with long, luxurious hair a light auburn in color. But it wasn't her physical attributes that interested him; it was her monetary ones. He looked all four ways before moving, as was his wont—left, right, back, forward—then quickly half-crawled behind a large, leafy bush alongside the house, again looking all four ways when he arrived. *So far, so good.*

He counted. He knew precisely how long it would take her to reach his hiding spot. When he had counted a third of the total, again there was the characteristic four-way glance followed by a quick shift to another overgrown bush and the follow-up glance. Still, no one else was in sight. He smiled in the darkness. *This is it!*

She was close enough that he could hear her shoes clacking against the sidewalk. He counted down the seconds to the surprise planned rendezvous. *Three... Two... One...* He scanned one last four-way and prepared to pounce.

* * *

The policeman smiled.

It wasn't the significant raise in pay he had received by joining up with Eddie's police force that made him smile; it wasn't the clear, cold drop they had on their suspect; it wasn't that he and his wife were no longer quarreling over money troubles; it wasn't even the pleasantly warm Nevada night. Any of them were good reasons to smile in and of themselves, and their combination made the evening all the more enjoyable. But what really filled his soul with joy was a feeling he hadn't experienced since he was a teenager, on the day that he swore an oath to his late mother that he would become a peace officer: it was the undeniable desire to help others, to do good and thwart evil, and to unfailingly deliver on that promise. That desire had propelled him to excel in school, and held firm through his rigorous training at the Police Academy. Given his powerful drive, it was no surprise he was the top of his class in every course; and when graduation day came, his pride burst forth and lit up the entire room, for he had been awarded the highest honor, Trainee of the Cycle, and not in the entire history of the Academy had there been such a stellar student.

Then, just like that, it was over. After so many years of preparation and dedicated effort, in much less than a month they took his dreams and smashed them to bits. They twisted his actions, his mind, and his very soul in unspeakable ways. Rather than enforcing the law, he found himself ordered to ignore it. Rather than an advocate for good, he had unwittingly been transformed into the involuntary agent of good's enemy. Faced with such unspeakable evil, he did what any red-blooded American of his day would do—he knuckled under. He did as he was told. He clipped his own wings. He got along to get along. The love of his career was perverted into a hatred of his job, a sorry trap from which there was no escape.

But that was then; this was now. The policeman smiled again. *Those days are gone forever!* Quietly excited, he sat in a comfortable chair in the third-story bedroom of a comfortable house across the street from the bandit's expected rendezvous point. From here he could scan the entire tableau and react to unexpected events as necessary. But he did not expect any complications—his trap was set; the bait, detected; and the rat was running through the maze, as planned.

"Do you want more tea, officer?" Silhouetted in the dark doorway of her bedroom, the busybody widow was all concern, expressing anxiety over the welfare of her temporary houseguest.

He smiled needlessly in the dark, his good nature unseen but plainly audible in his tone of voice. "No, thank you. It's almost time, and I need to be concentrating on my work."

She cooed her delight. She tiptoed across the bedroom to stand behind his chair—*her* chair, she should say!—from which she kept a near-constant watch over the neighborhood. For most of the day, every day, she would station herself behind the slatted blinds of her bedroom window and observe. Over time, she had come to know every one of her neighbors, their names, their families, their joys and sorrows—and their secrets. She was all but invisible behind her blinds, but the world outside could hide nothing from her prying eyes. When the teenaged boy up the street took up with a lady friend many years his senior, she knew about it before the boy's parents had any inkling. When the carpenter on the next block started a tryst with the courtesan who lived behind him, she was able to knowledgeably gossip about it long before the carpenter's wife learned the truth. Without a doubt, not a single event could take place anywhere within range of her lofty lookout post, no matter how insignificant, without her uncovering all the sordid details. So it was no surprise that when a strange young man began playing army games behind the abandoned house across the street in the middle of the night, she knew of it immediately. It was on his second practice run that she had divined his intent—and his target! He wasn't the only one who knew the behavior patterns of the residents. He was after the wealthiest of her neighbors, she was sure. Excited, she wasted not an instant more before calling the police, reporting in detail his movements, their timing, and her professional estimation of his intent. Now here it was, not twenty-four hours later, and they were ready for him. Her bosom swelled with pride for the service she was performing for her community. If only her late husband could see her now! He had always complained about her busybody ways, but tonight they would pay off handsomely—she had been promised the lion's share of the reward for the man's capture.

She touched the policeman gently on the shoulder. "That's nice. You have fun. I'll watch with you."

* * *

The quarry smiled.

She had seen the telltale, agreed-upon chalk mark scrawled on the sidewalk at the start of the block telling her that the police were in position. She told herself firmly that she had nothing to fear. *I hope!* she prayed, for she knew that the bandit would be armed.

As she proceeded up the block, she found that it was much more difficult to control her glance than she had expected. She knew specifically which bush he hid behind, exactly when he would appear, and precisely where he would confront her. Like a moth being drawn to the fire, the bush he hid behind pulled at her attention; but she dared not glance at his hiding place, lest she risk ruining the entire plan.

The police had gone over the bandit's *modus operandi* with her and the details of his strategy. "He's never hurt anyone, he only wants the money, so give it to him when he asks. That's all the evidence we'll need to move against him. Just give him the money. Leave it to us after that. Run home and lock your door."

Excited, she strode up the street, tossing her long hair back in anticipation, the beat of her high heels echoing in the dark.

\* \* \*

The time came.

The bandit sprang from the bushes. Unsurprisingly, the quarry was right where he expected her to be.

In the darkness, he confronted her, a small, silver revolver glistening dully in his hand. "Only the money," he hissed from behind his mask. "I only want the money."

On cue, on command, according to the plan, she complied, almost tossing her heavy purse at his chest. Freed of her burden, she spun on one foot and ran; and true to his word, the bandit did not pursue. Clutching the purse to his chest, he smiled, turned, and faced the combined weaponry of the Las Vegas Crime Prevention Unit, earning the honor of becoming its first victim. Outnumbered, outgunned, and scowling, he dropped the purse with a loud thump, the weapon with a smaller clunk, and raised his hands high as the tide of blue uniforms swept over him.

\* \* \*

Eddie hummed.

The simple tune, extracted from a complex concerto, rumbled gently in his throat, a pleasant undercurrent to the morning's labors. His hands were soiled, but with the clean stain of rich earth; it tightly filled the pores of his fingers appearing as tiny, undulating black whorls. The construction of his garden in the Transcontinental station cafeteria had been completed the day before, lacking only the seeds that were its purpose. Several varieties of them sat in carefully-labeled envelopes arranged neatly on the gleaming, chromium-trimmed table behind him, each seed waiting only on the farmer's enchanted touch that would bring them to life. Carefully, he poked a hole of deliberate depth into the soil, positioned the seed carefully inside, then gently tamped fertilized mulch into the dark cavity. A dash of water completed the cultivation before he moved on to the next planting. Unsurprisingly, his movements aligned with the beat of his humming, its rhythm adding an unconscious flourish to his every motion; the impression generated was that of a maestro conducting his orchestra. The last seed went into the ground as the last notes of the concerto rumbled within his chest, in the same instant.

He wiped his hands somewhat ineffectively on a battered towel as he stepped back to admire his handiwork. It was not all that impressive a sight to see: flat, damp earth pocked with petite piles of black mulch. Satisfied nonetheless, he gathered up his tools and returned them to their box, dropping the soiled towel on top. Idly, he reflected on his humming; the song that filled his mind had come to its impressive conclusion, and he felt hungry for more. That wasn't surprising; music was a rarity in Las Vegas, generally limited to the honky-tonk of the taproom pianos and the occasional amateur harmonica. There were no radio stations in town or even a record shop. Wistfully, he sighed. *There has to be something!* Perhaps he could ask around to see if anyone had any old records he could borrow—assuming he could find a phonograph.

He lifted the toolbox and was about to return it to its niche, but halted almost as soon as his motions began. Leaning in the doorway of the cafeteria, arms folded across his chest, was the policeman, his demeanor broadcasting a disconcerted mien.

"What's wrong?" asked Eddie without preamble.

The policeman unfolded his arms and stood straight. "It's our bandit."

"What? Your plan didn't work? You didn't nab him?"

"Quite the opposite—he's sitting comfortably in his cell."

Eddie's brow furrowed in bewilderment. "Shouldn't he be?"

"Well... yes and no."

He set down his toolbox on the corner of a table. "I don't follow you."

"Well, the man's got rights, doesn't he? Isn't he innocent until proven guilty? Shouldn't he have a trial or something?"

Two heartbeats passed. "Won't he?"

The policeman smiled without mirth. "City Hall is deserted, remember."

Light broke on Eddie's intellect. "Ah. No judges."

"Right. The last one we had left with the Mayor." As an afterthought, he added scornfully, "And good riddance, too, if you ask me!"

Eddie ignored the postscript. "You're right; the man deserves a fair trial, even though you caught him red handed."

The policeman nodded. "Exactly what I was thinking. These aren't the days of Mr. Wesley, you know."

"So where do we find a judge?"

"Actually..." The policeman paused, a mite disconcerted, as if he might be overstepping himself, but he plowed ahead nevertheless. "I was figuring that *you* might want to preside." He gained confidence as he spoke. "You're the one who set up the law enforcement here. It's only logical that you should be judge."

"Me? I'm no lawyer!"

The policeman laughed. "All the more reason why you should do it. And judging can't be that hard, or else lawyers wouldn't be able to do it! All you need is honesty and fairness, and you have that more than covered." He looked aside and continued in a sotto voice, "Not that this town has seen a whole lot of *that* in its judges!"

Eddie sighed. The policeman's logic stood to reason. "All right," he agreed resignedly. He thought it over for a moment, then added, "Can we do it first thing tomorrow morning?" He held out his stained hands, palms up. "'T'wer best done quickly,'" he quoted, "but I have things I need to finish up this afternoon."

"Nine tomorrow morning it is. 'So let it be written'...," the policeman quoted in turn as he turned to leave. "I'll spread the word."

\* \* \*

The bandit grinned.

He sat on a crude wooden cot in a bare cell down in the cool cellar of the jailhouse, but his predicament did not trouble him. He knew perfectly well that they had gotten the drop on him, but such details did not dissuade his mirth. That he had blundered was the cold truth, or else they would not have captured him so readily. He had been caught many, many times in the past, but had always managed to elude prison through bribes, political influence, legal chicanery, or a clever combination of the three, and there was no reason to think they wouldn't save him yet again, hence the grin.

Another part of his elation stemmed from the fact that they would have to reveal in open court exactly how they had caught him; as in the past, it would prove to be an invaluable education. He would listen carefully, examine his failure in all its aspects, then take steps to make sure it would never, ever happen again. He would transform his adversary from a determined enemy into a harsh tutor; and with every untoward encounter, he would improve himself and become even more invincible. Idly, he wondered who his judge could possibly be—all of them had left town, or so he heard. Perhaps it was a new judge; he hoped so. It would make things all the more interesting, plus there would be the added educational bonus of hearing a new and different viewpoint.

He heard footsteps coming down the stairs. It was time; they were coming for him. With relish, he anticipated his upcoming educational encounter.

\* \* \*

Eddie hesitated.

It was only a closet he faced, but the symbolism of the garments it held was overwhelming. Black robes, full length, hung from stout wooden hangers in the dark recesses. His hand had reached out to retrieve one of them, but his sense of self would not permit him to touch the fabric.

*I'm no judge!* he needlessly reminded himself, but found no courage in his unspoken defiance. Unbidden, dark warnings came to mind: *Judge not, lest thou shalt be judged!* The ancient wisdom handed down across the millennia stoked his disconcerted poise. He began to doubt the wisdom of involving himself in the entire affair in the first place, sorry that he had even bothered to even attempt to rebuild the rule of law; but he recognized his doubts for what they were—pure escapism—and as easily as they had come upon him, he just as readily shook them off. He was certain that throughout the entire affair his actions were necessary, right, and stood to reason, each and every step all along the way. That he found himself in this place, in front of this particular closet, being intimidated by a mere piece of cloth, was only the next phase of his convoluted journey toward making this town his home. Intellectually, he knew he should embrace the challenge, but still his emotions held him back.

Looking at the costumes arrayed in front of him, his jaw tightened; he realized that there was no reason why he should fear the traditional garb—or even need it, for that matter. His confidence returning, he firmly shut the closet door on the judicial robes and headed toward the courtroom. Flannel and denim would serve just as well.

\* \* \*

The gavel cracked.

"All rise!" the hastily-recruited bailiff called out as the door to the judge's chambers opened.

"No!" Eddie cried automatically, stopping in the doorway. In front of him the courtroom was populated with dozens of people; half were already standing, half still sitting, with a few caught midway in the act of rising, uncertain whether to complete the action in either direction.

"Sit down, please!" he called out. "It's only me. You don't have to get up."

The standees sat as one as Eddie strode with a confidence he did not feel to take his seat behind the large, ornate desk upon the raised dais. He looked around the room uncertainly, wondering if he had somehow been transported through a magical mirror and was now looking back through it into the normal world he had left behind. He shook off the fantasy, steeled himself, and took a deep breath.

"All right, this court will come to order."

"Objection!" It was the bandit. He was manacled to a burly policeman, wrist-to-wrist, co-joined Siamese twins seated at a table midway between Eddie and the audience.

"What?" Eddie blinked myopically. The unexpected interruption had taken him by surprise. "What's your objection?"

The bandit fixed a squinting gaze upon Eddie and jabbed an accusing index finger in his direction. "You're no judge! Where's your robe? You have no power over me!"

"You're right," he admitted lightly. "I'm no judge, I have no robe, and I have no power over you. But I promise you I'll do my best to make sure you get a fair hearing."

"No! It's the law! This trial cannot proceed without a real judge!"

"Sure it can," Eddie explained patiently. "Because it's not the judge who's important here, it's the jury. You're accused of robbing that woman—" He pointed to the stunningly pretty young lady in the front row. "—at gunpoint, and it'll be the jury who'll decide your guilt or innocence, not me. I'm only here acting as sort of a referee. I'll be doing no judging today."

"But that's not what the law says a judge does!"

"It's what I do," he said simply.

"But if there's no judge, then you have to set me free!"

"Why's that?"

"Because you're no judge!"

"I'll be the judge of that. Better yet..." Eddie turned to the audience. "How many of you accept me as judge here today?"

Every hand in the audience went up. At the table in front of Eddie, the burly policeman raised his own manacled wrist, dragging along with it the wrist of the bandit, lifting both their arms into the air. A satisfied, mischievous smile spread across his husky face.

The bandit threw the man an annoyed scowl before jerking both their arms back down.

Eddie scanned the crowd. "Okay, it looks unanimous. Let's get going." He quickly estimated the number of people in the room and divided by seven. "Starting with you..." He pointed to a teenager at one end of the front row. "...begin counting off. Every seventh person, please take a seat in the jury box."

A panicked buzz of conversation instantly filled the air as the members of the audience reacted to the unexpected duty that was being asked of them.

"Objection!"

Patiently, Eddie faced the bandit. "What is it this time?"

"You can't do that! I know the law—I'm allowed to interview each prospective juror!"

"Interview them? What for?"

"I get to reject the ones I don't like!"

Eddie blinked twice. "You mean you want to stack the jury?"

The bandit hesitated; he hadn't thought of it in quite those terms before. "But it's my right!"

Recovering, Eddie flatly replied, "No it isn't. Picking and choosing jurors like that wouldn't be fair. We'll just take every seventh person, no questions asked." To the audience, he repeated, "All right, start counting. Every seventh person to the jury box, please."

"Objection!"

Sternly, Eddie shook a finger at him. "Listen: I said I'm not going to let you stack the jury!"

"But it's the law!"

"Whose law?"

Again, the bandit hesitated. This trial definitely wasn't following along the normal lines. He didn't know whose law it was; all he knew were the gopher holes of procedure. But he wasn't going to let ignorance stop him. "The laws of America!" he guessed with forced conviction.

Intrigued but not impeded, Eddie asked, "Which law of America? Explain it to me. I'm no lawyer."

Hesitation and exasperation simultaneously burst forth. "How the hell should I know?"

"Or I," Eddie concurred. He sat in thought for a moment, then added, as if talking to himself, "You know, I'm not sure the laws of America would apply in any case. It's been over a month since the X Project exploded, and we've heard absolutely nothing from the rest of the nation since then. There doesn't seem to *be* any America any longer." He paused again briefly. "And besides, I'm not certain theft is a federal crime anyhow." With a start he realized the root of his uncertainty: he had never before read the Constitution, nor had it been taught in the schools he attended. He dismissed the random thought and returned to the matter at hand. "Regardless, if you or I don't know the law, how could we possibly follow it? How else would you suggest that we choose a jury?"

Seeing his chance, the bandit interjected, "That's why you have to let me go! You're no judge, you have no law, and you have no jury. You have no power over me!"

Eddie waved an arm across the courtroom. "These people have accepted me as their judge. They will be your jury."

"But you have no law!" he repeated.

Eddie hesitated. He could not deny that the bandit had a valid point. Given the total evaporation of government in Las Vegas—not to mention Nevada and the former United States!—where could a basis be found for any law? But there *had* to be some touchstone he could use that would provide a firm foundation for conducting a court of law. *But what might that principle be?* he asked himself. Unbidden, in his mind's eye Eddie recalled the bright sunlight of a summer morning when he was ten years old. On that day, in a clearing of the woods, he had told the young Dagny what he planned to do when he grew up: to reach for the best within himself, to do whatever is right. *Whatever is right!* For him it had always been a self-evident goal, one that he had pursued all of his life; he could never understand why men would ever want to do otherwise. That commitment made by the child Eddie reached across the decades to come to his aid today in this moment of need. He nodded to himself. He knew what to do, and more importantly, he *knew* he knew. Shaking himself out of his reverie, he asserted, "The law is that you must do whatever is right."

The bandit scoffed. "Yeah, right. And what does *right* mean?"

"A fair question. Here's a fair answer: it's the Golden Rule. Do unto others as you would have them do unto you—and isn't that enough law for any man? It's all about having the right to live your own life, but also respecting the rights and property of others. "

"Bah!" the bandit cried with a flourish of his free hand. "Mere words! Bromides! High-sounding, meaningless words!"

"They're not mean—," he began, but the bandit cut him off.

"Then what rights do I—or does anyone else!—have? Tell me that!"

Eddie did not hesitate. "All right, let me spell it out for you: you have the God-given, inalienable right to live your life your way, without interference, pro—"

"Then let me out of here!" he interrupted again. "I was living my own life my own way when you guys interfered!" He shook his manacled arm in defiant demonstration of the truth of his statement.

Eddie ignored the outburst and continued as if it had not happened. "You have the right... *provided*—do you hear me?—*provided* that you respect the rights and property of others. You did not respect this woman's right to live her life her own way, even though she was respecting yours."

"Respect?" he sneered. "Don't talk to me about respect! Your entire capitalist system lacks respect! If a man has no money, your system would just let him starve! Doesn't a man's privation give him the right to take what he needs?" He gestured unconsciously toward the victim he had robbed.

Eddie shook his head. "Not if she has a right to her own life and property, too. You have a responsibility to respect that right, or else you can't expect others to respect yours." After a second, he added, "And I would think that men are compassionate enough that they wouldn't let another man starve."

The bandit ignored the aside, and replied with mocking sarcasm. "Exactly where did I pick up this 'responsibility' to her?"

Eddie ignored his contempt and answered sincerely. "Responsibility is an integral, inseparable part of your rights. Because for every right you enjoy, you have a corresponding responsibility to respect that right in others. So, for example, you have the right to live your life—but you have the corresponding responsibility to respect her right to live her own life. You have the right to your property—but you have the corresponding responsibility to respect the property of others. Rights and responsibility are two sides of the same coin."

"And what coin is that?"

"Liberty."

For several seconds after the echoes of his word died away, not a sound could be heard.

The bandit was first to react. "So you're saying that my rights come with strings attached?"

"Not strings so much as intertwined obligations. I'd call it personal freedom tempered by personal responsibility."

"And how far does this responsibility extend?" he inquired derisively. "What limit do you place upon my rights?"

Eddie considered the question for a moment. "To use an analogy, your right to swing your fist ends where her nose begins." At a sudden thought, he corrected himself. "No, wait; that's not quite correct. Even swinging your fist at someone shows a lack of respect. It stands to reason that threats of violence cannot be considered respectful, now can they?" He stared off into space for a moment, surprised at the truth of his own words.

The bandit hesitated as well, but for different reasons. Granted, he had come here today expecting to receive an education—but not one in philosophy! What did he care about philosophy? Still, he had to grudgingly admit that what Eddie was saying made sense on some fundamental level. Regardless, he could not let it stand; he had to extricate himself from this courtroom as a free man, and he could see that he was quickly running out of options. He had walked free every time he had been in court before; he had fully expected to do so again today—except that he found the solid legal granite he stood upon was quickly turning to philosophical sand. "But I have a right!" he repeated with hollow conviction, not knowing what else to say, as if the mere repetition would make it true, while understanding fully that it wouldn't.

"I agree," Eddie replied simply. "You have a right." He pointed to the victim. "And so does she. We all do. But like I said, we also have the responsibility to respect the rights of others, lest we throw away our own rights in the process. Abdicating that responsibility is what you're essentially accused of having done."

"And that's another thing!" he cried, attempting to pull the philosophical argument back into the realm of the legal. "No one's told me exactly what crime it is I'm being accused of committing!"

Momentarily at a loss, Eddie responded uncertainly. "I thought I did." Recovering, he pointed a finger at the victim. "Yes I did. You're accused of stealing money from that woman at gunpoint. I said that."

The bandit leaned forward across the table and his voice became suavely derisive. "Yes, But what *kind* of stealing are you talking about? Larceny, burglary, robbery, or what? First, second, or third, degree? Petit or grand? Misdemeanor or felony?"

Still wearing a perplexed expression, he replied, "Does it really matter?"

"Huh? Of course it does!"

"Why is that?"

Once again, the bandit was brought up short. "Uh..."

Eddie waited him out. When it became apparent no further words were forthcoming, he picked up the thread. "I'd venture to say that part of the problem with trials in the past was that the lawyers and judges relied too much on the words rather than on the deeds. Who really cares what it's called? Why over-classify? You're accused of taking that woman's property under threat of force, and that's all that matters. You did not respect her right to her life and property. Understand?"

Silence.

Seeing again that no answer was imminent, Eddie sat up straight in his chair, and to the audience, he politely requested, "Okay, now that that's settled, let's proceed. Every seventh person to the jury box, please."

"But I have a right!" the bandit repeated yet again even less convincingly than before, almost whining. No one troubled to reply, and he did not—*could* not—pursue the matter further; he had no idea in which direction he might take it. Unschooled though he was, he was more than intelligent enough to recognize the wisdom in the words of Eddie, and he could plainly see that the audience saw it, too. Stripped of any philosophical, legal, or dramatic defense, he decided it best to bide his time for the moment, and wait for other opportunities to present themselves. He subsided moodily.

Uncertainly the count-off began and gathered confidence as it progressed. In short order, four men and three women took their new seats in the jury box. The bandit grumbled inaudibly at the table in front of him, not looking up.

"Okay, let's have the victim tell her side of it. Miss?"

At his behest, the woman stepped up to the witness stand demurely and took a seat. All eyes were upon her, and not merely because she was a newly-minted celebrity and a part of the show, but more so because she happened to be a stunningly beautiful woman. Only Eddie seemed to remain untouched and aloof. He nodded to her gravely. "All right, tell us what happened."

"Hey!" shouted the bandit. "Objection!"

"What now?" he asked patiently.

"She has to be sworn in!"

"Why is that?"

The bandit hesitated uncertainly. He was clearly not performing at his best this morning. "Uh... So that we know she's not lying?" He didn't sound too certain of his own assertion.

Eddie put a palm against his cheek, leaned on his elbow, and again looked perplexed. "But... But if she were going to lie, wouldn't she just lie about swearing to tell the truth? Either she's honest or she's not. It's up to the jury to take her at her word or not."

"Then what's to stop *me* from lying to *you*?"

"Nothing. Was there ever anything to stop you, except yourself?"

The bandit opened his mouth as if to say something, but no words came forth. His jaw closed and he wet his lips. The statement was true.

Eddie turned to the victim. "Proceed."

In an incongruently cheerful voice, she told her story of the evening in question exactly as it had happened, how she was walking home with the evening's receipts in her handbag, how the bandit had approached her and demanded the money at gunpoint, how she had complied and ran. In a minute, she was through.

"Do you have any questions for her?" Eddie asked the bandit.

"You bet I do!" The bandit stood and began to swagger around the table to approach the witness stand, but only made it as far as the length of the short chain on the manacles. Sporting a sardonic smile, the burly officer gently but insistently pulled him back to their table and into his chair; the bandit scowled at him menacingly but impotently. Regaining his poise somewhat, the bandit turned to the woman, addressing her from his seat.

"How did you catch me?"

She smiled prettily. "I didn't," she replied politely. "The police did."

"How did you know I was coming?" he pressed. "You guys were all ready for me!"

"The police did it," she replied, not the least bit put out for having to repeat herself. "They warned me you might try to rob me one night soon. And they were right!"

"How did *they* know?"

Smiling coyly, she replied, "You should probably ask them that."

"This is a waste of time," he grumbled. Turning to Eddie, he demanded, "I want to talk to the cops. Put the cops on the stand!"

"Have you any further questions for this woman?"

"No! Get the cops up there!"

Eddie dismissed the woman, and time stopped as she took her seat, every eye upon her. Again, only Eddie seemed above the delightful distraction.

Next he called up the policeman. With professional detachment, the man related how he had watched the entire incident from the third story bedroom of the busybody widow, how he had seen the masked bandit approach his victim, heard the demand for money, saw her throw her purse at him and run away, and how his men had stepped in and immediately apprehended the man. Finished with his tale, the policeman calmly sat there, hands folded in his lap, not offering any additional details.

Without waiting to be invited, the bandit demanded, "How come you were already there?"

"Me?" asked the policeman, a little too innocently. "You're asking me what I was doing in a woman's bedroom late at night?" He looked up to Eddie. "Do I have to answer that?"

Blushing, he replied. "No, of course not." To the bandit, he advised, "Let's stay on topic. Any other questions? Related to the trial, that is?"

The bandit felt trapped, an unusual circumstance for him. He was accustomed to being the man in command of every conceivable situation, yet he felt his grip on events loosening more and more with each passing second. "I... I...," he began, but could not finish. He nervously glanced right and left as if seeking escape. "I..." Something suddenly snapped within him and he brought both his fists down hard on the table in front of him, the resounding slam startling everyone. "How the hell did you know I was going to rob this woman?" he yelled. Someone at the back of the courtroom emitted a long whistle. Too late did the bandit realize his error— he had just admitted his guilt. Slack-jawed, he looked around him. The faces of the jurors were hard and closed. It was all over for him, he could tell.

Getting control of himself, he sat upright and folded his arms across his chest, his face blank, the manacles' chain pulled taut. They'd never tell him what he wanted to know, that was certain. There would be no education for him here today, no victory.

"Any other questions?"

The bandit did not reply. Arms folded, he stared straight ahead, eyes focused on nothing. The impression was that of a child pouting.

"Then we'll proceed."

Several other witnesses were called to testify, some of them police officers on the scene, others neighbors who had been watching from the safety of their own homes, each describing their viewpoint of the robbery.

Throughout it all, the bandit sat silent. For the first time in his nefarious career, he was at a complete loss; his mind raced, but it spun in circles; he simply could not think of any way out. There was no question he would be found guilty, irrespective of his blunt admission. He could not rely on esoteric errors of legal procedure, and he was certain he would not be able to bribe his way out; his only remaining chance was in fighting the sentencing.

The last witness completed his damning testimony, and Eddie addressed the bandit directly.

"Do you wish to call any witnesses?"

Sullen silence echoed across the room.

"I'll take that as a 'no.'" To the bailiff, he ordered, "Please take the jurors to the deliberation room so they can come to a verdict."

The bandit glimpsed another procedural avenue opening up to him, and without thinking, automatically took it. He sprang to life: "Objection!"

Again caught by surprise, Eddie could only reply, "What? What now?"

With a sinking feeling, the bandit realized that procedural objections fell upon deaf ears here; he may as well have remained silent. Nevertheless, the damage had been done, so he pressed on. "You're required to give them their instructions!"

"What instructions?" asked Eddie blankly.

The bandit snorted. "Lots of them! A big rigmarole about trying the facts and not the law. I've heard judges say it a thousand times!" He was interrupted by jeering laughter from the back of the room; the bandit ignored it.

Eddie was plainly confused. "Are you saying that I should try to influence the jury?"

Now it was the bandit's turn to be confused. "Huh?"

Patiently, Eddie explained. "They are the jury. They are the ones who must decide, and I'm not going to try to influence them in any way. As I said at the beginning, I'm a referee, not a participant. They listened to everything that was said, and now it's up to them to decide your guilt or innocence."

"Using your 'law?'" he sneered.

"That's up to them, too. I can't force my law or my opinions onto anyone. Nor should they listen to me, if I tried. That's what makes them the jury. They can judge both the law and the facts. If they believe it's all right for you to walk up to someone and demand money at gunpoint, then they'll acquit you. If not, they'll find you guilty. What is it I could possibly add to that? Or want to?"

"I..." He halted. Nothing further came out. Again, he was completely at sea. Deflated, he returned to his sullen pose.

After a respectful pause, Eddie turned to the bailiff. "Please take the jurors to the deliberation room." He gently clacked the gavel on the surface of his desk. "We'll recess until they decide."

As she left, one of the jurors called out over her shoulder, "You can bet it won't be long!"

The bandit sat up with a start, as if he were about to object to something, but thought better of it and subsided.

Standing up and stretching, Eddie commented, "In that case, I'll think we'll wait right here."

* * *

The jurors returned.

It could not have been more than three minutes; a bad sign for the bandit, to be sure. Their faces blank, the seven filed back into the jury box as the audience and Eddie reclaimed their own seats.

Once everyone had settled down, he asked, "Have you reached a verdict?"

One of the jurors stood up, the woman who had warned of a quick verdict. "Yes, Your Honor, we have."

Eddie could not help but wince at being addressed as "Your Honor," but tried not to let it show. "Well? What say you?"

"Guilty!"

The gallery sat silent. No one was surprised by either the verdict or the restrained reaction, but electric anticipation hung heavy in the air. They all knew what was coming next.

In the silence, Eddie locked eyes with the bandit. His words echoed clearly across the silent room. "You're one smart fellow, do you know that?" The bandit did not reply. "From what we've heard about how you planned out and executed your crime, and from what I saw of your defense, it's plain to me that you're more than a cut above your average crook." Still there was no reaction, so Eddie continued. "I spent a lot of time considering what sort of sentence might be appropriate if you were convicted, and until five minutes ago I still wasn't sure exactly what we should do. The idea of tossing you in jail is personally repugnant to me, not to mention the question of who pays the cost of keeping you there. Tell me: do you want to go to jail?"

The bandit remained silent at first, but then stirred in his seat. "No" was all he said.

Eddie nodded. "Then I think we can work out something that might be a little better for all of us." He sat up straight and assumed a more formal pose; the sentencing was about to begin. Many in the gallery straightened in unconscious imitation, sensing the moment of truth was at hand.

"Having been found guilty by a jury of your peers of not respecting the rights of another, I recommend the following sentence: by your actions you have demonstrated that you cannot be trusted to roam freely in our society, so I believe it appropriate that you be exiled from Las Vegas for the period of one year."

The audience murmured its surprise; it was not what they had expected to hear. The bandit did not react, and Eddie waited for silence before he continued.

"I further recommend that you spend your year confined to the vicinity of the Boulder Dam powerplant. While you are there, you will be presented with the opportunity to learn how the powerplant operates, and you shall be given the chance to apply your knowledge as a worker. If you choose to take the job, you will be paid a fair wage during your exile. But if you cause trouble, then the remainder of your year will be spent in jail here in town where you'll perform whatever menial labor is necessary to cover the cost of your board." He paused for a brief moment indicating he had finished, then added tentatively, "Okay?"

Caught off guard, the bandit gaped. "'Okay?' What do you mean, *okay?*"

"I mean, do you accept the sentence?" he explained succinctly, knowing full well he had no authority to impose it directly. As far as he was concerned, it was up to the bandit to accept it or not. He leaned slightly forward in his chair, attentively awaiting an answer. He fervently hoped the answer would be 'yes;' he wasn't entirely sure what he would do should the sentence be rejected.

The bandit did not react at first, but soon a small smile crossed his face. He had recognized the same absence of an alternative. "And what if I refuse?"

Eddie shrugged. "As I said, you're a smart fellow. I don't think you will."

The bandit sat for almost a full minute quietly considering his plight. Like Eddie, he was unsure of just what might happen, should he refuse. On the other hand, if he agreed, here was an opportunity to remove himself from the path of career criminal upon which he had long ago set himself. *Perhaps I should accept?* The bandit shrugged to himself. *And why not?* If it didn't work out, he could always return to a life of banditry. He silently reviewed his options one last time, and as the last of the minute began to die, he finally spoke: "I accept exile." He smiled to himself, thinking, *Once again I get off without a jail term! My record is intact!*

The audience burst into spontaneous applause. Rather than the somber moment which characterized most sentencing, the mood was one of unexpected jubilation. Many of the men had feared that a milquetoast Eddie might prove to be too lenient, while others feared the inexperienced judge would overreact with an unduly heavy-handed response; but having the bandit not only removed from the company of the law-abiding citizenry for a reasonable period and also set on a path to rehabilitation allayed all such doubts. Not only had vengeance been served this day, but justice as well.

Two members of the audience, obviously friends of the accused, rushed forward and shook the bandit's hand enthusiastically, slapping him on the back and laughing. The attractive woman who was the victim rested her two adoring eyes squarely upon Eddie, obviously pleased with the result. The jurors were shaking hands with one another, but each of them kept catching Eddie's eye as well, giving him a brief nod of appreciation. The policeman sat alone to one side, and when his eyes met Eddie's, he flashed him an energetic, two-fisted "thumbs up." Similar reactions came from every corner of the room. As with the defeat of the raiders, Eddie found himself once again cast in the role of the hero.

His work here done, Eddie rose to leave. To his surprise, as he did, all conversation came to a quick, abrupt halt. All eyes were upon him now; he felt self-consciously aware of their stares as he stood alone on the dais before them. He felt it incumbent upon himself to say something profound, but he retreated instead into the trite. To the bandit, he said simply, "Welcome aboard." Looking to the audience, he added, "This court is adjourned."

The crowd exploded into cheers as Eddie turned and left.

## Chapter 8 – The Wall

The hangar was packed.

Once again, people were crowded together on the temporary bleachers in Dwight's largest hangar. Again, virtually all of the residents of the valley—minus some hundred scabs—turned out to witness the oath-taking, but the atmosphere this time was markedly different. The strikers and soon-to-be strikers sat calmly in their seats under the glare of the white arc lights that beat down upon them, waiting patiently as the last stragglers took their seats. The only residents of the valley not in attendance were the scabs who had refused to take the oath, but had not yet been ferried back Outside. They had been permitted to attend the ceremony, but most opted to stay away, en masse.

Among the assembled residents were the almost five hundred newcomers who had arrived since the preceding summer. They included famous luminaries such as Hank, and relative non-entities such as his secretary Gwen. Also among them, ignored for now, sat the woman from Sacramento. Unlike the remainder of the assembly, she fidgeted nervously in her chair. At the first mass meeting eleven days ago, she had implemented the first stage of her ill-conceived plan: her taking the oath that night was a blatant lie. When she swore to the falsehood, she never suspected she would ever be called on it; but she hadn't counted on the philosophical tenacity of the valley's residents, nor their determination to purge all hints of the looter strain from their midst. Ragnar had revealed no hint beforehand that they would resort to a lie detector; now it was too late for her to retract her fraud. She felt trapped; she could neither accept the oath as truth, nor defend her deceit. She licked her lips nervously as she glanced surreptitiously around the audience to see if anyone noticed her unease. None did.

Her pilot friend was not among the assembled, he being one of the very first to walk out in refusal to take the oath. She had left him behind at *The Golden Touch* tonight to cater to the remaining scabs who had not yet been ferried out of the valley. As his luck would have it, he was slated to be a passenger on the very last load of scabs, some three weeks hence. The woman recalled how once she had asserted she would remain in the valley far beyond the March deadline, but that boast was starting to seem fragile and hollow.

Seated serenely in the chair next to her was the janitor who had brought her into the valley two weeks ago. She glanced at him out of the corner of her eye, jealous of his calm composure. If he noticed how edgy his former co-worker had become, he did not trouble to indicate it; in fact, if anything, he behaved as if she did not exist. Nervously, she pulled her attention away from him. Still fidgeting, she re-crossed her legs in the opposite direction for the fourth time in less than a minute.

Escaping her worried attention was Gwen, who also fidgeted nervously in her seat in the next row forward, also repeatedly re-crossing her legs. Gwen was also among the newcomers who had sworn the striker's oath eleven days earlier, and other than her nervousness, Gwen's frame of mind tonight remained unchanged. *It's all the same!* she kept reminding herself. *I can honestly swear! The oath means nothing, and I know that for a fact!* Gwen deliberately forced herself to examine visions of the looter society, sternly telling herself that this was not where her allegiance lay. She pictured the mills of Hank Steel, both the now-abandoned hulk near Philadelphia and the half-reborn mills she was helping to construct here in the valley, just as sternly telling herself that this was her future. If embracing that future included embracing the valley's philosophy, so be it. *Because it doesn't really matter! I may still create victims, but at least I'll be using good means!* Yet despite her visions, her conviction, and her stern reminders to herself, she still held grave reservations; she did not want to create any victims at all, but she could see no way to achieve her desire. She re-crossed her legs yet again, wishing it were over and settled, one way or the other. She glanced surreptitiously at Hank sitting quietly next to her, but his ascetic profile held no concern. He had no qualms about the oath, despite what Gwen had revealed to him about choosing victims and champions. Again, she re-crossed her legs.

Before long, Ragnar stepped up to the microphone. "Are we ready?" he called out excitedly, with a voice like a machine gun spitting smiles. "Are we ready?" he repeated loudly. The crowd responded enthusiastically; they were ready. "Then let's get to it!" he barked excitedly. Again, the audience cheered its consent.

"Okay, let's take it one row at a time," he suggested. "First the left side bleachers, then the right, then the chairs on the floor. When you come up, line up along the left side of the lectern here—" He indicated a location with a chopping motion of his hand, "—and come up one by one to give the oath. Remember to place your hands on the electrode plates of the lie detector. With an exaggerated wink, he added, "Looters need not apply!" The audience again roared its approval.

The first row of newcomers advanced to the front of the room and queued up in a ragged line stretching away from the lectern. Dr. Thomas sat in a chair alongside the lectern, a careful eye on several dials and gauges mounted on the lectern's side.

The hangar fell silent as the first man self-consciously stepped up to the lectern, placed his hands, and began his pledge. "I swear, by my life and my love of it, that I will never live for the sake of another man, nor ask another man to live for mine!" The green light on the face of the podium winked a bright green. The crowd roared its approval. Dr. Thomas did not react.

One by one the newcomers approached the lectern and gave their vow, the green light flashing its approval. Row after row came forward to repeat the feat, but before long the level of applause between each swearing diminished noticeably as the audience members wearied of their repetitious role. Still, they dutifully applauded each and every new striker.

Scores of oaths had been affirmed when suddenly the first miscue surfaced. A nondescript newcomer had sworn the oath in the same tone and with the same sincerity as the multitude that had preceded him, but the outcome this time was different: the lectern's light winked red. Dark murmurs swept the crowd, and a look of dread came over the young man's face.

From his station seated alongside the lectern, Dr. Thomas nodded to him. "Try again," he entreated the man with an avuncular smile.

Swallowing hard, the man repositioned his hands. "I swear...," he began, but his nerves would not let him finish. Again, the lectern winked red.

The smile was gone from Dr. Thomas' face, but he nodded reassuringly. "Relax," he suggested. "Once more, now."

Taking a deep breath, the man steeled himself and looked out over the faces of the crowd. This time he began firmly, and held his fear tightly in check. "I swear, by my life and my love of it, that I will never live for the sake of another man, nor ask another man to live for mine." He completed the recitation with a confident nod of his head.

The lectern winked red. Dr. Thomas did not react.

"Next," prompted the pirate, but the man at the lectern did not move.

"I swear—" he began again, a note of panic creeping into his voice.

"Next!" Ragnar repeated, more firmly.

Confused and ashamed, the man stumbled away from the lectern. Ragnar guided him to a cluster of empty seats behind the lectern that faced the audience, indicating he should wait there. Wide-eyed with panic clearly showing on his face, he complied. Ragnar strode up to the lectern, pointedly placing his hands on the electrodes.

"A man's word is his bond," he began, "And the worst sort of man is the one without integrity!" Murmurs of assent rippled across the hangar, and the lectern winked green. "Eleven days ago, in front of us all, this man swore to a lie!" His hand swept backward, momentarily off of the electrode plate, to indicate the panicked man sitting behind him. The crowd did not react. "Since he cannot swear to our striker's oath, he cannot remain in the valley. And since he cannot be trusted, he will be ferried to California with any others who prove unworthy of our trust!" The lectern winked green again, cold applause thundered from the audience, and Ragnar reclaimed his chair. He nodded to the man at the head of the line of waiting newcomers.

"I swear..." began the next supplicant; when he had finished, the light winked its approval, and the crowd applauded heartily, with all of its old energy returning.

With that, the routine resumed its rhythm: swear, wink, applause. Swear, wink, applause. Swear, wink, applause.

Still sitting in the audience awaiting her turn, the Sacramento woman sat in a state of shock: *Not California!* The life had drained out of her, her stomach fell to the floor, and her knees turned to water. She was so frightened that she feared she would begin to babble at any moment. The ceremonies continued, but she paid them no mind. Against her will, firmly-suppressed memories began to bubble to the surface.

She found herself sitting once again at her desk in her office in Sacramento, proofreading a paper she had just typed. Automatic gunfire echoed in the distance, but she unconsciously ignored it. Sounds of battle had lately become a routine part of California life; and as long as the noise remained in the distance, she knew there was no cause for concern. She continued with her proofreading.

Without warning or preamble, the door to her office burst open, and in poured several men wearing identical red robes sporting a stylized orange flame on the left breasts, each man bearing a frightening weapon of some kind.

"Repent, sinner!" one yelled at her, training the weapon hard on her.

"I'm sorry—," she began tersely, but that was as far as she got. She was about to add "—but I'll rot in your Hell forever before I *ever* agree to tolerate your sort of world!" but she never had the chance to say the rest of the words. The acolyte had only heard the word "sorry" before his attention moved on. He raced past the woman, calling out over his shoulder, "Bless you, then, for you are forgiven. Remain here!"

From a neighboring office, her supervisor heard the ruckus and came in to investigate.

"Repent, sinner!" another acolyte called as he entered.

"What? What?" he asked, in frightened perplexity.

"Repent!"

"Why should I repent?"

"Heathen!" The acolyte shot him dead.

Gunfire erupted from other portions of the building; women were screaming, men shouting, and through it all came the cry, "Repent! Repent!"

With a start, the distraught woman was pulled back to the real world and found herself sitting up straight in her seat in the hangar. Another scab, a woman this time, had triggered the red light, and the striker audience clucked its disapproval. The unfortunate scab was ushered to a seat alongside the other man of no integrity who was now openly weeping, not even attempting to control his panic. As she stared at the unfortunate man's face, his features underwent a metamorphosis before her eyes, melting into those of the janitor where she worked. In her mind's eye she saw his face and the tears he shed as the two of them huddled in her office, listening to the sounds of gunfire that were erupting all around them.

"They shot him! They shot him!" he repeated. "They shot my boss dead!"

"My supervisor, too! Just like that!"

"They told me to wait here," he whispered.

The woman nodded torpidly.

"Why did they spare us?" he wondered aloud.

"Shhh!" she warned. "They're coming back."

Into the office breezed three red-robed figures. One of them spoke to them. "This den of iniquity must be cleansed." He handed them two bright orange swatches crudely cut from cloth in the shape of a flame. "Pin these over your hearts to show the others that you have repented. Return to your homes and await further instructions."

Discretion being the better part of valor, the woman and the janitor donned the telltale icons and quickly left the office without a word. As they fled the conquered building, they passed many red-robed men, all armed, plus many bodies. From a room to their left came the screams of a woman; as they passed they glanced inside, but turned quickly away, their stomachs sick. They hastened their step to quit the murderous building and its red-robed—

*Red*, winked the light on the lectern. Again, the crowded hangar muttered their disapproval. But Dr. Thomas held up a hand to pause the proceedings, adjusted a knob, then nodded to the wide-eyed oath-taker to try again. *Green*, the light winked this time, and the audience applauded heartily.

Again, the reality of the present faded from the terrified woman's mind just as quickly as it had surfaced. She found herself walking down the streets of Sacramento, the janitor at her side, heading home as ordered. Red-robed figures were everywhere, but none paid them any mind. It was as if the acolytes knew from their own personal knowledge that the pair had repented, and allowed them to go on their way unmolested. It was a measure of the incredible level of organization and discipline of the acolyte army that the conjecture was a true one. The emblem pinned over their hearts said it all.

Presently, they reached his home. When they entered, he immediately ran upstairs, returning a moment later with a few random items in his hands, which he stuffed nervously into his pockets. "I've got to get away!" he whispered, as if fearful that someone might hear. His head jerked left then right, as if seeking out invisible spies.

"Get away where?" she cried in a whisper, mirroring his caution. "Where could we go?"

"The Gulch, if it's not too late!"

"Where?"

"The Gulch!" he repeated. "It's where I've been going every June when I go away for a month," he explained, still whispering. "I've got to go there! It's my only chance!"

"Where?" she repeated, but with different inflection.

"Colorado," he whispered, correctly divining the intent of her question. She stared up into his eyes with a hard resolve. "Take me with you!"

He hesitated and looked away uncomfortably. "I'm not sure I can do that," he admitted.

"*What?!* What do you mean, you're not sure?" As if on cue, gunfire sounded in the near distance. Her eyes widened in terror. "You can't leave me here! You can't! You saw what they were doing to that woman back there!"

The janitor hesitated again; it was obvious from his face that he was having some sort of an argument with himself. After several seconds, his face suddenly cleared; he had apparently come to a decision. "All right, you can come along, but we'll have to work out a few things once we get there.

Right now, though, we need to get away from here—and fast! Is there anything you need to get from your house? Anything you can't live without?"

"No, there— Wait! Yes there is! My cat!" she hissed.

"Damn your cat!" he whispered hoarsely.

"Damn your oath!" the scab called out from behind the red light on the lectern, eerily in time with the memories in her head, jerking her again back to the present. "Damn you all!"

"And damn you, too!" retorted a striker. The latest revealed scab of no integrity joined the first two.

"Damn you!" he called again.

"Damn!" echoed the janitor. "Will you look at that!" He and the woman had re-emerged from his Sacramento home, and in the near distance they saw billowing clouds of black smoke shooting skyward from their office. The building was fully engulfed in the cleansing flames, their undulating shape not unlike that of the garish icons which still adorned their breasts. Never again would the building be a party to the manufacture of evil electric toasters. "Come on," he prompted. "To the airfield! If there's still time!"

The two of them hurried off, but sounds of applause pulled her back to the reality of the hangar. The newcomers sitting in the row in front of her stood and filed forward to line up next to the lectern; her turn would come next. Her hands began to shake. Sitting next to her, the janitor still did not notice her agitated state. He was enjoying the swearing-in ceremonies and not paying the slightest bit of attention to her travails.

Among the newcomers heading for the front of the room walked Gwen, with Hank docilely following. *This is it!* she needlessly told herself. Standing in line, fretfully waiting her turn, a nervous smile flitted quickly across Gwen's lips. *I've always wanted to see California!* she kidded herself. But there was no time for wry humor; suddenly it was her turn at the lectern. Slowly she walked up to it to meet her fate.

From behind its protective arms, Gwen surveyed the crowded hangar. Two thousand pairs of eyes spared no idle thought, save for her. For what seemed an eternity, she stood in the rapture of their attention, then regained her focus. Reaching out with both hands, she placed them on the electrode plates of the lie detector. A faint tingle rippled through her arms; she couldn't be sure if it was the device or her own imagination that produced the mild shock. The electrodes were clammy with the fearful sweat of her predecessors.

She looked up from the lectern to the sea of faces. *It's all the same!* she reminded herself one final time, inhaled deeply, then began.

"I swear...," she intoned, her confident voice echoing across the vaulted space of the hangar. She stumbled mentally as she heard the echo of those words come bouncing back to her, for at that moment she realized that never before, not in her entire life, had she ever spoken those two words—her mother had raised her never to swear. The uniqueness of her words added an unanticipated solemnity to her oath.

"...by my life and my love of it..." Hearing her own words, she was suddenly aware of herself, not self-conscious, but rather conscious of self. She felt her life's blood coursing through her veins, the pressure of her hands on the electrodes, the strength of her legs holding her firmly and deliberately in place. In a single flash, she saw her whole life laid before her: as a little girl in New Jersey, as a teen on her first date, accepting her first job with pride at Hank Steel, the flight out West, the death of her father, everything in one giant, single burst.  Never had she been so aware of her life and its tremendous potential as she was in that moment.  Never before did she realize how much she loved her life.  *What a power there is in this oath!* she marveled.

"...that I will never again live for the sake of another man..."

Tears welled up in her eyes as her thoughts turned involuntarily toward her father.  His death was too recent and its cause too sudden that she could not control the wall of grief that rose within her, threatening to engulf her.  *He's gone!* she reminded herself.  There was no one left now to live her life for *except* herself.  She blinked her eyes several times to drive back the tears before concluding.

"...nor ask another man to live for mine!"

She knew these last words were meaningless in the grander scheme of things, but the power of her oath still struck her.  Without thinking, she turned to face Mr. Hank who stood in line behind her.  Their eyes locked.  She remembered his gallant attempt to save her father, and his calm manner of authority as he entreated Dr. Thomas to win the day.  She felt the invisible but undeniable protection of the figurative arm he had curled about her shoulders that night, taking her under his protection and guard, taming the forces of man just as deftly as his mills tamed the forces of nature.

As she focused on him, she became as aware of him and his own life force, just as she was aware of her own, in that moment.  She saw how the lines of his face were pulled tight, giving it a peculiar purity, a sharp precision of form, making it clean and young.  From the edges of her attention, she heard the crashing sounds of applause.  Hank smiled at her; she could do nothing but smile back, her eyes still shining with unshed tears and the power of her oath.  As she returned to her seat, behind her she heard his confident voice.  "I swear..."  Before she could reach her seat, another round of applause swept over them.  *But it's all the same, Mr. Hank!* she smiled.

*CRASH!*  One of the chairs had fallen over.  The members of the row behind Gwen had risen to step up to the front of the room, and one nervous-looking woman had accidentally upset her chair.  The man next to her righted the chair, set her fallen coat upon its seat, and took her arm to assist her.  They filed forward along with the rest of their row as Gwen sat down.

The nervous woman was grateful to have the janitor's arm to cling to.  Without his support, for certain she would have crumbled to the floor somewhere along the way.  As they stood in line waiting their turn, she knew he must have plainly felt her twitching muscles writhing in nervous anticipation.  But he merely smiled knowingly at her, saying nothing.  Nevertheless, the man was her only point of reassurance in a world rapidly dissolving around her.

With another mental jar, she suddenly found herself looking at his face in another setting; it was still in a hangar, but one in Sacramento, not Colorado.  He was busying himself with preparations for their departure.  The airplane he ministered was a tiny one, with only two miniature, close-spaced seats and no room for the luggage they didn't have anyway.  The steel-grey bulk of an extra fuel tank almost completely filled the space behind their tiny seats, topped by an undersized rear window with the vertical stabilizer bisecting the backward view.  From beyond the closed hangar door, they could hear the sounds of nearby gunfire.  She realized it must have been weeks since the sharp, staccato sound hadn't been a part of life's daily backdrop. But if what the janitor had said was true, they would soon be shut of it once and for all.

The sound of gunfire was suddenly drowned out by a yet-louder sound, that of the airplane's motor bursting to loud life within the close confines of the enclosed hangar. The janitor had to shout to make himself heard over its loud drone.

"Stand on that brake pedal and don't let go!" he yelled. "I'm going to open the hangar!" He opened the airplane's door, climbed out, and ran for the hangar doors. He pushed one open slightly, poked his head out, looked left, then right, and with a mighty shove, he pushed both doors open, the massive panels swinging wide out of the way of the idling aircraft. Without waiting for them to finish their outward journey, he was already running back to the airplane. Climbing in, he scrambled awkwardly in his panic, twice having to slam the airplane's door before it was secure. She could see his hands shaking as they pulled back on the throttle, but the motor purred into smooth, louder life as it spooled up to top speed. The sound inside the building was deafening, but it did not last long; the airplane shot from the hangar like an arrow from a bow.

The noise must have alerted the acolytes long before he had opened the hangar doors, for several of them were already running at top speed in the hangar's direction. When they saw the airplane hurtling down the taxiway, several of them fell to one knee, leveled their weapons, and began firing.

"Get down!" screamed the janitor. "For God's sake, get down!"

But there was no room to squat in the tiny cabin; she ended up merely twisted to one side to huddle fearfully against his shoulder as the airplane rocked and bounced along the uneven taxiway as it accelerated to rotation speed. With a loud crash that was followed by the naked drone of the airplane's motor, the rear window shattered into a thousand fragments, victim of a well-aimed shot. Wind buffeted them from behind and papers fluttered in the air, but the airplane continued accelerating unabated. Still jouncing along the taxiway rather than the smooth runway, the airplane bounced hard several times, each jolt jarring her spine as if she had jumped out of a tall tree. Suddenly, the roughness vanished as the airplane's wheels departed the taxiway and swung into the air. Over the roars of the wind and motor that were invading through the missing rear window, they could still hear the sounds of gunfire diminishing behind them. Foolishly, the woman turned to release one last blast of hatred at their tormentors.

"Not your kind of world!" she screamed at them defiantly, shaking her fist. But her words were whipped away by the wind and drowned out by the motor, and her gestures were too far away to be discernable.

The janitor swung the aircraft around to the east and turned to her and smiled, squeezing her hand once. She smiled in return, floating along on a cushion of air.

Without a break, she found herself letting go of his hand and walking up to the lectern. One knee buckled, but she caught herself from falling with an instinctive hand grasping the lectern's edge. She looked up to the amassed face of the valley's residents, and again her internal organs melted into liquid terror. Next to her she saw the fatherly face of Dr. Thomas; he was smiling encouragingly, nodding for her to proceed. She took heart from his encouragement, and stood up straight. She was surprised by the unexpected strength she suddenly found welling up within her. *I'm going to be all right!* she realized.

With head held high, she recited the striker's oath in a clear voice, then waited for the applause. But it never came. Murmurs rippled through the audience, dropping to a quick silence. Panicked, she looked to Dr. Thomas; but the man was still smiling, nodding for her to try again. He adjusted a knob slightly.

"I swear, by my life and my love of it...," she began again, but in her panic she forgot the rest of the words. Murmuring came louder from the audience; she knew the red light had illuminated yet again, if only from its reflection on the stern visage of Ragnar, sitting nearby. She had heard that the man was formerly a pirate who had once terrorized the high seas, but never believed that this handsome, golden-haired philosopher might have been the same man—not until that moment.

Turning back to face the audience, withering under their disapproving stares, she could withstand no more and her panic consumed her. Eyes wide, she stared down at her hands on the electrode plates, then snatched them back as if the plates were a thing diseased. Fingers outstretched, she examined her hands slowly, oblivious to the curious attention of the audience. She held one hand in front of her face, examining every detail, front and back, as if she were a young baby who for the first time realized that she possessed something called a hand. Between her outstretched fingers, she saw Ragnar rising, with the look of a man about to undertake an unpleasant, important duty. His motion jerked her back to reality.

"No!" she screamed. "No! I won't go back there! No! Not that kind of world!" She backed away from the pirate, her hands still outstretched in front of her, knees buckling under the strain of her terror. "No!" she screamed one last time, then turned and ran.

With battle-honed instincts, Ragnar immediately took flight in hot pursuit; but fortunately for the woman, he became momentarily entangled in the queue of would-be oath-takers, slowing his charge. With no one standing between her and the hangar's side door, she bolted across the open floor, paused momentarily to clumsily operate the door latch, then burst through it to freedom and the cold Colorado night.

The icy breeze blew right through her dress; in her panicked haste, she had not thought to fetch a coat. But the same panic that drove her unguided down random streets and pathways also left her numb to the cold. Unheeded, the frigid night air simply washed off her skin.

She ran for her life. Huge mounds of snow reared up on either side of her as she barreled first down one passageway, then another. She met no one in her flight; virtually the entire population of the valley was in the hangar she had just abandoned. She turned to look over her shoulder, finally feeling the cold wind as it whistled past her freezing ears. But it was a phantom cold: she was looking over her shoulder at the smashed rear pane of glass and the tall tail of an airplane beyond it. Seated next to her in the cold cockpit was the janitor.

"I've got the heater turned up as high as it'll go!" he shouted to be heard. "I think we'll be all right if I stay low and follow the valleys!"

Ahead of her, she saw the western slopes of the Colorado Rockies rearing up in front of them, their peaks ponderously clad in the late winter snows. As they approached, they found that the valleys oozed thick clouds, blocking their view of the dangerous mountain peaks that surrounded them.

"I'll have to go higher to get above this fog!" he warned. "It's going to get colder, but it's not much farther now!" Before long they burst out of the fog and into the bright sunshine, majestic mountains rearing up on all sides, when suddenly the vista vanished again as they penetrated another fluffy white cloud. There was no impact when the airplane pierced its pillowy surface, but there was one when the woman impacted the wall of snow in front of her. In her blind haste she had slipped on the snowy ground, and with a soundless *poof!* she tumbled into the massive, dusty collection of ice particles that paralleled her intended path.

At first she tried to stand, but the cold air had already deeply penetrated her exposed, unprotected skin, leaving her muscles flaccid and unresponsive. She wiggled weakly in the snow drift for a moment, like a dying fish out of water, then relaxed. Paradoxically, the snow drift warmed her skin, relaxing her panicked mind. With a small sigh, she nestled her head lower onto the soft, warm cushion of snow and drifted slowly off to sleep.

## CHAPTER 9 – COME AWAY WITH ME

The pilot swore.

"God *DAMN* it! One bomb," he stressed. "One bomb! All two thousand of them are sitting in one place—and at this very moment! All it would take would be one nice, big, fat bomb!" He dropped an ice cube into his whiskey in demonstration, its impact throwing a slight splash of golden liquid onto the surface of the bar. "Bo-o-o-o-o-om!" he rumbled.

A solitary patron sat at the bar in front of the pilot and shook his head scornfully. "What, and lose out on a free Yucatan vacation?"

"Free?" He snorted in derision. "It's not free for me, bud! They told me that since I brought myself into the valley, I've got to pay to get myself back out!"

"Ouch. Sorry. Call it a paid Yucatan vacation, then."

"Is that where you're going?"

The patron finished his own whiskey before answering. "Isn't everybody?"

"I hear New Orleans is still alive," confided the pilot. "*That's* the place to be!" *Just the sort of town where the glamorous, deep-voiced pilot can find a—*

"Still alive for now, you mean," the man retorted. He held up a hand and began ticking off his fingers, one by one. "Atlanta's gone, Chattanooga's gone, Knoxville's gone, Dallas is gone, everything else in the Old South is gone! How long is it going to take before ten thousand refugees—men just like you!—show up on New Orleans' doorstep? You'd burst their levees! No, I think all the American cities are done for. Where else is there to go but Mexico? Surely not to the People's State of Canada!"

"Yeah, but to the Yucatan Peninsula?"

"Why not? It's nicely out of the way, especially if you stay near the northern coast. Desert and mountains behind you, ocean in front, fishing's good, land's fertile, ample rainfall—and no ten-foot snowfalls!"

"No turning back, once you do that."

"Where would you want to turn back to?"

"Surely not this hell-hole!" swore the pilot. He was still mad, boiling mad, and it showed.

"What's eating you?" the man finally ventured to ask.

The truth immediately tumbled out of the pilot. "I can't find a buyer for *The Golden Touch!*"

"Can't find a buyer? I thought you turned a nice business here."

"I do! But those bastards know I'm leaving April 15th. So they sit and wait, then on April 16th they'll just waltz right in!"

"Ouch again. They must really like you!"

He scowled again. "Then why am I scheduled to be on the *last* goddamned airplane out of the valley?"

"Go on!"

"I'm serious. Check the manifests. I'm dead last."

"I wonder why?"

The pilot shrugged. "Luck of the draw, I guess."

The man stood and donned his overcoat. "Sounds like a lack of luck to me. I'm scheduled to go Friday morning, and I, for one, can't wait to leave Old Man Winter behind forever. Be seeing you!" He turned to leave.

"Or not," he called mockingly to the man's departing back. Alone, the pilot cleaned up the bar where the man had been sitting and pocketed the tip he had left, feeling the cold coin clink in his pocket as it joined its brother coins. Despite his sour mood, he smiled. Even if the bastards seized his taproom, he'd still walk away with a hefty amount of gold. Thinking of all that gold, it suddenly dawned on him: *Mexico might be a better place to go after all!* Pulling out a paper and pencil, he did some quick calculations based on his recollection of the value of the peso from his Mexican vacation the year before. Looking at the final totals, he whistled long and loud. *I could live like a king down there!* he realized. *Maybe Mexico really is the place for me!* Instantly he discarded the notion of holing up in someplace stodgy and safe like the Yucatan Peninsula. *Why not something a little more glamorous, someplace exciting, something more like... Aruba! Yeah, Aruba! Where a deep-voiced pilot—*

The front door opened again, interrupting his thoughts. In walked Ragnar.

The pilot did not immediately react, even though Ragnar had never visited the taproom before. "Welcome to *The Golden Touch*," he offered without animosity or cordiality.

"Where is she," demanded the pirate, his professional demeanor dominating.

"Where is who?" the pilot asked nonchalantly, as if playing a card game for high stakes. The pilot plainly understood who the pirate meant, but he'd had more than enough out of these philosophical Johnnies, and wasn't going to willingly play along any more than he had to.

"The woman with no integrity," Ragnar replied flatly.

"There's nobody here." He waved a hand across the empty taproom.

"She won't get far," he warned.

"What do you mean?" asked the pilot, feigning confusion, feeding him rope.

Ragnar eyed him levelly without blinking. "After twice swearing to a lie, your girl friend ran away. I thought she might have come here."

The news rattled the pilot, but his years of wagering had taught him not to let it show. "Nope. Haven't seen her."

Ragnar dumped a bundle of cloth on the bar's surface. "Would you be so kind as to return her coat when you do see her?" He set a copper penny deliberately upon the wooden surface of the bar. "Please."

The pilot's eyes dropped to the bundle, shifted to the coin, then back to the pirate. "Sure," he deadpanned, pocketing the coin.

Ragnar turned to leave, but stood in the doorway for another moment, looking around. Then without another word, he left.

"Hey! Where're you going?" the pilot called after his departing back. "Your first drink is free!" *Yeah, free drink of rat poison! Pie-rat poison!* If he weren't so angry, he would have laughed at his own joke.

Shrugging, he picked up the abandoned coat and hung it on a peg. Another customer entered, and he turned to serve him. "What can I get you?"

"Your best wine, whatever that may be. It's my last night in the valley!"

"Congratulations," he groused.

"Well, at least I'm not going to California!"

"Nobody is, from what I hear."

"Then maybe you ought to listen again! Didn't you hear? Four people got caught lying when they took the oath tonight. I was there. I saw it."

The pilot scoffed. "Yeah, right. How could anyone tell they were lying? I know for a fact that lie detectors do not work."

"Ha!" He flashed a knowing smile. "Not *this* lie detector!"

The pilot held onto his scorn. "And what's so special about *this* lie detector?" he mocked.

The man's eyes opened wide. "Because it was designed by Dr. Thomas!" he insisted awefully.

The pilot's silence spoke volumes.

Faced with the pilot's manifest disbelief, the man softened his stance. "Well... I don't know, but four people are heading to California nevertheless. I was there, I tell you."

The pilot shook his head in commiseration. "I sure wouldn't want to be any of them! I've heard some pretty frightening stuff about California."

"Me, too! And it's not just me and you—one of those liars must have heard those same stories. She screamed her head off when they caught her. Somebody said she just got here from Sacramento a few weeks ago; she probably has some of her own stories to tell—firsthand stuff." He shook his head. "Must've been pretty nasty out there." He stared for a moment at the pilot's blank face. "Hey, are you all right?"

"Where did she run away to?"

"Nobody knows. She just ran away."

"Was she wearing a coat?"

"Huh?" He was taken aback by the strange question. "Now that you mention it, she wasn't. She just turned and ran!"

"Isn't it around ten degrees outside?" the pilot asked needlessly.

"Hey: It's Colorado. It's March. It's dark. What else would the temperature be—except maybe lower?"

The pilot strode around from behind the bar and began shuffling the newcomer toward the door. "Closing time. Sorry."

"Hey, you can't close now! It's my last night in the valley!"

The pilot put on his best English butler accent, adding in extra baritone from his dust-damaged vocal chords, plus a dose of high-brow sarcasm. "Do have a good evening, sir!" He stood holding the door open, smiling and bowing, until the miffed man reluctantly departed.

As soon as he was gone, the pilot grabbed his own coat along with the woman's, doused the lights, then headed out into the night in search of her. His quest did not take long; there were only so many roads that led from the hangar at the airstrip. But he had also come into some luck, since she wasn't in the last place he could have looked. He found her embedded in a wall of snow at the top of a T-intersection, as if she had tried to make the turn at high speed but stumbled into the far wall. He pulled her out of the drift, ineffectually brushed the snow from her face and hair, and was relieved to find that she was still breathing. He clumsily stuffed her arms into her coat sleeves, flung her over his shoulder in a fireman's carry, and bore her back to

*The Golden Touch.* Turning the lights back on, he carried her up the stairs to his private apartment, laid her on his bed, and covered her with several blankets. Her breathing was regular; she appeared to be asleep, but her face was deathly pale.

He picked up the telephone on the nightstand next to his bed and called Dr. Thomas. The doctor wasn't in, a nurse explained; he had gone to the swearing ceremony and had not yet returned, but she would send for him right away. The pilot hung up the telephone and descended the steps, taking a seat at a random table. The only thing he could do now was wait.

But he did not have to wait long; Dr. Thomas showed up in less than ten minutes. He also brought along an entourage: Ragnar and a nondescript woman who he took to be a nurse, pushing an empty wheelchair.

"Where is she?" Dr. Thomas asked the pilot.

With a silent nod, the pilot indicated the staircase at the back of the taproom, and without another word, Dr. Thomas turned and climbed the steps. The three of them waited in heavy silence, and soon Dr. Thomas reappeared.

"She'll be fine. Just a little overexposure to the cold. No frostbite, thankfully. I gave her a sedative, and when she wakes up tomorrow morning, she'll be fine." He turned to the nurse. "Okay, let's go up and get her." The nurse turned to comply, wheelchair in the lead, the doctor at her side.

The pilot immediately reacted, moving to bar their path. "Get her? What do you mean, 'get her?' You leave her be!"

Uncertain, the pair stopped in their tracks.

Again assuming the mannerisms of a pirate born to command, hands on his hips, Ragnar intoned, "She has sworn to a lie. She must leave the valley immediately." He inclined his head briefly in the direction of Dr. Thomas. "As he said, she'll be fine when she wakes up. And when she does, she'll be in California!"

"Like hell she will!" retorted the pilot.

Ragnar looked down at the pilot with mild surprise, as if he were examining a piece of furniture that had inexplicably come to life and begun to speak. He held the pilot's eye firmly for a moment, then slowly rotated his head. Meaningfully, his gaze rested upon the scab petitions still tacked to the wall, then slowly turned back to the pilot. "Don't play any more of your games with me, tappy," he warned darkly. "You forget that you're living in *our* world now!"

The pilot did not answer, did not even move. In his mind, he evaluated and re-evaluated his options, but realized he had none.

Ignoring him, and without another word, doctor and nurse disappeared upstairs with the empty wheelchair, unmolested. Presently they reappeared with the sedated woman strapped firmly into the chair. Dr. Thomas rolled her sleeping form gently down the steps, one bump at a time, the nurse in tow. When they reached the ground floor, the nurse took over; she covered the woman up to her neck with a heavy woolen blanket, tucking in the corners conscientiously, then wheeled her charge out the front door, followed by Dr. Thomas. Last in line, Ragnar stood in the doorway for another moment, looking around. Then without another word, he left.

The optionless pilot did not move for a long time.

# Chapter 10 – Hotel California

The woman awoke.

At first, her mind could not focus; she felt as if she had been drugged. She could not discern whether she still remained in the valley's hangar, or was caught in reliving yet another one of her unbidden Sacramento memories. Listening, eyes still closed, she heard the drone of an airplane's motor, but the air around her face was warm and calm. From that, she concluded that it must not be a dream. She could also feel the familiar lightness of her drifting stomach confirming that she was airborne. Opening her eyes revealed that indeed she sat in an airplane, and that it was real. She squinted against the morning sunlight that brilliantly illuminated the interior of the aircraft from behind; and as her eyes became acclimated to the scene, she discovered the reason for the brilliance: the airplane was a sightseeing model, and the entire roof above her was a single paned canopy. She sat up with a start and looked around.

Six other people were in the cabin with her; she sat in the back seat close alongside a sleeping woman. In front of her were two men seated side by side, also dozing. In front of them, the pair of seats had been turned rearward, and in them sat two burly men, both armed, both awake; guards, apparently. Behind them, facing forward, was a slender, nervous woman with an angular face sitting alone at the controls; the pilot, obviously.

*What am I doing here?* the perplexed passenger asked herself, but her groggy thoughts came only sluggishly. She felt woozy, as if she were recovering from a bad hangover. Looking outside the window, beneath her she saw a featureless desert; turning to the rear, beyond the airplane's tail she recognized the familiar jagged peaks of the Colorado Rockies. Peering ahead over the pilot's shoulder, she saw another tall mountain range many miles ahead: the Sierra Nevadas. With a sickening start, her sluggish brain snapped into action and she finally realized where she was—and why. "Take us back!" she shrieked without preamble or warning. "Oh, God, take us back!"

Startled by the sudden scream, the woman next to her was instantly awake. The two men in front of her spun their heads around in unison to face her, then looked away. One of them sneered as he turned, mumbling some unheard insult. A guard elbowed his comrade, a mocking grin on his face; the other guard chuckled and returned the cruel smile.

She clutched the startled woman next to her, shaking her. "Make her take us back! Oh, please, make her take us back!"

The woman piloting the aircraft turned to face the unruly passenger, a sweep of her brown hair falling back, almost touching the line of her shoulders. "We don't allow men of no integrity to remain in our valley," the aviatrix explained needlessly, her gun-metal grey eyes flashing in anger. "Or women, either. You lied; all four of you lied. So it's Back For God for you!"

"Oh, God, take us back!" she repeated yet again, the irony of her statement lost on her panicked consciousness. "You have no idea what it's like there! No idea! Take us back!"

"Stop your whining, scab!" taunted one of the guards. "You're lucky you didn't freeze to death in that snow drift. If it were up to me, I'd have left you there to die! What kind of a woman are you anyway, swearing to lies? It's bad enough that you're a lousy scab, but to throw away your integrity—something no man can ever take from you!—why you're much worse than a measly scab!" Folding his arms across his chest, he let loose one final pitiless volley. "It's people like you who ruined this country and brought about its downfall! You deserve a whole lot worse than what you're getting!"

But the target of his scorn did not react to the verbal abuse, clinging instead to her mantra. "Turn back! You have to turn back!"

The guard smirked mockingly at the gaping, panicked passenger. "Look at your face! Even when you know you're in the wrong, you won't even repent!"

*Repent!* The guard's final word remained, resonating loudly inside the woman's skull, ballooning beyond belief to drown out all sights, sounds, and feelings. *Repent!* the word echoed in her mind. *Repent!* it echoed again, sounding like a drum beat of some savage's melody. *Repent!* Helpless, her jaw fell slack. *Repent!* But the drum would not stop. *Repent!*

As the unrelenting, cruel cadence continued to repeat itself, to her horror she saw that in time with each beat a tiny red-robed figure suddenly appeared, each the size of a child's crayon, its hair aflame with a brilliant orange glow, dancing on her arms, on her legs, becoming tangled in her hair. *Repent!* Screaming, she dug her nails into her scalp, pulling out tufts of her own hair in a vain attempt to sweep the tiny demons from her head. *Repent!* But as she pulled one off, another demon quickly took its place, worming up her sleeve and down the back of her neck, crawling into her ears, her mouth, and nose, wriggling around inside her clothes, and violating her in the most obscene ways. *Repent!*

"Noooooooo!" she cried out yet again in a panicked voice, her hands sweeping over her skin and swatting the empty air. "Get me out of here!" she cried, clawing like a trapped animal at the paned canopy that encased the passengers. Her hands flailed wildly back and forth in their panic, until one landed by sheer accident on the canopy's release latch. Her fingers tightened around it instinctively.

"Don't open it!" the guards called out almost in unison, but to no avail; their words could not reach her. Without pause, in a moment of clarity she deliberately flipped open the latch, and the section of canopy above her head cracked open slightly and was abruptly snatched out of her hand by the force of the wind and twirled away behind them. The deafening roar of the wind filled the cabin.

"No!" she screamed one final time over the shrieking gale, her disheveled hair whipping across her mouth. "No! Not your kind of world!"

With that, with no break, no moment of doubt, with full consciousness of acting in self-preservation, she unbuckled her safety harness and stood up in her seat to be snatched away by the wind, just as the canopy had been; and not stopping, she tumbled over into space.

## CHAPTER 11 – HERE COMES THE JUDGE

The gavel cracked.

"This court will please come to order!" called the bailiff, setting the gavel aside. Without being told, a number of the men and women in the audience stood automatically, but a sizeable majority pointedly retained their seats, veterans of the bandit's trial.

Self-consciously, Eddie stepped up to claim his seat behind the judge's bench, but halted halfway across the room. Sometime in the week since the bandit's trial, someone had affixed a large, wooden signboard high on the wall behind his seat. In ornate, carved capitals, it read: "YOU HAVE THE

GOD-GIVEN, INALIENABLE RIGHT TO LIVE YOUR LIFE YOUR WAY WITHOUT INTERFERENCE, PROVIDED YOU RESPECT THE RIGHTS AND PROPERTY OF OTHERS." At the paragraph's foot, one carved word stood out in even larger letters: "LIBERTY." Twice he read through the words before casting a curious glance across the assembled audience. He caught the eye of the policeman, who innocently cast his own gaze elsewhere, answering the obvious, unasked question.

"All right, let's get started," prompted Eddie as he finally took his seat. "What's the issue here?"

An elderly spinster rose in response. "Your Honor, there is a travesty taking place in our town that must be brought to a halt immediately!"

All concern, Eddie leaned forward attentively. "What? What's that?"

The spinster spit out her venomous reply. "Prostitution!" Behind her, almost filling the first three rows, a contingent of women of various ages burst into energetic applause. From behind them came the sound of tittering laughter. The spinster basked in one and ignored the other.

*Prostitution?* Eddie stared blankly across the sea of faces. While he would never consider consorting with a prostitute or even befriending one, similarly he could not find it in himself to condemn the man who might—or the ladies of the night themselves. In one sense, the ladies performed a service for the community by providing an outlet to those men whose needs could not otherwise be met. There was no denying they might keep a simple fellow out of jail. "What would you have me do?" he asked cautiously.

"Why, put an end to it, of course!" Again, the elderly contingent dutifully applauded.

"But...," he began hesitantly. "But how would I be able to do that?"

"Lock them all up!" she replied with a vehemence that belied her age, a response that brought more applause—and catcalls. "Run them out of town!" she added, giving both the demonstration and counter-demonstration new life.

"But why?" he persisted.

"Because they're prostitutes, that's why! It's self-evident!" More applause echoed among the laughter.

"Please!" he implored the audience. No one challenged his request; they subsided as he addressed the spinster. "I agree it's self-evident that there are prostitutes in town—this *is* Las Vegas, after all—but what is it they've done wrong? Are they robbing the men who come to see them?"

"They are robbing society!" she hissed.

"How so?"

"By their very existence, that's how!"

Eddie exhaled wearily and leaned back in his chair. *This is going to be a tough one to—* The thought came to a screeching halt. *Then again, maybe not!* He glanced quickly at the policeman, then back to the supplicant. "Ma'am, do you notice the carved statement on the wall behind me? Read it, please, if you will."

The woman's lips twitched; she remained silent.

"Much as you or I may agree or disagree with the way certain women have chosen to run their lives, there's no denying they do respect the rights and property of others. Un—"

"But—," she attempted to interrupt, but he did not let her finish.

"—less you know of an instance where they did not show such respect, how could I justify moving against them? And if I did so anyhow, I'd be demonstrating a lack of respect for them myself!"

"Well!" she sniffed haughtily. "*I* certainly have no respect for them!"

"Does that mean you would rob them or harm them?"

"No!" she retorted instantly. "Of course not!"

"Yet you would have *me* act as your agent and drive them out of town, lock them up, or worse." He stroked his chin and mused out loud. "You know, I'm not certain we mean the same thing by the word 'respect' here. What right is it the ladies are not respecting? Whose property?"

She did not hesitate. "They're not respecting their own bodies!"

Confused, Eddie replied, "But neither do the men who smoke and drink in the gambling halls. Would you want them locked up, too?"

Again there was no hesitation. "Yes!"

Loud applause came from her supporters in the audience, and mocking jeers came from the others; both groups cut themselves off instantly at the sight of Eddie's stern glance.

Returning his attention to the spinster, he nodded in understanding. "Ma'am, unless someone is not respecting the rights and property of others, there's nothing I can justify doing."

"Well!" she snorted angrily. "I was told you were an honorable man, but now we can all see the plain truth! You're no better than the scum of the Earth you're protecting!"

"But what can I properly do?"

"Oh, nothing! Nothing!" she replied testily as she picked up her handbag in obvious preparation to leave. "A body could as soon choke to death as say a word. Oh, you *men!*" Angrily she turned her back on him and stalked off toward the door; en masse her supporters in the audience stood in sympathy and followed noisily, their numerous tongues clucking in disapproval. Their spokesman halted briefly at the courtroom door to hurl a final, indignant warning: "You're not the only one in town who can play judge, you know!"

Calmly Eddie replied, "Feel free. Just be sure to respect the rights or property of others—or perhaps we shall meet here again."

Reddening, she scarcely contained her fury as she yanked the door open and stalked out, her numerous supporters in tow.

A pregnant silence hung in the air following their departure, but Eddie only shrugged. "This court is adjourned."

\* \* \*

The gavel cracked.

"This court will please come to order!" called the bailiff. Only a handful of men and women stood; the vast majority deliberately remained seated. They were learning.

Self-consciously, Eddie took his own seat behind the judge's bench. "All right," he started. "What's the issue here?"

"That man killed my husband!" cried a distraught woman, pointing a shaky finger at a slim, good-looking man.

"Look, lady!" protested the accused. "It was a duel, fought fair and square, and he lost big! You can ask his second!" He gestured to a man seated in the front row. "Or mine!" He waved the hand at another.

The woman was undeterred. "Duel or no duel, you killed my husband, and that's a fact!"

"But it was *him* who challenged *me!*"

"You didn't have to accept!" she retorted.

He drew himself up. "What, and have everyone think I'm some sort of coward?"

147

"Only a coward would gun down another man!"

"Bah!" he cried with a dismissive wave of the hand. "You talk some sense into her, Mr. Eddie!"

Hesitantly Eddie entered the fray. "Well, if it's a case of murder, that's really for a jury to decide, not me." He turned his attention to the woman. "Is what he says true? Did your husband challenge this man?"

"I hardly see how that matters!" she snapped.

"You are correct," he agreed solemnly. "It doesn't. Challenged or challenger, what really matters is whether or not both men willingly entered the duel. If your husband agreed, he must have known the risk he was taking."

"What?!" she cried. "A man was murdered! *That* is all that matters!"

He shook his head slowly. "If your husband had declined and was killed anyhow, or if he was killed by a wild shot, or if the bullet smashed a window and no one paid for the damage, then I could see how someone would have a grievance. But that's not the case here, is it?"

Astonished by the unexpected response, the woman did not reply.

Eddie turned to the dueler. "Where was the duel held?"

"In the desert south of town, out past the old silver mine."

Eddie nodded; he knew the place. "I'm glad to hear you weren't shooting off guns here in town. That's just not safe." He turned back to the woman. "Unless I'm missing something, it appears that everyone's rights were respected, don't you think?"

Angry tears began to stream down the woman's face. "So you'd let my husband's murderer get away?"

"Pardon me if what I'm about to say seems harsh; I don't mean it that way. But it sounds to me like this is more a case of elaborate suicide than one of murder." He reddened slightly.

"Then I *won't* ask you! Let's ask a jury!"

Eddie hesitated and glanced briefly at the policeman. "The costs of this court are paid by the law enforcement unit of the Las Vegas police." He waved a hand to the carved plaque over his shoulder. "And here is the law we enforce. But I can see no violation of—"

"Then *I* will pay for it!" she screamed. "How much do you want?" She clutched frantically at her purse and rummaged around inside it while muttering, "Where's my wallet? I've been in court before. I know how justice works..."

He shook his head. "I'm sorry if I confused you; that's not what I meant. I don't accept any payment for my time here. I'm a volunteer. But please let me finish what I was saying. No one violated our basic law, so there is no way I can legally intervene. In fact, I would be in trouble myself if I tried. If two men agree to a duel—or agree to anything else between them!—then it's a contract voluntarily entered. How could I interfere with a private contract? By what right? And if I did, I'd be guilty of not respecting their rights."

"But...," she began, but no further words came.

Eddie rose. "There are no 'buts.' While I do not approve of duels personally, my approval or disapproval means nothing here. Unless there was force, fraud, or some other violation of the rights or property of another, I cannot be a party to these proceedings." With that, he turned for the door.

"Wait! Come back here, you!" she yelled to his retreating form. "You can't leave! You're the judge!"

Two paces away from his vacated seat, he politely turned to face her. "My apologies again if my role here is still unclear to you." He pointed a finger again at the carved sign above his vacated seat. "That's all I do. You're asking me to do its opposite. It's like you're asking me to deliberately eat poison instead of food. But I can't. I won't."

The speechless woman gaped, recovered, and finally found her tongue, and it was an angry one. "How dare you! To Hell with you! I'll go out and find another judge! I'm sure there's a lot of men in this town who would not look kindly upon a man who makes widows!" With that, she stomped for the door.

"Please!" he warned her retreating back, a note of genuine concern in his voice. He opened his mouth as if to say more, but no words came forth. Slowly, deliberately, he closed it instead.

Her step faltered only slightly at his admonition, yet noticeably so, but she continued her exit without a backward glance. Even though she had not seen the hesitant, open mouth, in her mind she could nevertheless hear its unstated message: *Or perhaps we shall meet here again!* She slammed the door behind her. Almost unnoticed, a distinguished, olive-skinned gentleman followed her out.

In the silence that followed, Eddie looked around the room. The faces of the audience spanned the entire spectrum of human emotion: hate, anger, malice, shock, amazement, awe, joy, pride, delight, admiration, and a host of others; everything save indifference. Many emotions appeared on the same face simultaneously, shifting seamlessly from one into another; and adding to the emotional melee, the same array of emotions were being directed by some men at the closed door, and by others at Eddie.

"Just a moment, Mr. Eddie," interrupted the bailiff. "There's one more case."

"What? Oh, right. Sorry." He reclaimed his seat on the dais, asking, "All right, what's the next issue here?"

Two men stood, each at opposite sides of the room. One came forward, but the second gathered his belongings and headed for the door.

Bewildered, the first man called, "Hey! Just where do you think you're going?"

The second man halted at the door; he faced Eddie, but answered his questioner. "I can see there's no way I'll be able to get our contract annulled. Not here, anyway." With that, he turned and left.

A heavy silence hung over the room, until it was finally broken by Eddie. "This court is adjourned," he said simply.

\* \* \*

The widow was dubious.

"Let me get this straight," she contested. "You run your own court?"

The olive-skinned man sitting on the bench next to her nodded respectfully. "Yes, madam."

"And you'd be willing to hear my case *gratis*?"

Again he nodded. The man seemed genuinely interested in her plight. "Yes, madam. If you come to me asking for justice, you shall have it." After a brief pause, he added, "And it seems likely to me that your husband's murderer will be convicted."

"And sentenced?"

"And sentenced."

"But what about..." She waved a hand in an ambiguous direction. "...the other court?"

"Our sentences are compatible with those handed down by Mr. Eddie."

"Compatible?" Still dubious, her eye narrowed. "How so?"

He smiled congenially. "We practice the time-honored, religious art of shunning."

"'Shunning?'"

"Quite so. Those we convict are shunned by the friends of our court. That means we will not deal with convicted men, not in any capacity. It's that simple."

"But... But what good does that do?"

He held his amiable smile. "Our court has friends in many positions here in town, both high and low. Not everywhere, to be sure, but in enough places that those we convict may find their opportunities for a pleasant life... diminished, shall we say?"

"Diminished? In what way?"

"In any number of ways. They may be passed over for a job or a promotion. They might find there are some shopkeepers who are unwilling to conduct business with them. Some societies or congregations may not look favorably upon them when considering them for membership—or continuing their membership. The possibilities are literally endless."

"And you don't run afoul of..." Her hand waved again, less energetically. "Other courts?"

"The men of Las Vegas have freedom of association. That implies its opposite: the freedom not to associate." His warm smile broadened. "We have no quarrel with Mr. Eddie, nor him with us. We are quite within his law, and are quite happy to remain there. Even his police know that. We are not his competitor; we are his supporter."

She nodded; but her dubiousness remained. "And it's not going to cost me?"

"There is no cost," he assured her affably. "However..." His smile faded into one of serious concern. "Someday—and that day may never come—you may be called upon to help us to... diminish... an opportunity for some other criminal we have convicted."

"'Me? 'Diminish' someone else?"

"Yes. If you wish that we hear your case, we ask that you become another friend of our court."

"Yet you want me to do nothing..." This time her hand barely twitched. "...illegal?"

The cordial smile returned. "No, madam, of course not. It's just a favor we do for you today which you might have to return sometime in the future. Freely offered, and just as freely accepted." The smile did not falter as he added, "But you should know that we will never ask a second favor once we've been refused the first, nor grant a second favor—and neither will the friends of our court." He paused meaningfully. "Do you understand?"

She did. The woman rose jerkily to her feet and clumsily tucked her purse under her arm. "I'll think about it," she lied as she quickly took her leave.

"*Bene*," he called to her retreating figure.

\* \* \*

The gavel tapped daintily.

"This court will please come to order," the spinster croaked throatily from her seat behind the judge's bench on the dais in the courtroom, her stern gaze sweeping across the dozens of biddies who filled the first several rows in the audience. An equal number of nondescript townsfolk sat in the back rows, among them, the policeman. Sitting in the chair next to him was a large, coarse man smiling broadly through an unruly beard and several missing teeth. A sizeable number of the other onlookers were familiar faces in the courtroom, many of them men with an agenda to advance, hoping to be selected to serve on a jury.

Behind the spinster's head hung the carved wooden sign, but its message was covered snugly by a fitted pink sheet. Embroidered on the surface of the fabric were ornate, pastel letters proclaiming, "Ladies Court."

"What is our first case?" she demanded in a tone usually reserved for men who refused to tip their hats.

From her second row seat a lemon-faced nun rose, her flowing black habit cloaking her in a sinister regality. In a high-pitched, nasal whine she cried out, "Las Vegas versus prostitution!" The biddies surrounding her burst into animated applause.

The spinster-judge nodded. "I see," she said. Shifting her attention to the biddy-packed room, she commanded, "You there, in the front row! The first seven of you please proceed to the jury box."

The chosen few clutched their handbags close and eagerly scurried to claim their new seats. Most all of the men in the back scowled in disgust; a sizeable fraction took their leave, many of them in a huff.

"You may proceed," the spinster instructed the nun.

The nun maneuvered out from the midst of her peers and approached the bench. "Your Honor, there is a scourge loose upon our town," she began, "A foul scourge that...," and for the next twenty minutes she railed against the institution of prostitution, its purveyors, its clientele, and the society that permitted it to continue. The tone, delivery, and repetition exhibited in her words had the makings of an appalling, sixty-page speech. In dry detail she spoke of the unrelated evils the institution theoretically engendered, and how ending the vile practice would bring a swift end to all the world's ills. "...thus we are seeking judgment against the harlots and their ilk!" she finally concluded.

Looking around, the spinster inquired formally, "Do any of the accused wish to say anything in their defense?"

A general murmur rose from the audience, and the nun toyed with the beads that hung from her waist, nervously shifting her weight first onto one foot, then the other. "Your Honor," she finally admitted. "None of the accused are here."

"And why is that?" the spinster arrogantly demanded, as if their absence were some horrible personal affront.

"They all refused to come! They were told we were offering them a chance to repent for their sins, but they refused to take it!"

"That does not matter," decreed the spinster matter-of-factly. "Their presence here is not required. They can be sentenced in absentia."

"We'll see about that!" cried a male voice. All heads turned toward the source of the defiance; it came from the coarse man sitting next to the policeman.

Offended and flaunting it, the spinster challenged, "And just who do you think you are?"

"A bouncer at one of the brothels," he immediately replied, then drew himself up proudly. "*And* a founding member of the Bouncer's Union!" He

151

hooked a thumb at the policeman sitting alongside him. "My Union's one of his competitors, but only when it comes to the business of protecting our ladies. If anyone tries any funny-business, they'll have to deal with him and me both!—and all my union buddies, too! We union brothers stick together, no matter what. That's what makes us strong!"

"Sir!" The spinster assumed an astonished air. "Are you threatening me?"

He smiled broadly, revealing fully the extent of his inadequate dentistry. "No ma'am! I'm just saying that we union buddies always stick together to protect our ladies. Just something for you to keep in mind." He crossed his hairy arms over his chest, signifying he was finished speaking.

The spinster hesitated, but recovered quickly. "Well!" she retorted indignantly. "Don't interrupt again unless you have something of substance to add!" Waiting for neither reaction nor response, she turned her attention toward the jurors. "Do the ladies of the jury have any questions?"

Stone-faced, no one replied.

"In that case, I order the jury to retire and deliberate their verdict."

The jurors did not rise; rather they looked to one another inquisitively and began to nod at each another. One of them set her jaw and stood. "Your Honor, we have already reached a verdict!"

"What is your verdict?"

"Guilty!" she cried out. Again the biddies of the audience applauded, and this time the judge and jury joined them. Abruptly the approbation ended, as if the entire proceeding had been well rehearsed—which in truth, it had.

"And what sentence do you recommend?"

"Exile!" exclaimed the juror. "Exile forever!" Again the applause echoed.

"Pardon me!" came a call from the rear of the room, his voice rising to be heard over the din. An uncertain silence descended as all heads turned to see the policeman standing at his seat. Tipping his cap back on his head with the knuckle of a bent index finger and placing his hands on his hips, he inquired innocently, "I was wondering how you ladies were planning on carrying out that sentence."

Seconds ticked away in silence.

He gestured with one hand to the hairy man seated next to him and with the other to the distinguished, olive-skinned gentleman seated in the far corner of the room. "The other courts in town all make their sentences voluntary, you know."

The reminder was not necessary. They knew.

Lips pursed, the spinster regarded the blue-suited man several seconds longer. "And so are ours, of course," she finally admitted.

He touched his fingers to his cap in recognition and sat down, a friendly, satisfied smile on his face.

She shook an angry finger at him. "But see if the decent people of this town are ever caught associating with any of those fallen ladies or those who do!" Again her cheering section cheered, again stopping in unison as if on cue.

With another light tap of the gavel, the spinster added anticlimactically, "This court is adjourned."

\* \* \*

Government returned.

But most of the men of Las Vegas did not quite recognize that it had, especially since it was a much smaller, much simpler government—dramatically simpler, given the absence of the abused, ritualistic legalisms and institutionalized theft that had characterized its predecessor. Consequently, for the first time in history, individual citizens could finally, personally understand the precise role that government had in running their lives, specifically: none. Government was not there either to help them nor to hinder them; it was not a cornucopia to be mined for one's personal gain or a weapon to be wielded to beat down one's opponents. Instead its mission was to strictly restrict itself to defending the rights and property of men. Granted, there were still quibbles over what constituted a "right," and honest men could always come to disagree; but regardless, the seeds of a proper government had been planted, and as the weeks passed they quickly took root and blossomed.

Popular reaction to the coalescing of Eddie's laissez-faire government varied little, with the only differentiating mark being the swiftness with which each group climbed on board. Sitting squarely at the earliest end of that spectrum were the taprooms and brothels; it was no surprise that they were among the first to sing the praises of rights versus responsibilities, and they operated their premises accordingly. In the middle of the spectrum, the common man soon came to realize that he felt himself more secure, knowing that his home was truly his castle, that none could pass his door without his leave, and that there was an unlikely agent ready to help defend that right—his new government. At the far end of the spectrum were the meddling righteous who, outnumbered though they were, continued to voice a shrill insistence that things be done their way. But the vast majority of the citizens of Las Vegas paid the moralists no mind. Men refused to countenance so intolerant a message, or trade their newfound liberty for the unreasonable whims of an unreasoning minority. Grudgingly, the moralists eventually yielded to the inevitable and were compelled to capitulate—although not quietly.

Under the steadying influence of a simple, single body of law, numerous private courts and police services flourished, some providing general assistance, much as the Las Vegas police department did, while others specialized in certain aspects of prevention or enforcement, catering to specific niches of need. But, like having multiple hospitals in the same neighborhood, the men of Las Vegas were richer for it.

Still, not all was sweetness and light in town. An occasional crime still went unsolved, despite the best efforts of the various law enforcement units. An old, penniless widow had been discovered lying unconscious on her porch suffering from malnourishment; now that the social workers had all vanished, no one had noticed her plight until it had become dire. Fist fights still broke out late at night in the shadowed alleyways behind the taprooms, their sodden sands reeking of stale whiskey, vomit, and worse.

There had also been a time—once, to be exact—where an accused man had packed the audience of the courtroom with his own supporters, and against all evidence had been found innocent. Indignation at the miscarriage of justice had quickly swept the town, bringing an angry mob flocking to Eddie's doorstep. Patiently he pointed out how the outcome stemmed not from any flaw in either law or legal procedure, but rather from their own indifference toward the proceedings. What they had in Las Vegas was *self*-government, he reminded them, and that implied that they, them*selves*, must personally become involved in its administration. If other men were able to seize control of the machinery of justice, it was the citizens' own apathy which had let it happen. Chastised, the men of Las Vegas took the episode to heart, and attendance at court functions rose immediately and dramatically, and the more significant the trial, the greater was the number of honest citizens who attended, thus ending the possibility that a second, similar miscarriage of justice might ever occur.

Justice aside, there also remained the possibility that some malicious militia might spontaneously spring from among the citizenry and attempt to take over the town by force, but the geographical remoteness of Las Vegas engendered a strong camaraderie among the populace that encouraged a vigilant cooperation, a feeling fueled by the very-real perception that they were the last remnant of civilization remaining in America. Had they tried, those brutish men who cherished brawn over brain would find no toehold in Las Vegas. The town counted itself lucky to finally be rid of such men, and would damn well not accept their return now.

Despite its scattered failings and plethora of possible pitfalls, life in Las Vegas continued to improve almost exponentially, and as time passed, the citizens of town came to associate their improved lot in life not so much with their almost invisible, minarchist government, but rather with one particular man: Eddie—everyone except Eddie, that is.

## CHAPTER 12 – UNCHAIN MY HEART

The pilot scowled.

Here it was, April 15th, the day he was supposed to leave this stinking valley, yet here he sat. Aruba had beckoned to him, its native women called to him, enticed him with dreams of gold waiting to be well spent, but without warning the promise had been broken—nay, shattered! Instead of sitting on a sun-drenched beach surrounded by mindless pleasures, he found himself sitting among the remote peaks of Colorado behind the bar in *The Golden Touch*.

He had awoken that morning well prepared for his journey south. The last of the distilled spirits, beer kegs, and Richard's consigned wine had been returned to their respective owners the day before; the shelves of *The Golden Touch* were bare and cold. With a smile and without a backward glance, he had shut—and not locked—the door behind him, carrying a single, half-full suitcase containing the few personal items he would need in the new world. Heavy under his clothes was the money vest he had created for himself, with hundreds of tiny pockets sewn into its liner holding thousands of gold and silver coins, several layers deep, their bulk giving him a convincing illusion of plumpness.

He had deliberately arrived at the airstrip several minutes late for his ferry flight, a final act of defiance; but Dwight did not seem to notice or care. He sat at his desk in the expansive administration building filling out some paperwork, and looked up briefly as the pilot entered. The building was airily empty; with the departure of the scab population, the pressure on the valley's housing market had eased immensely and immediately, allowing Dwight to evict the fellow strikers who had shared his headquarters with him these last several months. Even the tents outside had vanished; only the pattern of now-pointless paths which once connected them remained trampled in the grass. And come summer, even that residual trace of the scabs would finally vanish.

"I'm ready for Aruba!" the pilot declared merrily to Dwight's bent back. "Now let's see if Aruba is ready for me!" He slapped his chest flatly with both hands, feeling the heft of the gold that lay hidden beneath.

Unhurried, Dwight made a few more notations on the paper in front of him, then stashed it in a cubbyhole above the desk. He pushed himself back from his work, spinning in his chair to face the pilot, his fingers locked behind his head. "I have some news for you," he began. "Maybe good, or maybe bad, depending."

The pilot did not react; he waited Dwight out, with not so much as a look of apprehension on his face. He refused to give Dwight the satisfaction.

"Fact is, we can't help you leave."

Still, the pilot did not react.

Dwight continued undismayed. "You're a dangerous man, do you know that?"

Cold silence faced him.

"Of all the scabs we've ferried out of here, *you* are the only one who could have any prayer of finding his way back. Tell me you don't know where we are!"

The pilot broke his stony silence. "38.02 degrees north latitude, 107.67 degrees west longitude."

Dwight nodded. "And you know how to fly an airplane, too. You'd be a tough man to keep under wraps, especially since you work for Dr. Floyd."

"But I promised not to reveal the secret!" protested the pilot, finally revealing the emotions that welled up within him. "I even passed Dr. Thomas' damn lie detector test!"

Dwight sighed. "True, but there are folks around here who have played cards with you. Some of them have their doubts about how well the device works on you—Dr. Thomas among them."

The pilot snorted in humorous derision and said nothing.

Dwight sighed again, taking the pilot's response as a confirmation. "That's what I thought," he observed.

"No wonder nobody bought my taproom."

"It was a well-kept secret you'd be staying—and it wouldn't have been proper for any of us to buy it from you under false pretenses."

"What if I tried to leave anyway?"

"Go ahead. Just don't use any of my airplanes."

"Why not rent me one? You can name your price." He slapped his golden gut in demonstration.

"No."

"No? But— Damn it! I need to get the hell out of here!"

"Be that as it may, I am under no obligation to provide you with the time of day, let alone rent you an airplane."

"To Hell with you, buddy!" he snapped. "I don't need your damn airplane anyhow!"

"You don't?" Dwight sounded unconvinced. "Why's that?"

An evil smile creased the pilot's face. "It must have taken a lot of cement trucks coming up here to build this airstrip," he observed, waving a hand theatrically at the tall window. "They'd need a good road, built to last. And that road still has to be out there somewhere!"

Dwight smiled in return. "Oh, it's out there all right—under several feet of snow and all the rockslides and avalanches that have buried it since it was last used... when? Ten years ago? Not to mention the damage Midas did to it once he was finished with it. And it's almost a hundred miles before you come to the first crossroad. That's a long walk, especially for someone who's used to flying such distances. And even if you reached the crossroad, where would you go from there? Everything this side of Washington is pulverized dust! Or were you thinking of heading to California?"

The pilot said nothing.

Dwight leaned back in his chair, hands still behind his head, waiting. The silent seconds slipped by.

Stymied, the pilot finally replied, "Okay, so what am I then? Your prisoner?"

"Oh, no! You're free to go where you like whenever you like. Just don't expect any striker to help you leave the valley; they won't. All the scabs are gone now—except for you, that is—so there'll be no help from that quarter. And I think you've already learned that a philosophy is not as easy to revolt against as a government might be."

"That doesn't leave me many alternatives, does it?"

"You could always take our striker's oath", Dwight pointed out. "In fact, a number of us have wondered why you haven't already done so. In the few months that you've been here, you've seemed to be living up to it in any case."

"Maybe I like to keep my options a little more open", he ventured grudgingly. "Besides, what makes you think I'd want to live here with you Johnnies at all? I've only stayed this long because I've had no other choice! And now you're telling me I'm stuck here forever?"

"No, no, your visit with us won't go on forever," Dwight reassured him, lowering his arms. "At some point in the not-too-distant future, we'll be returning Outside, and our secret will no longer matter. When we do, perhaps I'll sell your old airplane back to you, assuming you can afford it, and you can go to Aruba then. Or wherever you wish—even back to Dr. Floyd. But not today."

The pilot did not reply for over a minute. Finally, flatly, he made one final observation before stalking out the door.

"You bastards," he swore levelly.

# Section IV – The First Months

Mid-1953

# CHAPTER 1 – MONEY

Eddie's brow furrowed.

He had been busily trimming back unruly vegetables in his cafeteria garden and was getting ready to call it a night when the banker intruded, briefcase in hand. Given the late hour, there was no reason to expect any visitors, nor did Eddie usually lock the doors against the possibility. Thanks to his crime prevention and law enforcement efforts, crime in Las Vegas had become almost non-existent, so there was little need for paranoid precautions such as locks. But the lack of evil intent did not preclude a more innocent invasion of privacy, as the banker's unexpected appearance demonstrated.

"I'm sorry, I know it's late," he began without preamble, "but I was heading home and saw your lights were still on, and I needed to speak with you as soon as possible."

Setting aside his clippers, with unfeigned concern Eddie had to ask, "Why? What is it?"

The banker scratched the back of his head as if embarrassed. "Well..." He paused, clearly unsure how to proceed. "I know this is going to sound strange, but... I'm running out of money."

Eddie was perplexed. He wasn't sure he understood what the banker meant. "What? You need a loan?"

"No, no!" The banker laughed nervously. "Nothing like that!" He grew instantly somber again. "No, the problem is that there's no more money."

Eddie considered the statement, but was none the wiser. "What do you mean, no more money?"

"Just that!" replied the banker, becoming more agitated. "There's no money!" He pulled back a little, then corrected himself. "Not *no* money. Not yet. But we're running dangerously low."

"Low? Low on money?"

"On cash! We're running out of cash at the bank. Dollar bills, fives, tens, twenties. We're running out."

"Ah." While he understood the answer, he still did not grasp the significance of the banker's plight, and his continued lack of understanding reflected itself in his hesitant questioning. "Running out, you say?"

"Yes! Running out! The bank's rules call for a minimum amount of currency to be on hand at all times, and today my bank fell below that line." He set his briefcase down and gestured at it with one hand. "I just closed the books on the month, and discovered we've fallen below the required minimum."

Eddie nodded. Now he was beginning to understand.

"Ordinarily when this sort of thing happens, I just wire the main office in New York City and a couple of days later an armored car brings in what we need. But today..." He trailed off with a shrug. "There's no New York City—or anyplace else, it would seem! I'm on my own out here and I don't know what to do! You've helped solve a lot of other big problems here in town, so I figured I'd come talk to you first."

"I see," he said.

The banker literally wrung his hands. "Do you realize what will happen to me if someone comes in to make a withdrawal and I don't have the cash? Panic! That's what!" His eyes went wide, looking like some madman in a Saturday matinee. "A flood of people will be pounding on my door wanting all their deposits! I'll have to close down! It could wipe me out!"

Eddie nodded again. As the implications sank in, his eyes widened in unconscious imitation. "And it won't stop with you! It'll—"

"You're absolutely right!" interrupted the banker in a panicked voice. "People will lose faith in the entire system! Once my doors close, they'll flock to my competitor, then suck him dry, too! He'll follow me down the drain! I don't know what the situation is with respect to his own minimum requirements, but it's certain he only has so much cash on hand himself. We're the only two banks in town, both trapped on the same sinking ship, and at some point he's sure to face the same crisis. Why, he could be balancing his own books right now and wondering how to avert the same prospect of a run on his own bank!"

Scores of questions were boiling up in Eddie mind. He opened his mouth as if to say one thing, but stopped himself. He began again: "You're right. This is serious." He glanced around the cafeteria, then back to the banker. "Why don't we go someplace more comfortable where we can sit down and figure out what to do?"

"Please!"

He led the banker out of the cafeteria and across the brightly-lit, cavernous waiting room of the Transcontinental station, their lonely footsteps echoing hollowly, then down the long, slowly-sloping tunnel that led to the train platforms. Only a few scattered overhead bulbs illuminated the dim track area against the dark night, but gleaming waves of light streamed from the windows of the *Meteor's* observation car, a fiery orange ambiance that washed over the platform with cheerful warmth. They mounted the stairs at the squared end of the car and entered.

The banker had never been aboard the *Meteor* before, and he was taken aback by the unbelievable opulence of its observation car. From stem to stern it exuded luxury, starting with the polished brass doorknob set in a finely-lacquered mahogany door at its entrance, right on through to the shiny, curving brass railing of its rear balcony. They trod upon luxurious burgundy carpeting adorned with abstract patterns resembling leafy, golden vines. Along the walls, the wainscoting was dark mahogany with intricate inlays of silver birds nesting in golden vines; the upper wall was regularly punctuated with wide, tinted windows curtained and valenced in the same burgundy-and-gold motif. Between each pair of windows protruded a brass, two-armed lighting fixture in the style of an old-fashioned gas lamp in the same leaf-and-vine theme; each arm sported a raised, translucent-orange crystalline globe with a sparkling electric light burning within. On one wall of the near end of the car, a sizeable mirror ornately framed in carved mahogany vines was hung behind a polished mahogany bar with four tall barstools of the same dark wood uniformly positioned in front. Along the opposite wall sat a similarly-ornate, glass-fronted hutch filled with sparkling crystal glassware and gleaming ivory-colored dishes; it was flanked by a small, cubical refrigerator on the near side and a low server with an empty wine rack underneath on the other. The center of the car was dominated by a round mahogany table covered by an intricately crocheted tablecloth that almost reached its diameter; at its hub sat a tall lead crystal vase containing orchids native to the region—spotted coralroot—with the long, pointed petals of its pastel purple flowers tinged with spots of burgundy, and stems of the same deep reddish-brown as the walls. Four mahogany chairs sat at the compass points of the table; centered above it was a massive brass chandelier of many globes, in the same style as the wall lamps, hanging from a vaulted ceiling that ran the entire length of the car, an arched, golden surface that reflected soft, indirect lighting. Beyond the table was a sitting area, with a maroon, velvet-covered couch stretching along one wall and two overstuffed velvet wing-back chairs positioned along the other; a small, round table sat between them, its surface shielded by a crocheted doily of a pattern similar to that of the table's. A long, low-slung coffee table was positioned between chairs and couch, but closer to the couch, its polished surface bare. Beyond them was an expansive carpeted area running halfway to the base of a curved brass railing that was adorned with brass vines and bellied outward into space at the very end of the car; the arched ceiling bent down from above to shade it, its rounded edge aligned precisely above the curve of the railing. Midway between the sitting area and the railing, where the carpet ended, were glass-paned, folding mahogany doors that were collapsed, for the moment, against either wall, leaving the interior of the car open to the warm Nevada night. Beyond the railing he could see ruler-straight tracks disappearing to a vanishing point far out of town in the dark desert. The banker's head turned left and right as he took in the lavish magnificence, his mouth agape. The predominant thought in his mind was, *I'm jealous!* Aloud, he remarked, "This is fabulous! You live here?"

"It's my living room," he admitted. "I cook and sleep in the sleeper car next door."

"Is that car anything like this one?" he asked, the awe plain in his voice.

"Oh, no! That one is standard Transcontinental rolling stock. This one is a VIP car. I picked it up before I left San Francisco a few months back. There was a lot of fighting there, and I was worried it might get damaged. So I had them couple it to the end of the *Meteor* and brought it with me."

"Good thing you did," marveled the banker. "It's a beauty!"

"Thank you," he replied as he gestured to one of the velvet chairs. He took the other himself. "Getting back to your problem, I appreciate your confidence in my abilities, but I'm not sure there's anything I can do about currency shortages."

The banker set his briefcase on the floor, taking the indicated seat. "Well, at least we can talk it out and see if maybe we can come up with a few ideas."

"Again, I'm not so sure. Where could you possibly get more money?"

"Maybe we could print more?" the banker suggested weakly. "At least that was one idea I had."

Eddie considered it only briefly. "I'm not sure there's a printer in town who could handle that sort of a job."

The banker sighed. "You're probably right. Now that you mention it, I know for a fact there's not. And it's not just finding the printer, you'd need that special linen paper, too—and even regular paper is difficult enough to come by these days. The town newspaper went out of business almost a year ago because they couldn't get enough paper."

Eddie had known that no newspaper circulated in town, but he had not known why. "How about coins? Can you mint more?"

The banker slowly shook his head. "There's nothing to mint. There used to be a number of silver mines not too far out of town, but they all closed down. Between the taxes and regulations, they were far too expensive to run. And even if we could mint more, who would want to carry around pounds and pounds of coins all the time?"

They fell silent, thinking, and the minutes dragged by. "Checks!" the banker cried suddenly. "People can write checks!"

"Against what? There's no money!"

"Against their balances! We can use book entries to keep track of everything, and people can use their personal checks as currency."

"But there's no money behind the balances!"

The banker dismissed his objection with the wave of a hand. "That doesn't matter; I've never had a one hundred percent reserve for my demand deposits here, even though the bank did when you added up the cash in all our branch offices. Bank rules allow for a certain degree of latitude, so a book entry accounting system would be business as usual as far as everyone is concerned. If I tell a man he has money in the bank, he'll believe me."

This time it was Eddie who dismissed the thought. "Writing checks may stave off the current crisis for a little while, but it won't work for very long. You'll still reach a point where people will want cash, and that'll trigger your panic."

The banker sighed. "You're right, I suppose." He pulled at his chin pensively. "If only there were a way to convince people to accept script rather than real money, or poker chips instead of solid coins."

"It would be a sad day for this country if that were to ever happen," Eddie lamented solemnly.

The banker laughed dryly, a discordant counterpoint to Eddie's serious demeanor. "As if it isn't already a sad day for the country!" He shook his head in dismay.

Silence descended on the two men again, and lengthened into several minutes.

"You know...," Eddie began carefully, as if the thought hadn't quite taken shape in his own mind yet. He sat up straight, stared piercingly at the banker, and began again with confidence. "You know, there *is* a way to have enough currency to go around."

"How? We can't print it. We can't mint enough of it. We can't bring in more. Where else would you get it?"

"We already have it!" He reached into his pocket and pulled out a handful of coins. He shook them in his palm, the motion producing the pure, clear clinking of silver coin on silver coin. "We can use these!"

The banker scrunched up his face, not understanding. "But... But that's the problem! We don't have enough currency, coins included!"

"No! Not currency *and* coins! Just the coins!"

The look on the banker's face plainly revealed that he was not following.

"Look here," commanded Eddie, holding up a quarter. "How much is this worth?"

Still confused, the banker ventured uncertainly, "A quarter?" He felt silly naming it.

"All right..." He dug into his pocket for his wallet, opened it, and produced a dollar bill. "And how much is this worth?"

Plainly still at sea, the banker ventured. "A dollar?"

"Ah! But it doesn't have to be, does it? "

"If a dollar's not worth a dollar, then what *is* it worth?"

"I couldn't say for sure off the top of my head, but for the sake of argument, let's say it's worth ten quarters."

"But ten quarters are worth two-fifty!"

"No! Let me say it again: it doesn't have to be!"

The banker fidgeted irritably in his plush chair. "A quarter's not worth a quarter, and a dollar's not worth a dollar? What nonsense!" There was a frustrated edge to his voice.

Eddie could see that he wasn't piercing the banker's long-ingrained monetary prejudices, so he tried a different tack. "All right, let's start over again. What problem are we solving here?"

"We're running out of currency," the banker replied immediately and impatiently.

"And why is that a problem?"

"Because we're running out of currency!" he replied testily. "People will panic!"

"No, no! That's not what I mean. Let me rephrase the question: *Why* do you run out of currency?"

Subsiding somewhat, the banker thought for a moment, then sighed. "In theory, it could be for any of a number of reasons: old bills wear out, people hoard them, they get lost or destroyed, the economy grows and needs more money in circulation, things like that. But in this case, the culprit is obvious: inflation! More and more dollars have been chasing fewer and fewer goods for years. I've needed currency infusions every couple of months ever since Directive 289-10 went into effect. And it's been getting worse."

Eddie shook his head patiently. "I know all that. But you're still thinking of the physical paper—but what about money itself?"

"The money itself?" he echoed, not understanding.

"The money itself," he agreed. "This..." He held up the dollar bill. "...is not 'money,' is it?" When the banker did not respond, he stretched it out stiffly, pinching it at both ends between thumb and finger. "Here, read the fine print. It says, 'This certifies that there is on deposit in the Treasury of the United States of America one dollar in silver payable to the bearer on demand.' In other words, this paper is a debt, isn't it? It's not really money at all."

"Money is debt?" The unusual thought penetrated slowly. "I guess in some queer manner of thinking, money could be considered debt." He paused, then asserted with more confidence, "Yes, it is. Money is debt."

"No, no! Not the money... The *paper* is the debt! It's a promissory note, a warehouse receipt, or whatever you want to call it, but it's not 'money.' The actual money is in the Treasury of the United States—this paper even says so! And isn't that the root of our problem? That the debt this paper represents cannot be paid off? No one can go to Washington and convert this piece of paper into a silver dollar, now can they?"

"No, of course not. Not these days."

"So it was the United States Treasury that issued the debt, not you. But as the banker, you're the one left holding the bag, aren't you?"

The banker impatiently fidgeted almost pointedly and replied huffily. "What are you saying here? That I should be the one responsible for paying off that debt?"

"No! Why should you? It's not your debt! It's the United States Treasury's debt. But apparently there's no United States Treasury any longer, is there?"

Red-faced with anger, the banker repeated sternly, "Are you saying we should repudiate that debt? Not accept currency? I won't hear of it!"

"But it's not your debt!"

"But we must honor it!"

"You can't! Do you have the silver to exchange for it?"

"No, of course not!"

"Then what is it you must do?" Eddie waited expectantly for the answer, but none was forthcoming. He still had not pierced the banker's stubborn knowledge. Taking a deep breath, he decided to try again from yet another point of view. "All right. Think of it this way: if all trade was handled by barter, a currency shortage wouldn't be a problem, would it?"

Gruffly, the banker replied, "No, of course not. You wouldn't need currency at all."

"If all trade was handled by silver or gold coin, currency still wouldn't be a problem, would it?" he pressed.

The banker remained silent for a moment, his fingers drumming lightly on his cheek. He was finally starting to see a glimmer of where Eddie was leading. "No. It wouldn't," he replied slowly, a little more reasonably.

"In other words, we don't so much have a currency problem." He let the words sink in. "Unbacked debt is the real problem here, isn't it?"

Several seconds passed. "I see," he said finally, his gaze slowly slipping off to one side as he became lost in thought. His fingers continued to drum his cheek. "I see!" he repeated a little more firmly, staring at the carpet.

"Then the solution to this crisis is obvious, isn't it?"

Eddie could almost hear the gears turning in the banker's head. Presently, the drumming fingers stopped. The man understood.

Looking back up to Eddie, he warned darkly, "People will howl!"

"Some will. But most won't, not once they understand. And they won't panic."

Seconds passed as gears continued to turn. "No. Not panic." The banker nodded. "Some of them will surely get angry—especially the ones without any coins!—but the percentage of coins is probably insignificant in comparison anyway." He chuckled, adding, "Except the casinos. They stock lots of coins." The banker sat in silence for another moment considering, then stood up abruptly, grabbed his briefcase, and strode swiftly across the carpeted floor to take a seat on the couch. He tossed the briefcase onto the empty coffee table and popped it open. "All right, I'm with you now. I see where you're going. But the devil will definitely be in the details of exactly *how* we're going to pull this one off." He rifled around inside the briefcase for a moment. "I have all the numbers right here," he asserted, pulling out a sheaf of ledger paper. He let it plop onto the table and fanned out the pages with one hand.

Eddie could see they were filled with numbers written in a neat script of varying hand.

The banker held up a bound booklet. "I also have with me the supposed net worth of the bank as of the last annual report, but it's a tangled mess." He dropped it onto the table on top of the papers. "Unfortunately, it carries the cost of administering Directive 289-10, the Equalization of Opportunities Bill, and a lot of insane local directives as well. Given our current political climate..." He swept an arm across the documents. "...it's all junk. But the raw data is still in there somewhere, and we can use that to help us implement your scheme."

Eddie leaned back in his chair and eyed the splayed material warily, contemplatively rubbing a temple. He could see it was going to be a long night.

\* \* \*

The clock chimed four in the morning.

Wearily, the banker pushed himself back from the round mahogany table. The tablecloth and orchids had been set aside, and the table was instead covered with scattered papers heaped in disorderly piles, and the papers themselves covered with long columns of calculations annotated with circles and arrows, sometimes accompanied by an occasional paragraph. "That's it, then?"

Eddie had strength enough to nod, but none he felt he could spare for speech.

"Good! Based on the numbers we have here and on our extrapolations of my competitor's share of the town's business, I think we have a reasonably good estimate of how much money there is in circulation, how much of it is coins, and how much is paper money. Assuming we exchange all the paper in town for coins, we'll have to devalue the paper ninety-seven point three-three percent to make things balance out. Call it three cents on the dollar. Assuming everyone cashes in their paper currency, that should keep the net worth of the town's money supply roughly the same while completely eliminating the paper currency."

Weary though he was, Eddie marveled in wonder at the audacious gambit they were plotting. Eschewing paper currency in favor of commodity-backed barter would be a revolutionary transformation. His amazement burst to the surface. "Everything is going to change! Prices... Wages... It'll affect the whole economy!"

The banker nodded. "But at the same time it'll stay the same, too. Only the numbers will change. All we do is just multiply current values by three percent across the board, eliminate the paper bills, and retain the face value of the coins. If something cost a dollar before, it'll cost three cents afterwards. Likewise, if you're getting paid a dollar an hour for your wage, it'll drop to three cents an hour. It's all proportional." He pondered the idea for a moment, then added, "You know, we couldn't even consider doing this sort of changeover unless we were isolated from the rest of the nation." He chuckled dryly. "Count your blessings!"

Ignoring the aside, Eddie eyed him wearily. "Will the bank have enough coins to buy back all your deposits?"

"Easily! I have lots of coins in storage—prices have been so high lately that there's been a lot less demand for them, so they tend to pile up. Once we make the changeover, I'll be in a good position to lend money and still hold a one hundred percent reserve on all my demand deposits—and I'll make a pretty penny on it, too, if you'll pardon the pun."

Eddie ignored the banker's attempt at humor; he had never been a fan of puns. "How long will the changeover take?"

The banker considered the question. "If our population estimates are correct, it would take days just for people to line up at the tellers' windows and exchange their outstanding paper for coins. But there's no reason why that should slow us down. We just flip the switch whenever we're ready and buy back the outstanding paper at people's convenience. In fact I expect that the paper will continue to circulate for some time before it finally falls by the wayside. So long as the exchange rate remains relatively stable, there's no hurry. And since it'll be the bank doing the exchanging, we'll make sure the rate remains steady."

"Doesn't that mean that there'll have to be two prices for everything?"

"Yes, that's true. One price for things bought or sold with coins, another price for paper. But the three-to-one-hundred ratio will stay fixed, so it won't be so difficult to calculate. People will get used to it pretty quickly. You'll see."

"That'll be a pretty big drop in prices. Won't some things end up costing less than a penny?"

The banker fixed his gaze on Eddie. "How much is a pack of chewing gum? Or a candy bar?"

"Fifty cents at least, these days. Usually more."

"It'll be one or two cents once we're through. So where's the problem? Name something that costs less than a quarter."

Seconds passed. "I can't," he admitted.

"The lowly penny will make a comeback. Money will be worth something again." With a chuckle, he added, "And no one will need to carry around pounds and pounds of coins."

"What happens to the money in people's bank accounts?"

"Three for a hundred, the same as any paper asset. If something is not coin or commodity-backed one-for-one, its days are numbered." He smiled. "*Re*-numbered, I should say!"

Again, Eddie ignored the witticism. "And the bank will keep a stockpile of coins, then, just like you've stockpiled paper currency?"

"Indeed. The coins are the money and the money is the coin. Fractional reserve currencies will become a thing of the past—in fact, it'll be impossible. There'll be no more debt as money."

Eddie nodded. Being a banker sure made certain things much easier to accomplish. That thought triggered another: "How about your competitor? Do we need to let him know what we have planned?"

"We don't have to, but we should. Once we make our announcement, he'll have to toe the line. Otherwise he'll see a run on coins as people try to sneak in under the wire using the existing one-to-one ratio. If he's worth anything as a banker—and I'm not too sure that he is, mind you!—he'll realize the score. So we should tell him. It'll make our job of convincing the citizens that much easier if we can present a unified front." The banker hesitated uneasily. "But I'm not too sure he'll agree to help."

Overlooking the significance of that admonition, a weary Eddie took a long, tired breath and shifted the subject. "So when do we make the changeover?"

"Soon, that's for sure! There's no telling when we'll run out of paper currency, and we want the transition to be as orderly as possible. It would make things that much more difficult for everyone if a panic were to set in first. And it could get ugly. People can get pretty touchy when it comes to money, believe me!"

Eddie nodded absently; he was still only half listening to the answers. Rather, he was thinking ahead and trying to determine what the impact would be upon Transcontinental. He knew they had a good deal of cash in the station's basement vault to fund their daily operations, and a substantial portion of that was, out of necessity, in coin. In the days when trains regularly roamed the rails of the nation, Transcontinental station agents routinely made change when travelers purchased tickets. But he had no idea how much coin was on hand today—if any.

Shaking himself out of his reverie, he repeated his question. "Pardon me, I was woolgathering. When did you say the changeover would occur?"

"Well, I guess I didn't say." The banker thought for a moment before replying. "We'll need to speak with my competitor first, and that can't be done until at least tomorrow morning—later this morning, I should say!" He hesitated, still deep in thought. "Maybe we can change over tomorrow sometime?" he ventured. He thought a moment longer, then continued. "On second thought, to keep it simple we should do it while the banks are closed. That means the earliest we can make the changeover is tomorrow night." Nodding, he declared, "Let's do that, then. Tomorrow night it is. What do you think?"

"Can we do it that quickly?"

"We have to. And the sooner, the better. We don't want a panic, do we?"

Eddie considered a moment, then replied, "All right. But how do we get the news to the people? There's no newspaper or radio, and there's not much time."

"Good question! Handbills? Posters? A town crier?"

The look on Eddie's face was one of shocked concern. "You can't just hang up posters that say, 'We're devaluing your money!' We'd have to be a little more tactful than that."

The banker nodded. "You're right. We should probably tell them in person, convene a big town meeting, explain the situation, and let them ask questions. We can hold the meeting tomorrow after the banks close, the same time we make the changeover. At sunset, let's say."

"All right. But how do we get people to show up for the meeting?"

The banker laughed. "You underestimate your own importance, sir! Trust me. All it would take would be to have your name attached to it, and most men would come. You can call it a 'critically important town meeting' or something alluring like that. But you're right, it has to be done diplomatically—and above all, it has to be kept secret until the meeting. Not a word of this to anyone except you, me, and my competitor!"

"Of course not."

* * *

The tumblers fell.

The stationmaster hauled the huge, circular vault door open, its massive bulk swinging smoothly on thick, expertly-oiled hinges. He stepped inside the confined, cubical room and flicked a light switch, revealing tall racks of large stainless steel drawers along all three walls. Eddie followed him inside and pulled open one of the drawers; it was full of neat bundles of cash.

"And you know exactly how much is here?"

"Down to the penny, Mr. Eddie, to the penny!" In demonstration of his confidence, he reached behind him without looking and pulled open another drawer; it was full of small cylinders of rolled pennies. He smiled without a glance at the pennies and bumped the drawer closed with his elbow. "Back when we still ran trains, we used the money down here to keep our cash registers stocked. These days we only use it to cover the pay rolls."

"Do you know how much of it is in coins?"

The stationmaster hesitated. "In coins? Nope, can't say. Never bothered to keep track of the coins separately. All I know is the total dollar value."

"If you didn't keep track of the value of your coins, how would you know when you needed more of them?"

He pointed to the closed penny drawer. "When a drawer started running low, we sent someone to the bank to get more. When it got too full, we sent some back. I just kept track of the difference."

Eddie opened and closed a few more drawers at random, then faced the stationmaster. "I'm going to need an accurate count of the value of all our coins as soon as you can."

"The coins? How come?"

Eddie hesitated. "I hope you won't be offended if I wait until tonight to answer that question."

The stationmaster shrugged. "I was just asking."

"Let's get back upstairs to your office. There's something else that needs to be done right away." He flipped off the light and sealed the massive door. As he followed the stationmaster to the stairs, a tall rack of complex electronic equipment caught Eddie's eye. Its broad face was studded with jeweled indicator lights, calibrated knobs, rows of toggle switches and cryptically-labeled meters. The indicator lights were all dark; the meters registered nothing.

Curious, Eddie stopped to examine the equipment. "What's this?"

The stationmaster halted, one foot on the first step. "Oh, that? It's a transmitter from the town's old commercial radio station. They stopped broadcasting about a year ago when the owner disappeared unexpected-like. Been sitting there ever since."

"Does it work?"

"I guess so. At least it used to, before the owner vanished. And the tower is still there, out on the western side of the rail yard."

Eddie nodded. He had seen the tall radio tower many times, but had not given it any thought. To him it was nothing more than another seldom-noticed feature of the landscape.

"Do you know how it works?"

The stationmaster shook his head. "No, not in the sense of what all those buttons and knobs do. But I do know a couple of things. Back when they were still on the air I used to get calls to come down here and adjust the power level or turn it back on after a lightning strike would blow the breakers. Things like that. Uncomplicated things."

"Is there a microphone for it?" he asked eagerly, realizing that this might be just the vehicle for getting word out about the town meeting.

"No, no microphone or anything else here. They had a cable from their studio that would feed the signal directly."

"Where's the studio?"

Again, the stationmaster shook his head. "Burned down, Mr. Eddie, same time as when the owner disappeared. Lots of people think he did it himself then skipped town. Other folks suspect foul play. But who really knows? Who is John Galt?"

Deflated, Eddie's shoulders fell. He stared at the dark indicators and lifeless meters a moment longer, before turning to go. They ascended the steps and headed for the stationmaster's office behind the ticket booths. Once they arrived, Eddie informed him, "I'll need the help of you and your men to prepare a stack of posters and hang them up around town. And it needs to be done right away."

"Posters? About what?"

Eddie handed him a scrap of paper. "Here's what they should say. Make the letters big and dark so you can recognize them from a distance."

The stationmaster scanned the text twice, then looked up at Eddie from under his eyebrows. "A big town meeting? Tonight? What's this all about, Mr. Eddie?"

Again, Eddie hesitated. "If you don't mind, we can talk about that tonight, too."

The stationmaster gestured with the scrap of paper. "Before or after this meeting?"

Uncomfortably, not trusting himself to fabricate an answer, Eddie turned and left.

* * *

The stationmaster wondered.

The mindless activity of drawing up and hanging scores of posters around the town left the stationmaster with plenty of leftover brain power to consider what might be a possible topic for the upcoming town meeting. He was an intelligent man, but prone to a lack of initiative, a fortuitous combination which had originally secured him his lofty position as stationmaster. His superiors from the old days preferred such men; it dramatically reduced the chances of him interfering in their political scheming while allowing him to participate meaningfully—if only as their pawn. But his eyes were none the less seeing for not being self-directed, his mind none the less experienced and wise for being impassive.

He sat in his office with nothing else to do, waiting vacantly for the end of his workday still hours hence, wondering what could possibly be on the agenda for the grand gathering that evening. There was no information available to him other than what appeared on the posters, and that was sparse indeed; no one had the slightest clue what Mr. Eddie planned to talk about, least of all the stationmaster. Many was the man who had stopped him in his assignment of hanging the posters to ask what it was all about. Truthfully he had answered how he was just as much in the dark as everyone else. *Perhaps that had been Mr. Eddie's intent?* he wondered. An honest ignorance was difficult to feign; an unknown secret was impossible to spill.

The meeting was not the only mystery the stationmaster had on his mind. What could possibly have triggered Mr. Eddie's interest in the coins in the vault? Did he suspect thievery? The stationmaster and Mr. Eddie were the only people in town who knew the vault's combination, and since he knew *he* hadn't stolen any company money, it stood to reason that no one had. Besides, if there had been a theft, it would be more logical to steal those neat bundles of cash, not the heavy coins. Given that they were so much less valuable, what, then, was his interest in the coins? For not the first time that day, he shook his head ruefully. He could not figure it out.

His intuition told him that somehow the two mysteries were related. It was far too much of a coincidence that both undertakings came out of nowhere together, then needed to be completed by the same deadline—at which time Mr. Eddie promised to reveal all. The tasks were too tightly tied in time to be unrelated. *What is it about pennies that made for a "critically important town meeting,"* he pondered. Why was it important to know how many pennies were in the vault? Why not how many bills? What could be so critically important about knowing how many pennies you had, but not how many dollar bills? *Unless the coins were more valuable than the bills?* he pondered. He laughed to himself. Under what outrageous condition could metal money possibly hold more value than paper money? What could make mere pennies more valuable than real money? He almost tossed the question aside as unworthy of thought, when with a start he realized exactly what that condition was: *There's something wrong with the bills!* Without break, his mind leapt forward again. *There's a counterfeiter out there! And the big meeting tonight is to make the announcement!* He nodded to himself. It all made sense. Mr. Eddie had been working with the police quite a lot lately, and now they were working together on this problem as well. Someone was counterfeiting, for sure.

Curious, he fished his wallet from his pocket, pulled out the not-so-modest wad of cash he routinely carried with him, and examined each bill carefully. If any of them were counterfeit, he could not tell. He halted abruptly at a thought: *If I can't tell... then neither can anyone else!* Needlessly glancing left and right conspiratorially, he nervously secreted the stack of bills back in his wallet. He glanced at his desk clock; it was early afternoon. The banks were still open.

He pocketed his wallet and headed for the door.

\* \* \*

Eddie tried.

After ordering the posters be put up, he had gone to pay a visit to the banker's competitor. True to the banker's prediction, his competitor took a completely different point of view of the potential crisis.

"Who, me? Running low on currency?" He sported a friendly smile that reminded Eddie of a used car salesman. "Son, I started running low months ago."

"Don't your bank rules require you to report it?"

The smile vanished; he eyed him warily. "What's it to you?"

"What happens if you run out of currency?"

He shrugged. "I write IOU's until things balance out again. It wouldn't be the first time."

"But aren't you risking a run on your bank by doing that?"

"Naw. If I tell people they have money in the bank, they'll believe me."

A passing feeling of *déjà vu* ran through Eddie, but he ignored it. "Yes, but only for so long. Shouldn't you do something to shore up your position?"

He tilted his head back and gravely looked down his nose at Eddie. "Son," he began disdainfully, drawing out the word. "I don't tell you how to run your railroad. Don't you tell me how to run my bank."

Eddie strained to make himself understood. "But aren't you worried about a run on your bank?"

"Worried like my goodie-two-shoes competitor, you mean?"

"Like your competitor—yes."

He sighed. "I imagine that's the reason for your visit. He's finally hit the minimums, too, hasn't he?"

"Yes."

The man chortled. "And New York City's not going to be able to bail him out this time, will it?

"No."

"I bet he's not planning to write any IOU's either."

"No. We're going to do something very different than that." Patiently, Eddie began to explain the course of action that they planned to follow, but he never had a chance to finish half his exposition before he was rudely interrupted.

"What?! Eliminate paper currency? What are you, son, crazy? Don't you see that this is our golden opportunity? Uncoupling the currency from gold and silver leaves us in the driver's seat! We'll just print up more dollars any time we need them!"

Eddie was astonished. "But that's inflationary!"

"Why, sure," he replied easily, but his eyes narrowed, watching him suspiciously, as if he were wondering what motive prompted Eddie to make so explicit a statement.

"It reduces the value of everyone's money!"

"Not immediately, it doesn't. Every new dollar I issue is worth the same as everyone else's dollars. But once it gets into circulation, *then* it reduces oh-so-slightly the value of everyone else's dollars. I get the full value; everyone else pays for it."

"But that's theft! An insidious, invisible theft..." Inexplicably, the image of the hollowed core of an old oak tree came to mind, its splintered hulk shattered by lightning. He shook off the thought. "...but theft nonetheless!"

The man leaned back as if he had lost all further interest in the discussion. He waved a hand at Eddie in good-natured dismissal. "Go ahead and try to eliminate dollar bills. I don't care. It won't matter, because people won't go for it."

"What? Why not?"

He leaned forward intently, his eyes bright. "Haven't you studied economics, son? It's a well-known law that bad money drives out the good! It's held true all through history, and why shouldn't it hold true today? If you're going to tell people their dollars are only worth three cents, I guarantee you they won't listen to you—especially when I'm telling them their dollars are worth a hundred cents. It's basic economics!"

Eddie recalled having heard something along the same lines in his studies long ago, but he couldn't help but feel there was some flaw in the man's reasoning; yet he couldn't put his finger on it. Economics could be a tricky science at times, where a conclusion would seem to be absolutely correct when in actuality it was terribly wrong. His intuition told him that this was such a time. "So you won't join us?"

"Son, haven't you been listening? It's *you* who will be forced to join *me!* It's as undeniable as Adam Smith's invisible hand. And who are you to argue with Adam Smith?"

\* \* \*

The teller asked, too.

The stationmaster shook his head. "No, ma'am," he admitted. "Mr. Eddie didn't tell me anything about what he wants to talk about tonight, not a word."

"Well, I figured you might know, seeing how you work for him."

"Nope. I did ask, but he told me he'd tell me tonight, same time as you, and that's the God's honest truth!"

"Well, I'll be there to hear it, believe me! He's really gotten my curiosity up." One at a time, she plopped three canvas bank bags of coins between them on the countertop and managed to push the heavy load only slightly toward him, not even clearing the teller's iron grate. "Here you are, sir, the change you requested." Parenthetically, she added, "And most all of what we had handy. I'd have to go into our vault if you needed any more."

"This will do just fine, thanks."

"And please bring the bags back when you can—there aren't that many of them left."

"I will," he promised. Somewhat clumsily he gathered up the loot in his arms and left.

No one else had been waiting behind him in line, leaving the teller idle for the moment. She had brightened when the stationmaster had first entered the bank; she was certain he would be able tell her all the gossip about the upcoming meeting, but his lack of hard facts was beyond disappointing. He had told her nothing; all he had wanted was silver dollars, three bags full.

The thought gave her pause. *Now that's odd... What could he want with so many?* With a start, she quickly made a mental connection. *If Mr. Eddie's stationmaster is suddenly collecting silver dollars...* She left the thought incomplete, lacking both the ability and knowledge to complete it. But she did not need either knowledge or ability; imagination proved to be more than enough.

She turned to the teller at the window next to hers. "Say, the strangest thing just happened."

"What's that?" she asked eagerly.

"Well! Let me tell you all about it..."

\* \* \*

"The Panic" began.

It started modestly, but gathered steam quickly. At first, it followed the pattern set by the stationmaster. After he had left the bank, the two tellers immediately exchanged not only the cash in their purses for silver dollars but also the entire balance in their modest accounts. By mutual agreement, one teller covered the duties of the other while the first carried her heavy load home. But before the first teller returned to spell her colleague, the word was already out. When she entered the bank, over a dozen people were queued up waiting to convert their savings.

Worse yet, the questionable message of financial uncertainty morphed with each telling, becoming more grandiose by the moment, like the child's game of whispering a common phrase in someone's ear; by the time the message reached the end of the lane, it was horribly garbled. Within the hour, the dictum had transformed from "Transcontinental's stationmaster exchanged some bills for coins" to "Eddie withdrew all his money!" to "The banks have no money!" By the time the second teller had lugged her own haul home and returned to her post, the bank was mobbed. Before long the lines extended out into the street, then around the corners, left and right. Fistfights broke out as people jockeyed for position in the makeshift lines, and still the crowds grew.

When it came to banking, the term "panic" was one not lightly earned, and the word added another chevron to its infamous rank that afternoon. Less than an hour after the stationmaster had walked out of the bank, both of the town's banks were forced to close their doors. There was no more currency. Yet still the crowds grew—as did their anger. With the banks closed, they had only one destination left in mind, one outlet for their fury: Transcontinental Railroad's Las Vegas station.

\* \* \*

The sun set.

The broad boulevard in front of the Transcontinental station was jammed with people. The size of the crowd was difficult to estimate under the fading sky and uneven lighting supplied by the widely-spaced streetlights, but a conservative estimate placed it in the thousands.

Eddie and the banker watched from inside the darkened station behind locked doors. For once, the security precaution seemed prudent. The only other barrier separating the massive gathering from the men hiding inside was a lone hitching rail, its horizontal blockade providing woefully inadequate protection. Eddie knew he couldn't wait too much longer before facing their wrath. Angry though they were, for the moment the crowd retained enough civility not to break down his doors and demand an immediate accounting. They stood not-so-patiently on their side of the rail, touchy and raw, waiting in an edgy sort of mood for Eddie and the banker to appear.

As the two men listened, they could hear the cries from the crowd growing in volume as each person raised their own voice in order to be heard above that of their neighbors, creating a positive feedback that promised to reach a deafening crescendo in a very short while. They could put off facing the crowd no longer. Eddie turned to the banker. "Are you ready?"

The banker nodded gravely. "We practiced our speeches enough. If we're not ready now, we'll never be."

Displaying a confidence he did not feel, Eddie unlocked the door, pushed it open, and stepped outside, the banker close behind. Those nearest the door jumped back in surprise, falling silent. Eerily, the silence rapidly stretched across the crowd in an expanding bubble, as if some powerful wizard had cast a spreading spell stealing their power of speech. Within seconds, the stillness reached the farthest corners of the mob, leaving only the quietest rustle of cloth on cloth as people turned to face Eddie as he stood at the top of the station steps shielded solely by the hitching rail. But the silence only held for a few seconds before being replaced by a broad-based murmuring. Eddie could make out some of the words spoken by those closest to him.

"Look! There he is!"

"That banker fellow, too!"

"He's got a lot of gall coming here, after what he's done!"

"He doesn't look very contrite!"

"And to think we trusted him!"

Eddie surveyed the sea of faces apprehensively. He stood on a square landing at the top of the three steps that led from the sidewalk up to a pair of wide glass doors that were closely flanked by tall, imposing pillars, consigning him and the banker to a narrow stage a scant two feet higher than the crowd. From his modest vantage, the faces seemed endless as they stretched out of sight. The night before, he and the banker had estimated the town held roughly five or six thousand people, and it appeared to him that almost all of the thousands had zeroed in on the station. Eddie swallowed hard and raised a hand for silence. Again, the magic bubble reached across the crowd, stilling their voices.

He lowered his arm. "Thank you all for coming here tonight...," he began nervously, his voice shaking. Irrespective of the quality of its delivery, his speaking was enough to disturb the spell; it shattered. In a heap, a cacophony of angry words were thrown in his face from every direction.

"What did you do with my money!"

"Throw him in jail!"

"How will we eat?"

"Thief!"

This time it took his holding up both his hands in a patting motion to slowly reinstate the spell, and even then, much less effectively. The assembled multitude continued to emit a low growl, but it was uneven, shifting, and widely spread, making it more difficult for him to be heard. He took a deep breath; it would have to do.

"Thank you for coming," he called again as loud as he could, and this time his countrymen grudgingly lent him their ears. But the low growl remained. "I ask that you please hear me out first, then I'll answer your questions as best I can. All right?" He paused, not for effect, but rather because despite all his practice that afternoon, his mind went momentarily blank. He was no public speaker, and even if he were more practiced in the art, he had never before faced such a sea of contempt in his entire life, and its impact on his peace of mind was much more immense than he could ever have imagined. But his pause had an accidental, positive effect on the crowd; as the silence stretched out, many nodded grudgingly in quiet agreement to his unintended question, and others fell silent, giving the man his due. The growling subsided, replaced with a murmuring forbearance.

Buoyed, he recalled his opening line and leapt into the aural opening. In a loud, clear voice, he called out, "I asked you to come here tonight because our town is facing a financial crisis. We have a plan to overcome the crisis, but I'll need your help."

Growls swiftly rose and fell as the mob reacted to his pronouncements. His statement held both menace and promise; it left the crowd curious to hear more.

"What is the crisis?" he asked rhetorically. "The crisis is that the banks are running out of cash on hand. Since we're—" But he wasn't given the chance to complete his sentence. With his frank admission—he meant to say "running low"—the noise level instantly shot up, as if someone had opened the door on a raucous party. Women wailed and angry men shouted. In their midst, others were worriedly discussing his bald revelation among themselves: it was as bad as they had feared. There was no money. They had been wiped out. They were broke; destitute. Their worst fears had been confirmed.

A full fifteen seconds passed before Eddie could even attempt to speak once more, the level of confusion was so pronounced. "Since we're isolated...," he began again; the crowd subsided slowly. "Since we're isolated...," he repeated, then waited, giving the silence a chance to spread before continuing. He did not wait for it to perfect itself.

"Since we're isolated from the rest of the country, we can't bring in more money from out of town, and we don't have the ability to print more. But we do have a solution." He paused to let his words sink in before continuing. The hubbub did not rise appreciably; they were listening now.

"We do have a solution," he repeated firmly, "And no one will lose any money. Do you hear me?" A clamor began to rise again, but Eddie shouted over it. "No one will lose any money!" he bellowed, but the din swallowed his words. As their meaning finally took hold, a mixed bag of phrases reached his ears.

"Oh, thank God!"
"Yeah, sure!"
"Who's he fooling?"
"How does he plan to do that!"
"Quiet! Give the man a chance!"
"Haw, haw, haw!"
"With the banks closed?"

When the clamor subsided somewhat, he loudly repeated one more time, "No one will lose any money!" The voices became subdued. He had their attention again, and their tacit approval; it was news they had wanted to hear, even if most did not yet believe him. He proceeded cautiously.

"Our plan calls for us to return to a system of sound money..." He paused to let his words sink in, and for the first time since he had begun speaking, the crowd did not react unreasonably. Somewhat lifted by their reaction, he continued with some measure of confidence. "Sound money! We will return to the sound money of silver and gold coins. That means that starting tonight, the value of the coins in your pocket will tretrigenuple!"

To a man, the silent crowd stared at him blankly. Behind him, the banker hissed, "I *told* you no one would understand!"

Eddie waved him off and tried again. "Starting tonight, the coins in your pocket will multiply in value thirty-three times over!"

The crowd buzzed again, only this time there was no menace in the sound—disbelief, incredulity, and surprise, yes; but no menace. The words had their desired effect. Eddie and the banker momentarily met each other's glance; the message that passed between them was: *it worked!* In crafting the wording of their speech that afternoon, they had reasoned that it would be easier to sell the populace on multiplying the value of their coins rather than presenting their plan as a mammoth drop in the value of their paper script. But it amounted to the same thing mathematically, regardless of how it might be presented. Human nature was a peculiar thing, and not always pervious to logic.

The excited buzz faded, and Eddie continued. "By multiplying the value of your coins thirty-three times over, the total value of money in circulation will remain the same, but to do that successfully, only coins can circulate. Let me say that again: starting tomorrow morning, only coins will circulate! That will let us eliminate paper money entirely. The money shortage will vanish, because we won't need paper cash any longer."

The sheer absurdity of his statement set the crowd into a riotous frenzy. Many were angry, thinking that they were being played for a fool. Others laughed, taking his words as a joke. A very few nodded their heads in understanding, but the vast majority still had no idea exactly what it was that was being proposed. If it had taken the throng a long time to quiet down before, it was dwarfed by their reaction to his outrageous scheme. Eddie held both hands up pleading for silence, but it was long in coming. Minutes passed before the crowd raggedly ran down, and even then, not completely so. Four times Eddie began to speak before he finally reclaimed their attention.

"That's the plan. Tomorrow morning when the bank opens, your paper money will be purchased at a rate of three cents for each paper dollar. To make things balance out throughout the economy, the cost of all goods and services must also be multiplied by three percent. That means that something which costs a dollar today will cost three cents tomorrow morning. If you earned one hundred dollars a day today, you'll be earning three dollars a day tomorrow."

"Says who!" a loud voice called out. Eddie recognized the butcher from the south side of town.

The banker stepped forward, placing a restraining hand lightly on Eddie's arm. "Let me answer this," he whispered, then in a loud voice, he shouted, "Says *you*, that's who!" Silence met his words. "Nobody is going to force anyone to do this. But I'm telling you tonight that *I'm* going to do it! I run my bank my way, and starting right now I'm not doing business in paper money any longer. If you want to do business with my bank, you'll do it in coin. I don't care what you do with other people." He paused, taking in the eye of the crowd. "Who among you doesn't think it's the end of the line for paper money in Las Vegas?"

"I don't!" shouted another voice. "You're not the only bank in town!" It was the banker's competitor. He pushed his way through the throng, demanding, "Step aside! Let me through! Get the hell out of my way!" He vaulted over the hitching rail and bounded up the three stairs onto the impromptu stage. He turned to face the multitude. "Let them keep their outrageous scheme!" he bellowed. "We don't want it! My bank will open tomorrow morning and your dollars are more than welcome—at a hundred cents on the dollar, too!" He waved a hand in dismissal at the two men standing at his side. "Let these commoners count their pennies. You and I will count our dollars!" The crowd burst into applause, but a sizeable minority voiced a counter-demonstration of disapproval.

Eddie held up his hands in supplication. By now the throng had learned the rules; they knew his gesture meant that he wanted to speak, and they raggedly obliged him. Once he had acquired sufficient silence, he gestured toward the newcomer and warned, "You should all know something: this man does not have enough cash to continue operating a bank, and that he hasn't had enough cash on hand for months! He has been risking your deposits. And now he's telling you he wants even more of your deposits! Yet his bank also had to close its doors today. He is out of cash. He told me so himself! I want him to tell us what's going to happen to his customers now that he's run out of cash!" He turned to face his nemesis. "Well? What will you do? How will you solve this crisis? Where will you find more cash?"

"Become my customer," he roared to the crowd, arms open wide, the used-car salesman smile on his face, "and find out!"

Scattered cheers and catcalls could be heard. It wasn't clear who was being lauded or damned.

Eddie turned to face the assembled citizenry once more. "He hasn't any cash! If you deposit your money with him, it's likely to vanish! Solid coins are the only way to protect your savings. Paper currency—"

He was interrupted by a burly man not far from the stage. "Hey! I got a question for your banker friend!" he hollered. "I took all my savings out of your bank today, thousands of dollars. What happens if I deposit it back?"

"You'll get three cents in coin for each paper dollar, same as everyone else."

Interrupting in turn, his competitor retorted, "You can deposit it in my bank, dollar for dollar!"

A woman cried out angrily, "I couldn't get my money out before you closed! What happened to it?" It wasn't clear which banker she was addressing.

"You'll get it all when I open tomorrow," the competitor cried back.

"You'll get three cents in coin for every dollar you have on deposit with me," the banker cried back.

"That's theft!" she screamed.

"But, lady! What would you have me do?" pleaded the banker. "There's not enough cash in all Las Vegas to give everyone their deposits back. That's what made this a crisis!" He pointed to the butcher. "Shall I refuse to give him any cash at all, just so you can get yours?" He pointed to the burly man. "Should I confiscate his deposit, just to give you your withdrawal? Rob Peter to pay Paul? What, then, happens to poor Peter?" He pointed at his competitor. "Come tomorrow morning, that's exactly

175

what *he's* going to do! He's going to take your deposits and use them for someone else's withdrawal! Would you have me write IOU's—like he'll have to do!—then let you find out they're worthless once my bank fails from a lack of capital? Is that what you want? Madam, my honesty will not permit me to become a thief! The only way we can survive as a town, the only way we can keep our economy alive, is to burn all the old currency and shift to solid, safe, silver coins!"

A smattering of applause and cheers came from around the crowd. Slowly, more of the townsfolk were being won over. But there was still a long way to go.

Eddie took center stage once again. "Let me remind you that whether you took out your money today or not, it's all worth the same thing: three solid pennies per paper dollar. We're all in this together, and if we stay together, we can ride this out. I think the best way for you to understand how it will turn out is to let it run its course. As the banker says, you don't have to do this. But if you don't, I'm warning you that your paper money will soon be worthless. And if you do, your money will still be worth the same it was worth this morning, except that you won't be an easy victim to the first looter that comes blathering down the pike." Unconsciously he spread his arms, apparently gesturing to the banker's competitor who still stood at his side.

"What?!" he shrieked, the car-salesman friendliness vanishing. "Are you calling me a thief?" Without waiting for an answer, he cocked a tight fist and swung. The blow landed squarely on Eddie's jaw, and he fell to the steps unconscious. For Eddie, the night was over.

\* \* \*

Eddie came to.

His head throbbed painfully as he lay on his bed in the sleeper car. It was dark, but there was a tight, bright circle of white light emanating from the miniature lens of a focused reading lamp mounted in the ceiling. In its umbra, out of the corner of his eye he could make out the shapely torso of a woman sitting in a chair next to him, a book open in her lap. Her shadowed face lifted up toward him as he stirred. He opened his mouth to speak, but halted the motion as soon as it began, wincing sharply from the pain in his jaw.

"The doctor said he doesn't think it's broken," she reassured him in a bright tone.

"That's good to know," he slurred through unmoving teeth. He turned his head to see who it was who spoke, but she remained only partially visible. He could distinguish the last few inches of her long, light auburn hair splayed across her ample bosom, but her face was outside the circle of illumination emitted by the reading light. As he turned to better see her face, he halted the motion almost as soon as it started; the back of his head complained with a sharp pain. He raised a hand to gingerly rub a large lump.

"But he said you might have a mild concussion from banging your head when you fell." She set her book down in her lap and flicked a switch mounted on the wall. A dim, blue night light filled the compartment, its soft cerulean radiance gently banishing the shadows. "It's a good sign that you're awake. If you hadn't woken up soon by yourself, he said I was supposed to try to wake you."

Despite the murky, alien light, he immediately recognized his nurse—it was the woman who had been the victim of the bandit. He became aware of the great, absorbed eyes that rested so lightly upon his. He turned away, muttering, "Have you any aspirin?"

"Doctor says 'no,'" she replied cheerily. "It's not good for you after you've had a concussion. That ice pack is all he'd allow."

*Ice pack?* She was right; his head was resting on a cold, bumpy sock filled with ice. He hadn't noticed its presence until she had mentioned it. His confusion was itself confusing, leaving him to wonder, *I don't think I banged my head that hard!—Did I?*

"I hope you don't mind, but I found the ice in the refrigerator on board your train—it's a *beautiful* train by the way!—and the sock was in there." She pointed a blue finger at a closed drawer mounted flush inside the sleeper compartment's wall. "I put a towel under the ice so that it doesn't get your pillow so wet."

"Thank you," he murmured without moving his jaw.

"I brought you some lavender, too. My grandmother always used to use lavender oil to cure headaches. And I just love lavender, don't you? The doctor said it was okay, so I put some on the sock, if you don't mind."

As with the ice, he hadn't noticed the delicate scent until she mentioned it. Perhaps he *had* banged his head harder than he thought.

"If it makes you feel any better, that mean man who punched you is cooling his heels in jail at the moment. You'll be proud to know that once he knocked you down, a dozen men stormed up the steps to defend you, and held him down until our friend the policeman arrived. Looks like you'll get another chance to play judge, Your Honor, once you're back on your feet again."

He closed his eyes. "How long have I been unconscious?"

"Oh, not long. Not even an hour. There's still an awful lot of people outside arguing about your plan—can't you hear them?" She cocked an ear, but Eddie heard nothing. "Your banker friend is still out there talking it up, and he's convinced a lot of people. Me, I think it's a great idea. Kids'll have penny candy again! Isn't that sweet?"

He moved to sit up.

"Oh, no!" She laid a palm gently but firmly upon his chest. "Doctor's orders! You need to stay in bed, Your Honor! Anything you need, you just let me know."

"Thanks, but I'm all right. You can go home now."

"Let's not talk. You rest." She reached out and switched off the blue nightlight, strengthening the stark illumination that washed over the book on her lap while dramatically darkening the rest of the sleeper compartment. She lifted her book, and after one last glance and a half-seen, self-assured smile, pointedly resumed her reading. She was obviously done talking.

Eddie was in no mood to argue. He closed his eyes, and with the whisper of lavender drifting around him, he slept.

* * *

The economy shifted.

The morning following the crucial town meeting dawned with only a tad of confusion, but that was far outweighed by quite a bit of considered resolve. Shopkeepers were in the vanguard of Eddie's new economic order, which they embraced wholeheartedly. They knew the value of a paper dollar versus the value of the silver coins that no longer backed those dollars, and that knowledge was reflected in the prices of their wares. Existing prices remained, but only for those who chose to purchase goods with paper money; those who used coins alone were treated to the suggested one-thirty-third of a dollar price. No customers could complain, since they could use their preferred choice of money either at the existing price or at the new deep discount. It was as if two separate economies existed side by side; in short order silver and paper became like quarts and liters or miles and kilometers. People automatically understood the difference, and unconsciously acted accordingly.

Initially there were some few stubborn holdouts among the shopkeepers who continued to treat paper and metal money equally, but once word spread of their folly, customers would deliberately patronize their establishments and purchase goods in such amounts so as to maximize the amount of coins they would receive in change. Long before midmorning, the recalcitrant shopkeepers had no choice but to fall into line. It was either that or give away good money for bad—and at a steep premium, at that.

Another strong impetus driving the adoption of the silver standard was circumstantial: of the two banks that operated in Las Vegas, only one of them opened their doors that morning; the owner of the other bank remained in jail awaiting trial for assaulting Eddie. Citizens who wished to redeem their dollars for one hundred cents in coins were left with no place to go. But even had the paper banker opened his doors that morning, the outcome would have been the same for him as it was with the recalcitrant shopkeepers: choose to pursue an expensive folly or fall in line.

They fell in line.

\* \* \*

Eddie woke.

Despite the fact that his eyes were still closed, he knew breakfast had arrived. He squinted against the bright, late-morning sunshine angling steeply through the window of his sleeper car, and with trouble he focused on the shapely feminine form standing in the doorway. But vision was not needed to know she had brought along a piping hot omelet; the aroma was extraordinary. He rubbed his eyes and his vision cleared sufficiently to discern that she held a tray with two tall iced tumblers full of grapefruit juice and two plates graced not only with an aromatic heaping of egg, but also a fluffy muffin smothered in steaming sausage gravy.

"Good morning, Your Honor," she beamed. "Feel like some breakfast?"

He lifted himself up on one elbow. "You've been here all night?"

"Well," she replied smiling, "I'm used to staying up late because of work. And someone had to keep waking you every couple of hours to make sure you didn't die or something." She rolled her eyes playfully. "I slept in the compartment next door and used your alarm clock. I thought you wouldn't mind."

He nodded. He remembered being repeatedly woken, if not the waker.

She balanced the tray expertly on one hand while using the other to fold down the collapsible table from its recess in the wall, then set the tray upon it. "Mind if I join you?" she asked as she sat down uninvited in the chair she had occupied the night before.

"Please," he finally mustered.

"I hope you don't mind, but I made only soft food for you. I was worried your jaw might still be sore. How do you feel?"

Experimentally he sat up in bed and jiggled his jaw, but noticed no untoward effects. "Me? I feel fine."

"Good! Let's eat." She cautiously relocated the tray with their breakfasts onto his lap, then transferred her own plate, silverware, and glass from it back to the table.

After the second bite, Eddie paused; the omelet was excellent. She was obviously a skilled cook. He dug in with relish. It did not take long for the nourishment to reinvigorate his thought processes, bringing the details of the night before back into sharp focus. He sat up straight, dangerously unbalancing the tray on his lap. "What time is it?"

"Almost eleven."

"What's happening with the money?"

She set her fork down with feigned irritation. "Well, I haven't heard any gunshots, so I assume things must be going smoothly." She smiled, then added, "Don't worry. I've already talked with several people, and they all say it's going well. I'd suggest you get out there and talk with people yourself. The doctor said it's okay for you to be out and about, if you take it easy. But no horseback riding or anything rough for a couple of days, he said."

"But it's working?"

"It's working. As you knew it would." She smiled proudly, as if his achievement somehow reflected well upon her. "Now eat your breakfast before it gets cold."

They ate in silence, and when they had finished, she gathered up the dishes. "I'll take care of these and be on my way to work. But I'll stop in on you tonight after I get off, and see how you're doing. I get out of work late, you may recall, so don't hold dinner for me."

"Thanks, but I don't think it'll be necessary for you to bother."

"Oh, it's no bother! I work just up the street from here, so it'll be no problem to stop by. Besides..." She shook a playful finger at him. "I told the doctor I'd keep my eye on you!"

Two seconds passed. "I see," he said.

"And remember! Take it easy today, Your Honor. No big speeches!" With a small wave, she was gone.

Once she had left, with needless surreptitiousness Eddie snuck a glance under his blanket; except for an absence of shoes he was still dressed. He tossed back the covers and sat on the edge of the bed, sizing himself up physically. His head did not swim, nor did he feel the slightest bit weak. He rubbed the back of his skull gently; the lump remained, but not quite so tender or as large as the night before. He put on his shoes, left the sleeper car, and headed for the station's front door. Outside it was a typical morning in Las Vegas: hot, dry, and clear, but with a brisk wind blowing from the west. There was the usual amount of foot and horse traffic on the street; it did not appear that anything had overtly changed.

"Good morning, Mr. Eddie," a strange woman offered, a broad smile on her face. He nodded once in return.

"Morning, Eddie," an unknown man called from atop his horse with the tip of his hat. "Glad to see you're up and about. Feeling all right?"

"I'm fine, thanks," he responded. *What a difference a day makes!* he marveled. Their pleasant reactions laid to rest any initial doubts he may have had about their acceptance of his economic reforms. But he had to dig under the façade to make sure.

He entered the butcher shop to the sound of the tinkling bell affixed to the door, but before he could begin to close it, an unseen, angry voice called out, "No! I won't change a dollar! Go away!" A head popped up from behind the counter. "Oh, it's you! Come on in! Quick, close the door—the wind's making it dusty outside today. How are you feeling?"

"No permanent damage," he conceded. "I was more interested in how *you* were doing!"

"You mean the money thing? Of course you do!" He put his hands on his hips. "Let me tell you something: there are a lot of men wandering the streets looking for people to change a dollar for them." He barked a short laugh. "Flim flams, looking for a quick buck. Well, they won't get it here! And let me tell you another thing: they won't get it anywhere! Everyone who's come into my store already knows the score. Some of them pay with bills, some with coins, but no one makes a fuss. Excepting them scam artists, that is."

Eddie examined the contents of the refrigerated meat case through its angled front glass trimmed in gleaming chromium. Numerous cuts of meat were arrayed inside, each sporting skewers announcing two prices, one thirty-three-times higher than the other. He nodded in understanding. Looking up at the butcher, he instructed, "Since I'm here, I'll take that fat steak there."

"Sure thing!" He extracted the indicated slab of meat, weighed it, and wrapped it in brown paper. "That's one fine cut you picked there," he complimented. "Got something special going on tonight? Celebrating or something?"

"Not particularly."

"You should."

"Why? What's to celebrate?"

The butcher looked Eddie squarely in the eye, a mocking, sarcastic expression on his face. "Be that way," he retorted enigmatically. He set the wrapped victual on the countertop. "Will that be cash or coin?"

"Cash."

The butcher sighed. "You and everyone else! Seems everyone wants to get rid of their paper money pronto. But so what? Me, I'll just take it to the bank and turn it into silver. No sense holding onto bad money."

"I agree." He headed for the door and nodded on his way out. "Be seeing you."

"And you."

Eddie stopped in several other establishments on his walk back to the Transcontinental station, sometimes to make purchases, but mostly just to talk; he found all their stories to be similar to the butcher's. The revaluation of the currency had apparently gone over smoothly, but there was still one important place to check.

"It's working!" the banker announced when Eddie entered the bank. "There have been a few innocents wandering in here looking for too much change for a dollar, but other than that, it's gone off without a hitch. I've talked to many of my customers, and almost all of them are behind it one hundred percent. In fact, most people coming in today are here only to exchange their bills for coins." He frowned fleetingly. "I'm thinking we may have erred in setting the price at three cents on the dollar. Given the level of demand, I believe we could have gotten away with two. And soon, we will."

"You're the expert," he replied deferentially. "Just don't push it too hard or too fast."

"No, of course not." He let out a deep breath. "So that's it, then. We did it!"

"Yes we did," he agreed. "But there's still one question left hanging."

"What's that?"

"'The Panic'. How did word get out? I didn't tell anyone."

"Neither did I."

The silence between them stretched itself out. Neither man noticed the two tellers exchanging worried glances from behind their respective windows.

"Then how *did* word get out?" Eddie repeated.

The banker thought for a moment, then replied, "My competitor?"

"I think not! He was pretty convinced that we were going to fail. Besides, a panic wouldn't be in his interest. It would hurt him as much as it would you. Even more so, given his low cash reserves. He knew that. He wouldn't risk it."

"Then who?"

Silence.

Eddie sighed. "Well, let's not worry about it right now. We're over that hump, so it's not that important for the moment. But I imagine we'll find out eventually." He gestured with a bundle wrapped in brown paper. "If you'll excuse me, I need to get this home and into the refrigerator. We'll talk again soon."

Despite the needs of his provisions, he did not head directly home; he still had to pursue his last and largest concern. He walked the several blocks to the city jail.

"Good morning!" the policeman called cheerfully when he recognized his visitor, the relief plain in his voice. "No serious injuries, I take it?"

"Just a bit of a bump on the head, but I expect I'll live," he replied with a weak attempt at humor. "Where's our friend?"

"Downstairs in his cell, where he belongs."

"I want to see him."

The policeman eyed him curiously. "All right." He stood, retrieved the keys from their nail, and led the way downstairs. They found the pugilistic banker sitting on his cot idly staring at the floor, elbows on his legs, and hands folded between his knees, the perfect picture of a pitiful prisoner.

He rose at their approach. "So, the condemned man has a visitor, has he?" When neither man took the gambit, he continued contemptuously, "Or is it time for my impartial trial, Your Honor?"

Eddie's expression did not change. "There will be no trial."

The banker's eyebrows shot up in mock surprise. "What, you're just going to have me shot?"

Eddie turned to the policeman. "Let him out."

"What?!"

"Let him out. I don't want to press any charges."

Warily, the policeman swayed slightly where he was standing. "You sure?"

"Yes. Let him go."

"If you say so..." Slowly, almost theatrically, the policeman stepped forward, unlocked the cell, and swung the barred door wide.

The former prisoner did not move to leave the cell. "What's the deal, son?"

"No deal," he replied in a deadpan voice. "You're free to go. But before you re-open your bank, I'd suggest you stop by and talk to some of the merchants."

"It's working?" His voice dripped disdain.

"It's working," he replied, not deigning to notice the pointedly negative attitude. "I heard that there were a few shops that were making change dollar-for-dollar when they first opened up this morning, but not now. It's over. You won't be able to inflate your way to wealth." To the policeman, he asserted, "He's no threat any longer."

"If you say so!"

The banker's aloofness began to crack. "But... But what about Adam Smith? The invisible hand?"

Eddie shrugged. "It would appear that one of Mr. Smith's basic premises doesn't hold true."

"What? You must be joking! It's a law of economics!"

Again, Eddie shrugged. "I'm no economist, but it appears to me that given their own choice, people prefer to receive the best money available and give away the worst, not the other way around as you would have it. My guess is that in the absence of someone imposing a set value on their money, men will decide for themselves how much a given currency is actually worth, and they act accordingly. It's still the invisible hand, only it's setting the value of the currency rather than what that currency can buy."

Uncertainly, the former prisoner looked from one man to the other, and without another word angrily shouldered past them and bounded up the steps.

The policeman watched him leave, then turned to Eddie. "I hope you know what you're doing!"

He sighed. "Me, too."

\* \* \*

The stationmaster fretted.

He found it out of place that he should fret. He had just made the most profitable investment of his entire life, and ironically he had done it for all the wrong reasons. He felt he should be proud of his cunning, how he had predicted the future of Las Vegas from such slim information, gambled, and won. Instead, he felt somehow haunted. He knew that eventually the story of how he had swapped paper dollars for silver dollars would come out, but that was not what worried him. That he was personally responsible for The Panic was beyond a doubt, and all it would take would be for someone to connect the dots before he would be called on the carpet for his foolishness. He fretted over the reaction of the mob once they found out. He had witnessed their wrath firsthand the night before, and he knew he did not want to face it himself. He wished it were years later so that it would all be over and far behind him.

In the old days when the trains still plied the rails of the nation, he often fretted as he did now. Back then, the men of the Unificating Board held a great, unchecked power over the continued employment—and subsequently the lives—of every man, woman, and child, both the high and mighty and the lowliest laborer, and at any possible moment his comfortable position as stationmaster could become history. But once Mr. Eddie had come on the scene, those fretful days had come to an end. It was pleasant to work with an honest man for a change.

*An honest man!* The thought brought another bout of fear welling up within his knotted stomach. That he had somehow betrayed Mr. Eddie was obvious—not that he was any saint himself; the role of stationmaster had always held its opportunities for questionable perks and petty graft, and he had not been immune to their allure. In past years he had earned what amounted to a second salary by providing tickets to trains that were already full, or diverting railroad property to other, more personal uses. When motorized vehicles still roamed the highways he had collected a nice honorarium from tapping the forgotten tank cars full of diesel fuel. Siphoning off a few dozen gallons a week from a twenty-thousand-gallon tank car could continue for years before the level dropped to empty; not that anyone would notice or care. But with the disappearance of mechanized transportation he was forced to halt even that undetectable larceny. One or two working trucks in a stilled, fuel-less city would trigger too many questions.

The stationmaster tried valiantly to rationalize his actions at the bank. Tank cars aside, had he really done anything wrong? Since Mr. Eddie hadn't taken him into his confidence, there was really no confidence to betray. And the conclusion he had painfully teased out of less-than-meager information was plainly incorrect in any case, even though it may have been correct on another level. He had not intended to cause The Panic; his motives were pure. In retrospect, perhaps he should have swapped his currency for some of the coins stored safely in the terminal's vault; the intrinsic secrecy of the transaction would have shielded him from the public scrutiny he now feared. But what was there to fear? He had only attempted to protect himself from the possible effects of counterfeit money. Whether the coins originated from the bank's vault or the terminal's vault was of no matter; he had merely sought to cover his own assets, and had succeeded. The others be damned.

The stationmaster shrugged. There was no sense losing any sleep over the morality of his plight. Morality aside, he knew he was innocent. Besides, it was up to them to catch him; he'd save his worries for the day they did, if and when.

Confidently setting moral concerns behind him once and for all, for the fourth time that day he gleefully counted out each and every one of the silver dollars he had had the forethought to acquire.

\* \* \*

It was late.

Ignoring the hour and the advice of the doctor, Eddie was busily cleaning up around the cafeteria. Despite his best efforts, dirt somehow managed to escape from the garden's beds to lightly dust the floor of the cafeteria. Once there, it ended up getting tracked all over the station. Although he usually delegated cleanup chores to a Transcontinental employee, the cafeteria was off-limits to them. He could never consider ordering any of them to take a role in maintaining his garden. Somehow, it didn't seem proper tasking Transcontinental Railroad to look after his personal endeavors.

He heard the front door to the station open and close. "Hello!" a woman's echoing voice sang out musically. "Hello! I'm back!"

"In here," he called.

She entered the cafeteria, saw the broom in his hand and immediately donned a stern look of concern, hands on her broad hips. "Didn't I tell you the doctor said to take it easy?"

"Sweeping *is* easy," he countered.

"You shouldn't be taking the chance!"

"All right," he conceded, holding the broom off to one side. "I was only keeping myself busy until you got back. Otherwise I might have fallen asleep."

"And I would have just woken you up, like last night." She shook a playful finger at him. "And there's no hiding, because now I know where you sleep!"

"I see," he said, reddening.

Her mockingly stern visage softened. "I'm sorry it took me this long to get here, but I had to work late."

"Have you eaten?"

"Not dinner, no. I was going to grab something when I got home."

"I picked up a nice steak when I was out today. We can cook that, if you like." He paused, embarrassed. "I wanted to do something to thank you for helping me out last night."

Her eyes shone. "How sweet! I'd love to stay for dinner!" Her face darkened again. "But you're not allowed to cook! You still have to take it easy. Doctor's orders. Tell you what, though: I'll let you watch."

"All right," he surrendered. "You're a much better cook than I am anyhow. That breakfast this morning was superb!"

"Why thank you, Your Honor. I'll have you know I was trained as a gourmet chef in New York City and did my apprenticeship in the People's State of France." She grabbed the broom from his hand possessively and headed for the cafeteria door. "I'm sure I could teach you a trick or two, if you'd like."

"All right," he replied, following in her wake.

For the next half-hour, they busied themselves with preparations for their late meal. She relaxed her nursing orders enough to let him prepare a salad while she broiled the steak in the compact electric oven he had installed in the sleeper car. Before long they sat down at the round mahogany table in the observation car to enjoy the fruit of their labors, and the results were scrumptious.

"All we're missing is a nice red wine," she lamented. "And I mean wine made from real grapes, not one of those horrible fruit wines everybody serves these days."

The lack of variety did not make much difference to Eddie; as a rule, he did not drink.

Small talk punctuated their meal; and no surprise, the main topic on Eddie's mind was the local economy. "I must have spoken with dozens of people today about the changeover," he explained. "And every one of them was pretty happy with it. It went over much smoother than I would have expected."

"I heard almost all good things about it at work, too." She giggled. "But some people still need to change their thinking when it comes to tipping, though."

"What? What do you mean?"

"Well, a dollar bill isn't worth what it used to be, right? But some men keep tipping with them as if they were still worth the trouble of picking up off the street. It'd take at least a hundred dollar bill just to get my attention these days."

"I imagine it will be some time before people get a better feel for it," he admitted.

She sighed. "I, for one, can't wait."

He sat in thought for a moment. "You get tipped? You know, I don't know what it is you do for a living. The subject never came up when we were out to catch the bandit. All I know is that you work late."

"Oh," she replied demurely. "I'm a courtesan at the honky-tonk a block west of here."

Ten full seconds passed in absolute silence. "I see," he finally said.

"I also dance on Fridays and Saturdays," she picked up, not countenancing his hesitation. "Or anytime really, if someone tips me enough, and I'm in the mood. But I usually am. You ought to catch my act sometime. I really enjoy dancing—always have, even when I was a little girl." She smiled at the thought, but suddenly bristled in a mock anger; it appeared as if she didn't have the capacity for actual anger. "That's just what I was talking about. Some people still think a five-dollar tip is enough to get me dancing, but let me tell you: five dollars won't get you nearly as far as it used to!"

Eddie face colored. "I see," he repeated.

She shrugged, again not reacting to his discomfiture. "Oh, well. You warned us there would have to be a period of adjustment. I'm sure it'll all settle out soon enough—just like it did after you started your court." An amused smile crossed her face. "Speaking of which, I got another letter from the Ladies' Auxiliary today. It seems I've been exiled again—the second time this month!" She giggled. "I guess once wasn't enough for them." She reached out to momentarily touch his hand. "I'm *so* glad you made it voluntary to accept a court's sentence. Otherwise I might find myself sleeping with strangers in Boulder City."

"I see." The color deepened.

She rose with an air of finality. "And speaking of sleep, I should be on my way. I didn't get a good night's sleep last night, and it's been a long day today. No! Don't get up!" She leaned over and gave Eddie a quick peck on the cheek. Her long auburn hair tumbled off her shoulder and brushed lightly across his face, instantly imbuing his awareness with her subtle fragrance. "Let me put these dishes in the sink, then I'll find my own way out. Thank you for the dinner, Your Honor, and I'm glad to see you're doing so well. I'll stop by tomorrow and finish cleaning up."

"That won't be necessary." He reddened even more.

"Oh, it's my pleasure," she reminded him, once more not taking overt notice to his unease. With a final small wave, she left.

Eddie sat for a long time before finally retiring to his compartment, the delicate scent of lavender following him all the way.

* * *

Las Vegas changed.

Along with the arrival of the new economy came several unexpected ramifications, and the first revealed itself almost immediately: whenever a paper dollar purchase totaled to some fraction of a dollar, of course coins would no longer be given in change; instead, the price would be rounded up to the next nearest whole dollar amount, and change be damned. Fortunately this did not prove problematic; hardly any commodities were worth less than a paper dollar, and for those few that were, they became bundled in packages of two, three, or whatever was appropriate. In terms of respect, the dollar bill quickly became the penny of paper money.

Another unexpected fallout that developed over the course of the first week, one that quickly rendered rounding moot, was a new, undeniable pressure of an invisible hand on the prices of certain commodities. Since the days of Directive 289-10, the cost of virtually all goods had been fixed by public policy, not by market forces; but with their unleashing from both law and tradition, prices quickly rearranged themselves to settle each to their own proper level. Not only did this settling occur for commodities, it also affected the old paper dollar—now a commodity itself—which dropped in value to two cents within as many days, then to a penny within the week. It remained at that level for another week, then dropped to an ignominious two dollars to the penny. In an odd turnabout, paper dollars began to be used for making change of a copper penny, and, having broken the crucial level of one-to-one parity, its value deteriorated steadily over the course of the month until it finally settled at an even five dollars to the penny, a mere two mills each. There it sat, the almighty dollar, a shadow of its former glory, and a monument to the folly of fiat currency.

The upward revaluation of silver coins triggered yet another unexpected result: more than a few entrepreneurs discovered it was again profitable to operate some of the nearby silver mines; the silver in the ground was now worth quite a bit more than the effort required to extract and refine it, triggering a boom in the mining market. Within weeks, newly-minted silver dollars began to circulate. At first the coins were featureless disks, but—to Eddie's acute embarrassment—one of the silver miners began minting a silver dollar with a fair likeness of Eddie's face embossed upon one side, and a Diesel engine on the other, with the motto, *In Eddie We Trust* above his profile, and *Las Vegas* beneath. In jest, the miner christened the coin a "willie," and unsurprisingly the colloquial slang stuck, and soon replaced the old word completely. In common usage, *dollar* was reserved for paper; *willies* were always silver, regardless of whose countenance happened to grace a particular coin.

Along with prosperity, hobbies and other simple pleasures made a comeback, and Eddie decided he'd try his hand at an unusual one—for a very personal reason. Recalling the abandoned radio transmitter in the basement of the Transcontinental station, he decided he would try to bring it back to life. But he fretted over how to keep the equipment in repair. To the best of his knowledge, aside from the stationmaster's minimal empirical experience with the transmitter and the Dam technician's general knowledge of electricity, none of the town's residents possessed any detailed technical expertise with regards to either radio or television. He was acutely aware that all it would take would be one major failure of his equipment and he would be off the air for good. So his plan was to severely limit the amount of time that he kept the transmitter active in hopes of extending its life.

While equipment malfunctions were merely a potential problem, locating a phonograph was an actual one. Despite the variety of shops in town, there were few that sold electric appliances—virtually all second-hand, there being no factories to manufacture new ones—and none of the stores had any phonographs for sale. Undeterred, a driven Eddie pursued an alternative solution: he began a house-by-house search of the many vacant homes in Las Vegas to seek one out.

When he entered the first house, his heart sank; the place had been ransacked. In room after room, clothes, trash, and unrecognizable debris lay in tumbled heaps on the floor. The scene was much the same in the next several vacant homes he visited, but soon he began to find evidence of the existence of what he sought: one house possessed a meager collection of popular recordings which no one had thought worth removing from their dusty shelf. Eddie left them undisturbed as well, but it raised his hopes that he might find his phonograph, and perhaps more. Sure enough, the next home yielded a battered, but serviceable model, and his spirits rose further. It took some time, but before long his quest proved more than successful: not only did he locate several working phonographs of varying quality, he also found something just as precious: several large caches of recorded music. And not merely music; a good number of the recordings were classical symphonies and concertos, precisely the type of music he was seeking. He felt no guilt in rummaging through the abandoned homes; it was better that the music be heard rather than have it lying around ownerless collecting dust, especially given the goal he had in mind.

With the help of the Dam technician, he assembled a crude radio studio in the empty mail car of the *Meteor*, running a shielded copper wire from there to the transmitter in the station's basement. To assure pinpoint precision in the scheduling of his radio show, he purchased a vintage railroad pocket watch from a curio shop, then commissioned the town jeweler to clean and calibrate the timepiece; the man guaranteed its accuracy to within seconds each year, an exactitude that appealed to the railroadman in Eddie.

With everything finally in place, he put his station on the air for the pleasure of Las Vegas and the silent world beyond. For one solid hour he played songs that he knew to be among Dagny's favorites, beginning his broadcast at precisely nine o'clock each night except for those occasional evenings where business or social engagements would pre-empt his time.

The broadcasts represented a bittersweet joy in his life. As he prepared to spin his discs, he would imagine Dagny eagerly tuning in to hear them. In his mind's eye he would picture her smiling face as she listened to the songs he would choose for her pleasure, and the look of little-girl serenity on her face as they lulled her to sleep.

In his heart, he hoped that she heard them; but in his mind he knew she must be dead. With the catastrophic end of civilization in America, it seemed ludicrous to think that she alone could have survived whatever disaster had befallen New York City when apparently no one else had.

But still he serenaded her most every night, broadcasting from his makeshift studio in the mail car of the last *Meteor* she had ordered dispatched out onto the road. It was his musical gift to her, a memorial to her memory, from ocean to ocean forever.

## CHAPTER 2 – BLESSÈD

Ma sighed.

The pewless church was packed far beyond comfortable capacity, and the reek of unwashed bodies was oppressive. But better to suffer the olfactory assault than to be caught outdoors during the weekly prayer service—the Bishop's acolytes might suspect her "conversion" at the Golden Gate Bridge to be the farce it truly was. In the months since California had lost contact with the rest of the nation, all those who were unfortunate enough to have survived the fighting, famine, and fires now found themselves fallen under the crushing heel of the Bishop's religious dictatorship.

The sputtering, smoky fires on either side of the altar added their own musk to the giant room, bringing a stinging veneer of tears to her eyes. On the altar between the fires were the bound figures of those who the Bishop had decreed to be heretics, their crime being self-evident to all assembled. Ma recognized one of them: her lieutenant who was captured along with her after the fiery destruction of San Francisco. *He was never contrite enough,* she recalled, *and it finally caught up with him!*

She could see him casting his gaze about, trying to spot her standing among the crowd, to catch her eye, but she knew it was futile to try to find any one face in the teeming mass that filled the cavernous church. *Not that it would do either of us any good...*

The crowd surged and roared as the Bishop came up behind the altar to face the congregation. Ma cheered, too; there were watchers who were always on the lookout for new heretics, leaving her little choice.

"Amen to you, my brothers and sisters!" the Bishop called out, a broad smile on his face. Rather than the traditional red vestments of his sect, instead he wore a pure white robe with the stylized orange flame sewn over the left breast; his head was bare. Behind him, a dirty white banner hung on the back wall proclaiming, "Back For God" in large, crudely-painted red letters. The afternoon sun filtering through the recently-installed stained glass windows cast mottled colors across both banner and Bishop.

"*AMEN!*" the congregation called back with thundering vigor, but they all fell suddenly still, and a deathly quiet reigned in the church. The weekly service had now begun. Silence was the golden rule, and woe to anyone who made a noise that was not a scripted response. Ma didn't move a muscle; she knew that acolytes were certainly watching. They always did.

In the packed stillness of the church, the Bishop could be heard plainly to the farthest corner. "Let us pray!" he implored. "But before we humble ourselves before our God, we must first cleanse our souls. For it is written that the unbeliever shall be cast into the darkness for his sins." He swept a vestment-clad arm toward the bound figures. "And who are the unbelievers?"

"*HERETICS!*" replied the congregation. Ma joined in the chant wholeheartedly, letting feigned contempt show on her face. She definitely saw an acolyte off to her left studying her; she hoped her performance was sufficiently convincing.

Again, silence fell as quickly as if a curtain had fallen. Into the silence, the Bishop intoned his words.

"Thus it is written. Thus, they shall be banished."

"*FOR EVER AND EVER, AMEN!*"

"The Mark of the Beast be upon them!"

"*AND UPON THEIR SOULS!*"

On receiving his cue, an acolyte near the altar drew a branding iron from the fire; there was a rustle of movement among the heretics. A low murmur almost rose from the crowd, but died even as it began. Ma held her breath, as did the entire congregation.

The acolyte stepped up to the first heretic, cherry-red brand in hand, while two other acolytes held her arms and a third held her head. The silence in the church was absolute; the tension, electric. Ma closed her eyes; tears formed and leaked down her cheeks. The screams of the first heretic echoed through the church. She squeezed her eyes shut tighter.

"Ma! Ma!" cried a second, desperate voice. "Do something, Emma! Help me!"

She recognized the heretic's voice without seeing him, despite her best attempt to refuse to listen. But she couldn't help herself; she opened her eyes: it was her lieutenant, of course. She watched as the acolytes grabbed his arms, his head. Again, she shut her eyes tight; it was all she could do for him. More tears leaked. *Surely the acolytes have seen*, she feared. She managed to fabricate a smile in hopes of fooling them; but then she was past caring, for all she could perceive were his screams echoing inside her skull. When she opened her eyes, two acolytes were lifting her up, one on each arm. She had been on the floor.

"You fainted, sister," one of them whispered, his mouth close to her ear. Although the universal ban on speaking during services also applied to the acolytes, discreet words in the performance of their duties were grudgingly tolerated—but not words from the congregation.

"Let our strength be yours!" hissed the other.

They lifted her to her feet and held her vertical so that she could again clearly observe the ceremony at the altar. "Is that better, sister?" whispered one acolyte.

Tears continued to pour down her cheeks. "Yes. Bless you, brother," she managed to stammer. But more heretical shrieks filled the air, mercifully drowning out her forbidden words. Fortunately for her, the acolyte had not heard them.

The ceremony continued. One by one, the heretics were imprinted with the mark of the beast across their foreheads: a brand in the shape of a cleansing flame. Soon, all had received their due.

"The mark is upon them!" the Bishop called out once the grisly task was completed.

"*LET THEM BE BANISHED!*" rejoined the crowd.

Again on cue, the packed congregation packed themselves tighter still, opening a straight and narrow path from the altar at the front of the church to the main entrance far in the back. One by one, the heretics were freed of their bonds and prodded to walk down the human corridor, some with blood oozing from their fresh burns. As they passed, each member of the congregation spat upon them, as required by the ritual.

Ma stood too far from the makeshift corridor to participate in the ritualistic defiling, but not so far that she could not plainly observe the ghastly procession. Presently she saw her lieutenant: dirty, scarred, eyes downcast as he endured the constant stream of liquid indignities. Blood from his wounded forehead trickled down one cheek, staining his torn shirt. Never once looking up, he reached the door at the rear of the church and was gone.

After the last of them had departed, the Bishop called, "Let the doors be shut! The heretics have been purged, as it is written."

"*AS IT IS WRITTEN,*" replied the congregation.

"Let no man assist the evil ones who have been cast out, lest he share their fate!"

"*AMEN!*"

With that, the organ swelled up in a burst of music, and the congregation began to sing.

"*OUR GOD IS A MERCIFUL GOD...*" With the acolytes still flanking her, Ma had no choice but to join in with all her heart and soul. Again the tears began to cascade down her smiling cheeks as she proclaimed the blatant contradiction at the top of her musical lungs. She couldn't bear to listen to herself; the result was more tears.

The acolytes finally released their steadying grip, leaving her to stand on her own two feet once more. One of them left her side to mill about the crowd to search out volunteers for future services, but the second remained alongside her, joining her in song. They caught each other's eye for a moment, him taking deliberate note of the tears as they continued to course their way down her smiling cheeks.

"*...OUR LOVE IS STRONG, OUR GOD MOST KIND...*" Ma continued to smile at the acolyte as she sang; he smiled back. "*...THY PEACE UPON THE LAND!*" they concluded.

After several more hymns, homilies, and a fiery sermon, the service finally ended. The murmur of conversation followed the congregation as they streamed for the exits. The acolyte next to Ma bowed respectfully to her.

"Your love of God must be great indeed for you to shed such tears of joy!"

Ma pushed a dangling lock of damp grey hair back from her cheek before replying. "Our God is most kind," was all she could think to say. *But what kind?* she asked herself wryly from behind her artificial smile.

"Such devotion cannot go unrewarded," asserted the acolyte. "I am sure that the Bishop would be very interested in communing with one so holy as you."

"I am not worthy," she demurred. "Certainly the Bishop has far greater concerns than one old woman."

"That is for God to decide. Please come with me. I insist."

*Trapped!* Her feigned piety had obviously been *too* convincing. Ma reluctantly surrendered, and still sporting a sham smile, she accompanied the acolyte into the sacristy behind the altar.

\* \* \*

The Bishop smiled.

He was more than happy to escape his hot vestments. Since electricity had been outlawed as a sinful manifestation of Babylon, of necessity the church lacked adequate ventilation. Nor had the building been designed with humans in mind; it had previously served as a hangar for commercial airliners; installing looted stained glass windows and a steam-driven pipe organ were the only concessions to its new religious purpose. Despite its shortcomings, at least it was someplace out of the sun and rain; and the soaring, arched ceiling helped to moderate the oppressive temperature somewhat.

As he removed his vestments, he idly considered the fates of those banished. He wasn't sure where the heretics ultimately settled, but he had made sure there were not many places remaining in God's California where they could roost—certainly not in any of the cities! All of the once-proud metropolises of the West had been purified in the crusades by cleansing fire and now stood in charred ruins, deserted, and the southern farms surrounding them had promptly followed the abandoned warrens into oblivion. Too many aqueducts and dams had been destroyed in the fighting; and without electricity, modern irrigation methods, and the precision equipment they required, the farms quickly reverted into the deserts they once were. Only the central farming country and widely-scattered cattle ranches survived, now forming the backbone of the religious dictatorship's socialist granary.

The logistical nightmare of administrating the far-flung farm country proved at first to be problematic for the Bishop. Although a divine mandate tended to cut most dissent short, spreading that mandate was nigh on impossible in the absence of the web of modern communications, especially since the Californian farmsteads were scattered widely across an oval some two hundred miles long and fifty miles wide.

The solution grew of its own initiative rather than by conscious design, as if God Himself had ordained it. What started as a cadre of fleet messengers quickly evolved into an army of acolyte soldiers chosen exclusively for their piety and unswerving obedience to God and His servant, the Bishop. Before long they multiplied and poured across the land like locusts, spreading the word of the faithful and the justice of the righteous among the survivors. In short order, the ranks of the acolytes and their influence swelled exponentially until they had their holy grip on literally all aspects of California life, responsible only to the Bishop and their God. From the commandeered airfield they employed as their base of operations located at the western foot of the Sierras, the Bishop and his acolytes held total power over the lives and souls of the survivors—God's Unificating Board, as Ma's lieutenant dared to name them, that being their pretext for branding him a heretic. But in spite of the vast temporal power the Bishop wielded, he remained truly devout to his God; and his authentic piety augmented that power immensely, as well as the power of his acolytes, particularly the most pious ones.

The Bishop was hanging his sweaty vestments in the closet when the acolyte brought Ma into the sacristy unannounced. The Bishop turned and smiled at them. "May the peace of God be upon you!"

"And upon your soul," they replied in unison, giving the proper response.

"How may I serve you?" he asked deferentially.

The acolyte bowed. "Your Excellency, I have been watching this woman for weeks, and I am moved by her piety. I believe she possesses the soul of a saint, and would make a fitting addition to our order."

The Bishop accepted the recommendation without question; he knew the acolyte's faith was strong and sincere. The same could be said for any acolyte, or he would not long remain among the ranks of the acolytes—or of the unbanished. Similarly, he also assumed that Ma would welcome her elevation to the status of acolyte; to do otherwise would brand her the heretic.

Bowing to Ma, he smiled peacefully. "We joyously welcome the pious to join us in our mission."

"The joy is mine," she lied, the feigned smile still on her face. "Happy is my soul to rejoice!" Tears began to flow again as she realized the futility of her situation.

The acolyte looked from her tear-streaked face to his Bishop, then back again, smiling. He caught his Bishop's eye with a knowing glance which inferred, *didn't I tell you she was pious?*

The Bishop smiled even more broadly and nodded to the acolyte. *Indeed!* his smile replied. "Take the woman to the seminary for her instructions. My heart tells me that her destiny is with God."

The acolyte bowed again. "His will be done."

Ma's tears coursed down her cheeks, unabated.

\* \* \*

Ma's lieutenant ran.

His forehead ached terribly from the blistering branding he had just received, and every time his stride touched ground, the jarring would echo painfully in the fresh wound. But despite the intense discomfort his fast pace induced, he entertained no thoughts of slowing. The evening service would be ending soon, and he knew what sort of sport the acolytes made with the banished; worst of all, there was no protection from their holy sadism and no recourse to the ecclesiastical court, should he be foolish enough to complain. The banished had no standing and no rights. So he ran for his life, fast as he could, and hoped he was running fast enough.

With the weekly service still in progress, the roads were deserted for the moment, except for another branded heretic who matched his pace a moderate distance behind him, a woman, apparently heading for the same refuge as he: the high Sierras. The rough, wooded terrain would provide ample hiding places in the short term, and a secluded place to live in the longer term—assuming either of them made it that far, of course. Among the newly-banished, the chances for survival in the short term were exceedingly slim.

Lack of oxygen forced the lieutenant to a slower pace, his breath coming now in ragged gasps. Behind him, he saw that the woman had slowed as well, her stride no longer quite matching his; the distance between them had widened. He maintained a brisk walking pace until his breathing again approached a cadence closer to normal, then he resumed a slow trot. He did not consider waiting for the woman, or even turn his head to see if she still followed, let alone kept up. She was a stranger to him; and should acolytes appear, there was little he could do to help her in any event. He would be hard pressed to save himself, let alone her.

The moving tableau held for a short while, until behind him he heard the sound of expected, but definitely unwelcome voices in the near distance. He turned without slowing to see three acolytes in red robes running in hot pursuit, calling for the woman to halt. She wisely showed no signs of complying, but rather increased her pace and angled off into the undergrowth that stretched between the road and the base of the nearby foothills. All three acolytes hurried along her path in pursuit, not yet noticing, or perhaps not caring about the lieutenant; so he slowed to a halt and crouched down, taking the opportunity to rest a bit and catch his breath. He could well be needing all his stamina very soon.

From his vantage point further up the hill, he could see one of the three acolytes quickly closing in on the woman as she sprinted furiously but fruitlessly across the scrub. In no time the lead acolyte was upon her; he grabbed her by the arm, and together they spun to the ground, tumbling. The other two acolytes quickly caught up, then stood guard over them, not intent upon the carnal ritual about to take place on the ground, but rather scanning the fields and road instead. Disquietingly, one of them caught sight of the lieutenant, and they locked eyes. For a brief moment, the lieutenant could not bring himself to look away. He cursed under his breath at himself for having waited; he finally turned away brusquely, instantly assuming a getaway pace. There was nothing he could do for her now; and he would be fortunate indeed if he were able to elude the acolytes himself. Glancing back over his shoulder, he was relieved to see that they were not pursuing. But he was dismayed at the damage that had already been done, for they now knew the general direction in which he fled. They would be back, he knew.

Despite his faux pas, nightfall found him safely embraced in the protective arms of the forested foot of the mountains. A cheerful brook bubbled under his feet as he stumbled further into the dark woods, the sound and feel of the water serving as an invisible guide to lead him constantly higher into the mountains. The moving water would also help to mask his scent, should they decide to pursue him with hounds. It was an old survival trick he had learned during his Army days, a lesson he never expected to need or use, but which now paid an unanticipated dividend.

He splashed on in the dark for hours, stumbling occasionally as he continued his ascent. It wasn't until long after midnight that he caught the strong smell of pine hanging in the darkness around him. Calling upon another survival trick he had learned so long ago, he stepped out of the narrowing stream and fell to his knees in the soft needles that carpeted the ground. Using his arms as rakes, he scooped up a huge pile of pine needles to create a relatively soft bed. Burrowing deep into its insulating warmth, he fell immediately asleep, too drained of strength and heart to savor the sweet fact that he had somehow managed to elude his pursuers without further molestation. So far.

\* \* \*

An acolyte was created.

For the next several weeks, Ma alternated between her morning chores on the small farm where she lived, and her afternoon and evening education classes as an acolyte. In short order, she learned all she needed to know about life as an acolyte, and much of it amazed her.

She had had no idea that the Bishop's realm was so extensive and pervasive. Although there was no estimate of the number of members in the innumerable local congregations, the number of acolytes was known to the last detail, and there were thousands of them. There was no command structure or hierarchy; all of the acolytes reported directly to the Bishop, and he seemed to know each one of them personally. Whenever an undertaking required supervision, the Bishop merely chose one acolyte, apparently at random, to serve as straw boss.

Ma quickly learned those things that her new status required of her. They escorted her around the former airfield to familiarize her with its renovated facilities. In addition to the hangar that served as their church, other buildings had been adapted for ecclesiastical uses as well. Some served as storage areas for their communal food, others as armories, many as barracks for the acolytes. There were vast storehouses of red vestments, and scores of seamstresses always making more. But there were no jails or courts; branding, banishment, and blind obedience to the Bishop was all that was required to keep order.

Soon Ma assimilated the necessary knowledge, and with great fanfare was consecrated as a Holy Acolyte in the Order of God. She quickly became something of a celebrity among her fellow acolytes. Her smiling tears became her unwilling trademark, and because of them she was eagerly sought out to lead prayer vigils and other ceremonies. Her fellow acolytes strove to imitate her ability to cry on demand, and a few succeeded. But Ma could not say if their tears sprang from the same Earthly revulsion as hers, or from their own holy joy. She detested it all, not only her duties as an acolyte, but also how well she ultimately performed them. The result was more tears and more duties in endless, escalating repetition.

It was an inescapable, yet well-concealed fact that she despised being an acolyte. But of all her duties, there was one which she disliked less than all the rest. Despite the universal ban on electricity, there was one application that was deliberately retained. In the control tower of the former airfield was kept a shortwave transmitter, and for two hours every day it was Ma's duty to broadcast the Word of God to the sinners of the world, her tears invisible to the distant listeners, yet plainly evident in her voice. With the muted hum of an ungodly electric generator in the background, she would sing her false praises of the Bishop and his God. Despite the double hypocrisy, she preferred her broadcasts to any other acolyte duties, if only because she was left alone with her sorrow.

Occasionally, someone from the outside world would attempt to communicate with her via the shortwave, but the strict rules imposed upon her sinful use of electricity demanded that she never reply, and an acolyte was frequently posted in the control tower to ensure that every word she broadcast conformed with holy doctrine. But in the acolyte's absence, there was no prohibition on listening. As a result, she learned much about the destruction that had swept the nation, and the resulting shock waves that were still sweeping the world. She was devastated to discover that Mr. James, president of Transcontinental Railroad, had not only survived, but had somehow become the new Head of State. She couldn't forget that it was him and his railroad who had killed her son, Kip.

One evening on a whim, in her anger and anguish she penned a sermon denouncing Mr. James and the heathen world he represented, with Kip featured as the oppressed victim of James' ruthlessness. With some trepidation, she chanced presenting it to the Bishop fearing he might brand her a heretic for it. But the prelate was thrilled with what she had written. Not only was her sermon distributed to all of the congregations to be delivered at their next service, she was permitted to broadcast it herself to the world via shortwave.

For once, the tears in her eyes stemmed from her own righteousness and the venom in her voice came voluntarily as she blasted her own form of divine vengeance upon the forever-damned soul of Mr. James. It was a small consolation in compensation for the fraudulent role fate had forced her to play, but she accepted it gratefully; there were too few other blessings for her to count in this new world.

Besides, she had little other choice.

## CHAPTER 3 – STATIC ON THE RADIO

Dagny lighted another cigarette.

It was almost dark outside, the hour when the shrinking summer snowcaps seethed with an ultraviolet sheen, and the craggy peaks that surrounded the Gulch took on a purple haze. She sat on a bedroom windowsill seat admiring the splendor of the quickly gathering gloom, a beauty made more brilliant by leaving all of the interior house lights turned off.

She sat alone in the twilight. Her husband was out for the evening, and wasn't due back for at least another hour—likely longer. Philosophical discussions tended to stretch on and on sometimes; most times, in fact.

She frowned at the cigarette in her hand with some disdain. She wasn't sure she had really wanted one, but had lit it anyway. Despite its high quality, the tobacco tasted stale, leaving an off taste in her mouth. Wearing a sour expression that matched the foul flavor, she set the unwanted cigarette to smolder in the ashtray unsmoked.

Their house in the valley would have been quiet as a church, except for a constant background hiss of static that emanated from the ancient bakelite radio sitting on her nightstand. The volume was turned down, low enough that it was easy to ignore, but loud enough for her to notice the instant that the static might stop. With a hint of impatience obvious in her manner, her glance shot up to the clock. She had to squint as she peered through the gloom to discern the positions of the hands; it was quarter to nine. The broadcast was five minutes late, which meant that it was not going to air tonight. Her shoulders sagged almost imperceptibly. She was disappointed, as she always was on any night that the broadcast failed to air.

She had not felt entirely well for most of the day—perhaps she had the beginnings of a cold or some other minor malady—and she had been anticipating a quiet evening with her husband; that she felt out of sorts only added to that anticipation. But he had agreed at the last minute to hold a lecture on philosophy for some of the newcomers, leaving her alone in the twilit room with her incipient malady and her moody thoughts. He held such impromptu consultations often, so often that Dagny frequently felt that her role in married life revolved almost exclusively around bed and breakfast.

Sometimes, though, the breakfasts were themselves a major event. Earlier that summer, she had played hostess for the traditional breakfast held every June first for the last thirteen years, a meal always attended by Francisco, Ragnar, and her husband—and this year for the second time, her. Her husband still asleep, she had awakened with the dawn that morning to arrange for their repast, starting with a trip to Lawrence's Grocery Market to purchase the victuals it required. Upon her return, she busied herself with the domestic routine of preparing the bounty: squeezing oranges, slicing bread, filling the coffee pot, setting the table for the four of them, and more. At one time she considered such actions to be a simple joy, but tonight, sitting in the murk with only her disappointment for company, she found it difficult to recapture that delight.

Without warning, conscious thought, or effort, all of the feelings within her and the images surrounding her coalesced into one sharp emotion, one that reflected the overall mood, fostered by a combination of the gloomy darkness inside the house, the fading daylight outside, and her physical weariness from the illness, seasoned with the hollow taste in her mouth of a cigarette lit too soon, and now her disappointment. Surprisingly, she found herself experiencing an emotion she seldom encountered: tonight, Dagny felt lonely.

The darkness outside had gradually become complete. The only remaining lights were the tiny orange coal of her ignored cigarette still smoldering in the ashtray next to her, and the soft brown glow of the lighted radio dial against the far wall of the bedroom. She stood up in the blackness, cautiously felt her way across the darkened room, and switched on the lamp next to the radio, banishing the shadows. In its light, she studied the radio for a moment, listening to the quiet, meaningless sound of the static. She looked back to the clock: seven minutes late now. There would be no symphonies tonight, that was sure. She reached out for a knob and brusquely snapped off the current, spun around, and stalked back to the windowsill seat. As she sat back down, she impatiently crushed out the cigarette she had lit, but not smoked. She glanced outside, but her eyes met only her own reflection in the glass; nervously she turned away from her own visage.

Without the constant low drone of random static from the radio, the silence in the house became almost deafening, bluntly showcasing the missing music. *Of all times to skip broadcasting!* she protested. *This is surely not my lucky day!* Instantly her jaw tightened in angry irritation at herself that she would even presume to entertain such a thought. She did not believe in luck—except that men made their own luck. Exasperated, she abandoned the windowsill seat and nervously began pacing the floor. Sadly, there was no broadcast to soothe her savage mood.

Nobody knew the source of the broadcasts; the only thing that was certain was that they always started at exactly twenty minutes of nine—not every night, but most nights someone somewhere took pleasure in broadcasting an hour of music; no talking, no station call letters, no weather forecasts, advertising, or news, nothing but one hour of uninterrupted music.

The program had been discovered by chance by Quentin, a young scientist formerly employed by the Utah Technology Institute—and also formerly employed by Dagny, tasked with discovering the secret of the galtmotor—but now a sworn striker. He had accidentally discovered the radio program one evening in his lab when a short circuit captured the broadcast's carrier signal on an oscilloscope. Some quick measurements revealed that it was a station on the commercial radio band, something that was once very commonplace; but since the collapse of the world Outside, there was little electricity left to either broadcast or to listen.

At first, Quentin's discovery made him the brunt of a number of good-natured jokes; for by the time he was able to inform someone about the phantom station, it had ceased broadcasting, the oscilloscope showing only a flat line where just moments before a squiggly sine wave had hung immobile. But with the tenacity that marks all great scientists, Quentin commenced a methodical search for the mysterious signal. It took him only twenty-three hours before he found the broadcast—and an end to the jokes—and within a few days he had its pattern nailed down: it would always begin at the same moment, eight forty, with the precision of a railroad timetable, and last for exactly one hour plus the minute or two it would take for the last song to finish. He could not, however, determine which nights would see a broadcast and which nights would remain silent. When cornered, he'd opine that the broadcasts occurred on a "random majority" of evenings.

His interest piqued, Quentin constructed a primitive breadboard receiver to transform the radio waves into physical sounds, at first only out of curiosity, but soon found that he enjoyed listening to the music. Before long it became his custom to tune in regularly.

Although Dagny had heard the news of Quentin's discovery, it was several weeks later before she finally heard the program for herself. One evening when Dagny happened to be visiting the man, she heard the program for the first time and was taken aback. What nobody had mentioned to her was that it wasn't merely music; it wasn't waltzes or swing or jazz or gospel or mindless popular trash, but rather the broadcast consisted of nothing but symphonies interspersed with an occasional concerto, those being her favorite forms of music. There wasn't a large variety of recorded music in the valley, and despite Richard's frequent talented performances, the additional fare was both welcome and refreshing. Even better, the symphonies weren't merely symphonies, but rather some of the best ever performed, ones that she would personally single out to air, were she the program's host. As outlandish as it may seem, she felt as if someone were serenading her individually, someone who knew her moods, feelings, and heart. She became an instant fan.

The morning after first hearing the broadcast, she began a systematic search of the valley for a radio of her own. Her quest did not take very long: Midas had owned an old tabletop model which he had brought with him into the valley when he first arrived so many years earlier, a relic which had once belonged to Midas' father. She found that the radio still occupied its same old perch in Midas' attic, although its ownership had been transferred along with the remainder of the late magnate's estate. The new owner sold the heirloom to her for its scrap value, that being his estimation of its worth.

Beginning that night, Dagny made it a point to catch the broadcast whenever she could, always tuning in a little early so as not to miss a single note. But on too many nights, such as tonight—a "random minority" of nights—there were no notes at all, and a mild disappointment would instead become her theme song for the evening. As an added, unexpected and unwanted bonus, tonight she danced to the rare melody of loneliness.

She could not understand why she felt so all alone. With characteristic ruthlessness, she delved into the possible reasons. She thought of her husband, now a familiar presence in her everyday life, no longer the shadow he once played Outside. But thinking of him did not assuage the void within her; she still felt the sharp stab of loneliness. Her self-honesty forced her to delve deeper. *If not for him, then for whom or what am I lonely?* She thought of her former lovers, Hank and Francisco, two other now-constant presences in her life, again without discovering the cause. With the tendrils of her mind, she reached out to all the people, places, and achievements she could call to mind that might be the cause of the void. She called up memories of her parents, of the arduous pleasure of re-building Transcontinental's Rio branch, of vacationing with Hank, working at the Stockdale station as a teen, riding the *Meteor*, the quiet, continuous joy of running Transcontinental Railroad, and a long series of the other bright points in her life whose absence may now be the source of her loneliness; but to no avail. All that remained was that unprecedented, peculiar emptiness.

Exasperated, Dagny plopped down on the bed with a bounce, mussing the expertly-made bedspread. She was out of ideas. *What could it be?* she wondered. *Am I over-reacting to something?* Suddenly, she smiled; she had caught a brief glimpse of her own reflection in the dresser mirror: a wide-eyed and wondering expression hovering on her face for an instant before it changed to the small smile she now wore. She almost laughed aloud at the fleeting image of herself that she had glimpsed: one of honest, open, self-interrogation with an edge of bewilderment. *Just look at yourself!* she chided, locking eyes with the candid image in the mirror. *You remind me of Edd—*

And the room spun!

\* \* \*

The sign creaked.

Ignoring it and the warm night breeze that animated it, Dagny walked briskly along the brightly-lit street, hands swinging slightly at her side, her fingers naked to the tame August air, her heels clicking on the clean sidewalk in a fast rhythm sounding not unlike train wheels clattering over joints in the rail. As she walked, her glance turned left and right to better take in all of the sights; for the main road through the center of the Gulch had undergone a complete metamorphosis of late, courtesy of the local merchants. Not only had its surface been paved smooth and crossing lines neatly painted for the first time, but also a goodly number of new buildings had recently been constructed in the shadow of the golden dollar sign. Together, they formed a lively town center. Where once sat only the bank, grocery, and dry goods store now held dozens of different shops and restaurants offering for sale a wide variety of products and services. The sidewalk had been installed only a few days earlier, another joint effort of the merchants, and this was her first trip along its smooth, unyielding surface. Multi-colored neon signs competed with the brilliant street lamps against the black backdrop of the Colorado night to create a bubble of lively cheerfulness amidst the dark mountains. Here and there couples and small cliques of friends walked or loitered on the sidewalks, with numerous cars parked along the curbs. Ahead of her, a Lawrence limousine swung around a corner, expertly steered. Rumor had it that traffic lights would soon be needed at several of the town's intersections—there had been two accidents within the last month alone—but the issue of who would pay for the signals remained unresolved.

The brilliant scene stretched on for several blocks ahead of her before it dissipated into unending darkness. Dagny smiled. The lights of the town center were precisely the tonic she had been seeking to dispel her unexpected loneliness. The sights of the hustle and bustle of small-town life seasoned with big-city tastes appealed to her, not only for its apparent gaiety, but also for the philosophy which underpinned it and made that gaiety authentic. This was a society that no looter could touch. She continued to smile, nodding in recognition as a middle-aged couple walked by. Dagny noted in passing that it looked like the woman was pregnant. Briefly she considered the possibility of her and her husband raising children of their own, but she immediately rejected the notion. *Too busy for babies!*

Again, the wooden sign creaked behind her in the breeze, its metal eyes scraping against the rusting steel rod which held it outstretched. *"The Caged Bird,"* it proclaimed, with painted gilded letters carved against a red velvet background. The sign gave Dagny pause. She had thought the taproom was named *The Golden Touch*. On the wall underneath the sign hung a poster announcing, "Miss Kay, On Stage! Tonight Only!" and from within came the sounds of a ragtime piano. Curious, Dagny entered the dimly-lit taproom.

She hadn't been inside the building since the days when it had served as Midas' bank. From what she had heard, one of the scabs had purchased the property shortly after his arrival and converted it into a taproom, with the stage being the most recent addition. He had left most of the bank décor intact, cleverly adapting its furnishings to their new purpose. Even the taproom's original name—*The Golden Touch*—had retained a tribute to its former purpose and its late owner. Idly, she wondered what had made him change it.

She stood in the doorway a moment to let her eyes adapt to the dimmer lighting within. Cigarette smoke hung thickly in the air. Ahead of her, a raised stage filled the area behind the teller booths, their gratings and smoked glass serving to shield the glare of the footlights from the patrons. On her left, the tall, long tables formerly used by bank customers to prepare their deposits had been skillfully joined together to form a single, smooth surface to serve as the bar, and a low-slung bar rail had been added to its front face. High stools were arrayed in front of the makeshift bar, and oak shelves lined the wall behind it. Those shelves had once held bank records; today they held an array of wines and spirits, and a variety of glasses. Over a dozen round tables of varying sizes were sprinkled around the former bank lobby, each accompanied by two to four chairs around their circumference. All of the seats were occupied. Several more people sat in chairs lined up along the remaining walls, and a number were left standing. Dagny recognized fewer than half of the patrons; the pianist she recognized immediately: it was Richard. Some of the patrons spoke softly among themselves, but overall the air in the room was one of quiet expectation.

"Evening, Miss Dagny," the pilot rumbled politely and nodded deferentially from behind the bar. He succeeded in concealing his shock; Dagny had never before deigned to bless his establishment with her august presence. *Glad I hired Kay!* he congratulated himself. "What can I get for you?"

On a whim stemming from her melancholy, Dagny suggested the impossible. "French wine, please."

Without missing a beat, straight-faced the pilot replied, "Red or white?"

Caught by surprise, it took her a second to recover. "Red," she replied matter-of-factly, unconsciously mimicking his suave.

"Bordeaux, Merlot, or Cabernet?"

Her eyebrows went up. "Merlot," she replied after a pause, the expression on her face revealing a bewildered intrigue.

"What year?"

Dagny was completely taken aback. She had no idea that there was such a selection of wines available in the valley; she had no ready answer. But the poorly-suppressed mischievous grin on the pilot's face eventually broke through, exposing his game. Looking around, Dagny discovered that much of the room had been eavesdropping on their exchange. They burst into friendly laughter and light applause at her quiet, embarrassed smile.

"Welcome to *The Caged Bird*, Miss Dagny. I hope you're not offended. Seriously, I'm sorry to say that we have no French wines, only those which our friend and neighbor Richard puts down. But he does do a reasonable Baco Noir, if I say so myself." He flipped a wine glass up from under the bar and set it in front of her. "First one's always on the house." He turned to retrieve a smallish bottle of wine from the top shelf, popped its cork, and poured her glass full. As an afterthought, he produced a second glass for himself and drained the remainder of the split into it. He raised his glass and toasted, "Naz Drowie. To tak jest dobre."

As she reached for her glass, she raised an inquisitive eyebrow. "Meaning...?"

"Beats me," he admitted. "Something about a dog in your driveway, I think." The pilot shrugged. "No matter..." He took a rather large sip and added, "You're just in time—Kay goes on in about six minutes. And by the way, it's a fifty cent cover charge."

Dagny had just begun to sip her wine, but lowered the glass from her lips in shocked surprise. She attempted to speak around the wine in her mouth, but, "Fity cen—!" was all that came out.

"It's Miss Kay!" he explained with mock offense.

"I see," she said, recovering.

"Double that, and maybe I can get you a chair?" he offered, a too-innocent look on his face.

"That would be fine, thank you," she agreed, correctly reading his expression. Clearly, the room was already overbooked; he had no chair to offer. She searched briefly in her handbag and placed a one-dollar coin on the bar.

He took on a pained look, then brightened, and turned to comply, gaining speed as he left—he didn't fancy missing a moment of Kay's appearance. Seconds later, he returned with a chair, although it had clearly seen better days. He dithered for a moment as he searched for a place to place it, when a young woman's voice called out, "Dagny! Over here!"

It was Gwen, sitting alone at an uncomfortably small, round table. An empty chair sat across from her, but the foamy-yellow contents of a sparking glass mug that stood in front of it suggested the chair was spoken for. Gwen pushed the chair out of the way and scooted her own chair in the opposite direction. The pilot set Dagny's battered chair into the cleared space between them and hurried back to the bar. It was almost show time; and he had a role to fill.

Gwen slid the glasses and napkins aside to clear a space in front of Dagny. "I'm really looking forward to this," she gushed. "I've never seen Miss Kay in so intimate a venue."

"I didn't even know this was happening!" confessed Dagny.

"It was a last-minute thing," she explained. "Kay has been working up this new act with Richard and wanted to go through a full dress rehearsal, complete with audience reactions. Our host offered *The Caged Bird*'s new stage, and she accepted. It was planned only this afternoon, and news spread by word of mouth."

"I see," she said, taking a sip of wine. After a pause, she continued. "So how are plans for the wedding coming along?"

"Wonderfully! There's still another month to go, but everything is already just about ready!"

Dagny smiled. "I've worked alongside you too many times, Gwen—such as when we rebuilt the Rio branch—that I'm not surprised. I'm sure you've left nothing to chance."

"Of course, Miss Dagny," she replied formally, a playful tone in her clear, courteous voice.

Dagny's smile broadened. "I thought we agreed a long time ago it was just 'Dagny,'" she reminded her needlessly.

"Of course, Miss Dagny," she replied just as formally; and neither woman could suppress the laughter that followed. Subsiding, Gwen reached across the round surface of the table and placed a hand softly on Dagny's arm. On the third finger was an ornate engagement ring, replete with one large diamond flanked by two lesser brethren. Clearly, it was an expensive item, even by the standards of the old world Outside. "Seriously, Dagny, I'm *so* glad you consented to being my Maid of Honor. You're the closest thing to a sister that I have in this valley."

Smiling, Dagny took a sip of wine, her eyes bright. "Thank you, Gwen. I'd have to say the same thing myself about you."

"And I didn't ask you to be in our wedding just for your sake—" She caught herself. "—not that it matters! I'm also doing it for my fiancé, especially since you two have been working together for so long."

"He'll make a fine husband, Gwen. You can trust me on that."

"But should I?" murmured Gwen as an aside to herself, her philosophical slipup on top of her mind.

"What did you say?"

"Nothing. I was reminded of something… from philosophy class."

Dagny had no chance to probe further when Quentin returned.

"I'm glad I made it back in time!" he whispered excitedly to Gwen as he took his seat. "I'd hate to miss a minute of it!" He turned to face Dagny. "Hello, Miss Dagny. Glad you could make it, too."

"Thank you. As am I. I hadn't heard about this until just now."

"I heard about it early on," Quentin bragged good-naturedly. "Just after lunch, when it was first set up. But then…," he sighed, tossing up his hands in mock disgust, "I was so busy with the secret code, I almost forgot to come! I was—"

"Secret code?" interrupted Dagny. "What secret code?"

"The State's Science Institute's secret code. They've been sending a lot of coded broadcasts lately, and I was curious what it was all about."

"Curious about some looter's broadcasts?" she inquired mockingly. "What on Earth for?"

"No! About their code! I thought it would be fun to try to decipher it."

"And were you able to?"

He struck a pose. "Of course!" he beamed, then added playfully, "And after all the time you and I have worked together, how could you possibly start to doubt me now?" He leaned over the table and glanced at Gwen then back to Dagny conspiratorially. "Listen: I found out that Dr. Floyd is planning to attack Washington come November!" he whispered unnecessarily. "They have a small army hiding just outside of town, and they're going to try to restore Mr. Thomson as Head of State. I was able to break their code and find out all about it. Isn't that exciting?"

Dagny tossed her shoulder-length brown hair in dismissal. "To a looter, perhaps." She sipped her wine briefly, almost theatrically. "Who else could get excited about what happens Outside?"

"No! No! I meant breaking the code was exciting! It was a tough one, one of their best—and I had to decode it manually!" He paused for a moment, considering. "You know, now that I think of it, I bet I could build an automatic decoder out of relays and an electric typewriter..." His eyes glazed over as he considered the idea.

"Yes, but could you build a traffic light?" interrupted Gwen.

Taken by surprise, Quentin stared at her. "A what?"

"A traffic light! There was another automobile accident up the corner yesterday, the second one this month!"

"Well, sure I could build one. It wouldn't be too hard to make, even one that would stand up to our Colorado winters. But it wouldn't come cheap."

Dagny interjected flatly. "And just who do you expect to pay for it, Gwen?"

"Well, you'd think *someone* would—before they become a victim and get themselves killed out there!"

Nonchalantly Dagny took another sip of wine. "When it becomes important enough to enough men, it will get done."

"True enough," agreed Quentin. "And I'd bet the men who underwrite automobile insurance would be among the ones most interested in funding it. Or would they...?" His eyes took on a distant look. "Let's see, if the average cost of an accident repair is $X$ dollars and there are $Y$ accidents per month, how long would it take to amortize..." He drifted off, deep in thought, then paused, a questioning look on his face. "Gwen, how badly damaged were those automobiles?"

"They weren't," she admitted, somewhat reluctantly. "They were both made of Miracle Metal, so neither one was damaged."

"Then $X$ is zero! There's no cost!" He threw his hands in the air in exasperation. "All the equations fall apart when $X$ is a zero!"

"Now do you see why no one has bothered to put up a light?" Dagny interrupted again.

Gwen looked deflated. "I guess. But it's not only about the automobiles—what about the men? I just hope it's not going to be the life insurers who'll have to amortize the cost!"

Quentin was already calculating. "Well, that's an entirely different question. Let's see, then. If the average...," he began, but quickly shook himself out of it with a gay smile. "No! Enough of traffic lights for today! I'm here to see Kay! I've been looking forward to this all afternoon! Haven't you, Miss Dagny?"

"As I said, I just happened by," Dagny reminded him, not recalling, for the moment, how she happened to be in the area. "I saw the sign out front and came in to see what it was all about."

"Well, this must be your lucky day!"

Upon hearing his words, Dagny froze. The pang of loneliness that shot through her body was almost physical in its intensity. For several minutes now, she had not thought of Eddie; the care-free banter with her friends had momentarily masked her melancholy. But the reference to her luck sounded a shatteringly discordant note within her, instantly deflating her gay mood. Almost ashamed of herself, she recognized his words as her own.

Something of her state of mind must have shown on her face, for she saw concern reflected in Quentin's; its mate began to take form on Gwen's as well. But before either of them could formulate a spoken reply, the house lights dimmed, and the audience reacted excitedly. From behind the bar, the deep voice of the pilot boomed out.

"Ladies and gentlemen!" he rumbled, his bass timbre impressively resonating across and around the room. The patrons fell silent; electricity was in the air. He paused briefly and expertly to let its energy build before he continued. "*The Caged Bird...*" He paused. "Proudly presents..." He paused again. "Mr. Richard and..." Into the tense atmosphere he had created, he finally bellowed, "*Miss... KAY!*" The darkened stage lights suddenly burst into brilliance, revealing the lovely Miss Kay dressed in blue denim overalls sharply contrasting a feminine, lace-trimmed white blouse. Cheers and applause greeted her appearance, then the appreciative noises quickly dissipated into a church-like silence.

Richard began to play, and for the next half hour the audience was treated to a brilliant, personal performance by two of the immortals of entertainment. Tonight Kay danced alone to a piano accompaniment, and her recital was pure poetry in motion supported on the wings of Richard's imagination. With her well-trained body, her natural talent, and her mind's ability to translate complex thought into meaningful action, coupled with Richard's incomparable musical talent, in dance and music they presented to the audience a story of deliverance, a tale of joy, of woe, of rebirth, and restoration. It was the Phoenix rising from the ashes, the celebration of a life that could not be denied or defeated, clearly portrayed in seamlessly-complementary piano and choreography. Each motion, each facial expression, and each note that accompanied them blended together into a single, comprehensible, integrated whole.

When the finale had finally finished, the audience sat awestruck. The music was so uplifting, the timing so perfect, the message so clear, the score so perfect that it took several seconds for the performance to finish resonating within the minds of the audience. Then, to a man, the audience rose as one to their feet, thunderous applause rocking the old bank's walls to their granite roots as Kay and Richard took their bows. When it seemed as if the thunder would go on forever, Kay held up a single hand. As if by magic, the room fell instantly silent; yet none sat down. Truth be told, it was magic indeed; she still held the audience solidly under her thespian's spell, and they would have done most anything she would have commanded.

Into the silence she had created, Miss Kay dropped her words. "I call my performance, 'Hank Steel.' Could you tell?"

Again, the audience went wild, for her performance had been so accurate in its portrayal of that company's long history of overcoming all trials and tribulations that it couldn't have been called anything else. It was a tribute to the company and, out of necessity, to the man who had made the company real.

She held up her hand again, and again the audience recognized their cue. Even faster than before, the room fell silent. They hung on her every word.

"Remember! This is going to be a surprise for Hank to celebrate the re-opening of Hank Steel next week, so *don't give me away!* Can I count on you not to tell?" she asked coquettishly.

Again, the room cheered its assent. This time, all she needed to do was to open her mouth and the room fell instantly silent. "It will be held inside his new mills next Wednesday at noon sharp... and it's only a one dollar cover. See you there!" With that, Kay took a final bow and left the stage amidst a long-sustained roar of appreciation.

When the bedlam had finally quieted, Dagny turned to Quentin, her eyes wide and moist. "That was truly amazing!" she blurted, still held in thrall to the performance.

His expression reflected his own similar state of mind, as he replied, "Indeed! I can't wait to see the look on Hank's face!"

With that, again Dagny froze. She recalled all too well having said those very words to herself on innumerable occasions, back in the days when she had been Hank's mistress. But tonight it wasn't Hank whose memory was called to mind; it was Eddie.

"Miss Dagny? Are you all right?"

"Dagny?...," Gwen chimed in worriedly.

She needlessly pushed her hair back with one hand. "I believe I'm coming down with a cold. Perhaps I shouldn't have had the wine."

All concern, Gwen suggested, "Maybe you should stop by to see Dr. Thomas in the morning?"

"You're right" she replied wearily, standing up. "I will. But right now I should be on my way. My husband will be home in a little while and I'll need to cook him a late dinner." Without another word, Dagny took her leave, apparently not hearing their well-wishes.

She emerged from the taproom onto the new sidewalk lit by radiant tubing shining brightly in gay defiance of the dark night, but the gaiety was now lost on her. Kay's spell had been broken, and with its passing the pressure of thoughts not to be denied burst upon her. She strode quickly from the taproom, unconsciously increasing the speed of her step; she soon found herself running, then racing along the new sidewalk, around a corner, and hurtling into the darkness beyond the brightly-lit street. As she ran, she could see her own shadow from the receding streetlights growing longer and longer in front of her, a lengthening silhouette being pursued, but never surpassed. Eventually, she collapsed in fatigue, taking refuge to sit upon a wooden box behind some unnamed building. Soon, her breathing returned almost to normal. She bent over slowly into an almost fetal position, dropping her head onto her folded arms, arms against her knees. Huddled, she took one confident, deep breath, and broke down into tears. *Oh, Eddie!*

Involuntarily but unsurprisingly her thoughts retreated to the last time she had seen Eddie, perhaps a week before the lights of New York City had gone out forever. He was leaving for San Francisco, determined to herd one more *Meteor* across the nation back to New York. He had secured a spot on an Army airplane bound for California, and that same night it had carried him away. Then within the week the entire world had been carried away, with Eddie being swallowed up along with all the rest.

Dagny sighed through her sobs, recalling Eddie's last words: "Did you know... how I felt about you?"

"Yes," she had said softly, realizing in that moment that she had known it wordlessly for years.

With that, he had left. But the awareness of his long-held love for her had remained with her ever since. And tonight, the void his absence had created within her proved to be far too great for her to ignore any longer: finally, Dagny came to understand fully that she loved Eddie in return—and more importantly, she also understood why she loved him—*had* to love him.

She lifted her head, tears sparkling on her cheeks, staring at the silent, uncaring stars. Who was it that stood by her all her life? Who ran Transcontinental Railroad while she was off re-building the Rio branch? Who was it who helped to carry her load? Who was her constant partner in the never-ending battle against the looters? Who was always there for her, no matter what, no matter when? *Eddie! The unassuming hero!*

This was a longing she had never permitted herself to acknowledge, but she faced it openly now. She brusquely and inadequately brushed away the starlit tears. *I was a fool!* she told herself. *I should have seen!* But recriminations were of little use now; Eddie was surely dead. With all the death and destruction that had devastated the nation and the planet—especially given the stories that had come out of California!—it was ludicrous to believe that Eddie could have possibly survived. But even as she formulated that thought, her mind instinctively rebelled. She shot to her feet, standing stiffly straight.

"No!" she cried aloud to the dark, empty street. "No!" she screamed again. Her wits in a whirl, she ran off blindly into the black night, even though one part of her mind recognized her vain gesture for the folly it was. But the sputtering spark of reason was drowned out by the tide of tears; she ran on.

She was not aware of the passage of time, but presently her angry despair subsided. Finally taking note of her surroundings, she found herself at the valley's cemetery. She gently opened the gate she found in front of her and let herself in, needlessly careful to latch it behind her. Arrayed before her were the thirteen graves which inaugurated the use of the cemetery in the wake of Midas' Avalanche several months ago; no one else had been buried since. She walked among the headstones, reading each one slowly. Halfway through her study, she plopped down roughly to sit on one of the smaller stone markers. Again she dropped her head onto her knees, and again she began to sob softly. "Oh, Eddie!" was all she could say. "Oh, Eddie!"

She could not say how much time had passed before she finally sat up. She took a deep breath and rubbed both eyes before looking up at the dark sky. Only the impassive, immobile stars met her gaze. Again she sighed, only this time more resigned than sorrowful, then stood. The tears that remained on her cheeks still refracted the dim starlight, but they no longer flowed. With a final deep breath, Dagny faced her truth. Eddie was dead. It didn't matter anymore, *couldn't* matter anymore. She had to get on with her life. She still had her husband, and while he was no Eddie, he was at least a reasonable second. *But no Eddie*, she told herself one last time, realizing it, appreciating it and its dual meaning, understanding it fully, and silently accepting it.

With one final glance at the impersonal stars, again locking the gate needlessly carefully behind her, she left the graveyard behind, also leaving behind the memory of Eddie.

With the matter finally settled in her mind once and for all, she recovered her mental equilibrium quickly, as if some powerful narcotic had finally worn off. She turned toward home; eyes straight, chin high, step firm. *What shall I make for my husband's dinner tonight?* she wondered.

\* \* \*

Dr. Thomas smiled.

Across the desk from him sat Dagny, her face serious and calm, not reflecting Dr. Thomas' unexplained joviality.

He held up a manila folder thick with paperwork. "I have the results of the tests we ran the other day."

"So you said."

"They show that you're a normal, healthy woman."

"I'm glad."

"With normal, healthy consequences."

Dagny hesitated. "Meaning...?"

His smile broadened. "Congratulations, Dagny. You're pregnant."

Her expression did not change; only her eyes widened slightly. With calm precision, she replied, "Thank you for the news, doctor, but I really can't afford to make time for a baby right now. Hank and I are in the middle of building a branch line to his new copper mine halfway up the south mountain."

"The first railroad in the Gulch!"

"Yes—the Dagny Line. But it won't be finished for another three and a half months yet."

"Not until December?" His smile faltered. "But how can you run trains at that altitude once the winter snows begin?"

"Oh, the snow won't matter."

His eyebrows went up in surprise. "Won't matter?"

"No. If you run the right amount of electricity through Miracle Metal rails, the electrical resistance heats them up sufficiently to keep the entire right of way clear of ice and snow—except for the occasional avalanche, of course—and the difference in electrical potential between the rails can be used to power the train's engine, too. My husband is building a special galtmotor, just to run the Line."

"That's outstanding, Dagny! It sounds like you're pretty busy."

"Bored is more like it," she snapped unexpectedly, reaching for her package of cigarettes.

"Bored?" He was taken by surprise by the sudden change of subject, but he smiled at himself; given her condition, he should have expected it. "What do you mean, bored?"

Brusquely, Dagny lighted a cigarette. "Doctor Thomas," she began severely, blowing smoke into the air above their heads. "After running a transcontinental railroad for over a decade, how else do you think I would feel about building a local freight spur?"

He smiled in sympathy. "I see," he said.

She hesitated and glanced around uncertainly, then looked back to his face. "I assume I'd have to limit any strenuous activities?"

This time he was ready for the sudden shift of topic. "Of course. No mountain climbing or anything else too arduous. Given it's your first pregnancy, you shouldn't take any chances until you learn how your body handles it."

"It's not my first pregnancy," she replied flatly. "You know that."

"First baby, I should have said."

"And it's not going to be that, either. Not now."

"I see," he said again. "Then we ought to schedule some time very soon when we can address the situation."

"What about right now?"

"Don't you want to talk it over with your husband first?"

"No. The last time, he said it was my decision what I should do with the little parasite." She permitted herself a small smile. "I think we can safely assume his opinion has not changed."

Dr. Thomas glanced at his wristwatch and stood. "Fine. My next patient isn't due until late this afternoon. The procedure is a simple one, so I could squeeze it in right away with no problem."

Dagny stood as well. "All right. Let's have this over with. I have a railroad to build."

"Fine," he repeated. He extended a hand toward an examination room.

She spoke over her shoulder as she headed for the indicated door. "Those mood swings I've been experiencing lately suddenly make a lot more sense."

"Of course. Your hormone balance is way out of kilter right now. But it should return to normal in a month or so, and then you'll be over it."

Dagny paused at the door, her hand on its knob. Her eyes took on a distant gaze as if she were pondering some object far, far away.

"We shall see," she observed absently.

## CHAPTER 4 – CRAWL BACK UNDER MY STONE

The crook cowered.

The unfortunate man had little choice but to hide himself. The day had been pure hell for him, a damnation that had started early and continued to accelerate with each passing hour. Hence, he hid; he *had* to hide!

As with most damnations, his had sprouted from a combination of great pride and righteous determination. Standing in front of the Las Vegas jury that had just convicted him of theft, he flatly rejected the sentence of three months' exile they had decreed as his punishment. "I do not recognize this court's right to try me!" he had cried defiantly. If they needed his sanction to make the proceedings legal, he was not going to give it. "Go ahead and plaster my face around town on your 'exiled' posters; I will not help you pretend that you are administering justice!" he asserted brazenly. "I will have no part of it!" His brave words earned him the admiration of his criminal peers; and when he stalked out of the courtroom unmolested, they slapped him on the back and pumped his hand energetically. By now, everyone in town had heard how you need not accept the sentence of the jury, but in the months since the new brand of trials had begun, none had chosen to stand against their verdict—until today. The crook was riding high on top of his thieves' world as a man in sole control of his fate. Standing in the mid-morning sun in front of the courthouse, he snapped his fingers at the building in criminal contempt, to a backdrop of his contemporaries' raucous applause. *He* sure showed *them!*

But the initial glow of triumph did not last long. The first crack in his newfound renown arrived only a few hours later, innocently enough, on the wings of humor during lunch at the honky-tonk near the Transcontinental station. As he sat with his co-workers and related the proud tale of the morning's trial over a fat mug of foamy, yellow ale, on a whim one of his companions took on a mischievous grin and reached out to snatch the mug from in front of the unsuspecting crook.

"Hey!" the crook cried. "That was *my* beer!"

His friend laughed into the pilfered beer as he sipped it, spraying white foam across the tabletop. "You're right! It *was* your beer!" With that, he downed the drink in a single, gulping swig.

"Why, you—," the crook began, but his companions only laughed.

"Go tell it to the jury!" the friend jabbed as he wiped off his chin. "If they'll even bother to listen to you!"

The others at the table laughed in unison at the joke being played on the unfortunate crook; they knew for a fact the man could never call on the jury to defend his rights ever again. So the victimized crook found himself reluctantly joining in the laughter; and for the first time that day, he found he had little other choice.

"Just having a little fun," asserted his friend. "Hey, let me buy you another." He signaled to the lovely barmaid, and she brought the crook a fresh mug. But no sooner than the beverage hit the table when another man snatched it up before the thirsty crook could even begin to reach for it.

"Hey!" he cried again.

"Tell it to the jury!" the man echoed. Sipping noisily, in a single, fluid motion he rose and spun away from the table to escape with his booty.

The results were similar with the third, fourth, and fifth beers the hapless crook attempted to order. The joke had rapidly worn thin, and the crook was forced to retreat in anger from the table to take a seat at the bar. Moodily he claimed an empty stool and ordered yet another beer. The beverage arrived swiftly, and he slid a large silver coin across the surface of the bar in payment; the proprietor smiled, pocketed the gleaming disc, and walked away.

"Hey!" the crook called to the retreating man. "Where's my change, buddy? That was a willie, you know!"

"What change?" the proprietor inquired innocently, brazenly holding his gaze.

The tableau held for several seconds before the crook realized he was being had yet again, and worse yet, that he was again left without recourse. Stymied, he angrily dashed the contents of the mug into the proprietor's face and stormed away, heading for the door. But in his anger he did not notice the foot that unexpectedly shot out in front of his, and with a squawk he tumbled over it to fall hard onto the wooden floor. The patrons laughed, and several heckled the unfortunate crook as he clambered to his feet and continued his interrupted retreat, red-faced with impotent anger. He slammed the swinging doors wide and fled the scene, once again being left with no other choice.

The end of the afternoon found him progressing further down the road to damnation: when his employer paid him his day's wage, it was only half the amount that was due him.

"Where's the rest of my money?" he demanded.

"You spent the whole morning in court. You're lucky you're getting that much!"

"But the trial lasted less than an hour, and I was on the job before ten!" he protested. "I deserve more than a half day's pay!"

"Go cry to the jury," suggested the cheating employer. "If they'll listen, that is!" He knew they wouldn't; not now. The news of the mischievous escapade at lunch had spread quickly.

The short-changed crook had no choice but to head for home; and when he arrived, he discovered his troubles had ratcheted to a new level, for while he was away someone had kicked in his door and ransacked the house; a quick glance revealed that most everything of value was missing. Granted, he did not live in the best of neighborhoods, and his friends were all of the same moral caliber as he, but there used to be some modicum of honor among thieves. Yet in light of his refusal to accept the sentence of the jury, that negligible amount of honor had vanished in a flash.

Open-mouthed he stared at the devastation a moment longer before blind anger washed over him. "Damn them all to Hell!" he frothed, hurling his hat to the messy floor in exasperated rage, his curse spanning not only his so-called friends, but also the members of the morning's jury. Ignoring the mess, he stepped hatless out onto the street, leaving the breached door open behind him. There was no point in closing it now. *What next?* he snapped angrily at the unknown judges of his unwitnessed mood.

*BLAM!* The dust puffed at his feet where the bullet had hit. "Run, you lousy bastard!" a disembodied voice yelled. *BLAM!* the revolver reported again, this time shattering the door jamb alongside his head, scattering splinters painfully across his cheek.

The panicked crook immediately took the advice to heart. Crouching low, he scurried around the corner of his home anxiously awaiting a third bullet, which fortunately never came. Discharging firearms within the city limits of Las Vegas was itself a crime, regardless of the intended target, but such niceties apparently meant nothing to his unseen attacker.

"You stay away from my girl!" demanded the anonymous assailant of the fleeing crook. "Or else! Because it's open season on the likes of you, you damned Exile, you! Get out of town! *Now!* And *stay* out!"

The poor crook's mind was in a whirl as he fled; he had no idea which girl his invisible nemesis might have meant—or if any girl existed at all! But girl or no girl, the heart of his message was crystal clear.

Sunset found him cowering in the back room of an abandoned store on the seediest side of town. In mere hours, his status had devolved from that of a free citizen to apprehended suspect to convicted criminal to hunted animal, leaving him with all the rights of an animal, specifically: none. He was an outlaw—literally a man outside the law—and as such, no longer entitled to call upon the court for protection. Nor was there any viable alternative; even the former crime bosses in town obeyed the new rules. There was more profit in it.

"Damn!" he cursed under his breath, cautiously quiet lest he inadvertently give his presence away. *What do I do now?* he demanded of himself, yet full well knowing the answer.

With a sigh he came to the only decision possible: later on, in the very wee hours of the morning—which was the *only* time the streets of Las Vegas ever emptied out!—he would slink back to the police station, turn himself in, repent, and accept the sentence of the court. One final time, he found himself with no other choice. Yes, he'd have to move to Boulder City or take a job as a farmhand at one of the outlying ranches, but the three months of his exile would pass quickly—or so he hoped. And even if it didn't, his existence would surely improve over what had promptly become one of the worst days of his life.

## CHAPTER 5 – LIVING IN THE USA

Ma's lieutenant escaped.

The first days of his exile were much less difficult than he had feared. He began his new life by establishing a base camp at an icy spring high in a wooded mountain hollow, that being the source of the same creek that he had first followed into the mountains. The spring seeped to the surface in the middle of a shallow, pine-filled depression some fifty feet in diameter, its bowl forming an ideal location for him to set up his household. The raised rim of the hollow would shield the gleam of his campfire from prying eyes, and would also help to cut down the force of the coming winter winds.

Having determined a location for his home base, he spent most of his waking hours exploring the surrounding forest and foraging for food. Game was plentiful in the mountain forests, and he had little difficulty constructing effective traps out of vines and saplings, creating spring-loaded nooses to snare unwary animals. In fact, his springes were so successful that when he first placed them, within a single day he snagged three deer. It was more meat than he could possibly consume before it spoiled, so he was forced to set two of the animals free. But he found it heartening that his meat was so easy to come by; he was certainly not going to starve.

In his foraging trips, while he never encountered a living person, he did stumble across an occasional abandoned mountain dwelling. Although any of them were his for the taking, he wouldn't dare consider moving in. He made it a steadfast rule never to linger for long anyplace accessible by road, lest the acolytes discover him.

But that did not stop him from rummaging through every dwelling he found. From them, he quickly amassed the wealth he would need to survive in this new world, including several knives of varying sizes, a serviceable three-quarter axe, a rusted shovel, copper wire, kitchen matches, some stout hemp rope, cookery, ill-fitting winter clothes, and even an old, but serviceable bicycle. One of the dwellings possessed a garden of sorts, with a sprawling berry patch and a modest, long-abandoned orchard. It being late in the growing season, both these finds were heavily laden with fruit. He spent several days harvesting the boon and transporting the fruit back to his base camp in the hollow, all the time watching over his shoulder for the acolytes who never came.

With the food situation well in hand, building a sturdy shelter became his highest priority; he knew the high Sierras could be a harsh mistress in wintertime, and he wanted to be as prepared as possible before the winter snows blew in. Using building materials scavenged from abandoned dwellings, he was able to construct a modest, one-room shack in his hollow, and as the weeks passed, Ma's branded lieutenant settled into his new way of life with some degree of rustic comfort.

As autumn advanced, he traveled farther and wider from his hollow in a random search for any item that might potentially enhance his chances for survival. One afternoon, he was out foraging many miles to the north of his hollow, and was surprised to catch the scent of a campfire drifting on the breeze. With great stealth, he slowly crawled upwind toward the source of the smoke, and soon found it. Peering through the trees he saw a camp much like his own, except this one lay in a narrow wooded valley alongside a tumbling brook rather than in a secluded hollow. He shook his head in scorn at such a bad choice of location; he knew that the noisy water would mask the sound of any approaching intruders.

A crude hut, a good deal smaller than his own shack, sat near the creek, its low door opening onto a large, flat, moss-covered rock that bordered the creek. Squatting on the carpeted rock outside the hut was the lone figure of a man working intently at some task in his lap; and when he looked up from his work, the lieutenant was not surprised to recognize a familiar scar on his forehead. It was another branded heretic.

Satisfied that he understood the situation, the lieutenant withdrew immediately, just as silently as he had come, thinking it best to elude discovery. While it would have been pleasant to have some company, he would much rather have no one at all know that he existed, not even another heretic. Besides, it was entirely possible that this might be an elaborate trap set to capture someone just like himself. He marked the location on his mental map, more as a region to avoid on future forays rather than in expectation of any return visit.

As the weeks turned into months, the lieutenant saw or heard no signs of any other humans. The temperatures had been drifting lower and lower day by day as the winter neared, and he continued gathering firewood, trapping, and foraging in preparation for the cold days ahead.

A healthy paranoia convinced him to cache some of his wealth a decent distance from his base camp, just in case, so he bundled up a spare knife, some matches, and a few other items handy for emergency survival, then secreted them under a cairn of rock further up the mountainside. Having established one such stash, he found reason to establish several others, some being backup stockpiles similar to the first, only further away, while others were no more than a collection of relatively useless odds and ends he had gathered which may prove their worth someday, such as the copper wire and the bicycle, but in the meantime would only serve to clutter up his hollow.

Once winter arrived in force, the lieutenant was glad he had put so much effort into preparedness, for once they started, the snows fell with a vengeance. The forest surrounding his sheltered hollow was soon buried under several feet of snow, a heavy blanket which precluded travel not only because of the inherent difficulty of traversing its depths, but also for the risk of leaving telltale footprints which might lead the acolytes to his lair.

Fortunately, there were no signs of any patrols, leaving him with only the much bigger challenge of simply surviving.

## CHAPTER 6 – A WORLD OF OUR OWN

The teller fidgeted.

"Well, there were quite a number of people who came in the bank that day," she explained nervously.

Her discomfort did not go unnoticed by the banker. He reached across his desk and handed her a sheet of ledger paper. "Take a look at this log of deposits and withdrawals," he suggested. "What would you make of it?"

She knew exactly what to make of it, and was trying her best to conceal that knowledge. She scanned it nonchalantly. "It's just a list of deposits and withdrawals," she observed a little too innocently.

"Yes, but isn't there something interesting about it? Take a look at what happens around one thirty."

She pretended to read the suggested entries, the paper starting to shake slightly in her jittery hand. She made no comment.

He pointed to the quivering paper. "Don't you see how there were random deposits and withdrawals up until that time, then almost nothing but withdrawals afterwards?"

She continued to look at the paper unnecessarily. She already knew what it said. "How about that," she noted noncommittally. Her voice quavered.

"Do you recognize the bank account number of the first withdrawal?"

Of course she did. It was hers. But she said nothing.

"It seemed an odd time to withdraw all your cash—just before everyone else did. Don't you think?"

She did not answer. There was nothing to be said.

"And then your co-worker did the same."

The hapless teller stared unblinkingly at the paper, and the banker continued. "You had better tell me what you know..."

She sighed heavily, nervously. "It was the Transcontinental stationmaster," she began, her voice cracking. "He came in here and changed all his money into silver dollars."

"How many?"

"Over a thousand of them. I forget exactly how many. They filled three of our canvas coin bags."

He pointed to the sheet she still held in her shaking hand. "But he didn't withdraw any money."

"No, I guess not."

"But you did. Why?"

She took a ragged deep breath. "I don't rightly know!" The words started tumbling out. "Mr. Eddie had called for the big meeting to be held that night and no one knew what it was all about then in walks his stationmaster and exchanges all his money for silver dollars and I thought he must know what he was doing..." She hesitated, looked down, and spoke softly to her knees. "...and so I did it, too."

"Did you ask him why he did it?"

She shook her head. Tears began to leak down her cheeks.

"Did you tell anyone else what he had done?"

She nodded, still looking down. The tears shook from her chin to splash onto the paper. "My sister," she whispered.

The banker sighed, leaning back in his chair. *That's what did it!*

She looked up with large, wet eyes. "You're not going to have them fire me, are you?" She was terrified. She could only imagine what the all-powerful Unificating Board might do to her, but in her troubled state of mind, she had forgotten that the Board no longer existed. The power it once held over the employment of every American was a thing of the recent past, but the fear was current, deep seated, and not easily excised.

He coldly held her gaze several seconds before replying. "No, I'm not going to have them fire you—*I'm* going to do it myself. You know how much the bank depends on your trustworthiness. You tried to take a personal benefit based upon knowledge of one of our customer's banking habits. That's a breach of trust. For the sake of our customers, I have to let you go."

Her hands flew to her face and she burst into sobs.

"I could take legal proceedings against you to reclaim the silver you girls took, but I won't." He stood up, indicating the interview was ended. "You can consider it your severance pay. It's far more than either of you deserve." This time it was the banker's voice that shook. "Please gather up your personal belongings and go."

Crying, she fled his office.

Again, the banker sighed. He loved his work, but sometimes he absolutely hated his job. *And there's still one more teller to go!*

\* \* \*

The stationmaster interrupted.

"You wanted to see me, Mr. Eddie?"

Eddie was on the telephone. He abstractly held up an index finger indicating the stationmaster should wait; his concentration was on his conversation. "No more pepper? What do you mean there's no more pepper?... Really? I wasn't aware that it was all imported... What should I use instead?... You're right, that would work. It's close enough... All right, thanks for the advice... Good-bye." He hung up the telephone and glanced up. "Sorry."

The stationmaster's eyes flicked toward the telephone inquisitively. "There's no pepper left?"

"That's what she says," he replied, reddening slightly. "Unless someone somewhere in town is growing it, it looks like there'll be no more pepper until we can manage to import some." He shook his head and mused abstractly. "Who would have thought it! I wonder what we'll run out of next?"

The stationmaster had little interest in the spice. Not only was it bad for his stomach, he detested its taste. "You wanted to see me?" he repeated.

"Yes. Please have a seat." He took a deep breath. "Listen: I was talking with the banker a little while ago and he had some interesting news."

"Is that so?" *Uh oh! Here it comes!* His heartbeat increased its pace noticeably.

"Yes." Eddie was clearly uncomfortable. He was reluctant to meet the stationmaster's eyes. "He said you exchanged a lot of paper money for silver dollars the afternoon of the big town meeting."

The stationmaster did not reply.

"Can I ask why you did it?"

He let out a deep breath. He had erred in that he had no lie ready; there was nothing else to do but play it straight. "I'll be honest with you, Mr. Eddie. I thought my cash might have been counterfeit."

"What? Counterfeit? Who could possibly counterfeit money? There's not a printer in town who could handle that sort of a job." A mental hiccough of *déjà vu* shook him; he recognized the words as his own.

The stationmaster spread his pudgy hands wide. "Well, there was this town meeting coming up, and I figured you had some big announcement to make, and then you said you wanted me to count up all the coins. I put two and two together and figured you were going to warn people there was a counterfeiter in town."

Eddie wore a perplexed expression. "I don't see how those facts fit together."

The stationmaster shrugged. "They seemed to fit at the time, Mr. Eddie. So I figured I'd just be on the safe side and get rid of all my cash." He smiled uncomfortably. "Turned out to be a good move, even if it was for the wrong reasons."

"If you thought they were counterfeit, shouldn't you have contacted the police?"

He hesitated. "Never thought to."

"Didn't you think you might be doing something wrong?"

"How's that, Mr. Eddie?"

"If they were counterfeit, wouldn't you be giving the bank bad bills?"

"I figured they'd know what to do with them."

"Do *what* with them? They couldn't give them to their customers, could they?"

He considered the question for a moment. "No, I guess not."

Eddie sat silent for a moment, then asked, "Do you know it's a crime to pass bad money?"

"I wasn't sure it was bad money."

"But you suspected it was."

"But it wasn't!" he cried, starting to become agitated.

He let that pass. "Do you know it was your actions that started The Panic?"

The stationmaster looked away. "Maybe."

"Maybe? It was! Right after you exchanged your bills, the tellers did the same, then all their friends and family, then the whole town! You triggered it!"

"I can't control what no tellers do!" he replied vehemently. "They should have kept quiet—it's their job to keep quiet!"

"But it was still you who tipped them off. They knew I had called the town meeting for that night, and that you worked for Transcontinental Railroad. They assumed you knew what the meeting was about. They were only following your lead."

"That's as may be, but like I said, I can't control no tellers! And besides, the money wasn't even counterfeit! You said so yourself!"

"You used railroad information for your own personal gain—and started a panic! Let me ask you again: don't you think you did something wrong?" When the stationmaster did not reply immediately, Eddie sighed. "Well, you can take your time and think it over, because it'll all be hashed out at your trial."

"My trial?" he yelped, his voice cracking.

"I'm sorry. The banker is pressing charges against you. He went over his records and was able to pinpoint the exact transaction that started The Panic. It was yours."

The stationmaster grew angry. "I didn't rob nobody! I just had them make some change."

"Your dollars were only worth three cents each. You collected one hundred cents each."

"It's not my job to correct his employees' mistakes!"

Eddie blinked twice. He could not believe what he was hearing. "But... But they made a mistake in giving you the silver. Shouldn't you return it? It was a mistake!"

"People make mistakes all the time."

"That mistake cost the banker a great deal of money—money that you now have! Shouldn't you return it?"

"I don't see how it's my duty."

"As a Transcontinental employee, it's your duty to keep our business dealings confidential and not take personal advantage of them."

"If that's a Transcontinental rule," he replied defiantly, "I ain't never heard it before now. Besides, you never told me nothing about anything! What's there to take advantage of?"

Eddie hesitated; the man had two valid points. Still, it was obvious the stationmaster's moral code diverged from his own. "Regardless, if you're not going to return the money, you should turn yourself in to the police. They're expecting you, but I told them I wanted to talk with you first about giving it back."

He leapt to his feet. "I was just watchin' out for myself! I didn't do nothing wrong!"

"That's for a jury to decide now."

He stood there red-faced for another moment, then bolted from the room.

Eddie sighed audibly. He felt miserable.

\* \* \*

The trial began.

As with the other recent hearings, the legal proceedings were a far cry from the meaningless, over-stylized formality, pomp and circumstance of the fallen regime. However, while the new court's choreography was similar to that of recent trials, the audience was not—the room was packed to overflowing. People were curious to learn the details of how The Panic had come about—and what would be done about it.

Waiting upon the appointed hour, Eddie sat silently alongside the banker at the prosecutor's table located near the front of the courtroom midway between the judge's bench and the railing separating the audience from the legal machinery. When the time to convene arrived, without ceremony he stood and took the seat behind the judge's bench, the carved law hanging above his head. Self-consciously, he lightly banged the gavel twice in quick succession. "All right, let's get started." The room quieted quickly. "We're here today to talk about The Panic. The banker feels that my stationmaster acted out of line by asking for..." He consulted a paper. "...one thousand three hundred sixty nine silver dollars in exchange for the same number of paper dollars. He feels that the stationmaster's actions were not respectful of his rights and property, and so he wants his money back." He looked to the banker. "Is that it?"

"Yes, Your Honor."

Eddie winced. He could not imagine how he would ever become accustomed to being addressed in that manner. He looked at the stationmaster. "Do you understand what it is he's asking for?"

"Well, I hear what he says, Mr. Eddie, but I don't see as how it's my fault."

"That's fine. You'll each get your chance to explain." He glanced around the packed room and estimated the crowd at well over three hundred, perhaps as many as five hundred. Given its standing-room-only character, it was difficult to estimate its size. "All right, let's have a jury. Please start from here..." He indicated the woman sitting at one end of the front row. "...and count off. Every... uh... fiftieth person, let's say, please come up to the jury box."

There was an excited buzz as the audience members began enumerating. Word of Eddie's odd brand of justice had quickly spread throughout the town, and scores had come that day with a single goal, that of being selected to serve on the jury. A great many were disappointed; seven were not. The chosen few took their appointed seats, but one remained standing: a priest. He clasped his hands in front of his chest, and his gaze went to the window. "Please," he addressed it. "Grant Your servants wisdom. But Thy will be done. Amen." A thin scattering of amens chorused around the room.

With the jury seated, the banker took the witness stand and began his tale. In the patient, cut-and-dried, matter-of-fact manner of the businessman, as if reciting a balance sheet, he explained how he and Eddie had met the night before The Panic, hatched their strategy, and planned out its execution. He then laid out his retroactive research into the causes of The Panic, including the story told by his deposits log, the tearful revelations of the tellers, and of their subsequent firing, concluding with his assertion that the stationmaster should return his ill-gotten gains. There was much concurrence throughout the audience; many heads nodded in agreement, but many others did not.

Next came the stationmaster's turn on the stand. Using so much less detail that it sounded stark in light of the testimony that had preceded it, he related how he had been instructed to count the coins in Transcontinental's vault, and had come to the dubious conclusion that the town meeting being held that night might have something to do with the coins. Not knowing exactly what that might be, he chose to exchange his paper dollars for silver ones, just to be on the safe side. With that final, bald assertion, he stopped and sat there waiting.

Eddie took on his referee's role. "That pretty much matches up with my recollections." He faced to the banker. "Do you have any questions for him?"

The banker shook his head slowly and deliberately.

"You may step down," he directed the stationmaster, and scanned the sea of faces. "Does anyone in the audience have anything to add?" He paused, waiting.

"Give 'em hell, Eddie!" someone called out. The audience tittered in response.

Eddie ignore the aside and faced the jurors. "Does anyone from the jury have any questions?"

One juror raised a tentative hand. "Yes, I do." She hesitated, then asked, almost embarrassed, "Pardon me, but I don't understand. What was it the stationmaster did wrong?" The audience murmured its approval for her words—and some, their contempt.

"That's part of what we're here to find out," replied Eddie, not giving countenance to either group. "Speaking strictly from my point of view, he did not betray the responsibility entrusted to him as a Transcontinental stationmaster. But the question is not about his duty to the railroad, but rather to the bank."

The banker surged to his feet angrily and stood behind his table. "Well, I can't say my tellers were blameless! They violated the confidentiality of our customers. That's why I had to fire them."

Awkwardly, the juror hesitated. "I understand all that, but I don't see how the stationmaster did anything wrong in exchanging his money."

The banker was quick to reply. "Because those dollars were worth only three cents at the time. Less, today."

"But how was he to know that? The big meeting was held hours later!"

"He should not have acted on confidential railroad information. That's what triggered The Panic!"

"Well, if you didn't want your tellers to make change, shouldn't you have instructed them not to?"

"And tell them what we had planned? No, of course not! Two of us knowing were already two too many."

The juror shook her head. "You didn't have to reveal the whole plan. Why didn't you just tell them not to make change?"

Now it was the banker's turn to hesitate. "I did not think of it," he finally replied gruffly.

The juror sat back, satisfied.

Another juror leaned forward—the priest—to confront her. "Now wait a minute here," he interjected. "How can you suggest he mislead his tellers? 'Thou shalt not bear false witness,' remember! It's the telling of these half-truths that started The Panic in the first place." He gestured toward the banker. "Are you saying that he should have told the tellers more lies?"

Eddie interrupted. "Pardon me, but I think you should save that conversation for the deliberation room. Let's try to stick with asking questions of the defense and prosecution for now."

The priest turned to Eddie, an injured, officious look on his face. "I *was* asking questions. I think it *is* important that we find out their answers here and now. Because if acting on half-truths is a crime as well as a sin, then there are a lot of guilty people in this room!"

Eddie's confusion showed plainly on his face. "What? Like who?"

"Him!" He pointed an accusing finger at the banker who still stood at his table. "This man did not take reasonable steps to prevent The Panic! He's just as guilty as your stationmaster!"

The banker was stunned. "I? Now wait one minute! *I'm* not the one who's on trial here!"

"But you had a hand in causing The Panic!"

The banker turned to Eddie, a growing anger reflecting in his voice. "What is this, some sort of court arena where anyone can be skewered?"

Eddie shrugged. "The juror does have a point, though. You did have a hand in it. Wouldn't you agree?"

"Yes, I would—if the purpose of this trial were to determine the causes of The Panic. But it's not! I'm here to get my money back! And if what he said were true, then..." He paused, amazed at his own realization. He pointed a finger at Eddie. "...then *you're* guilty, too!"

"Me?"

The banker was openly angry now. "If I'm guilty because I did not say enough to my tellers, then *you're* guilty for not saying enough to your stationmaster!"

"But I said too much as it was!"

The priest jumped back in. "Or not enough, Mr. Eddie. It depends on how you look at it."

"This is ridiculous!" declared the banker. "We are *not* here to talk about The Panic." He jabbed a finger in the direction of the stationmaster, but tossed his angry words at the priest. "The issue here is that this man used privileged information to rob my bank!"

"He did *not* rob your bank!" the priest retorted. "It was a routine transaction. And you let it happen." He folded his arms over his chest with smug satisfaction and leaned back in his chair.

The woman juror was nodding her agreement and replied, "That's what I meant. The stationmaster didn't do anything wrong—it was the banker!"

"Balderdash!" shouted the banker. Angrily he turned to face Eddie. "I demand a new jury! One that can stick to the facts of the case, not run off in unwarranted directions!"

The turmoil in Eddie mind was plainly reflected in his expression. "But that's their job, isn't it? To judge the law as well as the facts? You can't keep changing the jury until you find one that agrees with you. How would that be respectful of the rights of the stationmaster?"

"And how did he respect mine?" he replied, red-faced.

Eddie sighed. He was not cut out to be a judge, and it was moments like this one that drove the fact solidly home. Fortunately, the decision would not be his; he was only the referee. "And that's why we have a jury." Turning to face them, he asked, "Do any of you have any more questions?" No one replied. He turned to the stationmaster. "Anything more you want to add?"

"No, Your Honor."

Suppressing the near-automatic wince, Eddie turned to the banker. "And you?"

His face still glowed red with his fury, but he did not reply. After several seconds, he demurred. "No, Your Honor."

This time Eddie did wince. He turned to the bailiff and politely asked, "Will you please escort the jury to the deliberation room?" He banged the gavel once—too hard, he thought—and declared, "This court is in recess."

Bedlam burst out as several hundred people excitedly began to talk all at once. Unnoticed, His Honor Eddie quickly abandoned the room to escape their eyes.

* * *

The jury returned.

"Have you reached a verdict?" Eddie asked formally.

Several hundred people held their collective breath.

The jury's foreman—the priest—rose and stood proudly, his head held high, appearing as if he were a prophet handing down the wisdom of the ages, his ecclesiastical costume adding to the sacred image. "Yes we have, Your Honor. That, and more."

He winced. "All right, let's have it."

"We find everyone guilty!" he announced in a clear, righteous voice. "Every single one of you!"

The silence screamed, and Eddie hesitated, clearly confused. "What do you mean, 'everyone?'"

"We find you, the stationmaster, the banker, and the two tellers all guilty of causing The Panic. Any one of you could have stopped it, but not one of you did. You're all guilty!"

The decorum of the courtroom vaporized into pandemonium. Some were cheering, others jeering, but most were excitedly engaged in spirited discussion with one another trying to divine the meaning of the priest's words and their possible repercussions. Several times Eddie banged his gavel in vain attempts to restore order; but this time the gavel's sharp sound seemed woefully inadequate, like snapping one's fingers at an onrushing hurricane. Order struggled to reassert itself, and eventually did.

Still standing, the priest continued. "And we have decided on several sentences we want to hand down as well. First..." He pointed at the banker. "You do not deserve to get your money back. Had you done the right thing early on and instructed your tellers properly, none of this would have happened." He twirled a finger in the air, indicating The Panic that had transpired. "You did not stop to think what the result of your actions would be on the rest of the town. You did not respect us. Next..." He brought the spiraling finger down and pointed at the stationmaster. "It's more than clear that you respected the rights of your employer and the property of the banker. Although your actions directly triggered The Panic, we must reluctantly agree: you betrayed no trust, nor is it a crime to ask someone to make change. You, sir, may keep your money." His eyes scanned the audience, and quickly found the object of his search—the two tellers, huddled together, wide-eyed with panic. The accusing digit picked them out of the crowd. "And you—you both deserved to be fired! But the jury cannot interfere in a private affair, nor is it you two who are on trial here today—" He tossed a quick glance at the banker. "—as your former boss has twice reminded us. But if you were, we would pronounce you guilty and affirm that as your sentence."

The priest was on a roll, and did not give any indication that he would soon slow down. "And you!" He whirled around to point at Eddie, startling him. "You're guilty as well! You're the man who started this whole chain in motion!" He paused theatrically, as if he were reaching the climax of a fiery sermon. The audience's patience was barely held in check as they anxiously waited for him to come to a conclusion. "However, by all accounts you also saved this town from total economic collapse. The fact that virtually no one lost any money in The Panic is thanks to your doing. You saved us once again, Mr. Eddie. In fact, you've done so much for this town, the last thing we'd want you to do is to stop. I know this jury has no power over you either, but we still find you guilty of triggering The Panic and will recommend a sentence." Maddeningly, he paused again; but mercifully, it was brief. "Your sentence is to keep on doing just what you've been doing, and may God bless your work!" He leaned toward Eddie, winked, and continued in a casual, conversational tone. "Just be a little more careful next time." He sat down to tumultuous applause that rocked the courtroom down to the sands that lay beneath it.

The ruckus continued for several minutes before Eddie's gavel finally pierced the wall of noise and regained control of the proceedings. But once the audience subsided, they subsided completely, as if someone had flipped a switch turning off a loud radio.

In the silence, Eddie turned to face the stationmaster. "Do you accept the sentence?"

The stationmaster snorted sarcastically. "Are you kidding? Of course I do!"

Eddie turned to the banker and asked, "How about you? Do you accept the sentence?"

The banker said nothing at first, but he wore an angry look and blood suffused his face; he glowed beet-red. Quite a lot of money was at stake—at current exchange rates, those willies were worth well over a half million old dollars, quite a tidy sum. He wasn't going to simply walk away from that! "And what if I don't?" he challenged defiantly, the anger plain in his voice.

Eddie nodded. He had heard the question several times before, starting with the bandit's trial. At that time, he had not thought the question all the way through, nor had it been necessary; the bandit had accepted the sentence willingly. But in the months since that trial, several other defendants had made the same challenge; by this time Eddie was ready with a confident answer. Deliberately avoiding mirroring the banker's defiant tone, he replied unemotionally, "You really don't have to accept it. Since the rest of the country seems to have abandoned us, we're pretty much on our own out here. I can't say categorically what sort of actual legal authority we have to impose any sentences at all, but I can say this: if you don't accept the sentence, you've effectively chosen not to participate in what we feel is justice in this town. So I'd say that if you don't accept our brand of justice, then you can't really expect to be able to call upon it in the future, should you find yourself somehow wronged. It's really up to you whether or not you choose to participate—and judging from what's happened to others who have refused, I'd advise that you choose carefully."

The banker was plainly not pleased with the answer. "So you're saying that if I refuse to accept the sentence, if my bank gets robbed tomorrow you won't prosecute the thief?"

He did not pause to think twice. "It stands to reason, doesn't it? Think of it this way: wouldn't it be hypocritical of you to spurn our system of justice when it applies to you, but embrace it when it comes to others? You need to decide which side you're on—ours or someone else's. Whether or not you accept your sentence would be a reflection of that decision."

The banker's mouth opened, then slowly closed; he could not refute the logic. The seconds passed. "How did I ever get myself into this?" he murmured to himself testily.

Eddie heard the aside and answered aloud. "You put yourself into it when you initiated the use of courts." Silent seconds passed, and Eddie pressed, "So do you accept your sentence?"

"Bah!" he shot back testily, looking away and folding his arms defiantly. "What's the point? I may as well just fight it in my appeal."

"Your... what?"

He whirled to face Eddie. "My appeal! I'll have their decision overturned at my appeal."

"But...," he began slowly, a bewildered look on his face.

"I *do* get an appeal, don't I?" demanded the banker, almost petulantly.

"But...," he began again, with only a minor amount of the uncertainty fading from his voice. "The jury has pronounced its verdict based on the facts presented here today, right? So if you were to appeal..." He paused a moment, in doubt about how to continue. More to himself than any listener, he pondered aloud, "Now that I think about it, I'm not sure how an appeal would work. I'm not even sure what form it might take—that of a new trial?" He hesitated again. "But wouldn't that be the same thing as asking for a new jury?" Shaking himself loose from his reverie, he faced the banker. "We've already established that you can't do that. It wouldn't be right."

"But I have the right to an appeal!"

"A right? What right?" He gestured to the wooden sign hanging behind his head. "Are you suggesting you can improve the law somehow? How would you change it? What should it say instead?"

The banker could already grasp the ultimate conclusion of Eddie's arguments, and his continued refusal to face that truth only served to stoke his anger. It boiled to the surface. "How the hell should I know?!"

"But that's all I do here—protect the rights and property of men!"

"Then I'll go to another court!" he huffed.

Eddie shook his head. "That's the same thing as asking for a new jury. And we already said that wouldn't be right. How would doing that be fair to the stationmaster?"

"How has this trial been fair to me?" snapped the banker.

"How has it been unfair?" countered Eddie.

The banker glowered defiantly for a moment, but his anger gradually ebbed and he awkwardly looked away. If anything, the proceedings had been fair almost to a fault, and everyone knew it.

A little more certain of himself, Eddie sat up straighter. "No, there can be no appeal. What's to appeal? There's nothing *to* appeal! On the other hand, if there were new evidence that would plainly influence the verdict, then we could simply reconvene the same trial—ideally with the same jury—present the new evidence, then let them decide if either the verdict or the sentence needed to be changed." More became clear to him as he spoke. "Or if someone didn't respect your rights in the trial somehow—say, a witness lied or somehow violated your rights in other ways—maybe that would merit another trial—of course it would be a completely different trial, one about whether or not that man violated your rights—and if he were found guilty, then I could see you might want to reconvene your original trial. But I hardly think you could really call any of those situations an appeal. It would either be a continuation of the original trial, or a new trial about new crimes."

The banker was reduced to desperation. "And why can't I just get a new trial as my appeal? Not a continuation. A new hearing instead."

Again Eddie shook his head. "I already said that asking for that is the same thing as asking for a new jury. And—"

"But—"

Eddie held up a finger in interruption. "Think of it this way: suppose you did have a new trial and let's say you won. Wouldn't we then need a third trial to break the tie? So wouldn't asking for a new trial really be the same thing as saying, 'Best out of three?' And if you lost again, what would stop it from becoming best out of five? Or seven? Or seven times seven times? It could go on forever! And that wouldn't be fair to anyone. It just wouldn't be right."

The banker's arms crossed his chest again. He was losing the logical argument, and he knew it. "So there's no such thing as an appeal, is that what you're saying?"

"I cannot imagine what its purpose would be."

"So the sentence... it's either take it or leave it, then? "

"I cannot imagine a third choice. Can you?"

The banker opened his mouth as if to speak, but he slowly closed it. He couldn't visualize any third path either.

After a moment, Eddie interrupted the silence. "So. Do you accept the sentence of the jury?"

Desperately the banker grasped at a final straw. "Wait a minute! The first time it was you who came up with the sentence. This time it was the jury. Whose justice is this anyhow?"

"I don't see why anyone can't suggest what the sentence might be. Many times it's been me; this time it was the jury; next time it may be someone in the audience—maybe even the defendant! But does it really matter? I think the jury's sentence a good one. It stands to reason, and it fits the crime—or lack thereof, I should say, given the verdict. Or do you have an alternative sentence you wish to offer?"

Seconds passed. The banker did not reply.

Eddie faced the audience. "Anyone have a suggestion for a different sentence?"

Seconds passed in pregnant silence.

He turned back to the banker. "There it is, then. Do you accept the sentence of the jury?"

No answer.

He repeated a little more forcefully, enunciating each word separately. "Do you accept the sentence of the jury?"

The silence dragged out several seconds longer. Finally, the banker mumbled a reply. "Yeah, I guess so."

Eddie nodded and looked out across the audience. "And so do I." He banged the gavel once. "This court is adjourned."

The audience released its collective breath and exploded in cheers and applause.

\* \* \*

Las Vegas changed again.

It was as if the sun had finally popped out from behind the last black cloud to brighten a storm-beaten land, and the transformation that overspread the town's economy occurred just as abruptly. With the establishment of sound money, prices for most commodities quickly stabilized, then fell. Without the drag of taxation, fiat currency, or the inflation they encouraged, wages rose. Given the low prices and high wages, the economy began to stretch in unusual directions: people began taking more time away from their work to pursue hobbies, charitable service, or just sit on their porch and enjoy life. Homes were better kept, yards neatly trimmed, and the streets proudly swept clean. Crime dropped dramatically, not only because of the judicial mechanisms Eddie had put in place, but also due to the plethora of opportunities for honest, well-paid work. With the reduced economic pressure also came a reduced psychological pressure; people seemed to tolerate each other's foibles more readily, and were also much more willing to help one another. For Las Vegas the day of the looter had finally ended.

But challenges still remained. Despite the surfeit of good tidings, their paradise was punctuated with random shortages induced by their isolation. Everyday commodities, long taken for granted, continued to disappear from the store shelves, and one of the first commodities to vanish was coffee, much to the agitated annoyance of the populace. Refined sugar was soon replaced with several coarser varieties. Chocolate, maple syrup, cinnamon, and other formerly-mundane wares also dwindled quickly. Fortunately, the staples of existence remained plentiful; men adjusted, and life moved on.

The occasional stranger would wander into town, most of them local ranchers who had abandoned their lonely farms in favor of the more civilized life and greater economic opportunities that the town offered. A few refugees from the fighting to the west still emigrated from time to time, but their sparse numbers trickled off to zero before very long. It was as if the world had forgotten that Las Vegas existed.

At least for the moment.

# SECTION V – THE FIRST YEARS

Mid-1950's

# CHAPTER 1 – WONDERFUL, WONDERFUL

The stars twinkled.

It was late evening in Starnesville, and stars overhead randomly pocked a black, moonless sky slashed by the off-center, pearly-white glow of the sprawling Milky Way. A man and woman sat on a makeshift glider seat on their front porch, rocking gently and admiring the beauty of it all. It was a warm, windless Wisconsin night—and a silent one now that their young children had stopped fidgeting and finally fallen asleep.

"This is the life!" the man asserted as he pulled his wife closer to him. The homemade glider rocked left and right in response to the shifting center of gravity, but it handled the conflicting forces with grace. He smiled, justifiably proud of his handiwork: he had constructed the glider out of a collection of scraps and junk scavenged from the old Factory up on the hill. The base of the glider had once been a part of a precision machine tool, specifically, the basin at its base which had collected oil before it was re-circulated to lubricate the complex mechanism. The oil pan was an ideal size: large enough to hold the floating seat of the glider, yet compact enough to fit conveniently on their front porch. Crucially, its flat bottom did not leak. The floating part of the glider's seat was constructed from the rectangular gas tank that had once been part of the old station wagon parked in their garage. A leather back seat salvaged from the same source was strapped to the tank's surface, completing the gliding portion. Filled only with air, the gas tank floated neatly on a bed of water within the oil pan, assuming its center of gravity remained pretty much near the center. Despite its somewhat cautious mode of operation, it was a unique product of the man's ingenuity, a dream made real, and a luxury no one else in Starnesville could envision until he had done it. In his wake, others began scavenging through the Factory and empty buildings in search of the makings for their own gliders; but he had done it first.

The man's wife sighed her contentment and laid her head on his shoulder. It was her legs, not his, that were propelling their rocking motion; her husband was just along for the ride, so to speak, not helping but not hindering. She smiled to herself as she counted her blessings: the new glider, a comfy place to live, food on the table, a clever man for a husband, three equally-clever children—*And a fourth on the way!* she reminded herself, a hand on her slightly bulging stomach. "This *is* the life!" she agreed.

A comfortable silence settled between them, neither of them feeling the necessity to speak; there was no need to name its facets; their life told its own story. Many years ago they had worked for the Century Motor Company in the Factory up on the hill, right up until the day it closed down. The owners' grand experiment had failed—as it must, they now realized, although at the time it had seemed the best of ideas. Century had been the top motor manufacturer in the country when the experiment began, but the firm had erroneously traded that enviable status for the shame of bankruptcy. The formula for failure was based on a simple credo: *From each according to his ability, to each according to his need.* The factory owners had tried to force that collectivist philosophy onto six thousand workers, but in less than a handful of short years it had ended in ignominious failure.

Recalling the arrogance of the factory owners, the man snorted his derision. *It went against human nature!* he now knew. *Of course it failed—it had to!* Aloud, he reminisced, "Remember the days of the Factory?"

"Mmm hmm," she replied dreamily.

"'From each according to his ability...'" he quoted.

The woman sniggered. "'To each according to their need!'" She twisted her head up to plant a kiss awkwardly on his chin. "My man of ability!" she praised. "You're all I need!"

He accepted the compliment in passing. "Remember how it all ended?"

"Mmm hmm."

Her agreement did not sidetrack his reminiscing. "What a mess! For years the Factory took care of all our worldly needs and then it went bust. All the cowards fled, like a blob of mercury hit with a hammer. There was no one left to loot here in Starnesville, no one to fix their derailed gravy train, so they all left."

"Almost all!" she hugged him gently yet pointedly. She knew he would not have forgotten how it was he who had devised their original strategy for staying in Starnesville. The two were the first resilient pioneers who had chosen to remain—and for good reason.

"Almost all," he agreed. "Those of us who valued our own ability and worth saw our chance. We recognized that there was no value left in the outside world, and that it would be counterproductive to support it with our labor. We were in the perfect position, out here in the middle of nowhere, to try our own grand experiment, not one based on looting, but on man's productive ability. With the weak looters gone, all that remained were us, the men of ability, we who could command Nature to obey us!"

She rocked the glider a little more deliberately; he could feel the subtle change of tempo in their glide, underscoring the excitement in his words. "Like commanding a glider to carry us!" she praised again. She gave him another gentle hug, her head sliding a little down his chest in the process.

Silently, she tried to chronicle all the other blessings he had bestowed upon their idyllic existence. She thought of the gas stove in their home, worthless as a stove now that natural gas no longer flowed through the zinc-plated pipes. But he had expertly converted it into a chest of drawers, its racks keeping her clean clothes organized and neat, its surface serving as an easy-to-clean porcelain changing table for the diapered children. She smiled at the thought of the warmth that came from the fireplace he had constructed in one corner of their home, keeping them comfortable through the cold Wisconsin winters. He had adeptly employed chunks of fire-resistant concrete salvaged from the paving of the old highway to line the hearth and chimney, protecting their home and children against the chance of a devastating fire. Even that salvaging had been a victory for his intellect, seeing as how the highway's cement was hardened and reinforced with thick iron rods. But he had conquered its indestructibility, first by cracking up the surface into manageable chunks using an old, oversized motor casing as a wrecking ball suspended by a complex array of chains and pulleys, then using the same mechanism to sever the reinforcing iron fingers through repeated bending. She recalled how he had worked on the hearth over the course of many weeks before it was finally complete. But the effort proved its worth; their home had been warm and safe for many a winter now. And it wasn't only their house; all the other men of ability in Starnesville had copied his process—and not for the first or last time! The torn-up highway leading into town stood as a silent testimonial to the popularity of his invention. All the homes in Starnesville were warm and safe now, too; and as an added value, the lack of a good road made the town even more inaccessible. The town was richer in many ways for her husband's resourcefulness.

"Mmm hmm," he replied, accepting her tribute to his worth. Not that he required her approval; he knew the value of his own achievements. In the days of the Factory's downward spiral, the cowards who had fled would have been foolish to acknowledge their own competence—in fact, even he had made that mistake once. He had devised a process that had saved his co-workers thousands of man-hours, but found himself sentenced to night work because of it. The owners believed that since he was so productive, they were justified in trying to extract even more from him. *From each according to his ability...* He shook his head, more at his own folly than the owners'.

But today in this new world, there was no reason to conceal the bright spark of intelligence. He well knew his own value, and so did his wife. But their relationship was not one-sided, he reminded himself—as if he needed to be reminded! He could never forget her value to him, not only as a loving wife and caring mother, but also because she was a wizard with her hands, possessing the ability to weave top quality cloth from the hemp that grew wild in the fields north of town. For work clothes she used a coarser strand for strength, but their finery, such as what they wore this evening, was soft and pliant to the touch. Her talent was widely recognized among the other hardy residents of Starnesville, tipping the balance of trade their way, to the benefit of their children and their comfort. He smiled, just as aware of the treasure that he owned as she was of hers. He was her number one value, and she, his.

He recalled how he, too, had once thought of leaving Starnesville, back before the Factory closed. He laughed quietly at the thought, causing his wife to glance up at him in curiosity.

"I thought of leaving, once," he explained.

"Me, too," she confessed. "But I couldn't."

"You couldn't get me to leave here today, even with old lady Ivy glaring in my face!"

His wife laughed out loud. "Remember her?"

"The Factory's co-owner whose face I spat in? How could I forget?! If ever there was a tighter-fisted sourpuss to have for a boss, she was it!"

"But Gerald was worse," she countered teasingly.

"Her diamond-studded brother?" he retorted in mock anger. "Mister Gerald 'Cigar Smoke in Your Face?'"

She giggled at the thought. "You're right! I forgot how he did that. It's been a while, now. What, three? No, four years?"

He patted her slightly-swollen stomach. "Four years, four babies, just as we planned it."

"Mmm hmm," she purred.

Crickets chirped in the tall grasses surrounding their house. He listened to them for a moment, then sighed in the darkness. "You know, there are a couple of people from the old days I'd sure like to meet up with again."

"Like who?"

"Oh, not sourpuss Ivy or any of those folks. I was thinking about some of my old co-workers from the research lab... What was his name? Bill... No, William! My old boss Mr. William. Now there's a man who was as smart as the day is long. He'd really appreciate what we've built here." After a pause, he continued, "And remember that night a couple of years ago when it rained mud?—I'd like to ask him about that. Strangest thing!"

"Yuckiest thing, you mean!"

He laughed in agreement. "Never saw anything like it before or since. If anybody would've known what it was all about, it would've been him. He was definitely the sharpest wrangler on the block."

"He wasn't around when the Factory closed, was he?" It was a statement more than a question.

"No, he left early on—the second man to quit, as I recall!—and most of the research staff followed suit." He laughed lightly. "Not me, though."

She snuggled more closely into his shoulder. "Such a gallant man!"

He hugged her in return. "How could I leave without you? Wouldn't think of it, not until you were back on your feet. You sure gave us all a scare..."

"It was touch and go there for a while," she admitted uneasily; she didn't like to talk about it.

"Three years of touch and go!" he exclaimed, knocking the glider a little off balance in his vehemence.

"But waiting turned out to be a blessing."

"True," he agreed. "It gave me the time to work out our plans for staying." He sat pensive for a moment, then resumed his remembrances. "And it's not just Mr. William. I wish my old buddy Johnnie were still around to see what we've built here. It's a shame, but Johnnie and I never kept in touch once he left. I bet he doesn't even know we're still living up here." He shook his head regretfully, a somber, invisible motion in the dark. "Yep. My old pal Johnnie. He and I were hired right around the same time. I remember back in the days when Mr. Jed still ran the Factory how Johnnie and I would go on and on about the sad state of the world. God, but how we'd argue! All night, sometimes! He kept looking for some way to fix things up, insisting there was some way to make the world somehow work better." He shook his head in the dark. "What a fool!"

The woman smiled unseen. She had heard this story many, many times before; it appeared as if she was going to hear it once more. Almost eagerly she waited for him to continue; despite the repetition it was a fascinating story—and their legacy to their children.

"It took a while, but I finally convinced him that the world wasn't worth saving—no, that's not quite right—that it was too far gone to *be* saved. I finally got him to realize that the only solution was to try and hole up in some unnoticed corner of the world someplace, then build your own sanctuary from scratch. Get rid of all the old assumptions, all the old prejudices and start over." He sat in thought for a moment, contemplating the conversations they had had. "At first he thought it couldn't work, if only for geographic reasons. And I admitted he had a point: where could you hide a secret settlement where it wouldn't be found? He thought you'd have to put it on some island someplace maybe, or high in the mountains. Bah! Why go through all that trouble? He'd already left before I figured out it'd be a lot easier to hide it right out in the open, like we ended up doing here in Starnesville. Since the Factory closed down, there isn't a man on Earth who'd think to come bother us here. They've abandoned us—forgotten about us!—and it's as good as if we never existed. Our secret is safe, even though we're sitting right out in the open."

The moments passed in blissful silence. A chortle escaped her nose.

He kissed her hair. "What's funny?"

She smiled invisibly in the darkness, but it was plainly reflected in her voice. "Our secret was tested once—only once! Remember those city slickers?"

"Couple of years back? In that big, black limo with the flat tire? Sure do! What a pair of losers! We sure convinced *them* there was nothing here to see! We just played dumb and off they went. They never saw what was right under their noses!"

"I still have that old hemp dress I put on for them," she added. "One of the first ones I ever made."

He laughed. "That old thing? It looks like a flour sack!"

"Of course it does! You've said often enough at our town meetings that we always have to be ready to mislead people in case someone comes snooping around. That dress is my costume. We can't let anyone think we have such a prosperous settlement here."

"All of us here in Starnesville know that," he agreed. "Don't want them meddling with our little piece of heaven on Earth. Next thing you know, they'll be all over us with their bureaucrats, tax collectors, preachers, and all."

She hugged him again. "Your grand experiment. It worked. And it's still working!"

"And it sure fooled those city slickers, didn't it?"

She chortled again. "They didn't know what to make of us, did they?"

"Well, I'm not surprised. That sort of person knows nothing of self-reliance, what with them living down there in the city. Don't know how to depend on themselves. Need others to help them to live. And *expecting* others to help them!" He shook his head in self-righteousness. "Remember how the neighborhood kids drove them off?"

"Mmm hmm," she agreed. "I saw them using the tactics you taught them. And they only needed to use the first part of the Stage One strategy. Woe be to anyone who comes sneaking around here meaning us harm!"

"Ah, those slickers were no threat. Just a couple of looters. Remember how they snuck up to the Factory and stole one of Johnnie's old motors? They wrapped it up in canvas and stuck it in their trunk, real secret-like, as if we couldn't see what they'd done. And then they couldn't even close the trunk lid on it! What do they think we are, stupid? If you're going to steal something, you should at least try to cover your tracks!"

"That motor didn't work anyhow."

"Nope. It was an early experimental model—never worked. Had the old kind of power receiver on it—impossible to tune. And that was before we separated the motor portion from the power converter portion. It was more efficient to generate electricity using the converter, then use the electricity to run a conventional motor. That's the way I built the converter I have mounted in the station wagon out in the garage."

"Good thing they didn't steal that one!"

He laughed at the thought. "They wouldn't realize the value of that motor if you handed it to them on a platter! Witness how the fools left all the best pickings from the Factory behind," he reminded her. "A couple of weeks afterward they sent in those two other clowns with this big truck and a crane that could have carted off anything they wanted! They crawled around the old Factory for days, but ended up taking nothing—and they left all the best receivers behind! To them, it probably looked like scrap: just some bits of heavy cable and lead conduit." He laughed derisively. "What kind of rotten looters are they? They didn't even know what to steal! How can you run the converter for Johnnie's motor without a decent lead conduit receiver?" He snorted. "More for us, then!"

She stopped rocking and turned to face him in the dark night. "Speaking of the Factory I hear tell your kid brother was up there the other night drinking again."

The man stirred uneasily. "Now, you know how he built his own still. Can't deny a man the fruits of his labors!"

"But he's only sixteen!"

"How old were you when you had your first drink?"

She did not answer; they both knew—and remembered how that night had ended. In the darkness, neither one noticed how the other smiled at the memory.

"And did you have the initiative and imagination to distill your own brew when you were sixteen?" he pressed. "In a still you built with your own two hands?"

"He was up there with Miss You-Know-Who again," she replied, moving the conversation to what she thought might be firmer ground.

"And...? The man's sixteen, isn't he? And she's what, seventeen now?"

His wife did not reply.

"And haven't you been teaching her how to work your miracles with weaving? She's also been learning healing from the old Factory nurse, hasn't she? And wasn't she the girl who figured out how to build Dutch ovens out of those old ceramic toilet tanks from the Factory?" He nodded vigorously in the dark, the glider jiggling in harmony. "She'd make a good wife for my brother. I dare you to deny it!"

"Perhaps you're right," she placated. "She's a good woman. I should let your brother grow up, I guess. He's—"

"Oh!" he exclaimed, interrupting, his arm flinging around to point heavenward, knocking the glider's center of balance off sufficiently that his end of the seat bottomed out in its pan of water, clunking hollowly. "A shooting star! Did you see it? Quick! Make a wish!"

She pulled him closer to her, not looking up. "The whole world could collapse and crumble into dust for all care. I have all I could ever wish for right here in good old Starnesville!"

He took a finger and placed it under her chin, drawing her face up to his. "Me, too," he whispered in the dark as their lips met.

## CHAPTER 2 – SOUTH CALIFORNIA PURPLES

Ma's lieutenant survived.

With the arrival of spring and the melting of the deep snow, he was relieved to find himself increasingly mobile once again, for it was becoming imperative that he resume his scavenging. Although game remained plentiful, his supply of kitchen matches was almost gone, and he was reluctant to tap into his cached reserves unless some sort of trouble made it critically necessary.

Unfortunately, before long that necessity came; but mercifully, at least it progressed in small steps. The first sign of trouble took the form of a black cloud of smoke in a clear blue sky, filtering the sunlight in uneven waves as it drifted high over his hollow on its way south. *The other heretic's fire?* he wondered as he studied the northern sky. *But why so smoky?* There was only one way to find out; he immediately stalked off into the woods to investigate.

It took hours for him to reach the vicinity of the fire, and by then the smoke had diminished to virtually nothing. But its aroma still clung to every tree, guiding him the last of the way. Not that it mattered; he recognized the lay of the land long before he arrived; nor was there any question about it: the fire had originated from the other heretic's camp.

He cautiously approached the narrow valley where the camp lay, crawling on his hands and knees to insure that he would not be seen. As he peered over the lip and down into the valley, he was stunned to see that the other heretic's camp lay in smoking ruin. Clothes, magazines, and other items were strewn about the area, some of them scorched. A large heap of rags was still smoking; it sat in the middle of what must have been a huge bonfire. *That explains all the smoke!* he thought.

An icon was crudely painted on the moss of the large flat rock between the creek and where the hut had once stood: it was the stylized flame of Back For God, its color more the brown of dried blood than the bright orange usually favored by the acolytes. With a shudder, he realized it *was* blood! Looking again to the smoldering heap of rags, in even greater horror he realized its true nature as well. Without a moment's delay, heart thumping, he slowly and stealthily retreated from the camp. Before very long, he found himself trembling. But despite his fears, he was careful not to panic; he took his time, and chose his path carefully. As a result, the return journey took almost twice as long due to the precautions he took: keeping off the roads and trails, crouching low as he walked, and halting frequently to listen. Even though he had not seen or heard any acolytes about, he couldn't afford to take any chances, especially now. But fortune smiled on him, and his journey home concluded without incident; he encountered no one. When several days had passed with no further signs of trouble, the lieutenant wrote off the acolyte attack as a random patrol not to be repeated, and counted himself lucky.

But the second sign of trouble came a few weeks later. He had traveled south to check his traps for captured game, but was having some difficulty in locating one of the springes. At first he suspected the problem was with his recollection, believing that he misremembered the wooded location where he had set it; but the truth became immediately obvious, once he saw it. While the trap itself was nowhere to be found, a short piece of his hemp rope remained firmly anchored to a sapling, its knot neatly severed as if by a sharp knife. *No animal chewed through this!* he knew. Apparently someone had stolen his trap. He looked around the woods nervously; *Another heretic?* he wondered. But he had never seen any signs of anyone else roaming the mountains to the south. He licked his lips nervously. It had to be the acolytes! He knew that a foraging heretic such as himself would never have abandoned the hemp.

To his credit, in the days following the disappearance of his trap, he exercised even more caution in his activities. He traveled less frequently, making it a point to consolidate several shorter trips into one longer one, and budgeting more travel time to accommodate the slower pace that his increased stealth required; and when he did travel, he timed his activities around dawn or sunset, the times he thought least likely for acolyte activity. Sometimes he would be gone for days on end, not only to enable him to forage further from home, but also to maintain an even lower level of human activity around the hollow.

His travel precautions may have saved him from personal discovery at one point or another; he could never know for certain. But he did discover how insufficient his precautions were for protecting the secrecy of his camp in the hollow; for he returned one evening from an overnight foraging trip to find it a charred ruin. His home base had been burned to the ground and destroyed.

Reconstructing events as best he could from the evidence, he surmised that acolytes had stumbled across one of his hunting paths and followed it through the forest back to his camp. Or perhaps they reached his hollow in the same manner as he originally had, by following the bubbling creek up the mountainside to its source. He cursed himself for his foolhardy negligence; but he also counted his blessings: at least he had not been at home when the attack had come.

Regardless of how it happened, there was no denying that the deed had been done. Acolytes had found his camp and destroyed it as completely as they had done with the other heretic's camp. They had likely arrived the day before, because the fires were all cold now.

The lieutenant surveyed the wreckage and his heart sank, not only from the distress of the immediate loss, but more from the deeper knowledge that the mountains were no longer safe for him. Yet his spirits lifted when he remembered how he had had the foresight to cache emergency supplies in several locations, and that most likely each of them was still waiting for him. But his heart fell again as he wondered, *Or did the acolytes find them, too?* He surely hoped not.

Regardless of whether his emergency supplies remained or not, there was no question that it was time to leave the forest. The only question that remained was where to go.

## CHAPTER 3 – TRAIN IN THE DISTANCE

The horse collapsed.

"God *DAMN it!*" swore the wagonmaster as he threw down the reins, furious in his anger. Heads popped out behind him from under the shade of the wagon's patched canvas bonnet; dread spread across their delicate faces when they saw the cause of the curse. There were few enough horses left alive pulling them across the desert. Now there was one fewer.

In a justifiably-foul temper, painfully the wagonmaster climbed down from the inadequately-padded driver's seat. He stood alongside the downed steed and for a moment glared pitilessly at its pathetic, pleading eyes. He had seen that look too many times before not to know what it meant; this one was never going to get back up. Not that he was surprised; it should have been a mule or an ox pulling that heavy wagon through the dry heat, but horses were all they had. *No sense in putting it off!* he griped to himself. He reached down and unhitched the unfortunate creature from the wagon's neck yoke and traces, removed the leather reins and balled them up in his hands. Ignoring the fallen horse, he stood for a moment scanning the featureless, desert horizon, and his rage exploded. "*DAMN* it!" he cursed again in a fit of pique and threw the tangled leather ball down onto the bleached surface of the old concrete highway. Leaving it there, he marched determinedly to the rear of the wagon and gruffly ordered, "Alright, everybody out! Come on, come on! Quit your dawdling! From here on you'll have to walk!"

Feeble, high-pitched protests could be heard from the shaded interior, but their dissent had all the impact of kittens meowing in a box, if not merely the tone. Lethargically, an even dozen women and children clambered out of the wagon and onto the hot surface of the concrete highway. From their midst, an almost pubescent teen with long, stringy hair stepped forward and faced the wagonmaster insolently, gesturing toward the front of the wagon. "There's still another horse!" she fumed, just as angry as he was. "Why are you making us walk?"

"Because one goddamn horse can't pull a wagon loaded with impudent scum like you!" he roared. "Maybe you want we should throw away the rest of the water instead? Or do you just want to see if you can kill the other horse, too? Gah!" He turned away in disgust. "Kids!" he muttered under his breath as he reluctantly returned to reclaim his uncomfortable perch. Even before he was seated, he grasped and shook the remaining set of reins none too gently. "Giddyup!" he cried. The overworked horse strained for a second against the off-balanced harness before the wagon slowly began to roll forward once more, with long, piercing squeaks shrieking from its under-lubricated wheels. The two wagons behind him followed in slow suit, each of them making the slight detour around the dying obstacle lying in the road.

"Heeyah!" shouted the wagonmaster, not as any command for the sole remaining animal in front of him, but rather to release some of his own pent-up feeling of hopelessness.

They were not going to make it; of that he was now certain. Their efforts had all been for nothing. A little over a year ago he had somehow survived the fiery death of Los Angeles and the subsequent, merciless attacks of the Party of the People that drove him and his sons first into the Imperial Valley, then back out of it. They had managed to avoid the mass exodus of refugees, and eventually found an isolated farm on the southwestern edge of California where they could finally settle down. Once there, they had successfully fought off raiders, buzzards, and the heat, only to ultimately be driven from their home once again, only this time by the religious zealots of Back For God. Somewhere several hundred miles behind him, his three strong sons were making their final stand alongside a woefully inadequate number of defenders, full well knowing their fate, selflessly cashing in the last ounce of their strength for the sole purpose of buying time for him and his charges to escape. Now he found himself leading a shabby, shrinking wagon train consisting of himself and thirty-eight women and children. They had started with many more, and he was convinced they'd end with many less—zero, to be exact. Even the portents bespoke of ill times ahead: a few days earlier they had to maneuver around a human skeleton lying in the middle of the highway, shards of shattered bone protruding at awkward angles from the corpse's shrunken, mummified skin. It was impossible to say what sort of horrible calamity had befallen the poor soul; it appeared that the body had been pummeled with some gigantic hammer, or fallen from a great height. He shook his head ruefully at the ill-omened memory, and what it foretold. Surely his sons were all dead by now; it had been weeks since they had parted company: a tearful farewell for the women, and a tight-jawed nod of the head for the men. You did what you had to do to survive, to press on, no matter how tough the going. The only alternative was to lie down and die, like some overstressed hor—

"*DAMN* it!" he cursed again; he had forgotten about the fallen horse! Pulling on the reins none too gently, he halted the wagon, and behind him the rest of the wagon train followed in painful suit. He steeled himself for the task that had to be done.

"What now?" came a plaintive whine from one usually-pleasant grandmother, her insubordination plainly demonstrating how irritable and edgy everyone had become.

He climbed down from the wagon without a word and retraced a path to the downed animal still lying in the road not far behind the two wagons that followed his own, each of them also pulled by a single horse. Only one of their wagons carried passengers: those who were too old, weak, or ill to walk on their own; the other two held the last of their food and water. Other than a cache of precious sacks of seeds, the refugees carried no luggage other than the clothes on their backs. The weight penalty was far too great to carry anything more; and losing one more horse would now also mean losing a wagon—and more importantly the food and water—or the people!—it carried.

The children jumped at the loud, sharp report from the wagonmaster's revolver. As he returned, they stared at him with wide, alarmed eyes, their frightened faces swiveling to track his progress as he passed. He did not look back at them or the dispatched animal, but rather without a word climbed back into his painfully-flat wooden seat. He shook the reins once and the tired gelding leaned into the weary task once more.

It was hopeless folly to have ever tried to make for Lake Meade, of that he was sure, but there had been no other choice. What the acolytes of Back For God did with their heathen prisoners—especially the women!—was well known to all. It was a kinder fate for them to attempt a journey of hundreds of miles and die as mummified skeletons under the scorching desert sun than to face such barbaric cruelty; and with each passing day, it was becoming more and more certain that the kinder fate would soon come to pass.

\* \* \*

The *Meteor* hurtled.

Like some superbly-trained athlete in a marathon race, the Diesel effortlessly barreled along the flat, ruler-straight track across the sparsely-settled desert south of Las Vegas. Eddie sat relaxed in the engineer's seat, one hand resting lightly on the throttle, his eyes studiously fixed on the track ahead. He did not expect any problems on the scheduled trip down to Boulder City. He had been piloting this run for half a year now without incident, but prudence dictated that he always keep a watchful eye. It was not too distant a journey to the deserted town—less than an hour each way—nor was the train a long one: it consisted of only the Diesel, a baggage car, and one day coach carrying a mere six passengers: four of them were members of the relief crew for the four men who were currently watching over the powerplant of the massive Boulder Dam; the other two passengers were wives.

Early in the morning of every third and fourth day Eddie and the *Meteor* would make the trip to Boulder City, that being the closest approach any track made to the Dam, then return to Las Vegas an hour later. Commuting on the *Meteor* not only saved the workers many hours of horseback riding in the hot desert sun, it also saved them the trouble of bringing additional horses to cart the several days' worth of food and other supplies that would be needed during their vigil, not to mention doing away with the bother and expense of feeding and caring for a small herd of horses. The run also served to bring in a reasonable amount of revenue to the coffers of Transcontinental Railroad. But none of these reasons were what drove Eddie to provide train service, even though he personally profited from the operation of both the railroad and the Dam. For him it was reason enough to keep the railroad running so that it could serve the men of ability, as it was always meant to do; and as with his radio broadcasts, keeping the *Meteor* alive also kept an important part of Eddie's past alive as well.

In addition to the men of ability, the *Meteor* also served their children: after returning from the morning trip to the Dam, Eddie would run an afternoon "Kids' Special" into the desert north of town, just for the fun of it. Unsurprisingly, the jaunts were a huge hit among the children and their parents alike. He refused to accept any payment from the children who rode these excursions; he felt he was amply rewarded by their laughter as they hung their heads out the windows of the day coach, and by the grateful, almost worshiping gaze of their parents. Not that it was any altruism on his part; Eddie had an ulterior motive for the joyrides: he wanted to instill in the hearts of the children the same love of the railroad that he held in his own heart. Someday, he knew, one of them would have to take his place in the Diesel. As proved to be the case with the bandit exiled to work at the Dam, among those children were several future Transcontinental Railroad employees.

The hurtling train swallowed the desert miles, soon encountering a darkened semaphore signal. Its lack of illumination was deliberate; given that the *Meteor* was the only train running anywhere within hundreds of miles—more likely thousands!—Eddie had not troubled to power up the signaling system. Despite its darkness, for him the semaphore was an important waypoint. From there, ahead in the distance he could begin to make out the squat, abandoned structures of Boulder City; the *Meteor* was almost there.

He had heard news that plans were in the offing to re-colonize the town; it was becoming more trouble for the Dam workers to commute than it would be to simply move in. Nor would bringing the lonely ghost town back to life be difficult. Being so close to the Dam, the town already had electricity aplenty; and telephone service had recently been restored to both the Dam and the abandoned town. Once the town's water supply was secured—an effort already well underway—re-colonization would be the next logical step.

The planned colonization was not all that unexpected; other areas surrounding Las Vegas were also being slowly re-populated as well. Private exploration parties had been ranging far and wide across the desert seeking out new opportunities for wealth, and they were finding them. Many farms and ranches, previously abandoned, were being brought back to life. Disregarded herds which had been left to roam freely were again corralled within vast fenced plains. Neglected orchards of fruit trees were reclaimed, pruned, and tended. The economic arms of Las Vegas stretched out to embrace them all. Within fifty miles of town civilization had been restored, and peace and tranquility reigned; but beyond that lay nothing but uninhabited, empty space—or so they imagined. No one had yet explored the wilderness out very far; nor had that wilderness intruded upon them.

Eddie sounded one long, mournful wail on the Diesel's triple-coned air horn to announce his approach to Boulder City, and began slowing the *Meteor*. Minutes later, he switched on its yard bell, and soon brought the train to a gentle halt at a makeshift station just short of the final track switch before the end of the line, studiously cautious not to foul its points. Waiting with their luggage were the four men and three of their wives that were to be his return passengers. Eddie recognized the reformed bandit standing proudly among them, no longer an exile, but now a productive citizen and the Dam's newly-promoted shift supervisor. Parked nearby was a compact battery-powered cart and its low, boxy trailer that the men used to haul their personal effects and supplies the remaining distance to and from the Dam.

The electric carts were a relatively new item on the Las Vegas scene. One clever lad had taken to scavenging electric motors of varying sizes from whatever source he could find, wiring them up to old batteries removed from stilled automobiles, and installing them on carriages, wagons, or any sort of wheeled contraption he could cobble together. The result was an array of unique carts that could travel for up to an hour on a single charge. Given that electricity was cheap and plentiful, the carts became an instant hit. Unsurprisingly, the lad had difficulty keeping up with demand, and before long a competitor established himself in the business as well. Each tried to out-do the other in terms of features, range, and style, but the winners of their competition were the citizens of Las Vegas who found themselves conveyed back to the age of motorized transportation.

While the arriving men transferred their supplies from the *Meteor's* baggage car to the cart, Eddie uncoupled the Diesel from the rest of the train and maneuvered around the triangle of sidings to position it in front of the coach for its return journey. By the time he was finished re-coupling the Diesel, the men had completed their task as well. Before long, at the appointed moment, he climbed the four steps to the top of the platform at the rear of the day coach and called "All aboard!" in a signature voice, then walked down the aisle and dutifully collected and punched their tickets. He emerged from the other end of the coach and was about to descend to the ground and head for the cab of the Diesel when movement in the near distance caught his eye. Coming up from the southwest making an apparent beeline in the direction of the train, was a long, large cloud of dust.

\* \* \*

The wagonmaster dozed.

That he could somehow manage to sleep at all in so uncomfortable a spot as the wagon's driver's seat was a clear indication of his deteriorating physical condition. Nor was he alone in his travails. He had presided over yet another burial that morning—the fifth in as many days—performing last rites for an elderly lady who had not managed to survive the night. Equally distressing, they had lost another horse two days before, reducing their train to a mere two wagons: one to carry the sick, and the other, the last of their water; and just yesterday the food had run out as well. He cursed himself for not having the forethought to butcher the fallen horses; he simply had not thought of it. He shook his head; the blunder may prove to be his final mistake. He pressed ahead unthinkingly, just marking time now, going through the motions of what he knew for certain to be their final days, doing what duty demanded of him until he would finally be relieved of both duty and life together, in the same instant.

He stirred in his restless sleep and squinted one eye open. Ahead in the distance he could see the squat structures of yet another town. Although he remained convinced they were on the correct road, he had little idea exactly where they were. Not that there weren't landmarks; every few days they would come upon some side road or an abandoned town duly identified by a faded sign at its outskirts; but lacking a map, the names yielded no information regarding their progress. So it was no surprise that coming across yet another town instilled no sense of excitement in him; it was just another unremarkable milestone in an unending journey. To be sure, the towns were universally useful for replenishing their water supply:

there was more than enough potable water trapped in every house's water pipes to meet their needs, waiting only to be drained into their buckets. The limiting factor was not the water in the pipes, but rather how much weight the remaining two horses could pull. Should luck smile upon them, they might even find a few morsels of food in the abandoned town; but such luck had been elusive.

In weariness, he closed his eyes again; but only for a split second. His posture snapped into a straight sitting position unlike any he had held in almost a week. His fading eyes narrowed as he peered into the distance; he tilted his head, listening. At first he feared he was hallucinating, but the reaction of the walkers around him confirmed the reality of the clear, sweet note of a train whistle blaring dimly in the near distance.

"Whoa! Whoa!" he cried, pulling fiercely on the reins, causing the tired horse to rear up on its hind legs despite its own great fatigue. Before the wagon could come to a stop, he was already down from his seat furiously working to unhitch the horse, but his stiff, weakened hands fumbled at the task. "Here! Here!" he cried over his shoulder. "Quick! Come help me!" Several pairs of hands joined in the effort, and in seconds the horse was free of its bindings.

"You!" he cried, pointing to the rebellious teen. "Get out there and STOP THAT TRAIN!" Without a word, she leapt onto the bare back of the freed animal and was off.

\* \* \*

The *Meteor* was ready.

The bandit-turned-supervisor had assumed command of their defense. He had sent the wives to take armed concealment in one of the abandoned buildings strategically located behind the shelter of the train, out of sight of the approaching cloud, and deployed the eight men for battle in numerous carefully-considered locations: behind the Diesel, under the wheels of the day coach, inside the cab, peering around either edge of the slightly-open door of the baggage car, and more, with each man armed and ready for action. Left, right, back, and forward the bandit glanced, assessing their defenses, then smiled. He was in his element; they were ready.

Eddie crouched behind the large steel coupler protruding from the snub nose of the Diesel, a worn pistol in hand. Typically he did not travel about armed, as was generally the custom in Las Vegas these days, but he kept an old, yet serviceable weapon in the Diesel's toolkit in case an emergency such as this should arise. With no small amount of trepidation, he waited.

As the dust cloud approached, details of its source began to resolve themselves. It was one person riding a horse. He was small. He... that is, *she* was wearing a dress that billowed behind her from the wind of her motion, her long, stringy hair streaming back almost horizontally, bouncing in tandem with the undulation of the horse beneath her. She slowed as she approached the train, then halted a score of feet away and dismounted from the badly-frothing horse. She couldn't have been much more than twelve or thirteen. Cautiously she took several steps toward the noisily-idling, apparently-abandoned train and halted. Behind her, the horse collapsed onto its side with a resounding thud.

"Hello?" she called dubiously, not looking back to the downed steed. Several seconds passed in silence.

"Could you raise your hands, please?" Eddie finally returned politely, still crouching behind the coupler.

"Huh? Oh, sure!" she complied, a wide grin on her grimy face.

Eddie emerged slowly from behind the *Meteor*, worn pistol in hand pointed carelessly at the ground. "Can I help you?" he asked uncertainly.

The girl theatrically faked a swoon, dramatically placing the back of a raised hand against her forehead. "Golly! Can you ever!"

\* \* \*

The refugees arrived.

It had taken almost an hour before the sole remaining horse and its wagon, flanked by weary walkers, finally reached the makeshift station in Boulder City, but it only required a few short minutes to transfer the sickly passengers from the covered wagon to the *Meteor*. The healthier refugees filled the seats of the day coach nearly to capacity, while the seriously ill were relegated to lying on the floor of the baggage car. The returning Dam workers and their wives did what they could to make the refugees comfortable as the *Meteor* barreled swiftly north.

The platform of the Las Vegas station of Transcontinental Railroad was jammed beyond capacity in numbers not seen in years. Many of them were children with their parents who were always there to meet the *Meteor*, eagerly awaiting the departure of the afternoon's Kids' Special. Adding to the throng were the curious; one of the workers had called ahead from the Dam with the news of the approaching refugees. The two groups mingled and buzzed with excitement. It had been years since so large a contingent of newcomers had arrived in town, and no one wanted to miss the occasion.

The waiting horde held its collective breath when they first heard the distant blast of the train's whistle, and jockeyed for the best positions on the platform once the yard bell's dead, off-key clanking heralded the *Meteor*'s incipient arrival. They watched gleefully as the bright headlight approached; then, with a loud hiss and an abrupt release of compressed air, the *Meteor* came to a solid halt and the animated mob swarmed in to crowd around the day coach. One by one the refugees stepped off the train with an expression as if they were stepping into a dream, while the unfortunates in the baggage car were borne out on makeshift stretchers; all were led out of the mid-day sun into the relative coolth of the station's waiting room. The natives had many questions, and all the while badgered the weary newcomers incessantly, yet good-naturedly. The waiting room echoed cheerfully with their chatter, but when Eddie emerged from the tunnel that led from the platforms, the room quickly fell silent. The wagonmaster stood and faced him deferentially, battered hat in hand.

Eddie spoke first. "Welcome to Las Vegas," he said simply, and the crowd burst into applause and cheers. The tumult reverberated impressively within the open confines of the vaulted ceiling of the Transcontinental station.

The wagonmaster managed a smile, the first one to grace his face in weeks. "Thank you," he replied hoarsely, taking in the entire assembly with the wave of his hat. "Thank you all!" Again, the crowd cheered.

Eddie faced the crowd. "Listen: some of his people need to see a doctor. All of them are tired and hungry. Would—"

"My wagon's out front!" one man interrupted. "Somebody help me get a couple of them sick folks on board. I'll take them over to the hospital."

"I have an electric cart!" someone else called out. "Let me help, too!"

"A couple of the children can stay with me tonight!" one woman called. "We have room."

"I do, too!" cried another.

In a torrent, one after the other, the good people of Las Vegas fell over each other as they opened up their hearts and homes to the refugees. Noisily the two groups mingled and merged, then headed for the door in small clusters with supportive arms slung around each others' shoulders.

Eddie walked over to the wagonmaster. "I'd be obliged if you'd stay with me for a while."

The wagonmaster eyed him warily. "I hope you're not going to ask for train fares," he asked, only half joking. "We have no money."

Eddie was momentarily taken aback. The idea had never so much as crossed his mind. Recovering, he tossed the question aside with the wave of a hand. "No, of course not. But I would like a chance to talk with you a little more and hear your story. As it was, I only caught a few snippets before we left Boulder City."

The wagonmaster did not immediately reply; his mind was concerned with other things. He was a proud man, not accustomed to accepting charity; but in his position he was left with little choice—again. Reluctantly, he grumbled, "Is there someplace I can maybe get something to eat first? Then rest up a little? Would you mind?"

"Not at all. There's no hurry. I'm about to take the *Meteor* back out on the road anyhow. But before I do, let me get you a sandwich and find you a bed."

He led the man to an unused compartment in the sleeper car and showed him where the shower and other amenities were located. He left him there momentarily, then returned presently with a tray holding a thick sandwich and a tall, chilled glass of fresh milk. The hungry man took pains not to wolf down the food, yet still finished the snack in barely a minute. He did not think to use the starched white napkin that Eddie had provided.

"Thanks," he muttered. "I needed that."

"You're certainly welcome." Eddie glanced at his wristwatch and suggested, "It's a little after noon. Tell you what: how about I come wake you for dinner around six. Or would that be too soon? I'm dying to hear your story."

"I guess," he replied wearily. "But I'm not too sure you'll enjoy hearing it."

\* \* \*

The telephone rang.

Eddie was in the cafeteria picking vegetables for their evening meal when the call came in. Fortunately, he had recently had an extension telephone installed in the station's cafeteria so that he need not walk all the way back to the stationmaster's office to take a call. He was able to pick it up halfway through the second ring rather than on the tenth.

"Hello, Mr. Eddie?" the tinny voice came. "I'm the head nurse at the hospital, and we have a situation here that I need to speak with you about."

"Regarding our newcomers?" he asked anxiously.

Recognizing his tone of voice, thoughtfully she anticipated, "Yes, but not about their medical condition. Considering what they've been through, they're in remarkably good shape, or at least not as bad as they might have been. The doctors think that most of them will be just fine after a few meals and a little rest. There are only four really questionable patients, and one of them is a pregnant women. Weeks of being shaken around in the back of a covered wagon didn't do her baby any good—or her. She may still lose it—and we may even lose her!"

"Oh! I'm sorry to hear that."

"Thank you, but that's not exactly what I'm calling about."

"What? What is it, then?"

She hesitated, then began awkwardly, "Well, I'm calling to find out if you knew who is going to be paying for their medical care?"

As with the wagonmaster's question of train fares, it was an issue that Eddie hadn't even remotely considered. "I see," he said.

"As I said, most of them are only going to need some bed rest and a minor amount of attention, but others, such as our pregnant friend, is going to require a substantial degree of care, and that's going to run into a lot of willies."

"I see," he repeated, his face coloring with an unseen blush.

"We'll do what we can for them all, but it's something that will need to be addressed soon."

"All right. Let me get back to you."

"Thank you, Mr. Eddie."

He hung up and stood there for several seconds with his hand still on the instrument, thinking. It was only fair that the hospital be paid for services rendered, but who is it that should be paying it? His first notion was that the refugees should pay for it themselves, but as the wagonmaster had already pointed out, they had no money. Perhaps someone could lend them the money until they were able to pay it back, but that implied that someone had to be the source of the loan. Certainly it would not be right to leave the hospital holding that bag; but if not them, who? He sighed. It looked like it was going to be another one of those fundamental quandaries that kept sneaking up on Las Vegas every now and again. Civilization could be so complicated!

The question itself was not a new one. The town had its own share of the poor, mostly elderly widows and widowers, but in these days of heightened prosperity, their needs were pretty much taken care of by their family, friends, and neighbors. The police even had a special "adopt a neighbor" rate where for a modest, additional fee one could add a destitute friend to the list of those who were entitled to police protection. But this new situation would surely prove to be more expensive and difficult to solve than a random widow's meals or an occasional burial, if only because of its suddenly-larger constituency.

He mulled over who he might be able to call for advice. There were several people who had helped him solve other town problems in the past, such as the banker, the policeman, and the butcher, among many others, but none of them seemed right for this sort of a question. Perhaps a social worker might be of some assistance, but he was not aware of any who remained in the town; he had assumed that all of them had left with the Mayor. Even if any had remained, with the collapse of the Las Vegas government, there was no one left to pay them. They would have long since moved on to other vocations, increasing the difficulty of tracking them down.

*Who else cares for the needy?* he asked himself, and the metaphorical light bulb instantly illuminated over his head. *Churches!* He glanced up at the large, electric clock that hung over the cafeteria door. There was plenty of time for him to do a little research before he had to start preparing dinner.

He realized he still had his hand on the telephone. He released it and headed for the door.

* * *

The priest knelt.

Respectfully, Eddie removed his wide-brimmed hat as he closed the towering, ornate church door behind him. His eyes adjusted to the dim, candle-lit interior sufficiently to allow him to discern the priest kneeling in the first pew. He walked up the aisle; the priest turned at hearing his echoing footsteps, stood, and faced him.

"Do you have a few minutes, shepherd?"

"Of course, Mr. Eddie. My time is yours."

"Thank you." With a start, Eddie recognized the man: he was the juror who pronounced sentence upon him and the banker; but he said nothing about it. "You're aware that we took in thirty-three refugees earlier today?"

"One of them is napping in my rectory," he replied with a smile. "A young boy."

"Good! I wanted—" Eddie glanced awkwardly around at the sacred surroundings as the echo of his voice slowly died away. "Is there a more comfortable place we can talk?" he whispered self-consciously. "I have some questions I'd like to ask."

"Of course. Come with me." He led him to the small, sunlit sacristy behind the altar. The room was not large; the walls were bare, and several plain wooden chairs were positioned around a table of the same stark style, a large book at its center. The priest extended a hand to one chair and took another. "Now how can I be of service to you, Mr. Eddie?"

"I'm looking for advice."

"Regarding our newcomers?"

"Regarding our newcomers. Right now they're living on our charity, but I can't say how much longer that can continue." Briefly, he related the details of his conversation with the head nurse. "I was wondering what your church does in circumstances like these."

"We do what we can, Mr. Eddie, and all too often that's not nearly enough." He sighed heavily. "Charity is a cordial but fickle friend. You and I both saw its good side at your station this morning: people lined up gladly to help those unfortunate women and children. But I can promise you that in much less than a week that charity will start to wear thin. Such has always been the nature of charity."

"Are you saying people will throw them out?"

"'Edge them out' might be a better way of putting it. But yes, it will happen nevertheless. Even with the young one that I have taken on, for my means are meager, and the boy should have a decent home."

"There has to be an alternative!"

"Oh, there is, there is! Otherwise..." He turned his gaze heavenward. "...I would not have been so blessed as to serve my congregation for so many years." He made a complex series of motions with his hands, clearly choreographed.

Confused, Eddie asked, "But where does your income come from?" He cast an uncertain, fleeting glance upward questioningly.

The priest laughed. It was a cheerful, friendly laugh. "No, no pennies from heaven, if that's what you mean. Typically I pass the plate at our services and people give what they can, each according to their ability. If there's some special need, such as the new roof we put on the church last year, I go from door to door asking for a special contribution—and not only from members of my congregation, but from everyone."

"And strangers will give?"

He laughed again. "No, Mr. Eddie. Generally speaking, they don't. Maybe one out of a hundred might."

"Is that enough?"

Again, his gaze went heavenward, although the subject of his glance was much closer at hand this time. "Well, we do have our new roof—but the builder insisted on a weekly mention during my sermon before giving me the discounted price. When it comes to charity, it's often a two-way street."

"What if there's not enough charity to go around?"

"Then you do without," he said flatly.

"Some of the refugees in the hospital have life-threatening injuries. How can they possibly 'do without?'"

"Write that down!" the priest commanded emphatically. "That's a wonderful appeal to use when you go door-to-door!"

Eddie did not react. He could not picture himself going from door to door begging for money. He had done something similar when he first established the town's police force, but then he was offering a needed, valuable service; this time, he would merely be a moocher looking for a handout.

The priest took no notice of his silence. "Another thing you can do is hold some sort of a fundraiser. Dance socials are always a winner. There's little enough innocent fun in this wicked town that you'd probably get a good number of people to come out. I hold one here once a month, and the turnout is fairly good. Once I get them in the door, I hit them with raffles, games, and prizes, and that raises the take. Bake sales are another way to pull in money, although you do need to first convince the ladies to bake for you. In the old days, if you had the right connections you could get a government grant, but in these new days that's no longer an option." He thought for a minute, then added, "Speaking of government, since you're pretty much in charge of the town, why don't you just levy a temporary tax? To help the refugees. It's a good cause. People would pay it, I'm telling you."

Eddie's eyes widened in horror. "A tax? What right do I have to take someone's money without their permission?"

"Governments tax all the time." He gestured at the book in the middle of the table. "'Render unto Caesar' and all that," he quoted. "It's the price we pay for living in a civilized society."

"I would hardly call it 'civilized' when you take money from people at the point of a gun."

The priest shrugged. "It's the way of the world."

"Not my sort of world."

"But you'd be helping people!"

"I can't justify doing evil in the name of doing good."

"Ah, yes. No evil means, regardless of the goodness of the ends. Very laudable." The priest considered for a moment longer and chuckled good-naturedly. "Then I sentence you to bake sales, dances, and knocking on doors!"

Eddie did not smile. "Or do without?"

"Or do without."

The silence dragged out for a moment, then Eddie stood up and extended a hand. "Thank you for your time and the ideas."

The priest shook his hand warmly in both of his. "Really, you should think about a tax."

Again, Eddie did not smile. "I think not."

* * *

Dinner ended.

"That was without a doubt the best meal I have had in many a week!" the wagonmaster praised. He chuckled dryly. "Not meaning to denigrate my own compliment, but I really haven't had much more than trail food for weeks either. Seriously, though, this was really good!"

"I've had the benefit of a good teacher who trained in Paris to be a chef."

"He taught you well."

"She." He reddened slightly.

"Ah. Sorry."

"Not a problem." They sat at the round mahogany table in the ornate observation car, and Eddie leaned back in his chair. "So you're from Los Angeles?"

"Yep. While it was still there, I should say."

"It's gone now?"

He laughed dryly again. "Ashes and bones. Dust and rot. That's all it is now."

"Why? What happened?"

"It burned to the ground... what? Over a year ago," he explained without emotion. After a short, pensive silence, he continued. "You might recall how things had been getting progressively worse in California for quite some time, even back in the days when things were still somewhat civilized. There had been a lot of fighting, even though it was pretty much kept out of the newspapers—back when there were still newspapers!" He laughed without mirth; it seemed to be a defining characteristic for the man. "I remember how Washington just kept sending more and more troops, but it wasn't doing anyone any good. It just added to the number of men who were running around shooting guns." He shook his head sadly at the thought. "It was pretty bad."

Eddie nodded. "I was in San Francisco toward the end, and it was pretty much the same thing there, too."

"Then you know what I mean. It wasn't too long after we heard the news about the X Project exploding that some troublemakers with their backs against the wall decided to pull their own doomsday scenario and set their slum on fire. The winds had been blowing pretty hard for days, and it just fanned that fire so big that the firemen couldn't hold the line. Next thing you knew, the whole damn city goes up in flames and thousands of people were running for their lives." He paused, reliving the scenario in his mind, as a haunted, distant look crept into his eyes.

Eddie found himself on the edge of his seat. He took a deep breath and tried to relax. "How did you escape?"

He held Eddie's gaze firmly. "I didn't." He waited a moment to let that sink in before continuing. "My sons and I headed south to get out of the way of the fires when we were captured by some paramilitary group calling themselves the 'Party of the People.' They kept us penned up inside an old Army base and used us as forced laborers."

"What?! Slavery? In America!"

Seeing the shocked expression on Eddie's face, he chuckled. "Thanks, but it actually turned out to be a good thing for me and my boys, because that was during the time when the refugee problem was at its worst. The Party of the People kept up a pretty solid defense, so most of the homeless folk were pushed south into Mexico. Did us a favor by capturing us, they did. Kept us alive."

"Was your wife with you?"

He snorted. "She got lucky—died in childbirth about fifteen years ago." He shook his head. "She would never have survived what me and our boys went through."

"I'm sorry." Awkwardly, he tried to change the subject. "And your sons are here in town?"

He stared hard at Eddie. Seconds passed. "No." He looked away, then back. "I'm getting to that."

"I'm sorry," he repeated, reddening brightly at his obvious faux pas.

The wagonmaster took a deep breath before continuing. "Well, we had been prisoners about a month when one day we got our big chance. We were in a chain gang out on a work detail and this one guy decided he'd make a break for it. He had gotten his hands on a key for the leg irons—don't ask me where!—and he unlocked his own, real sneaky-like, then handed one of my boys the key, and when no one was looking he just turned tail and ran. Well, the guards noticed pretty quick, and all of them went off chasing after him, leaving the rest of us behind. And why not? We were all chained up to each other, so we couldn't have gotten very far even if we tried. But they didn't count on my boy having that key. All of us got ourselves loose, the whole chain gang, and we lit off like bats out of Hell! Don't know what happened with the guy who gave us the key, or the guards. We never saw any of them again. Least not those guards."

"You were captured by other guards?" he anticipated apprehensively.

"Hey, who's telling this story?" Angrily the wagonmaster turned away for a moment, then resumed his tale. "We figured our best bet was to get away from the coast and all the refugees deserting the populated areas, so we headed east across the desert. It took us a lot of hungry days, but we eventually made it out to the Imperial Valley. Things were still pretty normal there—if you can call living with no electricity normal!—because by then the X Project had already blown up and people had lost contact with the rest of the country."

"Do you have any news about what happened to New York City?" Eddie interrupted anxiously. The memories stung when they came on too fast.

"Nothing since the X Project blew up."

His face fell. "I see," he said.

"In any case, there weren't a whole lot of people in the Imperial Valley, and that suited us just fine, as we had had more than enough of other people right then. We took on jobs as farmhands and it started to look like things were going to work out, but it didn't last not two weeks before the army of the Party of the People waltzed right in and took over. Maybe they were looking for us in particular, maybe not. Didn't matter. You didn't have to ask me and the boys twice—we were on our way that same day, abandoning most everything we owned and heading further east across the desert before they could catch us again. Couple of days later we reached the farms on the Colorado River along the Arizona border and took work as farmhands again. Things were pretty nice for quite a while—months!—and by the time last year's harvest was in we had saved up enough to set up our own farm further up the river, maybe a hundred miles north of Yuma—which, by the way, was already burned to the ground by then; all the cities are." He snorted cynically. "The farm was nothing fancy: just a barn and an old farmhouse, but more than enough to keep us alive." At that point he halted his narrative; he appeared to be lost in thought.

Eddie let him drift along for a short while, then prompted, "That was over six months ago. What happened next?"

He didn't respond for almost another minute, and this time Eddie waited him out. Apparently this was a man who could not be rushed. When he finally resumed, he did not look up. "Eight months, it was. Eight beautiful months like no time in my life had ever been before, at least not since my wife passed." He halted again, his head down and face blank. "Then a few weeks ago... they appeared."

"Who appeared?"

He looked up, wild eyed. "Back For God!" Eddie sat up in fearful empathy with the wagonmaster's anxiety. "Thousands of them! They poured up the Colorado Valley like a plague of locusts. We'd first heard about them from some of the newer arrivals, and by all accounts they were nothing but bad news! A ruthless, religious sect that controls the whole middle of California, they say."

Eddie nodded uneasily. "We've heard about them." He shivered involuntarily.

"Well, we hadn't. The first that me and the boys saw of them was the smoke from other folks' farms downriver being burned. Next came the first wave of farmers running away, mostly women and children, some in wagons, others on horses, but most of them just running on foot. They were pretty hysterical, some of them—and when I heard what Back For God does to heathen women, I can understand why! And anybody who could defeat a well-organized bunch like the Party of the People would have to be pretty powerful." He paused. "Now where was I? Oh, yes: the women. From what we could get out of them, their men had set up a defensive line and were going to try and hold the acolytes back. Turned out it didn't work, because less than a day later the men came high-tailing it up the river, tails between their legs. What was left of them, that is. Almost half never made it." He sighed mournfully, then shifted his weight in the chair before continuing. "Now, our farm was situated a little upstream from a narrow part of the river valley with mountains on both sides which we figured could serve as a natural blockade. For almost two days the lot of us worked like madmen fortifying the spot as best we could, when without warning the first of them red-robed bastards came into sight. Our defenses weren't organized, our plans weren't finished, nothing was ready, but here they came. Only a couple at first, and we managed to hold them off, but we knew the main body couldn't be far behind."

He took a deep, shaking breath before continuing. "We got all the women and children aboard a half-dozen wagons and a couple of carriages, hitched up what horses we could find, threw in some barrels of water, hardtack, salted meats, and several sacks of seeds, and within the hour I went off with them heading north. My boys stayed behind with the rest of the men to help man the ramparts along the south end of our farm." He paused dejectedly. "Last I saw them, they were waiting, watching." He stopped again, his mind's eye hundreds of miles to the south. His expression was flat, as if he could no longer feel any emotion; only his eyes burned bright with the memory. Abruptly, he stood and turned away from

Eddie, walked to the rear balcony of the observation car, and leaned on the ornate railing. Still facing away, he resumed his tale.

"That was about three weeks ago. My boys must have done their job well, because no one's caught up with us—and we were moving pretty slow at the end, there. The last week or so we were traveling at walking speed, so if they wanted to catch us, a single man on a horse could've had us, just like that!" He snapped his fingers over the railing at the setting sun. Slowly, he turned back to face Eddie. "But they didn't. My boys did their job." His voice did not break, but it somehow felt as if it had. "And now here we are, thirty-three of us with just two wagons, a few sacks of seeds, and one malnourished horse to our name, where forty-two of us started out with six wagons, two carriages, and fifteen horses." He walked back to the table that still held the remnants of their dinner and leaned heavily on the back of his chair. "Two hundred miles, Mr. Eddie. Three weeks' ride by wagon, one or two by horse. That's all that separates you from a living Hell."

Eddie could think of nothing to say. The man's saga had been a sobering one.

Incongruously, the wagonmaster smiled. "But you folks have nothing to worry about."

"What? What do you mean?" His question was almost a cry.

"No one knows you're here! It's been... what, two years since the country fell apart? And everything's all so much a torn patchwork now. All the reports I've heard from other refugees like me say that all the cities are dead. Los Angeles... San Diego... Bakersfield...—I've seen the body. Phoenix... Tucson... Flagstaff...—I've heard firsthand obituaries." He lifted his gaze thoughtfully. "Ah, what other places am I forgetting? Yuma..." He looked back down to Eddie and waved a hand in dismissal. "Lots. Doesn't matter. They're all dead. Everyone knows that. All the cities are dead—all except lonely Las Vegas, that is!" He chuckled. "And no one knows. Even I thought Las Vegas was dead. Every other city died—why not you, too?" He paused, then added, "Did I tell you our goal was really Lake Meade, not Las Vegas? We hoped we could get some farming going again... Me and thirty-two women and children..." He shook his head somberly, and stood for a moment in silence. "Fools, all of us," he finally murmured, and reclaimed his seat. Unexpectedly shifting the subject, out of the blue he asked, "How many people you have here in town, Mr. Eddie?"

"We're not sure. We're guessing about five thousand. Could be three or seven. We have no way of knowing."

"And you're well armed?"

"Sir! In Nevada?"

"Sorry. Stupid of me to ask."

"There's also an Army base not far north of here that has a lot of materiel. If we were forced to mount a defense, I think we could do a serviceable job of it."

The wagonmaster cast him a stern eye. "Could you do it on two days' warning?"

Eddie did not so much as pause. "No. It would take at least that long to transport what we'd need from the Army base, and no one is really trained to use that kind of weaponry, or in tactics."

"You ought to correct that."

Eddie did not reply.

"Soon," he stressed. "Very soon. If I could find a lost city, it's certain that sooner or later others will, too."

* * *

Sleep would not come.

Eddie lay on his back in bed, troubled. Images of religious fanatics dominated one part of his overactive mind and Dickensian waifs another, both visions feeding a deep-seated unease that was new to him. In the old days when he was merely the Special Assistant to the Vice-President of Operations for Transcontinental Railroad, the trials and tribulations of his job had merely been frustrating rather than troubling, and any anxiety he may have felt had been kept handily at bay by his confidence in the superlative ability of the Vice-President of Operations herself, Dagny. But in these new days there was no one to whom he could turn for counsel and assistance; in fact, the situation had somehow, inexplicably reversed itself: he found himself the one to whom others turned. He was left with only himself to rely upon, and he felt himself nowhere nearly up to the task.

He had already resigned himself to following two separate courses of action come the morning. The first was to send men up to the abandoned Army base north of town to take steps to better equip the town's makeshift militia. The second was to start knocking on doors to beg for money for the unfortunate refugees. The first task was trivial; he'd make the suggestion to the militia commander, explain his reasons, and that would be that; the chain of command they had established would take it from there. But the second task was more than Eddie could personally handle—or wanted to. To assist him in his begging, he considered wielding the men under his command who still worked for Transcontinental. Of the dozen whom he had inherited when he first arrived in town, only five remained, and there were few enough duties for them to perform even though scheduled train service had been revived many months ago. But today, facing so daunting a charitable effort, he now wished he had retained the other seven as well. Yet even as the wish formed in his mind, he tossed it aside. It would not have been fair to either the men or to Transcontinental to have kept them on the pay rolls standing idle the last year waiting only for this troubling day to arrive. In fact, it was ethically questionable whether he should order Transcontinental employees to help at all. And he had learned his lesson well regarding ordering railroad personnel to perform any task whose purpose might be misconstrued.

He sighed aloud in the dark. That he needed more help was clear; and not just the help of more hands, but also the help of more minds. He needed the brawn of many people multiplied by the power of their intellects, each man working of his own initiative toward solving the town's problems. However, creating such a partnership in itself would give rise to yet another state of affairs that would require his attention, namely, that of defining, designing, and developing that organization. Not for the first time he wished he had some sort of a roadmap to create such an association, some tried-and-true formula that he knew would produce predictable solutions, like some mathematical equation whose truth had long since been hammered out and proven, and was now taken for granted. Sadly, in the realm of forming a helping society, no such roadmap existed.

*Or did it?* His eyes widened in the dark, seeing nothing yet seeing more. There *had* been many examples of formulaic organizations throughout history that dealt with societal problems—they were called "governments." They routinely dealt with crises of charity—not always efficiently, but at least adequately. *No, not even adequately*, he corrected himself; the current state of the world plainly reflected a flawed approach. Still, it was a start, an obvious, yet crucial clue to developing a solution. The next morning, he would visit the public library and read up on how governments handled charity.

Satisfied for the moment, he rolled over in bed and instantly fell into a dreamless sleep.

* * *

Governments forced.

After spending several long hours in the deserted library tracking down the details of one governmental charitable solution after another, Eddie came to the universal conclusion that governments dealt with that warmest of human actions—charity—by means of one of the coldest—force. In example after example, while the ends varied widely, the means were woefully the same. He had fully expected to encounter such shabby stories when he examined the politics of charity within the various People's States of the world, and in that he was not disappointed. Despite their avowed purpose to serve the common man, the reality was always the inverse; they uniformly made life worse for their citizens despite any high-sounding goals. But one unexpected discovery that shook him to the core was how his own purportedly-capitalist nation had addressed the question of charity.

He started that investigation with the ultimate authority, the Constitution for the United States of America. He had never before read his nation's highest law—it had been only superficially taught in the government-run public school he had attended—and his long-overdue initial reading was an eye opener. Having read it all the way through, he came away somewhat perplexed—he had somehow missed seeing the part about charity. He re-read it more carefully, but only managed to convince himself that the topic was not mentioned. Worse yet, it was clear that the Tenth Amendment bluntly forbade the national government from exercising any power not explicitly granted: *The powers not delegated to the United States by the Constitution, nor prohibited by it to the States, are reserved to the States respectively, or to the people.* He sat up straight when the import of those words sank in. Since charity was not one of the delegated powers, it followed logically that the federal government had *no authority* to perform charity! The meaning of the Tenth Amendment was crystal clear: charity belonged in the realm of the States and the people. Eddie was both stunned and perplexed. How, then, could the Supreme Court have countenanced all of the innumerable social programs, grants, subsidies, and thousands of other handouts the government offered? The Constitution only authorized the federal government to do seventeen things, all enumerated in Article 1 Section 8, such as coining money and organizing the militia—responsibilities which, Eddie ironically noted, he had taken charge of in Las Vegas—but charity was not listed among them.

Since charity was reserved to the States, it was clear he should turn next to the Nevada Constitution. This time, he found the salient words on his first pass; however, governmental charity in Nevada was strictly limited to *Institutions for the benefit of the Insane, Blind and Deaf and Dumb.* To his knowledge, none of the refugees were either insane, blind, deaf, or dumb, so apparently there was nothing the state could legally do for them—*Not that there was any state government left!* he reminded himself.

Curiously, a footnote revealed that at one time Nevada possessed the constitutional authority to do much more for its indigents, but the authorizing clause had been repealed many years ago. According to the footnote, the elided phrase read: *The respective counties of the State shall provide as may be prescribed by law, for those inhabitants who, by reason of age and infirmity or misfortunes, may have claim upon the sympathy and aid of Society.* Now *this* was the sort of authorizing clause he had expected to find in the national Constitution!—but didn't.

Certainly the refugees were the victims of egregious misfortunes, but the charitable constitutional provision had been repealed; aid was no longer permitted. Eddie wondered what had convinced the citizens of Nevada to revoke such a plainly-humanitarian power; it could very well have a bearing on his quest. Intrigued, he searched the library for information on the topic, and soon found a pamphlet containing a brief history of public charity, not only in Nevada, but historically as well.

Eddie found it to be an interesting exposition. He learned that since ancient times charity had been the exclusive realm of religious groups, but had become secularized beginning with the first Poor Tax levied centuries ago in England. Government-sponsored charity had never existed in the young United States, but a few individual states did opt to provide for some measure of charity, with Nevada being one of the first. The pamphlet also answered Eddie's question as to why the provision was repealed—the responsibility had been relinquished to Washington as a condition for receiving a federal subsidy. Eddie shook his head; the good people of Nevada had thrown away a constitutional state charity and sold it for an *un*-constitutional national charity!

Following up further, he searched the library looking for the text of the law which controlled the distribution of charity nationally, but could not locate it. No surprise; the library could only hold so many books—or perhaps that particular treatise did not exist? However, he did accidentally stumble across a slim pamphlet on charity containing an excellent essay penned by an American patriot of the highest renown, Davy Crockett, chronicling his experiences with governmental charity while he served as a United States Congressman. His essay provided Eddie with numerous irrefutable reasons to avoid any dalliance with the idea of government-controlled charity, for it was replete with warnings and admonitions, crowned by Crockett's most damning passage: *The power of collecting and disbursing money at pleasure is the most dangerous power that can be intrusted to man, particularly under our system of collecting revenue by a tariff... If you had the right to give to one, you have the right to give to all, and as the Constitution neither defines charity nor stipulates the amount, you are at liberty to give to any and everything which you may believe, or profess to believe, is a charity, and to any amount you may think proper. You will very easily perceive what a wide door this would open for fraud and corruption and favoritism on the one hand, and for robbing the people on the other.*

For the second time since entering the library that morning, Eddie was stunned. The observation was so precisely accurate, so true to reality, it seemed as if Davy Crockett had personally visited the America of Eddie's time, examined the actual workings of government, then returned to his own era to pen the pamphlet. That eminent patriot's voice reached out across the years to dash Eddie's hopes of finding any brand of viable, government-sponsored benevolence.

Apparently he had reached a dead end. In fact, his search had come up worse than empty; for not only was a comprehensive government charity forbidden by the constitutions, any attempt was fraught with peril. What, then, was to be done with the refugees? Were the only options left open to him bake sales, Saturday night dances, and knocking on doors? But that approach had its own major shortcoming: while it may take care of the needs of the moment, what about the needs of tomorrow? He did not fancy himself knocking on doors for the rest of his days, chained to the never-ending demands of the indigent, a slave to charity.

He sighed aloud, because he knew the issue to be a much wider one than mere hospitalized refugees; they were not the only possible objects of charity, merely the ones at hand. What of the less crucial needs of society? As a clear example also at hand, Eddie considered the empty library in which he sat. There was no librarian to greet him, no staff to care for the wealth of knowledge it contained, no one to add new knowledge—such as information about the national charity laws—and no one to keep the older knowledge up to date. The front door had not even been locked against the possibility of theft or vandalism; Eddie had simply walked into the abandoned building. Having once been funded through the taxes of the now-defunct Las Vegas government, a dependable sponsorship for the library had vanished along with the Mayor and his entourage. Unless a new patron could be found, before very much longer the library would become a heritage lost; someone was needed to step in and take the trouble to knock on the closed doors of strangers in order to retain the open doors of the library.

Again, Eddie sighed. Wearily, he surveyed the various books and pamphlets arrayed on the table in front of him. He was ready to admit defeat. If it was only a government that possessed the resources to adequately tackle charity, yet that agent lay acutely vulnerable to widespread "fraud and corruption and favoritism," then there could be no answer. Indeed, it was that very trio of sins which had ultimately brought down the once-great United States of America. There was no denying that public charity was a monster that consumed all within sight, for charity was a commodity never out of demand. The conundrum was an ancient one that pre-dated the original Poor Tax from centuries ago. Even the priest's sacred book, many millennia old, foretold, "The poor you will always have with you." Against the wisdom of the ages, what chance had someone like Eddie? *But what can you do when you have to deal with people?* he asked himself. He had no answer.

In theory, he knew what was needed: some custom or law limiting charity, a societal contrivance analogous to the mechanical governors found on the electric turbines in the Boulder Dam powerplant which prevented their armatures from over-speeding. Perhaps a like construct could be placed upon government charity to prevent its spinning out of control? The priest had suggested he levy a tax; but what could prevent the bottomless need for public charity from eventually draining the pockets of the productive men who made charity possible in the first place? Aside from his own personal moral qualms, any attempt at re-establishing taxation would set a dangerous precedent, and coupling the coercive power of taxation with the insatiable demands of charity guaranteed its own destruction, much as would connecting a tank of oxygen to the vacuum of space; the oxygen would be instantly dispersed, but the vacuum would still remain—and all those dependent upon the life-giving gas would perish.

The only rational conclusion possible was that if the vacuum would always be there—and surely it would!—then a coercive tax was the *last* thing that should be considered—better yet, not even considered at all! *But if not the coercive power of taxation,* he wondered, *what could be used to fund public charity—perhaps a more general, non-coercive tax, similar to what was being done with the police force?* He almost smiled at the oxymoronic idea, but suddenly his mind halted. Stunned yet again, sitting in silence, his mind leapt into high gear. *But why not a broad-based, non-coercive tax?* he asked himself, *a voluntary tax earmarked solely for governmental charity?* He was frozen into immobility at the immense import of his simple insight: all that would be necessary would be to strip the government of its power of coercive taxation when it came to charity. It would be warm charity without the chilling use of force.

Moments passed as he absorbed the ramifications of the peculiar concept. Forbidding the government from using coercive taxation for charitable purposes would constrain a governmental charity to live within its means; it would have available only that money which the citizens might choose to voluntarily donate. Such scarcity would act as an analogous governor, keeping charity within reasonable bounds such that it would neither be completely ineffective nor stop the motor of the world. If there was not enough money to cure all the world's ills, then it stood to reason that the world would either be forced to prioritize its needs so as to remain within its means, knock on more doors to raise more money, or do without. He foresaw how a library could temporarily cut back on its services until some unfortunate refugees were healed.

At first blush, it appeared as if the concept might be made to work. But how would the cautionary wisdom of Davy Crockett mesh with voluntary taxation? Could it still lead to the same evils that had destroyed America? *Probably*, he admitted glumly. What's to stop unscrupulous lawmakers from ignoring the restriction against using tax monies for charity? Who's to force errant judges to enforce the restriction? Witness how these very men had routinely ignored the plain language of the Constitution on all too many occasions; and given the opportunity, doubtless they would do so again. When lawmakers and judges conspired to ignore their solemn oath to uphold the Constitution, short of armed revolution, how could anyone stop them?

With another sudden leap, Eddie realized that the answer was again simple. Given how Crockett had argued it should never be within the realm of government to provide charity, then the solution was obvious: don't have the oath-breaking lawmakers and judges involved at all! Someone else besides government must provide the charity instead; to wit: it must be made a separate, societal responsibility, as it originally once was. With rapid crystallization, the answer fell squarely into the lap of his brain. Why not separate Society and State, and render unto Caesar the things that were Caesar's, but to Society the things that were Society's?

He nodded to himself. That was it. He was convinced. He had found the solution. A formulaic approach could be established, yet avoid the pitfalls which had doomed the nation. Society would be that formula. Better yet, there would be no need to reinvent from scratch the organization that would administer charity; an excellent blueprint already existed.

Surveying the papers and books scattered across the table, he shuffled through the jumbled clutter until he came across the United States Constitution. Scanning it quickly, he found the section he was looking for: the seventeen enumerated powers of the now-defunct national government. It would be trivial to excise those powers and replace them with a new mission, one suited *not* to a coercive government, but rather one suited to a voluntary Society. The resulting document would effectively become the oft-mentioned but never-seen "social contract," except that its tenets would be optional, not mandatory. One need not sign it, but even having done so, would still not be bound by it.

He retrieved a blank sheet of the library's dwindling supply of scrap paper and began to transcribe what he imagined should be the enumerated powers for this new Society, a new Article 1 Section 8. The first power was obvious: *To make voluntary Guidelines regarding requesting donations and making expenditures toward the common good and the good of others, from each according to his ability, to each according to his need.* He stared into space for a moment, pencil in hand, considering what other powers might be needed by Society. But could not conceive of any others; the one clause apparently covered it all.

No blind fool, he readily recognized the collectivist creed he had just penned for what it was. Including those twelve final words in Society's Constitution justifiably troubled him at first; but in the end he was forced to admit there were none better to capture the concept. The phrase did not imply any sanctioning of theft by a People's State, nor did it impose a ruinous burden upon men—after all, by definition a man could only act according to his ability—which rendered the first six words, in essence, a tautology. But despite their stating the obvious, those six words fulfilled their goal by clearly naming the source of Society's wealth outright: *from each according to his ability*, with that ability being characterized by each individual man. Similarly, the final six named its target: *to each according to his need*, with that need being determined by circumstance. And standing squarely between ability and need would be the Guidelines of Society. Given that those Guidelines were defined by a sympathetic Society, not by predatory looters, the producer could never be milked for the benefit of the needy, nor would the needy have a claim on the resources of the producer. The key feature differentiating Society from a People's State was that Society held no coercive powers, none at all. So despite his initial misgivings, ultimately Eddie let the collectivist phrase remain intact, despite its less-than-glorious history. In a voluntary Society, the mantra was proper and apt.

Deciding he may as well formalize what he had been doing in the courtroom, he drew a double line across the middle of the paper and penned a second clause below it, quoting the carved sign: *All men have the God-given, inalienable right to live their own lives their own way without interference, provided they respect the rights and property of others.* Considering how justice was being practiced in Las Vegas, he decided to chronicle a few important details based upon his own experiences as judge. *Individuals can only be tried once for a given crime. Those convicted by a randomly-selected jury of their peers of violating this Constitution are sentenced to a punishment that is appropriate for the crime and stands to reason, and have the option of accepting or not accepting the sentence. Those who do not accept their sentence are no longer entitled to receive any benefits granted under this Constitution.*

But before he had even finished transcribing the concept, he began to have second thoughts about including the clause as a part of Society's powers. Defending the rights and property of citizens was clearly a governmental responsibility, not a societal one; and he had learned just this day exactly how dangerous it was to ever consider mixing the two. It would be crucial—nay, a *sine qua non*—that they be kept utterly and totally separate.

Giving that thought a tangible manifestation, he carefully tore the paper in half along the lines he had drawn, fittingly physically separating the powers of Society from the powers of the State. He set aside, for the moment, the bottom half of the page; once he finished with the Constitution for Society, he'd insert the text into its own Constitution for the State.

That done, he returned his hand to adapting the rest of the realigned Constitution to serve Society's needs. One after the other, he made note of those sections that could be omitted as being irrelevant—such as the power of coercive taxation—and others that needed minor modification—such as the jurisdiction of the courts—but he kept intact the bulk of the organizational structure it outlined. It did not take long to shift the paradigm; soon he was finished.

He re-read his notes once, then again, and with every passing second, he became more firmly convinced. It would work. The eleemosynous entity known as Society would become a rallying point for the caring people of Las Vegas, bringing together the medley of helping hands and minds that Eddie had been seeking. It was a formulaic response—a *non-governmental* response—that could not possibly spin out of control. The vacuum of space would still exist, but there would be a self-controlled regulator which would limit the rate at which the oxygen might be expelled. There was no chance it would stop the motor of the world, nor was there any need to.

Satisfied, he carefully set his notes on Society to one side. Turning his hand to the Constitution of the State with the goal of repeating the same task, he was surprised to find that the process progressed very differently than it had with Society's creation: the text of the Constitution literally melted in his hands, like cotton candy in a laughing child's mouth. He began the process in the same manner, first replacing the seventeen enumerated powers with his new rules of court, but from there the progression diverged rapidly, starting with the venerable document's very first words. Gone was the Legislature and its law-making ability; it had been over a year since the bandit's trial, and since that day there had been no rational reason to add any new law beyond the twenty-three carved words which still hung over the judge's bench in the courtroom. Gone also was the Head of State; without a legislature, why have a leader? In an organization without powers, what need is there to charge an executive with executing those non-existent laws? And without a Congress to pass laws, what was the need for someone to sign or veto non-existent bills? Rules regarding elections and succession were similarly useless, given that no man needed to be elected or succeeded. The courts would remain, of course, but given the communal nature of the new court system, the bulk of even that section of constitutional text melted away.

Turning finally to the numerous constitutional amendments, one by one the guarantees of the Bill of Rights fell by the wayside as being unnecessary. All of their restrictions upon the power of government were either currently covered by the concise commandment carved in the courtroom, or the powers that the amendments were meant to balance no longer existed. The only amendment he felt worthy of keeping was a foreshortened rendering of the Tenth, the one reserving all rights to the people.

In the end, so many words had vanished that when he finally finished drafting the Constitution for the State, little was left beyond his new rules of court, a means for amendments, and the reservation of rights to the people. The rest had simply evaporated as being either redundant or unnecessary. Where there were once three branches of government, he was left with only one, the judicial branch—less than one, actually, since anyone could establish a court, not just the State.

Although he was convinced it was complete, one part of Eddie remained dubious. How could so much of the exalted Constitution prove to be so superfluous to running the necessary functions of a government? Returning to the top of the document, he carefully reviewed his edits, but he could make no justification for including any more of its text, nor removing any of that which he had left intact. While his instincts told him that his wording might possibly be tightened up to make it more precise, intellectually he could not imagine how. To his eye it was all correct and complete.

Sitting alone in the library, he nodded to himself, satisfied. Against all odds and the misguided wisdom of the ages, he had accomplished his goal. He leaned over the table, holding the two sets of scribbled notes side by side, the Constitution for Society in one hand and the Constitution for the State in the other. As he bent over the few scraps of paper which would make it possible for thousands of men to live together in peace, he considered the implications of what he had wrought: the separation of Society and State. Like some modern-day Solomon, he had taken the powers long assumed to be the province of the State and had ordered them to be divided, giving most to Society and reserving very few for the original holder. While the result would be a radically different political world, it would also remain hauntingly the same. Where the old governments had passed laws, Society would now suggest Guidelines. Where governments had set mandatory tax rates, Society would instead recommend voluntary contributions. Like a traditional government, Society would have its Congress, its courts, and its Head of State—Head of Society, actually. The new Legislature would suggest and enact Guidelines for Society designed to help those less fortunate, then solicit, collect, and distribute charitable funds as could best be done; and where there were disagreements, Society's court would decide the Societal issue. Other than that, Society would have no power over men; its edicts would be completely voluntary. It was a perfect solution, for it would provide a disciplined vehicle for the kind-hearted people of the world who wished to help their fellow man, but not for the scoundrels who wished to rob that same fellow man. Although those who would abuse the system could not be stopped or eliminated entirely, the damage they might be able to do would be strictly limited.

Pleased with the results of his labors, Eddie prepared to leave. He conscientiously re-shelved the books and pamphlets he had accumulated, cleared the other clutter from the table, and folded almost reverently his notes for the new Constitutions, placing one in his left pocket and the other in his right.

He departed the library. There was much to be done.

*  *  *

The priest hesitated.

"You did what?" he inquired uncertainly.

"I separated Society and State."

He scratched an ear abstractly. "My apologies, but I'm still none the wiser for you repeating it."

Eddie was almost excited. "Remember our discussions about charity?"

"Of course," he replied without rancor. "It was only yesterday."

"Well there's another solution aside from the ones you mentioned."

"I'm sure there is. I'm no Solomon, just a humble servant of his Master."

"That's what I'm telling you! There *is* another way! You can separate Society and State."

It was a measure of the priest's patience that he held his smile. "Yes. You mentioned that."

"Let me explain..." Pulling two carefully-folded sheets of paper from his pockets, Eddie briefed the priest on his idea. The exposition did not take long, as there was not much to tell. He felt that its simplicity was its most salient feature. "...and it avoids all the pitfalls that Davy Crockett warned of," he concluded.

The priest had listened carefully out of professional habit, then he started in with the questions, intrigued. "And how many people would run this Society?"

"Let me see... There would be one Head of Society and an Assistant Head of Society, two Senators representing all of Nevada, and I figure on starting out with three Congressmen so as to avoid ties when voting. Add three Supreme Court Justices for the same reason, and that brings it up to ten people. Not too many."

"And they'd pass laws?"

"Yes, but I thought 'Guidelines' would probably be a better word. Whatever it is they pass would have no force of law."

"Then what's to make people follow them?"

"Nothing. They're only Guidelines."

Confused, the priest stammered, "But... How would that work, if people don't have to follow them?"

"Easily! Take the case of helping our refugee friends. Let's assume their medical care costs a hundred willies in total." His face colored momentarily. "Given that there are about five thousand residents here in town, each person's share comes out to..." Briefly, he calculated in his head. "What, two cents?"

"But what if someone doesn't want to contribute? You said the laws were only guidelines."

"They are. I was getting to that. As you say, not everyone will want to contribute, but you just have to take that into account. I don't know what the actual percentage would be, but let's use your number from yesterday and say that only one in a hundred wants to help. That means the suggested fair share is two willies each." Again, he colored; diplomatically, the priest did not comment. "So, assuming the Guideline gets passed, everyone in town would be asked to contribute two willies to Society." The color deepened. "One in a hundred contributes, and the bills are paid. And there would always be people who'd be more than happy to give more than their fair share, so their actual donation might even be higher."

"That's certainly true. I see the same sort of generosity within my congregation." He pondered Eddie's words for a moment. "But 'assuming the Guidelines get passed,' you say? Why wouldn't they?"

"I couldn't say. Any number of reasons. Maybe the Congress or Senate doesn't like how a given scheme operates and votes it down. Or the Head of Society vetoes it because it's too expensive. It would work just like the United States government. And that's part of the beauty of Society—everyone already knows how it operates." Recalling his own ignorance of the Constitution, he quickly added, "At least they *should* know how it operates." Again, he corrected himself. "'Operated,' I should say."

"So your legislature would have to vote on every request for help?" he asked, the concern plain on his face. "There are a lot of charity cases out there, believe me. You'd be voting twenty-four hours a day!"

"No, no, that's not how it would work." He gestured with his notes. "This is only the framework, not the actual mechanism. Once Society authorizes some Guideline, you'd set up an individual Societal agency to administer the actual spending, such as an Agency of Meals, and Agency of Medicine, and so forth. The Head of Society would propose an annual budget to fund the various Agencies, just like the Head of State does—uh, used to do. Society would estimate the anticipated costs of all the Agencies, divide it by the number of people who they think will contribute, statistically speaking, and that would be the tax they'd be asked to pay."

"Tithe," prompted the priest.

"What?"

"Not taxes; tithes. Taxes aren't voluntary; tithes are."

"I see your point, but I'm not sure tithes is the right word either. And I doubt the contribution rate would be as high as the traditional ten percent."

"Then what would you want to call it? A contribution? Alms? How about a duty?" He smiled pleasantly. "I like that one, especially given its double meaning."

"I'm not so sure that's the best word either. A duty is really a tax, and we would really want to stress the voluntary nature of the contribution."

"Philanthropy, then? Patronage? Benefaction?"

Eddie waved him off. "Call it what you will; the idea is what's important."

"Very true," he agreed. The priest stroked his chin contemplatively. "You know, it might be difficult coming up with that budget, Mr. Eddie. I can tell you from my own experience that it's not easy to predict when someone will need help. Just look at the case with our newcomers!"

Eddie nodded. "That's one of the reasons I came to see you. Before I go public with this plan, I'd like to have an idea of how much we can expect to ask people to pay. I was hoping we could use your numbers and extrapolate from there to estimate what the entire town would need, and how much they might contribute." *Like the banker and I did with the money supply*, he realized. *Only today it's the charity supply!*

"Wouldn't your budget depend on what Guidelines get passed?"

"That's another thing I'd hope you'd be able to tell me. What Guidelines do you think we should have?"

"More than you'd imagine. The needs are great."

"You know, I just had an interesting idea."

"I do now. What's that?"

Eddie held his gaze. "Since you're such an expert on charity, would you consider serving as the first Head of Society?"

Without hesitation, the priest laughed in his clear, friendly manner. "No, sir! In fact, let me turn the tables on you: this whole Society concept is your idea—and pardon me if I borrow one of your favorite phrases—I believe it *stands to reason* that there is none other who so clearly understands that vision any better than you. You're a natural to be the leader!"

Eddie did not reply. There was no argument he could offer. The holy man's belief did indeed stand to reason.

The priest let him consider the proposition for a moment, then added, "Tell you what, though. I understand and support what you're trying to accomplish. I'd be honored to serve as your Assistant Head of Society instead and help make your idea a reality. But you'd have to be the man in command. Besides, this town wouldn't want anyone else."

Eddie remained silent for a moment. Again, there was no argument he could offer. "All right—at least for now." Solemnly, he held out his hand. "Deal."

The two men shook hands.

\* \* \*

Society formed.

Although the road to its creation was littered with many bumps, they were minor and quickly overcome.

The first bump was in the explaining. It was fortunate for Eddie that there was much less urgency to decide the issue, unlike the night they restructured the local economy. This time it took three town meetings, one per week, before Eddie was satisfied that the people of Las Vegas sufficiently understood what it was he was proposing. There were two indications that his message was finally getting through: the first was that men no longer kept asking the same questions over and over again, and the second was that campaign signs began to appear around town touting one prominent citizen or another for a post in Society's Legislature.

Another bump was the election itself. Rather than going through the elaborate effort of establishing polling places and creating ballots, a fourth town meeting was scheduled to select Society's leaders through shows of hands. Eddie and the priest were running unopposed for the top two posts, and when the big night arrived they were elected by loud acclamation. But there were many more candidates for Senator and Congressman than available billets, so Eddie held successive ballots; the candidate who received the least number of votes was dropped from the balloting, then another round of voting would occur. It was the only way that seemed fair to him. In short order, enough candidates were eliminated leaving five victors standing: three Congressmen and two Senators. One of the new Senators was a rich casino owner who had made his fortune in the coin conversion; the other, Eddie's banker friend.

Meeting in the cavernous confines of the waiting room of Transcontinental Railroad's Las Vegas station, it took the new Head of Society and his Legislature less than a week to populate their Supreme Court and hammer out a budget, and one week later the first notice of benefaction was posted. Much to the surprise of both Eddie and the priest, the appeal brought in many times the amount their austere budget required. The hospital was promptly repaid for the expenses incurred in caring for the refugees, leaving quite a tidy sum of cash in Society's coffers for future charitable purposes.

Flush with willies, the Legislature quickly passed a succession of Guidelines which provided pensions for the aged, soup kitchens for the hungry, and electric carts for the crippled. Eddie promptly vetoed each one. He still retained in his mind the unpleasant vision of knocking on doors, and tapping too heavily into the available charity of the town was his constant fear; besides, there was always the possibility of incurring an unanticipated, unexpectedly large charitable expenditure. After the vetoes, he explained to the Legislature that he felt it better to stockpile reserves and to build up a track record of potential expenditures over the course of many months, perhaps years, before committing to such bold initiatives. The suggestions made sense; his vetoes were not overridden.

Caution became the watchword of Eddie's administration. Aside from the appropriation to repay the initial bills of the refugees, the only Guideline he consented to signing in the first month of his tenure was a modest appropriation for the public library.

## Chapter 4 – Stairway to Heaven

Francisco squealed.

As he rolled across the bed, the woman seized his naked body with both hands and pulled him toward her, rolling him onto his back. "Lay still until I'm done!" she scolded, but Francisco just smiled at her.

Lifting both of Francisco's legs with one hand, Gwen slid a diaper under the baby's bottom with the other, and expertly pinned it snug. She kept up a one-sided dialogue with the six-month-old child as she dressed him.

"No time for your antics today, young man. Your father is very busy with their big test flight, and Mommy promised to have lunch ready for him when he gets here. They're going to *fly like the birds*...," she crooned, lifting Francisco high over her head. He gurgled in appreciation as she swooped him to a safe landing back on the bed. "...in their new Miracle Metal airplane." She winced as her shoulder complained mildly at the exertion— she had not noticed until now, but apparently in a moment of passion the night before, her husband had somehow wrenched it. She ignored the twinges, as she always did; they usually soon faded. "Now hold still while I fasten these buttons. You want to look handsome for your father, don't you?" Her soliloquy was interrupted by the ringing of the telephone.

"Sanction telephone answer," she called to the air. An electronic click sounded from speakers cleverly concealed in the bedroom walls. "Hello?" she continued.

"Hello, darling."

"Hi, Hank!" she replied, smiling broadly at the empty air.

"I just wanted to let you know we'll be grabbing something to eat here at the airstrip, so I won't be coming home for lunch. We're almost ready to do our first high-Mach tests, and no one wants to take time off to eat."

"I could bring you something," she offered.

"All right," he agreed, "But I'm not sure I'll have the time to eat it!" The excitement was clearly evident in Hank's voice, even without her seeing his image.

"I will anyway. And tell the boys I'll bring something for them, too. No charge." She heard his pause and understood its significance; her chronic generosity constantly raised eyebrows among the strikers. "You just tell them I'll be there in a little while," she finished.

"Okay. Thanks, Gwen."

"Yes, Mr. Hank," she replied formally, then called out, "Sanction telephone hangup." She heard the click as the line disconnected.

"Come on, you!" she cooed to Francisco. "Let's make your Daddy's lunch and go for a walk. The autumn colors are so pretty, and it's a beautiful day to *fly!*" She lifted him high into the air once again, spinning as she did, and again ignoring the hint of a twinge in her shoulder. Francisco let out a happy shriek.

She pirouetted from the bedroom humming a tune to herself, the laughing babe held high over her head.

\* \* \*

Francisco concentrated.

He sat strapped into the cockpit of the odd-shaped craft, three of its four seats empty. One hand held his preflight checklist while the other adjusted knobs and snapped switches according to the carefully-planned sequence outlined by the list's author. He wore slim headphones with an attached boom microphone into which he spoke, verifying each step vocally as he completed it.

He slowly turned a dial on the control panel in front of him, a gauge moving in simpatico; he halted when the needle floated into a green zone. An adjacent green indicator light illuminated. "Main galtmotor converter activated," he reported. He flicked a switch over his head. "Hull pressurization commenced..." The sound of pumps throbbed in the background. Presently, a green indicator light winked on overhead. "Hull pressurization complete." Simultaneously pressing a pair of buttons along the left side of the cockpit, he reported, "Engaging main turbine power." He heard the whine of the electric turbines begin to hum all around him. Another green light flashed its approval. "Power engaged," he confirmed.

Sitting in the tall control tower, looking conspicuously out of place in his bright cowboy shirt, Dwight set aside his checklist, a duplicate of the one in Francisco's hand, and spoke into a large microphone on the control panel in front of him. The microphone was greenish-blue. "That does it, Francisco. She's ready to roll."

"Acknowledged," Francisco replied crisply. Looking out the curved quartz windshield, he could see Hank watching him from his vantage behind the high control tower window. Francisco grinned at him and flashed a "thumbs up" gesture. Hank replied in kind.

Dwight and Hank watched as the strange-shaped craft began to travel down the taxiway toward the upwind end of the runway. The sun glinted off its greenish-blue hull as it rolled gracefully along the taxiway on its five-wheel landing gear. As it rolled away from them, they could see the two broad, circular exhaust ports for the twin electric turbines along the flat rear face of the hypercraft. Cradled in a deep hollow between the turbines was a complex set of antennae constructed of lead conduit and heavy cable: the power receiver for the hypercraft's galtmotor.

Francisco reached the far end of the taxiway and turned toward the main runway. Viewed from the side, the hypercraft little resembled any airplane yet devised by the hand of Man. There was no fuselage or tailfin; its profile resembled an extended teardrop, rounded end forward, with the tear's rear point truncated flat. No exhaust could be seen coming from it, as its twin high-speed turbines merely pumped ambient air at ludicrous speed for its propulsion. Francisco brought the hypercraft around to face down the long concrete runway.

Viewed straight on, the craft looked even stranger, sitting on its five wheels: an elevated, fat tube that flattened out to a rounded tip at either end. Two intake ports for the turbines presented the vague illusion of two eyes in the middle of an oversized, rounded mask. If any correlation could be made to a standard aircraft, it could only be called a flying wing; but even then, the broad, sweeping curves of the hull belied the analogy.

"Throttling up," they heard Francisco's voice over the control tower's speakers.

"Go for throttle up," confirmed Dwight. In the background, he could plainly hear the whine of the turbines as they spooled up to takeoff speeds.

Releasing the wheel brakes, Francisco started the hypercraft on its takeoff roll, accelerating slowly at first, then quickly faster and faster. In no time the nose wheel and front pair of wing wheels simultaneously lifted from the Earth, and the ship continued to roll for the moment on only the rear two wing wheels. Still accelerating, Francisco completed the rotation, and the craft swiftly took to the air, gracefully soaring into the clear autumn sky. In unison, the five wheels retracted into recesses in the bottom of the craft, with five doors simultaneously sliding shut to seal its skin into a smooth, unbroken whole. With the towering, colorful mountains of

Colorado as a backdrop, the craft banked northward and briskly gained altitude.

"All systems nominal," they heard Francisco's disembodied voice announce over the control tower's speakers.

Dwight and Hank looked at each other and smiled. This was the ninth test flight of the Dwight-Hank hypercraft, and it continued to perform flawlessly. All of the flights had. The first few proved the performance within the basic flight envelope at low speed, but once they had the craft in the sky, the clouds became their test chamber, the swirling white mist revealing the vortex flows across the greenish-blue skin of the hypercraft, confirming the aerodynamic configuration as well as suggesting a few minor improvements. So successful were their early trials that on only the seventh flight had Francisco taken it supersonic for the first time, and they aimed to expand its flight envelope with each subsequent flight. Today's test was targeted to reach Mach four, and at the rate they were progressing Dwight calculated they should reach the design maximum velocity of Mach seven within the week, assuming no major modifications were required—not that they expected any. The design seemed virtually flawless.

"Climbing to test altitude," Francisco informed them. They watched as the craft angled off to the north, the sun glinting again off the greenish-blue hull. For several minutes it continued to climb against the mountain scene. "Approaching Mach zero point nine; I'm slowing my acceleration," advised Francisco.

Dwight consulted the Doppler radar at his elbow. "I confirm your speed at Mach zero point nine."

"Good. I'll get aligned on the test flight path, flight level two hundred." He banked the craft in a wide turn to come about to head due south, back toward the valley. "All right, I'm aligned on the flight path. All systems nominal. I'm ready to begin."

"Okay, Francisco. Let's see what she's got."

"Roger. Accelerating to Mach one point five."

Through the speakers, Dwight heard the pitch increase as the gulping turbines tossed greater and greater quantities of air rearwards, spooling up to speeds inconceivable for bearings made of anything but Miracle Metal II. Hank, the metal's inventor, squinted at the sky, following the craft's progress with fatherly pride.

"About to break the sound barrier," Francisco notified them without emotion. No surprise; this was his third flight to have done so. "Mach one," he confirmed. "Mach one point one... Hull temperature rising... One point two... Point three..."

The control tower rumbled impressively as the sonic boom reached the airstrip in the valley. Again, Hank and Dwight looked at each other and grinned. Francisco had insisted that the test flight path always begin over the valley, just so the residents could hear the boom. "The sound of progress," he called it. In the distance outside the control tower, through its open windows they could hear the din of scattered cheers.

"Mach one point four... Hull temperature rising as expected," Francisco's calm voice apprised them, finally reporting, "Mach one point five and holding. Hull temperature leveling, eleven hundred degrees Fahrenheit on the leading edges, seven hundred on the control surfaces. Altitude steady at flight level two hundred. All systems remain nominal."

"Hey, I don't want to hear that 'nominal' stuff, Francisco," Dwight radioed, his impatient enthusiasm obvious. "That doesn't tell me anything. What I want to know is: how does she *feel*?"

"She feels great!" Francisco replied excitedly. "Just like the first flight, only faster. This ship loves to fly; I can't wait to open her up all the way to see what she can really do!"

"Just go easy on her for the moment, please. I don't want you damaging my latest creation!"

"Don't worry; I'll be careful," Francisco assured him with a laugh. His voice regained a businesslike edge. "Approaching the southern turn point; all systems remain nominal." With a practiced hand, Francisco brought the craft around in a broad arc to head back north toward the airstrip in the valley. "Straightening out... On course, now. Ready to begin the run-up to Mach two."

"Go for it, Francisco!"

"Roger. Accelerating to Mach two..."

They could hear the whine of the turbines increase in pitch again as Francisco advanced the throttle. Slowly, cautiously, he nudged the craft to higher and higher speeds, extended its flight envelope beyond Mach one point five for the first time.

"Mach one point six..." Long pause. "Point seven..." Another long pause. "Point eight. Hull temperature rising; leading edges at thirteen hundred degrees now..." Pause again. "Point nine. Thirteen fifty..." A final pause; "Mach two!" he announced. "All systems still nominal. Hull temperature just under fourteen hundred degrees and steady. Flies like a dream, Dwight. Well done!"

"Congratulations, Francisco!" Dwight replied in return. "Think of it! You're the fastest man who's ever lived!"

"Thank you, Dwight. I am honored." They could hear the deferential tone in his voice, as if he were bowing before them.

"Okay, let's go through the handling tests," suggested Dwight.

"Roger. Initiating banking maneuvers..." With practiced precision, Francisco took the craft through its planned paces, banking slightly left then right in arcs of decreasing chord across the cloudless sky, expanding the flight envelope. "Banking is smooth with minimal sideslip, easily countered by the trim thrusters," he reported. "All systems still nominal."

Dwight and Hank both turned at the sound of the control tower door opening; it was Gwen with baby Francisco in one arm, and a picnic basket hanging from the other. "Ready for lunch?" she asked.

Hank walked over and kissed her. "Francisco's in the middle of the latest test flight. We'll eat when he lands." He laid his hand across young Francisco's brow; the baby squirmed out from under his father with a displeased whine, recalling the less-than-gentle discipline he had received at those hands. Hank smiled at both baby and mother.

Dwight scowled good-naturedly. "You could not have picked a worse time, Gwen," then added, "and speaking of 'time,' that reminds me: you and I should make some time sometime soon to finalize the delivery schedule for the next hypercraft."

"At your convenience, Mr. Dwight," she replied formally. "Just please give me a half-hour's notice before you come over."

"All systems still nominal," Francisco's voice announced, interrupting. "I think we can call the Mach two handling tests a success, Dwight. Ready for the straight run-up to Mach four?"

Turning from Gwen with a "We'll talk about it later, you and I," to the microphone he replied, "Roger. Take her up, Francisco."

"Will do. I'm about to come over the valley again. See if you can catch sight of me!"

They all moved closer to the tower window and searched the sky.

"There he is," called Gwen, pointing to the south.

"Where?" the two men asked in unison. Gwen's outstretched arm swept quickly across the sky. "You missed him! Goodness, but that's fast!"

"Mach two," Hank told her matter-of-factly. "That's over a thousand miles an hour at that altitude." The tower rumbled deeply again with the sonic boom from Francisco's passage. The baby peered about in curiosity at the sound. More cheers could be heard outside.

"That's your Uncle Francisco!" Gwen told the child, pointing at the sky. "See?"

"The fastest man on Earth!" Dwight added with enthusiastic pride.

"Accelerating...," came Francisco's voice again. Mach two point one... Point two... Hull temperature rising again. Fifteen hundred degrees. Point three..."

Gwen looked at her husband. "Fifteen hundred degrees? That sounds hot!"

"No, not really. Regular Miracle Metal melts at over four thousand degrees, but this new MM-II alloy won't even begin to lose its strength at that temperature. The fused quartz windshield could withstand a lot more heat, too, if I added an active cooling system, but it never gets hot enough to need one. The limiting factor is actually the passenger cabin's air cooler, and we think it can handle a mean hull temperature of well over two thousand degrees, and even higher on the leading edges. That's one of the parameters that Francisco will be verifying—"

"Mach two point five and holding for system checks," interrupted the radio. There was a brief pause, then he continued, "Hull temperature seventeen hundred degrees up front, nine hundred behind. All systems nominal."

"How's the internal temperature, Francisco?" inquired Dwight, more for Gwen's benefit than his own.

"A comfortable sixty-nine Fahrenheit and holding steady. I'll let you know if it changes." Francisco held the speed for a moment longer, then announced, "Accelerating again..."

"Roger, Francisco. Take her up to Mach three."

Through the speakers, they could hear the whine of the turbines grow higher and louder still. Dwight made a mental note to increase the acoustic shielding before the next flight.

"Mach two point six... Point seven... Hull temperature eighteen hundred and climbing... Point eight... Point nine... Mach three! Hull temperature eighteen fifty and steady, right where we expected it to be. Internal is still sixty-nine. The turbine coolant temperature is rising, but it's high by less than a hundred degrees, and that's no show-stopper. All other systems are nominal."

Hank and Dwight looked at each other. "Is that coolant temperature going to be a problem?" asked Hank, a tinge of concern in his voice.

"I don't think so. Not yet, anyway. But you're right—we did expect it to remain flat through at least Mach six." He thought a moment before shrugging it off. "No, I'm not worried. There's lots of margin left. Besides, Francisco and Ellis concocted the coolant formula themselves. If anyone knows its limits, Francisco does."

"Coming up on the plains of Wyoming," reported Francisco. "Got here pretty fast! Two thousand miles an hour is a nice pace, don't you think?

"Don't get lost!" joked Dwight, then added in a more serious voice. "Francisco, I'm not worried yet, but keep an eye on that turbine coolant temperature. If it goes up another fifty degrees or so, you should probably shed some speed until it drops."

"Roger. One hundred fifty degrees over nominal on the turbines and I cut back the speed," repeated Francisco. "Shouldn't it have held steady through Mach six?" he added.

"Yes. Hank and I were just discussing that. I'm not sure why it's rising."

"Do you think we should abort the test?" Francisco asked in a no-nonsense tone.

After a brief pause, Dwight drawled slowly, "Y-e-e-s-s-s-s. I'd say we'd better. No sense taking a chance until we know the reason for the temperature spike. Take her back down to Mach one point five and come on back."

"Roger. Mach one point five and home for lunch. Decelerating now... Mach two point nine... Point eight... Dwight, the coolant temperature is still going up. It's nominal plus one twenty... make that a plus one twenty-five now... Velocity still slowing, Mach two point six now... Hull temperature dropping to seventeen hundred... Turbine coolant temperatures still rising... Plus one forty... It's rising faster, now... Plus one fifty..."

From the look on his face, it was obvious that Dwight was thinking hard. "Francisco," he radioed. "What's your coolant level?"

"One point one," he replied. "A little high, but still within spec. It must be expanding with the heat. I'm at plus one seventy degrees on the coolant. Repeat: plus one seventy on the turbine coolant. All other readings nominal. I'm down to Mach one point five. Hull temperature fifteen hundred and dropping. I'm starting my turn for home. So long, Wyoming!"

For several minutes, the only sound in the control tower was the whine of the turbines coming over the radio, and occasional gibberish from baby Francisco. But there was a tension in the air that communicated itself without words.

"Coolant temperature nominal plus one eighty," reported Francisco, then added, "I wish we had a pressure gauge on it."

"Drop to subsonic speed, Francisco. That's way too high a temperature."

"Roger. Dropping to Mach zero point nine," he confirmed. "Speed now Mach one point four... Point three... Coolant plus one-eighty-five and rising. Point two... Point—"

The speakers let out a loud bang followed by a piercing screech, interrupting Francisco; then all was silent.

"Mayday. Mayday," Francisco radioed, his voice calm. "Coolant levels have dropped to zero. Both turbines are out. Repeat: both turbines out. Speed, Mach one point one and dropping. I still have main power and attitude control, but no thrust. Altitude dropping, flight level is one eighty and dropping."

Francisco's friends in the control tower looked to each other in horror.

"Francisco! What happened?" Dwight called into his microphone.

"It's the coolant," he replied, his voice confident and calm contrasting starkly with Dwight's agitation. "Looks like it built up too much pressure from the high temperature and blew out the seals. Mach one point zero and falling... That was the loud bang you heard; I'm assuming that the screech afterwards was the bearings on the turbines seizing up from too much heat. Mach zero point nine and falling, hull temperature nine fifty and falling... If those turbines were made of anything other than MM-II, they probably would have torn the ship apart. Zero point eight, flight level one sixty and dropping... There must be an expansion coefficient in the coolant formula we didn't uncover in the lab tests. Mach zero point seven, flight level one fifty. Mountains coming up on my right. Tell Ellis that if he uses the next higher cracking level on the coolant distillation process, it should add to the coefficient enough to prevent the excessive thermal expansion that blew the seals. Zero point five and falling... Flight level one hundred ten and falling... Dwight, if you add pressure relief hardware to the turbine cooling system, the next time something like this happens the thermal expansion won't result in the seals blowing. Matter of fact, you may want to install a secondary reservoir to hold the expanded coolant, then feed it back into the system when it contracts, and the hell with changing the coolant formula! Mach zero point three, flight level ninety. Trees coming up from below. Hank, you might want to try adding some beryllium to the MM-II bearings. It ought to help reduce the bearings' thermal expansion, too. Zero point two, flight lev—"

There was a burst of static and the speakers went dead.

"Francisco!" cried Dwight, clutching the microphone. "Come in, Francisco!" There was no reply.

The sudden silence in the control room was absolute. No one spoke. Hank was still watching the sky, his face taut and closed. Dwight's head was drooped just a little, as if he were studying the microphone in his hand. Gwen still stood near the window, mouth open wide in disbelief. Baby Francisco gooed once, unconcerned; he was playing with his mother's necklace.

Hank turned to Dwight. "Do you have any idea where he went down?"

He straightened up immediately and consulted an instrument. "Not exactly. Looks like he was still over Wyoming, maybe near the border."

"Sanction telephone call Dr. Thomas!" Hank announced to the air. A click came over the tower speakers, then a confident voice spoke, "Dr. Thomas speaking."

"Doctor!" cried Hank. "This is Hank calling from the airstrip. Francisco's airplane just crashed near the Wyoming border!"

"What?! Francisco's crashed?"

"Yes! You've got to get out there immediately! And if he's not on retainer, send me the bill! I'll pay for it!"

"Don't worry; he is. Let me get my gear assembled and I'll be over right away. Give me five minutes."

"Doctor!" interrupted Dwight. "This is Dwight. I'll have your airplane ready for flight by the time you get here. Seeing how it's Francisco, I'll cut in half the standard surcharge for expedited service."

"I'd appreciate that, Dwight. Sanction telephone hangup."

Before the telephone connection was severed, Dwight was already running out of the tower, sprinting toward the hangar to ready Dr. Thomas' airplane.

"Let me help," Hank cried as he hurried after him.

Gwen remained where she was, baby in one arm, picnic basket on the other, mouth still agape.

* * *

The setting sun shone.

Gwen lay on her back in the tall grass outside the control tower watching crimson clouds drifting across the early evening sky. Alongside her, baby Francisco sat chewing on a toy in the last rays of the sinking sun. Dr. Thomas had taken off to the north hours ago to race to Francisco's aid, and not only was she waiting on some word from him, so also were a substantial number of the valley's residents. The terrible news traveled quickly, and the atmosphere in the valley was one of disbelief and shock; Francisco was well loved.

Her anxious repose was interrupted by the sight of Dwight emerging from the control tower. As she sat up, a hush fell over the onlookers as all eyes immediately focused on him.

He stood self-consciously in the doorway, with an air of a man with a mission. He scanned the scattered strikers. "No news, folks," he called out. "Dr. Thomas just checked in and he told me he hasn't found any sign of Francisco's airplane yet, so he's landed for the night on some highway somewhere in Wyoming. He says he'll continue the search first thing in the morning, and several of us are going to fly up there to join him." Dwight paused awkwardly in the ruddy orange light. "Don't worry," he added. "We'll find him." He hesitated another moment, then turned and re-entered the tower, closing the door behind him. Among those waiting outside, none spoke.

Gwen turned away and stared into the setting sun, a blood red orb dimmed by diffraction such that she could gaze directly into its disc without discomfort. It nestled between two snow-capped peaks, slowly sinking into the cleavage between them. As she watched, one edge of the sun touched the snowy slope of the left peak and gradually began to settle behind it, little by little becoming more and more occluded. In concert, the light levels dimmed noticeably as the life ebbed out of the day's radiance. Man-made lights began to twinkle among the dwellings in the valley below the airstrip, pinpoints of brilliance scattered across a spreading darkness. A chill breeze drifted gently over mother and child, and protectively she pulled him closer to her warmth. Absorbed, she watched intently as the sun shrank from a half circle to a quarter, to an ever-shrinking sliver. At the moment the sun vanished entirely behind the mountain peak, she closed her eyes and tenderly pressed her cheek to baby Francisco's fuzzy crop of thin hair. With a unintentionally-loud sob, Gwen broke down and cried.

## CHAPTER 5 – I'D LOVE TO CHANGE THE WORLD

Eddie cooked.

Like some general proudly reviewing his troops, he stood watch over a bevy of steaming pots and sizzling pans, their aromatic mélange drifting through the air already tinged with the delicate scent of lavender.

"You see?" the woman applauded, her voice brightly cheerful. "I told you it wasn't all that difficult."

He had to agree. "I never thought I'd be able to put together such a complicated meal. It smells wonderful!"

"Well, it's not over yet," she warned. "You still have to get it onto the table before it burns... boils... scorches..." She looked toward the ceiling, playfully pondering all of the possible calamities that could still befall their dinner, ticking them off on an insufficient number of fingers. "...melts... falls... smolders... bursts into flames..." He threw her a dark glance and she burst out laughing.

"Help me get this into the serving dishes, will you?"

"Oh, no!" she exclaimed, the laughter still in her voice. "You wanted to do a French dinner all on your own, and that's just what you're going to do. Presentation is just as important as the preparation, remember. You've gotten this far without my help, Edwin, and now that it's almost done, I'm not going to start interfering."

He had not waited for her to finish her admonition before taking action. He turned off two of the burners and pulled the pans from the stove, swinging around to place them on their waiting trivets as she squirmed lithely out of his way. He tried not to notice how attractive her motions were; he did not succeed. "I'll let you set the table," he compromised, "if it'll keep you out of my way."

"My pleasure, Your Honor."

Before long they sat down to a fine dinner, and Eddie had to admit it was beyond excellent, even if he did say so himself. He could hardly believe he had done so superb a job on his own. Granted, it was her recipe which he had mastered under her tutelage, but the glory of the master reflected in the accomplishments of the student was just as much a burnished triumph for the student as it was for the master.

Nor was this the first masterpiece he had prepared. In the nearly two years since she had first cooked his breakfast on that memorable morning following his concussion, she had taught him much about the finer points of cooking; in fact, she had generally become something of a fixture in his life. Not that he sought her out; rather, she had, in effect, adopted him. Aside from their weekly cooking lessons, she would drop by unannounced at all hours several times a week, "just to say 'hello.'" No clueless prude, Eddie suspected she held some ulterior motive of a romantic nature; but she had never pushed the matter beyond a routine peck on his cheek whenever they parted. Nor had he pursued her, despite her stunning attractiveness; he feared that if he showed the slightest interest, the situation would transform itself in an instant, of its own accord, to a very personal one. Given the nature of her profession, he took embarrassed pains to keep their relationship on a strictly social basis; nevertheless it was no secret that he enjoyed her company as much as she enjoyed his, yet there remained a wall between them that he hesitated to peer over.

After dinner, in what had become another ritual for them, they took repose in the wing-back chairs overlooking the rear railing of the observation car enjoying the warm evening over glasses of a sweet cordial she had brought along. It was there that the banker found them.

"Ah!" he exclaimed when he noticed Eddie's lovely guest. "I'm sorry to interrupt! I didn't think you'd still have company this late."

Blushing furiously, Eddie literally leapt out of his chair. "No! You're not interrupting! We were just relaxing after dinner." He held up his cordial. "Can I get you a glass?"

"No, no thank you." He glanced briefly at the woman. "I won't be staying that long. I was on my way home and needed to speak with you about a Societal matter as soon as possible." He glanced again at the woman. "Perhaps it should wait until the morning?"

The woman spoke up, deferentially stressing his title. "That's quite all right, Senator. It's getting late, and I really should be going." She set her glass down, stood up, and faced Eddie. "Thank you for the fine dinner."

"And you, for teaching me how to cook it."

She flashed a bright smile. "My pleasure, Your Honor." She gave him her usual peck on the cheek and descended the four steps from the balcony to the platform. Entranced, the two men watched her walk away until she was out of sight.

A few seconds later the distracted banker turned toward Eddie. "Where were we?"

"Ah..." He rummaged about in his mind, trying to focus. "Something important you had to speak with me about?"

"Oh! Yes, there was." He ascended the steps and took the woman's vacated seat, setting his briefcase on his lap. "I'm sorry to trouble you."

Eddie sat down. "Not at all. What is it?"

He sighed. "I think we have another problem." He opened the brief case and pulled out a thick sheaf of papers. "I was doing some analysis on the value of our paper money to see if we should consider devaluing it further when I noticed some anomalies." He paused dramatically, holding up the sheaf, waiting to be encouraged.

"Anomalies? Such as?" he prompted.

The banker dropped his bombshell. "It appears the value of the paper money is rising."

Eddie eyebrows shot up. "Rising? Why should it be rising? It's only paper."

"That's what got me wondering." He produced a graph littered with spiked lines of various colors. "Notice how its value has been dropping ever since we shifted to a silver-backed economy a few years ago." He slid a finger along a dark red line on the graph. "It dropped quickly at first, then more slowly, then flattened out. But as you can see..." He paused again.

"...it's rising again," Eddie finished. "What would cause that?"

"It could be any of several factors. I won't bore you with all the ins and outs, but I have a strong suspicion as to what it might be." For a third time, he paused; it was obvious he was again waiting to be prompted.

"Well? What do you think?"

Smiling, the banker dropped a second bombshell. "I don't believe it's the value of the paper that's rising. It's the value of silver that's dropping." He leaned back in his chair, smug.

Eddie hesitated, confused. "Well... Doesn't that make sense? A good number of mines have re-opened over the last year and added a lot of silver to the money supply. Wouldn't that drive down its value?"

"Yes, but not nearly so much" He pointed to a rising green line. "I took that into account. Here's the estimated output of the mines, and this..." He indicated a falling dashed green line, "...is the value of silver. You'll notice that it's falling much faster than the value of paper is rising. If you look at the fundamentals, such as the velocity of money..." He began flipping through his papers, but stopped himself. "I do apologize. I promised to avoid the ins and outs, so let me cut to the chase: it appears to me that someone is circulating silver that doesn't exist. Quite a bit of it, too. That's why its value is dropping as fast as it is."

Two seconds passed before Eddie reacted. "You're making a joke? How can one circulate silver that doesn't exist?"

"It's not that difficult. Stop and think—isn't non-existent silver exactly what the old paper money represented? Silver in Washington that, for all intents and purposes, did not exist?"

"You're saying someone is counterfeiting paper money?"

"In a way. 'Writing' is probably a better term for it."

"I don't follow you. What do you mean, 'writing' money? And who could be doing it?"

"I believe it's my competitor. My guess is that he's writing IOU's against silver he doesn't own—in other words, he's practicing fractional reserve banking." He pointed to the graph. "No one else is in a position to have so big an impact on the money supply—" He flashed a self-conscious smile. "—except me, of course."

"You mean he's handing out people's deposits as his own money?"

The banker nodded gravely. "I suspect that if everyone went to his bank all at once and withdrew their demand deposits, he would not have enough silver on hand to cover the withdrawals." He pointed to a bright red line on his graph. It was rising, and the slope was steepening. "If I read my numbers right, he's already over-lent almost twenty percent of his silver assets."

"And no one's noticed?"

"Well, I noticed!" The banker shook his graph testily at Eddie in demonstration. "But you're right. Usually people won't notice anything because most of their deposits just sit around in the vault collecting dust. But it looks to me like he's either lending it out to earn interest, or just stealing it and hoping no one notices. If he goes too far, he risks the stability of his bank."

Eddie angled his head toward the graph with concern. "Does this mean another panic?"

"Yes, eventually. And some of his depositors could surely lose money. In fact, they may already have."

"So what do we do?"

"Well, first we have to confirm that my calculations are correct, and if they are, we have to get him to stop."

"How would you do that?"

The banker took a deep breath. "I have no idea. That's why I'm here."

Eddie sighed glumly. "Here we go again."

"At least there's no tremendous hurry this time. We can take a little while to think it through. We probably should convene a special session of Society's Legislature to deal with it."

"Not so quickly," countered Eddie. "If he's stealing depositors' money, it's not a Societal issue; it's for a court to decide. But before we take that step, let me pay our friend a visit tomorrow morning. His bank is just around the corner."

"And do what?" the banker challenged sarcastically. "Ask him if he's stealing from his depositors? Or merely risking their deposits? Bah!" He rose to his feet "Trust me; he won't answer. And there's no way I can force him to answer—not without me ending up paying an involuntary visit to your courtroom for 'lacking respect for his rights.'" He lifted his briefcase. "What we need in this town are some laws with teeth in them!"

Eddie looked momentarily perplexed. Putting on a mantle of formality, he inquired, "You're inviting Society to forcibly regulate your bank, Senator?"

"No, of course not," he backpedaled. "But there has to be something we can do!"

"Let me talk to him first."

"Good luck!" he replied gruffly, and strode off into the night.

* * *

The banker's competitor scoffed.

"Son, if you think I'm going to let you paw through my books, you are out of your mind!" His eyes narrowed at Eddie suspiciously. "What business is it of yours to be meddling anyway?"

Another man may have been able to fabricate a plausible excuse on the spot, perhaps sidestep the question entirely; but Eddie was not the type of person to dissemble or dodge; it was not in his character. Instead, he gave a forthright reply. "Then let me ask you outright: are you retaining a one hundred percent reserve on your demand deposits?"

"That's none of your business!"

"But if you're not, then it could threaten people's deposits! Wasn't one panic enough?"

"Son, you may be Head of Society, but you're not the head of this bank." He rose to his feet. "I'm a busy man. If that's all you wanted to see me about, then good day, sir!"

Eddie sat a moment longer, trying without success to think of some way to reach the man.

"Good day, sir!" repeated the banker.

Defeated for the moment, Eddie stood and left.

\* \* \*

Eddie stepped outside.

The wide boulevard in front of the bank was full of activity. Shoppers strolled along the sidewalks, mounted horses ambled up and down the street, and laughing children ran weaving in and out amongst all of them.

He joined the unconscious dance in a dejected mood. He had to admit that the man was well within his rights; he deserved to have his privacy respected. But did that mean that the town had to wait until his bank crashed before they were able to take action? That was akin to closing the gate after the horse had escaped. At what point did a suspicion become a reason to disrespect someone's privacy? And upon what authority? It seemed to be a slippery slope with no clear answer, when what was needed was a black-and-white differentiation. But he could not imagine what that might be.

His glum reverie was interrupted by some sort of commotion brewing ahead of him: he could hear a man yelling, a rearing horse neighing, and other angry voices. It did not take long for Eddie to pick out the cause of the uproar: a young teenaged girl was careening down the street at a good clip straddling an odd-shaped electric cart, leaving dust and curses in her wake. Close on her heels were two more carts, similarly piloted by a pair of her peers. As the lead girl neared Eddie, so did the commotion; a shopper stepped sideways to avoid a reined horse, accidentally bumping into him. Knocked momentarily off balance, Eddie began to take a step backward; but his foot never completed the motion: close behind his heel was the curb. His foot abruptly stopped, and the momentum and inertia of his backward step propelled him over the curb, arching backward. Arms flailing, down he went, and with a sharp crack, his head impacted the unyielding sidewalk, then all went dark.

\* \* \*

Eddie came to.

His head throbbed painfully as he lay on his bed in the sleeper car. He squinted open one eye, and the agonizingly bright morning sunlight forced him to quickly close it.

"We have to stop meeting like this," a woman's voice suggested in a playfully mocking tone.

He didn't have to look to see who it was who spoke; the delicate scent in the air gave her away. Slowly, he forced one eye open, then the other. He squinted at her as he raised a hand to his head and gingerly rubbed a small lump. He closed his eyes with a soft sigh.

"At least no one punched you this time ," she offered helpfully.

"Small blessings," he murmured. He moved to sit up.

"No, no!" she warned, a hand pressing upon his chest. "You should know the routine by now. You lay still!"

Gently, he shoved her hand away. "I'm all right," he ventured, ignoring a slight swoon to his surroundings. He sat up, swung his legs to the floor, and took a deep breath. "I'm all right," he repeated, a little more firmly.

"Are you sure?" she asked, all concern.

He ignored her question, instead focusing on her as if seeing her for the first time. "What are *you* doing here?"

"When you fell, I happened to be walking by, lucky for you. I deputized a few strong men to carry you in here—I figured it was just around the corner and a lot closer than the hospital. I already called the doctor. He's on his way."

Eddie stood up somewhat successfully. He held his arms wide, palms up. "See? I'm all right," he reaffirmed. "I don't need a doctor."

"We'll let the doctor be the judge of that, Your Honor." She turned her head at the sound of footsteps climbing into the sleeper car. "That's probably him now."

It was. "Hello?" a masculine voice called out.

"In here!" Eddie and the woman replied simultaneously.

The doctor entered the compartment and his glance went from one to the other. "Who's the patient?"

"I am," admitted Eddie. "But I'm all right."

"Let me check you out anyway. It's never good to bang your head." With rapid efficiency, the doctor examined his injury. When he had finished, he proclaimed, "It appears that no real damage was done, but you should take it easy for a while anyway."

"If I'm careful and move slowly, I'll be all right."

"You ought to rest."

"I'm all right," he repeated.

The doctor sighed. "Pardon the pun, but on your head be it. Just try to take it easy for the next day or so." He turned to leave, and Eddie immediately followed.

"Where do you think you're going," the woman asked sternly.

He turned at the door to face her. "I need to see the priest."

"The priest?" Her mouth hung open slightly in confusion. "But the doctor said you'd be all right!"

"I need to speak with him about how this happened," he explained, raising a hand to his cranium. "One sore head is enough."

"Oh, you're not that grumpy," she replied with a clever smile.

Without another word, he turned to leave. Puns had never been among his favorite things, and two in a row exceeded his quota by a similar amount.

"I'll stop back around noon," she called to his retreating back. "I have a new recipe I want to try for lunch."

"Okay," his diminishing voice agreed. Calling over his shoulder, he added, "I might be a bit late, though. I need to talk with the policeman, too."

* * *

Eddie stared.

The policeman waited him out.

"But they're just kids!" cried Eddie. "I don't want them locked up!"

"You are—" The policeman held up a clipboard clamping together several sheets of paper. "—the thirteenth person to come in here today complaining about those kids and their driving. Kids or not, something has to be done!" He tossed the clipboard back onto his desk with a clatter. "Or are you saying we should do nothing?"

"No, no," he retreated. "But why do you insist that we toss them in jail? Isn't that... well... a bit heavy-handed?"

The policeman pushed the clipboard aside and leaned over the desk. "What would you suggest we do then?"

"Lots of things! Have you spoken with their parents yet?"

"I've already looked into that option. Only one of the kids has parents here in town. The other two came in with your trainload of refugees. Legally speaking, they have no parents."

"Well, have you contacted the orphanage then?"

"Of course. But from what I understand, they're not living at the orphanage."

Eddie blinked. It was not an answer he had expected. "Where do they sleep, then?"

The policeman shrugged. "You'd have to ask them that."

"What?! How old are they? Eleven? Twelve?"

"Thereabouts. I couldn't say for sure, but looking at them, my guess is that puberty is waiting for each of them just around the next corner."

Eddie reddened faintly.

Ignoring his unease, the policeman persisted. "Orphans or not, shouldn't children be required to respect the rights and property of others? That is the town law, you know—as if I have to explain that to *you* of all people!"

"Yes, but..." Again, Eddie hesitated. "...They're just kids! Shouldn't we be cutting them a little slack?"

"Slack? Are you saying kids should be able to violate the law whenever they like?"

"No, no, of course not."

"But that's my point: they should be respecting the rights and property of others. That's not something you can slack on; it's either all or nothing."

"Yes, but...," Eddie repeated, again hesitating.

"But what?"

He sighed aloud. "But should you be talking right away about jail? Isn't there some authority figure we can appeal to first? Someone a bit more compassionate?"

"Like who?"

"Like the person who is supposed to be responsible for those kids."

"Two of them are orphans, I tell you. No one is responsible for them."

269

Eddie shook his head in negation, ignoring the slight swoon it induced. "That can't be right. The way I see it, someone has to be responsible for a given child: it could be their parents, a relative, guardians; you know: *someone*. I know I'm repeating myself, but they *are* just kids after all. Somebody's got to be looking out for them."

"I would agree. But, at the risk of repeating myself as well, who?"

Eddie sat in silent thought for a moment, then ventured, "Well, let's look at it logically. Who is responsible for anyone?"

Now it was the policeman's turn to hesitate. "I'm not sure I follow you."

"Think of it this way." Eddie pointed at the policeman. "Who is responsible for you?"

"I am." The answer was as swift as it was proud.

"And what about when you were a baby?"

"My father," came the reply, just as quickly. Conceding he owed Eddie more of an explanation, he added, "My mother died in childbirth."

Eddie reddened. "Oh! I didn't know. I'm sorry."

"Thank you, but what was your point?"

As his color slowly returned to normal, he concluded, "My point is that somewhere between then and now, you assumed control over your own life. But regardless of when that point was, there was always someone responsible: first it was your father, then it was you."

"Ah, I see," the policeman anticipated. "The question is: when is it that a man—or an orphan—becomes responsible for himself? What marks that line?"

"Precisely!"

Attentively, the policeman leaned forward. "And where *do* you draw that line?"

Eddie held the policeman's eye for a moment, then looked away uneasily. "I'm not certain," he admitted.

"Not certain?" He leaned back dismayed, almost scornful. "You seemed pretty certain a half a second ago!"

"I *am* certain there's a line," he quickly clarified, then paused. "But I'm not sure how one would recognize it."

The policeman chuckled. "Well, wherever it is, I know a lot of grown men who've never crossed it."

Eddie nodded. "And so do I—we've certainly seen enough of them in court. They're like children in that they don't act as if they were responsible for themselves."

"Leaving the State to be responsible for them," he groused. "Jail or exile, mostly. Restitution, when possible."

"That is true—" Eddie agreed, but cut himself off abruptly. "Is that the line we're looking for, then?"

"What, jail?" The policeman stared at him blankly. The statement made no sense. "I thought you said—"

"No!" he interrupted impatiently. "Self-responsibility! That's the line we're looking for!" Eddie's mind had already shot far ahead of the policeman's. He paused momentarily as he mentally pursued the ramifications. "Yes," he asserted confidently. "That's the answer. The line is drawn at the point where each person decides to draw it."

The policeman's stare remained blank. "But... How does that mean anything, if everyone defines it for themselves? Didn't we just say how some men never get around to drawing it?"

"Exactly!" he agreed. "That's when you and I have to step in and draw it for them—the State, I should say. And isn't that just what we've been doing in court?"

The policeman heard the words, but he was not following the reasoning. "But I thought you just said that men must decide for themselves where to draw that line. What if they don't?"

"But they do, even if they don't. Failure to make a decision is still a decision, you know. It's a decision not to decide. And *that* is what defines your line."

The policeman paused in thought; the enigmatic assertion made perfect sense. "I think I'm with you now. If a man has crossed that line, it's reflected in his responsible behavior; and if he hasn't, it's reflected in his irresponsible behavior."

"Yes! And it's not the responsible men that you and I meet in court, it's the irresponsible ones; and the State has to take responsibility for them. The incorrigibles, we exile; the... corrigibles...?" He waved the word aside. "Whatever you call them, we merely punish. We make them realize they need to draw that line for themselves, and we give them the chance to better themselves. As we did with your first bandit a few years ago."

"A chance to mature?" the policeman suggested with a smile.

Eddie nodded. "That's the word. Men choose to respect the rights of others—to act mature—or they don't. It's a self-selected group."

"I'm with you now," agreed the policeman. "And I also see how this applies to our three rapscallions."

"That's right," Eddie agreed in turn. "It's obvious which side of the line they're on, or else we wouldn't be thinking of initiating the use of courts against them. Since they aren't taking responsibility for themselves to respect the rights of others, it's up to the State to assume that responsibility."

Again the policeman nodded. "With grown men, who could disagree? But with children, wouldn't the State come second? I'd say it's their parents who are primarily responsible."

"Of course!" Eddie retorted testily, as if the idea was not open to question. "And that prioritization will determine how we handle sentencing for them. We don't just throw them in jail, like you're suggesting. Rather, since the kids obviously aren't acting responsibly themselves, it's a much better idea to remand them to the custody of someone who will assume that responsibility: the obvious choice is their parents."

"And what about the other two? The refugee orphans? They have no parents." Even as he asked the question, the policeman realized the answer. He and Eddie spoke in unison: "The orphanage!"

Eddie raised a halting hand. "Assuming they'll take them in, that is. They can only afford to take care of so many children, you know, even with the stipend Society has been giving them."

"Well, it doesn't necessarily have to be the orphanage, does it?"

"That's true. Anyone could step in and adopt them..." Eddie hesitated, as if he did not want to name his thoughts aloud. "But if no one wants them or can't take them, for whatever reason..." He faltered again, still not wanting to name the logical conclusion.

The policeman did him the favor of finishing the sentence for him. "Then the State takes over. We'd have no choice but to treat them as an adult. And that means..."

Eddie nodded and looked away uneasily. "Ultimately jail or exile," he answered matter-of-factly, understanding fully how those were the only choices remaining; but either option was infinitely better than letting the little hellions run wild. Although his face remained sadly distraught, it was clear he finally accepted such solutions as the last resort—but only as the last resort. He fervently wished there were a better alternative, but the possible direction of any third path eluded him. After a moment, he faced the policeman unapologetically. "It would appear your initial premise was correct; we are indeed forced to arrest them. And try them. And sentence them, if they're guilty." He took a deep breath. "And ultimately jail them if we must."

The policeman tactfully acknowledged the reluctant acquiescence. "As you say, unless someone steps up to assume responsibility, what other choice is there except to have the State assume it?"

Eddie nodded gravely. "And the same would hold true if the parents or the orphanage could not effectively exercise their responsibility—if the poor kid kept on getting into trouble, for example—at some point responsibility would have to fall back upon the State."

The policeman nodded in turn, just as gravely. "Then it would be a jail term for that poor kid. Or exile, in the worst cases."

"Exile a child!" Eddie sighed loudly. "It would be a pity if that were ever to come to pass."

The policeman held Eddie's eye boldly. "But it *is* my duty to keep the streets safe, remember—even from children."

Eddie did not shy away from the policeman's steady gaze. "And respecting the rights and property of others is everyone's duty—kids and grownups alike." With a resigned sigh he finally looked away. "But you're right: enforcing the fulfillment of that duty is the responsibility of the State—even when it comes to children."

"When and as needed, sorry to say," agreed the policeman. After a short pause, he added, "But I still have some questions. About practical applications."

"Such as?"

"Well..." The policeman hesitated, knowing he might be borrowing trouble, but after another brief pause he resumed. He knew the issue would arise sooner or later in any case; they may as well deal with it now. "Some call this a wicked town, and for good reason. Wouldn't you want us to protect our children from its pitfalls?"

"Such as?"

"Well..." He considered the question for a moment. "Don't you think there should be a minimum drinking age, for example?"

"Why, no," Eddie stated flatly.

"No?"

"No," he repeated. "Most men drink responsibly, but there are always some men who simply should not drink alcohol. I'm sure the same can be said for children. Again: it's a self-selecting group. If an adult—or a child—drinks responsibly, what business is it of the State? But if they cannot control themselves when they drink such that they don't respect the rights or property of others, then the State can and should move against them. That's the law for adults today. Why wouldn't it work for children, too?"

"But what if the parents don't want their child to drink?" He knew the question sounded academic, but the policeman was actually speaking for himself. Like most people, he did not condone widespread drinking among children; but, again like most people, his own introduction to alcohol pre-dated the legal drinking age by many a year. In light of that personal experience, he suddenly realized that eliminating the drinking age would not significantly alter that pattern. Kids would still be kids, regardless of any artificial statutory requirement—and creating one would only serve to criminalize typical adolescent behavior.

Eddie hesitated, as if he didn't understand the question. "If the parents don't want their child to drink alcohol, then wouldn't that be a private matter between them and their child?" He nodded his head gently and answered his own question. "That's right; family matters are none of the State's business. Because once you start down that path, you might as well have the State enforcing bedtimes, or deciding what kids should eat for dinner, or where and when they go to school. Those are all issues best decided within the family."

The policeman paused pensively. "I believe I see. It's not a public issue; it's a family issue. So long as the children are respecting the rights and property of others, the State never has a role."

Eddie nodded emphatically, but winced at a sudden pain. Apparently he still wasn't completely his normal self. "Correct! Neither State nor Society has a role. How could anyone justify standing between parents and their children? Or forcing policemen like you to enforce their personal edicts?"

The policeman was finally catching up with Eddie's train of thought. "Then I assume the same premise would hold true for, say, tobacco and gambling?"

"Of course. It's not for the State to say. Parents are responsible for raising their children as they see fit, until the time the children successfully assume that burden. That would include any vice, I would say."

"Prostitution, too?" interjected the policeman.

"Prostitution!" Inexplicably, Eddie glanced quickly at his wristwatch and blushed a beet red. "You mean..." He swallowed uneasily. "With a... a..." He could not vocalize the thought.

The policeman bluntly obliged. "Yes. Sex. With a child. Or a child prostitute, for that matter. And to make it black and white, let's say the child has the parents' permission, unlikely as that may seem." He folded his arms across his chest and stared coldly, waiting for an answer. Veteran policeman though he was, he was loath to hear what might come next.

A horror-struck Eddie opened and closed his mouth several times, but no sounds came forth. He paused to take a deep breath, then managed to blurt out, "But if someone tried to do something like that to a child, he wouldn't be respecting the rights of the child! Not at all! Even if the child agreed! It's not the child's choice that's the issue, it's the man's!" He took another deep breath. Exhaling shakily, he concluded, "Besides, a child is too young to know any better anyway."

"Too true," agreed the policeman. "If you left all the important decisions to children, they'd be living on a diet of ice cream and candy!" He smiled at the thought.

Eddie remained too rattled to react to the policeman's mirth, especially in light of the horrid images that dominated his consciousness. With a voice that still shook, he added, "And what sort of man would even *consider* doing that sort of thing to a child?" His eyes misted over, forcing him to blink repeatedly.

Grimly, the policeman lowered his folded arms. "I could tell you... except I that don't use that sort of language!" He appraised poor Eddie's distress. "Sorry, but I had to ask. Professional habit."

Still red-faced, Eddie could only nod.

"One more question, and I'll let this one go: how old would you think the child should be, before... you know."

"Past puberty!" he immediately cried, reddening anew. "That's for sure!" He took another deep breath before finishing. "—and older is better!"

"How much older? Where exactly would you draw that line?"

Eddie was clearly uncomfortable with the continued questioning, but managed to hold his voice steady. "That's why we have a jury: to examine the borderline cases and make a ruling based on the individual situation, just as we do today. If you ask me, two fourteen-year-olds would be one thing; but a fourteen-year-old and a forty-year-old... That could be something else entirely."

The policeman relaxed; he had his answer. Even better, he understood the principle underlying it. *There's a lot of law hiding behind those twenty-three carved words!* he marveled to himself; but aloud, he commended, "Those are good answers." Diplomatically, he added, "I was concerned we might have to amend our town law to account for children."

Finally recovering, Eddie replied, "Why should the rules be any different for children as they are for adults?"

"So I'm learning."

Eddie's eyes widened slightly at a sudden thought. "You know, I just realized all this would apply not only to children, but also to those men who live in the town's asylum. They can be like children in a lot of ways."

"A very good point," agreed the policeman. In the course of performing his duties, he had dealt with such men from time to time. They needed protection under the law as much as any child—maybe even more so. "So the law is the same for everyone."

"For everyone," he agreed. "It stands to reason."

The policeman chuckled at a sudden, random thought. "Dogs, too?" he joked.

Eddie's eyebrows shot up, not recognizing the capricious question as humor. "And why not? There are a lot of well-behaved dogs who walk alongside their masters without the need of a leash, yet there are others that shouldn't be let out of their cages even for a moment."

"Or some men," the policeman mumbled ominously; Eddie ignored the aside.

Neither man spoke for a lengthening pause until the policeman finally broke the silence. "So, getting back to the matter at hand, our first order of business is to arrest those kids. Correct?"

Reluctantly, Eddie nodded—more gently this time. It stood to reason.

"And when we get them into court, I assume you'll be sentencing them to the custody of their parents and the orphanage?"

Eddie stood. "It does seem a logical first step. And a compassionate one, too."

The policeman stood in turn. "All right. Let me get things rolling."

\* \* \*

The priest listened attentively.

"It hasn't been the best of days," confessed Eddie as he sat across the sacristy's table from the holy man. "First, I couldn't get any information out of that banker, then some rambunctious teen almost ran me over."

"Perhaps. But kids will be kids," the priest needlessly observed.

"Yes, but driving one of those carts that way can mean trouble!" Unconsciously he reached up and rubbed the back of his head. The lump had already begun to subside.

"True, but what can one do about the exuberance of youth?" he offered philosophically.

"That's one of the things I wanted to speak with you about. We can't have kids running wild like that in the streets. There has to be something we can do."

The priest shrugged. "Pass a law?"

"We already have a law: live your life your way, so long as you respect the rights and property of others. But those kids weren't respecting the rights of anyone, driving like that. I was lucky it wasn't worse!" After a pause, he added with a sigh, "I suppose it had to end up in court sooner or later, and now is probably the best time. In fact, I was just talking with the police about having them arrested. Certainly those kids are guilty of not respecting the rights of others, especially that girl in the lead cart. It was her fault that I was knocked over."

"Your sore head testifies to that," agreed the priest. "And it's a certainty she'll accept the sentence of the court. I don't think there's a person in town foolish enough not to."

"Too true. But what sort of sentence might we impose? I was thinking about remanding them to custody of their parents or the orphanage."

"Why not bring back the good old driver's license so you can take it away from her?"

Eddie shook his head emphatically, noting in passing that his abused cranium did not complain so much—at least not as much as before. "I've already considered that, but came to the conclusion that a driver's license is a terrible idea."

"Maybe," the priest conceded diplomatically, "But at least it would have stopped that girl."

"Would it?" Eddie tilted his bruised head inquisitively. "How would having a license have stopped her?"

"I already told you: because you could take it away from her, and then she couldn't drive."

He shook his head more gently this time. "And what's to stop her from just driving without the license?"

"The police," the priest replied matter-of-factly, automatically, and without thought.

"How? Would you have them stop everyone driving a cart just to see if they had a license? Or make people pay for a license plate? And it's not just carts that would need a license—what about horses? Remember that incident a few weeks ago?"

The priest nodded grimly. Everyone in Las Vegas knew about the impromptu noontime race through the center of town—especially the terrified people who had to scramble out of the way. "Yes, I do. We were lucky no one was hurt. When you got them into court, you ruled that they should apologize and promise not to pull that sort of stunt again."

"That's the only sentence anyone could think of at the time," he admitted. "Jail or exile didn't seem to be warranted—they were just a bunch of good boys having some fun they shouldn't have been having. But do you really think making them apologize was effective?"

The priest considered for hardly a brief moment. "No. I know human nature, and apologies are easy when they mean nothing."

Eddie gave him a satisfied nod. "You see?"

"That's why you should think about requiring driver's licenses."

He shook his head gently. "As I said, that would be a terrible idea."

The priest cocked his head. "True. But you have not said why."

"Because you're punishing everyone for the actions of a few troublemakers." He leveled a finger at the priest. "Look at you—you always ride your horse responsibly. Why should I saddle you with a license?"

The priest smiled. "Clever humor."

Eddie stopped. "What?"

"Horse...? Saddle...? I thought you were making a joke."

He waved him off with uncharacteristic impatience; three puns within an hour were three too many for him. "No, no. My point is, why should you pay for the misdeeds of others? And think of the cost! Who would pay to administer it?"

The priest shrugged. "Society?"

Eddie folded his arms determinedly. "By what right? Where would Society get the authority to pass such a Guideline?"

The priest smiled broadly. "There are two Senators, remember. As Assistant Head of Society I get to vote to break any ties. If you can't convince both of them that driver's licenses are a bad idea, you may find yourself having to convince me. And right now, I'm not convinced."

Eddie again waved him off, an edge of impatience still clinging to his actions. "No, no! Society can't pass that sort of a Guideline at all! How could Society mandate a driver's license? Where would that power come from? Since no man has the ability to mandate any sort of coercion, how could he possibly delegate that ability to Society or to anyone else?"

"But what about—"

"There are no buts! Society can't mandate anything at all, not even something as trivial as a driver's license. It just stands to reason."

"So you're saying Society does nothing? You'd just let people run red lights and such?"

"Of course you don't let people run red lights—not that we've had the traffic lights turned on for the last year!—because it wouldn't be very respectful of the right of others to travel, now would it? However, you are correct. Society does nothing. Dealing with that sort of thing would be up to the State."

The priest opened his mouth to protest; but seeing the objection written plainly on the man's face, Eddie anticipated, "No, I tell you. This cannot be a matter for Society to decide. Otherwise you're saying we should give Society the power to force people to do things—like getting a driver's license or stopping for red lights—but it's never been the case for Society to force men to act. In fact, it would demonstrate our lack of respect for the innocent if we did. Society and State are completely different entities with completely different powers and spheres of influence, and we know it's critical to keep them separate."

"All right." The priest spread his hands in friendly capitulation. "I see I can't argue with your logic. Which leaves us... Where?"

"Which leaves us right where we were—without a solution." Eddie sighed glumly. He sat silently for some seconds, considering. "If only there were some way to ride herd only on the troublemakers without inconveniencing the innocent."

"Then you'd be the first man to turn that particular fact of life on its head."

Eddie halted abruptly; he stared at the priest.

Seconds passed, and the priest smiled self-consciously under Eddie's wide-eyed scrutiny, squirming uncertainly in his seat. "What's the matter?" he finally asked.

"And why *not* turn it on its head?"

The priest held his awkward smile. "Turn what on its head?"

"The driver's license!"

"What in heaven's name do you mean?"

He was becoming excited now. "Rather than a driver's license—how about a *can't*-drive license?"

"A what?"

"A can't-drive license! Rather than sentencing that teen to meaningless apologies, let's give her a can't-drive license instead!"

"What would that mean?"

"It means just what it says: she can't drive. And if we do catch her driving, we up the punishment—maybe a night in jail or something for the first offense, then two nights for the second. You get the idea!"

The priest gradually lost his smile as the idea sank in. "You might be onto something there..." The smile slowly returned as his excitement grew along with his understanding. "You definitely might! Using that scheme, you wouldn't be bothering the innocent at all, only the guilty!"

"That's right! So the police wouldn't have to stop everyone. They'd only have to interfere if a man was not respecting the peace in the first place. Like our horse racers. We can even post their pictures around town, like we're already doing with the men who get themselves exiled."

A can't-drive license," pondered the priest, nodding. "I like it!" He snorted a short laugh and added, "Even if it does sound so very oxymoronic."

At a sudden thought, Eddie reached across the table and touched the priest's shoulder. "And that'll take care of our errant banker, too!"

"What," the priest anticipated, "a can't-bank license?"

"Yes! Yes! We give him a warning to stop garnishing other men's deposits on the sly—that's theft, you know—then if he continues anyway, the jury can sentence him to shut his bank down! Not Society, but the State!"

The priest stroked his chin. "That would also work with that miner east of town who's been fouling the stream. We can give him a can't-mine license."

"Yes, that's right. Polluting like that is akin to trespassing, because that's a violation of the property rights of everyone downstream."

"Agreed." After a brief pause the priest laughed abruptly. "And I can think of more than a few men in this town who well deserve a can't-drink license!"

Lost in thought, Eddie could only nod absently.

"And a can't-carry license for that fellow whose gun always seems to be going off at the wrong times inside the city limits."

Eddie continued to nod distractedly. "It would work against a whole host of problems," he mused aloud. "Particularly those where there's no particular person injured, such as with the miner and that banker."

"So you're saying he'll never be able to bank again?"

"No, no. We can sentence him to a reasonable duration that fits the situation."

"Such as six months of a can't-drive license for your rambunctious teens?"

"Yes, something like that. But it need not be permanent."

"You know," the priest ventured at a sudden thought. "Sentencing someone to a year's exile can be considered akin to a can't-live-here license—and exiles already have a duration."

Still only half listening, Eddie sat in thought for a moment longer, then replied. "Yes, that's true. And another good feature: we don't have to put someone in jail as our only option. They get a chance to mend their ways before we need to get serious with them."

The priest could only nod. Such forgiving charity appealed to him.

Eddie nodded in turn. "I think we have our answer: the can't license." He hesitated. "But one thing still troubles me."

"And that is...?"

"I was thinking this morning—just before I fell and hit my head!—that waiting for trouble to happen may not be the best idea, especially if you can see the problem coming, like we can with that bad banker. Fractional banking isn't necessarily a bad thing, if it's managed well. It's the misuse of it that's bad. The same can be said of the silver mines—all of them leave some sort of scars upon the land. But how much damage is acceptable? How much is too much? Where do you draw the line?"

"I understand what you're saying. Fractional banking might not cause any problems if, say, ninety percent of the deposits were always available. But if it were only ten percent available..."

Eddie nodded. "You understand. There have to be standards, and I'm thinking that it should be Society who sets them."

"You would have Society mandate there be no fractional banking? But you just said it wasn't necessarily a bad thing."

"And it's not—provided it's managed well and people know that it's being done and what risks they're taking." Again he waved a hand, tossing his own words aside. "But that's not the point either, because Society can mandate *nothing*! Nor would we want to start over-regulating business again. When I suggested last night that Society might want to regulate the banks, our banker-Senator did not take well to the idea at all."

The priest laughed. "I can see why! Especially since he suffered for so many years under the whims of one Mister Wesley! No one wants a return to those good old days."

"I agree. Which is why Society must do it—and that means the regulations must be voluntary."

The priest laughed again. "What?! Voluntary regulations? That's as extraordinary as your 'voluntary taxation' brainchild." The smile faltering, he dubiously added, "But how would regulations like that work? If they're voluntary, I mean."

"Easily! Society would set the Guidelines, and businesses would adhere to them—or not, as they see fit. If they meet the Guidelines, they could advertise the fact. If they don't, they can't. That way, people would be aware that a particular business might be using risky practices—or at least unorthodox ones."

"I think I see," he ventured. "So if we passed a Guideline saying not to practice fractional banking, a bank could still do that, only they couldn't say they meet Society's standards."

"Exactly! So in a questionable situation like that, people could make up their own minds whether or not they wanted to take on the risk."

"Ah, but what if the banker claimed he met the Guideline, but didn't?"

"Then he'd be guilty of not respecting the rights and property of others—that would be fraud, you know—and the courts could move against him."

"And give him a can't-bank license," asserted the priest almost merrily. He understood.

"That's right."

The priest smiled. "Looks like we'll have to amend Society's constitution after all."

"Yes, it does. Something like, 'Society shall have the power to set voluntary Guidelines for the conduct of business and other affairs of men.'"

The priest's smile broadened. "Including marriage?"

Eddie shrugged. "Why not? You're probably the best man to write the Guideline for that."

"I am only the messenger," he demurred, gesturing to the tome that lay between them on the sacristy's table.

The two men sat in silence contemplating the ramifications of the proposed change. Finally Eddie spoke. "Yes, that ought to do it. Once we pass the banking Guideline, one banker will be able to say he meets it, and the other will not—or he can choose to mend his ways and meet it. After that, people can make up their own mind where they want to put their money."

The priest snorted with a wry smile. "I know where *I* would put *my* congregation's money!"

"And I, mine." He recalled another aspect of his conversation with the errant banker that morning. "We should add an audit requirement, too. That would give us access to the bank's books to ensure compliance."

"But that's something that would go into the Guideline," the priest pointed out. "Not the constitution."

"That's right. I think our one short sentence should do it."

"Agreed."

Eddie let out a deep breath. "All right. That's it, then. I'll start the wheels turning to amend Society's constitution." He placed his hands on the arms of the chair, elbows out, in preparation to stand.

The priest studied him silently for a moment and shook his head slowly and pensively, his expression reflecting disbelief.

Eddie momentarily relaxed his grip on the chair and remained seated. He threw the priest a perplexed glance. "What? What's the matter?"

The priest rose from the table and idly ambled over to the sacristy's window, speaking as he walked. "It's all these remarkable ideas you keep coming up with. Voluntary regulations... Can't licenses... Society... And more... So many blessings!" He lifted his attention to the sky outside the window, saying nothing, then raised his hands to chest level, his fingers tightly intertwining; he assumed a serious demeanor. After holding the pose a moment, he addressed the sky. "You work in mysterious ways", he called out; it was obvious he was no longer addressing Eddie. "You saved Your people from Armageddon, yet continue to test them at every turn. But time after time Your hand draws us back from the precipice. I thank You for Your intercession and mercy—but please..." He paused, turning his head away from the window only slightly, awkwardly, almost apologetically toward Eddie, then back to the sky. "I only want to know: who is this man? Who is this man who always respects the rights and property of others, this man who does not sacrifice his love or his values, this man who eschews death and taxes, leaving only life and production in his wake? I pray You will answer my plea. Tell me! Who is this man? Who is Eddie Willers?!"

A shock like an electric bolt shot through a thunderstruck Eddie; he had not seen the final question coming. His chair squeaked loudly as it shifted under his startled weight. He did not speak.

The priest continued unabated. "Who is Eddie Willers?" he repeated firmly. "What senses do we lack that we cannot see another world all around us, yet he does? From whence comes this fountainhead of life, this sighted one in the kingdom of the blind? Please. Enlighten Your servant. But Thy will be done. Amen."

After a respectful pause, the priest turned completely from the window to face the town's stunned savior and continued in a more conventional tone. "I hope you don't mind the interruption." He inclined his head toward the window. "But I had to stop and ask." With a quick smile, he added, "Professional habit." He paused in thought, the more serious demeanor returning to his face, then continued. "I trust you recognized the fictional reference, and it's obvious association with you. You see, I could not help but think of the correlation between my question about Eddie Willers and that cheap piece of slang the world has echoed so much of late: 'Who is John Galt?' Because when men ask that senseless question, they ask it out of fear and futility. They mean it as a cry of surrender to calamity, to bad luck. It's a plea for help against a doom they know cannot be stopped. That question has become the final refuge of the incompetent, with this John Galt person being nothing less than despair personified. But here—" He held out both hands, palms up, toward Eddie. "—we have its opposite: hope. No, not hope," he corrected himself. "It's much more than mere hope: it's certainty. A certainty that life is *good*, that it can and will be better still; that men can and do respect one another and care for one another, that doom is not inevitable; rather, it is a fate that can be thwarted. Life is not reduced to a choice among unrelenting miseries; rather, the choice is how wonderful that life can become. No, no; please don't gape, Mr. Eddie. I've seen you do it so many times here in Las Vegas, the answers you keep coming up with, one after the other. And I just realized what one question sums up all those answers: 'Who is Eddie Willers?'"

There was not so much as a flicker of a pause on Eddie's flushed face. "I'll tell you who he is: just this guy. An ordinary man who always tries to do whatever is right."

The priest's broad smile broadened even further. "So we agree, then!"

Without another word, the thoroughly embarrassed subject in question leapt from his chair and headed for the door.

"Admit it, Mr. Eddie," the priest called after him jovially. "It *stands to reason*, doesn't it?"

Eddie did not reply; the answer was obvious. As he reached for the knob, the priest called out to him insistently, "Mr. Eddie..."

Hand on the doorknob, slowly he turned. "Yes?"

Still smiling broadly, the priest teased, "Must I be forced to give you a can't-hide license?"

Without another word, he left.

* * *

Fractional reserve banking ended.

With the passing of the new Guideline setting banking standards, informed depositors began pulling their money out of the bank that did not meet the standard, and promptly placed their money with the bank that did. The run was slow at first, but gathered steam quickly. Fortuitously for the town, the errant bank owner was able to make good on all of the depositors' withdrawal demands, although it did turn out to be a close thing: the man was almost wiped out by the run and was forced to close his bank as a result. But Las Vegas had dodged a disaster. Secretly, Eddie suspected that the man had simply embezzled the missing silver, and repaid the depositors out of the pilfered assets. But Eddie had no proof of any misdeed; nor was any required for justice to be done since full restitution had been made. He felt that being forced to close his bank was punishment enough for the man.

Close on the heels of the voluntary banking regulations came many others: one defining the metal content of coins, another the cleanliness of restaurants and grocery stores, a third regulating how buildings were constructed and repaired. Each guideline was written with the advice and participation of those affected by it, thereby insuring its acceptability. Labels were standardized, contract content regulated, even the courtesans wrote their own "Johns' Bill of Rights"—which Eddie blushingly signed. A few well-intentioned but ill-advised Guidelines were passed over the objection of those who would be affected by them, but the flawed rules did no damage: since no one agreed with them, no one bothered following them, and they were soon repealed as being moot. Even if they had remained on the books, it would not have mattered since no one troubled to cite them in their advertising, nor did the general public care. All in all, the end result was that the people of Las Vegas gained a more informed confidence in their business dealings, and the town's prosperity was able to grow more quickly as a result.

If the constitutional change had calmed the roiled waters of business, the sentencing change had a similar effect on the unruly behavior of the troublesome. The number of cases heard by the courts slowly declined in direct proportion to the number of can't licenses issued, and the town's tranquility increased in response. Nor did the new sentencing philosophy place an added burden on the police. Whenever an offender's picture was posted in the courtroom lobby, word would quickly spread around town that a can't license had been issued, thereby creating thousands of ad hoc deputies to ensure the sentence's enforcement. Several civic-minded citizens took to duplicating the sentencing notices and displaying them publicly around town, further expanding the enforcement effort.

With the pair of changes in place, the result was that few people ever knew that either Society or State even existed, since both stayed quietly out of the way of men until and unless intervention was required. Only when someone was in need, or when the rights or property of others was not respected, would either entity rear its respective, righteous head.

As the months passed, by all accounts life in Las Vegas waxed very good indeed; and Eddie's only hope was that it would stay that way. But there was still a great, wide world out there, and he knew it was only a matter of time before that world would reassert itself upon their idyllic existence.

Of course, one day, it did.

# Book Two:
# Who Is Eddie Willers?

# Section I – The Final Days

# Chapter 1 – Break on Through to the Other Side

The acolytes gathered.

In theory, all acolytes in the hierarchy of the army of Back For God were equal; only the Bishop stood above them. In practice, however, different acolytes performed vastly divergent functions. Some worked as menials on assembly lines in the numerous mills that produced their trademark red garments. Others filled the role of bookkeepers, maintaining meticulous inventory of their weaponry, robes, and communal food. Some were skilled warriors, others compassionate healers, but regardless of their position all of them were directly responsible to their Bishop. Despite the overtly egalitarian structure of the holy hierarchy, out of necessity some acolytes held positions of greater authority. They were the overseers of larger projects, coordinating the efforts of dozens, hundreds, even thousands of other acolytes. These minions were not mere acolytes; they were the right and left hands of the Bishop himself. As such, it became necessary that he and they coordinate their activities more closely; and toward that end, once a month the most devout gathered at the Bishop's residence in the center of God's California to report on their dealings, and to receive new assignments as necessary.

The agenda for their gatherings was always the same. It began with an extended period of silent prayer followed by a free-wheeling dialogue between the Bishop and any one or group of acolytes, continuing at the pleasure of the Bishop until he dismissed them. No one took notes or kept minutes, but all were expected to fulfill God's commands verbatim as revealed to them through His Bishop—although paradoxically there was much latitude in how those commands might be implemented. In practice, that freedom proved to be a mixed blessing. Although employing so decentralized an approach allowed for many more initiatives to come to simultaneous fruition, it also allowed for religious excesses to go unnoticed. So it was no surprise that perceived atrocities might be committed in their God's name, especially when it came to unbelievers and the banished heretics—and above all, their women. But even had these crimes been chronicled in fine detail and presented before an ecclesiastical court, nothing would have been done about them; no holy sentence would be handed down. Such uncouth behavior constituted no sin, for the saved owed no morality to the damned.

It was the damned who were the topic at hand this day. "These heretics infest the eastern mountains, Your Eminence," observed one acolyte. "They foul the Earth and leech its bounty to maintain their damnable existence. They are an evil pestilence upon God's holy land."

"Surely their numbers cannot be so great," countered the Bishop. "For the winters have been harsh and few can survive there."

"Ah, but survive they do, Eminence. And they thrive! Our patrols continually discover their camps, their traps, and their trails—and all too infrequently, the heretics themselves."

"And when you do find these abominations, you cleanse the land?"

"Of course, Eminence! But for every camp we cleanse, for every trap we dismantle, for every heretic we drive off, scores elude us."

The Bishop pondered a moment. "Do we need more patrols, then?"

"Eminence, I believe we are past the time for patrols."

"What?! Shall we just leave the heretics there, you say?"

"Not at all! We must do the opposite, Your Eminence. We must sweep the mountains clean of this pestilence!"

"And how do you propose we do that?"

The acolyte smiled. "Meticulously."

## CHAPTER 2 – SOMETHING IN THE AIR

Dr. Floyd ducked.

*That bastard Jimmy is attacking again!* he thought accusingly as he rolled under his desk. The cold marble building rumbled impressively all around him.

He cowered there for several minutes, but when there was no second volley immediately forthcoming, he gingerly poked his head out from under the desk and peered up out the window. All he could see from his vantage on the floor of his office was an overcast sky that promised an early spring snow before dark. Incongruously, he heard the muted chime of a doorbell sounding somewhere beyond his office door. Ignoring it, he climbed to his feet, straightened his heavy coat and loose-fitting clothes, and took a better look outside. From what he could see of the treeless grounds behind the State's Science Institute, everything appeared to be normal.

Smiling now, he chided himself for his foolishness. *A minor earthquake*, he assured himself. Earthquakes were rare, but not unheard of in New Hampshire. There was a seismograph in one wing of the Institute; later he would have a technician determine just how big an earthquake it was, maybe even locate its epicenter. The device required electricity to operate, but coincidentally it was the time of day when the generators were active and electricity flowed, as evidenced by the unexplained chiming of the doorbell. Odds were that the seismograph had dutifully captured the tremor. *But why bother?* he shrugged.

He reclaimed his seat again and was about to resume his interrupted task when the massive building shook again, top to bottom. Dr. Floyd was instantly on the floor under his desk. *He IS attacking!* Several silent moments went by, but this time Dr. Floyd refused to emerge. He was certain that a third bomb was about to be dropped, and he wanted at least a little protection around him. More minutes passed in silence as Dr. Floyd fretted under his desk. With a sudden start, he banged his head on the underside of the desk, startled into involuntary motion by the unexpected, almost cheerful ringing of the telephone that was sitting on top of it directly above him. Given that the telephone system was usually shut off, it was rare that the device rang at all, adding to the intensity of his startled reaction.

Rubbing his sore cranium, Dr. Floyd reached around from under the desk to grab the telephone. He pulled the instrument into his makeshift shelter and held the receiver to his aching head.

"Hello," he answered grumpily. " Dr. Floyd here."

But his mood changed quickly. Eyes wide, he listened in disbelief. Apparently it wasn't an attack after all.

## CHAPTER 3 – SHAPE OF THINGS TO COME

The airbase tower controller gasped.

"Good God, what the hell is that?" he cried to no one. His long-range detection equipment had duly noted an aircraft approaching from the north.

His surprise was understandable, if only because it had been years since the last unexpected flight had come into the Washington area. But the bulk of his surprise was precipitated primarily by the object's velocity—Mach four!—several times the speed of sound.

His brow furrowed; he was immediately suspicious of his equipment. No such airplane had ever existed, and its sudden appearance could not be explained by anything other than a malfunction. Without hesitation he rolled his chair across the floor of the cramped tower to the backup detector. He ineffectually brushed some of the dust from the console, then switched it on. During the few moments it took for it to power up to operational status, he kept a disbelieving eye on his main detector as the approaching bogie swiftly swallowed half the distance to Washington.

When the "ready" light finally illuminated on his backup equipment, he deftly manipulated the dusty knobs and switches to train the backup detector on the intruder. It readily confirmed the aircraft's presence; however, it conceded that its speed was actually somewhat slower now—a mere Mach three. He snatched the telephone and dialed his commander's home.

"Colonel, we have a bogie coming in at one o'clock, velocity Mach three."

"Mach three?" gasped the Colonel incredulously. "Three times the speed of sound? Soldier, your equipment must be malfunctioning! Go to your backup detector."

"I did that, sir, and the backup equipment confirms it. The bogie is slowing; he was at Mach four when I first detected him, and he's at Mach two now. No, wait; he's gone subsonic. And he's heading right for the main runway. It looks like he's coming in to land, sir!" Through the telephone, the Colonel heard the rumble of the aircraft's sonic boom as it engulfed the control tower, its glass panes tinkling in bass harmony.

The Colonel felt a dizzying sensation of *déjà vu*—when Mr. Thomson first returned to Washington two years ago, the pattern of events was very similar. His first reaction this time was that he was the brunt of a practical joke, except that *nothing* could travel at Mach four near ground level. At that speed, the heat from friction with the air would melt any airplane in an instant, not to mention ripping its wings off.

He opened his mouth, about to give the order to the controller to attempt communications, when his unformed words were interrupted by the rumble of the same sonic boom thundering over his own house. Mouth still open, his eyes drifted slowly ceilingward in amazement. No practical joke, this. Before he could recover, the controller spoke again.

"Sir, he's landed. And—it's not an airplane! It's... It's... Hell, Colonel; I don't know *what* it is! It looks like a sideways sewer pipe that melted! I've seen a lot of airplanes in my day, sir, but to the best of my knowledge, I'd say that aircraft was not made anywhere on Earth!"

*A melted sewer pipe?* The Colonel was at a complete loss. "Are you feeling all right, soldier?" he ventured. But he could have been addressing himself, given the way he felt.

"I'm fine, sir. But you ought to see this! It's all metallic, colored some kind of greenish blue. And it looks like a hatch is opening! No, wait! Now it's closing... The thing is moving again—it's taking off! Sir, it's in the air and accelerating. God, but he's accelerating! He's already at Mach one! Mach two! Let me check the backup detector..." The controller set the telephone down; through it, the Colonel heard the rumbling of another sonic boom trailing the departing aircraft.

Picking the telephone back up, the controller reported, "Sir, he's already out of detection range—just like that! You're not going to believe this, but he was traveling at Mach six when I lost him. Mach six! And he was still accelerating!"

The Colonel did not speak. He was listening to the second sonic boom rumbling over his house.

"Colonel, did you hear me?"

"Soldier, have someone relieve you immediately. Meet me at the White House as soon as you can. I'm sure the Head of State himself will want to speak with you."

"Yes sir!" He hung up the phone, but did not immediately move to follow the Colonel's orders. *They'll think me insane!* he fretted. *And there's no evidence the bogie was even here!* But it was too late for such concerns. He set aside his paranoia for the moment and summoned his replacement.

It took close to a half an hour for his relief to finally appear. The barracks were over a mile away from the control tower on the other side of the runway; and his relief had to be roused from a sound sleep, adding to the delay. It was no surprise that he was none too pleased when he eventually arrived.

"What's the big deal?" he groused, still not quite fully awake.

"You don't want to know," warned the controller, not wanting to waste more time—or have fantasy stories about Men from Mars spreading too far. "I have to report to the White House for a briefing."

"Now? In the middle of your shift? You'd think someone would have the decency to warn me, or schedule it while you weren't on duty!"

"Hey, I only work here!" he called over his shoulder as he headed out the door.

As he was traversing the broad tarmac, he wished in vain that they still had use of their jeeps. It was a long walk from the airbase to the White House, and he expected it would take him the better part of an hour to get there. But there was precious little fuel to spare for the sake of an enlisted man's convenience. A bicycle would have speeded his trip, but they were few in number and reserved exclusively for commissioned officers. "Damn that John Galt!" he swore reflexively.

Out of professional habit, he scanned the skies left and right before crossing the main runway. Regardless of any Mach six aircraft flitting about their airspace, his deeply-ingrained airman's habits would not let him take any chances. He was halfway across the runway and still scanning the skies anxiously when a small object glinting on the centerline caught his attention. At first he thought it was merely a piece of debris; but a chill ran up his spine when he realized it lay where the unknown bogie had halted.

As he slowly approached it, he could discern that it was a metal cube some four inches square; and like the bogie, it was metallic with a greenish-blue luster. In another dozen paces he was standing over it, then dropped to his hands and knees to cautiously examine it. The cube's edges were rounded rather than sharp, and its surface was full of tiny holes, resembling the fine mesh of a window screen. On all four faces, a series of larger holes in the mesh outlined the image of a large dollar sign. On top, a single greenish-blue pushbutton protruded, a legend engraved on its face in tiny letters. It said simply, "Push To Talk."

The controller stood and took a step back. He looked apprehensively at the cloudless blue sky, then back at the metal box. *Talk to whom?* he wondered. Another chill ran up his spine.

He extended a tentative foot and kicked gingerly at the side of the box; it slid slightly along the runway, but nothing else happened. He crouched, then cautiously poked the box lightly with one finger. Again, nothing happened. Incautiously, he picked the box up; it was feathery light. He held it up to the sun and examined it from all sides, pointlessly careful not to tip it. Peering through its mesh walls, he could discern little of its internal detail. All he could see were several tiny, interconnected greenish-blue components, plus a complex array of dull grey wires that vaguely resembled an antenna. There were no instructions, no manufacturer's name, no power cord, no screws or access panels; nothing except the four outlined dollar signs and a solitary, labeled stud. Otherwise it was a single, unbroken whole.

"No way I'm pushing that button!" he announced to the air.

Holding the box outstretched far in front of him, as if it were infected with a deadly disease, he resumed his trek to the White House. His heart was pounding fast, but on another level he was relieved. *At least they won't think I'm crazy!*

## CHAPTER 4 – SYMPATHY FOR THE DEVIL

Ma was startled.

The sun was shining brightly outside, so the rumble of thunder was completely unexpected. Looking out the window, she saw that the spring sky was a cloudless blue. Mystified, she abandoned her chair in front of the shortwave's microphone and stepped outside. *An explosion?* she wondered. Looking around her on all sides, she saw no telltale smoke or other indications of any detonation.

She was about to shrug it off and return to her daily broadcast when a flash of light in the sky caught her eye. *It can't be an airplane!* she objected, disputing the evidence of her own eyes.

But that's what it looked like, sort of. Ma was far from being any kind of an expert on technology, but still she knew that she had never seen anything remotely similar to what was now approaching. It was strangely shaped, and constructed of greenish-blue metal. It flew in a deliberate line, coming in for a landing on the old airstrip next to the church. In what seemed too brief a roll, the odd-shaped aircraft touched down and abruptly halted, as if it had landed in molasses.

She watched in mounting fear as a hatch opened in the belly of the aircraft. A man's arm extended from the opening, his hand holding a small box. Behind the hand, a head and shoulder followed as he deposited the box on the runway. The visitor looked around quickly, and noticed her watching him. He smiled and waved in a friendly fashion, then disappeared inside. The hatch closed, and in seconds the aircraft took back to the air and was gone. Again, the rumble of thunder washed over her.

Her curiosity overcoming her fear, Ma walked over to examine the unexpected gift. Like the aircraft, it was made of a greenish-blue metal, but its surface was a fine mesh rather than a solid artifact. It was otherwise featureless, except for a large dollar sign on all four sides and a labeled button on top. It took her old eyes a moment to focus on the inscription: "Push To Talk," it said.

Her former fright suddenly flooding back, Ma ran to find the Bishop, her shortwave broadcast forgotten.

## Chapter 5 – Don't Pass Me By

Eddie frowned.

He scrutinized the desert sky above him. Unsurprisingly, it was a perfect blue bowl inverted over the broad, flat Earth. He looked down along the railroad track, past where the Diesel stood idling, then up the track toward Las Vegas; there was nothing to see. *Where could thunder possibly have come from?* he wondered. He studied the empty sky a moment longer, shrugged, then returned his attention to greasing the track switch in front of him. *Probably just heat lightning*, he told himself.

The maintenance task completed, Eddie climbed back aboard the *Meteor*. He gave the lone, anomalous rumble no further thought.

## Chapter 6 – Reach Out in the Darkness

The time came.

As with Moses bringing down the Ten Commandments from Mount Sinai, a new commandment had been handed down from the highest peaks of the Colorado Rockies to the denizens of the Gulch below: it was time to return to the world Outside.

The first fallout of the pronouncement befell the pilot in the form of a hand-delivered letter from the Judge left on his doorstep informing him that he had thirty days in which to either take the striker's oath or wrap up his affairs and move out of the valley for good. The pilot stared at the letter for a long time, not certain if he should feel elated or annoyed. He had been living in the Gulch for over two years, and in spite of the shunning he still received at the hands of some of the strikers, it had come to be his home nevertheless. Apparently the time had come to seek a new one.

It was early in the day when he discovered the letter, and he would not need to open his doors for the lunch crowd for a few hours yet; there was time for him to take this particular travesty up with its author. He donned the leather flight jacket he had worn on the day he arrived in the valley, pocketed the letter, and walked out the door of *The Caged Bird* onto the cool, breezy street. A few minutes later, he was facing the open door and closed face of the Judge.

"What's the idea?" demanded the pilot, waving the envelope angrily.

"Is the letter not clear?"

"Why do I have to leave?"

"You don't. You're free to take our oath."

"What if I don't want to?"

The Judge's marble-hard visage cracked; he sighed. "Oh, for Galt's sake! I've been through this too many times before—and not just with you, but with all the other scabs who faced the same choice a couple of years ago." His face closed again and took on the cold countenance of justice. "This valley is our private property, and we ask that you respect that. We've respected your property, and will continue to do so, even though you've refused to take the striker's oath. We were under no duty to begin, let alone continue our practice of allowing you to live here. Your needs and wants are not a claim on us. So unless you agree to join our strike, you cannot stay." Again, the stern mien diminished, but only slightly. "Really!" he repeated. "I know for a fact that you're already aware of all this."

"This is pointless," the pilot muttered to himself, angrily stuffing the letter back in his pocket.

"Indeed," agreed the Judge. He placed a hand high on the door jamb dismissively. "Is there anything else I can do for you?" his tone of voice belying the courteous request. He started to swing the door slowly closed.

The pilot spun on his heel and cried over his shoulder without looking back. "You can rot in Hell!"

The Judge smiled grimly at the retreating form. "If I believed in such a myth," he said softly, "it would not be I who would be heading there, scab." Shaking his head gently in reproach, he finished closing the door.

* * *

Owen shrugged.

"You knew this day was coming," he admonished, his deep voice lending an apocalyptic tone to his words. "Personally, I'm surprised they let you stay this long. What's it been, two years?"

"More!" The pilot stretched out his hands, palms up. "Don't they give any preference to seniority or to historical precedence?" he implored, his own equally-deep voice giving him the authoritative presence of a newsreel commentator.

"No. It's dog-eat-dog around here." Owen smiled, as if at some private joke.

The pilot's arms fell to his side with a slap. "What am I going to do then?"

Holding his smile, Owen replied, "Swear, or leave here swearing." When the pilot didn't respond to his witticism, he added, "Listen: why not just take the oath?"

The pilot shrugged. "Principle, I guess. Besides, I like to keep my options open." He scowled. "And maybe I'm still a little more than annoyed by what they did with their California nonsense and that Sacramento girl." Again, he stretched out his hands in supplication. "Tell me why can't I live my life my own way?"

"Because it's not your valley."

"Who am I hurting by staying?"

Owen shrugged in turn. "That's not the issue. You have to remember that we—us, that is, not you—were treated pretty shabbily by society Outside. Now that we're opening our doors to the rest of the world, it's going to become an even greater badge of honor for someone to be living here. We don't call this place Atlantis for nothing. It's the place of heroes, and we mean to keep it that way."

"'We?'" the pilot challenged sardonically.

Owen paused, both hurt and offended. "Yes, 'we,'" he had to say. "I've suffered more than my own share of shabby treatment at the hands of your philosophical brethren." He shook his head. "I've had enough."

"I thought we were friends! You saved my life!"

"We are and I did. But neither of those facts represent any sort of claim upon me or my actions."

He scowled again. "You sound just like that jerk Judge."

"I daresay everyone in this valley does. Except for you, that is."

"A good reason for me to leave this goddamn Hell hole in a lot fewer than thirty days," he muttered.

The two men stood silently, awkwardly not catching each other's eye. The moment was a rough one for both of them.

The silence lengthened, then finally Owen spoke. "Listen: there may be some way to turn this mess to our advantage."

"Oh, you think so?" the pilot asked disdainfully. "How?"

"You and I could go into business together. It's been a while since I've flown any scavenger missions—there's not much in the way of pickings left Outside that we can use. But now that the gates to the Gulch have opened up, there will be commerce. We can tap that market, you and I. We're both still pilots, remember."

"Who the hell would want to visit this God-forsaken valley?" contested the pilot, still angry and not pausing to think.

"No, not visitors—commerce! Trade alone! It is strong enough."

"Trade? Trade what?"

"There are a lot of things we can sell—Miracle Metal, galtmotors, Richard's music, lots of things people Outside would want."

The pilot snorted. "You really think these prima donnas would actually agree to soil their souls by dealing with unclean commoners?"

"Yes—but only on our own terms. That was the whole idea behind our strike, to bring the world around to the point where they would deal with us on our own terms, not theirs. They had to first realize our value to them and respect it. Now they will. And someone has to fly out there and make contact, who better than a rotten scab?" The last he said playfully, to take the sting out of his words.

But the pilot heard neither the tone nor the words—he had heard nothing beyond the phrase, "fly out there." His eyes took on a distant gaze and for several seconds his mouth hung slightly open. Coming back down to Earth, he met Owen's eyes. "Do you think Dwight will sell me my airplane back?" he asked incongruously, almost eagerly.

Owen half-turned in the direction of the airfield and extended a palm. "Shall we go see?"

The pilot was off like a shot, leaving his friend in his wake, smiling.

\* \* \*

The pilot dickered.

In the end he got what he wanted: his old airplane back. But the price Dwight charged him was a steep one, and for good reason. For starters, the airplane's aluminum skin had been replaced completely with a thin sheathing of Miracle Metal, lighter and stronger, and reinforced throughout with internal members of the same remarkable material. The old-fashioned internal combustion engines had both been replaced by high-powered electric motors whose coils were wound with wire made of Miracle Metal, plus a new pair of oversized propellers of the same alloy that could take full advantage of the motors' tremendous might. The fuel tanks in the wings had been removed, the volume converted to storage space, and a galtmotor had been mounted in the nose as the new power source. The avionics had been completely revamped; the new radio was powerful enough to broadcast thousands of miles. It was, in almost every respect, a brand new airplane; only its outlines remained the same. Although its price was a dear one, the pilot was able to cover the purchase exclusively from his savings; *The Caged Bird* remained unmortgaged.

The ink had hardly dried on the agreement of sale before the pilot took to the sky; not to escape the valley, but only for the sheer joy of it. Two years he had been grounded, two long years trapped as a caged bird with clipped wings and feet stuck in the mud, but the torture of the hiatus was swept away with the ease of sugar dissolving in boiling water, and the feeling was superb. At first he amused himself by soaring among the granite peaks that surrounded the valley, but little by little he expanded the envelope of possible maneuvers until he felt himself the master of his airplane's new configuration. With its greater power and strengthened wings, the pilot was able to perform aerobatic feats unheard of in any airplane that ever existed before. More than once he hurled its mass at high speed directly toward the Earth, only to pull out of the dive at the last minute with centrifugal forces several times the pull of gravity threatening to blacken out his consciousness. He behaved as if he had much to get out of his system; he did, and he did.

Satisfied with its performance and his mastery of it, he brought his reborn lady to a feather-soft landing at the airstrip, and for a long time he sat at the controls doing nothing, merely sitting, soaking up the feel of being back in the seat where he truly belonged. His love of flying washed away the contempt and anger he felt towards the Atlanteans; he knew he had already found his new home; the only question remaining was where he would sleep between flights. Reluctantly, he climbed out of the cockpit to open his taproom for lunch.

While the pilot was busy joyously reacquainting himself with his lost love, Owen kept busy as well. He approached Roger, the electronics wizard who ran Roger Electric, and commissioned the design and construction of a set of two-way radios to be used to communicate with their future customers. In both design and operation, the radios were simple: each was a four-inch cube constructed of a mesh of Miracle Metal appropriately emblazoned with the sign of the dollar on each side. The mesh served both as an aerial for the transceiver, and as an impenetrable container encasing a tiny galtmotor and other components. On its top was an activation stud, a simple pushbutton made of Miracle Metal engraved with the legend, "Push To Talk." As a base station for the remote units, Roger was to construct a companion device of the same size, but with an additional rotary switch on top which allowed selective communication with one or all of the remote stations, plus a bank of sixteen lights ringed in an arc around the switch indicating the source of a particular signal. Owen ordered eight of the remote radios be built immediately, with an option to purchase eight more at the same price any time prior to the year's end. Owing to their simplicity, Roger was able to promise to complete the initial order within only a few weeks, perhaps even sooner, leaving a reasonable cushion of time to distribute the radios before the pilot's imminent expulsion.

In the days following the receipt of his eviction notice, the pilot continued to conduct business as usual at *The Caged Bird*, despite his impending departure. As the Judge had affirmed, while the pilot's physical presence may no longer be appreciated within the valley, there could be no objection to him retaining ownership of the popular establishment. Relieved, the pilot hired Owen as general manager to conduct the taproom's affairs during his upcoming exile in return for a percentage of the profits. Out of necessity, he and Owen arranged their import-export business such that Owen would conduct affairs inside the valley, and the pilot those on the Outside.

The terms satisfied the pilot immensely. He had his lady back, would retain most of the revenue stream from *The Caged Bird*, and, best of all, would be finally free of those philosophically-prissy Johnnies forever. In high spirits, he began preparations for his permanent departure. The first order of business was to change the name of his taproom; appropriately, it became *The Empty Nest*.

\* \* \*

The radios were ready.

The pilot planned to personally fly them to their four targeted markets: the State's Science Institute, Washington, California, and that part of Yucatan where the bulk of the scabs had been exiled—and do it all in one trip. Since his airplane had been converted to galtmotor technology, he no longer had to concern himself with such mundane worries as fuel or range; his plan was to fly one large circle around the western hemisphere to deliver the radios. But while the airplane's range was not an issue, he quickly realized that his own personal limits might be. The top speed of his enhanced craft had been increased to almost the speed of sound, but even at that prodigious velocity his great circle would require most of a day to complete—longer, actually, once ground time was considered. Although it would require a good deal of stamina on his part, he was ready to attempt it nonetheless. Fortunately, the Earth-bound intervals promised to be short; besides, he was chary of spending any amount of time at any of his destinations until he was able to ascertain the political situation there; a quick circuit would be the prudent approach. The last thing he would want would be for some local yokel to confiscate his airplane, especially after his having spent so many years grounded.

In preparation for the upcoming journey, he stopped by the airfield administration building to purchase the maps he would need. As usual, Dwight was on duty.

"Ah, the caged bird himself," Dwight hailed mockingly. "What can I do for you?"

"Maps," he explained tersely. "I need maps."

"Sure! Got just what you need." He stood and walked to a file cabinet on the other side of the spacious room. "Where to?"

"The State's Science Institute, Washington, Yucatan, and California."

"That all?" he joked. "Why not Japan as well?"

The pilot did not reply. He had never taken a liking to Dwight, despite their shared love of flying. He still felt a good deal of resentment at the cold treatment he had received when he first arrived in the valley, and at least for him, it had colored their relationship ever since.

Dwight took no notice of his sulky silence. He rummaged through the drawer and produced several charts which would fill the bill. "What do you have in mind," he asked conversationally, the mocking tone still prominent. "An extended vacation?"

The pilot replied with an edge in his voice. "You know as well as every other Johnnie in this valley that I have to be out of here in a couple more weeks." Grudgingly, he let slip the real answer. "Besides, Owen and I are going into the import-export business, and I need to pay a visit to our future customers."

For his part, Dwight did not care for the pilot either. The man was a scab, and as far as he was concerned that was reason enough to distance himself. But he was not so strict in his interpretation of their philosophy as some, that he wouldn't deal with the pilot as a customer—barely—but he did take every opportunity to overcharge him. He handed the pilot the maps. "Seventy-five cents for the lot of them."

"Yeah, yeah," he grumbled, snatching the maps from his outstretched hand.

"Looks like you'll be gone for at least a week, given that itinerary," he commented. "Are you sure you'll be back in time for us to throw you out?"

"Very funny," retorted the pilot. "As it so happens, I plan to do the entire circle in one shot. And it'll only be a short stay at each stop—I just need to drop off the radios and be on my way."

"One shot?" His eyebrows went up. "In *your* airplane?"

"Well, I wasn't planning to walk!"

"Seems a tough row to hoe."

"What's it to you?"

"Well, since you ask, let me remind you that I'm also in the business of renting airplanes."

"I already have an airplane, thank you,", he observed dryly.

"Yes, but why not rent my hypercraft? It'd take you a lot less time, that's for sure."

The pilot stopped cold, all animosity forgotten. "Your hypercraft?" he asked eagerly.

"Yep. It's just sitting in the hangar. Might as well make some money off it." He definitely had the pilot's skeptical attention.

"But I don't know how to fly it."

"No problem. Either you can hire me as a pilot or I can sell you lessons. Your choice." Dwight could see the gears turning in the pilot's mind; he laughed to himself about how some very formidable men were so very easy to manipulate.

"Lessons? How long would that take?"

"Oh, we could be done with them long before you'd have to leave the valley. But if you want to make that trip in the next week or so, I'd suggest you hire me to fly you."

The pilot never hesitated. "All right. How much for the whole trip?"

"Ah..." Dwight hemmed, calculating. He named a price.

"Done," replied the pilot, apparently without thinking. The price seemed far too low, and he wanted to leave no chance for Dwight to change his mind. "When can we leave?"

"Anytime, really. It should only take us a couple of hours to hit all your destinations."

The pilot stared. *A couple of hours! It's almost ten thousand miles!*

Knowing what the pilot was thinking, he replied offhandedly. "She tops out at Mach seven, remember. Over four thousand miles an hour. If you keep the acceleration to a tolerable level, you can rev her up to top speed in about half a minute."

The pilot gaped. "It's not easy to get used to the idea of traveling so fast," he stammered. It was no wonder the price was so low; it represented only a couple hours of Dwight's time. In fact, now that he thought about it, the price was actually significantly on the high side.

Dwight smiled like a proud parent. "Agreed. It took some effort for *me* to get used to it myself—and I built the damned thing!"

At a sudden thought, the pilot asked, "Speaking of the hypercraft, has there been any more news about Francisco?"

Instantly, Dwight's smile vanished. "No," he replied flatly. He turned away from the pilot and slammed the open map drawer shut.

"Not even the wreck?"

"No. Nothing." He took a deep breath. "God knows we searched!"

"I'm sorry," offered the pilot, bowing his head. He meant it. The brotherhood among pilots ran deep, despite any personal issues that might separate its individual members.

Dwight did not reply.

After a respectful moment, the pilot resumed his usual mind-set. "You sure you have all the kinks worked out of this new ship?"

Anger flashed briefly in Dwight eyes, but faded quickly. "Yes. We learned a lot from the prototype. We fixed the problem that brought down Francisco, and added a crash-proof homing beacon, survival kit and a lot more. Next time things go wrong, we'll be much better prepared." He took a deep breath; a hopeful sound. "But no need to worry—it appears I did everything right this time, even though building the replacement took a lot more money than I could afford. But it's been worth it! I've already flown it from coast to coast at top speed several times, just for the heck of it." He smiled slightly. "I've been considering a 'round the world trip, but it seems too risky right now. Maybe after I get around to building another craft, I'll give it a try. That way if I have a problem, someone can come to my rescue." He sighed. "Someday, perhaps. But not today."

The pilot smiled, despite his dislike for the man. "I'd be happy to play chase for you."

Dwight smiled in turn. "I may just take you up on that."

"How much for lessons?"

Dwight paused, eyes unfocused, then looked back to the pilot. "Tell you what," he suggested. "Let me work up a training plan and a number and get back to you on that." At a sudden thought, he added, "Come to think of it, there's no reason our trip out to Washington and all can't be combined with your first lessons. That'll save you time and money. You should even be able to get some time in as pilot in command."

"Deal!" asserted the pilot, extending a hand. "Looks like I'll get to see Japan soon enough."

The two men shook hands solemnly.

* * *

The hypercraft circled.

"Looks pretty beat up down there," observed the pilot. "Look at that runway!" Below them, the tarmac behind the State's Science Institute was punctuated with blackened craters and white patches of snow. "There's no way we'll be landing there!"

"Yep," agreed Dwight. "Washington sure bombed the hell out of this place."

"Where'll we land, then?" he asked anxiously.

Dwight banked the craft to get a better look. "How about the driveway out front?" he suggested.

The pilot eyed him suspiciously. "You're joking," he finally answered, suspecting he wasn't.

"Nope. If we can go from zero to Mach seven in thirty-three seconds, that implies we can do the opposite. Since this baby generates enough lift to fly at forty miles an hour and rotates at fifty, using wheel brakes alone we'd only need about a hundred feet of runway. Assuming no trees and using reverse thrust, a good pilot could get away with fifty. I'm a good pilot—" He gestured out the window to the barren landscape; every tree in sight had been cut down. "—and trees don't seem to be a problem."

"I don't know," the pilot replied dubiously. "Fifty feet seems like some sort of pipe dream. But you're the expert, I guess."

"That I am," he agreed nonchalantly. He banked the craft around and brought it in for a quick landing, as predicted. Both men were pressed forward against the straps of their seat harnesses as the craft came to an abrupt halt far short of the end of the driveway.

"Looks like about forty feet," Dwight bragged good-naturedly.

The pilot ignored him. He unbuckled his harness and pulled a greenish-blue cube out of his backpack. "Hang on a moment while I drop this off." He opened the rear hatch, climbed out, and trotted toward the front door of the State's Science Institute. Far above his head, etched into the marble edifice of the building, read the words, "To the Fearless Mind. To the Inviolate Truth." *Yeah, sure!* scoffed the pilot. *Not in your wildest dreams, Dr. Floyd!* He swiftly traversed the distance from airplane to Institute, and like some school boy pulling a mischievous prank, he set the radio down on the doorstep, rang the doorbell, turned and ran. Seconds later, he was strapped back in.

Dwight taxied to the far end of the driveway, turned the craft around, and blasted back into the sky, going supersonic seconds later. "One down, three to go!" he called merrily. "Better dig out your next radio—we'll be in Washington in a few minutes."

The pilot shook his head. It was tough enough on his flying instincts that they had reached New Hampshire in much less than an hour. Clearly, he had to recalibrate those instincts.

Dwight broke in on his reverie. "Where in California will you want to drop off the radio?"

"Good question. Anyplace there's someone with a forty-foot driveway, I'd guess."

"Hey, I have an idea..." Dwight fiddled with the knobs on the hypercraft's shortwave radio. From the speaker came a woman's tearful voice extolling the vision that comes from a blind faith in God. "I suspected she'd be on the air right about now," he congratulated himself. "She usually is." He turned to the pilot, a silly grin on his face. "How about we give it to her?"

At first the pilot looked on with confusion, but it quickly gave way to the same, roguish smile. "Why not!" His smile wavered at a discouraging thought. "Do you know where she is?"

"No. But that's not a problem. We can triangulate on her signal..." He was already manipulating the controls. Satisfied with what he saw, he wrote down some numbers. "When we get to Washington we'll take another reading on her. That'll bring us pretty close. If she's still broadcasting when we reach Yucatan that'll nail it."

"Will she, do you think?"

He tapped the craft's chronometer. "If she's true to form, she'll be on the air for another hour and a half. Plenty of time!" He glanced out the window. "There's the Chesapeake. Here comes Washington!" Minutes later, he was aligning the craft along the main runway at the airbase south of town.

"Is this the right airfield?" the pilot asked uncertainly.

"Yep. I monitor their tower transmissions as a regular thing, even though there aren't too many flights in or out of here. That's how I knew our evangelist would be broadcasting—I monitor all the established stations." As an afterthought, he added conversationally, "You know, if you want to keep up on what's going on in the world, you ought to talk with Quentin sometime. He's been eavesdropping on the State's Science Institute—he's even cracked their secret code! Washington's, too. We had ourselves a ringside seat during their big war last year." He chuckled. "That Dr. Floyd is no strategist, that's for sure!"

297

"No wonder his runway got all bombed up."

"Well, to be fair, Washington's still got a good number of military men at their disposal, so Dr. Floyd never stood much of a chance." His words came out somewhat distorted as the two men were pressed by deceleration against their seat harnesses. "Alright! Second stop! All out!"

Looking around, the pilot could see that the control tower was some distance away. Without a word, he unbuckled himself and reached down to open the craft's belly hatch. "Tell you what," he called over his shoulder. "I'm just going to leave it here on the runway. I don't hanker to be that far away from safety just to make a personal delivery." He leaned out of the open hatch and set the radio on the tarmac. "Besides," he grunted as he pulled the hatch closed, "all those military men you mentioned may try to make me stay." The pilot plopped into his seat and strapped back in. "Let's git!"

"Roger," Dwight replied indifferently. With a muffled whine, the turbines spooled up to maximum safe thrust and the craft leapt back into the sky. He fiddled with the radio dials and jotted down some more numbers. "That should be enough to get us in her general vicinity. One more reading ought to do it within a hundred feet." Absently, he added, "If it were later in the day, maybe we could get a fix on whoever is broadcasting those old symphonies that Dagny likes so much."

The pilot looked at him. "You telling me you don't know where they're coming from?"

"Never thought to try to find out before now."

"Any guesses?"

"Nope. Could be anywhere. I'd have to fly out at night while he's broadcasting to get a good bearing, but I can't do that. No lights on the runway at the Gulch, you know."

"Yes, yes," he replied testily. "Owen and I were discussing that last week when we were setting up our flight schedules. You ought to fix that, you know."

Smiling, he kept his eyes on the sky ahead. "Never had any reason to. But anytime you want to pay to install them..." He turned his smile on the pilot, then returned his attention out the windshield.

"Yeah, yeah," he groused again. "That's what Owen said. You Johnnies are all alike!"

"But of course! A is A."

Before very long they were crossing the blue waters of the Gulf of Mexico, and the Yucatan Peninsula lay dead ahead. "Better do this now in case she signs off early," muttered Dwight as he fiddled with the radio. He jotted down several more numbers and handed his notes to the pilot. "Can you do the triangulation, or should I?"

The pilot snatched the paper out of Dwight's hand. "I can do it," he grumbled, peeved. "But are you sure you know where we're supposed to be landing?"

"Not to worry, boss! I flew out here over a dozen times when we ferried the rest of you scabs out of the valley. I could do this one in my sleep!"

Land quickly overtook them, and he brought them around in a sweeping, descending turn. Not a minute later, the craft sat motionless on a dirt runway on a broad plain at the foot of some rugged mountains. Outside the windshield they could plainly see the charred ruins that lined the rough airstrip.

Dwight silently scanned the ruins nonchalantly, as if the scene were nothing out of the ordinary.

Slowly, as if he were overly careful not to disturb a fragile mechanism, the pilot unbuckled his seat harness and gingerly set the straps aside. Ignoring the cautious motions of his hands, he kept all his attention riveted on the scene outside. With wary deliberation, he stood and leaned his face close to the quartz windshield. His mind balked at the destruction; it seemed too matter-of-fact to be real. Left, then right he scanned the devastation. After a moment, he turned from the window to face Dwight. "Do you have a weapon aboard?"

Dwight drew himself up, "After what happened to Francisco? Of course! I already told you I took steps to be ready for whatever calamity might possibly befall me in my travels." He held up a fist and began extending fingers, one by one, in cadence with his itemization: "I have one rifle. One revolver. One hundred rounds for each of them. One spare shortwave radio. One collapsible galtcart." He held up the other fist. "One month's rations of food. One doctor's bag, suitably equipped. One—"

The pilot cut him off. "Spare me the merit badge review. Just let me have the revolver."

"Not the rifle?"

"No, thanks. I'm only interested in defending myself, not the entire neighborhood. Besides, whatever happened to those men must have happened a long time ago."

"True." He gestured out the windshield. "None of the embers are still smoking." He rose and stepped to the rear wall of the cabin and opened a small panel. From inside he pulled out a greenish-blue revolver, then reached in with his other hand and produced a box of ammunition. "All yours," he offered, holding out the armament. "A nickel for the gun rental, and one cent for each bullet you fire."

The pilot did not reach for the proffered items. "You bastard," he said levelly, without emotion. He knew for a fact that ammunition in the valley cost a tenth that price.

Dwight withdrew the weaponry a few inches; but without another word, the pilot snatched the revolver and ammunition out of Dwight's hands and began loading the handgun's chambers, one by one.

Dwight laughed irritatingly. "I'll wait here and hold the fort, if you don't mind—and to be perfectly honest, I'm not overly interested in what might have happened to a bunch of scabs."

The pilot continued his task without looking up. *Double bastard!* Upon finishing, again without a word, he opened the rear hatch and stepped outside, revolver in hand, hammer cocked, finger on the trigger.

"Knock twice, wait, then knock three times," Dwight called to his departing back, "so I know that it's you."

The pilot was not surprised to hear the hatch slam tightly shut behind him. He had to admit it was a prudent precaution. Mere lead bullets were impotent against Miracle Metal; Dwight would be completely safe behind the greenish-blue hull.

Looking around, the pilot saw no one about, and no structure left intact. What was obviously once a bustling village had been reduced to ruins. Cautiously he moved down one dirt street after another, but the scene did not change. Poking around amid the fire-scarred rubble he found no surviving man-made items—nor any bodies. The destruction was complete; it also looked purposeful, as if someone had deliberately chosen to burn the village to the ground, house by house, then pick over the remains, removing anything salvageable.

"Hello?" he called dubiously; there was no answer. "I wonder where the hell everybody went?" he mused aloud to himself. "HELLO!" he bellowed to the world at large in his deep, stentorian voice. He heard a faint echo bounce back from the nearer mountains, but nothing more. He waited a moment longer listening for a reply. When none came, he shrugged, uncocked the revolver's hammer, and trotted back to the waiting hypercraft. Rhythmically he knocked on the hatch with the butt of the weapon. After a moment, he could hear Dwight manipulating the latch mechanism and the hatch swung open.

"Nobody home," the pilot reported as he shouldered past Dwight and buckled himself in.

"Looks like no radio for them!" joked Dwight as he sealed the hatch. He took the revolver from the pilot, unloaded it, and returned it to its niche.

The pilot ignored the remark. "I wonder what happened here?"

"Can't say I care," he asserted carelessly as he reclaimed his own seat. He had already put the ruined village out of his mind. He reached out to engage the hypercraft's turbines, but halted halfway through the motion. Turning to the pilot, he suggested, "No, wait: it's your turn. I've already explained how this baby flies, and you've seen me take off a couple of times. It's not that tough to pilot." He sat back and deliberately folded his hands in his lap. "Your airplane, Captain!"

Surprised, but not wanting to show it, the pilot replied calmly, "I have the airplane, sir," thereby finishing the airman's formal protocol for transferring control of an aircraft. "But let me do the triangulation before I take off. Wouldn't want to divide my attention."

"Suit yourself."

The pilot busied himself with calculations, and moments later reached for the chart. Expertly using a straightedge, he carefully drew three lines across the map; they intersected in west-central California. "And there she is," he announced. He handed the chart to Dwight and reached out to start the turbines. "Play navigator for me, would you?"

Dwight smiled mockingly. "I thought this was supposed to be your show, Captain."

"Then just do me the favor this one time," he called out sarcastically over the increasing whine of the turbines spooling up to speed. "Or is that considered a sin for you Johnnies?"

Refusing to be baited, Dwight capitulated with sarcastic grace. "Yes sir, Captain! Whatever you say, sir! But it'll cost you another nickel."

The pilot ignored him. Abruptly, with rude, natural competence, he smoothly launched the hypercraft into the air and immediately banked into a supersonic turn to the northwest, the growing G-force pulling both men downward and to one side. The pilot's pulse quickened; he was excited. *This ship is a dream!* he told himself needlessly. *And SO easy to fly!* His face was pulled into a slight grimace from their acceleration, slurring his words. "Mach seven, you say?"

"Yep." Dwight smiled. He knew how the pilot must feel. "And don't worry about overstressing her—the safeties will kick in before you can do any damage."

"We'll see about that..." The whine of the turbines grew along with the size of the pilot's smile as the craft barreled across the Mexican skies, swiftly reaching the hypercraft's top speed. "California, here I come!" he sang in his deep bass voice.

"Better be careful or you may miss it!" Dwight warned playfully, only half joking.

The pilot smiled, clasping the controls with both hands and holding his attention on the sky ahead. "I need to get me one of these babies," he mused absently. "Yes sir-ee!"

Dwight laughed aloud. "Trade you one for *The Caged Bird*?"

The pilot froze. Slowly, he turned his gaze to Dwight and held it there. "One does not joke about certain subjects," he warned darkly.

"Sorry. I forgot how you feel about taprooms."

"That's *not* what I meant!"

Dwight smiled annoyingly. "I must admit that I was aware of that."

"I should say 'yes' just to make you eat your words!"

"Go ahead."

He held eye contact. "You're serious."

"Yep."

The pilot did not reply immediately, even though the offer was far too good to turn down. It wasn't that he did not want to become the proud owner of a Dwight-Hank hypercraft; what gave him pause was that he couldn't just abandon his lady, his old aircraft he had just redeemed. He *couldn't!* It would be like Dagny jilting her husband for... for... He couldn't imagine who, but the idea was the same. Regardless; the temptation was undeniable and irrefutable.

By his simple act of trying on the thought of owning it, the hypercraft suddenly took on a surreal reality for him. He became acutely aware of his hands and how each finger clutched the controls, of his feet on the rudder pedals. He could feel the cushioned seat pressing up against him with the immutable force of gravity behind it, gently transmitting the subliminal whine of the turbines into his very soul. He heard the muted rush of the air around them as they careened at thousands of miles an hour through the atmosphere, the Earth beneath them spinning through outer space at a mere fraction of their immense velocity. He smelled the dry, conditioned air blowing coolly gentle against his cheek as the sun glinted a bright greenish-blue spark off the metal trim around the thick windshield. He sensed all these things and more as undercurrents to his love of flying, of himself, and of life itself—no, more than life itself! It was the meaning of life, of its underlying values that defined everything as right or wrong, and it was undeniably right that he could do nothing else but accept Dwight's offer on the spot, regardless of the price, because possessing so fine a craft would be priceless itself—no, not priceless, but beyond any possible price. The question of whether or not he would make the trade was a rhetorical one, irrespective of price, for the answer was obvious.

Still holding Dwight's eyes, his hands resting lightly on the controls, offhandedly the pilot deadpanned, "Since you mention it, I might consider trading a half interest in *The Caged Bird* for the hypercraft. Depends on what else you'd be willing to throw into the bargain."

Dwight burst out laughing. "Half interest?! You cad!"

Poker-faced, the pilot said nothing. He pointedly returned his attention to his flying.

"You're not serious!" he exclaimed.

The pilot glanced briefly in his direction. "Yep."

"No! There's been no airplane like this in the history of Man! It's a marvel of science and engineering!"

"And yet you offer no warranty?" he asked innocently. "Have you no faith in your own product?"

Dwight huffed, looking away. "Of course I do." He paused, then glanced back at the pilot. "A year."

"Three."

"Two."

The pilot allowed the silence to drag out for several seconds. "And no landing fees."

"Oh! Are those three-cent landings really going to break you?"

"Should I be asking you the same question?"

Looking away, Dwight scowled and folded his arms. Presently he nodded curtly without facing his questioner. "All right. Half interest, two years' warranty, and no landing fees." He finally turned to the pilot and wagged an angry finger at him. "But that's it!"

Nonchalantly the pilot threw him another brief glance. "Done," he rumbled. "When can I take delivery?"

"Ah... Let me check my production schedule with Hank before I get back to you with a firm date. I'd guess I could deliver in about three, maybe four months."

"I can't wait too long, you know. Or else the price will start going down."

"Oh, it won't be that long. It took about three months to build this one, so it shouldn't take me quite that long to build another."

"I assume I get to use this one in the meantime." It was a statement, not a question.

Dwight started, then stared at the pilot wide-eyed. "Do you always drive this hard a bargain?"

The pilot smiled derisively, a caustic edge to his mirth. "It's something I learned in your valley, I must admit," he lied.

"I bet. No deal. But I'll agree to rent it to you, same terms as today."

"You're too kind—and I'm not going to say what kind."

"You'll be the kind of person who flies to Japan if you don't pay attention to where we're headed," he warned. "You'd better turn the controls back over to me for the landing. We're almost there."

"As you wish." He released his grip. "Your airplane, Dwight."

"I have the airplane," he agreed.

With practiced precision, Dwight banked the hypercraft over the triangulation point. Surprisingly, there was an airstrip there; it appeared the source of the broadcast was the control tower or perhaps one of the hangars that flanked it. Bringing the craft around one more time, he landed and taxied to a quick halt alongside the tower.

"Make it short," Dwight suggested worriedly. "Remember where we are."

"That's for sure!" The pilot unstrapped himself and opened the craft's smaller belly hatch rather than the man-sized one behind the wing, thinking it prudent to present a smaller target. As he set the radio down on the runway, he looked around and saw an elderly woman standing open-mouthed in front of the control tower. Friendly-like, he waved and flashed her a smile before disappearing back inside. He slammed the hatch and scrambled into his seat. "Let's get the hell out of here before they try to convert us!"

"Fat chance for that," Dwight mumbled to himself as they bolted back into the sky.

Moments later they were hurtling eastward, the tan desert streaking miles beneath them and the granite, snow-capped mountains quickly approaching ahead. "Time to set course for home!" exclaimed Dwight. He pointed excitedly at the craft's chronometer. "Around the continent in two hours." His justified pride in his ship burst to the surface. "What an airplane!"

The pilot stretched noisily, arms extended high in the air, paying Dwight no mind. "Now it remains to be seen if Owen and I can eke any business out of this crumbled country."

## SECTION II – THE FINAL WEEKS

# Chapter 1 – A Horse With No Name

The ground dropped.

From his vantage point high in the mountain pass, Ma's banished lieutenant straddled his bicycle and stared down across the vast expanse of Death Valley. It was with great apprehension that he faced the next phase of his journey.

In the year since he was forced to abandon his home in the hollow, he had cautiously and methodically worked his way south and east through the Sierras, his zigzagging course carefully chosen to avoid the twin threats of the acolytes of Back For God to the west, and the scorching heat of the desert to the east.

That year spent on the run had been uninteresting and unexciting—fortunately. After the acolytes had laid waste to his camp, he became a wanderer among the mountain passes, never remaining longer than a month in any single location lest the unavoidable scars he left upon the land once again betray him. During the harsh winter months he traveled along the eastern foothills closer to Death Valley, not only for the milder clime, but more so to reduce the odds of stumbling upon another human being. He emerged victorious on both counts, for not only did he manage to avoid the deep snows and frigid temperatures he encountered the prior winter, he also discovered no trace of another living man. The blessings allowed him to spend significantly less time on those tasks necessary for his very survival, and more time preparing for the upcoming desert crossing.

Now he stood among the last sequoia groves before they gave way to the arid eastern slopes of the southern Sierra Nevada mountains. The breeze was pleasant enough at this high altitude, but in a few short hours his bicycle would bring him down into that vast, scorching desert. He was only waiting for the merciless sun to set before beginning; from here on, he planned to travel always at night.

He considered checking his provisions and maps one more time, but decided it was not necessary. He had calculated his travel time, food supplies, water requirements, and other parameters over and over again so many times that he could recite them in his sleep. Besides, there was no way he would be able to carry any more weight if he wanted to. He was loaded with as much gear and provisions as he and his bicycle could possibly carry, and in four days he would either reach Las Vegas, or surely die in the attempt.

He had chosen his destination out of desperation. From his own experience, he knew that all of the coastal cities had perished in the fighting well over a year ago, and he had heard first-hand accounts that the inland Californian cities had all died a similar death; so there was no salvation in fleeing to any of them. His experiences also told him that remaining anywhere in God's California was definitely out of the question, especially with the brand of the heretic permanently emblazoned across his forehead. That eliminated most all of his possible destinations, save one: he could not recall anyone ever speaking of the fate of Las Vegas, so by process of elimination, it became his only choice; and the more he thought about it, the more certain he became that the town had to have survived. He reasoned that its remote location must have spared it from the fighting; he couldn't say for sure, but for good or for bad he was determined to find out.

Before long, the shadow of the Sierras was stretching far across Death Valley; it was time for him to go. He needlessly checked the hemp bindings holding his provisions on the bicycle one last time, and with a final glance at the setting sun over his shoulder, he started the long downhill glide to meet his fate.

* * *

Ma's lieutenant grinned.

He was sunburned, dehydrated, banged up, and just plain tired after his five-day, two-wheeled marathon across Death Valley. But none of that could hold any sway over his attitude; for as he crested the final ridge before reaching Las Vegas, he saw what he had hoped beyond hope that he would see: widespread signs of life. The town lay stretched out in the valley before him, thin lines of smoke rising from scattered, tiny smokestacks to merge into a smeared haze impossibly high in the clear afternoon sky. He could make out microscopic dots as they moved sluggishly along threadlike strings of highways that laced the desert floor—even a miniature train rolling down the tracks from the distant north. Ma's lieutenant had gambled and won. Las Vegas lived!

With a will, he leaned his weight into the pedals of his bicycle, ignoring the ubiquitous pains crackling from his sunburned skin and tortured muscles, flying at dangerous speeds as he descended the treacherous, twisting, unpaved mountain back road. He was already more than a day behind schedule, and he should have been hiding from the burning afternoon sun at this hour. But with his destination in sight, he threw caution to the wind; besides, he wasn't certain he could survive another day in the desert; his water was almost gone.

As he approached the town, he began to encounter humanity. Some were on horseback, others in horse-drawn carriages and wagons, most on foot, even a few riding small, motorized contraptions of varying design, but no automobiles, trucks, or buses. The neighborhood he cycled through was pleasant and spacious. Occasional passers-by waved to him in friendly fashion or nodded in his direction, while others unconsciously ignored him, more intent on their own personal business than one sunburned bicycle rider. The easygoing atmosphere was markedly different from the religious busybodies in God's California where everyone eyed everyone else with holy suspicion. He smiled at the tremendous philosophical differences between the two cultures. *Things are going to be all right*, he declared to himself.

Buoyed by the non-hostile non-reception, the lieutenant decided to push his luck and make contact; it would be the first person he'd spoken to in almost two years. Ahead, he saw a tall middle-aged woman with long, luxurious grey hair walking along the sidewalk carrying a brown sack, groceries bulging from its top. He slowed, then pulled up alongside her, one foot extended to prop himself up alongside the curb.

"Pardon me, ma'am. I just got into town. Know anyplace a man might find a room?"

She eyed him with wonder rather than suspicion, noting his beet red complexion and obvious lack of recent bathing. "Apparently you have. Welcome to Las Vegas! You must be the first person I've seen coming into town since the refugees. Getting to your question, no I don't. There's no hotel or any such thing around these parts. As I say, we don't see many folks coming into town these days, so why have a hotel? But if you're looking for someplace to stay that's a little more permanent, I'd suggest you do what everybody else has done: find yourself a nice empty place in a nice neighborhood, move in, and make yourself at home. Who is Eddie Willers?" She smiled at him. "But there aren't that many homes still empty, though." After a brief pause, she added wryly, "At least not in the neighborhoods worth living in!" She paused for another moment, then suggested, "You know, speaking of Eddie, maybe you should talk to him first. He's usually at the Transcontinental station. He'd know the best places left available, or if anybody's taking on boarders. And anyway, he's always a good person to ask whenever you need anything."

Something about the man's name tickled at the edge of his awareness, but he let it pass. "All right, I will. Which way to the station?"

She pondered a bit before answering, "Now that, I don't rightly know. Out that way, somewhere." She waved a hand offhandedly, then pointed. "Take this road as far as the big power lines, then stop and ask someone else. It's somewhere the other side of them, to the right, I think. Sorry I can't be more help; I've never been there myself where someone else wasn't leading, and I haven't been there in a long time. Not that many people travel by train these days. Besides the kids, that is."

He thanked her kindly and pedaled off in the indicated direction, not wanting to waste any more time; the sun remained high in the sky, and he had had more than enough exposure to its blistering rays to last a lifetime. Soon he reached the power line, passed under it, and continued pedaling deeper into town. Presently he overtook another pedestrian.

"Morning. Can you direct me to the train station?"

"Morning," echoed the pedestrian. "Off to see Eddie, are you? Just keep heading the way you're heading, turn right at the church, cross over the tracks, then follow them to the right. You'll get there. Big building with granite pillars. Can't miss it."

"Thanks."

"My best to Eddie."

"Right."

The lieutenant resumed his journey, and soon came to the expected railroad crossing. Between his pain and fatigue, colored by so many months living alone in the wild, he foolishly paid no heed to the rhythmic off-key clanking of a nearby bell. But as his bicycle tires rumbled across the rails, his heart stopped cold. Blaring in his left ear was the incredible, deep blast of an immense air horn. Flustered beyond belief, he lost his balance; the bicycle wobbled off the paved roadway where he crashed into the pebbly sand alongside the track in a painful, sunburned heap. He rolled over and looked up as a deafening metal behemoth bore down on him like a giant dragon snagging its prey. Wide-eyed and ignoring his pain, he vainly scrambled across the rough ground in a futile attempt to escape from the beast that swept down upon him, but his foot was inextricably tangled up between the spokes of his bicycle and the chain, mercilessly holding him in place—fortunately alongside the track rather than astride it. Scant feet in front of his face the Diesel rumbled past, its raucous roar washing over his consciousness like a huge tidal wave, paralyzing him with fear. The Diesel's thunder dropped off quickly, only to be replaced by the incongruous laughter of children. Over a dozen of them hung out the windows of the day coach, waving and laughing at him and his plight. In a few seconds the train was past, slowly shrinking into the distance, small arms dangling from both sides. But his heart still kept up a beat so loud that he could hear the blood rushing in his ears, drowning out every third word of the concerned passers-by who came to his assistance. With their help, he extricated himself from his machinery, dusted himself off painfully, and resumed the final leg of his journey.

He was in the city proper now, with block after block of homes, stores, and other buildings lining streets that were busy with horse and foot traffic, plus more of those self-propelled carts of improbable design. The turbulent afternoon streetscape was a medley of contradictory impressions. Although the streets bustled with activity, a number of the premises which lined them were vacant. Above the intersections, all the traffic signals stood dark, as if the town were experiencing a widespread power failure, but at the same time neon signs glowed gaily from the windows of the occasional taproom and other stores. Since little of the traffic was motorized, the lack of traffic lights was understandable, although disquieting. Despite the plentiful traffic, it was sparse enough that he progressed through town quickly, and not once did he have to come to a complete halt to avoid cross traffic.

There was no mistaking it when he arrived: the Las Vegas station of Transcontinental Railroad. The huge, columned granite edifice remained a monument to the days when railroads were the kings of the West, bringing settlers, trade, and the rule of law to a wild country. But he remembered with much trepidation the wild country and lack of law he encountered the last time he visited a train station, in San Francisco, and how he and Ma were driven from the place amid a hail of gunfire and flames. His bicycle slowed in reaction to the troubling memory, and he was forced to halt less than a block away from the station, his heart racing once again. *What's the matter with me?* He scowled at himself for his childish reaction. *It's just a train station*, he tried to reassure himself, but with limited success. It had been over two years since he fled San Francisco, and until today he hadn't seen a train; no surprise, his close brush with the Diesel coupled with his past experiences conspired to turn his knees to water. Slowly he wheeled up to a hitching rail in front of the impressive building and dismounted clumsily, nervously letting his bicycle drop noisily to the ground. He cursed as it scraped against the raw skin of his leg, and he rubbed it gently as he hobbled up the few steps to the station's entrance, pulled the unlocked door open, and walked in.

The interior of the station was as impressive as its façade: a huge vaulted ceiling soared high over his head, encompassing a bright, cavernous marble waiting room. The air possessed a natural coolness that emanated from the heavy stones of its construction, relieving some of the omnipresent pain from his scraped, sun-parched skin. Abandoned ticket booths lined the far wall, with numbered passageways on either side that led, presumably, to the train platforms. Rows of facing benches took up much of the floor, with wide aisles separating them from each other. On the left side of the waiting room was a double glass door leading into the station's cafeteria, a large electric clock centered over the entrance; on his right were tall, expansive windows that took up the entire wall. The giant room was brilliant with the diffuse afternoon light, and completely uninhabited.

"Hello?" he called, his voice echoing hollowly in the vast chamber. "Hello?" he called again. There was no answer. He walked over to the cafeteria, his footsteps reverberating quietly off the walls until they abruptly muted with the change of acoustics as he passed through the double doors. Although the cafeteria, too, was uninhabited, it did possess a very distinct, yet prosaic sign of life: an extensive vegetable garden arrayed against the tall windows occupied almost half the cafeteria's floor space.

"Hello?" Still no answer. He exited the cafeteria and headed down the first passageway to the track platforms. An arrowed sign posted along the left wall proclaimed in large letters, "To The Trains." He had hardly entered the tunnel's mouth when ahead of him he heard a cacophony of shrieks and screams quickly bearing down upon him. Panic-stricken, he flattened against the wall barely in time to dodge the tide of overexcited children spilling out of the tunnel. Close in their wake were a pack of pursuing women, presumably their parents. None of them paid him any mind beyond an occasional smile or nod. Within the minute, they had passed, leaving him alone at the tunnel's entrance. Again with some trepidation, he progressed down the gently sloping passageway toward its far end.

As he emerged from the tunnel and onto the platform, his breath was stolen away as he was once again stunned into open-mouthed immobility; for there, towering over his head, was the Transcontinental *Meteor* in all its glory: headlamp blazing brightly ahead, its Diesel engine loudly idling, and its compressors hissing intermittently amid a medley of all the assorted noises that modern trains are apt to make. Wide-eyed, he staggered back a few half steps from an almost religious intimidation of the belching behemoth looming above him. A movement behind the Diesel's windshield caught his eye—there was someone aboard.

"*TOOT! TOOT!*" blasted the horn, impossibly loud at such close range, but accompanied by a friendly wave from behind the glass. The hatch on the side of the Diesel swung open, and a middle-aged man in coveralls descended the ladder to the platform. Wiping his hands on a rag, the man walked briskly toward the filthy red man, then extended his hand. "You look like a newcomer. Welcome to Las Vegas. I'm Eddie."

"Hey, I know you!" the lieutenant blurted, realizing why the name had seemed familiar to him. "I was with Ma at your station back in 'Frisco. We negotiated a treaty... with you..." His excitement dulled quickly as he spoke the last words; he shook his head at the memory and smiled ruefully. "Just before the whole damned city burned to the ground." He barked a short, mirthless laugh, then shook his head again.

On hearing the news, Eddie's shoulder's drooped and his eyes fell. "Then it did burn." He sighed. "Rumor had it, but we weren't really sure. No one that anyone had spoken with had seen it for themselves."

"Well, I was there. I saw it. God, but I saw it! It's burnt, burnt to a cold cinder and abandoned. So are all the cities out West. All burnt, every one. All gone. The only settlements left are some tiny villages surrounded by acres and acres and acres of God's farms. I've seen those, too. Pretty places, if you like that sort of thing—and can stand kowtowing to the acolytes all the time."

Eddie eyed the newcomer carefully, searching his memory for a recollection of the man. He found it, then recoiled in horror from the contrast between his memory and the rugged, hard-boiled reality standing in front of him. "I do remember you," admitted Eddie, backing up a half a step. "You were the cynic."

Ma's lieutenant laughed a dry chuckle. "Right. That's me: the cynic. My epithet!" He chuckled again and shook his head. "Still am, too. That's what earned me this!" He pulled off his headband, revealing the flame-shaped scar emblazoned on his forehead.

Eddie winced. "We'd heard about that. Yours is the first one I've actually seen, though."

"There are no other heretics here?"

"No. In fact, you're the first Californian who's come into town in almost a year."

The lieutenant grinned theatrically as he replaced the bandana. "Maybe nobody's coming because you're not running trains out of town anymore?"

Missing the humor in his voice, Eddie turned to admire the idling Diesel behind him, then turned back to face the lieutenant. "Sure they're running—" He turned again to face the throbbing Diesel, reciting a familiar formula more to himself than to the lieutenant. "—from ocean to ocean forever." He let several seconds pass in silence before he returned his attention to the lieutenant. "Sorry. I was woolgathering." He cleared his throat. "What can I do for you?"

"I was looking for a place to stay."

"You're in luck. There are still a number of nice homes in town left vacant. You can pick any one that suits your liking and move in. Later on I'll get out a map and show you where the best ones are, but right now you should get someone to take a look at that sunburn. There's a hospital not too far away; let me walk you over. Are you hungry? There's a nice diner across the street where we could catch an early dinner and talk. Society's treat."

"Some water would be great before we head out." The lieutenant looked ruefully at the blistering skin on the backs of his hands. "But let's see what the hospital can do before we talk about food."

"The water fountains in the station work. Help yourself."

The lieutenant's eyebrows went up at Eddie's last words as he realized his pauper status. "But... How will I pay for the hospital visit?"

"I'd guess the medical care should only cost a couple of willies, and dinner about the same." He colored faintly. "Not too much. It doesn't matter, though—Society will pay for it."

"Willies? Society?"

Eddie hesitated, inexplicably blushing a deeper red. "We'll talk about it later, you and I."

\* \* \*

Eddie listened.

He barely touched the meal that sat in front of him. Instead he listened intently as Ma's lieutenant related the horrifying saga of the battle for California. His fresh, copious hospital bandages oozed ointment from their wraps, but that did not restrain either his capacity to deliver the story with sweeping gestures, or the dark mood revealed in its reporting. He spoke of unimaginably-huge fires engulfing entire cities, about the massive swarms of refugees, the desperate fighting, the famines, the roving gangs of thugs, and an unbelievable, inconceivable number of deaths.

It was heartbreaking for Eddie to listen to the gruesome details surrounding the ultimate fate of Transcontinental's San Francisco terminal, not merely for the blow it had dealt to his life's work, but more so for the human tragedy it entailed. He again found it miraculous that Las Vegas had been spared the horrors that had befallen the rest of the nation. Against such a chaotic backdrop, Eddie could well understand how a religious dictatorship such as Back For God could rise to power. Between the promise of peace in this world and peace in the all-too-near afterlife, it came as no surprise their business would boom.

"And electricity is forbidden, you say?" Eddie asked.

"An instrument of Babylon!" exclaimed the lieutenant, the mockery plain in his voice. "But I think that fable was invented as a convenience for the Bishop. It would have taken an awful lot of work to generate the electricity in the first place, let alone the effort of re-electrifying all those farms. I was a radio technician in the Army, so I know. Hell, some of those farms were never electrified in the first place. The Bishop is no fool. Best to focus efforts where they give the best return." He rubbed the bandana on his forehead reflectively, unconsciously.

Not for the first time, Eddie changed the subject; only this time he changed it reluctantly, fearing a familiar response. "Do you have any news of what happened to New York City?" It was a question he asked every newcomer; he had never received a proper answer.

"Without electricity? How would we get it?" demanded the lieutenant, tossing his bandaged hands in the air. "By carrier pigeon?" He paused thoughtfully. "So you don't know what happened to New York either?"

Eddie did not answer right away, and when he did, he spoke in a choked voice, as if speaking around a long-held, deep-felt emotion. "No. The last news we received was that an explosion at the X Project in Iowa destroyed Transcontinental Bridge over the Mississippi. That was the same night that all the television and radio stations went off the air."

"Off the air? What happened to them?"

He inhaled deeply and let out a shaking breath. "No one knows."

"Haven't you asked?"

Eddie looked at him blankly. "Asked? Asked whom?"

"The radio! Haven't you tried using the shortwave?" His hands were in the air again.

"Oh! Yes, we tried. There are a lot of shortwave radios up at the Army base north of town—at least that's what we think they are—but we could never get any of them to work. Nobody in town really understands radio, and with all the nation's commercial stations dead, we figured the problem wasn't with the radio, but rather with the nation."

"Nonsense! I know there have to still be shortwave stations broadcasting somewhere on the planet. There used to be thousands! Some must have survived. Like I said, I was a radio tech back when I was in the Army. I'm sure I'd be able to figure out how to get something hooked up, even though it's been ten years since I last touched a shortwave. And maybe we can find out what's what with New York." A thought occurred to him; he smiled his sarcastic half grin and added sardonically, "At least I won't face banishment for using sinful electricity!"

Eddie did not react. "Which road did you come into town on?" he asked abruptly, again changing the subject.

"Road?" He laughed dryly. "I'm not sure you could rightfully call that dirt track a road. I crossed Death Valley at Stovepipe Wells, then dropped down through the Pahrump Valley—passed by a real fine rifle range there, too. Better than anything we ever had in the Army, that's for sure! Deserted, though. Why do you ask?"

Eddie hesitated before answering; he was embarrassed to say. "We maintain sentry posts a couple of miles outside of town on all the roads—the paved ones, that is. I was wondering why none of the sentries reported your approach." His face reddened slightly. "Now I know."

"Sounds like you have some holes in your defenses to patch up, friend—and before someone else decides to follow me."

Eddie sat bolt upright in his seat, eyes wide. "You were followed? By Back For God?" The thought terrified him. He had heard more than enough California stories over the years to frighten even the most stout-hearted man; and this newcomer had just given him a fresh set of fears.

311

"No..." The lieutenant dropped his gaze uncomfortably, hesitating in turn before finally answering, "At least I don't think anyone followed me. The acolytes certainly knew that heretics were living in the high Sierras, but I'd wager they never laid eyes on me." He chuckled his dry laugh again. "In fact, I'm certain. If they had, I'd be a dead man."

"Then you're sure you weren't followed?"

"It would be pretty difficult for any pursuers to hide in that desert. I'd have seen them for sure. And they would have certainly seen me. And caught up with me. And killed me—if I was lucky, that is."

Eddie shuddered. He could not escape the truth that it was only a matter of time before Back For God discovered Las Vegas. If the lieutenant was able to correctly surmise from the available evidence that the town might not be dead—as many others had before him!—then the acolytes should be able to make the same mental leap. But he couldn't imagine what he or Las Vegas would be able to do about it, except redouble their vigilance—and fret.

*  *  *

The radio hissed.

Eddie watched intently as the lieutenant adjusted various knobs on the shortwave radio, seemingly at random. "Is it working?" he asked anxiously, uncharacteristically impatient, hoping yet dreading that he would finally learn what fate befell New York City. He had already waited more than a week while the man had led an expedition up to the abandoned Army base to retrieve the shortwave radio and its supporting gear, then waited longer still while it was wired up to the tall radio tower still standing guard on the western edge of the rail yard. Now that the moment of truth was upon him, Eddie's trepidation skyrocketed.

Several seconds passed without a word as the lieutenant delicately adjusted two knobs simultaneously. He studied a meter as its thin, black needle slowly drifted toward the green-marked zone, his head tilted back and eyes cast downward as if he were accustomed to peering through reading glasses. "It is working," he agreed as the needle crossed the crucial line. He pushed his chair back from the mail car's table where the radio sat, spun around to face Eddie, and announced triumphantly, "We are on the air!" He waved a disdainful hand at Eddie's makeshift radio station. "And we can reach a hell of a lot further than any puny commercial station."

"Puny? That's fifty thousand watts!" he cried defensively. "Clear channel!"

"Yes, yes; the flagship station of Transcontinental Railroad," he mocked. "But it doesn't hold a candle to this baby!" He reached out and patted the hissing shortwave affectionately.

"Can you find a station?"

He spun back to face the radio. "Let's see..." He began manipulating the frequency selector; for a moment all that could be heard was meaningless static when suddenly a man's authoritative voice burst out. Both men jumped, startled. Such was their discomfiture that a moment passed before either of them realized the language was not their own. The lieutenant smiled sheepishly and shrugged, lowered the volume, and resumed his manipulations. Another voice jumped from the radio speaker; this time it was a woman's tearful voice, the words understandable. Her voice sounded as if it were falling in drops, not of water, but of mayonnaise. They caught her sobbing in mid-sentence.

"—sible for their sins. They must repent. Atone. Beg for God's mercy. And until they do—"

"Hey!" cried the lieutenant, pointing. "I know that voice!" He spun in his chair toward Eddie, his eyes wide. "And so do you! That's Ma, for sure!"

"Your what?" he asked, perplexed.

"No, no! Ma, as in Emma! Remember? I told you about how you brokered a treaty with us back in San Francisco. She was there with us!"

Eddie blinked once, then again, trying to place the woman. He turned to face the lieutenant. "Elderly woman? Grey hair?"

"And cries a lot!" he added, pointing again to the speaker for substantiation. "I'd recognize that sob story anywhere. She and I go back a lo-o-o-o-o-ong way." At his gesture, both men stopped to listen.

"—has been the daily broadcast brought to you by the faithful souls of Back For God here in the hills of God's California. Until tomorrow, may God keep you lovingly in His protective hands. Over and out."

"Yep. That's Ma!" repeated the lieutenant as he swiveled toward his equipment. Without preamble, he picked up the microphone, flipped a toggle switch, and began to speak. "Emma!" he intoned with a mockingly authoritative voice. "'What makes a person so poisonously righteous that they'd think less of anyone who just disagreed?'" He turned to Eddie and grinned mischievously, then whispered in a sotto aside, "That was one of her favorite quotations!"

He spoke into the microphone again. "Yes, Ma. It is I, returned from banishment to haunt you!" Turning back to Eddie, his eyes twinkled with mirth. It was all he could do to keep from bursting out laughing. Still watching Eddie, he spoke into the microphone. "Repent, Ma. Atone. Beg for—" He could contain himself no longer; the guffaws burst out as if they would never cease. Once, then again, he theatrically banged a fist gently on the desk, pleased with himself and the joke. He may have gone on laughing forever had not Ma interrupted.

"It can't be you!" announced the radio. "Over."

"Oh, yes it can!" His smile was evident in his voice. "Over."

"You survived?" The surprise was plain in hers. "Over."

"Of course," he replied, a haughty, hurt tone in his words. "And I didn't even have to repent!" he added playfully. "Over."

"But— Where are you? Over."

"Las Vegas," he replied casually. "The town's full of people! I just got here last week and—"

The sound of the radio equipment crashing to the floor was earsplitting within the confines of the mail car. Sparks shot from the smashed remnant of the shortwave radio lying on its side on the wooden floor as a thick column of acrid smoke surged to the ceiling. Standing over its wreckage, eyes aflame, was Eddie, his arms still extended in front of him, fingers intertwined, as if ready to sweep another radio off a table if need be. His breath came in shallow, short bursts. Slowly he lifted a wild gaze to the lieutenant. "Nobody knows we're here!" he whispered tensely, as if spies lurked everywhere and secrecy were paramount. "Nobody *knew* we were here!"

The import of Eddie's words penetrated quickly, and was immediately reflected in a look of panic on the face of the lieutenant. "She'd never turn me in!" he blurted. "Never!"

His words hung in the air for several seconds as the tableau held, the reek of ozone and burnt copper wires underscoring their portent.

Instantly Eddie regained his composure, as if someone had flipped a switch. He reached for the telephone. "Let's hope she was alone, then..." He dialed the militia commander. "...but I'm not counting on it."

* * *

The acolyte gaped.
Ma gaped back.
"Las Vegas lives!" he rasped.
Ma gaped still, only now for a different reason.
"The Bishop must hear of this immediately," proclaimed the acolyte as he darted for the door. "Well done, sister," he called over his shoulder. "You have flushed out the nest of sinners."
Agape, she began to cry.

## CHAPTER 2 – TAKING CARE OF BUSINESS

The first light winked on.
Owen sat at a corner table in the newly-renamed taproom with a sharpened pencil in his hand, a pad of blank paper on his right, and a greenish-blue cube sitting in front of him, one of its sixteen jeweled indicators glowing. He had been anticipating this moment ever since the pilot had departed with Dwight on their grand tour not an hour earlier. Assuming the pilot hadn't jumbled the sequence of his deliveries, the position of the light indicated that it would be the State's Science Institute on the line. He spun the selector switch to align its pointer with the illuminated light.
"Hello?" came a clear voice from inside the cube. "Hello?"
Owen pressed the button on top of the cube. "Hello," he agreed. "How may I help you?"
"Who is this?" the voice demanded angrily.
"My name is Owen, co-proprietor of the Virtuous Scab Import-Export Company of Colorado. And with whom do I have the pleasure of speaking?"
Several seconds elapsed before a response came. "This is Dr. Floyd at the State's Science Institute in New Hampshire. Who did you say you were?"
"Owen, co-proprietor of the Virtuous Scab Import-Export Company of Colorado." *And I'm the virtuous half of the company*, he noted silently.
The light winked out, and another long pause ensued; Dr. Floyd had obviously released the pressure on his stud. Owen had the impression that Dr. Floyd was discussing what he had heard with someone else in the room before replying.
Presently the light lit again. "What is it you import and export?"
"Whatever it is you need. How can I be of service?"
The light died. He waited out another long pause before it came back on. "Fruit? Do you export fruit?"
"Certainly. What kind would you like?"
This time there was no delay. "Anything! Anything with vitamin C in it! I am *so* tired of cedar bark!"
Owen chuckled, politely remembering to momentarily release the gentle pressure on the talk button so as not to offend his customer. "It would be my pleasure to serve you, doctor. How much would you like?"

314

The indicator light winked out, and another, longer pause ensued. Presently it came back on. "Can we get other types of food, too?"

"Of course. What would you like?"

Without pause, the words tumbled out of the greenish-blue cube, a long list of victuals ranging from vegetables to spices, meats to beverages, and everything in between, even wine. Owen's hand flew at top speed to transcribe the list. He smiled broadly; this was going to be one very profitable trip!

Finally, Dr. Floyd ran down. "And I'm sure there's a lot more we need, but that's at least a start."

"That's fine. And how would you like to pay for this, doctor?" he asked deferentially.

"*Pay* for it?" There was a brief pause. "Listen, Owen: we're in desperate need! The harvest last year was meager, and our food supplies are dangerously low. Hunting has been terrible, and people here are dying!"

After two seconds passed, Owen prompted, "Yes...? And...?"

"And what?" came the angry reply.

"People are dying, and..."

"And we need food!"

"I understand that. And we'll send it. My question was: how would you like to pay for it?"

Silence met his question. Several seconds later, the indicator light winked out. A full minute passed, then another. Smiling, Owen laughed to himself. *Looters!*

Finally, the light came back on. "What's the matter with you?" a different voice whined plaintively. "Why won't you help us?"

"I'd be happy to help you. That's why I'm here." He was baiting them, he knew; but he couldn't resist. The Worker's strike had been a whopping success, and now it was time to reap its rewards. The time had come for the world to dance to the tune of the men of the mind, not the other way around.

"Then how can you talk about payment? Aren't there higher considerations than money?"

"No."

The light went instantly dark. Chuckling, Owen shook his head. He was enjoying this. After thousands of years, the shoe was finally on the other foot.

The light came back on. Seconds passed, but no words were forthcoming. He waited patiently; he suspected what was coming next. Finally, reluctantly, it came. The voice was Dr. Floyd's again.

"What would you want for payment? We don't use money, and I'm not sure how much cash might still be lying around."

*Hallelujah!* he screamed triumphantly in his mind. *We've won!* Setting his jubilation aside, Owen gave the answer he and the pilot had prepared. "I'm sure the Institute has a good number of precision instruments in its inventory. There are many things you could use in barter, such as centrifuges, micrometers, spectrometers, vacuum tubes, that sort of thing. You still have them?"

"Oh, yes!" he replied excitedly. "We have all sorts of equipment we no longer need or use."

"Excellent! If I may, could I ask you to please put together a list of equipment you'd be willing to part with, and then we can settle on a price."

"Yes! Yes! We'd be happy to!"

"Good! We can talk again tomorrow right around this time and come to an agreement."

"That's fine." Dr. Floyd paused expectantly. "But how soon can you deliver the food?"

He was ready for that question as well. "You'll have to give us a day to get everything together, then we can fly it out there the next day, let's say around noon. We may be able pick up the equipment on the same trip, maybe not. Our pilot will probably be heading down to Washington after he leaves the Institute, and depending on what they order, it could be that he'll have to stop by on his way back to pick up payment from you."

"That's fine, so long as we get the food as soon as possible."

"You will. That raises the question: how close is the nearest airfield?"

The light went dark; he expected it to. Soon, it came back on. "Uh... That's going to be a problem. Those bastards in Washington destroyed our airstrip!"

Owen nodded. He knew that, and was ready with an alternative. "Is there a decent highway nearby that runs in a straight line for a half a mile or so?"

"I'm sure there is. Maybe the river road will do? I'll have to check and get back to you. And if it won't..." He heard what sounded like a sinister chuckle. "...we'll see what we can do about patching up the airstrip."

Owen wasn't sure what the chuckle might have meant. "All right. You can let me know the landing spot tomorrow when you get back to me with your inventory list."

"I will," Dr. Floyd promised. After a pause, a thought occurred to him. "Let me ask you a question, Owen. Why is it you waited until now to contact us? We've been short on food for months!"

"My apologies for not contacting you sooner, doctor, but it was just a few weeks ago that the Worker announced that our strike was over and that we're returning to the world Outside. You're literally the first person Outside to find out about our return."

"The Worker? In Colorado? He's there with you?"

"That's right. This is the Worker's home."

"And he's alive?"

"Very much so, doctor."

"And you're one of his strikers?"

"Not any more, doctor. As I said, our strike is over, which is why the Virtuous Scab Import-Export Company has contacted you."

"I see," he said. The light remained illuminated, but Dr. Floyd had ceased speaking.

Courteously, Owen spoke up. "Will that be all for now, then?"

After a pause, the reply came, "For now."

"Thank you for your order, Dr. Floyd. I'll speak with you again tomorrow, and I expect we'll have our man out there around noon the day after."

"Yes! Thank you!"

The light went dark. Owen held up his notepad to examine the order and smiled. Food was cheap in the Gulch; precision scientific equipment was not. *Most profitable indeed!* He set the pad down, folded his hands, and waited patiently for the next customer to call.

It took almost an hour longer than he had expected before the call came in. According to the indicator light, this would be Washington calling. As a long-time employee of Transcontinental Railroad, Owen immediately recognized the voice of his former employer at the other end. It was Mr. James, erstwhile president of the now-defunct railroad.

"Hello? Hello?", the cube inquired. "Is this the Worker?"

"No, Mr. James. The Worker is not available at the moment. This is Owen of the Virtuous Scab Import-Export Company of Colorado. I salute you for recognizing the origin of our communications device."

"Thank you, but the dollar signs made it pretty obvious. And not many people in today's world know how to fabricate devices out of—" Owen heard a gasp; Mr. James must have realized more of the obvious. "Is he there, too? Is Hank there?"

"Yes he is, although he is not currently available, either. I would guess he's working at his mills."

Mr. James chuckled. "And not the ones in Philadelphia, I assume."

"No, not in Philadelphia," he agreed with a smile. In passing, Owen marveled at the product of Roger's ingenuity that sat on the table in front of him. Washington was thousands of miles away, yet the signal was so clear and true to life that he could easily detect the nuances of tone of voice. With a start, he realized that he might be able to set up his own radio station; he could not only sell advertising, he could also sell radios! Roger's radios were of higher quality than any other radio he had ever heard before. He reluctantly forced the idea aside for later consideration and returned his attention to the matter at hand.

"The Worker's not available either, you say?" continued the voice emanating from the cube. "When might I get a chance to speak with him?"

Owen could easily discern the suppressed excitement in Mr. James' voice, and it took him aback. Like everyone else in the valley, he had heard how James had suddenly appointed himself the stepfather of the Constitution, adopting it as his own; and like most strikers, Owen harbored more than a little doubt as to the sincerity of that newfound paternity. But hearing the guileless tone in that one question dispelled all doubts. "I will inquire and get back to you, Mr. James. Shall we say the same time tomorrow?"

"Yes! Thank you! That would be fine." He paused, then spoke again. "Now what is it I can do for you, Mr. Owen? Why have you sent us this device?"

"As I said, I'm with the Virtuous Scab Import-Export Company. We've just opened for business, and I was wondering if you needed anything."

"Such as?"

"You name it, and I'll tell you if we have it. Food? Miracle Metal? Radios?"

"Food isn't a problem. There's an Amish community south of Annapolis that also survived, and we do a lot of trading with them. But there's surely a plethora of other things we can use."

A new voice broke in. "This is General Whittington. What can you do with our air force? We're desperately short on certain spare parts."

Owen laughed. "General, you will be amazed when you see what we could do with your airplanes!"

Another new voice interrupted. "How about gasoline for our jeeps?"

Yet another voice sternly ordered, "Shut up, soldier!"

Owen laughed aloud. "We have something much better than gasoline for your jeeps." He marveled how well the interview was progressing, much better than he had ever dared to hope. There were an incredible number of needs that the valley could fill, and he and the pilot stood to profit enormously. He glanced at the clock; another call would be coming in soon. "Mr. James, not meaning to cut you off, but I'm expecting another call in a few minutes. My partner will be flying out your way the day after tomorrow. Since your needs aren't dire, perhaps it would be best if I asked him to pay you a visit and you could discuss things with him at length, and in more detail?"

"Yes, that would be fine."

"Would it be in that strange-looking airplane?" the new voice burst in. "Nobody here believes me when I tell them about it!"

Owen laughed. "No it won't, but let me assure you that the hypercraft truly does exist."

"And it flies at Mach four?"

"It flies much faster than that."

He clearly heard the expletive damning the Worker, and the admonition that followed.

"I think that ought to do it for now, Mr. Owen," interrupted James. "I'll speak with you again tomorrow, and watch for your partner the day after tomorrow."

"Feel free to get in touch in the meantime if you have any questions."

"I shall. Over and out." The light winked off.

Owen rubbed his palms together gleefully. He glanced at the clock again; almost time for Yucatan! He waited happily in impatient anticipation as the minutes dragged by.

Too many minutes dragged by, and there was no word. In fact, it was almost an hour after Washington signed off that the next light finally illuminated—the wrong one. A light in the sequence had been skipped. Either the pilot had distributed the radios out of order, or more likely, Yucatan did not yet choose to respond. No matter; he turned the selector to the proper channel to listen. *California or Yucatan?* he wondered.

He caught the speaker, a tearful woman, in mid-sentence: "—cast you into the eternal flames of that place which has been created for your evil likes! May your flesh burn for all eternity in wretched anguish! May pestilence destroy your crops and vile diseases corrupt your blood! May the—" He rotated the switch to the "off" position. *California!* He smiled to himself. *No business coming from there!*

He rose from his seat while happily examining the laundry list of items needed by the State's Science Institute, absently picking up the greenish-blue cube as he headed for the door. He had an order to fill.

## CHAPTER 3 – GET READY

Dwight pondered.

The sun had long since set over the Gulch, and his stomach was reminding him just how late he was for dinner.

It had already been a long day for him. He had spent the bulk of it pouring over plans for constructing the new hypercraft for the scab pilot, placing orders, arranging schedules, and hiring the temporary help its fabrication would require. He had stopped by the airfield's administration building shortly after sunset "only for a moment" to retrieve some paperwork when he had been interrupted by a panicked call over the shortwave from some nameless scientist at the State's Science Institute. There was a big battle brewing in the mountains of Massachusetts, the man had insisted, with the Institute playing the part of the belligerent. Ordinarily,

Dwight—or any striker, for that matter—wouldn't spare a second thought to what went on in the world Outside, except that the target of the Institute's pugilism was reportedly a strikers' enclave flying the sign of the dollar! Apparently the scientist was himself a sworn striker, intimately familiar with the details of the Worker's epic speech, but trapped among the looters at the Institute. At first the man's story had seemed fantastic, but it had held up under a long, grueling cross-examination. Dwight believed him. But belief alone wasn't required; some parts of the man's tale he could easily verify using data available to him. Given that the fate of a strikers' enclave may hang in the balance, dinner would just have to wait a little longer. "Sanction telephone call Quentin," Dwight announced to the air.

After a brief pause, a disembodied voice replied, "Quentin here."

"Quentin? Dwight. Listen: are you still eavesdropping on those coded transmissions from the State's Science Institute?"

"Yes, I am. Remember that relay-controlled typewriter I built last year to keep up with their war against Washington? It automatically captures everything."

"Good. Might you have a copy of the latest transmissions?"

"Uh... Probably, but I'm not sure. Assuming the beast is still operational, I do. But I'd have to check in the lab to be sure. That's where the electric typewriter is."

"Can you do me a favor and take a look? It might be important."

"Sure! Hold on..." Less than a minute passed. "Dwight? Yes. I have them right here. Several dozen transmissions over the last three weeks. These guys have been busy!"

"Is it the code or the plaintext?"

"Both. Which do you want?"

"Just the plaintext for now. Can you read them to me and tell me what they say?"

"Dwight... There are dozens of them!"

"Mind if I stop by and pick them up?"

"Not at all. Fifty cents for the lot of them."

"Okay. I'll see you in a few minutes, then. Sanction telephone hangup."

\* \* \*

Dwight read.

When he had finished, he nodded; the text matched the scientist's story to the finest detail. Looking up to Quentin, he sighed. "It appears we have a problem."

"How's that? I read through them before you got here, and it looks to me like just another squabble among the looters."

"Not this time." He shook the papers in his hand. "Something not mentioned in these messages is that the latest object of the State's Science Institute's wrath is most likely an enclave flying the sign of the dollar."

His eyes went wide. "Oh, no!"

"Oh, yes! I just had a long discussion over the shortwave with some scientist from the Institute, supposedly one of our philosophical brethren. He claims he's the radio man who's been sending these transmissions." Again he rattled the papers at Quentin. "He's been traveling with their army, and he says they're planning to attack the enclave at sunset tomorrow."

"So I read. If it's truly a strikers' enclave, that would not be good," he observed needlessly.

"No it wouldn't," Dwight agreed, equally needlessly. He took a deep breath and added solemnly, "You know what? I'm thinking I might want to take a hand in this battle."

"What?" Quentin chuckled mockingly "Altruism, Dwight?"

He chuckled good-naturedly in return. "No, sir! Merely fighting for our kind of world."

Quentin's mirth transformed into a smile of approval. "Well put. So what are you planning to do? Massachusetts is a long way away."

"Not really—I can take the hypercraft, and that will get me there well ahead of the attackers. But my first order of business is to make sure the men of the enclave really are strikers. Because if they're not..." Dwight shrugged.

"And if they are?"

He smiled grimly. "I've devised an interesting plan of action to pressure the Institute's army using my hypercraft."

"Pressure them how?"

"'Overpressure' them, I should say."

Instantly understanding, Quentin laughed aloud. "Clever tactic!"

Dwight nodded. He shook the fistful of papers yet again. "And these are the key to using it effectively. They describe the entire order of battle—deployments, troop strength, everything!"

"Excellent! How soon do you leave?"

"No reason to rush out the door. I have until nightfall tomorrow to stop the Institute's army. I guess I'd aim to leave around nine tomorrow morning. That would put me there before noon, their time, and leave me more than enough time to verify they're a bona fide enclave and still stop the attack."

"I can think of someone else who'd surely be interested in this news."

"You're right. He might even want to come along." Dwight raised his voice slightly. "Sanction telephone call Worker," he began.

A few seconds later, a woman's voice answered. "Hello?"

"Hi, Dagny! Dwight. Is the man of the house at home?"

"I'm sorry; he's at the powerhouse. But he should be back any moment. Is there something I can help you with?"

"Yes! Tell him that we've received word that there may be a strikers' enclave out in Massachusetts, and—"

"A strikers' enclave!" she interrupted excitedly.

"So it seems," he agreed. "But the bad news is that the State's Science Institute is about to attack them. I'll be flying out there in the morning to see what I can do to help—assuming I should do anything at all, that is. It may turn out that it's not an enclave, but I have reason to believe it is."

"Well, if it truly is an enclave I'm certain he would want to pay them a visit."

"That's what I was thinking."

"Would you have room for a couple of passengers?"

"Sure! Ten dollars each. And I'd appreciate the company."

"All right. While we're out there, would we be able to stop by Washington for a bit? I'd like to get a look at our Transcontinental station there and see about re-establishing train service now that we're returning Outside."

"I can't see why not. Only a dollar more; it's pretty much on the way."

"Fine. When are you leaving?"

"Nine tomorrow morning."

"We'll meet you at the airfield. Sanction telephone hangup."

Dwight turned to Quentin. "That's that!" he confirmed. He dug in his pocket and tossed Quentin a shiny copper penny. "Thanks for the use of your telephone."

"Don't mention it."

## CHAPTER 4 – WHEN THE MUSIC'S OVER

The Bishop prayed.

Surrounding him in the otherwise-empty, unfurnished upper room knelt a score of acolytes, knees on the hard floor, heads bowed and hands clasped in silent prayer, bathed in the afternoon sunlight slanting in from a single west-facing window of the Bishop's residence. The acolytes had gathered from all corners of the sacred realm for their monthly convocation, which always began with an hour's prayer. The religious fervor of the perfect silence continued until it was broken by the Bishop's sudden "Amen!"

"Amen!" they intoned in unison. With that cue, the assembly rose as one from their knees, and not a sigh could be heard among them. It was their pride to serve their God and His Bishop.

"Let God guide us!" exclaimed the Bishop, a smile on his face.

"That we may walk in His footsteps," they rejoined.

"Forever and ever."

"Amen!"

The Bishop stood in turn and faced his acolytes, his hands held wide apart. "Let us begin." He brought his hands together in front of his chest, fingers intertwined, and nodded to one of the red-robed acolytes. "It has been a month since you began your holy mission. Tell us of your progress."

"Yes, Your Eminence." The acolyte bowed to the Bishop and faced his fellow zealots. "The cleansing of the eastern mountain range is more than half complete. Thousands of our brothers and sisters are stretched out in a broad line that crosses the mountain, from our farms here in God's California to the heathen desert beyond. Since their holy journey began, they have flushed out dozens of heretics who had been living alone in the mountains in secrecy, and we have found a hitherto-unknown settlement of almost fifty heretics. All of them have been driven into the desert, as God has commanded, and the land they defiled cleansed."

The Bishop nodded his approval. "Are you certain none are slipping through your net?"

"They cannot, Eminence. As our brothers and sisters advance, they stay close enough that they can see the ones on their left and right. That way the noose is tight. None shall evade them."

"Good!" The Bishop smiled and nodded. "Very good! And when can we expect the cleansing to be complete?"

"Eminence, the line moves slowly because of the rough terrain and the need to keep them provided with sustenance, and many of the highest places are still covered in snow. But our brethren are progressing at a rate of about ten miles a day. So far, almost two hundred miles of the mountains have been cleansed. Perhaps another hundred more remain. If they can maintain their pace, God willing, they should be completed within the month."

"Excellent! And what about your flanks?"

"Your Eminence, if any heretic tries to flank us to the west, they must enter our farming lands, and we will know of it. If they try to flank us to the east, they must enter the desert, which is exactly where God commands them to be. In fact—"

The acolyte did not have a chance to reveal his fact; the door burst open, interrupting him. All eyes turned toward the intruder; it was another acolyte. Several of the acolytes momentarily assumed an offended look that broadcast the timeless question, "What is the meaning of this?" but the Bishop held his smile. Cordially, he inquired, "Yes, my son?"

"Your Eminence! I beg forgiveness for the intrusion, but we have just received word of a nest of sinners!"

"In the mountains?" He waved a hand across the assembled acolytes with a broad smile. "We were just discussing them when you arrived. I'm told that the settlement has been cleansed."

"No! Not in the mountains—in Las Vegas!"

"Las Vegas?" Confused, the Bishop looked at him askance. "But all of the sinful cities have long since perished!"

"Apparently not, Eminence! Sister Emma just finished her daily shortwave broadcast a few moments ago, and a heretic contacted her claiming he had made it to Las Vegas. He says the town is 'full of men.' I was there and heard it myself!" He paused briefly, then added in postscript, "It was very masterful how she maneuvered him into confessing his location."

Again, the bishop smiled broadly. "Indeed, Sister Emma is a very holy woman." He turned to the interrupted acolyte. "It is a sign from God. He has commanded that we drive the heretics into the desert, and now one of them has led us to this new nest of sinners." He paused a moment in thought. "Our duty is clear: we must act. You must call our brethren out of the mountains. Have them assemble at the desert's edge three days hence."

The acolyte's eyes widened. "All of them? There are thousands!"

"Yes. All of them. Have them adjust their supply lines as well. Be certain that our brethren are prepared to cross the desert. I will meet them at the gathering point and lead the crusade against this nest of sinners myself. We shall crush them once and for all."

The acolyte bowed. "God's will be done!"

## Chapter 5 – Lonely Days

The lookout yawned.

He positively hated guard duty, and counted himself lucky that his turn came only once every other month. Still, twelve long, boring hours alone up at the mountain pass was a lot for him to bear. He much preferred it when he was off with the Las Vegas militia on maneuvers practicing tactics to drive off imaginary invaders. That no one had attempted to invade the town in almost two years did not diminish his ardor in practicing; he enjoyed being a militiaman. It was only this infernal monthly guard duty that rankled him.

He stepped outside of the abandoned restaurant that served as his outpost and into the hazy mid-day sun. The restaurant was perched on a rocky ledge which offered a majestic view of both the town to the east and the desert to the west. But the splendor of the view was lost on him; he just wanted to be back home with his wife and kids. Adding to his annoyance, it was the worst of days for him to be pulling guard duty—the rest of his family would be out riding the Kids' Special and hanging out at Camp all afternoon, and he would much prefer to be enjoying the day with them. He had heard that Eddie recently added a playroom to the Special, actually a former baggage car converted to a new use where the kids could engage in any number of board games, or simply run around playing tag and burning off the excess energy children always seem to have. He hadn't seen it for himself yet, and it looked like it would be a couple of days still before he'd get the chance.

He brought the battered field glasses up to his eyes and scanned the town. To its south he could plainly see the *Meteor* approaching, returning from the morning's run down to Boulder City. In his mind's eye he could visualize the scene currently unfolding at the Transcontinental station: the crowded train platform bristling with excited children and their shepherding mothers—not to mention Eddie's lovely girl friend!—all anxiously awaiting the arrival of the Kids' Special. *Who is Eddie Willers?* he asked himself with a longing smile. He sighed and lowered the field glasses, feeling again the pangs of separation from his family. It'd be another three days before the Special ran again; or was it four? He would surely go out of his way to make sure he and his kids were on board that one.

He turned to head back inside the relative coolness of the restaurant and offhandedly cast a brief glance to the empty desert to the west—and froze. His stomach knotted and his blood ran cold; for on the horizon was a red ribbon that had not been on the road the last time he looked. His hands shaking, he raised the field glasses to his eyes and clumsily focused their lenses, revealing the individual members of what had to be a red-clad army of thousands! He stood paralyzed with a fear that struck to his very core. Las Vegas' worst nightmare had come true. Back For God was on the march. He bolted inside the restaurant to telephone his commander.

\* \* \*

The *Meteor* halted.

Eddie left the massive Diesel idling noisily, opened its hatch, and climbed down its side. Dozens of children excitedly stood on the platform, impatiently fidgeting while they waited for the Dam workers to disembark and unload so they could clamber aboard. At the crowd's head, herding them somewhat successfully, stood a shapely woman. She smiled at Eddie brightly when he turned her way. He blushed, tossed her a small wave of an index finger from waist level, and turned away to head inside the station for a moment. By the time he returned, he knew she would have the kids all aboard, waiting only for him to take command of the train for an afternoon's fun of tooling around the desert countryside. He was looking forward to it; he always did, as did she. It had become another ritual in their lives, another point of bonding between them, much like their long-standing dinner engagements.

Embarrassments aside, he was happy to have her assistance on the twice-weekly run. She acted as conductor, chaperone, and surrogate mother for the children, making his job of running the Kids' Special all the easier. On the Special's first run he had tried to handle the entire train all by himself, as he routinely did for the run down to Boulder City, but it immediately became clear to him that a conductor was necessary, not only to keep the kids in line, but more importantly to watch out for their safety. That night over dinner, he had mentioned to her the difficulties he had had with the children, and she cheerfully volunteered to help, as she had in so many other situations, whether it was catching a bandit, caring for him when he was injured, teaching him to cook, or any of the many other little favors she constantly went out of her way to perform. He gratefully accepted her offer to assist with running the railroad and immediately placed her name on the pay rolls, but he had to admit he felt some measure of guilt that she should be so very helpful to him while he did so little to reciprocate—certainly Transcontinental paid her as well as any employee, but that wasn't the issue; rather, he was well aware of how he pointedly did not reciprocate on any personal level. Although he could not deny that he enjoyed her company and could not help but be attracted by her uncommon beauty, he had not yet managed to successfully navigate around two apparently-insurmountable obstacles that derailed any possibility of a romantic relationship: her profession, and Dagny.

Eddie sighed. Intellectually he had long since accepted the fact that Dagny was gone forever, but emotionally he was not sure if he would ever get over her loss. He had loved her for far too long to stop now, even when his feelings so obviously got in the way of establishing a new relationship with his courtesan friend, a fine woman who deserved much more attention than Eddie was able to give her. Having known the woman for almost two years now, he was finally beginning to accept the fact that she was a working girl; but it was the chasm that remained in the wake of Dagny's loss that proved to be the larger obstacle, impossible to bridge. Yet he could see within himself that the healing process had finally begun, although only somewhat, and his ruthless self-honesty forced him to admit silently to himself that one day he might find that chasm bridged, but not today nor anytime soon; hence the guilt. It wasn't fair to her to leave so ripe a fruit hanging on the vine unplucked, but he could not divine any way which might hurry the process along—nor was he sure that he should... or wanted to.

Looking beyond his immediate romantic consternation, ironically Eddie had to admit that overall his life had taken a tremendous turn for the better in the years since the world ended. He acknowledged that to a large degree the improvement followed from the anomalous situations and roles in which he continually found himself immersed: judge, de facto mayor, militia organizer, financial wizard, and more, making his responsibilities as a railroadman seem almost prosaic in comparison. He increasingly felt as if he were a character in some convoluted philosophical novel where all of the plot twists served only to enhance the quality of his life, whether it was providing him with a lovely companion, an enviable social standing, even the geographic isolation which brought him peace in the midst of a ruined, shattered nation. He recognized his suspicion for the fantasy it was, but the recognition forced him to count his blessings, which in turn fed his guilt all the more. Who is Eddie Willers? What right does anyone have to be so happy? Why had he fared so well while the rest of the world crumbled? He had once functioned well enough in a world populated by men like Hank, Francisco, and Dagny; he would have guessed he would have no chance in a world without them. Why, then, had he succeeded beyond his wildest dreams?

He had no answers; but regardless of how well he was faring in this satisfying sequel, he could not help but wonder what sort of foul man would have penned the primitive vulgarity of this existence's cruel prequel, a sad tale of a spiteful, vindictive world dominated by looters where a destroyer moved soundless throughout the country, its lights dying at his touch, leaving uncounted millions to die—Eddie's beloved Dagny among them.

Granted, a worthy replacement for her lay easily within his grasp, but still he hesitated to reach out to claim the prize. Pretty and talented though she was, she was certainly no Dagny.

Once again, he set romantic matters aside unresolved and turned his attention to the task at hand. Emerging from the tunnel and back onto the platform, he felt a surge of pride when he saw the Diesel's headlight blazing bright above the silver shield bearing the stylized "TR" that was the coat of arms of Transcontinental Railroad. A few mothers still stood on the platform, obviously not coming along for the ride, waving farewell to their children. He climbed aboard the waiting Diesel, sealed the hatch, turned on the yard bell, and to the tune of its off-key warning, piloted the *Meteor* out for the afternoon's joy ride. The remaining mothers took their leave, and in the silence left in their wake could be heard the insistent ringing of a telephone left ignored and unanswered.

## CHAPTER 6 – WELCOME TO MY NIGHTMARE

The lieutenant panicked.

"Back For God? Back For God! An *army*? On their way *here?!*" His eyes bulged with terror. "Dear God, say it isn't so!"

Slightly more composed but no less frightened, the militia commander nodded his head. "I wish! But they are on their way and they'll be here in a matter of hours. The latest estimate puts the size of their forces at around three thousand, but there's a sizeable margin of error in that number. It could be a lot more. It could be a whole lot less. Or it might only be the first wave of thousands more."

"Three thousand!" The lieutenant's eyes darted back and forth, as if seeking escape. "And how big is your militia?"

The commander barked a short, mirthless laugh. "Around three hundred—and half of them are support personnel. There are only about five or six thousand people in the entire town!"

"Did anyone tell Eddie?"

"Mr. Eddie is not available," he replied stiffly. "Today's the day he takes the kids out on the train."

"When's he coming back?"

The commander eyed him levelly. "About the same time Back For God is supposed to reach here."

"My God, my God!" He ran his fingers roughly through his hair, automatically missing dislodging his scar-covering headband. "What are you going to do?"

"Me?" The commander drew himself up. "Defend the town, of course."

"With just three hundred men?"

"With whatever I can. And that's why I came to see you."

The lieutenant paused. "I see," he said finally, sitting up a little straighter. "I've served in the Army," he nodded self-assuredly. "I know how to use a weapon."

"You may get your chance, but what I really want you to use is that shortwave."

The lieutenant was taken aback by the sudden shift of subject. "The shortwave?" he repeated stupidly.

"Yes! You have to call for help!"

"Call for help?" he repeated. "Call whom?"

325

Exasperated, the commander threw up his hands in despair, some of his own fear edging out into the open. "How the hell should I know? Anyone! *You* tell *me* who to call! You're the goddamned radio man!"

"Listen, mister, I've only been in town a week or so, and haven't had that much time to do very much eavesdropping on the world. As far as I know, the only stations on the entire continent are in California and Washington."

"Then call Washington!"

"But they're thousands of miles away! What good could that possibly do?"

"What other choice do we have? We have to try!"

Awkwardly, the lieutenant admitted, "Uh... One thing... Eddie told me not to speak with anyone by radio—"

"What?" he interrupted, an edge of panic entering his voice.

"—but he couldn't have known something like this was going to come up," he backpedaled.

"I should say!"

The lieutenant scrambled to his feet. "The radio is at the Transcontinental station."

"Let's roll!"

\* \* \*

The two men ran.

They were not alone in their haste. The terrible news had spread like wildfire; panic had already begun to affect the townsfolk, and a great number of them had taken to the streets. Some dragged frightened children in their wake, others bore armloads of weapons and ammunition. Electric carts swerved in and out of the darting pedestrians and whinnying horses—and not always successfully navigating the melee. Something clipped the lieutenant's leg almost bringing him to the ground, but he paid no heed nor slackened his speed. There was no time.

Breathless, they entered the station and ran down the tunnel to the platform area where the mail car with the radio was parked. As they emerged from the tunnel, they were not surprised to see the platform packed with people, virtually all of them women, waiting in anxious terror for their children to return. Most of the women were armed—some of them heavily armed.

"Your militia may number a whole lot more than just three hundred," the lieutenant observed grimly.

"We're going to need it!"

The two men avoided the crowd and headed straight for the mail car. They bounded up the steps, the lieutenant in the lead, and ducked inside. Without stopping to take a seat, the lieutenant powered up the equipment, and fidgeted nervously as he waited for it to warm up. The commander pushed a chair at him with his foot; he took the seat, clutching the microphone tightly in anticipation. In a moment a green indictor light winked on, and the lieutenant began fiddling with knobs and switches.

"CQ, CQ, Las Vegas calling Washington!" He was almost screaming into the device. "Las Vegas calling Washington! Do you read me Washington, over?"

He paused for only a few seconds before the crisp reply came.

"Las Vegas, this is the White House in Washington. Go ahead. Over."

The two men glanced at each other in surprise. "What?!" exclaimed the lieutenant. "Was he just sitting there waiting for me to call?"

"Seems it," the commander replied in disbelief. "But that doesn't matter now—you talk!"

"Right." He turned his attention back to the microphone. "Washington, we are under attack and request immediate assistance. Repeat: we are under attack and request immediate assistance. Over."

In spite of the outrageous nature of the plea coming from a city not suspected to exist, the voice replied calmly, "Understood, Las Vegas. Please stand by. Over."

The two men continued to fidget as they waited. Fortunately for their tortured peace of mind, the wait was not a long one.

"Las Vegas, please stand by for Mr. James. Over."

The two men glanced at each other in confusion.

"The railroad guy James?" asked the commander, the incredulity plain in his voice.

The lieutenant shrugged, a mischievous smile creasing his face. "You did say 'anyone,' didn't you?" the mocking sarcasm dripping from every word. "And we're not in a position to be very picky, now are we? I'd talk to the devil himself if he were going to help—"

"This is Mr. James," the radio interrupted. "Over."

He had to ask. "The railroad guy James? Over."

They could hear the small smile reflected in his voice. "The former railroad guy James, yes. I'm Head of State now, the successor to Mr. Thomson. What can I do for you? Over."

"Please stand by," replied the lieutenant. "I'm going to pass the microphone over to the commander of the Las Vegas militia." He vacated the seat and the commander promptly claimed it.

"For the love of God, Mr. James, I hope you can do something!" the commander cried into the ether. Quickly, he gave James a succinct outline of their tactical situation. "I can't imagine what you may be able to do to help, but unless someone does something soon..." His words trailed off to silence, until he recalled he had not completed the protocol. "Over."

"I understand. Please stand by. Over."

Seconds passed. Minutes passed. Ten minutes elapsed before the lieutenant's patience finally wore out. He pulled the microphone from the commander's hand. "Washington, this is Las Vegas. What's the holdup? We haven't much time! Over."

The voice that answered was not Mr. James, but rather that of the first person they had spoken with. "Please stand by, Las Vegas," he replied calmly. "Over."

"Bah!" yelled the lieutenant, angrily pushing the microphone away from him. "This is pointless!"

"So is entering a battle at the wrong end of ten-to-one odds!" snapped the commander. "But what other choice do we have?"

"We can get ready for battle!"

"We *are* ready," he retorted proudly. "We've been practicing for something like this for over a year."

His eyes ran up and down the commander; his only weapon was a sidearm. "And where are the rest of your weapons?"

"At the armory, a couple of blocks from here. We still have a few hours before they reach us, so there's really no more reason to hurry." He pointed at the radio. "Either they can help us or they can't. Once they let us know what's what, we'll head over the armory and arm ourselves, then head into the desert to meet our fates."

"At ten-to-one odds?" he demanded.

"Well..." The commander scratched an ear and smiled. "Who is Eddie Willers? As you noticed, there are a lot more than three hundred people armed. And it may be that we're a lot better armed than they are—we've tapped a good deal of heavy-duty materiel from the Army base north of town. Then again, until we make contact with the enemy we have no way of telling who has the superior weaponry. But once we do know, it'll—"

A voice blaring from the radio's speaker interrupted him. "Las Vegas, this is Washington. Come in, over!"

Eagerly, the commander replied. "Las Vegas here. Go ahead, Washington. Over."

"Please stand by for Mr. Dwight. Over."

The commander turned to the lieutenant, perplexed. "The airplane guy, Dwight?"

The lieutenant shrugged. "How many Mr. Dwights are there in the world? And what does it matter anyhow? 'Anyone,' remember?"

"Good point." He turned back to the microphone. "Las Vegas standing by, Washington. Over."

## CHAPTER 7 – QUESTIONS 67 AND 68

Dwight looked up.

The red annunciator light was flashing on the control panel of the hypercraft, each flash accompanied by a soft chime sounding in synch. Someone was trying to telephone him, and the call was being automatically relayed to him at the enclave in Massachusetts. "Sanction telephone answer," he called to the air. He heard a click, then the voice of Dagny filled the craft's cabin. "Hello, darling!"

"Hi, Dagny! Sorry, this is Dwight. Your husband's still at the enclave's reception for our friend from the State's Science Institute. I'm sitting here in my hypercraft waiting for them to finish up with the celebrations."

"You're not attending their reception?" she asked incredulously. "After all, it was your tactics and your execution that defeated the Institute's army. You're as much a hero as the man who radioed you for help."

"You know I never cared for all that pageantry," he replied, the disapproval plain in his voice. Quickly changing the subject, he added, "Are you ready for me to come pick you up already? I didn't think you'd be done looking over the Washington station so soon. I just dropped you off not an hour ago!"

"No, not yet."

"Then what can I do for you?"

"You're going to find this hard to believe, Dwight, but Washington just received a call for help on the shortwave—from Las Vegas!"

Unseen by his listener, Dwight's jaw dropped. "Las Vegas? There's someone living in Las Vegas?"

"Yes—and they're about to be attacked by Back For God! They're looking for help."

"Ah! I see." He paused, then ventured, "Do you think that it might be another enclave."

"Who knows? It may be—or maybe not—which is why I called. If it is an enclave, the last thing we'd want is to have it overrun by those mystic thugs."

"Too true!" He gathered his thoughts for a second, then continued. "Tell you what: let me speak with the men in Las Vegas and find out if they're for real. I went through the same routine with my friend from the Institute, then with the men here at this enclave. I'm an expert at uncovering philosophical truth!"

"Thank you, Dwight. You do that. They're standing by and monitoring the emergency channel on the shortwave."

"I'll get in contact with them right away, Dagny. Sanction telephone hangup."

He sat for a moment bathed in wonder, smiling broadly. *Another enclave!* But his smile slowly faded as he realized how unlikely that was—and perhaps it wasn't even Back For God. But enclave or not, he sincerely hoped it was the red-robed army attacking, because sooner or later, he knew, the men of the mind were going to have to come to terms with the men of the soul. Back For God's imminent attack on Las Vegas could prove to be a golden opportunity for him to dispatch those bloody mystics, perhaps once and for all. But first, he had to make sure he had his facts straight, and— more importantly!—that he would be fighting for the correct side, philosophically speaking. There would be no sense in defending Las Vegas if it were inhabited merely by a pack of lousy looters. He had to allow for the possibility that the valley's interests might best be served by allowing the town to be overrun. *Well, let's see what's what...* He manipulated a few switches and knobs on the hypercraft's control panel, then picked up the microphone from its mounting on the panel. "CQ, CQ, Dwight in Massachusetts calling Las Vegas. Dwight in Massachusetts calling Las Vegas. Come in Las Vegas! " After a second, he remembered to add, "Over."

The reply came virtually instantly. "This is Las Vegas, receiving you loud and clear, Mr. Dwight. Over."

"Oh, you don't need to say 'over,'" he began. "I have a nifty gadget attached to my shortwave that tells me when you've released your transmit key. And I can still hear you even when I'm talking; another neat invention I have."

"If you say so!"

"That I do." He leaned back in his seat, settling in for what he suspected would be a long conversation. "So I hear you boys are having a little religious troubles."

"*That's* putting it mildly! There are about three thousand of the red-robed bastards about ten miles away, and they're not slowing down. They'll be here in about two or three hours! Is there anything you can do to help us out?"

"We-e-e-e-ell, not so fast. Maybe there is, but I have a few questions first. We wouldn't want to get involved in this if it didn't somehow involve our own interests."

"Mister, you can ask all the questions you want if it means you're going to help us. But remember we don't have much time—they're only a few hours away!"

"That's plenty of time; but let's begin. How many people in your enclave?"

"Maybe five or six thousand? We're not exactly sure. Could be more. Could be less."

Dwight eyebrows shot up. *Five or six thousand? How could we have missed a town that large? And right on our doorstep, too!* "What kind of government do you have?"

"Nothing much, really. We're pretty laissez-faire."

"I assume that you have no Unificating Board then?"

"None at all. Not since the Mayor left town."

"And when did the Mayor leave?"

"Over two years ago, on the night of the Worker's television show, if you remember when that was."

"Indeed I do!" smiled Dwight. He found it telling that the commander had referred to the Worker first. Part of Dwight's inquisition plan was to deliberately avoid any mention of the Worker, because if asked, any hamlet could claim to be a Worker enclave just to receive the benefits. But he wasn't going to fall into that sort of a trap; his line of questioning was more subtle, more philosophical, and there was still much ground to be covered. "In a town that large, I assume you have some criminals. With a laissez-faire government, how do you deal with them?"

"Crime is pretty much non-existent here these days, but it wasn't always like that. We set up our own court process where a jury gets to hear all the facts and ask questions, then someone suggests a sentence."

"What sort of sentence?"

"Well, one bandit got himself exiled. A thieving banker was driven out of business, that sort of thing. One guy who made a real killing in silver was tried, but the jury said he was allowed to keep his profits since he didn't cheat or steal from anyone."

Dwight nodded. It sure sounded like an enclave so far. Deciding to go for the philosophical jugular, he asked a key question. "What do you use for money?"

"Silver and gold. Silver, mostly."

"What about paper money? Don't you use that?"

"Not for over a year. It was too easy to steal from people when we had it. That's what that stinking banker was doing—circulating money he didn't own. People stopped dealing with him, and it drove him out of business."

"Do you regulate businesses?"

"Nope. They regulate themselves."

"How's that?"

"Well, I just told you about the banker. Regulated himself right out of business!" He barked an odd-sounding laugh. "Other businessmen, they came up with their own Guidelines and Society accepts them. Those that don't live up to the Guidelines don't stay in business too long."

"Can people other than businessmen come up with guidelines for them to follow?"

"Sure they can, but the businessmen are free to follow them or not, as they see fit. That's freedom, isn't it? They're only Guidelines, you know. But if the people don't like how a business follows the Guidelines, they don't deal with them." He paused a second, then added, "That's what happened to that banker fellow."

Dwight nodded to himself, recalling how a significant number of strikers had refused to transact any business with the scabs while they remained in the valley. He tallied another mental point in the town's favor. "Don't you have business licenses or official permission to go into business?"

"Nope. Matter of fact, we have the opposite. What we have are licenses that say you *can't* do certain things, and not just in business. The jury hands them out if you're being a real jerk about something. One of our former town drunks has a can't-drink license, and now no one will serve him any booze. If we catch him drunk, we lock him up for a couple of days, just to teach him a lesson. A crazy teenaged girl has a can't-drive license, and no one will let her drive a cart. She did it anyway—once—and she spent a night in the clinker as punishment. Sure set her straight, believe me!"

Again, Dwight's eyebrows went up. *What an approach! We could have used that against the scabs when they were still in the valley!* It appeared there might be a thing or two they could learn from this enclave.

He moved on to his next question. Remembering the day that Dr. Floyd's pilot had crash-landed in the valley, he wondered how this enclave would deal with that sort of situation. "What about charity?"

"What about it?"

"I take it that there are poor people among your thousands. Who takes care of them?"

"Mostly it's their neighbors who pitch in to help. But if the person has no money and no friends or if they're new in town, Society will help. Even pay for court costs, if necessary."

"Society?"

"Yep. People contribute money to Society and Society helps those who can't help themselves."

"Your society has taxes?"

"Nope. I said 'contribute,' mister, and that's what I meant. It's all voluntary. We have no taxes here."

With that admission, Dwight felt convinced; it was a philosophically-correct enclave. However he found himself intrigued by some of the ingenious answers, and was curious to hear more. Besides, it was always still possible he might be misjudging them; additional questions would strengthen his confidence as well as satisfying his curiosity. "Do you still have gambling in town?"

"Oh, yes. Wouldn't be Las Vegas without it, now would it?" He chucked again, an odd sound when reproduced by the radio. "The gambling halls came up with their own Guidelines, of course, and all of them live up to them. Wouldn't last long as a gambling hall if they didn't! That banker taught everyone how you can't get away with cheating your customers."

"Still have prostitution, too?"

"Of course. The ladies came up with their own set of Guidelines as well, and they stick to them. In fact, our Head of Society is pretty tight with one of the prostitutes, although she did give up the trade once she started to pal around with him. He's got a real sweet deal there, that's for sure!"

"Huh! And no one complains about that?" Dwight heard a garbled laugh burst from the speaker. For some reason, the man's laughter did not translate well via shortwave.

"It definitely made a lot of men jealous at first, but these days most everyone is pretty comfortable with the idea—except maybe Eddie! Still, you know how it is; there are always a few busybodies who like to complain about anything. People will be people."

"So the ladies are free to just go about their business, then?"

"If they're following proper Guidelines, what's there to complain about?"

"I heartily agree!" He took a deep breath. "All right, I'm convinced. You sound like a bona fide enclave to me. Let's talk about the military situation. You say Back For God has sent an army of about three thousand marching on you?"

"That's right."

Dwight asked what he felt was another crucial question. "How do you know it's Back For God?"

Again the strange sound came from the speaker that did not resemble a laugh. "Mister! There's no one west of us except California, no group of people so large except in California, and no crowd of thousands who'd all be wearing red robes and heading for Las Vegas!"

He smiled at the certainty; there could be no argument. "Point taken, sir. From exactly where are they approaching town?"

"They're following the main highway down from the northwest. My guess is that they came around the north side of Death Valley from central California."

Dwight unfurled a map and laid it across his knees. "Are you sure they're not coming down from Reno?"

There was a brief hesitation, then the reply. "I guess it's possible, but I couldn't rightly say. Nobody's been up that far north since the world ended. Reno's pretty close to California, so I'd guess it all belongs to Back For God anyhow, assuming Reno's still there, which I doubt. But what does it matter? The point is, there're a-coming!"

"Might they be coming up from Los Angeles and trying to throw you a curve by swinging in from the northwest?"

"Mister," he began testily, "We've had multiple eyewitness reports that say Los Angeles burned to the ground years ago. The gentleman sitting next to me saw San Francisco burn to the ground himself. So far as we know, all the California cities are gone. Does it really matter where they started from? They're red robes, damn it, and that's all that matters! You think I'm making all this up?"

"I already said I believed you. I was only speculating so as to better prepare my attack."

"Sorry. We're all pretty nervous here at the moment."

"I can understand!"

"And I truly appreciate that, Mr. Dwight." Over the speakers there came what sounded like a deep sigh. "So what is it you can do for us?"

"You say they're still two or three hours away from town? What's that, maybe ten miles?"

"That'd be just about right. Our lookouts say that except for horses pulling some supply wagons, the army is all on foot. The sun's not a killer today, but still: they couldn't get here much faster than that, and you can't run very fast or far across that desert, believe me!"

"And where are your troops positioned?"

"At the edge of town. We have an observation post about five miles out. We'll have to abandon it pretty soon."

Dwight pondered his tactics a moment. "All right. I think I can handle this. Listen up, because this is extremely important! Call back your men from the observation post right now, and keep the rest of them at the edge of town where you already have them. And whatever you do, *don't let anyone leave town!* Stay put until I get there, which should be in about an hour and a half. Where shall I meet you?"

"You should probably meet with our Head of Society. He's supposed to be at the Transcontinental station right around the time you get here, maybe a half hour later." There was a brief pause, followed by an incredulous question. "Did you say you'd be here in an hour and a half? I thought you said you were in Massachusetts!"

"Yep," Dwight replied baldly, then added mischievously, "Not too far away."

"An hour and a half from Massachusetts?" the commander repeated incredulously. That emotion was somehow transmitted flawlessly by the radio equipment.

"Yep!" he repeated, laughing. He understood the poor man's confusion, and he basked in it. He was proud of his creation. "Anything else?"

"No sir, except let me thank you on behalf of all Las Vegas!"

Dwight laughed again. "You should realize that I'm not doing this for you, sir. I'm doing this for me!"

"If you say so!"

"That I do. I'll see you in a few hours. Over and out." Dwight reached out, flipped a switch to put the shortwave back on standby, and leaned back in his chair, the grin still on his face. "So Back For God will soon be going back to God," he joked to himself. "This is going to be fun!" He rose from the captain's chair and headed for the reception hall; he needed to speak with the Worker. He assumed that the Worker would want to come along, and they could stop to pick up Dagny on the way, assuming she was done surveying Washington's Transcontinental station.

*Two enclaves in two days!* he cheered to himself. *And one great day for the forces of reason!*

## CHAPTER 8 – DAY BY DAY

The acolytes marched.

Never before had so large an acolyte army assembled, let alone marched, although none could say for certain exactly how large an army it was. Because of the decentralized nature of their command structure, short of an on-site head count—which had not been done—no accounting was humanly possible; and fortunately, since each group of acolytes had their own chain of command and supply lines, no accounting was tactically necessary. Numbers aside, if any acolyte had the temerity to question the logistics of their holy mission, the answer would invariably be the same: "God will provide." Indeed, their God had already provided them with an impressive force, arguably the largest on the continent: virtually every acolyte had been mustered for the campaign, and at its head was no less a personage than God's Bishop himself. He rode a pure white horse with a bright crimson saddle blanket; his vestments were similarly white and topped off, incongruously, with a tan ten-gallon hat sporting a crimson ribbon, its stampede string pulled snug under his chin. The hat was a holdover from the Bishop's former life as an oil man. It had served him well when he had traveled the desert tending oil derricks; he saw no reason it could not continue to travel the desert as he tended souls. Adding the crimson ribbon had been his sole concession to decorum.

The army had been advancing at a walking speed for several days, the slow pace allowing the horse-drawn supply chain to keep their food and water—a great deal of water—adequately replenished. They did not march in any sort of formation, but rather as a random collection of informal cliques with constantly-shifting membership spread out across the width of the old cement highway and stretching more than a half mile along its length. The most devout among them migrated to the front of the advancing army, politely elbowing one another out of the way so as to demonstrate their devotion to God and His Bishop. Their God had smiled on their journey; the early April weather remained relatively cool and slightly cloudy.

Far ahead, a lone figure could be seen approaching the army from the direction of Las Vegas, his red robe plainly visible even from so great a distance. Before long, the figure came alongside the Bishop.

"Report what you have seen, my son!" commanded the Bishop, reining his white steed to a halt.

"Your Eminence! I have been living in the hills the last two nights watching. The town lives! It burns with sinful electricity at night!"

"And how many do you believe may live there?"

"Hundreds, certainly. Thousands possibly. Not tens of thousands, surely."

"Do they defend themselves?"

"No, Your Eminence! That's the best part! They have a sentry—one single sentry!—a few miles outside of town. We will be upon them before they know we are coming!"

"And where is this sentry?"

The acolyte pointed to a shoulder of mountain in the near distance. "Once you walk out from behind that ridge, you will be in his sight."

The Bishop glanced down meaningfully at the acolyte's bright red garment. "And did he see you?"

"No, Eminence. Only now did I don my blessed robe when I saw my brethren approaching." He smiled sardonically. "I did not want God's warriors to confuse me for a heathen."

"Prudent," observed the Bishop. Raising his eyes to the ridge ahead, he asked, "And Las Vegas is not far beyond?"

"It is only three or four hours' journey from where we stand, Eminence."

The bishop glanced needlessly at the sky and nodded. The sun was plainly visible through the thin veil of clouds. "Then we would be arriving long before nightfall..." He paused, deep in thought. "Yes, it is better that we fight in God's daylight rather than in the Devil's darkness. He that doeth evil hateth the light, and the daylight makes it harder for them to hide." His face darkened with righteous anger. "Before tonight, their sinful lights will be extinguished forever!"

The acolyte bowed. "God's will be done!"

Without a word the Bishop spurred his horse in the direction of town.

* * *

Las Vegas brooded.

At least that's how it seemed to the Bishop. His army was close enough now that they could unmistakably see the town lying at their feet. The road they traveled slowly dropped out of the mountains, a straight line terminating at the edge of town—a heathen town waiting to be cleansed and its sinful ways put to an end. Although it still lay several miles distant, in the clear desert air it seemed close enough to grasp. Unconsciously, the Bishop nudged his horse to an increased pace; he was eager to reach the city. Behind him, the acolytes picked up their own pace as well, but without the benefit of a powerful horse beneath them, they soon tired and resumed their former speed. The Bishop continued ahead, unmindful of the growing lead he held; but no acolyte would have the impertinence to call him back, or even bring the situation to his attention. He was, after all, God's Bishop.

As he rode closer to the city, the Bishop's thoughts turned inward in prayer. He was not frightened, at least not conspicuously so, for he had led his acolytes into battles against many a city over the last few years. Bullets and bombs had zipped close, but none had ever scored so much as a scratch on his holy personage; he always traveled unarmed, and he fully expected his God to once again protect him in this upcoming battle. *Unless it is my time!* he reminded himself. The thought unnerved him slightly, but he shook it off. *If God were to call me, it would be directly into heaven! And who would not want so signal an honor?* The thought buoyed his courage; he sat up straight in his saddle, head held high, presenting the perfect picture of a warrior prophet marching against heathen sinners. Still, a smidgen of uncertainty remained deep in his soul; he knew he must take steps to purge it, lest a false heart betray them all. *Dear God!* he prayed. *I am not worthy! But I beseech You to reveal a sign of Your pleasure in the labors of Your servant! Not my will, but Thine be done!*

Much to his astonishment—he knew how precocious his Deity could be—the sign immediately presented itself. Suddenly there came from the heavens a great clap of thunder, a physical force that filled, then painfully stole the air from his lungs. Together, he and his steed were flung to the ground, an agonizing buzz ringing deafeningly in his ears, like some great voice drowning out all thoughts and actions. He came to a painful rest on the unyielding surface of the cement highway sitting upright on his buttocks a short distance from his capsized mount, legs splayed out in front of him, spun around and facing his acolyte army, its vanguard almost a thousand paces behind him. In rhythm with his posterior coming in agonizing contact with the highway's surface, the sea of red robes before him were tossed aside as if by some strong wind. En masse they tumbled to the ground and did not rise.

Stunned at the sight, the Bishop rose painfully to his feet, wide-eyed, refusing to even blink lest he chance missing some sign of movement among his acolytes. In the near distance, he could see there was none; but farther back the host of red robes were in full retreat, a crimson tide surging back up the old highway toward whence they came. The Bishop took an uncertain step in their direction and halted, his mind unable to accept the scene that confronted him. Stupidly, he looked again for any sort of movement from the fallen acolytes closest to him. But none came.

*Dear God!* he cried within the confines of his mind. *Surely this is not Your sign! Give me Your sign!* Uncannily, again as if in answer to his unspoken prayer, once more a deafening crescendo washed over him, again knocking him to the highway with a crippling slam. Despite his breath being stolen away and the aching which spread over every inch of his body, it did not seem as devastating as the first blow; he was able to roll over immediately to behold his army. But there was nothing to see. Laboriously, agonizingly, he sat up so as to get a better view, but still he saw nothing. Ascending first to his knees, then unsteadily to his feet, he scanned the rising land in front of him. The highway was littered with scattered bundles of red rags. Among them, nothing moved.

For many minutes the Bishop stood immobile facing the destruction, his mind a blank slate refusing to function. He was finally brought back to the here and now by the prosaic nuzzling of his horse's worried muzzle rubbing against his shoulder. He turned to the frightened animal, a confused expression gracing his own face, appearing as if he had never before encountered a horse in his entire life. Numbly, absently, he stroked the animal's long nose, his attention on nothing, not even his stroking.

Slowly his mind began to operate again, but the confusion stubbornly remained. Holding the reins, he took several steps toward the defeated army, jaw slack, his horse dutifully following, but it was several minutes longer before his jaw finally closed and his eyes focused; the look of confusion was replaced with one of resignation. There could be no misreading the sign: God was not at all pleased with His servant. It was obvious. But the Bishop still could not—*would not!*—accept it. He lifted his head to the dim, cloud-veiled sun.

"My God!" he screamed at the air, tears welling up in his eyes. "My God!" he repeated. "How could You do this? How can You kill so many good men, just to give me a mere sign? I am not worthy!" He flung the reins aside in anger, startling the poor, rattled horse. "And without an army, how do You expect me to possibly enforce Your will when You toss aside the instrument of Your vengeance?" Angrily he waved an irate hand across the flattened army and stared at the murky sky waiting on an answer; only this time, none came. As the seconds dragged into minutes, the obvious answer finally coalesced in his consciousness. *Unless there is to be no vengeance?* His mind rebelled at the thought, as it contradicted everything he had devoted his life to for the last three years. But the thought would not be denied, and others quickly followed. *God is not pleased with His servant... Las Vegas is not to be cleansed... I have been pursuing a false idol...* Thinking of the long trail of dead that lay between him and God's California, his head fell and his shoulders slumped. *So many dead! All, just for a sign? What sort of cruel God is He?* More tears filled his eyes, but there was no denying his God's message.

Finally coming to grips with the truth, the Bishop took a deep breath, at last understanding his God's sign fully, and fully accepting it. Clearly, God's California was lost to him now. With so blunt a repudiation of his dogma, there could be no going back, even had he sufficient food and water to chance re-crossing Death Valley. Climbing back astride his steed, he turned toward Las Vegas as his only remaining option. He paused a moment to cast his gaze one last time across the carnage that was once a red-robed army. *All those deaths, only to make a point?*

"Ah, well," he sighed softly before spurring the horse toward town. "Who is John Galt?"

## Chapter 9 – Out In The Country

The Diesel roared.

The throttle felt alive under Eddie's hand. It rumbled with a reflection of the vital forces that lay tamed behind it: a motive power which catapulted the hundreds of tons of metal and wood across the open desert on twin thin strips of shining steel glinting brightly in the mid-day sun.

They were approaching his favorite section of the Kids' Special run: a ten-mile straightaway rebuilt shortly before the world's collapse with fresh wooden crossties and rail made of now-irreplaceable Miracle Metal, making this stretch of track the best one anywhere in the vicinity of Las Vegas, capable of handling incredible loads and extraordinary track speeds. That knowledge encouraged a certain amount of reasoned recklessness on his part; for there was a caprice in which Eddie would always indulge himself, some boisterous fun that had quickly developed into a routine—if such a mundane word could be used to describe what had become the highest of the high points of the twice-weekly run.

The kids loved it, too. Eddie would always begin it with a series of blaring warning blasts on the triple-coned air horn, a sound followed by the rising roar of the massive motors that would drive the Diesel faster and faster down the greenish-blue straightaway until the *Meteor* was barreling along at a cool one hundred thirty-three miles an hour—that being the highest velocity its speedometer would register. He knew they could have gone faster still, but he was reluctant to accelerate further without the gauge's metered guidance. He knew from personal experience that high speed was hypnotizing; it was far too easy to misjudge the extent of their swiftness, and thereby invite disaster. But their current velocity proved to be more than adequate; for child and parent alike, it was the fastest that any of them had ever traveled and probably ever would. The novelty of it never wore off, neither for them nor for Eddie, because for him, it was along this particular stretch of rail that the *Meteor* felt the most alive, screaming with mechanical life as it faithfully followed the whimsical will of its master. The incredible motion melted the crossties beneath the *Meteor* into a single dark mass, as if they were not individual wooden logs, but rather a massively-long, seven-foot-wide board reinforced and ornamented by two gleaming strips of greenish-blue metal. Adding a bittersweet taint to his joy was the knowledge that the immense velocity would swallow up the ten miles in no time at all; the delight could only last a few short minutes before he would have to check his speed in anticipation of the rapidly-approaching bend. Dutifully, if reluctantly, he began to return the *Meteor* to a more prosaic velocity, once again toasting the moment with another series of blasts on the train's whistle, again according to the routine. Regardless of its ephemeral nature, the capricious sprint would always leave Eddie a happy man; happy for what had just transpired, and also in anticipation: he knew they still had to return this way.

He turned around at the gentle touch of a hand on his shoulder as the scent of lavender drifted up to him, mixing with the oiled, mechanical redolence of the Diesel's cab. He had not heard the sound of her approach over the various noises that the Diesel made: the low drone of the motors, the sharper clicking of the many parts that rang in varied cries of metal, and the high, thin chimes of trembling glass panes.

"That was *fun!*" she gushed, a childlike grin splitting her face, and her voice straining to be heard above the melee of the Diesel's song. Her eyes were bright with excitement.

Eddie nodded almost solemnly, returning his attention to the track ahead. "Yes," he replied calmly, his own voice unnaturally loud. "It always is."

"You should be back there to listen to the kids screaming! They love it, too!"

He nodded again, eyes on the track. "That's a part of my purpose in having these trips. I want the children to learn to love the railroad, too. Like I do."

"And me," she smiled, squeezing his shoulder lightly. She let her hand remain there. "But I don't know how you'll ever get to hear the kids if you spend all your time up here!"

He turned to glance at her briefly, as if she had stated the obvious, then looked away. "There's no one else who knows how to operate a Diesel," he reminded her, naming it.

"And what did you do with Boulder Dam's powerplant, Your Honor? Only one person knew how to operate that—until you stepped in, that is."

"That's not the same thing!" he protested, his eyes firmly on the track ahead.

"Of course, of course," she kidded, squeezing his shoulder gently one more time. This time she lowered her hand. "Maybe you could teach me?"

Slowly, Eddie turned to face her, hesitating before asking, "Teach you what?"

She gestured at the control panel. "How to drive a train," she said simply.

"'Operate a train', you mean."

"See?" she asked brightly. "I'm learning already!"

"There's a lot more than that you'd need to learn than just the terminology."

"Oh, pooh. How difficult was it for you to teach me how to become a conductor?"

"Operating a Diesel is a completely different subject! It's not something you can learn overnight."

"Of course!" she agreed quickly. "I know it won't be easy. But I'm willing... and I'm sure you can teach me—" She gestured again at the control panel. "—to do whatever is right." She smiled eagerly. "Would you give me a chance?"

His eyes widened at her proposition, leaving him momentarily speechless; not only did he recognize her words as his own, he could think of only one other woman in his experience who would have the audacity to aspire to run a train—or a railroad.

She did not give him the chance to recover, nor to reply. "We don't have to do it right now, though" she insisted. "I should be getting back with the kids." She pecked his cheek in farewell as she always did, but this time she held her lips against his cheek a half second longer than usual.

The impact the brief delay had upon poor Eddie was immense. He could not help but notice how her lips lingered, if only because of the almost electric shock that shot through his skin. In that short instant, his sense of touch sharpened and reeled under the plump softness of her lips; he could almost feel her every pore and the tenderness that lay behind each one of them; his will was wiped out, leaving him helpless and speechless.

Not giving countenance to the turmoil she had intentionally instilled within him, she added one final blow: "And wait until you see my new bathing suit!" With that, she turned to leave, calling over her shoulder, "See you at Camp!"

Eddie watched her depart, speechless still. Had he put his frozen thoughts to words, part of his mind would remark upon the ironic juxtaposition—before, it was he who was helping a beautiful woman to run a railroad, not the other way around. But the remainder of his frozen thoughts could only coalesce instinctively around one very-personal notion, almost as if she had planned it that way.

\* \* \*

Children screamed.

One after the other, they clambered up the wide, rough-hewn shallow steps along the rocky cliff face, clutched the hanging rope tightly, and launched themselves into the air out over the suitably-wide creek that flowed through the deep gulch beneath the graceful arch of a steel truss railroad bridge, each of them dutifully swinging back and forth two or three times before finally releasing their grip and splashing into the deep, still water below, screaming all the way. From the shore their mothers watched with half an eye as they gossiped among themselves. The delicious aroma of grilled meats drifted through the air, the smoke of the fires swirling among the greenish-blue girders of the bridge. Hanging under the center of its artistic steel span was a wide, polished wooden sign with large, neatly-carved capital letters: *CAMP DAGNY*.

Not too high above the creek, perched on the track at one end of the graceful arch idled the *Meteor*; and leaning on folded arms out of a cab window on the Diesel's shadowed side was Eddie surveying the scene below, his face reflecting a quiet pride. Constructing the Camp had surely been among his best ideas ever. The location was ideal for a picnic grove: the gulch was deep enough that its western wall shielded the afternoon sun, protecting the picnickers from the worst of its scorching desert rays. The creek at its bottom flowed deep and cool as it meandered along its sluggish path to Lake Meade. At water's edge, a flat, gravelly shelf situated between cliff and creek formed a natural mesa for holding the wooden picnic tables and metal fire pits. That the Camp sat beneath one of Transcontinental's most attractive truss arch bridges rounded out the perfection of the place.

The bridge itself was a scaled-down twin of the original Miracle Metal bridge which spanned the chasm immediately north of the former Ellis oil fields along Transcontinental's Rio branch. That bridge had been designed by Hank himself using a revolutionary approach that would have been impossible if it were constructed out of mere steel. But by combining a truss with an arch and employing the unique capabilities of Miracle Metal, the bridge was strong enough to carry four trains at once and last hundreds of years, not to mention costing less than their cheapest culvert. It was a true showpiece, one of dozens scattered across the country, and the best possible sentry to stand guard over Camp Dagny.

Colonizing the Camp took much less time and effort than Eddie would have imagined; he and his handful of Transcontinental employees had assembled the entire infrastructure in much less than a week, the most complicated aspect being the construction of a modest bathhouse with a simple privy. Once Camp opened, ridership on the Kids' Special skyrocketed; but then, that was its purpose. It was a rare day that the train wasn't full to capacity. Eddie felt bad whenever he needed to turn someone away; at this rate, he would soon have to bring back into service the bullet-riddled day coach that had sat idle since his arrival in Las Vegas so many years ago. Unfortunately, in this new age the tempered glass panes that its windows required were impossible to find. If the coach were to take to the road once more, he would have to first board up the shattered glass and caulk the bullet holes that pocked its metal flanks. And given the burgeoning ridership, there was no denying it would have to be soon.

He watched absently as the children flung themselves one by one into the waiting water, but his attention was constantly being pulled aside by the sight of a beautiful woman in a skimpy, bright red bathing suit. At the moment, she was waiting in line for her turn at the rope; and even though he was dozens of feet above her, he could almost convince himself that he could smell her fragrance drifting on the air. She turned her head up to him as he watched, as if she had unexpectedly become aware of his attention, and for several seconds they held each other's gaze. Suddenly uncharacteristically self-conscious, she brushed a loose strand of hair back from her face, flashed an embarrassed smile, and turned to take her chance at the swing.

Unable to look away, Eddie watched captivated as she stretched her arms high over her head to grasp the rope, the reaching accentuating the curved beauty of her lithe figure. Without hesitation she swung out over the water, legs straight and toes pointed, her long auburn hair trailing alluringly in the breeze of her passage. Once, twice, three times she oscillated, bending her shapely, rigid legs back and forth at the hip to increase the degree of her arc. On the upward stroke of the fourth swing she released her grip, spinning slightly to face him, arms still held high over her head, her long legs arrow straight, her toes pointed at the water, appearing like some ballerina caught in mid pirouette, mid-air. She held the artful pose for the half-second it took gravity to reassert itself, squawked awkwardly, then with arms and legs flailing plummeted toward the water below as her hair swirled around to entangle her face. With a loud splash she was gone, leaving only expanding concentric rings to mark the spot where she had entered the pool. A moment later, a dark mass of soggy hair emerged from their center, seeming much like some surfacing sea monster streaming with stringy seaweed. Momentarily treading water, she used her fingers as a comb to reveal her face, then swam gracefully toward shore. Wriggling out of the water and onto the mesa, she paused to adjust the shoulder straps on her swimsuit one by one, the motion lifting each of her breasts in turn to settle them into a more comfortable position within. Without pausing, she slid her hands down her sides to reach behind her to snap the suit's elastic on each side of the bottom of her derriere for a more comfortable fit. She tossed her head back and bent over backwards, breasts pointed skyward, her wet hair falling behind her before she gathered it up in her hands and leaned to one side to wring some of the water from it. Hands still holding her hair high, elbows alongside her face, she walked gingerly across the gravel to retrieve an oversized, fluffy towel and wrapped herself in its bulk.

Had the fate of the entire world depended upon his immediate action, Eddie could not have torn his attention from her. Nor was he alone; almost every eye had been upon her. Several teenaged boys stood slack-jawed as they waited in line for their turn at the rope that swung unoccupied and limp over the water. Most of the mothers pointedly ignored her performance; a few smiled, while some others scowled their displeasure. The few fathers in attendance were understandably captivated as well, but the younger children simply paid no attention to the grown-ups, as children were always wont to do.

"Oh, golly!" cried a young teen as she shouldered past several stupefied young men to clutch at the ignored rope. "Get the hell out of my way!" With that, the trance was broken; together, the upstaged teens turned their angry attention to the girl on the rope, not in another bout of helpless admiration, but rather in impatient annoyance for being upstaged in line.

"Hey! Wait your turn!" screamed one lad.

"Get the hell out of *MY* way!" cried another.

"We'll give you a can't-swim license to go with your can't-drive license!" protested a third.

"Who is Eddie Willers!" she laughed as she launched herself into space.

Eddie found himself incapable of smiling at the human comedy unfolding in the scene below, having been as much a victim of the woman's charms as the upstaged young men. Shaking himself free from their spell, he reached into his pocket and pulled out the precision railroad watch he always carried when operating a scheduled run; his eyebrows went up in surprise—

they were late, an unthinkable sin for a railroadman. Reaching over his head, he grasped the hemp rope that activated the Diesel's horn and pulled one long blast, a signal to the picnickers to begin their preparations to leave. Even over the noise of the idling Diesel he could hear the collective cry of dismay from the children—and from their parents. Their reactions were uniformly the same; no one wanted to leave. The thought brought a great deal of satisfaction to Eddie; it was precisely the feeling he had intended Camp Dagny to instill in its guests.

* * *

The *Meteor* slowed.

Eddie sounded the train's mighty horn repeatedly to mark the end of the fleeting sprint down the greenish-blue straightaway, and in less than a half hour they would be back in Las Vegas, albeit a half hour late. He sincerely hoped their delay was causing no consternation among the mothers waiting at the station; certainly those on board did not feel the slightest bit put out. Had he insisted they remain at Camp for another hour, there would likely be no dissent. Still, he felt that he had somehow let his passengers down through his careless inattention to the passage of time. Punctuality was a carefully cultivated trait of the true railroadman, a professional habit not easily overcome. But his ruthless self-honesty would not let him evade responsibility; he well knew the root cause of his tardiness.

He sighed in resignation, a soft sound inaudible within the loud confines of the Diesel's cab. It would appear that there was no way he could avoid educating a new railroadman—railroadwoman, to be more precise. Eddie fully realized that her interest in operating the Diesel would be no passing fancy. He knew for a fact that when the tendrils of her mind wrapped themselves around an idea, not all the force in the universe could dissuade her. It was one of the many traits he admired in her: she was intelligently headstrong. He knew that his only recourse would be to capitulate with good grace; yet within himself he could sense a deep-seated resistance to relenting, a stubborn refusal that was firmly grounded in an irrefutable two-worded argument: *Miss Dagny*.

For the umpteenth time he reminded himself sternly that Dagny was dead and gone, and that he should simply move on with his life. But that argument was an old one which he never seemed to win. Just when he felt he had finally put her memory behind him once and for all, some new quirk of circumstance would arise which would force him to face the incontrovertible truth: that he could never, ever let go of her, not even for so desirable a prize as his future student. And what a prize she was! Her new bathing suit only showcased that fact, a tactic he was sure she adopted only to capture his attention. *Well, it worked*, he admitted, thinking of his tardiness, *and it captured a lot of other folks' attention, too!* he recalled, thinking of the stupefied young men.

He marveled anew at the ironic juxtaposition inherent in her offer. *Her helping me to run the railroad!* Not that the concept of her assistance was a startling one; as conductor of the Kids' Special she was already helping him to run the railroad, and teaching her to operate the Diesel would only be another rung up that same ladder. But having climbed one rung, the next would be lying tantalizingly close to her hand, inviting her to take hold and lift herself up to the next level. And then there would be another rung within reach, then another, and another, leading her... where? But even as he posed the question, he realized he already knew the answer: she would be there by his side, his professional partner, sharing his love of the railroad—and perhaps more?  Again, instinctively his mind balked, once more backing away from the lovely vision of the future for the same two-worded reason: *Miss Dagny!*  But Dagny aside, he knew he would teach her railroading regardless of where the rungs might lead.  There was no denying that her premise was correct: someone else needed to know how to operate the Diesel—and run the railroad.

He remembered when he was a young child how the slightly older Dagny had first instructed him regarding the rules of the railroad: "Always look both ways before crossing the tracks," she'd told him.  "Stop, look, and listen."  "Never step on top of the rail—it might have grease on it, and you'll slip and fall!"  "Long-long-short-long on the horn means a grade crossing is coming."   As young adults the lessons became more important: "Never exceed the gross tonnage painted on the side of the boxcar, or else the journal boxes might catch fire."  "Never shut down a Diesel motor right away after a run; you extend its life if you leave it idling for a while instead."  "The safety of the passenger is paramount."  As railroad executives, the lessons became more complicated still: "How quickly can we turn around these freight cars so as to maximize our profits?"  "What is the best way to allocate train crews to trains such that you don't have one waiting for the other?"  "What level of revenue will justify running a train at all?"  He remembered how Dagny had been his patient tutor over the years, instilling her knowledge into him so expertly that today he found himself just as expertly capable of running the railroad in her absence, knowledgeable to the point where he could confidently take on a new student and school her in the industrial arts of commercial railroading.

*And why not?* he asked himself, almost defiantly.  *It would be so easy!*  Juxtaposing his own internal focus, he imagined himself schooling a younger, inexperienced Dagny.  In his mind's eye, he could see her looking up at him with an awe reserved for great men, the same worshipful gaze a young Eddie had once bestowed upon her.  In response, he pictured himself as the seasoned veteran, survivor of innumerable battles, passing his life-saving wisdom along to a new generation of fighters represented in Dagny's glowing gaze.   He felt the pride of accomplishment in watching his apprentice grow in knowledge and ability, soon an apprentice no longer, but rather an equal, a partner, an indispensable ally in keeping the well-oiled machinery of a transcontinental railroad operating smoothly.

By juxtaposing their roles, he could readily recognize how Dagny had helped him to climb his own ladder, to the benefit of both of them, the railroad, and the nation.  But benefits aside, visualizing that contrast also placed him in an unexpectedly unique situation: that of having Dagny looking up to him in wondrous admiration, a whimsical state of affairs which he had never imagined before.  He found the image astonishingly appealing, almost awe-inspiring, as if he had been walking an unknown path and chanced upon some magnificent view that laid the entire world at his feet.  Because in recognizing the Dagny within himself, he was finally able to appreciate in its full context not only his former position with Transcontinental Railroad, but more importantly his current position in Las Vegas.

His shoulders squared at the thought; for today he was no longer merely a successful railroad executive; rather he was the highly-respected ad hoc leader of the Lost City of Las Vegas, the seasoned veteran fighting the town's battles, shoring up its defenses, coinage, justice—and heart—to the best of his ability.  Unconsciously he sat up a little straighter in the engineer's seat, a little more proud of himself, not a pride based on what others might think of him, but on his own assessment of his own worth and for the values that he knew he brought to bear. Without emotion he faced and accepted the long line of successes that he had left in his wake. He felt the living beat of the Diesel under his fingers. *I did this!* he affirmed, his hand almost caressing the throttle, feeling through it the throb of the vital force of the train, a force he had brought back to life and kept alive to this day. He studied the hand that softly gripped the living throttle, considering how the *Meteor* would have been a rotting hulk stranded in an Arizona desert if not for him—or a burned out hulk in the former city of San Francisco, for that matter.

And there were many other achievements that stretched far beyond that of the *Meteor's* survival. The powerplant of Boulder Dam would be only so much weathered cement and scrap copper wire. A bandit would still be roaming the streets, refugees would be going hungry, and the town's economy would have collapsed; that, and so much more. *It's all my doing!* he grasped. *All of it!*

The blunt truth of that summation only served to further convince Eddie to face and accept his own true worth, the incredible value of his knowledge, and the life-giving results of its application. He lifted his chin a little higher still as a justified pride in himself swept through him. Ahead he could make out the first outlines of Las Vegas approaching; *I made that town what it is!* he told himself without a trace of boast or modesty, simply as a facet of reality, merely another fact he could face boldly, as well as facing his role in its cause. Again he looked down at his hand resting on the throttle, feeling the mechanical life behind it. *I am in control of my world!* he proclaimed inside his head, *and it was Dagny who gave me this ability!*

He still held the juxtaposed image of the worshiping Dagny in his mind's eye, but the image was beginning to slowly reshape itself. Dagny's shoulder-length brown hair lengthened and lightened to an elegant auburn; her finely-tailored dress changed color to a bright red and slowly shrank to the skimpy proportions of an alluring bathing suit while her breasts and hips swelled entrancingly larger within. But the transformation was not merely physical, for the beauty he beheld was no hollow shell. Behind it was a keen intelligence, one with a zest and joy for living topped off with a love of the railroad that rivaled his own. Speaking silently of the beautiful, red-suited image in his mind, he affirmed, *I deserve the affection she gives me.* Unsurprisingly, at that thought he felt the warm echo of his own feelings for her edging out into the open.

*And what of her?* he asked himself point blank, and not for the first time. *Shall I claim her for my own? Shall we share not only our working lives as Dagny and I once did, but also our personal lives, as Dagny and I did not?* Once again Eddie reflexively retreated from the notion. Despite the fondness he felt for her, the thought of sharing himself with any woman other than Dagny proved to be anathema to him, almost abhorrent. *Give up Dagny?* he asked himself rhetorically; and the inevitable answer was as clear as it was swift. *Never!*

He was not surprised by his immediate gut reaction, not at all, because this was how all of his discussions with himself about Dagny had always ended. *Then why do I continue to have them?* he demanded of himself almost testily. Despite the question's petulant nature, again the response was swift and clear. *I shouldn't!* Immediately on the heels of that obvious answer came the equally-obvious decision: *Then I won't.*

His jaw tightened as he boldly faced the manifest truth he had always known and would always know, and he faced it full on, only this time he embraced it, gathered it in, and took it for his own. With a solemn, reverent clarity, as if he stood in front of some sacred altar, within the confines of the Diesel's cab he loudly proclaimed, "I... Will... Never... Let... Her... Go!" It was a final seal of words for a vow that had never been necessary to take. But it was his pronouncing the words aloud that made the vow real.

That was that. The decision was made. Dagny came first, now and forever, period. His jaw still set firm, he slowly nodded to himself, finally accepting the state of affairs fully, thereby settling the two-worded argument with himself once and for all, with the verdict returned in favor of Dagny and her memory. It was a sentence he could readily accept, and with pleasure.

He looked over his shoulder; there was no one there. But the next time there was, he knew what he had to do, why he had to do it, where it would lead—and where it would *not* lead! It simply wouldn't be fair to her to keep her hanging any longer and hoping on a romantic commitment from him. They would still remain friends, to be sure, but no longer would their get-togethers end with a peck on the cheek. Nor could he think any less of her. While she was a noble prize indeed, she was no Dagny.

He pulled the throttle gently closer to his chest, almost lovingly, the action slowing the *Meteor* to restricted speed as it approached the Las Vegas station. Once he arrived, he told himself, there were going to be some fundamental changes in his life, that was certain. After all, it was *his* life, and that meant it was his to control.

Despite the import of his resolve, Eddie felt relaxed and at ease. His coming to a final decision did not feel as if some great weight had been lifted from his shoulders, nor did he experience any sort of an immense deliverance. Rather it was a quiet realization within him, a sensation which told him this was something he'd always known. Along in its wake came the calm certainty of knowing he was in control of his world—even the parts of it that came in red swimsuits! But regardless of the specific incarnation at hand, he also knew he would always be able to fulfill his childhood promise to Dagny—to do whatever is right—even in her absence, now and forever.

## CHAPTER 10 – HERE, THERE, AND EVERYWHERE

The hypercraft banked.

Dwight admired the broad expanse of scenic desert canted beneath him. To one side lay the town of Las Vegas; on the other he could plainly see the ragged red-robed formation trailing off into the mountains. *Back For God!* he asserted excitedly. The old highway that lay between army and town was deserted, as he had requested, leaving him the wiggle room he knew he'd be needing. Precision flying at Mach seven wasn't all that precise in practice; others would do well to stand well back.

For several days running, Dwight had been having the time of his life, purposefully flitting about the former nation like some hyperactive migratory bird. But his actions were driven by intellect, not instinct, in an attempt to come to the defense of his kind of world: the nascent nation of rational men. Less than two hours ago he had been in Massachusetts; one hour earlier he and the Worker were in Washington to pick up Dagny; fifteen minutes ago, he had dropped them off at the south end of Las Vegas to meet with the enclave's leader. Now he was alone, again in the air and ready to repeat the deadly tactic he had used so successfully in defense of the Massachusetts enclave against the army of the State's Science Institute. The incredible amount of overpressure that the hypercraft could generate at Mach seven—thousands of pounds per square inch at close range—was more than enough to implode the lungs of the attackers, provided he flew close enough to his targets. The Institute had done him a favor by aligning their troops along a ridgetop, making Dwight's mission all the easier to execute. Similarly, the broad expanse of open desert with its arrow-straight ribbon of highway should prove to be a target even easier still, especially since there were no trees to trouble him.

He leveled out the hypercraft and pointed it directly into the vanguard of the approaching army. He decreased his altitude to the point where he was only a few dozen feet above the desert floor, aimed the nose of the hypercraft only slightly above the horizon, and slammed the throttle forward. Governor safeties instantly kicked in, limiting his forward acceleration to a cool ten gravities—the maximum safe level for a human passenger—and within seconds he burst through the sound barrier. "Woooo hoooo!" he screamed as the incredible acceleration forced the air out of his lungs. Mach two, three, four, he accelerated, crossing each successive milestone every four seconds. In much less than a minute, the safeties cut in again as the craft achieved Mach seven, its movement swallowing more than a mile every second. Before he could even glance downward, he had long since passed over the entire red army. Slowing half as quickly as he had accelerated, a few moments later he brought the craft up and around in a broad semicircle to view his handiwork. A scattering of red robes revealed that more than half the army was clearly down, and the remainder were taking flight back up the highway, scurrying away from Las Vegas like a pack of frightened rats.

"Oh no you don't!" he cried as he brought the craft around for a second pass. "You don't, you don't!" he repeated ominously, grinning grimly. Obviously he had been a little off course with his first pass, and the lethal cone of high-pressure air had drifted off to one side of the highway. In confirmation of his conjecture, he could see its scar as an elongated dust cloud swirling over the desert.

Banking, he positioned his craft along the proper heading, leveled out, and again slammed the throttle forward, pressing himself once again into the padded depths of the seat. Not many seconds later he reached top speed; he slowed and circled for one last pass to insure he had gotten them all. But there was no need to follow through with a subsequent go-around; it was plain that the attackers were all down. *Two strikes and they're out!* he cheered to himself.

Satisfied, he banked the craft and headed for Las Vegas. Once the Worker and Dagny were finished meeting with the enclave's leader, he'd ferry them home. With luck, they'd make it back in time for dinner.

Dwight smiled. It had been a busy trip—and a happy one, if only because he spent so much of it in the air. Defeating two looter armies in as many days merely added icing to that sweet, sweet cake.

## CHAPTER 11 – GREEN FIELDS

Dagny reminisced.

It had been many years since the last time she visited the Transcontinental station in Las Vegas, and from what she remembered of it, very little had changed. Upon entering, she noted that the vaulted marble waiting room still held the same old wooden pews for the comfort of waiting passengers, the same art deco ticket booths, and the same chromium-and-plastic tables in the cafeteria—although half that cafeteria had been given up to various plantings.

    She and her husband had arrived in town not an hour earlier. Dwight had landed their craft on an empty highway south of town, then taxied up the old road to the town's edge. There, they disembarked; Dwight immediately took to the air to face the acolyte army of Back For God while his passengers rented a pair of horses from a local butcher and headed into town to find the Transcontinental station and meet with the leader of the enclave. Dagny was surprised she still remembered how to handle a horse; she hadn't ridden one since she was a child. When they arrived at the station, unsurprisingly they found it deserted; Dwight had warned them that they may have to wait a short while before the leader arrived. Her husband established himself at a corner table among the cafeteria's plantings in patient vigil, a slowly-filling ash tray at his elbow; Dagny decided she would do some exploring.

    She left the cafeteria behind to wander around and inspect the various nooks and crannies of the station, casting her professional gaze upon its artifacts. Peering over the ticket booth's counter, she could see that fresh paper punches littered the floor. She smiled sadly; the melancholy she felt was part a sense of anachronism and part homesickness. She found it ironic that the station appeared to be in regular use even though it had been years since trains last ran. The agent's stamp lay next to its inking pad, as if ready for use, waiting only on the agent's need. Idly, Dagny picked it up and examined the setting on its changeable rubber imprint. Her eyebrows rose in disbelief; the date it held was the correct one: year, month, and day. Somewhat apprehensively, she opened the lid of the inking pad and touched her finger to its cloth surface; the red mark it left behind told her the years had not dried the pad out. She glanced around curiously; the delicate scent of lavender hung in the air. *Have children been playing in the ticket booth?* she wondered, but quickly dismissed the thought: when she tried the booth's doorknob, she found it securely locked. Intrigued, she ambled down a sloping tunnel, following an arrowed sign reading, "To The Trains."

    When she emerged from the tunnel onto the platform, she halted in surprise; the platform was crowded with people, mostly women. She felt a dizzying sensation of *déjà vu*; the tableau resembled a typical Transcontinental station from the past, back in the days when trains still routinely plied the rails of the nation. But it had been years since she had seen such a scene. *Why are so many people gathered on an abandoned train platform?* she wondered. And it had to be abandoned, she knew, because to her knowledge the only railroad running anywhere in the country today was the Dagny Line, a steep, winding track that led from Hank's new mills up to his mines in the mountains overlooking the Gulch. The ore trains did not carry passengers, but there would soon be other trains that did, she reminded herself; while she was in Washington, she had had sufficient time to examine the Transcontinental station, and although the track itself was still intact and serviceable, it was going to take a lot of effort before that showcase station could be put back into full operation. But the Las Vegas station had not only survived intact, its premises even retained the look and feel of an active train station, right down to the punch-littered floor and crowded platform.

    Recovering her poise quickly, she headed in the direction of the crowd; she simply *had* to ask one of its members what the big draw might be. But she had only taken a few steps before she halted once again in stunned surprise at the hint of a sound. At first she suspected it to be her imagination, some illusion triggered by her nostalgic tour of the old station, but the reactions of the crowd confirmed the reality of the sound: dimly in the distance there came the off-key clanking of the yard bell of an approaching train. *A train? It can't be!* Her feet froze to the ground, immobile; her eyes stared, unblinking; her ears strained to confirm that she was really hearing what she thought she heard. In a short moment she was certain; it was definitely a yard bell. There was no mistaking its rhythmic clanking. *Who would be ringing a yard bell?* Soon she had her answer, for a short way down the track, coming into sight from around a bend, was a brilliant headlamp with sparkling spikes of light shooting from its center, like some dazzlingly bright star being refracted by shards of a shattered crystal. There was no room for doubt in her mind: it was a train, and it was pulling into the station. As it came closer, Dagny could hear the throbbing of its powerful motor, and she swooned at the sound. She stretched out a hand to clasp a nearby pillar for support, feeling the resonant rumbling of the massive Diesel traveling through the ground, up the pillar, and into her very bones. She moaned softly. Closer it came, looming larger, its headlight lifting itself proudly higher and higher above her as it approached. No one noticed her leaning there against the pillar; all eyes were fixated worriedly on the approaching train, and Dagny had no desire except to do the same. Her will was wiped out; and while one part of her consciousness reeled helplessly with astonishment and amazement, the deepest core of her being reveled in anticipation. It was a train—an actual, honest-to-God, moving, living, smoking, breathing train; and not merely a train, but one led by a huge Diesel of the sort that once pulled their transcontinental passenger trains across the nation, a sight she had not seen in years! Adding to her astonishment, as the train neared, on its rounded nose beneath the brilliant headlight, she could make out an image that had been burned into her brain since she was a little girl, a logo she was able to draw before she had learned to write. It was nothing less than the coat of arms of Transcontinental Railroad: the stylized "TR" emblazoned on a silver shield. Tears welled up in her eyes at the beautiful sight, one she had once thought she would never again behold. But here it was, incarnate. It was a snapshot of the past, a living image of her life and her love. It was a train—*a train!*—and a Transcontinental train, no less, pulled by the biggest of their Diesels, a king of the road. There had been only twelve like it in the fleet, she recalled.

With a sudden, sharp hiss of dumped air, the train came to a soft halt and the waiting multitude swarmed all over it. Laughing children and their smiling mothers bounded down the steps of the day coach while others boiled out of the baggage car, its side door flung wide. Panicked conversations ensued, instantly wiping out the mothers' smiles but not even denting the children's laughter. Dagny blinked her eyes several times to clear the tears in order to get the best possible view of the unanticipated scene unfolding in front of her. But her excitement got the better of her, and she burst into tears of joy, smiling and laughing while crying, feeling nothing but the naked joy of confronting one's love, a feeling made more special by the disproven certainty that she would never encounter a scene like this one ever again. It was like meeting an old friend long-thought to be dead. If there was a heaven possible on Earth, for Miss Dagny, former Vice-President of Operations for Transcontinental Railroad, this was it.

Mothers and their children began to shuffle past her, heading back up the tunnel and into the station, surging past her with the true indifference of disconnected crowds anywhere. None of them paid her tears of joy any mind; she was effectively alone. Still leaning a hand on the pillar for support, she let the joyous experience wash over her like the caress of a lover, soaking in the ambiance for future remembrance. She was smiling with the excitement of a child when she noticed the hatch on the Diesel swing open, and watched enthralled as a coveralled engineer climbed down the side. Idly, she wondered if it could be Logan or some other railroadman she might know.

Without warning, the pillar suddenly provided insufficient support to keep her on her feet. Instinctively, she reached out a second hand to clutch the stout pole, but her numb, weak grip found no purchase on its smooth surface; she started sliding slowly down its side. She, who placed all her faith in her own judgment, in reality, and in the validity of her senses, could not believe what her eyes were reporting. Standing a score of feet in front of her, casually wiping his hands on a rag, was none other than Eddie.

## Chapter 12 – Long Train Runnin'

The *Meteor* halted.

Looking out the windshield, Eddie could see that the platform was unusually crowded, mostly with women. He could make out their worried faces as they swarmed toward the stopped train. *I'm sorry I'm late!* he apologized silently to the multitude. He felt bad for having caused any consternation, mainly because he couldn't think of any way he could make it up to them other than to strive to do better in the future. And he knew he would; the feeling that he could overcome any obstacle remained strong within him.

Setting recriminations aside for the moment, he stood up and stretched, first pulling one way, then the other, a guttural grunt punctuating each of his motions. After a moment, he unlatched the safety release on the cab's hatch, swung the door open, and climbed down the idling Diesel's side. He stepped onto the platform, pulled a rag from his belt, and began wiping his hands as two men detached themselves from the crowd of women and approached him. In the lead was the militia commander, a large-caliber weapon strung casually over his shoulder, followed by the headbanded newcomer, similarly armed.

"Mr. Eddie!" cried the commander. "Thank God you're all right! We were so worried!"

Eddie eyed him uncertainly. "Worried? What do you mean?" Unconsciously he felt for the watch in his pocket. "We were only thirty-three minutes late," he explained, not understanding the source of the concern in the commander's voice. "I lost track of time, and we stayed out a little longer than usual."

The commander grinned. "That's the best news I've heard all day!"

"What, that I was late?"

"Yes!" He looked in both directions, and licked his lips. "Listen, none of that matters right now. We were worried about you because Back For God sent an army here to attack us!"

"Back For God!" His blood ran cold. His confidence in himself wavered. The feeling he could overcome any obstacle vanished. He felt as if he were about to burst into blubbery tears, but he managed to hold his voice steady. "An army, you say?"

"Thousands of them! We feared they may have gotten to you!"

"No, we never saw anyone." His heart was beating noticeably faster. For a long time he had dreaded that Las Vegas would someday come to the attention of the brutal theocracy to their west, and apparently today was the day. His worst fear had come to pass. *Thousands of them!* He took a deep breath, and was proud to note that it did not quaver. *This is Las Vegas*, he reminded himself, reaffirming his sense of self. *We'll get through these troubles, too!* He became all business. "Have you deployed the militia?"

"Yes sir, but it didn't matter."

Eddie hesitated. "Didn't matter?" he echoed cautiously, fearing the worst.

The commander shook his head. "Nope, not at all. The strangers from Colorado took care of that Back For God-damned army. Wiped 'em right out!"

"Who wiped them out? How?"

"Beats me. Them Colorado folks have some kind of weapon that wipes out entire armies, I guess. But the only thing that matters is that they're all dead."

"Back For God's army was defeated?" Eddie was clearly having difficulty keeping up.

"Yep! Every red-robed one of 'em! The road north of town is a real mess. You ought to see it!" He shook his head with a rueful smile. "Society's going to have one hell of a cleanup bill on its hands," he chuckled.

Eddie stared at him for a moment. "Defeated by strangers from Colorado, you say?" His confidence ebbed and flowed with each answer he heard. "Who are they?"

"I'm not rightly sure. When the lookout spotted the army approaching, we called for help on the shortwave, and these people from Colorado came flying in."

"They actually flew in? In an airplane?" he ebbed.

"That's what folks tell me, although I didn't see it for myself. And a strange-looking one at that, they say."

"And Back For God is defeated?" he flowed.

"That's right. And two of them Colorado folks are inside waiting to speak with you." He hooked a thumb in the direction of the station. "I was telling them how—"

Automatically Eddie turned his head to glance briefly in the indicated direction, began to turn back—and froze. Not twenty feet down the platform, slumped against a pillar, her astonished grey eyes locked firmly on his, hung a slight, beautiful woman. It was Dagny.

The commander was still speaking, but Eddie did not hear a word the man said. Slowly he turned to face her full on, their locked gazes as firm as a steel rod joining them solidly together into a single entity. Slowly he began to walk toward her—much to the surprise of the commander who found himself ignored while still in mid-sentence. She did not move as he approached; the steel of his gaze held her motionless. After what seemed an eternity for each of them, he finally closed the last of the distance and stood over her, his face unreadable. For several seconds the tableau held, neither believing the presence of the other, yet it was impossible to deny it. Finally, Eddie reached out a hand.

"Dagny?" he asked softly, already knowing the answer.

She took his hand and he gently helped her to her feet. "Eddie," she whispered in turn, placing her other hand flat against his chest, as if to feel the living force that lay within.

Still holding her hand, he gently brushed a fallen strand of her short brown hair back from her face, and tenderly caressed her cheek with the back of a finger, a rare break in the formality that had always existed between them. "Dagny," he replied with a firm finality.

For many seconds neither one moved, then with a soft sigh she fell forward and melted in his arms, breaking down into tears. "Eddie, you're alive!" she cried into his chest. "You're alive!" Sobs shook her.

"Dagny, Dagny," he uttered as he stroked her hair, tears starting to pour down his own cheeks.

"Oh, Ed—," she began, but her words broke off and she began laughing though her tears.

He held her out at arm's length, a hand on each shoulder, a confused look on his tear-streaked face. "Dagny!" he cried. "What's the matter?"

She looked up at him with wet, laughing eyes. "You smell like a *train!*"

He stared at her blankly, not knowing what to say.

"And it smells *wonderful!*" She buried her face back into his chest, clutching him tightly with both arms. "Oh, Eddie," she moaned softly.

For a long time they stood there in tight embrace as if neither would ever let go; it was Dagny who finally regained her poise. She drew back a little and studied him with mild amusement. "You're the one," she asserted. "You're the leader here. The man we're supposed to meet." It was a statement, not a question.

"Yes."

She lifted her head to look past him at the idling Diesel. Several seconds passed before she continued. "And that's the final *Meteor* out of San Francisco." Again, it was a not a question.

"Yes."

"And there's still train service in Las Vegas?" This time a slight question mark made itself felt.

"Twice a week," he replied, the quiet pride plain in his voice. "Down to Boulder City in the morning, and up to Camp Dagny in the afternoon."

"Camp Dagny?" she inquired, a small smile appearing on her lips.

"Yes," he replied somewhat defiantly, then more softly, "It's a pretty place. You'll like it, I think. The kids sure do."

Her eyes widened. "You have... kids?"

Eddie blushed furiously. "No, of course not. The kids on the train, I mean. I carry them and their mothers to Camp Dagny. It's a picnic grove we built to promote ticket sales."

"I see," she said. She looked around. "All this..." She waved an arm slowly. "All this time you've been living here..." She looked back to him. "Leading a normal life..."

He looked around them in turn. "I wouldn't quite call it a normal life," he countered, a slight tone of amusement creeping into his voice. "And you... You've been—"

"—in Colorado," she finished for him, gently pushing herself back from his embrace. She looked up into his eyes. "With my husband."

He held her at arms' length, a perplexed, wounded expression crossing his face. "You have... a husband?"

She nodded. "And you already know him—he's your old friend from Transcontinental's cafeteria in New York, the Worker. He and Midas set up an enclave in a secluded valley up in the Rockies, and all of the men of the mind retreated there before the world collapsed. Me, Francisco, Hank, Quentin, and lots of others you know. There are over two thousand of us living up there."

He held her eye for a moment. "But not me."

"No, not you," she echoed, looking away. "Everything you've ever said demonstrated how you weren't ready for it."

Several silent seconds slid past as he assimilated the news. "I see," he said.

"He's here with me now."

"Your husband? Here?" Eddie's eyes widened, a slight furrow gracing his brow as his eyes slowly scanned the platform area. "Where?"

She gestured lightly with her head toward the station building. "In the cafeteria."

Eddie glanced in the same direction. *How appropriate!* With the gesture of an owner, he took Dagny's hand and led her away from the platform, up the tunnel, and into the station. He hung back as they approached the cafeteria door, pulling her hand backward slightly so that she turned to face him. "Please. I need to sort this out with him alone."

"All right."

She had not hesitated before answering, nor had he waited for her response. Releasing her hand, he turned to open the cafeteria door.

## CHAPTER 13 – KILLER QUEEN

*It's time!*

*It's taken me... what, two years almost? But I have him! I finally have him right where I want him! The hook's sunk, he's on the line, and today—today!—today is the day I start to reel him in... No, that's not quite true. My Eddie will reel himself in, that's what. Everything is ready—ready for Eddie! He'll come. He's been one tough customer, my toughest ever, but he'll come. Today. For years I've used my skill and charms for the pleasure of others. Today, I'm going to use them for mine. It's time!*

She turned her head against the scented silk pillow and glanced at the softly-ticking clock; 9:02, its hands read, and she smiled. *See? It's time!* she joked to herself. Throwing off the lone flannel top sheet that covered her nakedness, she rose and busied herself with her morning chores, followed by an impromptu, inelegantly elegant breakfast: leftovers from her gourmet dinner with Eddie the night before. She smiled broadly at the memory. *He's finally comfortable coming up here to the house. He's become so much more relaxed with me. Finally! So today we up the stakes. Go for broke. Reel him in. It's time.* She finished her breakfast in a fine humor, although it was unexpectedly tainted with a rarely-felt pang of disappointment that she was still without her morning newspaper. *Years! Years with no newspaper!* Resignedly she shrugged good-naturedly. *I suppose I'll just have to start printing my own*, she lamented. *And maybe I will! The gossip I hear just from the folks on my block every day is more than enough to fill a book!* She pondered the possibility as she cleaned up her breakfast table, but put her fancies behind her as she headed for the shower. She had much more important matters on her mind. *Kids' Special day!* she twinkled. She glanced down at her still-naked body with a mocking smile. *Got to look my best for Eddie!* Reaching up to the shower curtain rod, she pulled down two scraps of bright red cloth and held them up appreciably, one in each hand, admiring the skimpy results of her fashionable handiwork at the sewing machine these last few days. *And you, my fine friends, are my rod and reel!*

\* \* \*

"All aboard!"

Following the safety rule Eddie had taught her, she hung her torso precipitously out into space, her feet firmly planted on the penultimate stair of the day coach and each hand wrapped tightly around a pair of opposing grab irons that flanked the steps. She turned her head right then left to make sure no one was making a last-minute attempt to board or disembark; and seeing no one, she waved her hand slowly to signal the *all's clear* to the engineer. With his head and elbow hanging outside the Diesel's cab, Eddie returned the signal, then vanished inside. The train began to move; after a moment she pulled herself in from her precarious perch and entered the baggage car. As she opened the door, a wall of noise pressed boisterously against her. Excited children scurried around the voluminous car, energized and eager to be finally underway, waiting impatiently for the long, straight stretch of rail where "Eddie's *Meteor*" would soon blast off.

"Tickets, tickets," she called, her cheerful voice cutting smartly across the din. She snicked her ticket punch several times in quick succession to punctuate her request. *I love this job!* she declared to herself as she collected the adults' tickets—but none from the kids; they rode free. Reaching down, she tousled one child's hair affectionately. *And I just love people! Big people, little people, men, women... and Eddie!"* she added. *And today's the day!* she reminded herself, tossing a quick glance ahead toward the unseen Diesel.

She stuffed the punched tickets in her pocket. Unsurprisingly, none of them mentioned Camp Dagny; rather, they sported destinations unreachable in today's world: San Diego, St. Paul, Atlanta, Denver, Miami, New York City, and more. Paper remained an uncommon commodity in Las Vegas, necessitating the use of whatever old tickets had happened to be in the station's vault at the time of civilization's collapse. Although a small amount of paper could be produced from the desert scrub that grew locally, it was far too brittle to withstand the handling a typical ticket received; worse, its muddy coloration defied the strongest bleaches available, thereby complicating the printing process. This marriage of ills disqualified the domestic paper from employment in everyday items, such as newspapers and train tickets, relegating it instead to the yeomen tasks of packaging, wrappings, and industrial uses.

Moving forward from the baggage car, she entered the day coach to face a similar scene of boisterous bedlam, and she loved to hear it. Efficiently she completed her conductor's duties and stood for a moment at the front end of the coach, her hand holding lightly onto an overhead strap, surveying the scene and waiting. She knew that as loud as her passengers already were, they were about to become a great deal louder. True to her surmising, the day coach instantly bursts into screams, harmonizing with the repeated blasts of the *Meteor*'s horn. They knew what was coming. Unconsciously, she tightened her grip; she knew, too. She smiled broadly as the *Meteor* accelerated faster and faster, her slender body reflexively leaning into the rapidly-lengthening velocity vector. Outside the windows, all became a blur as the train's speed quickly topped out at almost one-quarter the speed of sound; but all too soon it was over, and she leaned against the deceleration to the tune of the children's disorderly dismay.

She scanned her charges once more. *It's time. They'll hold out a few moments without me.* She turned around and left the car, heading forward, stepping across the gap between the day coach and the Diesel. *It's time!* she repeated to herself. *Time for step one!* She passed through the skinny door at the rear of the Diesel and maneuvered along the narrow passageway between engines and wall, paying no attention to the three thunderous motor units, their mechanical intricacies, or the powerful roar of their rising, falling, rising scream. She would be their master soon enough, if things went according to plan. *Which they will!* she confidently assured herself. Reaching the other end, she ascended the two metal steps, pushed open the door to the cab with the casual, unannounced right of an owner, and entered. The door had been ajar, inadequately sealing off the thunder of the continuous explosion thrown off by the motors; unsurprisingly, he did not notice her entrance. *Guess who?* she sang to herself, suppressing an urge to place her hands over his eyes from behind. Instead, she touched his shoulder gently. *Step one...*

"That was *fun!*" she gushed, a childlike grin splitting her face, and her voice straining to be heard above the Diesel's roar. Her eyes were bright with excitement, and her heart raced with anticipation at the sight of her hand on his shoulder. *Me of all people! Nervous about touching a man!* But she left her hand remain where it was, covering her unease with small talk and waiting for her opening to come. She did not have long to wait; he asked the question she had maneuvered him into asking.

"Teach you what?" he obliged.

She gestured at the control panel. "How to drive a train," she said simply.

"'Operate a train', you mean."

"See?" she asked brightly. "I'm learning already!" She paused to allow him to interject an expected, feeble objection, and again he obliged her. *Men are so predictable!* she observed. *But they're sweet, too.* She patiently waited for his protestations to taper off, then demurely tossed off a well-practiced line. "But you can teach me—" She gestured again at the control panel in front of him, quoting his own words against him: "—to do whatever is right." She almost swooned when she saw his reaction. *It worked! He must have told me that story a dozen times... Why is he so surprised when I repeat it back? Doesn't he think I actually listened?* She smiled brightly, half in pleased response to his surprise, and half in reply to her own elation. *That may already be more than enough shocks for my Eddie, but there are more coming!* Without giving him the chance to recover or reply, she asserted, "We don't have to do it right now, though. I should be getting back with the kids." *But not without a few more zingers first!* She leaned forward and pecked his cheek as usual, but this time she intentionally held her lips to his skin for a substantial fraction of a second longer than normal.

She pulled back slowly, and could see the glassy look in his eyes that affirmed he had noticed the deliberate delay. *Now for the pièce de résistance!* "And wait until you see me in my new bathing suit!" she exclaimed, calling in farewell over her shoulder. Without waiting to see his reaction, she opened the cab door leading back into the bowels of the Diesel and vanished.

Closing the door firmly behind her, she allowed herself a quick jig of joy, her feet tapping on the metal floor unheard above the cacophony of the motor units. *Got him, got him, GOT HIM!* she exalted as she re-entered the much-quieter day coach noisy with the laughter of the children.

Noticing her return, one little boy separated himself from the other children and approached her. "Are we there yet?" he asked innocently, his eyes wide.

"Almost!" she quickly replied, her word answering not only the little boy's direct question, but also one unasked pertaining to herself and her quest.

"Hooray!" he cheered. "Who is Eddie Willers!"

\* \* \*

Heads turned.

She had expected that, given the flashy color and meager proportions of her bathing suit; but then, that was its purpose. *Step two...*, she reminded herself as she ambled gracefully across the flat, pebbly mesa. Although eyes followed her, she would not chance turning her own eyes up toward the idling Diesel; *he* was supposed to be watching *her*, not the other way around; but against her will she found her glance pulled up. She had to know: *Is he seeing it?* But he was not watching her amble; he was mindful only of the children diving from the rope swing. Quickly she looked away disappointed, not wanting him to notice her noticing him, not yet. *Why can't he see me? How blind can he be?* But it was a blatant fact that most of her fellow picnickers did notice her. She could sense the various reactions of those around her without having to look; the female contingent was annoyed, jealous, aloof, shocked, and more, but the males were of a single mind, and singularly attentive. *Look at me!* she pleaded to the averted face above, ignoring the reactions of the scores around her, and struggling to keep her eyes off the idling Diesel to confirm compliance, a struggle she increasingly feared she would lose.

She did. She raised her head and found his eyes firmly upon her, his face expressionless. The sudden, unexpected awareness of his attention completely flustered her composure, leaving her mentally discombobulated. All of her careful planning and rehearsals went for naught; all the practiced details of her well-planned strategy vanished. Her mind reeled; she was unable to pull her gaze away. Awkwardly she brushed a loose strand of hair back from her face. *Well, this is what you wanted him to do! Now what?* For several seconds they held each other's eyes, but still she did nothing. *So much for step two!* Finally, uncertainly, she flashed him an embarrassed smile and looked away; she didn't know what else to do. Mercifully, the line advanced, and it was her turn at the swing. Grasping the rope, she lost no time swinging out into space, and with an awkward splash she landed in the water and swam to shore. *Well, I really muffed that one!* she scolded herself as she wrapped herself in a large, fluffy towel. *I try to solicit some sort of reaction from him, and what do I get? Nothing?!*

As if on cue, the triple-coned horn of the Diesel blared out one long echoing blast, startling her out of her wits. Alarmed, her grip on the towel loosened and it accidentally—and enticingly—slipped to the ground. Again involuntarily, her eyes shot up to the Diesel, but the watcher had vanished within. She could see from his profile that he was busily engaged in some task in front of him; her moment had come and gone. Frustrated, she snatched the towel from the pebbly ground and stalked off in the direction of the bath house to change, oblivious to the helpless adoration of the young men she left in her wake.

\* \* \*

The *Meteor* slowed.

She had postponed visiting the Diesel during their return journey, waiting until she felt she had sufficiently recaptured her poise and realigned the reality of the situation with her planning, but by then it was too late; they were almost back to town. *Well*, she sighed philosophically, *at least the foundation has been laid. I can always pick up from here. There's no big hurry, and it's not like I'm about to lose him for good!*

As the train pulled into the station, she assumed her usual position on the penultimate step of the day coach leaning outward. Looking ahead, she was surprised to see the enormity of the crowd that packed the platform. Granted, the *Special* was running a little later than usual, but that had happened before without causing nearly so much consternation. As the train came to a halt, she could make out the worried expressions on the waiting faces, looking as if they feared some disaster may have befallen the *Meteor,* mixed with relief that those fears had apparently been misplaced.

"Las Vegas!" she called out ritualistically and unnecessarily. "This station stop for Las Vegas!" She stood to one side of the vestibule as the laughing children and their mothers streamed down the steps and off the train. Over the din she caught a mélange of frightened phrases.

"...coming to attack us!"

"...here's your pistol!"

"...thank God you're safe!"

Confused and curious but mindful of her responsibilities as conductor, she waited for the day coach to empty, then walked through the vacant cars scanning left and right for forgotten possessions, possible maintenance issues, or anything else that might prove amiss. Finding all in order, she returned to the steps and leaned out of the car, her perch several feet above the dispersing crowd giving her a clear vantage of the goings on. Eddie was descending the ladder down the side of the Diesel; and waiting for him at its base was the militia commander—heavily armed, no less!—accompanied by that new man in town, the one who always wore a headband. She had seen him around the honky-tonk a few times, but they had never spoken. From the platform at her feet arose the conversations of those still lagging behind, quickly giving her the general idea of what it was that had triggered their distress—Back For God was attacking! The thought froze her feet to the steps, for she knew *precisely* where her kind stood in *their* pecking order! She watched numbly as Eddie assimilated the commander's briefing, likely hearing the same terrible news she had just overheard. Oddly, rather than reacting to the news as she had, Eddie turned and simply walked away from the commander, blithely abandoning him to exchanging perplexed glances with the new man. *What the heck?* she wondered, adding a third perplexed person to the milieu. She took one uncertain step down the stairs and hesitated as she watched Eddie walk deliberately and slowly toward the tunnel leading back into the station; but he did not choose to enter it. Rather, he paused to stand over what appeared to be a distraught woman, someone she did not recognize. *A newcomer?* she wondered. Eddie looked down at the woman for a moment before extending a hand to help her to her feet.

Simultaneously several things happened: Eddie and the woman embraced each other almost desperately; she finally recognized the woman in his arms—Miss Dagny!—and the reason behind the naming of the picnic grove, plus the fatal impact her appearance would have on the now-doomed step three. Her knees turned to water; she swooned; her numb legs gave way. She stumbled heavily down the steps of the day coach, and found herself sitting unceremoniously on the unyielding surface of the platform, her legs folded awkwardly beneath her and her arms leaning tenaciously on the bottom step for dubious support.

*It's over!* she realized with a well-founded horror. *It's all over! No steps three or four... or five!* Tears welled up in her eyes. *He's lost to me!* She felt hollow and drained. *It's obvious, now! Oh, so obvious!* A brittle laugh escaped her. *All the while I thought I knew what I was doing, why he was so distant, so difficult, so shy! I thought it was me—I did all I could to put my past behind me, but it was her all along! Her memory! It's obvious they had been lovers!* As she stared, she felt as if she were somehow violating their privacy, even though they stood openly in public view; and even though she could not tear her eyes away from the tearful reunion, she wanted nothing more than to blot it out of her consciousness. *Oh, Eddie, my Eddie!* Tears trickled down her cheeks to splash on the steps of the *Meteor*. Of its own accord, her head slumped onto her arms, finally and mercifully blocking her view.

"Miss?" a concerned voice broke through her grief. "Are you all right, miss?"

Ineffectively blinking to clear her tear-blurred vision, she looked up at her questioner, but his face swam in her view. "I... I...," she began, but could manage no more.

"Let me help you up!" he responded worriedly, taking her hand.

She let herself be lifted until she was on her feet. With her free hand she wiped one eye clear to regard her benefactor; it was the new man.

"Are you all right?" he repeated.

"Yes," she lied. "Just a dizzy spell." She took a ragged, deep breath; the man's eyes involuntarily dropped to her swelling chest, then back to her face. "I'll be all right," she assured him unconvincingly.

"Are you sure?"

"Yes, yes," she insisted, feigning a little more confidence. "I'm fine."

"Listen—you ought to sit down for a minute and take it easy." He gestured to a nearby bench.

Her eyes turned toward Eddie and Miss Dagny; he was leading her into the station, her hand in his.

"That's okay. I'm fine, thanks," she persisted, her eyes still on the departing couple. "Besides, I have to get back to my other job."

"Is it far? Let me walk you over," he persisted in turn, the concern plain in his voice.

"It's just a block away from here," she countered. "I'll be okay."

"Please! Just in case."

Her hesitation lengthened into a deliberate pause as she considered the man and his request. "All right," she finally replied, smiling through her tears.

## CHAPTER 14 – DIALOGUE

Eddie halted.

As he stood in the doorway of the cafeteria of Transcontinental Railroad's Las Vegas station, the sense of *déjà vu* was overwhelming. At the corner table, a cigarette between two fingers, sat the Worker. Eddie could think of him in no other terms than just "the Worker;" that was what he had always been to Eddie, a nameless character in the novel of his life, back in the days when they both worked for Transcontinental in New York City. But while Eddie well knew his name—in fact, the whole *world* knew his name!—to Eddie he would forever remain simply "the Worker."

The Worker was dressed in ordinary slacks and shirt, not the rough, grease-stained clothing that Eddie was accustomed to seeing him wear; but it was obvious that it was still the same man nonetheless, because although his clothes may have been different, his mien had not changed one iota. Behind a twisting blue curl of rising cigarette smoke, the face without guilt or pain or fear faced him with the same enormous intensity of interest it had always held. He watched Eddie from under a crown of copper hair with a pitiless gaze reminiscent of the prairie dog who had once barred the way of the motionless *Meteor* as it lay disabled in an Arizona desert.

It had been many a year since Eddie and the Worker had last crossed paths, since before civilization collapsed and the lights of New York City had gone out forever, before the Worker's long radio speech to the world, even before Dagny's airplane had crashed high in the Rockies, back in the days when the world had still lived and breathed with modern industrial life. But the years had not aged the Worker a day; his steady stare remained irresolutely the same as it ever was.

Eddie suppressed an impulse to fetch a tray of food, as he had always done at their past meetings. He could not help but note the irony that no Transcontinental diner car had served food in almost as many years as had elapsed since their previous encounter. Certainly he had not reintroduced meal service in the meantime. Incongruously, a thought surfaced: *Perhaps I should?* but he pushed it aside.

With an unintentionally sonorous pace, Eddie slowly and deliberately crossed the room to stand behind the chair opposite the Worker and looked down at him. They watched each other across the chrome-trimmed, plastic tabletop in silence for a long time, long enough for one of the Worker's cigarettes to expire and a new one to be lighted.

When Eddie finally spoke, the emotional indignation was manifestly evident in his shaking voice. He took a half step backward, stretched an accusing finger in the Worker's direction, held it for two long seconds, then cried out, "*You left me to DIE!*" as if the accusation were torn from him. He held the apocalyptic pose for several seconds longer, his eyes misting over with unshed tears, his breath coming in short gasps.

The Worker did not reply; his eyes remained intently fixed upon Eddie's.

Eddie took a deep breath, regaining some of his composure and letting his arm drop before continuing. "Our conversations always meant a lot to me. *You* meant a lot to me! I always assumed that I meant something to you, too... I did? Well, you sure picked a strange way to show it! Why did you decide to leave me behind?..." Eddie sighed deeply, regaining more of his composure as he did. "You're right; it *was* my choice. I did want to hold onto my job—I had to! I couldn't let it go!" He waved an arm around him, encompassing the cafeteria, the station, and beyond. "Not Transcontinental Railroad! From ocean to ocean forever!... No, they didn't say 'forever;' I added that part myself. Didn't I mention that to you once before?" With a toss of his hand, he waved off the aside. "Regardless! How was I to know that another choice existed? You never told me about your valley, never asked me to go with you... What do you mean, 'not in so many words?' You never mentioned it at all!... You did?..."

Straining to understand, Eddie listened in rapt attention as the Worker tried to explain, starting from the very beginning. He spoke of sanctions, of looters and mystics, of a flawed moral code that was guaranteed to bring about its own downfall, and how Eddie had been a willing participant in that destruction because he had continued to support his destroyers even in the face of knowing them for what they were. He spoke of the looters and called them by name: James, Orren, Mr. Thomson, Chick, Ma, Dr. Floyd, Fred, and more, and how each of them were strengthened by Eddie's ill-bestowed efforts, all to the nation's detriment. Then the Worker spoke of a new moral code, something he called a code of life, where a man pledged never to live his life for another. He spoke of his strike, of enclaves, of the

Gulch, and what sort of person it took to enter Atlantis. The quiet pride in his tone of voice was unmistakable.

Try as he might, Eddie could not comprehend fully, even though much of it he had heard years before during the Worker's overly-long radio address to the nation; and while he did understand and agree with much of what the Worker explained, other parts made no sense at all. Finally he shook his head, not so much in negation, but more to clear all the obfuscation the Worker's words were generating.

"No!" he interrupted. "Stop trying to confuse me! I'm no philosopher, I'm just this guy, you know? I can't argue with you on your own terms. But I do know that people do make mistakes—we are only human, after all... What? Stop trying to confuse me, I said! We *are* 'only' human. As I was saying, we all make mistakes—and I know I do, too! But even though I've made my share of them, I know one thing's no mistake: friends don't leave friends to die... Yes, even when they've made a really big mistake. *Especially* when they make a really big mistake! Don't you think it's a much, much bigger mistake for you to leave them to die?... What?! What do you mean, 'it depends?' What does it depend on? We're talking life or death here! Does my survival depend on your whims?... What do you mean, on *my* whims? But it was your own whim that stopped you from telling me about your valley, *yours!*... Yes, yes, you're right—you did tell a lot of others, from what I hear. But what about the rest of us? Men like me and all the other men of the world you left to die?... No duty? Oh, come on! You know you don't mean that! There are times when you have no choice but to help others—and this was one of them! Friends don't leave friends to die!... Yes, and I always thought you were my friend, too, but don't you think it's your duty?... Now you wait one minute here! You can't just give me a flat 'no!'... But that's my point! You should *want* to help others—especially your friends!—whenever they're in trouble. That's what friends are for... No, *no!* No one has to support anyone's destroyers. There are lots of other ways you can help without either compromising with a destroyer or stonewalling a friend. Just take a look at what we've accomplished here in Las Vegas. Thousands of people living together in peace. And this is Las Vegas, remember, a town that boasts a substantial number of those same looters and mystics you say you despise. Yet we all get along well enough without looting or despising each another." Eddie paused and shook his head at a thought. "'Despise,'" he repeated softly to himself, his anger subsiding. "That's a strong word to use to describe your feelings for a man with whom you merely happen to disagree... Don't say that!" he cried, angry again. "They are *not* all looters! That's simply not true! Most men are basically good at heart... Yes, yes; you're right. Some truly are looters. But they are few in number—*very* few! And there are ways of dealing with them besides leaving them and everybody else to die... Like what we've done here in Las Vegas, that's what. I was just trying to tell you: our Society doesn't tell people to hide in the mountains and stand aside while their fellow men perish. Instead we help them as best we can whenever we can... No, not paid by taxation. We have no taxes here. The rule is "from each according to his ability, to each according to his need. It's— Are you all right?... Because you suddenly looked ill, that's why..."

"That's right; we don't have taxes here. People give voluntarily to Society, and it's Society who helps those who can't help themselves... Stop trying to confuse me! I don't know what 'reification' means... No, no. There truly *is* something called Society, it really does exist, and I was elected its Head... Very funny, but no: Society's nothing like that, although women are free to participate. We have a Congress with Senators and Representatives. They pass Guidelines that I sign, and men are left free to follow them or not... No, no! Didn't you listen to what I just said? The Guidelines are voluntary. Society does nothing to men if they don't follow them. But if you're running a business it's best if you do, or else you won't stay in business very long... Because people won't deal with you, that's why. Let me tell you what happened to a man here who chose not to follow them..." He spoke in detail of their banking Guidelines and how failing to follow them forced the failed banker out of business.

"So you see, no one is forced to follow the Guidelines. We believe in the complete separation of economy and State, but more importantly, we believe in the separation of Society and State. You *have* to keep them separate! Otherwise the needs of charity will overwhelm everyone... No, Society has no responsibility toward anyone. It has nothing to do, properly speaking, with the life of any one person. Society just keeps out of the way and gives men a chance. But when men falter—for whatever reason— Society is there to lend them a hand... No, it's more of a hand up rather than a handout... No, Society's not just another name for government. I already told you we have complete separation of Society and State here. Governments are all about force; Society is all about cooperation, about helping... That's true; governments have traditionally been the ones to provide most of the charity, but without a functioning Society to whom else could men turn? Parents *care* whether or not their children get educated, so they let the government do it. Caring people *want* to help the indigent elderly. Education, charity—these are great goals for a man to have; or, more precisely, 'good ends'... You are correct in that; until recently even I never stopped to ask: by what means? Because with government, it's always been by forced taxation!... Government by looting? I guess you could call it that. Taxation is surely a form of theft... Well, at last we finally agree on *something!*...

"Yes, we do still have some crime in this town. Where on Earth doesn't?... Okay, if you say so!... Well, yes, there are a few things that have worked for us against criminals: one punishment for not respecting the rights and property of others is that the town withdraws its protection from the criminal. If a man doesn't want to play by our rules and respect the rights of others, he can't call on us to come defend his rights... That's right; someone could steal from him and he'd have no recourse through the courts. It only stands to reason... Yes, that might tend to escalate the violence, so another punishment we've used is outright exile in the worst cases... Ah, so you like the idea of exile? It appears we agree on something else, too. For how long do you exile men?..." Eddie harrumphed. "Why am I not surprised? But you can't cut yourself off from them forever. We've found that it's a rare man who takes well to exile. Instead, we've found it to be a powerful motivational force to convince them to take their lumps and rejoin society... Yes, it can work—and it *has* worked! Let me explain how we handle it here in Las Vegas..." He related the story of the bandit from two years earlier. "And now he's a productive citizen and a shift supervisor at Boulder Dam with a great future ahead of him. Should we have just sent him off forever to die in the desert?... Oh, come on! You know you don't mean that! Especially in his case—men who have the ability to understand high-voltage electrical systems are very hard to come by these days, in case you haven't noticed... What's so funny?... Oh, that's right— you're an engineer, too. Sorry. In any case, our former bandit has come around to a civilized way of thinking, and he's a bandit no longer...

359

Civilized? It means that so long as a man respects the rights and property of others, he can live his own life his own way. That's the only rule we really have here. Live and let live is the law of the land. Didn't I already tell you that? It's only when someone doesn't respect the rights or property of others that the courts need to step in. So our enforcement only affect the criminal, not the honest man... Of course we have the right to step in—since the offender isn't respecting the rights of others, why should anyone respect his? He's the one who's setting the rules; we're just following them. Like I said, it stands to reason... That's right; that's the only time we can move against them. Other than that, no man has a pure right over the person or property of others—except when they concede that right, of course... Yes, an individual could still step in, especially for self-defense—this is Nevada, remember!—nor is private charity forbidden. Nothing is, other than not respecting the rights and property of others... That's right. The use of retaliatory force is always left to individual men... No, the State has no monopoly on any use of force, either retaliatory or offensive. Where would it get such a power? Not from men... But no man possesses a monopoly on anything! So how could he delegate to the State a right that he, himself, does not possess? Isn't it true that the State has no rights except those delegated to it by men for a specific purpose?... So where does the State get it, then?... Yes, an individual man could always agree to hand away his right to defend himself, but why in God's name would anyone ever want to do that?..." Eddie sighed aloud. "Listen, stop making bald statements and just answer me: why do you insist that men surrender their right to self defense?... I'll tell you why it's a bad idea: because if the state has a monopoly on the defensive use of force, that monopoly has to be enforced, doesn't it? And how is it enforced? By force, obviously! And that opens the door to the state initiating force! And once they initiate force for one reason, you can bet your bottom willie they'll find other reasons as well. Surrendering your right to defend yourself is surrendering yourself into the hands of force!...

"No, Society has nothing to do with it. Law enforcement and the courts are completely separate from Society. I already told you we have total separation of Society and State here. That is key. We dare not let the State handle Societal matters—that's what helped kill this country in the first place! Instead what we have is an organized, voluntary charity as compared to the forced charity that America and the other People's States traditionally followed... Ah, but I disagree with you there. My Assistant Head of Society is a priest, and he has records demonstrating how individual charity is a lot less dependable... Because it's completely uncoordinated, that's why. It's sort of like living with anarchy as compared to having a proper government." He paused, considering the words he had just uttered. "Charitable anarchy?" he muttered to himself and nodded. "Yes, that's just what it is: anarchy in charity! And the effect it has on charity is the same effect that anarchy has on justice: it's unevenly applied, mostly randomly, usually inefficiently, where benefactors often end up acting at cross purposes, and the men most in need are the ones who fall between the cracks... What?! You can't mean that!... I don't care if you do! Stop saying it! If you can't be kind, at least have the decency to be vague!"

Eddie took a shaking deep breath before continuing. "Come on, man! Have a heart! Haven't you ever stopped to look at charity from the other side? Haven't you ever been in need?... Yes, you're right. Everyone has at some point, I guess. But I mean desperately in need, say a man suffered a bad accident where he didn't have the ability or money to put himself back on his feet. Who would take care of him?... Yes, I agree with you there. Too often men are irresponsible in life and squander whatever money they have... That's true, too, but you have to admit that sometimes it's a real lifesaver for the soul for a man to scrimp and save a few pennies out of his meager budget so that he can forget his troubles for a while and take in a movie show with his family, or maybe just get out of the house for a few hours and drop by the local taproom... Well, yes; but that's of no account, because that's not what I was talking about. I meant someone with absolutely no money or with really big troubles—or a whole bunch of regular men with lots of small troubles! Let me give you an example from here in town..." He related the story of the group of homeless refugees the town had taken in the year before. "That was the trigger that showed us how necessary an organized Society really is—and how badly the needy could suffer in its absence... Yes, the men of Las Vegas were eager to help, but the devil was in the details of how to do it... But that's just what I've been saying: maybe random charity would work that one time, but what about the next? You can't just leave it all to chance, because what if no one bothered to help? I remember a case here—pre-Society, of course. It couldn't happen today—where a lonely widow almost starved to death because no one stepped up... You know you can't mean that!... Because I can't believe a man would ever say what you just said, that's why I keep asking! Most people would not simply leave another man to die!—especially a destitute old widow!... Only because she doesn't agree with you?" He took a step closer to the Worker's table, his eyes widening in realization. "Is that how it was with me? I don't completely agree with your philosophy, but I'm no looter! Yet you left me to die anyway!" Eddie hesitated, a vacant stare revealing that something else had just occurred to him. He returned his attention to the Worker. "Let me ask you something: Hank quit his job a couple of years ago in—what, November? And then the nation collapsed before that winter was over. Had it taken him a couple of months longer to come around to your way of thinking, would you have left him behind to die, too?... You can't mean that! It's Hank we're talking about here! The great industrialist and inventor Hank!..." He shook his head slowly; he could not escape understanding the Worker's reasoning. "That explains why you'd leave *me* behind. You'd leave your friends to die simply because they don't think *exactly* like you do... No, no, *NO!* Stop saying that! We were *not* supporting our own destroyers! I already told you: Hank and I trying to keep our world afloat is *not* the same thing as us helping a looter to loot!... No! It's a completely different thing when you're fighting to save your own sort of world; it's the *right* thing to do. But what you did, to stand idly aside and leave everyone else—including your friends!—to die! Can't you see that's wrong?..."

Even as he asked the question, he realized what answer the Worker would proffer—which the Worker obligingly did. Little by little Eddie was being driven into a corner where he could not help but understand that the Worker simply did not care about the fate of those who thought the slightest bit differently from him. But Eddie refused to be driven quietly into his corner, for each of the Worker's outrageous answers was driving him further and further into a state of righteous anger, a fact that was becoming increasingly evident in his voice, his mannerisms, and his flushed face.

"Oh, come on! Our moral code did not kill us; and we did *not* kill ourselves!... No, maybe you didn't pull the trigger, but had you reacted differently your world might not have fallen apart as badly as it has... What do you mean, 'it's not your world?' *Will* you stop trying to confuse me? It *was* your world—what other world is there, the moon?—but you chose to abandon it anyway, and abandon *me!* Didn't you realize what would happen to the world you left behind?..."

Eddie was stunned into an astonished silence. He stared in wide-eyed disbelief at the Worker, drifting back a few paces until he bumped into another table. "You did?" he echoed in a bewildered whisper. As if in a dream, he added gently, "What do you mean, you knew?..."

Aghast, Eddie listened in horror as the Worker briefed him on the destruction that had devastated the planet, not merely the cold, blunt facts of that destruction, but more critically the reasons why it happened—*had* to happen—and how the strikers had worked diligently for over a decade to hasten the process along. He spoke of the many ways they had targeted key industries and key men at key moments, and the frightful fallout of each encounter. As he listened, Eddie's face plainly revealed the emotion he felt: it was disgust.

"Well, you predicted right," he agreed bitterly, once the Worker had concluded his exposition. "You got your wish. The nation's collapsed. The whole planet's probably collapsed! And as a result, millions died because you and your friends chose to vandalize the economic world! Didn't you ever stop to think how many men could die?..."

The cafeteria seemed to reel around Eddie's head. Even more aghast, once more poor Eddie did not—*could* not—reply. "You did," he finally repeated numbly, almost to himself. He turned away, stunned, placing a steadying hand on a table for support. "You really did," he muttered to the air. It was incomprehensible to him that anyone would even *consider* so deadly a course of action, let alone choose to follow it, then hustle it along on its deadly, downward slide. He stood silent, head averted, for several seconds as the horrendous ramifications of the strikers' sadistic strategy settled in.

When Eddie finally did reply, his voice was choked with horrid, indignant emotion. "And so you stood by and just—" He halted, at a complete loss for words. "...just let it happen?" he finally finished prosaically. "Let it all collapse? *Made* it all collapse? Let all those men die? And even helped to make sure they all died?" Tears began to leak from the corners of his eyes. He shook his head sadly and lifted both arms and let them slap resignedly to his sides, accompanied by a loud, shivering sigh. "I guess I should take back what I said a moment ago—it *was* you who pulled the trigger!... By organizing your strike, that's how! Earlier today I was thinking that I felt like I was a character in some horrible book—and here I find out it's you—*you!* One of my best friends!—who's the author!... Yes, you! You! Look what you've done to your fellow man! You're the worst thing that's happened to humanity since the bubonic plague!"

The Worker tried to interrupt, but Eddie brusquely brushed his words aside. "And the worst part is that all those deaths won't make one bit of difference... Because human nature will not change, that's why! Think for yourself, man! Even if you did manage to kill off all the looters—which you most certainly did not do!—what made you think new ones wouldn't arise to take their place? It may take five, ten, fifty years, but the looters will return. Guaranteed! And what will you do then, kill them all off again? And again? And again? And what trick will you use as your weapon of vengeance next time? Will you withhold food and let them starve? Refuse to rescue them from an army of religious fanatics? Or will you be merciful and just shoot them outright?..." Again he waved the Worker's words aside. "Yes, you did rescue us today, but that's not the point! Don't you see? *Can't* you see?

Your strike solved *nothing!* You're still left with the same problem you started with: what to do with looters! And the looters you shall always have with you. You've caught yourself in a cruel, vicious cycle of death that will repeat itself without end, forever and ever! At least here in Las Vegas we've devised a way that honest men and looters can coexist. We don't need to kill them off without any warning... Deserve it! What do you mean, they *deserve* it? How can you even think that?... But how can you call it 'justice' when you mete out a death penalty without trial, evidence, or conviction, with no chance for a man to face his accuser?... But we're talking about basic human decency here! How can you turn the blind eye to the suffering you deliberately caused?... Oh, come on! You *did* cause it! You just finished telling me how! And in detail! Don't give me any more of that 'your moral code did it' malarkey! YOU *did it!*"

His patience wearing unusually thin, Eddie brusquely strode from the table, unconsciously shoving the chair away from him forcibly as he moved away; it clattered noisily as it bounced hard against the table's gleaming chromium edge, leaving a noticeable dent. Turning back to face his nemesis, again he flung an accusing finger at the seated Worker.

"You say that man is the measure, so long as he doesn't initiate force against another. Well, you're right, but only to a degree. There's a lot more to right and wrong than just promising not to pick fights. There's also how you react when a man picks a fight with you!... Yes, you do have the right to your own life, and to defend it—didn't I already say that?—but there are ways to defend yourself against them without also killing off innocent bystanders!" He took a step closer to the seated Worker, his anger barely held in check. "Let me ask you a question: you say you knew from the start how much suffering and death your strike would cause; but if you knew, *why* would you even *think* about instigating such a harebrained scheme?... What?! Just so you could call *your* life your own? Even at the expense of millions of deaths?... What do you mean, worth it? *Worth it?!*" He came another step closer, his eyes widening in horror. "How can you say it was worth killing millions? What kind of horrible monster are you! Just because of a difference of opinion, you'd go beyond simply ignoring a man, to taking the steps necessary to physically destroy him and his world?—and not just the guilty, but the good and the bad together, the wheat and the chaff?... Stop trying to dodge it. It *was* you who destroyed the world, not our moral code! It was *your* code that killed them! Yours! You devised this supposed 'code of life,' you started the strike, you established your valley hideout, you talked men out of their jobs, you pushed the economy over the edge, you did it all! *Your* plan, *your* actions, *your* execution! *You* were the man responsible!... Yes, the strikers did join you of their own volition, but does that make you any less culpable for having organized it and led it? Does it become right because you were able to prosper by seeking the destruction of the world? Or because you were able to live by holding death as your standard of value? Didn't you stop and think what the results would be?... Yes, you're right; I did already ask you that. I'm just upset, that's all. But that doesn't change the basic issue... It's obvious what the basic issue is—haven't we been talking about it for the last half-hour or more? Yours was supposed to be a code of life. If that was your goal, did you achieve it? Well, did you? Why do you just sit there and stare at me like that? Answer me, damn you! Did you achieve it?"

Eddie was breathing hard, his face red, his hands clutching the back of the chair in front of him in a white-knuckled death-grip, leaning far over the table's worn surface to better throw his anger in the Worker's face. But the Worker chose not to reply.

"You're starting to see it now, aren't you? I can see it in your eyes. You're beginning to see how precise your aim was, yet how badly you missed the mark. Go on—take a good look at what you dared to call a moral code! If your so-called 'code of life' is the best that your engineer's talent could devise, I'd say it's time for you to go back to the drawing board. A 'code of life,' you call it? I'd sooner call it a Morality of Death! Because *death* is the premise at the root of your theory! You, who would not allow one percent of impurity into your valley, what sort of horror have you unleashed upon the world?... What do you mean, 'you have to leave?' Don't you turn away from me! I asked you a question! How could any so-called 'code of life' countenance knowingly triggering millions of deaths? If your goal was life, did you achieve it? Well, did you? Answer me, damn you, answer me! Because you know damn well you *didn't* achieve it! All you achieved was *death! DEATH!* Hey! Don't leave! Come back here! I want an answer! Come back! Oh God!—what's the matter with you?... What do you mean, 'I'm not ready to hear it yet?' To hear what? Don't go! Where are you going?"

## CHAPTER 15 – WHEN THE MUSIC'S OVER

The Worker burst out.

The doors of the cafeteria banged against their stops as he did so. Startled, Dagny could only sit on the hard wooden bench in the waiting room and watch as he stalked past, her cigarette poised halfway between the ashtray and her still-open mouth; but she recovered quickly. Tossing the cigarette impatiently to the floor, she hurried after him.

"Wait!" she cried. "What is it? What happened?" The Worker did not answer or slow his pace; with an echoing bang, he simultaneously slammed open both of the station's front doors and strode down the steps and into the street. He untied his horse, mounted, took the reins, and promptly galloped away, the horse under his hand exhibiting the same uncharacteristic impatience the rider revealed. Dagny stood on the station steps watching as he and his horse began shrinking in the distance, not comprehending. Before she could decide on a course of action, the door opened behind her, only this time in a more casual, conventional manner. Eddie stepped out slowly and deliberately, letting the door swing shut behind him, his attention more on the vanishing back of the Worker than any door.

"Eddie! What happened?"

Eddie did not reply at once. His pose was one of supreme confidence: head held high, shoulders back, one foot forward, and a hard countenance, eyes focused on the target in the distance. In that moment, Dagny felt he resembled a statue of an ancient Greek god more than the mere mortal he was. He held the pose for several seconds longer before the image slowly began to dissipate; first from the eyes, then his face. His shoulders slumped imperceptibly, but the action was more than enough to destroy the last remnant of the godlike illusion entirely; and like a child's soap bubble, it popped. When he turned to face her, he was merely Eddie again.

"Eddie? Are you all right? What happened?"

Eddie sighed, a deep, drawn out sigh that rose up from the core of his being. Some of his confident poise returned.

"I asked him why he left me to die." Seeing from her face that she did not comprehend, he went on. "Back before the end of the world, I mean. I asked why he had to kill so many men with his strike."

"But he didn't kill them," she recited. "It was their moral code that killed them."

Eddie snorted and shook his head, as if what she said were somehow funny, yet not worthy of laughter. "No, Dagny. He did kill them, he and his strike. He knew full well what would happen, took great pains to make *sure* it happened, then stood by and watched gleefully as the world collapsed. He even prodded it along, kicking good, honest men when they were down."

"But they could have joined us!"

Eddie looked to the hazy sky, as if calling upon the strength to continue. Again, he sighed. "Dagny, that's exactly the sort of thinking that got the world into the mess it's in—and is still in!" He swept an arm across the desert street before them. "Isn't that exactly what Back For God says? Repent and join us—or die! But why should anyone be forced to join anyone? Dagny, I'd welcome Back For God's Bishop himself into Las Vegas with open arms if only he promised to just leave men be! You can't insist a man think exactly as you do; and if he doesn't, take steps to deliberately destroy his world and leave him to die. That's just what I told your husband. I said that we couldn't leave it all to die. We couldn't let it go! Not Transcontinental Railroad, and certainly not the men who depended upon us."

"Yes, but—"

"No!" he interrupted. "There are no 'buts!' Not when it comes to letting a man die!"

With a bright fire in her eyes, Dagny inhaled sharply in preparation to lash out in response, but he never gave her the chance.

"No! Listen to me first!" Slowly, patiently, he explained to her the details of the exchange he had had with the Worker. As she listened, he saw her eyes glow darkly with the angry ardor of disagreement. Before long, though, her attitude began to shift; it seemed to him as if she were listening to him with an increasing, greater attentiveness, as if she were hearing much more than his words and seeing much more than his face, even though her eyes remained attentively fixed on his. She appeared as if she were studying some revelation within herself which she had never confronted before; but in truth, it was an old one once considered and long since tossed aside, like some burnt-out cigarette. But his words were bringing the butt back to life, making its ashes whole once more, kindling its spark aflame once again. She continued watching and listening; and as he spoke, Eddie could see first the shock slowly vanishing, the look of disagreement gradually transforming into one of wonder, then her face smoothing into a strange serenity that seemed simultaneously both quiet and glittering.

When he finally finished, she remained silent for several moments as she assimilated his words, her eyes occasionally darting unconsciously left and right as her mind chased down each of the ramifications of his values and beliefs, and their import. He watched in silence for several moments, when, like a flock of beautiful birds being released from their cruel cage, the words came tumbling out of her.

"Oh, Eddie," she cried. "You're absolutely right!"

He drew back in stunned surprise. "I am?"

"Yes!"

He hesitated. "But... But how could I convince you so quickly? It took me... what, close to an hour I was in there? But I didn't manage to convince *him!*" He snapped his head in the direction of the vanished Worker.

Her face held a deadly serious look. "No, Eddie. You didn't need so much to convince me as to remind me. What you've said is nothing new to me. It's the same belief I had lived by all my life—until recently. That belief was what prompted me to reject the Gulch the first time I was there, back in the days before civilization collapsed. I knew then I couldn't abandon the greatness of the world Outside to destruction, or abandon achievements such as Transcontinental Railroad and all those things that were yours and mine. I refused to believe that men would always refuse to see, to deliberately choose to be blind and deaf to the truth. Before I left the valley that time, I told the strikers that men do love their lives, and that so long as they desire to live, I cannot lose my battle."

"Then you felt it, too?"

"Yes Eddie. I've always felt it. I've known it wordlessly for years. And just now you've made me realize—no, made me *remember!*—how it was wrong for me to leave it all behind. I should never have let it go! *You* never let it go!" She waved an arm at the massive station behind them. "You've kept the last droplet of *our* sort of world alive. And you're still living it."

He nodded. "Of course I had to stay, Dagny. So long as men are engaged in productive effort, so long as they are depending on us to deliver on our promises, so long as we are alive to make and keep those promises, what else ought one man do? Sure, there are always looters like your brother and Mr. Wesley who take advantage of people like us, but most men are basically good and honest. How can we abandon them? Or set them up like chumps to suffer a horrible death?"

"Yet I did," she confessed. "I abandoned them." Abruptly, as if tossing off some dark thought, she lifted her chin and her eyes opened wide. "But you didn't, Eddie. You didn't—you *wouldn't!*" Her steely gaze held his firmly. "I was wrong to give it all up—and wrong to leave you behind, too, Eddie."

Eddie drew back again in stunned surprise. "Me?"

"Yes, you, Eddie. I had always known what Transcontinental Railroad meant to me, but I never realized what *you* meant to me until that evening we parted in New York City. Do you remember that night?"

Eddie's eyes misted over as he recalled the much-handled memory. "Of course I do."

"In that one moment, everything I already knew about you crystallized into its proper place. That night, I realized everything I'd ever lived my life for, you lived your life for it, too." Her voice became increasingly strident, as if she were lashing herself with words long suppressed. "Every dream I ever had, you shared it. Every battle I ever fought, it was you who fought at my side. Who was it who helped me to re-build the Rio branch against all odds? Who ran Transcontinental Railroad when I couldn't or wouldn't? And whose heart and soul was it that arrived here in Las Vegas on the very last *Meteor*? It was *yours*, Eddie! You and yours! And it could have been mine as well. *Should* have been mine, I should say! Yet I walked away from Transcontinental Railroad... and from you."

Dagny was openly, eagerly excited now, partly from the realization of the veracity of her words, and partly from the giddiness of freely experiencing an emotion she had not dared to let loose since that night in the cemetery almost two years ago, and her eyes brilliantly reflected its fire. "You! The man of ability who expertly executed my every order! And it wasn't just all the capable things you *did* do for me all those years, it was also what unspeakable things you *didn't* do." Her face clouded darkly at the memory. "You never walked out on me and pretended to be a playboy, never giving me a single *clue*—" She snapped her fingers angrily at the air. "—as to what was going on, or why you had done it." She huffed once and leaned forward intently. "Do you know what that man told me? 'Knowing what I was doing to you made me suffer!' Well, pardon *me!*" Her breaths came faster now. "And you didn't sneak out on a spiteful wife you despised to share a few fleeting hours of intimacy, then leave me battered and bruised! Or put me through the Hell of a national broadcast counteracting *your* cowardly capitulation to government blackmail you never needed to pay—and then telling me you did it in the name of *your* love for *me?*" She harrumphed mockingly. "I can't possibly imagine what worse that man would have done if he *didn't* love me!" Her voice had been rising in cadence with her anger, and now became almost shrill. "And you never played some cruel form of hide and seek, lurking in dark, dank tunnels like some perverted voyeur, groping me with furtive, pusillanimous eyes every time I'd chance to walk by! Scheming in secret to deliberately make my life as hard as possible while telling me that love is not served by torture! Setting up my railroad and the entire country for destruction, and then standing idly by with an arrogant, misplaced righteousness as millions of men—*millions!*— DIED!"

With the scream of her final word, she spun away from him to throw an upraised arm against one of the huge granite pillars and fell against it as massive sobs wracked her body. Jerkily she slowly sank to the station's steps to settle softly on her side. "Oh, Eddie!" she moaned, fists clenched tight against her temples as she rocked slightly on the unyielding slab of stone, back and forth, back and forth. "Oh, Eddie."

Eddie knelt at her side from behind, one hand lightly on her shoulder, the other stroking her hair. "Oh, Dagny," he replied in unconscious imitation, unaware of how prosaic his words sounded. He didn't know what else to say. "Oh, Dagny," he repeated.

The tableau held for some time, Dagny's remorse and Eddie's comforting, before finally fading into an extended, motionless silence.

Eddie's eyebrows suddenly shot up, and he brightened slightly. "Dagny..." He squeezed her shoulder lightly. "Dagny?" he repeated. "Come on. Get up. I'd like you to come with me."

She turned her reddened eyes toward him, confused. "What?"

Eddie stood and extended a hand to her. "Come with me."

"What?" she repeated, taking his hand and standing, almost as if she were moving in a trance.

"I'd like to show you something. A surprise. Something to brighten you up, make you feel better."

She eyed him warily, the tears no longer leaking down her face. Much of her composure had returned, as if a switch had been thrown. "Show me what?" she inquired warily.

"Well, it hasn't been all work and no play here in Las Vegas. I want to show you one of my hobbies."

"What, your garden?" She reached for a cigarette and paused to light it. "I saw that."

"No, no. Something much better. Come on." Still holding her hand, he led her through the station and out onto the empty train platform where the *Meteor* waited, its Diesel still idling noisily. They crossed the track behind the protruding balcony of the observation car, walked its length, and continued past the sleeper car coupled behind it. Just beyond it, they reached the steps leading into the mail car.

Eddie turned to Dagny. "Wait here a moment."

Her red eyes continued to regard him warily and without comprehension as he climbed the steps and disappeared inside the car. She heard some muffled noises coming through the half-open door: the snapping of switches, the hum of cooling fans, then one single, scratchy rasp.

Presently, Eddie emerged. "Okay, come on in." He extended a hand down to her.

She took it, tossed her cigarette aside, and ascended the steps. Together they entered the mail car, but from what met her eye, it no longer resembled any Transcontinental mail car she had ever seen. The entire left wall was taken up with rack after rack of phonograph records, and the right was lined with shelves that held piles and piles of papers. Above her, copper wires were suspended by ceramic insulators hanging from the ceiling, dropping at various points to connect with one device or another. In the middle of the car, sitting atop one side of the broad clerk's desk was what looked like a shortwave radio; on the other sat an old phonograph; it held a shiny black, grooved platter spinning swiftly on its turntable. Eddie lifted and gently dropped the stylus onto the edge of the disc, adjusted the volume, and stood back to face her as the music began.

Dagny's eyes again went wide, but this time from pleasant surprise rather than personal disaster. It was one of "those symphonies"; in fact, it was one of her favorites: Richard's Fourth Concerto. The Concerto was a great cry of rebellion, a resounding "No!" flung at some vast process of torture, a denial of suffering, a denial that held the agony of the struggle to break free. The sounds were like a disembodied voice saying: *There is no necessity for worldwide death—why, then, is the worst pain reserved for those who will not accept such wide-ranging death as a necessity? We who hold the love and the secret of joy, to what punishment have we been sentenced for it, and by whom?*

"How apropos!" She smiled broadly, the cheerful expression contrasting sharply with her red eyes and damp cheeks. "You were right, Eddie. This is just the song I needed to hear."

He basked in her pleasure. "And it's not just music for you and me here in the train." He gestured at the overhead cables. "It's going out to all of Las Vegas—these wires lead to a radio transmitter out near the yard limit."

"You're broadcasting that? Right now?" She inclined her head toward the spinning platter.

"Yes."

Her mind leapt to the obvious conclusion. "It's *you!*" she laughed, holding an astonished hand to her mouth. "It's you who's been broadcasting those symphonies for the last two years!" It was a statement, not a question.

Now it was Eddie's turn to be surprised. "What? You mean you heard them?"

"Yes! I've been listening to them every chance I could! Twenty to nine, almost every night."

Eddie hesitated, unconsciously feeling for the precision watch still sitting in his pocket. "I thought it was always at nine o'clock sharp," he ventured, half to himself, but shrugged it off.

Dagny laughed again and clapped her hands once, holding the palms together in front of her chin, smiling broadly as her eyes became unfocused while she listened to the music.

After a moment, Eddie faced her, bowed formally, and held out his hand. Dagny took it, smiled, curtsied almost theatrically, and the two began to dance.

Thinking about it, at first Dagny couldn't remember the last time she had danced... It had to be twenty years if it was a day! She brought her shoulders back from Eddie and looked him in the face. Eddie smiled, and Dagny smiled back, bringing herself closer to him again. Around and around the mail car they danced. With a start, she suddenly remembered the last time she had danced. She stopped short and held Eddie at arm's length. "It was *you!*" she laughed again.

Again, Eddie showed surprise. "Well, yes. I already told you it was me."

"No, not the broadcasts. The dancing! Do you know when the last time I danced was?"

Eddie drew her closer to him, resuming the cadence of the music. "Of course I remember—it was the last time for me, too. And when you're lucky enough to share the final dance of the evening with the seventeen-year-old debutante at her coming-out party, you don't easily forget that sort of thing."

She remained silent as they swayed to the music, then sadly added. "You were even there for me then, Eddie. Even then."

"I know."

"I've been a fool."

"No you haven't." He halted and held her at arm's length. "What is it you regret? What would you have done instead, or undone?"

"I would undo the..." She paused, her eyes moist with fresh, unshed tears, then steeled herself to continue, "...the *pain* that I know I've caused you all these years."

"Yes, there *was* pain, Dagny, but it was worth it because we were together. You were there with me all those years. We shared our lives, our dreams. Together we built a railroad and kept it running against all odds. It was so much, so very much just to be able to share it all with you! And now I find out you're still alive! I know I shouldn't dare to ask for more, but... Oh, Dagny..." His eyes were bright with his own unshed tears of joy. "...I wish you never had to go away ever again!" He hesitated, momentarily uncertain, but the self-assurance returned instantly, driven by a single certainty: *I am in control of my world!* He drew himself up and looked her confidently in the eye, lightly holding onto her shoulders. "Dagny...," he began, his voice steady, his eyes clear. "Would you stay here? Here in Las Vegas? Here with me?" He tossed his head slightly, indicating the train in which they stood and the station that surrounded it. "Stay here with me so we can rebuild a transcontinental railroad? Together? Please."

The song had come to an end, the stylus echoing its repetitious *bupp-bupp... bupp-bupp...* They had ceased their rhythmic sway, yet still held each other at arm's length. His face possessed a peculiar purity; hers, a joyous awe; and from her face, he could recognize her answer without her having to name it. Nor was there any need to. Two heartbeats passed, and they seized one another, the bupping phonograph ignored and forgotten.

# Chapter 16 – The Times They Are A-Changin'

The Bishop arrived.

When he entered Las Vegas sans army, of course no one recognized him for who he was; none of the town's citizens had ever met him face to face save Ma's lieutenant, but that potential accuser was off performing a very personal undertaking and had no opportunity to witness his adversary's arrival or to testify to his identity. Not that first-hand knowledge was needed to determine the newcomer's allegiance; his flowing white vestments with the fist-sized, stylized orange flame stitched over his heart readily betrayed his citizenship. That he calmly rode into town alone and unarmed allayed hardly at all the fears of those he passed; no surprise, they eyed him warily. It wasn't until he was several blocks inside the town before one brave soul had the temerity to approach him.

"You new in town?" an elderly woman inquired guardedly of the oddly-attired man perched on the white steed. A score of hard-faced men stood within earshot, hands on their holsters, listening, ready.

The Bishop tipped his hat. "Yes, my sister." He wasn't sure what else to say other than to confess—he certainly wasn't going to *lie!* Besides, being abandoned by his God coupled with the utter defeat of his army conspired to bring out the meek side of him—not that he was seeking to inherit the Earth in his God's name any longer.

"Welcome to Las Vegas, then," she replied in a more conversational tone, but her protectors did not alter their heightened states of alertness. "You should probably pay a visit to Eddie, seeing how you're new here."

"Eddie? Who is Eddie?"

She smiled at his inadvertent joke. "He's our Head of Society. Eddie's a good person to talk to when you first hit town. He knows where everything is and can get you set up with a nice place to stay." Looking up at the mounted Bishop, she shielded her eyes from the cloud-veiled sun with one hand, giving the appearance that she was saluting him. "Or don't you plan to stay on?"

The Bishop was taken aback by the cordiality of her welcome; he had expected to be treated harshly as a prisoner of war. *Perhaps my God is not so angry with His servant?* "I cannot rightly say," he ventured; that was unsurprising, as he had no plan. "Let us meet with your Mr. Eddie first and find out from him what is to be."

"Fine! He's usually in the Transcontinental train station. Just keep heading the way you're heading, turn right at the church, cross over the tracks, then follow them to the right. You'll get there. Can't miss it. Big granite columns out front."

"Bless you, sister."

"Thanks. My best to Eddie."

"Surely."

\* \* \*

The Bishop dismounted.

A lone horse was already tied up at a hitching rail in front of the imposing façade of the Transcontinental station; he secured his steed alongside it, and with some holy trepidation entered the heathen structure.

"Hello?" he called nervously. His voice echoed majestically within its cool marble confines, but no answer came. Slowly he advanced across the cavernous waiting room, pausing at the cafeteria door to peer inside; no one was in sight. All there was were some plantings along the windowed side and some tables and chairs along the other. The room reeked of stale, sinful tobacco smoke, the first he had smelled in years.

Still exercising caution—for he knew it to be a wicked place—he entered the tunnel alongside the deserted ticket booths following the advice of a sign that read, "To The Trains." True to its word, at the foot of the tunnel sat a huge Diesel idling noisily, a day coach and baggage car coupled behind it. He walked along the train's length and peered inside the windows of the coach and through the wide-open door of the baggage car as he passed. The train was as deserted as the rest of the station.

On the adjacent track sat other rolling stock. He crossed over the track behind the train to get a closer look, slipping slightly as he stepped on top of one of the rails. The first car he came to was another baggage car, except its door was tightly shut; it was coupled to a mail car, its doors similarly sealed, followed by a sleeper with curtained windows, and ending with an ornate observation car. He advanced along the silent platform, passing each of the sealed cars, not attempting to breach their privacy. When he reached the far end of the observation car, he stepped a little more cautiously over the rail and stood behind the protruding curve of the car's polished brass railing. Inside the car he saw two people: a man sat in a luxurious, velvet wing-back chair lacing his boots, and a woman stood behind a bar in front of a large, ornate mirror brushing her hair. The end of the observation car where the Bishop stood was open to the air, its doors folded back against either wall. "Hello?" he called uncertainly. Two startled heads spun his way.

"Hello?" the man inside asked in turn, a measure of anxiety in his own voice. His gaze dropped to take in the Bishop's vestments, and his eyes widened.

"Are you Eddie?"

"Yes, I am," he replied nervously. "Can I help you?"

The Bishop smiled uneasily. *This is very difficult for me, my God! But Thy will be done!* "Yes. I'm new in town, and a kind sister said I should come see you first."

He nodded in understanding, his fears subsiding somewhat. Undoubtedly this was a refugee from the crushed army of Back For God seeking to defect—not that it mattered where the man had come from, so long as he behaved himself. "Are you looking for a place to live? If you are, I can make a few suggestions."

The question took the Bishop aback. For heathens, the people of Las Vegas appeared to be very hospitable. "For a short while, perhaps. I have not yet reflected upon my journey's end."

"Well, you're more than welcome to stay, so long as you respect the rights and property of others."

Involuntarily, his eyebrows shot up. *Isn't that the essence of the Golden Rule? I thought these people were heathens!* He had to make sure. "Do you mean I should do unto others as I would have them do to me?"

"Yes, that's the spirit of it. Be excellent to each other."

The Bishop was startled by the man's response. *And coming from a heathen no less!* Close on the heels of the thought, with an unexpected mental crash, came a new revelation—surely divinely inspired, given its import. *No wonder my God stopped His army! These are no heathens at all, but rather a very holy people!* With the realization came relief, as if a great weight had been lifted from his shoulders. These were men he could deal with, despite the sinful, materialistic trinkets they surrounded themselves with. Obviously it was not the trinkets that mattered, but rather the heart. His God had not led him astray after all; rather, He had led him here and instructed him to live among these people and fit right in with their sinful way of life—difficult though that may initially be. God had not forsaken His Bishop after all. Everything was going to be all right. His penance would be to serve in Purgatory, not in Hell. He had apparently been spared to perform a new mission—whatever that might eventually turn out to be. But he knew he would find out soon enough. He prayed he was up to the task, one he would willingly perform to the best of his ability—until his God revealed to him a new mission, that is. In the meantime, he would masquerade as a man of Las Vegas. "Thank you, Mr. Eddie," smiled the Bishop. "Thank you very much. Perhaps I shall stay on."

"What line of work are you in?" inquired the woman, interrupting.

The Bishop's head spun in her direction and quickly spun away; the unanticipated questioning and question flustered his already-fragile state of mind. *Line of work? I'm a bishop without a congregation, that's what! But surely I cannot tell her that! A bishop without his congregation is no bishop at all! But I cannot lie to her, either...* He considered for a moment before replying. "Oil man," he finally confessed. *At least that's what I used to be before my God revealed Himself to me.*

The man's ears perked up at the response. "An oil man? How so?"

"Prior to God's Judgment Day, I was a wildcatter out in these parts."

"Are you thinking of getting back into the business?"

*A sign? Is this another sign?* "For what use have men for oil these days?" he asked guardedly, for it was a sinful profession that stained the Earth with its unholy unwholesomeness.

Eddie raised both his arms, hands extended, indicating the train in which he stood. "Trains use a great deal of diesel fuel. We still have a goodly supply, but it won't last forever. We could also use gasoline for our automobiles, trucks, and buses."

To the Bishop, Eddie's preacher-like pose took on stark religious overtones. *A sign indeed! This is one very holy man!* He hesitated a moment longer before coming to a decision. "Perhaps I could end my retirement," he finally replied. "I know of some wells not too distant a journey from here that one might be able to resurrect, God willing."

The woman interrupted again. "But even if you could drill for the oil, how would you go about refining it?"

He studied her for a moment before answering. To his intuitively attentive eyes, he could plainly see that she would always react with a measure of impertinent impatience; she was the sort of woman who would constantly drive herself boldly forward to achieve her goals. Her strength of will and determination reminded the Bishop of some of his most devout acolytes. He instantly took a liking to her.

Smiling at her, he replied, "God has made diesel fuel one of the easiest to extract, my sister, much easier than His gasoline. I once worked at a small refinery southwest of here. Perhaps it is still there and could be put back into—" *My God! Give Your servant strength!* He choked on the next words, but managed to pronounce them clearly. "—back into working order." He returned his attention to the man. "And as I recall, there was a rail spur serving it. That would make it easier to—" He hesitated again. "—transport the fuel."

"Excellent!" the man exclaimed. "Once you get yourself settled in, we'll take a ride out there and see what can be salvaged."

"As God wills, my son."

The man faced the woman. "Would you please excuse me for a minute while I escort our new immigrant over to the rectory?"

"Rectory?" interjected the Bishop.

"Yes." He glanced down at the Bishop's vestments. "I thought you might be a little more comfortable if you stayed your first few days with another man of the cloth."

The Bishop smiled warmly. *Thank You, my God!* "Bless you, my son."

"Welcome to Las Vegas."

## CHAPTER 17 – I'M FROM NEW JERSEY

The Gulch buzzed.

Not since Midas' Avalanche had there been so much earthshaking news, and it appeared the strikers would never tire of repeating the details or exploring their ramifications.

Of course the foremost news item was Dagny's expatriation to Las Vegas. In spite of its import, there was not that much of a tale to tell, for the particulars were sparse indeed. According to Dwight, as they were waiting on Dagny's return, Transcontinental stationmaster had approached the hypercraft parked on the empty highway south of Las Vegas and briefly addressed the two men waiting in its shadow. In concise terms, reading from notes scribbled on a scrap of paper, he delivered Dagny's farewell message: she would not be returning to the Gulch, he explained succinctly. Not that she was renouncing her striker's oath—"Whatever that is!" the stationmaster added as an editorial aside—rather, she was moving to Las Vegas to reclaim her former position as Vice-President in Charge of Operations for Transcontinental Railroad—"My new boss!" he proudly added—and while she would still retain ownership of the Dagny Line in the Gulch—"Wherever that is!"—for the time being she would be entrusting its day-to-day operation to its employees. Further, and most crucially, she was immediately sending for all of her personal belongings. Eddie had asked for her hand in marriage, and she had consented. If the men of the mind wished for more information than that, the stationmaster ended, they should feel free to come visit her at the Transcontinental station in Las Vegas to discuss it.

The stationmaster handed Dwight a coin-laden envelope addressed to Gwen, plus a single, loose willie. "It's instructions about Miss Dagny's belongings," he explained. "Plus payment for the envelope's delivery."

Awkwardly, Dwight had accepted both coin and envelope, thanked the railroadman for the news, laid a sympathetic hand on his companion's shoulder, and without another word the two men climbed aboard the hypercraft, sealed the hatch, and in a rumble of man-made thunder took to the sky and hastened for home.

If the startling news regarding Dagny was sparse, in contrast Dwight's multifaceted tale of high adventure more than made up for it in variety, length, and depth. Time after time he found himself relating the exciting details of the discovery of the strikers' enclave in Massachusetts and the defeat of the State's Science Institute's army; in fact, he told the tale so often that he considered charging for the telling, and perhaps writing a treatise on the subject, if only in the interest of saving himself the time consumed in the repeated re-telling.

On the other hand—and as could be expected—the popular reaction among the strikers to the discovery of the not-an-enclave in Las Vegas varied little: most cared as much about the desert scabs and the dead zealots that Dwight left lying on their doorstep as they did about the demented doings of some looter king two thousand miles away, which is to say: not at all. For some it may have proved to be an interesting tidbit, but little more.

Yet there was one aspect of Dwight's adventures which was considerably more significant than either excitement or indifference, for his captivating chronicle was not merely one of battles won or brethren rescued. Inextricably intertwined were many serious unanswered questions, and chief among them was Dwight's erroneous reasoning that the lost city of Las Vegas was somehow a strikers' enclave of the same pedigree as the one in Massachusetts. More often than he cared to—out of necessity and at no charge—he found himself explaining almost apologetically about his mistaken motivation for intervening; but taking his cue from Dagny's tale, he tended to limit the particulars to the bare facts and let others draw what conclusions they may. A was A, after all. But his terse explanations could not blank out the implication that he possessed at least one crucial blind spot that left him colorblind when presented with an enclave such as Las Vegas, that there was some new, as-yet unnamed color he lacked the ability to readily perceive. The town had shown itself to be some sort of newarchy ruled by a moral code beyond his knowledge and experience.

Regardless of how often or how deeply his fellow strikers may have questioned—or ignored questioning—his reasons, none questioned his ends. The value of initiating an unprovoked attack against such a threat as Back For God was universally recognized. Whether it was a true enclave he was defending or it wasn't, the Atlanteans unanimously agreed that he was more than justified nonetheless, regardless of who may have benefited. It was collectively accepted throughout the valley that they owed no morality to those who held men under a gun. It wasn't so much that Dwight had come to the aid of Las Vegas; it was sufficient and more noteworthy that he had acted against Back For God.

Despite such universal agreement over the efficacy of Dwight's pugilism, it came as no surprise at all that there was nigh on none when it came to defending Dagny's departure, for the consensus was virtually unanimous that Dagny was making some horrible mistake. That consensus even stretched to include the more tolerant strikers, men such as Richard and Owen. But in defiance of that unanimity, situated plainly outside the mainstream of public opinion silently stood a single striker: Gwen. Unlike literally every other resident of the valley, she was not the least bit surprised by Dagny's decision. Gwen had been associating with Dagny for almost a decade, first as executive secretary for Hank Steel in Philadelphia, then in the Gulch, and now as one of Dagny's best friends. She knew firsthand how close Dagny and Eddie had always been, not only as co-workers in the railroad business, but also as childhood friends—even their parents and grandparents had known each other! Eddie had always loved Dagny, that was plain for anyone to see, but Gwen could never say for certain whether Dagny had ever reciprocated—at least not until now; Dagny had always been a difficult woman to read.

There had once been a time years before when Gwen had suffered the sharp pangs of disappointment upon realizing how deeply infatuated Eddie was with his superior, a fact of reality that snicked off the nascent flower of romance within her scarcely moments after the appearance of its first bloom. Despite the unanticipated disenchantment, the experience had opened a window for Gwen into the soul of Eddie; she understood fully what Dagny saw in the man, for she had clearly seen it as well. *But that was many years ago*, she firmly reminded herself in a somewhat successful attempt to head off any emotional relapse. Regardless of the bittersweet taste the memories conjured up, thinking of Eddie made her smile. She was happy to learn he had survived.

Gwen found it somewhat ironic to discover she still harbored sweet feelings for Dagny's latest husband, for doubtless Dagny still harbored such feelings for Gwen's husband as well. Fully a year before the news had broken upon the world, Gwen had been well aware that Dagny and Hank had been an item. Dagny's nationally-broadcast, scandalous confession had revealed nothing new; given Gwen's position as Hank's personal secretary, there was no way she could possibly help but already know all the intimate details. Nevertheless, it wasn't until after Gwen had arrived in the valley that she discovered Dagny had taken on another man as her latest lover. And given Dagny's past history it was understandable—even predictable—that her amorous interest would have moved on. And so it had—and had now done so once again—and it was that latest refocusing of the heart which triggered Gwen's undertaking of the sympathetic task she found before her.

She stood in front of Dagny's dresser in her friend's former bedroom in the Gulch, transferring clothing, toiletries, and other personal items into one of several yawning suitcases and trunks lying wide open on and around the pine-posted double bed, appearing like a collection of giant oysters proudly showing off their pearls. She was alone in the house—which was all for the better, as far as she was concerned. Despite her usually imperturbable nature, she wasn't sure she could function as smoothly under that cold, watchful gaze without pain, fear, or guilt; worse yet, he might have started talking philosophy! He was the *last* person with whom she wanted to talk philosophy; not only did the emotional context of the moment make the timing all wrong for it, she still couldn't completely trust her own answers to be "correct" enough to suit the strikers—especially him!—even after all the years she had lived in the valley.

In her letter to Gwen, Dagny had asked that she commission Lawrence and the owner of the taproom to help ferry Dagny's possessions to Las Vegas, and Gwen was more than happy to help—and at no charge, of course. *What were friends for?* she asked herself needlessly. She noted with some amount of disdain that it wasn't a needless question among some people.

The first stage of her charitable task was soon completed. One by one she snapped each piece of luggage shut and lugged them in a similar serial fashion out to the front porch, and sat down on one stout trunk to await the arrival of Lawrence. It was a pleasant wait; spring was in the air, a welcome change from the harsh Colorado winter that had ushered it in.

Unsurprisingly, she did not have long to wait. Given her long experience orchestrating complex, interrelated tasks, Gwen had timed this straightforward, simple one well. Not three minutes after she emerged—and exactly two minutes late—from behind a hillock materialized Lawrence's mobile crawler, its bulbous, oversized cab perched on six articulated, gangly legs with a boxy cargo area protruding from its rear, seemingly suspended in space. The contraption made a bobbing beeline to where she waited, with each leg's splayed, foot-long greenish-blue fingers extended horizontally in the shape of a star to form a broad, flat, bony foot. Gwen was impressed with the contrivance Lawrence had constructed; its needle-tipped, almost indestructible claws could theoretically grab onto any surface, even climb sheer mountain faces, it was said. The device was a marvel of metallurgy and engineering, yet Lawrence called it, simply, his "pick-up truck."

The windows were folded down exposing the two seats within to the sweet spring air, and through the opening he called, "Hi, Gwen! All set?" As he spoke, the vehicle settled slowly to the ground on smoothly swiveling joints, like some oversized spider lowering itself onto its prey.

Gwen surveyed the luggage scattered at her feet. "I sure hope so!" she replied as she stood, allowing a playful note of exasperation to color her voice. "If I wasn't a woman myself I'd wonder how anyone could accumulate so much *stuff!*" She waved a hand across the objects of her wonderment.

"Well, let me get it all into the truck. I'm running a few minutes late, sorry to say, and I'll bet your pilot's already waiting at the airstrip."

"Let me help, then," she offered, reaching for one of the smaller valises.

"No, no!" he insisted testily. "You read that letter, same as me. You know what she said! Dagny's paid me good money to help move her things out of the valley, not you, so you're not responsible for carrying anything beyond this point!"

"But—"

"No! I don't want to have to be paying you!" He shooed her away impatiently. "Come on, come on! A contract's a contract! I have it. You don't."

"Yes, Mr. Lawrence," she replied formally, tactfully remembering to first remove the exasperation from her voice. But hidden behind her outward civility, two angry words echoed silently within the private confines of her mind: *These people!* It was moments like this that drove home for her how much she envied Dagny for having abandoned the valley altogether. Too often—such as right now!—these men of the mind could prove to be a bit too much for her liking. She was looking forward to visiting Las Vegas, not only for the chance to see Eddie and Dagny, but also for the welcome change of philosophical backdrop. Having spent almost three years among the strikers, she was more than ready for a brief sabbatical—or an extended one, for that matter! But she had willingly taken on many responsibilities here in the valley—a child, a husband, and a career—that precluded any thoughts of her own emigration.

Lawrence quickly finished loading the luggage into the cargo section of his truck. "All right, let's go, Gwen!" he called, gallantly holding the crawler's door open for her.

She climbed in, taking wry, silent exception to the fact that he did not charge her for the favor. She was no longer surprised at her cynical reaction; long ago she had recognized how she was becoming more and more jaded in her opinion of the strikers as time passed.

Lawrence took his own seat, manipulated the controls, and the odd vehicle lurched into motion. Gwen found the ride far from comfortable: the crawler bobbed and weaved on its multitudinous legs and flattened claws, pitching her to and fro in her padded seat. Given the amplitude of the lurching, some sort of seat harness or other restraint would have been welcome, but the cab's design did not include one. While Lawrence was clearly a genius when it came to constructing mobile devices, he could still learn a trick or two when it came to providing a more reasonable ride for their passengers. She was thankful that they quickly reached the airfield; not only was her stomach beginning to grow queasy, several hidden bruises, mementos of past passions, were making themselves felt.

Upon reaching the valley's airfield, they halted alongside the greenish-blue hypercraft waiting on the taxiway and climbed out. The pilot stood in the open doorway of the craft leaning on the jamb, arms folded across his chest reflecting his impatience. "Took you guys long enough," he rumbled, his deep voice adding to the impression of annoyance.

But Lawrence just smiled. "What; we're only a few minutes late. Why so impatient?"

"Impatient to get the hell out of the valley," he muttered quietly to himself.

"What's that?" Lawrence inquired innocuously. He had heard, but chose instead to play the innocent. He did not like scabs, and took every opportunity to give his dislike an outlet, even petty ones—and he was by far not the only striker who took pleasure in pursuing that pastime.

"Nothing," sighed the pilot, refusing to be baited. "Let's get these suitcases aboard." Quickly and expertly the two men transferred the gear from one greenish-blue conveyance to the other. "All right, Gwen," rumbled the pilot, deliberately pitching his voice louder for Lawrence's benefit. "Let's get the hell out of here!"

Excitedly she entered the craft and he sealed the door firmly behind them. It would be only the second time in her life she had ever flown, the first being when she first arrived in the valley years before. She was relieved to see that this conveyance indeed had seat harnesses. "Will we be traveling faster than sound?" she asked eagerly as she fastened herself in.

The pilot took his seat and grinned. "Just try to stop me!" He began manipulating the controls.

Gwen smiled broadly in return and scrunched her shoulders excitedly as the turbines spooled up to speed. "I feel like a little girl on my first roller coaster ride!"

"A roller coaster is *nothing* compared with *THIS!*" he cried, and on the final word he slammed the throttle forward. With a sudden high-pitched whine the craft sprang to life, hurtling itself down the runway like a cunning fox chasing a frightened rabbit. "Wooo-hooo!" sang the pilot as the hypercraft shot into the clear sky of the spring afternoon.

The instantaneous acceleration forced her firmly back into her seat and took her breath away, as if a giant hand were powerfully pressing against the entire front of her body and squeezing her firmly into her seat, pinning her arms and legs in place, flattening her breasts, and pulling the shape of her mouth from grin to grimace. As the immense pressure held steady, she began to wonder if her mother's milk might come down and her breasts start to leak. Not that it mattered; such physical manifestations induced by their mad dash could do nothing to dampen her enthusiasm for it. "I'll say!" she agreed heartily, her words slurred by the force of their acceleration.

They rocketed into the air, and mere seconds later they cleared the massive granite peaks that encircled the Gulch, trailing the deep rumble of the craft's sonic boom. Within the minute, the pilot leveled out their flight path several miles above the granite peaks and checked their speed. "Mach two is plenty fast enough, don't you think? We wouldn't want to overshoot and land in California!"

Gwen did not answer, but her wide grin spoke volumes. The mountains rolled quickly beneath them as the craft hurtled west, spreading its massive cone of sound to echo majestically in their wake.

After a few moments, Gwen spoke. "I appreciate your taking the time to fly me out to visit with Dagny and Eddie."

Smiling, the pilot instinctively turned on the charm. "Anything for a pretty lady."

She smiled in return at the unexpected compliment. "Thank you, kind sir," then jokingly added, "but aren't you here more because Dagny's paying you?"

The pilot froze, his smile suddenly gone. Slowly he turned to face her. "I don't talk that kind of striker's language, Gwen—and I don't think you do either!" He held her gaze boldly, as if challenging her to dispute his statement.

Briefly, reflexively, she considered doing just that; but then she remembered that the man had never taken the striker's oath—and not only was he a scab, but one who harbored a deep distaste for the average striker. And for her part, she was not your average striker; so rather than automatically attempting to rectify a perceived philosophical gaffe, as she had been doing for years now, instead she decided this was a man who she could trust with the naked truth. "That's true," she finally admitted. "I was only joking. If you took offense, my apologies." She nonchalantly turned away from him to watch the scenery flow past.

The pilot looked away in turn, successfully concealing how much he had been taken aback by the answer; hers was the sort of reaction he had long since fallen out of the habit of expecting from any striker. "That's okay," he replied smoothly, covering his surprise even more so by simply answering her question. "I was planning on heading out Vegas way anyhow, once I heard they were out there. I'm being kicked out of the valley in a couple of weeks, remember—and a place like Las Vegas is certainly worth checking out!" Conversationally, he added with a smile, "You know, it was like a gift from God when I heard that Las Vegas had survived." He whistled enthusiastically. "Las Vegas! If it's half the town it used to be, I could gladly make it my new base of operations!" *Just the sort of place where a glamorous, deep-voiced pilot can relax all night long in a fine saloon in the company of a beautiful woman—or three!* His smile broadened. "And what a base it would be! Not too far from *The Empty Nest*—and not too close, either!" He shook his head theatrically. "I have *so* had it with those Johnnies!"

"Me, too," Gwen admitted quietly without hesitation, her voice barely a whisper above the muted whine of the turbines.

But the pilot had heard; he turned to her and said nothing for a long moment before looking away. Twice in a row she had given the philosophically-incorrect answer. *What kind of Johnnie is this vixen?* He turned to face her again, deciding it was no longer the time to play it so circumspectly. "I thought you took the oath," he asserted bluntly.

She sighed. "I did."

He hesitated, waiting for a real answer. "What's the deal then?" he finally prompted. "Change your mind?"

"The deal?" Again she sighed, followed immediately by a mirthless laugh. "No, nothing's changed. It's just that the oath is no deal, that's what."

"Huh? What do you mean, 'no deal?'"

"It's 'no deal' because the oath doesn't mean anything!"

"What?" Cleary he was at a loss, an uncommon occurrence, and equally uncommonly, it showed.

"It doesn't mean anything," she repeated. "Listen to the words: it only says what you *shouldn't* do, not what you *should* do. It's meaningless as a guide for choosing a course of action. It's only a recipe for inaction."

*Hah! She's right!* he thought with a start; he said nothing aloud in reply, but his eyes spoke volumes as they held hers.

Under their astounded scrutiny, she felt compelled to explain further, even though no explanation was necessary. Speaking unemotionally in the dry tone of a banker, she related her reasoning; and as she spoke, she noticed that while he always retained a portion of his attention on flying the craft, she could also tell that the larger part of his awareness embraced her every word. Denying the detached mood spawned by her deadpan delivery and his divided attention, she clung to what attention there was like a drowning man would cling to a tossed life preserver. Here was a mind—a *normal* mind!—that could appreciate her explanations, a man who could understand. It came as no surprise that before long she found herself revealing much more than she had originally planned: she explained at length about negatives, about victims and champions, about how the men of the valley were no different than Back For God or Washington or Dr. Floyd; they merely chose victims differently—but they still chose them nonetheless. She spoke about her efforts to discover a third way and chart a philosophical course where it wasn't necessary to create any victims at all.

Every now and again the pilot would turn to her wide eyed when she made some particular point that struck a resonant chord within him—for he had too often felt himself being played for the unwilling victim. Several times he nodded his agreement, sometimes vigorously; *This woman knows what she's talking about!* his silent mien broadcast. He listened intently, soaking up her every word like a thirsty sponge; but presently she stopped.

"Well?" he demanded, his bass voice cutting across the muted whine of the turbines. He stared deeply and intently into her eyes.

"Well, what?"

"Well, what's the alternative? The third path?"

"I..." She hesitated and tore her gaze away, embarrassed. "I don't know," she finally admitted, lowering her head.

Stunned and showing it, his eyes never left hers. "You don't," he finally replied flatly.

"No."

"Had me fooled," he admitted, chuckling, breaking the mood. He returned the bulk of his attention to his piloting; the craft began to slowly descend. Eyes still on the sky ahead, he sighed. "My lady, that had to be the best speech I have heard since my Sacramento friend first suggested we revolt." He turned to face Gwen again. "But she didn't have the answer either. The right answer, that is."

Gwen didn't know what to say. "I'm sorry," she finally compromised.

"Not your fault," he replied causally, as if talking about the weather. He wasn't sure if she was sorry about not having an answer or about the cruel fate that had ultimately befallen the troubled woman. *And I still don't know what for. Doesn't matter anymore.* "Not anyone's fault," he reflected aloud. *That's how philosophy is!* he appended, but he kept that final thought to himself.

They continued their descent in silence. The pilot swung their craft around to the south of Las Vegas, slowed, aligned their flight path with the old cement highway stretching straight across the desert, and brought the hypercraft in for a smooth landing. He taxied up to the edge of town and shut down the turbines. Consulting the chronometer, he saw that while the entire trip had taken less than half an hour, somehow the conversation had made it seem quite a lot longer. He shook his head at himself. *Me of all people! Expecting answers to the deep questions of the Universe from such a pretty young thing!* He quickly shook off his disheartened reaction. *Cheer up!* he told himself. *You're in Las Vegas!* Regaining his normal sense of self, he slapped the release on the seat harness loudly with theatrical gusto and grinned wickedly. "C'mon, Gwen. Time's a-wasting!" He swept an arm across the windshield. "It's Las Vegas out there! Let's get a move on!"

When they stepped off the airplane, they hadn't walked ten feet into town before they were stopped by a nasty-looking fellow with an unruly beard framing bad teeth. "New in town?" he asked eagerly, his voice raspy and low. Several other townsfolk paused to listen to the exchange.

"Yes!" boomed the pilot in an attempt to out-bass the townsman—and hopefully intimidating the man as well. He suddenly realized that somehow he had lacked the forethought to bring a sidearm. *Damn!*

But the grizzly man didn't react as a man bested; rather, he beamed a gap-toothed grin as if he had won a sizeable wager, held out a large hand, and rasped, "Well, then! Welcome to Las Vegas!" He shook each of their hands heartily, then added, "You folks hungry? There's a honky-tonk I know what's got some fine chili—" He backhanded the pilot's upper arm friendly-like. "—and some fine whiskey, too, if that's to your liking."

"Whiskey!"

Gwen felt it time to interrupt. "We have a job to finish," she reminded the pilot, attempting to discourage any diversion. "And I'm sure we don't have whatever it is they use for money here."

"That's okay, ma'am," the resident replied quickly. "Society'll pay for it."

"Who?" Gwen and the pilot replied in unison.

"Society! Anyone who's new in town gets all their bills paid for a little while... until they get themselves set up, that is." He looked from one face to the other. "Speaking of which... You folks looking for a nice quiet place to spend the night, maybe?"

Gwen blushed awkwardly and turned away, lifting one hand to cover an embarrassed cheek. The pilot quickly interjected, "Hey, she's not my wife!"

The man glanced at the huge engagement ring sparkling on Gwen's finger alongside a gleaming gold wedding band and smiled with an air of knowing slyness. "So I suspected. Those dime-store rings gave you folks away in a second!"

The pilot waved his words aside. "Actually, she's only here for the night visiting friends. Me, though, I'd be looking for a place to stay, permanent-like." He hooked a thumb over his shoulder. "But like the lady says, first we have a stack of suitcases that have to get to the Transcontinental station. Know where we could rent an automobile or something?"

"An automobile!" The man laughed heartily. "Nope! Ain't been no automobiles around these parts for quite a while. Not for years! You might be able to find a cart big enough to fit you and the lady, but not the suitcases, too." He turned and pointed; over a garage next to a butcher shop hung a large sign that read, "For Rent: Horses, Wagons, Tack." "You'll probably do best to rent a wagon—," then quickly added, "—and Society'll pay for that, too, by the way."

Eager to move on, Gwen took a few steps in the indicated direction, but the pilot did not follow. She turned back and glanced at him questioningly.

"What's the hurry, Gwen?" he boomed in a loud voice. "This man here's talking about free whiskey!" His eyes were wide with anticipation.

"Have you any idea how long it's been since I've had a decent drink? Or a *free* one, for that matter?"

"Later. Let's get Dagny's things to her first." She resumed her trek, leaving the men behind.

The pilot turned to their chance companion and shrugged resignedly. "She's the boss. Maybe later?"

The man smiled. "No problem! I can wait." His smile broadened. "Better yet, let me help you move your things. Once we're done, we can get that whiskey."

Some of the pilot's suspicions still remained. "And it's free?"

"Free! Yes! Society pays for it!"

"Why is it you're so eager to help us?"

He winked knowingly. "Because Society'll cover my bar bill, too, you know, seeing how I'm part of your welcoming committee. Eddie set it up that way on purpose to encourage men like me to help new folks like you." He grinned broadly. "And I'm helping you!"

The pilot was still not sure he understood. "So you're saying this Society'll cover the cost to rent the wagon?"

The man nodded.

"And the whiskey?"

Nod.

Remembering which town it was where he stood, the pilot's mind raced ahead; he smiled evilly. "And what else?"

The man grinned broadly and punched him playfully on the arm. "You dog!" He looked him in the eye, his irregular smile faltering only slightly. "Really... Whiskey's okay, but maybe we shouldn't push it too far?" He sounded unsure of the veracity of his own advice.

The pilot eyed him askance, but before he had a chance to form a reply, the man laughed heartily and whacked the pilot on the arm. "But now that you mention it, it's definitely worth a try!"

The pilot grinned like a child on Christmas morning and tossed his head toward Gwen. "Come on, then! Let's get that wagon rented!" The two men trotted to catch up with her; she did not react to their presence as they came up alongside her and matched her pace.

"Know how to drive a wagon?" inquired their host, as if he already knew the answer.

The pilot and Gwen exchanged blank glances.

"Didn't think so. That's all right. I can drive you." He elbowed the pilot gently. "And Society'll pay me to do that, too!"

Gwen cast a perplexed glance upon the coarse man. "What is this, some sort of People's State?"

The man guffawed wholeheartedly. Clearly he had a zest for living. "Exactly the opposite, lady, exactly the opposite. Who is Eddie Willers?" Recognizing their blank stares for what they were, the man prompted, "You'll find out what I mean soon enough. There'll be lots of time for talking later..." He turned to the pilot and, with a smile and a wink, nudged him. "...over whiskey!" He turned to Gwen then back to the pilot. "But right now let's respect the rights of the charming lady who is not your wife and get your things to the station."

They approached the garage advertising rentals; the closed doors were papered with portraits and securely sealed by an oversized padlock.

"Wait here," suggested their host. "I'll get the owner." Without waiting for their assent, he turned and entered the butcher shop next door.

As they waited, the pilot idly examined the garage doors. Virtually all of the available surface area was covered by hand-drawn, brown-hued posters about a foot square, each fashioned by a different hand. Despite their artistic dissimilarities, they were identical in layout. The top of each poster proclaimed some slogan in large letters, including "EXILED," "CAN'T DRINK," "CAN'T DRIVE," and more. Beneath the title came the hand-drawn picture, presumably of the miscreant—some of them were very artistically rendered, but others, beyond crude—followed by a paragraph giving a brief summary of why the pictured villain deserved their punishment. A final line, also in large letters, began with a bold "UNTIL" and ended with a date. Most of the dates were scattered over the course of the next several months, but a few were years in the future.

"It looks like something out of the wild, wild West," mused the pilot as he examined the rogues' gallery, "Except for these..." He indicated a line of rose-colored posters along the bottom of the door. They were similar in layout to the other posters, except that rather than a verb phrase at the top, a noun appeared instead. Most read "PROSTITUTE," "GAMBLER," and "ROMEO," and while the paragraph detailing their "crime" was vague at best, the final line was clear as glass: "UNTIL FOREVER!"

"I'm not so sure I'm going to like this town...," the pilot observed glumly.

Gwen stood alongside the pilot surveying the posters. "Maybe the pink crimes are supposed to be religious prohibitions?" she hazarded.

The pilot snorted derisively, waving a hand at the pastel announcements. "If that's so, I'm going to be in big trouble!" he predicted, grinning evilly. He turned his head, chin held proudly high, to show Gwen his profile. "Do you know how to draw?" he inquired innocently.

Gwen giggled into her hands; but before she could reply, their impromptu host returned, a balding shopkeeper in tow.

"Damn it!" swore the shopkeeper as he approached. "Them goddamn bitches are at it again!" With the vengeance of a saint, he made a beeline for the garage door, shouldered the pilot and Gwen aside, and one by one angrily tore down the pastel posters. "Whatever happened to live and let live!" he demanded rhetorically as he finished his righteous task. "And respect for the property of others?" He balled the offending papers into a huge pink wad and finally recognized his customers. "All right, folks. Welcome to Las Vegas. Let's get your wagon outfitted. Society's treat!"

The pilot leaned toward Gwen and spoke in a hushed voice. "I think I'm going to like this town!"

* * *

The Transcontinental station loomed.

The pilot bounced painfully on the hard wooden seat of the horse-drawn wagon. Gwen sat snugly on one side of him, and their welcoming committee-of-one a little less so on the other. Idly the pilot considered the majesty of the station's massive granite pillars, but the bulk of his attention was decidedly elsewhere: he was still trying to figure out exactly what the hell was going on here. He wasn't sure who was paying for what; all he knew was that it wasn't him. Nevertheless he was patient about reaching an understanding, especially since there was the promise of free whiskey along the way—and perhaps more! This was definitely *not* the sort of reception he'd met when he first came to the Gulch.

"Whoa!" their host called out as they came abreast of the station's front door. The wagon creaked to a halt.

Instantly the pilot jumped down from his painful perch and seized the handles of the two nearest suitcases. Taken aback by his sudden leap into action, his traveling companions could only remain in place and watch, matching bewildered expressions plain on their faces. Without setting down either piece of luggage, the pilot flew up the few steps and clumsily opened the front door with two free fingers, swung the door wide with a toe, and deposited one suitcase inside; the other he used to prop open the door. Trotting hurriedly down the steps, he returned to the wagon and manhandled the larger of the two trunks to the ground; he dropped it with a thud and a puff onto the dusty street. He looked up briefly, began to reach for the trunk's handles, then stopped. "What's the matter?" he asked abruptly, seeing their faces. Not waiting for an answer, he returned to his task.

"Where's the fire?" a bewildered Gwen asked of the retreating pilot. "Only a moment ago you were willing to let the suitcases wait."

The pilot set his burden down before the open door and shoved the trunk inside impatiently with his foot. In a second he was back at the wagon reaching for the smaller trunk. "Not merely 'fire,' Gwen," he rumbled with a deep grunt as he dropped the second trunk to the street. "Fire *water!*" He grabbed the handle at one end and dragged it bouncing up the steps and slid it quickly inside. Their host threw his head back and laughed loud and long.

Not comprehending, Gwen looked from one man to the other. "What...?" she began, but thought it better to wait until she had their combined attention. "What—," she began again when the pilot returned for the last two suitcases, but he did not let her finish.

"Gwen, that man's talking about free whiskey!" He grabbed two handles and swung the suitcases into the air, maneuvering them expertly to the ground at either side of him. "Free! And you know how things work in the valley—I haven't had anything free in *years!* And the sooner we get this buggy unloaded—" He spun around impatiently, bounded up the station's steps, and deposited the last of the luggage with its mates as he finished his sentence. "—the sooner we get to drinking!" He kicked the makeshift door prop inside, and the front door swooped shut behind it.

Their grisly host laughed all the louder. "Now *there* is a man who knows his priorities!"

"Right you are!" he rumbled in reply as he hastily returned to the wagon. "Never stand between a thirsty man and his drink!" He hurriedly clambered back aboard and reclaimed his stiff seat between them. Turning to Gwen, he asked unhurriedly, "Coming?"

She finally recovered her composure. "Thank you, but no. I'd like to visit with Dagny and Eddie first." She stepped demurely from the wagon to the street.

The pilot shook his head slowly and playfully, then turned to their host. "I just do *not* understand some folks' priorities!" Turning to Gwen, he warned, "Don't expect to see me until at least nine tomorrow morning, but no later than ten. I promise I'll get you home by noon, like we planned." Without waiting for a reply, he turned his attention back to the laughing man. "Come on, come on! Let's get this party *rolling!*"

Still laughing, the man shook the reins. "Giddyup!" he bellowed.

Gwen watched as the wagon rolled swiftly away, a wry smile on her face. "At least he's consistent in the practice of his philosophy," she observed aloud to no one.

"Do you know how long it's been since I've had any descent whiskey?" she heard the pilot asking, his deep voice fading as the distance between them increased. "Years!" She heard loud laughter from the chauffer. "Tonight, you'll be enjoying the finest Las Vegas has to offer!" he replied, his voice fading in turn.

*Nine o'clock?* she wondered. *We shall see!* Smiling, she shook her head in mock displeasure and headed inside.

* * *

Gwen relaxed.

She sat comfortably in the luxurious wing back chair in the *Meteor's* observation car, a sweet cordial half filling the fine crystal stemware she held lightly between her fingers. So engrossed was she in Eddie's tales that she repeatedly neglected to notice she still held it in her hand.

The dinner they had just finished was nothing short of scrumptious. She had had no idea that Eddie was such a fine cook. When she asked him where he had acquired such amazing culinary skills, oddly he seemed ill at ease. "From a friend here in town," he had replied tersely, his face reddening perceptibly. Taking her cue from his discomfort, she did not pursue the subject; obviously, it was a touchy one.

While he was busily preparing their dinner, Gwen had taken the opportunity to question Dagny discretely about her decision to leave the valley, but discretion was not necessary; Dagny was openly matter-of-fact about her reasons. In the clear, monotonous voice of a military report, looking straight at Gwen, Dagny recited the litany of abuses she had endured all her life at the hands of the men who professed to love her, while in stark contrast, her association with Eddie had enriched her life at every turn. "I was a fool not to have seen it sooner," she concluded. Gwen had sympathized, tactfully leaving out any mention of her own similar conclusions, and deferring, for the moment, dwelling upon any impact Dagny's revelations about Hank might have upon her own marriage. Apparently Gwen was not the only woman who bruised easily.

With dinner done, they had retired to the more comfortable seating in the opulent observation car. Dagny and Eddie sat hand-in-hand on the couch while Gwen occupied one of the two wing back chairs that faced them. Entranced, the two women listened intently as Eddie related his tale in spell-binding detail. He spoke of the horrors of the battle for San Francisco and the truce he had brokered which allowed the final *Meteor* to depart unmolested. He expounded upon the fatal mechanical failure that brought down the Diesel, stranding him for uncounted days on end to slowly starve in the blazing Arizona desert.

Several times during the telling, Dagny would look up at Eddie with heartfelt concern plain on her face, concern for both the man and the railroad; it was the first time she had heard the saga in all its frightening detail, and she was as captivated by its telling as was Gwen.

Eddie's eyes lit up with pride as he described for the two women how he had ultimately saved the stalled train and returned to Las Vegas as his only option. Dagny smiled at the image of the *Meteor* being pulled across the desert with an inverted engine, while Gwen shivered at the mere thought of bare-handedly attacking then devouring a poor, defenseless prairie dog.

He spoke of marauders, bandits, and more, and how the town had triumphed over each and every challenge. With worried empathy plainly etched on his face, he told them of the arrival of refugees fleeing the fighting in the West, and the large influx of them which had led to the creation of Society.

At the mention of the word, Gwen's ears perked up. "Society?" she interrupted. "The man who helped us bring Dagny's luggage mentioned Society several times."

"Yes, I can understand why. Society pays the way for newcomers until they can get themselves settled," he explained. "And as your host, he's entitled to a few perquisites for himself as well. A free meal or two, minor expenses paid, that sort of thing. Most men won't bother to ask for any reimbursement, but there are always a few individuals who like to push things to the limit—and beyond!"

Gwen nodded. "That explains why he was so eager to help."

Eddie nodded in turn. "We men of Las Vegas help everyone we can—everyone who needs it, that is. It's part of our Constitution for Society: 'From each according to his ability, to each according to his need.' If newcomers in town need help, they get it. Long-term residents, too. It's their need that's paramount."

At his words, Gwen instantly froze, rebelling almost instinctively against the socialistic credo—she knew for a fact that it was the altruistic societies that created the most—and the worst!—victims. It was a reflection of her imperturbable nature that outwardly she reacted calmly; yet that did not stop her from asking what to her was the key question. "And whom does your Society force to play the victim?"

"What? What victim? What do you mean?"

"Well," she began, almost impatiently, as if repeating an obvious truth. "If you give the unearned to one person, doesn't it have to come at the expense of another?"

"That's true," Dagny chimed in, mirroring Gwen's challenging tone.

Eddie looked from one woman to the other, still retaining his perplexed expression. "Why, no." He glanced down to the carpeted floor, considering, then looked back up to Gwen, then to Dagny. "Why would it have to be that way?"

This time it was Gwen who took on the perplexed look. "Because—" she began, but interrupted herself to begin anew. "Let me ask this: who is it that's paying for my pilot's whiskey?"

"Anyone who wants to."

"And the wagon we rented?"

"Yes."

"Yes?"

"Yes. That, too."

"'Who,' I meant."

"Anyone who wants to," he repeated. Eddie shifted his weight on the sofa, pulling Dagny's hand toward him slightly as he moved. He recognized the source of the women's confusion; he had encountered it quite frequently in Society's early days. "Let me explain," he began. "As I said, Society helps those who can't help themselves, as is usually the case when someone first arrives in town. Sometimes all they need to get them started are a few meals and a place to stay; in other cases, such as with some of the refugees we've taken in, they may also need a doctor or some other critical help. Rather than leave it all to random charity—which operates poorly at best—we've created Society. Men donate voluntarily to Society, and Society distributes their charity in an organized, disciplined fashion."

"And what if men do not wish to donate?" asked Gwen in a clear, patient voice.

Eddie shrugged. "Then they don't. In fact, most men don't. But it's also a fact that those who do choose to contribute give far more than what's necessary to meet the needs of Las Vegas."

"And who decides what is necessary?" Gwen riposted. "What organization—"

"Society," he interrupted accidentally, answering her first question as she began the next. "Sorry. And the organization is Society, too," he finished, anticipating her interrupted question with an embarrassed downward glance.

"And exactly how does that work?"

"We have a written Constitution for Society that defines its organizational makeup. It works a lot like the United States government did. There's a Senate and a House of Representatives who vote on voluntary Guidelines that the Head of Society signs or vetoes..." He went on at length, first about the process, then about its execution, citing example after example of how men could help their fellow man without holding a gun to anyone's head. "The key is that Society is completely divorced from the State," he finished. "Society has no coercive powers, none at all, not even the power to tax."

"The power to tax is the power to destroy," interjected Dagny. "Witness the travesties Wesley and his cronies once perpetrated upon us."

Eddie squeezed her hand gently and smiled at her. "That's right," he replied. They held each other's eyes for several seconds, their thoughts written plainly on their faces, before he turned back to Gwen. When he did, the look on Gwen's face was one of astonishment.

"Except there's no reason to destroy anyone!" she cried, finally understanding. Her eyes unfocused as her mind pursued the ramifications. "No reason to create victims," she realized, speaking aloud to herself. "None at all!"

"Yes," he agreed. "None at all."

Gwen whirled to face Dagny. "And that's the answer!"

"The answer to what?"

"To who'll pay for traffic lights in the valley! Society!"

After a brief bout of astonishment, Dagny nodded at the non-sequitur. "I see," she said. "And I also see how it could also address many similar funding conundrums."

Gwen nodded abstractly, only half listening. Abruptly, she giggled. "Yes!" she added enthusiastically. "Such as plowing snow from all the streets!" Her face abruptly fell somber as she remembered her father's last hours and the fate of his ignored cellar-mate. *And other necessities, too...* Her eyes misted over; she raised a hand to clear them only to find it still held the stemware. Distractedly she took a sip, feeling the motion of the sweet liquid coursing warmly down her throat and into her veins. Her eyelids drooped in animal appreciation.

Misreading her overlapping reactions, Eddie was suddenly all concern. "I am so sorry! I've been talking entirely too much! You ladies must be tired—it's getting late and it's already been such a long day for you." He stood, releasing Dagny's hand. "Let me show you to your compartment, Gwen. It's not so roomy as the one Dagny and I are staying in, but I trust you'll find it to your liking."

She rose to face him. "And your Society will pay for that as well?"

He looked at her in silence for a moment. "It would...," he finally replied slowly, "...if I were to ask. But I'm happy to do this myself, to do it out of friendship, as my personal favor to you." He held her eyes causally but steadily for several seconds, and she, his.

Abruptly, Gwen turned away blushing as Eddie did the same, in the same instant, his face coloring to match hers. In that moment, each of them had seen in the eyes of the other more than either had intended to reveal. It had been a moment between them which was not to be mentioned.

* * *

Gwen lay.

Sleep would not come. As she stared at the darkened ceiling of the sleeper, her mind raced with innumerable thoughts that would not be denied. Many of them revolved around the ramifications of Eddie's Society and how it perfectly addressed her own long-standing questions about victims versus champions, while other thoughts held her in awe as she marveled at the twists and turns in the tale of the town's travails. All these concepts and more tugged at her attention; but one kept resurfacing and, when it did, it obliterated all the rest. Lying there in her compartment hours after the fact, she could still feel the deep warmth of his gaze at the moment they had briefly locked eyes and locked souls, unleashing an immense power that had instantly blasted apart the physical connection between them in a flurry of blushing embarrassment. No clueless fool, she plainly realized what had happened—and why—and more crucially, that the unstated feelings were mutual.

Such a discovery could easily have torn many a man apart; yet Gwen felt no conflict within her, and in the dark she smiled warmly at the tender feelings that filled her. Without question, she deeply loved her own husband and their son, and felt no diminishing of her affection toward them or any impetus to shirk the duties she owed them, nor any reluctance to bestow upon them the gifts she gladly gave. Rather, she felt richer for tonight's discovery, like a millionaire who had unexpectedly doubled his fortune through some chance investment.

With a slight gasp in the dark, a break tainted with both torment and promise, she recalled how Dagny's romantic relationships seldom lasted more than a few years. *Eddie might one day soon become more approachable...*, she told herself cautiously as her pulse quickened. In spite of how that frighteningly fascinating thought gave her pause, she immediately tossed it aside. *No, Dagny won't let it happen this time!* she knew. Her friend had finally found her ideal man, one of the highest moral caliber who shared all of her loves as well as every aspect of her life, the man who never abandoned his beliefs even in the face of an entire world crumbling around him, the man who refused to let it go, refused to give up, refused to give in: a true hero, without fear and above reproach. *So very much like my Hank!* she realized, the awareness simultaneously fueling her affection for both men.

In its wake, another, even more significant thought struck her racing, tumultuous mind: although she might not be free to openly express her feelings for Eddie in one arena, she suddenly realized how that restriction would not preclude her from expressing them in another. Lying there in the sleeper compartment staring at the dark ceiling, she suddenly realized what it was she could to do—no, *had* to do!—to consummate her new-found bond with Eddie. If she could not share his life as a lover or wife, then she would share it in another, more productive way: she would share his truth with the world.

Lying on her bed, in a moment of dedication more sacred than any wedding vow, to herself she silently affirmed, *I will put an end to victimhood. I will become an Apostle of Society!* She pressed her lips together tightly in silent determination: when she left Las Vegas come morning, along with her she would carry Eddie's Society back to the Gulch. She would exemplify by her own actions the one key issue which strikers had always overlooked—the victim. She would become the victim's champion, and let the damn strikers think of her what they may. Striker though she was, it was long past time she quit pretending where her allegiance truly lay. And if they threw her out on her ear as a result, at least she now had a place to go—one more exciting than Wildwood ever was.

In the darkness, she nodded without moving. It would be both easy and natural for her to turn her superlative ability as an executive secretary toward the goal of establishing and administering Eddie's Society in the Gulch. She was confident she could—no, *would!*—make it a success.

With that realization, a quiet peace settled over her, as if some great weight had been lifted from her shoulders; her racing mind slowed and her eyes gradually fluttered shut. Slowly, surely, she began to drift off; and the last thing to cross her notice before the sweetness of sleep engulfed her was the sensation of an almost imperceptible rocking of the sleeper compartment beneath her. Sharing in it, a small smile touched her lips; and finally, happily, she slept.

* * *

The pilot returned.

With eyes that were only somewhat bleary, he squinted at the bright morning sun slanting through the tall windows into the station's cavernous waiting room while regarding coolly the apprehensive appraisal the sunlit Gwen threw his way. The sunshine notwithstanding, her luminous face appeared to shine with an inner glow of its own; but he dismissed the impression as something of his own fancy, a reflection of the incredible bacchanalian revelry in which he had overindulged the night before—and all at Society's expense, too!

"I'm fine!" he protested, not at all convincingly.

"I see," she said, not at all convinced.

"Unless you want us to stay here another night?" he asked hopefully.

"No, thank you." With that, she lifted her suitcase and headed for the door, not waiting for him to follow.

"I'm fine!" he repeated to her retreating back, a resonating echo of his deep voice booming across the waiting room, but she paid him no mind. Shrugging, he followed quickly in her wake, taking the suitcase from her hand as he caught up to her. He held the door open for her, and the two of them walked outside to face the busy street.

Gwen hesitated at the top of the few steps leading down to street level and turned her head left and right, searching. "What happened to our wagon?" she finally asked.

"Oh! What's-his-name returned it for us."

"'What's-his-name?'" she blinked uncomprehendingly.

"Yes. What's-his-name, our dentally-deficient host."

"Ah." She hesitated uncertainly. "You know, now that you mention it, I don't recall asking his name. What was it?"

The pilot stood in silence a few seconds before replying. "You know, I don't recall having asked, either."

Gwen threw the pilot a hard glance. "You mean you partied all night long with this man and you never once even asked him his *name?*"

The pilot shrugged. "What's in a name?"

She hesitated, then shrugged in turn. "I guess I'm as guilty as you are since I never asked him, either." She paused in reflection. "Next time I meet the man—" *Or any stranger*, she resolved. "—I'll make it a point to ask him his name."

"An excuse to come back," he consoled, then added as an aside, "As if we needed one!"

"Too true," she admitted with a warm, genuine sincerity in her voice that submerged as quickly as it had surfaced. "But right now we have every reason to take our leave." Again without waiting for his assent, she descended the steps and headed south along the busy street; the pilot quickly caught up and walked along side her.

"Lots of opportunity here!" he exclaimed, waving an arm expansively to include the entire desert town. "The food is cheaper here than in the valley, but manufactured goods are a whole lot more expensive. If I set up a trade route for both commodities, I bet I could pocket a fine spread!" He rubbed his hands together as he walked. "And not only will I make a fortune, this fine, fine town will make a fine, fine home for this wayward scab!"

"Don't call yourself that!" she protested with uncharacteristic vehemence. She seemed genuinely perturbed. "You're a good man and have no claim to run yourself down like that!"

This time the pilot felt no surprise at hearing such heresy coming from the mouth of a striker. Rather, he bowed respectfully. "You are much too kind," he rejoined, speaking in his faux British accent, his deep voice adding warmth to the foreign compliment.

"Thank you," she responded tersely, not looking his way. Presently she sighed. "I'm sorry. I shouldn't have been so short with you."

"No offense taken, milady," he replied with stately dignity, still speaking with a British burr. Guardedly, he added, "Methinks there's something troubling Your Grace?"

For most of a minute she walked silently at his side before finally confessing, "You know, I can name many excellent reasons why I can't wait to get home—but I must admit I'm not quite ready to return to the valley."

The pilot laughed aloud. "I know *exactly* what you mean!"

She flashed him a knowing, secret smile. "Of course I'd expect you to understand. Las Vegas is so..." She waved a hand vaguely. "So *different!*"

"*Vive la différence!*" he cheered loudly in his deep voice. Several passers-by tossed curious glances their way.

"It is refreshing," she agreed. "Especially after spending so many years in the valley."

"Amen!" rejoined the pilot, mentally marveling at her continued candid comments. *If only I had met this one before Hank did!* he lamented. But recalling the revelry of the night before, he smiled openly. *Then again, maybe not!*

Seeing his thoughts written, for once, plainly upon his face, she had to ask: "Why the big smile?"

Dissembling, he pointed ahead; in the near distance sat the waiting hypercraft. "It's show time!" he cried, stepping up his pace in feigned, yet authentic anticipation.

Leaving the town behind, they advanced upon the odd-shaped, greenish-blue craft. The pilot opened the rear hatch and they climbed inside; he sealed it securely behind them. Gwen took her seat—and recalling their previous wild departure, dutifully latched her harness. Expectantly, she watched as the pilot manipulated the controls in preparation for takeoff. Her excitement was understandable, seeing how it would only be her third flight ever. Abstractly, she began to glance around the cabin, as if searching for something.

Noticing her scrutiny, the pilot looked up at her and asked uncertainly, "What's the matter?"

She wrinkled her nose slightly, unintentionally engendering a delightful coquettish expression. "Do you smell lavender?"

The pilot grinned and slammed the throttle forward; and with a powerful lurch the hypercraft shot into the sky.

"Wooo hooo!" he boomed, as he set course for home. "Do I ever!"

## CHAPTER 18 – HIT THE ROAD, JACK

Owen gasped.

Andrew folded his soot-stained arms across his chest. "Don't you look at me that way, Owen. I refuse, I tell you!"

"But—"

"But nothing!" he interrupted. "We didn't go on strike just to capitulate to the looters once we finally won!"

"But I'm not saying anyone should cap—"

"I don't give a damn *what* you're saying!" he insisted angrily. "I don't support my own destroyers!"

Slack-jawed, Owen stared at the beet-red face incredulously. "Your destroyers?"

"Yes!"

"But... But our strike was successful! We've won! Our destroyers have destroyed themselves! It's time to return Outside—the Worker even said so! I don't understand why you'd refuse me."

"It can be put in perspective easily enough." Andrew waved at the blueprints that Owen had laid out on one of the foundry's drafting tables. "You're asking me to cast precision titanium parts—for a *looter's* air force? Why the hell should I want to work for a stinking looter?"

"But it's for Mr. James! He's no looter. He's taken the oath!"

"That's as may be, but *Washington*, hasn't! I have no problem casting parts for James' new jeep, so long as it's for his personal use, but rebuilding Washington's air force for use by looters? That's something else entirely! Especially since their elections are coming up! Who knows who might win? And word has it that it likely *won't* be our boy James!"

"But—"

"No!" He clumsily gathered the blueprints into a crinkled bunch and thrust the bundle into Owen's chest. "No looter air force! Now get out—and don't come back! Not ever!" Without waiting for Owen to leave, he stalked away muttering under his breath. "Stinking looter lover!"

Chastised, Owen beat a hasty retreat. He stood in front of the foundry for a moment collecting his rattled wits and re-rolled the blueprints in a more orderly fashion than had Andrew. *Now what am I to do? Andrew operates the only foundry in the valley!* Hank might have been able to cast the parts, even though the job was clearly outside the man's specialty; these days he produced nothing but ingots, structural shapes, and other artifacts made exclusively of Miracle Metal. Precision titanium castings were something else entirely. Regardless, even though the man had the ability to do it, in this situation ability played no part; Hank had already given Owen the same bum's rush he had just been handed by Andrew. His shoulders slumped glumly. Where else in this new world was there to go for precision-cast aircraft parts? *Nowhere!*

He sighed. Until a moment ago, he was convinced that the lucrative agreement he and the pilot had signed with Mr. James was his ticket to an early retirement from the import-export business, thereby providing him with the capital and free time necessary to expand his personal horizons by pursuing yet another career. But without the skills that men like Andrew and Hank brought to the table, that agreement was only so much ink-stained paper. Their point-blank refusal had blasted the ground right out from under his feet—and he knew for certain his own disappointment would pale alongside the reaction he expected to receive from his partner once he and Gwen returned from Las Vegas that afternoon. Owen was not looking forward to that reunion.

He hurried along the road that wound though the grassy hillocks that separated the industrial corner of the valley from the town center. If he didn't hustle, he'd end up being late for work, and that would be bad indeed. In the pilot's absence he was fully responsible for the operation of *The Empty Nest* and would soon have to open its doors for the lunch crowd. Rushed though he was, he still had one more stop to make, Lawrence's Grocery Market, to purchase the taproom's provisions for the day. Fortunately, the grocer's shop was on his way, so the delay inspired by that interlude would be minimal.

The bell affixed to the door of Lawrence's shop tinkled merrily as he entered. Behind the counter stood Lawrence, bent over a large sheet of paper intent on some calculations. In front of the counter stood the fishwife impatiently puffing on a cigarette as she waited for him to finish. Between them on the countertop sat an oversized, screen-capped bucket full of water containing a number of lively fish which she had caught; the fishwife was one of the many producers who kept the Market stocked. Occasional thrashing noises sounded from within the bucket, each one tossing a minor spatter through the screen and onto the countertop. Ignoring the fish and their frenzied swimming, Lawrence completed his calculations, opened the cash drawer, and counted out the fishwife's due. She accepted the meager pile of silver coins, took a step back from the counter, and began counting them out for herself.

Lawrence smiled at him. "Morning, Owen. What'll it be, the usual?"

"That should do for starters," he agreed, his bass voice complementing the chorus of crystalline splashes coming from the bucket. He handed Lawrence a long list of victuals. "And here's a special order I'll need for tomorrow morning. I thought you'd appreciate the heads up."

"A second load for the State's Science Institute, eh?" he inquired idly, his attention more on scanning the list than on small talk.

"Yes. And likely a third, fourth, and fifth will be coming along as well."

At the mention of the Institute, the fishwife pointedly halted her counting. Slowly and deliberately, she shifted her large eyes from one man to the other and back again. Her gaze finally settled on Owen. "You're selling food to looters?" she asked flatly, a foreign accent coloring her words.

There was something about her tone of voice aside from the accent that gave him pause. "Yes," he finally admitted, wondering why he felt so apprehensive.

The large eyes swiveled to Lawrence. "And you're selling him food to sell to looters?"

Lawrence was still distracted with reading his list. "Uh-huh," he agreed absently.

She slapped the half-counted pile of coins back onto the counter. "Not me," she announced as she grabbed the bucket's handle with both hands. She hefted the heavy load to the floor, sloshing a little water in the process, adjusted her grip before lifting it again, and without another word headed for the door.

"Hey, wait!" cried Lawrence, his attention finally wrenched from his reading.

She halted at the door, waiting, bucket in hand, a mocking frown creasing her face, letting the silence speak for her.

Lawrence paused a moment. He understood. "Commendable," he praised, nodding to the woman. Turning to Owen, he politely handed him back his list. "Thanks, Owen, but I think I'll pass this time around."

"What?"

"I said I'll pass," he repeated a little more pointedly, and after a pause he added, "And come to think of it, I'll have to pass on your regular order as well."

"Wh——," he began again, but interrupted himself in mid-word. He understood.

With a satisfied smile, the fishwife set the heavy bucket on the floor, reclaimed the pile of silver still sitting on the counter, concluded her counting, and with a cold nod to Lawrence and a fiery glare at Owen, marched out the door sans bucket, the door's bell tinkling cheerfully in her wake.

Taking his cue from her lead, Lawrence let the silence lengthen.

Checkmated, Owen let the silence stand, turned, and left. There was nothing he could say, and everyone knew it.

\* \* \*

The schism waxed.

Heretic by heretic, it escalated and intensified almost by the minute. Spurred by the machinations of the fishwife, within a few short hours the atmosphere of the Gulch re-crystallized around its proper premises with the swiftness of the jerk of a pickpocket's hand caught dead in the act.

It was an odd crystallization, to be sure. From the point of view of a casual observer, there was nothing overt to be seen. Two men would be talking about business or something equally mundane, when suddenly both would fall silent. They would hold each other's eye for a moment longer, then simply walk away, never to speak again. It was disquieting to witness, to say the least.

Yet despite the schism's apparent low profile, in its wake households split, businesses fractured, and lifelong friends bid one another a stony farewell. Like it or not, it was evident to all that the valley was poised to lose scores of residents. It was either that or lose its soul.

\* \* \*

The pilot returned.

*The Empty Nest* was packed with patrons—almost as many as had attended Miss Kay's performance almost two years ago—but none were there for lunch. Owen had temporarily suspended all dining service, for food had suddenly become a priceless commodity. He knew they would soon be needing all the food they could get, but no idea where they might get it, short of importing it from Outside—assuming Dwight would let any of them use the airstrip!

With conscious intent, virtually all of the newly-minted *personae non gratae* had gravitated to the lair of the only man in the entire valley who they knew would still willingly associate with them: the sole scab remaining in all of the Gulch: the pilot. Unsurprisingly, among the *personae* were most of the taproom's regular patrons, most notably Richard, and least notably an unpublished author, the kind of writer who could only be popular Outside, the sort of man who believed that when you dealt with words, you must first try to be entertaining, and only secondarily informative, if at all.

For the most part, the patrons sat in silence or spoke softly among themselves; several nursed drinks, and of course none were eating. Owen stood behind the bar catering to their modest needs; and as the crowd swelled through the lunchless lunch hour, correspondingly his troubled thoughts increased in intensity as well, so much so that by the time the pilot arrived, Owen's train of thought had reached the point where his concern, bordering on panic, showed plainly on his face.

"What's wrong?" demanded the pilot not two seconds after he walked in the door.

At his entrance, *The Empty Nest* fell quiet as a church. From behind the bar, Owen sighed aloud. "Everything!"

The pilot scanned the crowded room, taking note that despite the hour, not a single person was eating. "What the hell's going on here? Did we run out of food or something?"

Owen shrugged. "'Or something,'" he explained tersely.

Silence dragged for a moment, and it was Richard who finally stood. "If I may explain..."

"Please!"

"In short: we—" He waved his hands in opposite directions, indicating the occupants of the room "—have been branded as evil. And I fear we will have to abandon this valley."

"Evil?" Idly, the pilot wondered why he had not been included in Richard's honor roll. After all, he was a scab, therefore evil by definition—at least in the eyes of these Johnnies. "How so?"

"Our fellow strikers feel we have committed an unforgivable sin," he explained, "the sin of condoning the willfully irrational."

The pilot's expression did not change; not that he was hiding anything behind what looked like his best poker face; rather he did not realize that Richard had made his point and finished speaking. Several seconds dragged by before he comprehended that it must be incumbent upon him to get the discussion rolling again. "Meaning...?" he finally prompted.

Richard eyebrows went up in surprise, as if it were something not open to question. "I mean just what I said: our sin is that we have chosen to associate with evil men."

It was obvious to the pilot that Richard was waiting to be prompted again. But in frustration over his own lack of understanding coupled with Richard's typical, maddeningly-piecemeal presentation, he decided upon an ironic method of showing it: he remained silent in return.

The silence dragged on for several more seconds before Richard recognized his own incumbency. "My apologies!" he exclaimed humbly, finally realizing his error. "I've been living among rational men for so long that I assumed everyone shared the same philosophical base as I. Please let me explain..." He hesitated, then amended, "No, there is too much. Let me sum up: what they say we have done wrong—our evil—was to support our own destroyers, even though we know them for what they actually are: evil!"

The pilot was plainly perplexed. "Who are these evil destroyers you're supporting?"

Richard smiled. "You." He gestured to Owen. "Washington. The State's Science Institute." He looked around the room for a moment, his eyes deliberately seeking out several of his closest friends, businessmen with newly-established contacts Outside. "Among others." Pensively, he fell silent.

Again the pilot held his tongue, but his invisible exasperation ran deep. *Maybe sooner or later this Johnnie will discover the proper premises for how to hold a conversation!* Or so he hoped. The silence dragged until the pilot grudgingly raised an eyebrow questioningly. "Evil how?"

"You have not taken our oath," explained Richard, not noticing the pause. "And since you have not, we cannot know what your moral code may be—or even if you have one! The same thing goes for all the scabs Outside. And until we discover it—and find it is correct—we are morally-bound not to deal with you, for if you do not share our philosophy, then you could easily be one of our destroyers." He smiled genially, belying his accusation. "And in your case that wasn't too difficult a determination—clearly you're not one of us."

*Sometimes I do things right!* the pilot congratulated himself. He smiled mockingly and remained silent.

"Don't you see?" continued Richard. "Because we knowingly support you and your ilk, our fellow strikers feel that we are knowingly supporting evil—our destroyers, that is; the willfully irrational—hence, our sin."

All around the room many heads nodded.

"And they are correct, of course," he conceded, "but only up to a point."

Seeing Richard pause yet again, in protest the exasperated pilot abruptly turned away to busy himself elsewhere. *Enough is enough!* He nonchalantly walked behind the bar, retrieved a bottle of his best wine, deliberately from a difficult-to-access shelf, opened it, and poured his glass full—and took his own good time doing it.

Gentleman that he was, Richard waited without comment as the pilot performed his chore.

The pilot gulped an impatient mouthful before succumbing to prodding again. "Well, oh Evil One? What is your point?"

Richard did not react to the baiting, but rather continued calmly. "As I said, since we have chosen to deal with you and other scabs Outside, many strikers feel we have not followed this valley's philosophy faithfully. We, however, feel that we *have* followed it faithfully. We deal with men such as you because we believe that your refusal to accept our philosophy is simply an error of knowledge on your part, not a mark of irredeemable immorality, and that sooner or later you will recognize the wisdom of our code. We are patient men. On the other hand, our fellow strikers believe such a refusal to be incontrovertible proof of your evil—even though we feel it is logically impossible for them to divine your true intentions without a thorough investigation of its full context. And since they view us as supporters of purportedly-evil men such as you, we ourselves are therefore similarly tainted. Further, they believe if any of them were to treat with us, they themselves would also become fouled by our malevolence. That is why I fear we will be forced to leave this valley, because of that misconception. None of them will ever deal with us again until we have confessed to our evil and sincerely repented—which we cannot do, in clear conscience, since we believe that we are right!"

"Well, it sure took them long enough to notice you sinners," the pilot groused, finally breaking his silence. "But why did they wait until now to force the issue? No one's ever mentioned it before. At least no one seemed to mind my presence, or condemn my customers." He gestured with his glass around the room before taking another healthy swig.

"Ah, but with all the other scabs gone these last few years, few noticed your existence," explained Richard. "And those who did could rightfully excuse those of us who dealt with you, seeing how we only sought to purchase food and drink for our own comfort and pleasure. Technically, that is not 'supporting our destroyers;' it's the same logic which permitted Ragnar to aid Hank prior to his taking the oath, or for the Worker to hire Dagny as his servant while she was still a scab. So the issue lay dormant until this week when you, Owen and others began to actively treat with the scabs Outside for much more than your mere personal comfort. It's not so much that the other strikers finally noticed you, it's more that they have noticed us noticing the scabs Outside."

"So now you're getting the silent treatment?" Recalling the many times he had suffered it himself, he was pleased—smugly pleased—to see how that shoe finally rested so snugly on the other foot.

Richard sighed. "That about sums it up. Now it seems I'll have to pack my bags and go."

An awkward silence hovered over the taproom, lasting until a troubled look crossed the pilot's face. "Hey, wait," he rumbled, his deep voice puncturing the silence. "Let me ask a practical question: does this eviction—or whatever you call it!—does it mean that you Johnnies don't have to honor your signed agreements with me?"

Horror fell upon the audience. They mumbled indignant murmurs among themselves and shook their heads forlornly. "You're forgetting the sanctity of the contract!" an unidentified woman's voice cried out huffily. The philosophical bromide sounded as if it were forced from her lungs by a righteous anger.

The pilot smiled. That was answer enough for him, and very good news indeed. It was just yesterday morning that Dwight had apparently-unwittingly signed the paperwork requiring him to deliver to the pilot a Dwight-Hank hypercraft some three months hence—including unlimited free use of the airfield—in exchange for half interest in his taproom. The order for James' jeep had also been signed with Lawrence, so his substantial commission from that error of knowledge would remain intact as well.

But the pilot still held some doubts, and this was obviously the time to raise them—especially since he was quitting the valley for good as soon as he could! In a fit of pique, he decided he'd cast that doubt as menace, starting with a question he already knew the answer to. "And when I'm evicted, what happens to my taproom...?" he inquired ominously in his deep voice, casting a sinister glance around the room. "Will they just... *take it?*"

Horror again swept the listeners; they understood the menace fully, but missed completely the mocking sarcasm. "The sanctity of private property!" the same woman hissed indignantly, as if he had cursed her god. After a brief pause, she snapped, "Exactly *how* long have you been living here?"

"Too long!" he snapped back. "Next question!"

"Who is John Galt?" quipped the author.

"That's what I want to know!" the pilot demanded angrily, deliberately taking the droll question seriously. "You guys seem to consider him some sort of god whose edicts are never to be questioned! But he's a man. He's just a man!"

"But it is not the messenger," Richard pointed out patiently. "It's the message—in this case, our philosophy. It's axiomatic, you must realize, so it all fits together of its own accord, irrespective of any man."

"Axiomatic, is it?" rumbled the pilot, then chuckled. "Does that mean you're guaranteed to make the same mistake every time?" He cast a twinkling eye around the taproom; no one smiled back. "So it would seem," he murmured to himself. Remembering his Sacramento friend's contribution to past philosophical challenges, aloud he proposed, "Then why don't you just revolt?"

Again Richard sighed. "I'm afraid that wouldn't work any better this time than the last." He glanced to the empty spot on the wall which once held the alternative oaths of the long-vanished scabs. "Our philosophy is what it is: integrated, axiomatic, and complete. You cannot just replace it on a whim—or any piece of it, for that matter!—without turning it into some other philosophy."

"Replace it?" The pilot scowled. "I was thinking more of armed revolt against it!"

"But we cannot initiate the use of force!" cried Richard. A shudder ran through the crowd; obviously he spoke for them all.

"Okay, okay," the pilot capitulated—not that he really cared. He would soon be shut of this town anyway. Still, he felt a debt of gratitude to the musician for having helped him establish his taproom, and to Owen for having saved his life. At the very least he owed it to these two to suggest a few other solutions. "Why not simply ignore those finicky Johnnies? Just go about your lives, like I've been doing these last couple of years."

Richard shook his head sadly. "It's not that simple, I'm afraid." He fell silent once again.

*Yes...? And...?* the pilot testily brooded, but still he said nothing. *This man is infuriatingly exasperating! Why can't he finish a thought?* Again he recalled with satisfaction that he would soon be rid of this valley and its contemptible Johnnies forever. Despite his anger, he smiled openly at the thought.

Mistakenly taking the smile as encouragement, Richard continued amicably. "In theory we could remain here in the valley, except that none would treat with us. While we would still have our homes and other personal possessions, how would we eat?" He gestured to the packed room. "You're the only one of us who owns an airplane, and I doubt you could ferry enough food to keep us all alive."

"Too true," agreed the pilot. "I'd spend the rest of my life chained to your stomachs."

"On the other hand," continued Richard, unprompted, "it would take far too long before we could replicate our food needs for ourselves."

"Would it, really?" The pilot turned to face the crowd. "How many of you folks are farmers?" Two hands went up. Turning back to Richard, he proclaimed, "There's your food, Richard."

"I'm not so sure you'd want to eat my tobacco," one of the farmers opined dryly.

"Or my cotton," the other pointed out with a laugh.

"Unless maybe if you coated your cotton in chocolate?" suggested the author. No one paid his playful proposition any mind.

"You could eat sour grapes out of my vineyards—," suggested Richard, smirking at his own witticism. "—or wait until they ripen come autumn. Either way it might get to be monotonous eating, assuming there would be enough to last us all until next year's harvest. Which I know there isn't." He exhaled noisily. "Face it, my friend: we simply haven't enough food to survive long enough to get enough food. We're left with no choice but to evacuate immediately."

With that depressing thought, the room fell still. This time the silence dragged on for several minutes.

"So what will you folks do?" the pilot finally prompted, facing the rest of the strikers. A buzz of answers rose from all parts of the audience.

"Move out."

"Establish a new valley someplace."

"Abandon my family."

"Sell my business and go."

"Dump my girl friend, unless she wants to come with me—which I doubt!"

On and on they went, and every one of them seemed to have a different story, none of them pleasant. Oddly, despite their dire words, the pilot could sense no semblance of remorse or guilt in any of their voices. It was as if the philosophical calamity that had befallen them were a force of nature, a random happenstance not to be questioned, like one of the valley's huge snowstorms, a mere inconvenience to be borne for the while then tossed aside, like some snake's shed skin.

Raggedly, they ran down, and Richard again took the fore—mercifully without being prompted. "Speaking for myself, I'm hoping I could find a nice, abandoned vineyard somewhere in the northern part of God's California that I could claim for my own." He smiled. "And who knows? Now that their theocracy has been defeated, perhaps I could spur their philosophical education along in the proper direction—with a more rational interpretation of the rules of association, of course."

"And now that I think of it," added Owen, "Dagny's letter did say that she and Eddie will be rebuilding Transcontinental Railroad. Perhaps I could claim the post of Division Superintendent that she once offered me—on the very day I first went on strike, by the way." He smiled at the memory, and glanced at Richard. "And I could become your educational counterpart in Las Vegas."

"Las Vegas!" exalted the pilot. "*Now* you're talking! Gwen and I got a good look at the place, and I'm definitely shifting my base of operations there just as soon as I can." He rubbed his hands together gleefully. "You'll love it there, Owen! Friendly people, no snowstorms, and I know this taproom there that puts this place to shame! Great whiskey, beautiful women, excellent beer, and more! It's a place where a deep-voiced, single guy like you could—"

"Save me the sales pitch," he interrupted, grudgingly grinning. "Looks like I have no other choice anyway."

"Nor would you want one. Trust me!" After a pause, he continued. "And I'm told there are entire neighborhoods still standing vacant. There's no reason you all couldn't take one over and make it your new valley."

"And we could call the neighborhood 'Sin City!'" gibed the author.

The pilot snorted a quick mocking laugh; but in contrast, a sizeable number of strikers averted their eyes in embarrassment.

Again the room fell silent; there was obviously nothing more to be said. Everyone understood.

The pilot finally broke the silence. "All right! Who wants to buy a one-way ticket to Las Vegas? Besides me, that is?"

# SECTION III – THE FINAL MONTHS

## Chapter 1 – It's a Beautiful Morning

Heads turned.

That was to be expected, since strangers were still a rare sight in the Gulch, but the man would have turned heads on any road. His easy gait reflected the assurance of royalty, yet his garb was of a dramatically simpler cut. His tanned, muscular arms and legs were naked to the warm June sunshine; his pants, shirt, and boots were each expertly crafted from the same, supple leather. One leg bore a wicked scar; it, appeared as if he had suffered a serious compound fracture in the not-too-distant past, but it did not reflect itself in his steady pace. In his hand he bore a tall, intricately-carved wooden staff, and slung on his back was an enormous pack, similarly of leather, but he carried its bulk with astonishing ease, as if it were stuffed merely with cotton candy. The improbable individual wore a wide-brimmed, skillfully-woven straw hat that shaded and half occluded his heavily-bearded face.

His direction of travel indicated he had come from a road seldom traveled, for behind him was the terminus of the old access road constructed at the behest of Midas over a decade earlier when the valley was first settled. But the road had long since been abandoned and deliberately rendered impassable to discourage intruders—but apparently insufficiently so.

Such was the stranger's self-assurance that no one challenged his presence; the strikers observed passively as the third surprise visitor in the history of the valley walked among them.

"Pardon me, stranger," one striker finally had the temerity to inquire, "But can I help you?" His words were friendly but his tone was that of a policeman addressing a thug.

Without slowing down, and with only a hint of a smile, the stranger replied politely, "No, thank you. I have an appointment I must keep." He left his questioner wondering in his wake.

"What sort of appointment?" he called after the retreating figure, a demand more than a question.

"Come see," he returned, calling over his shoulder, a hint of friendly humor echoing in his voice.

His questioner followed. So also did three other strikers who overheard their brief exchange.

Heads continued to turn as the stranger entered the town proper, and the number of followers began to swell. When the stranger paused near the floating golden dollar sign, they paused as well, as if some invisible cord married their step to his. They watched in silence as he cast his gaze upon it; his expression was one of near adulation, as if he had discovered some holy shrine long ago lost. He lingered a little longer, and when he resumed his journey, so also did they. He paused again in the center of town, standing on the smooth concrete sidewalk and marveling at the sight of several sleek, new traffic lights. As he approached one of the lights, its expertly-oiled mechanism hummed to life and changed the signal to red, stopping the entourage on the edge of a curb; in a moment the signal turned green, and they dutifully proceeded across the street en masse, their movement calling to mind that of Christmas crowds in New York City.

Two more times along his trek did a striker approach him to inquire about his business, both in a tone similar to the first; both times the answer was the same: that he had an appointment to keep, and that they should feel free to follow. By the time he had reached the far side of town, dozens trailed in his wake, with more adhering to the crowd as it passed, drawn not only by the odd stranger, but also by the mere spectacle of the moving mob.

Presently a woman detached herself from the crowd to match step with the stranger. "Welcome to the Gulch," she began with a kindly smile. In stark contrast to the men who had confronted the stranger thus far, her tone was such that it seemed she actually meant it.

He bowed in her general direction without slowing his pace. "Thank you," he replied with grace. "It's good to be here."

"Are you hungry? Or need a place to stay?"

This time the stranger halted. He hooked his thumbs under the shoulder straps of his pack and hefted it once. Taking a moment to consider her question, he did not appear so much confused as he did surprised. "Thank you for your offer of hospitality, but I believe I'll be all right." He smiled jovially for a moment, until finally he found himself forced to ask, "Pardon me, but this *is* the Gulch, isn't it?"

The woman smiled. "That is what we've named it."

Concern clouded his tanned face. "But what I mean is: you're not trying to be altruistic, are you?"

"Judge for yourself. Your needs are not a claim on me or on anyone else. Rather, it is someone else who is claiming the privilege of filling your needs. There is no coercion, no sacrifice, hence no altruism."

"I see," he said. "And who is it that is seeking this privilege?"

"Society."

"Society," he repeated, mimicking her inflection, but it was obvious it was a question nonetheless.

"Yes. The Society of Colorado." Still smiling, she paused briefly. "Think of it as a voluntary charity." She paused another breath before continuing. "So let me ask again: is there anything you need?"

He hesitated only briefly before replying. "Yes, there is. Later on, after I have finished with my appointment, I ask the favor of conversation. I have many questions for you about this Society you speak of."

"My pleasure, Mister...?"

"Addams," he replied after a short pause, a small smile on his lips. "Frankie Addams."

Dumbfounded, the woman suddenly recognized the name—and the man! Her jaw hung limply; her hands rose slowly to her face to inadequately cover her astonished surprise.

Mischievously, the man silently held an extended index finger up to his lips, requesting confidence. Wide-eyed, the woman nodded dazedly and drifted back into the crowd, her hands still covering her face as if she had forgotten she held them there, her tear-filled eyes peeking out from between limp fingertips.

The stranger and his entourage continued their journey among the hillocks of the valley, and it should have come as no surprise that he made a beeline for the home of the Worker, as if the path were familiar to him. He ascended the few steps to its porch, then turned to face his followers. With a grand sweep, he removed the hat from his head and bowed to them with a flourish. "Thank you all for the pleasure of your company," he called, his face toward the porch floor. Slowly he rose from his bow; he smiled gaily from within the depths of his bushy beard, turned, and entered the house with the casual manner of an owner, without knocking.

Inside, two men sat at a breakfast table set for three. Their demeanor was not that of men freshly awoken, well rested, and ready to face the challenges of a new day, but rather of those attending the funeral of a dear friend who had passed before his time. Their lowered heads turned and studied his bearded face in stunned fascination for a short moment before one of them recognized their long-absent friend, long presumed dead.

Ragnar leapt to his feet "Francisco!"

"Hi, Ragnar," he replied casually, as if their meeting were nothing out of the ordinary.

It was a rarity that Ragnar would be at such a loss for words, but, given the reason, could be expected and excused. "What...? What...?" he started, but could not finish.

"What's the matter?" he replied innocently. "It is the first of June, is it not? And don't the three of us always meet here in this room for breakfast on this day, at this time? I could hardly be so rude as to remain away, could I?" His eyes sparkled with mirth.

"But... But...," replied Ragnar in a further demonstration of his disheveled oratory skills.

"Have ye so little faith, my friends?"

"But your airplane crashed!" he finally managed to blurt.

"Yes, it did. A true inconvenience, that. And I'm not surprised that you couldn't find its wreckage. Not only was I about a hundred miles off to one side of my flight path when I finally came down, the craft wedged itself under an overhanging ledge of rock. It was all but impossible for anyone to find me by air—or even by foot, given the unforgiving terrain." Francisco shrugged; an interesting feat, given that he still carried his bulbous pack. "No matter. The radio was damaged beyond repair in the crash, but fortunately I wasn't too badly hurt." He gestured casually toward his scarred leg. "And the galtmotor still functioned, so I had light and heat—which, by the way, made it much easier to survive the winter that high in the mountains. I was able to trap my food and make my clothing—" He swept a hand across his attire. "—while I waited for the spring thaw to arrive. Once it did, I was all ready with provisions and pack." He paused with a slight air of embarrassment. "Speaking of which... Excuse me a moment." He grasped a pack strap and swung the large load from his back, setting it down gently on the floor behind him as if it were merely a feather-stuffed pillow. "In any case, I followed the streams down out of the mountains, hiked south until I came to the far end of the old road that Midas had built, then followed it back up here." He scratched an ear abstractly. "To be honest, I could have been here three weeks ago, but I thought it would be much more dramatic if I waited until today."

"Three weeks!"

"And why not?" Francisco shrugged mirthfully, adding, "I was camped the entire time not a mile away from my own house." A serious demeanor darkened his tanned face; he looked from one man to the other. "We should really be keeping a better watch on our borders, you know, although I haven't considered who would be responsible for paying for it."

"Well!" cried Ragnar, finally understanding and accepting. "Welcome home! Won't you join us for breakfast then?"

Francisco bowed. "I would be honored, my friends!" He took two steps toward the table, then paused.

"What's the matter, Francisco?"

He glanced around the room inquisitively. "Where's Dagny?"

# Chapter 2 – Who'll Stop The Reign?

Ma packed.

Time seemed to pass so quickly! It felt as if she had just returned from the last monthly gathering of the United Societies of America, yet here another one was already approaching. Not that she minded the trips or the other obligations which came along with her title of Head of Society for God's California. She had always enjoyed helping people, and riding in the hypercraft to and from the monthly meetings was a unique joy in and of itself. Rather, it was merely the subjective acceleration of the passage of time that afflicted many a woman her age.

Only half her mind was concentrated on her packing; not that her lack of attention mattered. The weather in Las Vegas this time of year was typically, monotonously hot, requiring that she bring along only the lightest of clothing; the vast remainder of her wardrobe would be less than worthless in that dry heat. Besides, she would only be staying the weekend; packing was trivial.

Rather than fashion issues, the bulk of her attention centered on how, over the course of the next two days, she would cajole the other Heads of Society converging on Society's capital city to support her humanitarian agenda—just as the other Heads would be bringing their own issues to the table. Some of the meeting's formal agenda would surely prove dry, such as the final report on how they had finally evacuated the last of the residents of the former State's Science Institute, fortunately before another winter set in. It had taken months and over one hundred flights to transplant all of them, and the final cost was astounding, so much so that it took the resources of a national Society to orchestrate so large an exodus—and even then, all of the bills were not yet paid in full. But regardless of the cost, they were compelled by compassion to act lest the tiny clot of humanity perish in the harshness of the upcoming New England winter.

And if that incredible expense wasn't enough, last month a hurricane had unexpectedly smashed into Washington, flooding the city and knocking out power for several days. Out of humanitarian necessity Society had come to the rescue with shipments of food, water, ice, and manpower. Necessary though it was, it only added to their bills. Projections were that the next round of benefactions and associated special fundraisers would cover the debt for both efforts—if only barely. She would learn within the day if that were so. Confoundingly, the unplanned costs were having an impact on Society's expenditures. Already they had to shelve expensive plans for emissaries of the United Societies to visit the People's States of Europe and South America. No one knew anything of conditions overseas, hence the need for the visits. But if conditions there were anything like those in the New United States, the situation was dire indeed, and ripe for the aid of the United Societies.

She sighed as she snapped her suitcase shut. The debt already hanging over Society's collective head would dampen enthusiasm for many new incentives, such as her planned soybean project. It had been straightforward to convince the residents of God's California to establish soybean farms as a way to feed more men for less effort—"The greatest food for the greatest number," she would always say—but there would be little enough money to take the project nationwide. Fortunately for her, Orren still owed her numerous favors, and this was definitely the time to call some of them in. As Head of Society for Washington, he had little else to offer other than his vote. Certainly Washington had the money—silver and gold money, at that!—but for some unfathomable reason their Society remained chronically poor. Why else would their participation seldom amount to anything more than a purely symbolic contribution? It seemed as if the men of Washington held no interest in providing for their fellow men—a failing she laid firmly on the doorstep of their former Head of State, that cold-hearted bastard Mr. James, the man whose railroad had killed her son, Kip! Even before that sad day, she and James had never gotten along, and their relationship had not improved in the days since the lights of New York City had gone out forever. More than once she had approached him—against her better judgment!—to solicit governmental support for one Societal project or another, but he always fell back on the same deliberately-pronounced mantra: "Is it Constitutional?" *Bah!* She had been more than overjoyed that hot July day when she learned he had resigned his position; but sadly, the assistant Head of State who had succeeded him was no better. She could hardly wait for the elections to be held come November. Popular wisdom had it that the man would be summarily sacked, along with the equally coldhearted Congress that Mr. James had appointed. *About time, too!*

With pursed lips, she swung her suitcase off the bed and dropped it angrily onto the bare wooden floor of her bedroom. It was so much simpler to seek help among the caring men here in God's California. Their recently-supplanted moral code had inculcated a strong sense of duty regarding the plight of their fellow man, a sense that had somehow held its own following the collapse of the religious dictatorship that once ruled the West with a red-robed fist. If anything, making charity optional had strangely enough strengthened it.

Again, she sighed. Regardless of the support of the former faithful, too many national benevolent incentives languished, and not merely those of her own agenda. The trouble was that there wasn't enough money to pay for all the things that Society sorely needed—which reminded her: she was going to have to speak with the national Head of Society about amending Society's Constitution to allow for some sort of taxation. If she was going to effectively care for the downtrodden disadvantaged of the nation, she was going to need wider powers! Who was Eddie to stand in her way? Orren would support her on that one, she was sure—and without her having to call in any favors. If she could only convince Chick to take on the role of Head of Society for Tennessee! Pockets of people had been found scattered across that state whom he could represent, but it wouldn't matter to her if he were the only man left alive in the entire nation! She only wanted another vote in her own pocket. If she could then repeat that sort of trick with a few other states—and New Hampshire had just slipped through her fingers—perhaps she could muster enough votes to get her Guidelines passed, and maybe even force the change to Society's Constitution. But it would take time.

*Ah well,* she sighed as she walked out into the sunshine. *If not this weekend, there's always next month. Or the next. Time marches on!*

## Section IV – The Final Years

# CHAPTER 1 – SCHOOL'S OUT

Peace returned.

Following the destruction of the armies of two of the remaining totalitarian holdouts in America, discernible discord finally departed the formerly-great nation; and unbeknownst as yet to the survivors of those conflicts, peace had also broken out abroad, extending to all four corners of the world.

But global peace was not achieved by conquest, treaty, or appeasement. No army was needed to bring about the peace, no diplomat to broker it, no pacifist to compromise for it; rather, it was brought about of its own accord on the wings of death. Absent the miracles that made modern life possible—electricity, mechanized farming, medicine, and so much more—the cities of the world promptly perished along with the men who once inhabited them, leaving behind only a woefully-tiny number of self-sustaining villages. Fortunately for peace, these villages were spaced so far apart as to preclude any meaningful warring and so poor as to preclude any worthwhile looting, let alone any trading. Travel, for any reason, ceased; there was nothing to be gained from it, and much to be lost. Left to themselves, it would take several generations before the villages would once again come in contact.

To the world outside America the Dark Ages had returned in force, replete with its kinglets, viziers, councils, and chieftains scrabbling pathetically for survival among the ruins. The simple act of remaining alive required so much effort that there was little left over for risky adventuring, not to mention too few men; it would take many decades—and a good deal of luck—before population levels would rise to the point where standing armies could again be sustained. Consequently, the militias shriveled into hunting parties, businessmen reverted into farmers, and intellectuals vanished. For the second time in humanity's history, the formula for making cement was lost. Literacy held its own for the moment—it would be at least a generation or two hence before that skill would disappear forever—but reading had already become a sterile study: there were few enough books remaining in existence to be read, but, more ominously, writing supplies had also dwindled. Scrap paper could still be found, if one knew where to look, but few men had realized the international complexity required to manufacture even the lowly pencil. Now they were reaping the harvest of that lack. Crude characters chalked with charcoal were all they had left.

Culture and language suffered horribly as well. A number of the less-utilized tongues vanished entirely from the face of the Earth along with the men who once spoke them; and even among the other, more fortunate survivors, vocabularies dwindled. In many cases, the contraction in the variety of spoken word was accidental, an innocent victim of now-limited circumstances in which men found themselves; but in other cases the decimation was deliberate, as some realms went so far as to forbid the use of the singular personal pronoun. Those men who violated the oral ban found themselves exiled, their houses carefully and deliberately burned to the ground—as had happened in Yucatan—and some offenders even threatened with death. Because whether ruled by King or Council, the unschooled leaders of this brave new world well knew what philosophical archetype had destroyed the planet: the unbridled individual. Indeed, everyone acknowledged it was that worst of individuals, the Worker, whose deadly strike had triggered the demise of modern civilization and hurtled humanity in a single blow back to the times before the Roman Empire; and in the process, inadvertently inspiring global peace.

But it was a different sort of peace than mankind had ever known: it was the peace of isolation, the peace of poverty, the peace of the grave. And given the world's unbridled animosity toward the men of the mind who had deliberately and calculatingly ruined the planet, the *Pax Galt* promised to be an enduring one.

# CHAPTER 2 – THE END

Eddie smiled.

The stark Nevada landscape streamed endlessly past the windshield of the *Meteor* under an equally-endless crystal blue sky. Greenish-blue rail stretched in a perfectly straight line ahead of him, diverting neither left nor right before vanishing in the far distance. Eddie's head protruded only slightly from the fireman's window on the left side of the old Diesel, and the warm, late-February wind whipped his thinning blonde hair along the exposed side. He was conscious of little else other than the pleasure it gave him. Behind his chair stood his wife, her hands resting lightly on his shoulders, enjoying the view and the feel of her man beneath her hands. A graying strand of hair blew across her eyes, tickling a wrinkled cheek; she reached up with one hand to tuck it behind an ear.

Beneath their feet they felt the growl of the old Diesel gathering strength, rumbling louder, firmer, and harder as the young engineer steadily advanced the throttle. Eddie recognized his cue from innumerable repetitions. Reaching overhead, his arthritic fingers closed achingly but tightly about the stout hemp cord and he tugged. Once, twice, three times the triple-coned horn bleated, screaming its mournful, drawn-out harmony while the massive Diesel barreled faster and faster down the straightaway suspended above a blur of brown crossties trimmed with twin ribbons of greenish-blue garnish.

His wife looked down at him and smiled. The run up to one hundred thirty-three miles per hour still exhilarated her, even after so many decades of riding the Kids' Special. The desert scenery alongside the train quickly melted into a blur where only the more distant mountains retained their definition. Out of the corner of her eye, she noted that the engineer had pulled back on the throttle; they had reached their peak velocity. This was the moment she loved best! She took an immense pleasure in the tableau that lay before her: the handsome young engineer, the starkly beautiful desert scene, their enormous velocity, her husband at her side, and the *Meteor* pulsing powerfully beneath her feet. Her hands squeezed Eddie's shoulders affectionately, absent-mindedly, yet deliberately.

Eddie looked up at her and smiled. He was just as thrilled by their journey as she was. It was a rare day that he rode in the cab of the *Meteor's* Diesel anymore, not since he had retired from Transcontinental Railroad so many years before. Nor was the aging Diesel often called upon for revenue service. But today was a special occasion that called for the presence of both man and machine. It was Eddie's birthday—or at least it was the day that Las Vegas chose to celebrate as his birthday—his seventieth—and a tremendous outdoor party was being held in his honor at Camp Dagny. Dozens of building-sized tents had been erected there to shield the partygoers from the winter sun, and an extravagant amount of food and drink had been prepared for the gala event. Scores of locomotives, day coaches, and sleepers had come clicking from across the country to help carry the crowds, drawing upon old, reclaimed Transcontinental rolling stock from all corners of the re-settled continent to descend upon the Las Vegas station. Fourteen thousand revelers had jammed the town for his sixty-fifth birthday; fifteen thousand were expected today, with virtually all of them arriving on a Transcontinental train.

Despite the decades of rebuilding that had taken place since the fall of the Old United States, those Transcontinental trains still remained the most efficient means of travel available to the common man. Not that there weren't fleets of aircraft filling the skies; there were. However their possible passengers were strictly restricted to sworn strikers only, an immutable condition laid down by the men who designed the airplanes, built their motors, and smelted the Miracle Metal which made their swift flight possible. If any man desired ever again to live in such an advanced industrial society, it would have to be on the producer's moral terms. Fellow strikers they welcomed with open arms, but the rest of mankind they snubbed.

Eddie did not so much as sigh at the thought; after so many years it was no longer worth the effort. The situation was a long-standing one that did not promise to change; not now, not ever. The strikers simply refused to deal with anyone who did not live up to their striker's oath, and that was that. Not that the uncompromising, obdurate strikers remained recluses within their valley; they hosted a lively trading empire among the scattered enclaves which flew the sign of the dollar. They also continued their long-running quest to search out other men of the mind who might be living among the scabs, men of ability who could be persuaded to take the striker's oath and emigrate to an enclave. For a striker it was a high calling indeed to effect the search, and among them such men were respectfully named "envoys" and were afforded every encouragement and act of cooperation—sometimes even without charge. But to the common man Outside, they were derisively named "missionaries," and not always treated in the kindly fashion that men of the cloth could typically expect. Assaults were not uncommon. In fact, on occasion an envoy might set out to make contact with a new town—especially one overseas—never to return. Yet regardless of the risk, their crusades continued unabated; they felt their quest more than worthwhile, no matter how often they might find themselves snubbed.

None of the strikers were expected to attend the celebration in Las Vegas, of course. They were too engrossed in holding their own massive celebration in their Colorado valley in joyful remembrance of the day that the lights of New York City had gone out forever. Nevertheless, there were several missionaries prowling around Las Vegas at that very moment seeking out new converts—although for some unspoken reason they studiously avoided the deed-restricted neighborhood known as Sin City. Ominously, only the night before, Eddie had encountered a pair of missionaries engaged in earnest conversation with the *Meteor's* young engineer. *Wasting their time!* Eddie hoped. When he had mentioned the episode to his wife that morning, she echoed both his apprehension, and his sentiment. They both had long ago learned of the false allure the striker's philosophy possessed, especially among the young.

As if aware of his thoughts, the young engineer turned to Eddie and nodded once; but his non-verbal agreement had nothing to do with the missionaries or their mission. Rather, the time had come.

Feeling both elated and a little deflated, Eddie reached up once more to grasp the rough hemp cord and sound the conclusion of the flight of "Eddie's *Meteor*," again, three long, mournful blasts. He turned his gaze upward to his wife, a firm, competent smile on his face, his elation easily edging out any trace of the disappointment he may have felt. "It simply does *not* get any better than life here in Las Vegas!"

His wife smiled down at him. "But of course," she agreed with a bright smile. As she leaned over to kiss the top of his head, her long, graying tresses tumbled enticingly across his face, a hint of lavender lurking among the locks. She lifted her head and glanced to the young engineer, a handsome lad tall and strong, a by-product of Eddie's fleeting first marriage whom she had raised as her own. She positively loved looking at his angular profile framed by the window, and her pride in him was manifestly evident on her face, for it was obvious that the young man shared their love of the railroad. His years at the controls of the Kids' Special affirmed that love beyond any doubt.

"Tell us," she called to him, a parent's pride plain in her voice. "Don't you agree with your father? Or have those mean missionaries finally gotten through to you?"

The young engineer turned his gun-metal grey eyes to face his stepmother and briefly glance at his father. They were singing the praises of Las Vegas again, and like always, it seemed as if they would never tire of the subject. But he could not deny the truth of their premises, nor countenance the arrogant, misplaced certitude spewed by the Worker's missionaries—in fact, he had learned more about the meaning of life from the old pilot who ran *The Soaring Eagle* taproom than he ever would from any of those missionary Johnnies. By any measure, life in the Society of Las Vegas was undoubtedly the best. Still, he hesitated to instantly agree; the old pilot had long ago taught him how it was always best to keep one's options open.

When the engineer did not immediately reply, his stepmother precipitately prompted, "Well, Atlas? Is he right?"

Surveying his parents from behind his best poker face, Atlas shrugged.

# Who Is Ken Krawchuk?

Ken V. Krawchuk was born and raised in the Feltonville section of Philadelphia, Pennsylvania, the grandson of five immigrant Eastern Europeans. He attended Roman Catholic elementary and high school, and graduated from a Jesuit university with a B.S. in Physics. He began his career as a professional computer programmer at the age of seventeen, and at thirty-five he founded a multi-million dollar computer consulting firm. Seven years later he was awarded the first of three United States patents pertaining to computer database theory.

Mr. Krawchuk read *Atlas Shrugged* for the first time at the age of thirty, and the ideas portrayed in the book transformed him from a life-long liberal Democrat into an eight-time Libertarian Party candidate for public office, including two record-breaking campaigns for Governor of Pennsylvania.

Mr. Krawchuk has been a member of Toastmasters International since 1997, and has been a professional public speaker almost as long. He is still married to his first wife Roberta, and they have been blessed with three daughters and two grandchildren (so far), and currently live in suburban Philadelphia.

# About the Book
(NO SPOILERS)

Reduced to its essential premises, *Atlas Snubbed* is a pastiche parody sequel to Ayn Rand's epic novel, *Atlas Shrugged*.

I call it a pastiche parody for several reasons. First off, it is pastiche in every sense of the word; for not only is the book meant to be a tribute to Ayn Rand and written in her style (at least to the limits of my meager ability), it is also a patchwork of "sampled" phrases and situations excerpted from her novels and other writings. Devoted fans of Atlas Shrugged will recognize how I relish taking the words of one character and placing them plausibly into the mouth of another, usually one who is likely to be a philosophical opposite, much like parents who hear their own words coming from the mouths of their babes—and not always in the most complimentary way. No surprise, then, that this novel is also a parody; and not merely a lampooning of Ayn Rand's writings and writing style—replete with long sentences sporting several semicolons, em dashes, and adjectives—but also an extrapolation, a sighting along the philosophical lines drawn out by her that end in some surely-unintended, yet plainly-foreseeable consequences. In other words, it's as much a lampooning of the philosophy portrayed in the novel as it is of the novel itself. So while there may be wry humor, poor puns, and alotta alliteration liberally littered throughout the book, overall it is a respectfully serious parody, oxymoronic though the concept may seem.

The genesis of this novel came on the heels of my 2002 campaign for Pennsylvania Governor under the Libertarian Party's banner, spawned and spurred by the combination of two key factors:

Firstly, Ayn Rand is the philosophical matriarch of the Libertarian Party. In fact, in order to be a card-carrying member of the party, it has always been required that one must sign the following oath: "*I swear, by my life and my love of it...*" Uh, sorry. Just kidding. Actually, the oath is: "*I hereby certify that I do not advocate the initiation of force or fraud to achieve political or social goals*," a pledge paraphrased—do you hear me? Paraphrased—from John Galt's epic speech in *Atlas Shrugged*.

Secondly, and more importantly, as the Libertarian candidate for Governor, I repeatedly found myself in a position where I was forced to defend Miss Rand's philosophy to the public at large, a task I ultimately found in part to be impossible. Not that I wasn't up to the philosophical challenge; rather my experiences drove home for me time and time again that some of her ideas are simply indefensible.

And so *Atlas Snubbed* was born. As envisioned, it would highlight some of the philosophical problems I encountered during the campaign and provide the story of their political solutions as I saw them. That statement bears repeating: this is a story of *political solutions*, not a philosophical treatise. I leave such justifications to those who are enamored of them.

Enough background; let's talk about the book. (No spoilers, as I promised.) Looking at the table of contents, you'll see that this parody is divided into Sections representing the first hours, the first days, the first weeks, etc. of the experiences of numerous selected characters—numerous, but far, far fewer than the hundred-plus that Miss Rand originally enlisted—followed by the story of their final hours, days, weeks, and years. The storyline commences with the state of affairs that existed exactly at the conclusion of *Atlas Shrugged*. Thus, the first hours for Eddie commence on the stalled *Meteor* in an Arizona desert, the first hours Dwight begin in the Gulch shortly after the lights of New York City go out forever, the first hours for Ma occur during the height the religious civil war raging in Rand's California, and so on. Like *Atlas Shrugged*, it is set in a fictional 1950s era where global Socialism is prevalent. The first chapter of this epic opens at 7:33 AM on a notional February 25, 1953—coincidentally my moment of birth.

It doesn't take a lot of perspicacity to note that the chapter titles are all taken from the titles of popular music of the last fifty years, most of them being among my personal favorites (with a few very-notable exceptions). The titles and the songs themselves are intended to present a fitting commentary upon the events of their respective chapters. Of course some hit that mark clearly, while others only strike a glancing blow. Regardless, playing the song as the chapter is being read provides an interesting backdrop, to say the least.

Many people who knew of my intent to create this parody were concerned about its legal aspects, because given the... uh... let us say "legendary intransigence" of your average Objectivist, the odds of receiving official permission to pen a critical parody of the greatest novel ever written would appear to be precisely zero. Fortunately, the legal minefield had already been cleared by a woman having an interesting coincidence of name, one Alice Randall. In 2001, Ms. Randall released a parody of Martha Mitchell's epic tale, *Gone With The Wind*, cleverly titled, *The Wind Done Gone*, which tells the exact same story during the exact same time frame, even including many of the novel's characters and passages—except the story is told from the slaves' point of view. (I toyed with the idea of naming this tome *Atlas Done Shrugged*, but concluded that the title was insufficiently on topic.) As you would expect, the Margaret Mitchell estate took frenzied exception to the apparent infringement, but after a protracted legal battle (ending with Suntrust v Houghton Mifflin, 252 F. 3d 1165, 11th Cir. 2001) the courts ruled that the parody was permissible without permission, as is this one, and the thousands of other creative works of critical fan fiction that have proliferated in Ms. Randall's wake. The literary world is a richer place for her courage.

I would be remiss in my appreciation if I did not take a moment to thank the folks who helped to make this book a reality, starting with my patient editors, Janet Easlea and Henry Whitney. Among those who reviewed the final draft version were Don Baldino, Dean and Julie DePue, Michele Guerin, Thomas Charles Marcy, Dave Nesom, Steve Scheetz, and my youngest daughter Carissa. Those who were unfortunate enough to also review the early draft of Book One a few years earlier included David Easlea, Rich Goldman, Eric Lucas, Bart Smith, Henry Whitney, and Marilyn Zonis. And I offer my sincerest condolences to my dear wife Roberta who had to listen to me ramble on and on and on for years on end as I wrestled with one plot complication after another. Without all of these good people and their invaluable feedback and unanimous support, I would never have gotten beyond the third chapter.

In any case, after eight political campaigns, dozens of readings of *Atlas Shrugged*, and nine years of occasionally uncompromising literary effort, you finally hold the results of my self-sacrifice in your hands. But please keep in mind that this critique is only my opinion; and the truth, as Arthur C. Clarke reminds us, will always prove far stranger.

- Ken
3:33 PM, November 27, 2011

Made in the USA
Charleston, SC
11 February 2012